A TIME TO DIE

Wilbur Smith was born in Central Africa in 1933. He was educated at Michaelhouse and Rhodes University. He became a full-time writer in 1964 after the successful publication of *When the Lion Feeds*, and has since written over thirty novels, all meticulously researched on his numerous expeditions worldwide. His books are now translated into twenty-six languages.

Find out more about Wilbur Smith
by visiting his author website,
www.wilbursmithbooks.com

THE NOVELS OF WILBUR SMITH

THE COURTNEYS

When the Lion Feeds   The Sound of Thunder

A Sparrow Falls   Birds of Prey   Monsoon

Blue Horizon   The Triumph of the Sun

THE COURTNEYS OF AFRICA

The Burning Shore   Power of the Sword   Rage

A Time to Die   Golden Fox   Assegai

THE BALLANTYNE NOVELS

A Falcon Flies   Men of Men   The Angels Weep

The Leopard Hunts in Darkness

THE EGYPTIAN NOVELS

River God   The Seventh Scroll

Warlock   The Quest

Also

The Dark of the Sun   Shout at the Devil

Gold Mine   The Diamond Hunters   The Sunbird

Eagle in the Sky   The Eye of the Tiger

Cry Wolf   Hungry as the Sea   Wild Justice

Elephant Song   Those in Peril

Vicious Circle

WILBUR SMITH

A TIME TO DIE

PAN BOOKS

First published 1989 by William Heinemann Ltd

This edition published 2014 by Pan Books
an imprint of Pan Macmillan, a division of Macmillan Publishers Limited
Pan Macmillan, 20 New Wharf Road, London N1 9RR
Basingstoke and Oxford
Associated companies throughout the world
www.panmacmillan.com

ISBN 978-1-4472-2177-7

Copyright © Wilbur Smith 1989

The right of Wilbur Smith to be identified as the
author of this work has been asserted by him in accordance
with the Copyright, Designs and Patents Act 1988.

1 3 5 7 9 8 6 4 2

A CIP catalogue record for this book is available from the British Library.

Typeset by Palimpsest Book Production Limited, Falkirk, Stirlingshire
Printed and bound by CPI Group (UK) Ltd, Croydon, CR0 4YY

Visit www.panmacmillan.com to read more about all our books
and to buy them. You will also find features, author interviews and
news of any author events, and you can sign up for e-newsletters
so that you're always first to hear about our new releases.

This book is for my wife

MOKHINISO

*who is the best thing
that has ever happened to me*

She had sat for well over two hours without moving, and the need to do so was an almost unbearable affliction. Every muscle in her body seemed to quiver with the craving for movement. Her buttocks were numb and despite being advised to do so, she had not emptied her bladder before they had gone into hiding, for she had been embarrassed by the masculine company and still too nervous in the African bush to go off alone to find a private place. She regretted her modesty and her timidity now.

She was staring out through the eye-slit in the rude grass structure of the hide, down a narrow open tunnel that the gunbearers had meticulously cleared through the thick bush, for even a tiny twig might deflect a bullet flying at 3000 feet a second. The tunnel was sixty yards long, paced out so that the telescopic sight of the rifle could be zeroed on precisely.

Without moving her head, Claudia swivelled her eyes towards where her father waited in the hide beside her. His rifle was propped in the vee of a branch in front of him and his right hand rested lightly on the stock. He needed to lift it mere inches to his cheek to be aiming and ready to fire.

Even in her physical discomfort the thought of her father firing that sinister glistening weapon made her angry. Yet he had always filled her with violent and conflicting emotions, nothing he ever did or said seemed to leave her untouched. He dominated her life and she hated him and loved him for it. Always she was trying to break away, and always he drew her effortlessly back. She knew that the main reason that she was still unmarried at twenty-six years

1

of age, despite the way she looked, despite her own singular achievements, despite having had countless proposals, at least two from men with whom she had believed herself in love at the time, the reason for all this was this man who sat beside her. She had never found another to compare with her papa.

Colonel Riccardo Monterro, soldier, engineer, scholar, gourmet, multi-millionaire businessman, athlete, *bon-vivant*, lady-killer, sportsman – how many descriptions fitted him perfectly and yet did not describe him as she knew him. They did not describe the kindness and the strength that made her love him, nor the cruelty and ruthlessness which made her hate him. They did not describe what he had done to her mother that had turned her into a discarded alcoholic shell. Claudia knew he was as capable of destroying her if she let herself be run down by him. He was the bull and she the matador. He was a dangerous man, and therein lay most of his appeal.

Someone had once told her, 'Some women always fall for real bastards.' She had immediately scoffed at the idea, but then thought about it later and came partially to accept it. The Lord knew, Papa was one. A great rumbustious bastard, with all the charm and flashing golden-brown eyes and shining teeth of his Latin origins, he could sing like Caruso and eat all the pasta she could heap on his plate. But although he had been born in Milano, the greater part of him was American for Claudia's grandparents had emigrated to Seattle from Mussolini's Italy when Riccardo was a child.

She had inherited his physical characteristics, the eyes and teeth and glowing olive skin, but she tried to reject every value of his that offended her and to take the opposite path to his. She had chosen to study law as a direct defiance of the lawless streak in him, and because he was a Republican she had decided long before she could understand what politics meant, that she was a Democrat. Because he set so much store by wealth and possessions, Claudia had deliberately turned down the $200,000 job she was offered after graduating fifth in her law class and had taken instead one at $40,000 in the civil rights agency. Because Papa had commanded a battalion of engineers in Vietnam and still talked of 'gooks', her work with the indigenous Inuit people of Alaska gave her satisfaction enhanced by his disapproval. He called the Eskimos 'gooks' as well. Yet here she was in Africa at his request, and the true horror of it was that he was here to kill animals and that she was in collusion with him.

At home what spare time she had was devoted to working without remuneration for the Alaskan Nature and Wildlife Conservation Society. The Society devoted most of its resources and efforts to fighting the oil exploration companies and their depredations on the environment. Her father's company, Anchorage Tool and Engineering, was a major supplier of hardware to the drilling rigs and pipeline contractors. The choices she had made had been calculated and deliberate.

Yet here she was in a foreign land waiting submissively for him to assassinate some beautiful wild animal. Her own duplicity sickened her. They called this expedition a safari. She would never have even contemplated becoming an accomplice in such a heinous enterprise, in fact she had indignantly refused the invitations he had made to her in previous years, but for the secret she had learned a scant few days before her father had invited her. This might be the last time, the very last time, she would be alone with him. That thought appalled her more even than the dirty business in which they were engaged.

'Oh God,' she thought, 'what will I do without him? What will my world be without him?'

As the thought struck her she turned her head, her first movement in two hours, and looked over her shoulder. Another man sat close behind her in the small thatch-walled hide. He was the professional hunter. Although her father had hunted with this man on a dozen other safaris, Claudia had met him for the first time only four days previously when they had disembarked from the South African Airways commercial flight at Harare, the capital city of Zimbabwe. The hunter had flown them out from there in his twin-engined Beechcraft Baron to this vast and remote hunting concession near the Mozambique border which he chartered from the Zimbabwe government.

His name was Sean Courtney. She had known him four days but already she loathed him as if she had known him a lifetime. Not strange that thinking of her father had led her instinctively to look back at him. Here was another dangerous man. Hard, ruthless and so devilishly good looking that her every instinct shrieked a warning at her.

He frowned sharply at her with clear bright green eyes in the darkly tanned face, and the crow's-feet at the corners of his eyes puckered with annoyance at her movement. He touched her on the hip with one finger, cautioning her to stillness again. The touch was light, but she felt the discon-certing male strength in his single finger. She had noticed his hands before, trying not to be impressed by their graceful form. 'The hands of an artist or a surgeon or a killer,' she had thought then, but now that peremptory touch offended her. She felt as though she had been sexually violated. She stared fixedly ahead again, through the eye-slit in the grass wall, and she fumed with indignation. How dare he touch her. The spot on her hip burned, as though he had branded her with his finger.

That afternoon before they had left camp, Sean had insisted that each of them shower and bathe with special unscented soap that he provided. He had cautioned Claudia to use no perfume and one of the camp servants had laid out freshly washed and ironed khaki shirt and slacks on her cot in the tent when she returned from the shower.

'Those big cats can smell you from two miles downwind,'

Sean had told her. Yet now after two hours in the heat of the Zambezi valley, she could faintly smell him sitting up close behind her, almost but not quite touching her, fresh, male sweat, and she felt an almost irresistible urge to move in the canvas camp chair. He made her feel restless, but she forced herself to sit perfectly still. She found herself breathing deeply, trying to pick up the faint intermittent wafts of his odour, then stopped herself angrily as soon as she realized what she was doing.

Inches in front of her eyes a single green leaf, hanging down into the opening in the grass wall, spiralled slowly on its stalk like a weathercock and almost immediately she felt the shift of the light evening breeze.

Sean had sited the blind below the prevailing wind, and now as the breeze came down to them, it brought a new odour, the stench of the carcass. The bait was an old buffalo cow. Sean had selected her from a herd of two hundred of the huge black animals.

'That old girl is way past breeding,' he had pointed her out. 'Take her low on the shoulder, through the heart,' he had ordered Papa.

It was the first animal Claudia had ever seen killed deliberately. The crash of the heavy rifle had shocked her, but not as deeply as the scarlet gush of blood in the bright African sunlight and the mournful death bellow of the old cow. She had walked back to where they had left the open Toyota hunting car and sat alone in the front seat in a cold sweat of nausea while Sean and his trackers had butchered the carcass.

They had hauled the carcass up into the lower branches of the wild fig tree with the power winch on the front of the Toyota, positioning it with much debate between Sean and his trackers at the exact height which would enable a full grown lion standing on his back legs to reach up and partially satisfy his hunger without enabling a large pride of cats to consume all of it at a sitting and so move on to find other fare.

5

That had been four days previously, but even then as they worked the metallic-green blow-flies had come swarming to the smell of fresh blood. Now the heat and the flies had done their work, Claudia wrinkled her nose and grimaced at the stench that came down to her on the breeze. The smell seemed to coat her tongue and the back of her throat like slime, and staring at the carcass in the tree, she imagined she could see the black hide undulating softly as the maggots seethed and burrowed into the putrid flesh beneath it.

'Lovely,' Sean had sniffed it before they entered the hide. 'Just like a ripe Camembert. No cat within ten miles will be able to resist it.' While they waited the sun sagged wearily down the sky, and the colours of the bush now glowed with the richer light, in contrast to the washed-out glare of noon.

The faint coolness in the evening breeze seemed to awaken the wild birds from their heat-drugged stupor. In the undergrowth down on the banks of the stream a lourie called 'Kok! Kok! Kok!' as raucously as a parrot, and in the branches directly over their heads a pair of glistening metallic sunbirds flitted busily, with fluttering wings, hanging upside down from the fluffy blooms to suck up the nectar. Claudia lifted her head slowly to watch them with intense pleasure. Though she was so close that she could see their thin tubular tongues thrusting deeply into the yellow flowers, the little creatures ignored her as though she was part of the tree.

She was still watching the birds when she became aware of a sudden tension in the hide. Her father had stiffened, his hand on the buttstock of the rifle clenched slightly. His sense of excitement was almost palpable. He was staring through his peephole, but though she stared as hard she could not see what had excited him. From the corner of her eye, she saw Sean Courtney reach forward between them, his hand moving with infinite stealth, to grasp her father's elbow in a cautionary restraining grip.

Then she heard Sean's whisper, softer than the breeze. 'Wait!' he said.

So they waited, deathly still, as the minutes drew out slowly and became ten and then twenty.

'On the left,' Sean said, and it was so unexpected that she started at the barely audible murmur. Her eyes swivelled left. She saw nothing, just grass and bush and shadows. She stared unblinkingly until her eyes smarted and swam with tears and she had to blink rapidly and then look again, and this time she saw something move like mist or smoke, a drift of brown in the long sun-seared grass.

Then abruptly, dramatically, an animal stepped out into the open killing ground below the reeking carcass in the fig tree.

Despite herself, Claudia gasped, and then her breath choked in her throat. It was the most beautiful beast she had ever seen, a great cat, much larger than she had ever expected, sleek and glossy and golden. It turned its head and looked directly at her. She saw that its throat was a soft cream, and sunlight gleamed on the long white whiskers. Its ears were round and tipped with black and held erect, listening. The eyes were yellow, as implacable and glowing as moonstones, the pupils reduced to black arrowheads as it stared up the long clearing at the wall of the hide.

Still Claudia could not breathe. She was frozen with excitement and dread as the cat stared at her. Only when it turned its head away and looked up at the carcass in the tree, could she let out her breath in a soft ragged sigh.

'Don't kill it. Please, don't kill it,' she almost cried aloud. With relief she saw that her father had not moved a muscle and Sean's hand was still on his elbow restraining him.

Only then did she realize that it was a female, there was no mane, a lioness, and she had listened to the camp-fire conversation enough to know that they were hunting only a full-maned lion and that there were heavy penalties, huge fines and even imprisonment for the killing of a female.

She relaxed slightly and gave herself over to the full enjoyment of the moment, to the stunning beauty of this beast. Claudia's pleasure had only just begun, for the lioness looked around her once more and then, satisfied that it was safe, she opened her mouth and gave a low mewling call.

Almost immediately, her cubs came tumbling into the clearing. There were three of them, fluffy as children's toys and dappled with their kitten spots. They tripped over paws that were too large for the tiny bodies, and after a few moments of hesitation during which their mother placed no restraint on them, they launched into boisterous mock combat, wrestling and falling over each other with ferocious baby growls.

The lioness ignored them and rose up on her hind legs to the dangling carcass. She thrust her head into the open belly from which the entrails had been plucked, and she began to feed. The row of black nipples down her belly were sucked out prominently and the fur around them matted with the saliva of her offspring. She had not yet weaned them and the cubs took no notice of her feeding and went on with their play.

Then a second lioness stepped into the clearing, followed by two half-grown cubs. This lioness was much darker in colour, almost blue along the spine and her pelt was crisscrossed with old healed scars, the legacy of a lifetime of hard hunting, the marks of hoof and horn and claw. Half of one ear was torn off and her ribs showed through the scarred hide. She was old. The two half-grown cubs that followed her into the clearing would probably be her last litter. Next year, when the cubs had deserted her and she was too weak to keep up with the pride, the hyena would take her, but now she was still living on her store of cunning and experience.

She had let the young lioness go in first to the bait, for she had seen two mates killed in just such a situation, beneath a succulent carcass dangling from a tree, and she mistrusted it. She did not begin to feed, but prowled restlessly around the clearing, her tail flicking with agitation and every so often she stopped and stared intently down the open lane to the grass wall of the hide at the far end.

Her two older cubs gazed up at the carcass, sitting on their haunches and growling with hunger and frustration for the meat was obviously beyond their reach. At last, the bolder of the two backed off then made a running leap at the bait. Hooking on with its front claws, its back legs swinging free, it tried to grab a hasty mouthful, but the young lioness turned on it viciously, snarling and cuffing it heavily until it fell on its back, scrambled to its feet and slunk away.

The older of the two lionesses made no effort to protect her cub. This was the pride law: the full-grown hunters, the most valuable members of the pride, must feed first. The pride survived on their strength. Only after they had gorged could the young ones feed. In the lean times, when game was scarce or when open terrain made hunting difficult, the young might starve to death, and the adult females would not come into season again until game was once more plentiful. In this way, the survival of the pride was ensured.

The chastened cub crept back to join its sibling beneath the carcass and then to compete eagerly with it for the scraps that the lioness ripped out of the buffalo's belly cavity and unintentionally let fall.

Once the young lioness dropped back on all fours in obvious discomfort, and Claudia was horrified to see that her whole head was swarming with white maggots that had crawled out of the meat as she fed. The lioness shook her head, scattering maggots like rice grains. She pawed frantically at her own head to be rid of the fat worms that were trying to crawl into the furry openings of her ears. Then she extended her neck and sneezed violently, blowing live maggots out of her nostrils.

Her young cubs took this as an invitation to play, or to

feed. Two of them launched themselves at her head, trying to hang on to her ears, while the third rushed under her belly and attached himself to a nipple like a tubby brown leech. The lioness ignored them and rose once more on her hind legs to continue eating. The cub at her nipple managed to hang on a few seconds longer and then fell under her back paws, and his dignity was trampled as she tugged and heaved at the bait. He crawled out between her legs crestfallen, dusty and dishevelled.

Claudia giggled, she could not help herself, she tried to muffle it with both hands. Immediately Sean dug her hard in the short ribs.

Only the old lioness reacted to her giggle. The rest of the pride were too preoccupied, but the lioness crouched and flattened her ears against her skull, staring fixedly down the opening at the hide. With these eyes on her, Claudia lost any urge to giggle again and she held her breath.

'She can't see me,' she told herself without conviction. 'Surely she can't see me?' But for long seconds, those eyes bored into hers.

Then abruptly, the old lioness rose and slid away into the thick undergrowth beyond the bait tree. She moved like a serpent, a sinuous flowing and gliding of the brown body. Claudia let out her breath slowly, and gulped with relief.

While the rest of the pride romped and tussled and fed beneath the bait tree, the sun slid below the tree-tops and the short African twilight was on them.

'If there is a tom with them, he will come in now,' Sean breathed softly. The night was the time of the cats, the darkness made them bold and fierce. The light was going even as they watched.

Claudia heard something beyond the grass wall beside her, a furtive brush of some creature in long grass, but the bush was full of such small sounds and she did not even turn her head. Then she heard a distinct and unmistakable sound. The footfall of some heavy creature, soft and stealthy, but very close, and she felt her skin crawl with the insects of fear and the prickle of it up the back of her neck. Quickly she turned her head.

Her left shoulder was pressed up against the thatch wall of the hide, and there was a chink in the thatch an inch wide. Her eyes were at the same level as the hole, and through it, she saw movement. For a moment, she did not recognize what she was seeing, and then she knew that it was a tiny expanse of smooth tawny hide, filling the chink, only inches on the far side. As she stared in horror, the tawny pelt slid past her eyes, and now she heard something else, an animal breathing, snuffling at the far side of the thatch wall.

Instinctively, she reached behind her with her free hand, but never taking her eyes from the chink. Her hand was seized in a hard cool grip. The touch that had offended her only minutes before, now gave her more comfort than she had ever believed possible. She did not even marvel that she had reached for Sean's hand, rather than her own papa's.

She stared into the chink, and suddenly, there was another eye beyond, a huge round eye, glistening like yellow agate, a terrible inhuman eye, unblinking, burning into hers with a dead black pupil in its centre, a hand's span from her face.

She wanted to scream, but her throat was closed. She wanted to leap to her feet, but her legs were dead. Her swollen bladder was like a stone in her lower belly, and before she could control it, she felt a few warm drops escape. That checked her, the humiliation was greater than her terror and she tightened her thighs and buttocks and clung to Sean's hand, still staring into that terrible yellow eye.

The lioness sniffed again loudly, and Claudia started silently but held on. 'I won't scream,' she told herself.

Again the lioness snuffled beyond the grass wall, and her nostrils were filled with the man odour and she let out an

11

explosive grunt that seemed to rock the flimsy grass walls. Claudia caught the scream in her throat before it could escape. Then the yellow eye was gone from the chink, and she heard the pad of great paws circling back round the hide.

Claudia swivelled her head to follow the sound, and she looked straight into Sean's face. He was smiling. That was what shocked her after what she had just lived through, there was that devil-may-care grin on his lips and mockery in those green eyes. He was laughing at her. Her terror subsided, and her anger flared.

'The swine,' she thought. 'The arrogant bloody swine.' And she knew that her face was bloodless and that her eyes were dark and wide with terror. She hated herself for it and she hated him for being witness to it.

She wanted to jerk her hand out of his grip, but she could still hear that great cat out there, still very close, circling them and though she loathed him, she knew that without his grip she would not be able to control herself. So she held on, but she turned her face away, following the furtive sounds of the lioness, so that Sean could not see her face.

The lioness passed in front of the blind. Through the peephole she saw the blur of its golden body, quickly gone, and she saw also that the young lioness and the cubs, alerted by the warning grunt, had disappeared into the undergrowth. The killing ground below the bait tree was deserted.

The light was going swiftly now. Within minutes it would be dark, and the thought of that brute in the darkness was almost too much to bear. Sean reached over her shoulder and pressed something small and hard against her lips. For a moment, she resisted and then she opened and let him slide it into her mouth. It was a cube of chewing-gum.

'The man has gone mad,' She was bewildered. 'Chewing-gum at a time like this?'

Then as she crunched down on to the cube she realized that her saliva had dried out and that the inside of her mouth was seared and puckered as though she had bitten into a green persimmon. At the taste of spearmint, her saliva flowed again, but she was so angry with him that she felt no gratitude. He had known that her mouth was dry with terror and she resented that fiercely.

The lioness growled in the semi-darkness behind the hide, and Claudia thought longingly of the Toyota that was parked a mile back up the track. Almost echoing her thought, her father asked softly. 'When did you tell the gunbearers to bring the truck?'

'After the last of the shooting light,' Sean answered him quietly. 'Another fifteen or twenty minutes.'

The lioness heard their voices and growled again threateningly.

'Cheeky bitch,' Sean said cheerfully. 'Snarly Sue in person.'

'Shut up!' Claudia hissed at him. 'She'll find us.'

'Oh, she knows we are here now,' Sean replied, and then raised his voice and called. 'Get away with you, you silly old bitch, go on back to your babies.'

Claudia jerked her hand out of his grip. 'Damn you! You'll get us all killed.'

But the loud human voice had alarmed the cat, and for minutes, there was silence beyond the grass wall. Sean took up the short ugly double-barrelled rifle that was propped against the wall beside him and placed it across his lap. He opened the breech of the .577 Nitro Express, and slid the fat brass cartridges out of the chambers, changing them for two others from the loops on the left breast of his jacket. It was a little superstitious ritual of his, that changing of cartridges, he always performed it at the beginning of a hunt.

'Now, listen to me, Capo,' he addressed Riccardo. 'If we kill that old whore without good reason, the game department is going to pull my licence. "Good reason" is when she has already chewed somebody's arm off, not before. Do you hear me?'

'I hear you,' Riccardo nodded.

'All right, don't shoot until I tell you, or by God, I'll shoot you.'

They grinned at each other in the half light, and Claudia realized with disbelief that the two of them were enjoying themselves. These two crazy oafs were actually having fun.

'By the time Job arrives with the truck, it will be pitch dark, and Job can't get the truck up to the hide. We'll have to go down to it in the riverbed. You go first, Capo, and then Claudia between us. Stay close together, and whatever you do, don't run! For the love of God, don't anybody run!'

Then they heard the lioness again, padding softly around them. She growled once more and almost immediately her growl was answered from the far side of the hide. The young lioness was out there now.

'The gang's all here,' Sean commented. The sound of voices and the old lioness's growls had summoned the rest of the pride, and the hunters had become the hunted. They were trapped in the hide. The darkness was almost complete. The sunset was merely a dull red furnace glow on the western horizon.

'Where is the truck?' Claudia whispered.

Sean said, 'It's coming.' Then his voice changed. 'Down!' he said sharply. 'Get down!' And though she had heard nothing, she dropped out of the canvas chair and crouched on the ground.

The lioness had crept up to the front wall again, almost soundlessly, and now she flung herself at it, roaring furiously as she tore at the flimsy structure with her front claws. With horror, Claudia realized that it was coming in on top of her.

'Keep your heads down,' Sean shouted urgently and lifted the double-barrelled rifle just as the wall burst open.

He fired, a stunning burst of sound as the muzzle blast swept through the hide and lit the interior with flame, brilliant as a flashbulb.

'He's killed the brute.' Despite her hatred of blood

sport, Claudia felt a guilty relief, but it was short-lived. The shot had merely startled the cat and driven her off for the moment. Claudia heard the lioness gallop away into the undergrowth snarling viciously.

'You missed,' she accused him breathlessly, with the stink of burnt gunpowder in her nostrils.

'Wasn't trying to hurt her.' Sean opened the rifle and reloaded from the cartridge loops on his breast. 'Just a warning shot over her bows.'

'There's the truck coming.' Riccardo's voice was level and unconcerned. Claudia's ears were still singing from the crash of gunfire, but she could make out the distant beat of the Toyota's diesel engine through it.

'Job heard the shot.' Sean stood up. 'He's coming early. All right, let's get ready to move out.'

Claudia scrambled up eagerly, and then looked over the low grass wall of the roofless hide into the dark forbidding forest around her, and remembered the track that led down to the dry riverbed that served as a road. They would have to travel almost a quarter of a mile in the night to reach the safety of the truck. Her spirit quailed at the prospect.

In the trees not fifty yards away, the lioness roared again.

'Noisy blighter,' Sean chuckled, and took her elbow to guide Claudia to the door. This time she did not try to pull away, but instead found herself clinging to his arm.

'Take hold of Capo's belt.' Gently he disengaged her hand and guided it to her father's belt at the small of his back.

'Hold on,' he told her. 'And remember, whatever happens, don't run. It will pull them onto you instantly. Cat with mouse, they can't resist it.'

Sean switched on the flashlight. It was a big black Maglite, but even that powerful beam seemed puny and yellow in the immensity of the forest as he played it in a circle around them. There were eyes reflected in the beam, they glowed like menacing stars, many eyes out there in the dark bush, impossible to tell cubs from full-grown lionesses.

'Let's go,' Sean said quietly, and Riccardo started down the rough narrow track, dragging Claudia with him.

They went slowly, bunched up tightly. Riccardo covering the van with his lighter rifle and Sean in the rearguard, with the heavy rifle and the flashlight.

Each time the torch beam picked up the flash of cat's eyes in the night, they seemed closer, until Claudia could make out the body of the animal behind the glowing eyes. They were pale as moths in the torchlight, nimble and restless, as they circled, both lionesses closing in now, pacing swiftly through the undergrowth, watching them intently, but turning their heads away whenever the powerful light hit their eyes.

The track was steep and rough, and oh, so long. Each step was an agony of impatience for Claudia as she stumbled along behind her father, not watching her footing, but watching instead those pale feline shapes that paraded around them.

'Here comes Snarly Sue!' Sean warned quietly as the old lioness screwed up her courage and came at them out of the night, grunting like a steam locomotive, deafening gusts of sound surging up her throat and out of her open mouth, her long tail lashing from side to side like a hippo-hide whip. They stopped in a tight group, and Sean swung the torch and the rifle on to the charging animal.

'Get out of it!' he yelled at her. 'Go on, scat!' And the lioness came on, her ears flattened against her skull, long yellow fangs and pink tongue curling between her gaping jaws.

'Yah! Snarly Sue!' Sean howled. 'I'll blow your stupid head off!'

She broke her charge at the last possible moment, skidding to a halt on stiff front legs, ten feet from where they were bunched and the dust swirled around her in the torch-light.

'Piss off!' Sean ordered her sternly, and her ears came erect and she turned and trotted obediently back into the forest.

'That was a game of chicken chicken,' Sean chuckled. 'She was just trying it on.'

'How did you know that?' Claudia's voice was cracked and shrill in her own ears.

'Her tail. As long as she keeps waving it, she's only kidding. When she holds it stiff, then look out!'

'Here's the truck,' Riccardo said, and they could see the Toyota's headlights through the trees as it bumped up the dry riverbed below them.

'Praise the Lord,' Claudia whispered.

'It's not over yet,' Sean warned as they moved off down the track once more. 'There is still Growly Gertie to deal with.'

Claudia had forgotten the younger lioness and now she glanced around fearfully, as she stumbled after her father, hanging onto his belt.

Then at last, they were on the bank of the riverbed, fully lit by the headlights of the parked truck which was standing only thirty yards away with its engine running. She could make out the heads of the trackers in the front seat beyond the blaze of headlights. So close, so very close, and she could not help herself. Claudia let go of her father's belt, and ran for the truck, pelting wildly through the thick loose white sand of the riverbed.

She heard Sean shout behind her, 'You bloody idiot!'

And immediately afterwards the fearsome grunting roar of the lioness as she charged. Claudia glanced sideways as she ran, and the great cat was almost on her, coming in at an angle out of the tall reeds that lined the open riverbed. She was huge and pale in the headlights of the Toyota, snake-swift, and her roaring cramped Claudia's belly and her feet dragged in the thick white sand.

Claudia saw that the charging lioness carried her tail high

17

and stiff as a steel ramrod, and even in her terror, she remembered what Sean had said and she thought with icy clarity. 'This time she's not going to stop, she's going to kill me.'

For a vital instant, Sean had not realized that the girl had run. He was backing carefully down the steep path into the riverbed, with the flashlight in his left hand and the double rifle in his right. He held the rifle by the grip with the barrels tilted up over his shoulder and his thumb on the slide of the safety-catch and he was watching the old lioness out there on the edge of the reed bed as she crawled on her belly towards them. But he was sure that she was now merely going through the motions of aggression since he had stared down her mock charge. There were two of the cubs well back behind her, sitting up in the grass and watching the performance with huge eyes and candid fascination, but too timid to take part. He had lost sight of the younger lioness, although he was sure that she was now the main threat, but the river reeds were dense and tall.

He had felt Claudia bump against his hip, but he thought she had stumbled, not realizing that she had bumped him as she turned to run. He was still searching for the younger lioness, probing the reed-beds with the torch beam, when he heard the crunch of Claudia's running feet in the sugary river sand, and he whirled and saw her out there in the dry riverbed alone.

'You bloody idiot!' he yelled in fury. The girl had been a constant source of irritation and dissent since she had arrived four days ago. Now she had flagrantly disobeyed his order, and he knew in an instant, even before the lioness launched her charge, that he was going to lose her. Getting a client killed or mauled was the blackest disgrace that could befall a professional hunter. It meant the end of his career, the end of twenty years of work and striving.

'You bloody idiot!' he vented all his bitterness on the running figure. He barged past Riccardo, who was still standing frozen with shock on the path below him, and at that moment, the lioness burst out of the edge of the reed bed where she had been lying.

The riverbed was brilliantly lit by the lights of the truck, so Sean dropped the torch and swung up the rifle with both hands, but he could not fire. The angle was wrong, the girl was between him and the lioness. Claudia ran awkwardly in the clinging sand, her head twisted away from him to watch the charge, her arms pumping frantically out of time with her legs.

'Down!' Sean shouted. 'Fall flat!' But she kept running, blocking his shot and the lioness swept in on her, sand spurting under her paws from which the curved yellow claws were already fully extended. She was grunting and roaring with each stride and her tail was carried stiff and straight.

In the headlights, the shadows of girl and cat on the stark white sand were grotesque and black, coming together swiftly, and Sean saw the lioness gather herself for the leap and he watched helplessly over the open iron sights of the rifle, impossible to separate them, impossible to fire without hitting the girl.

At the last moment Claudia tripped, her legs weak with fear collapsed under her and with a despairing wail, she sprawled face down in the sand.

Instantly, Sean zeroed his aim on the creamy chest of the lioness. With this rifle, he could hit two penny coins flipped simultaneously into the air at a range of thirty paces, left and right, both coins before they fell to earth. With this rifle, he had killed leopard, lion, rhino, buffalo, elephant by the hundred – and men, many men in the days of the Rhodesian bush war. He never needed a second shot. Now the target was open, he could with supreme confidence send a 750-grain soft-nosed mushrooming bullet through the lioness from her chest to the root of her tail. It would be the end of the cat, and of the safari, and probably his licence. At the least, it would mean months of investigation and trial. A dead lioness would bring all the wrath of the government, and the game department, down upon him.

The lioness was almost on top of the fallen girl, only a scant few feet of white sand between them, and Sean dropped his aim. It was a terrible risk, but he thrived on risk. He was gambling with the girl's life, but she had infuriated him, she deserved to take her chance.

He fired into the sand two feet in front of the lioness' open jaws. The huge heavy bullet ploughed in, sending up an eruption of sand, a solid fountain of flying white grains that for a moment, completely enveloped the animal. Sand filled its mouth and was sucked into its lungs as it roared, sand drove into its nostrils clogging them, and sand lashed into its open yellow eyes, tearing, raking, blinding the lioness, disorientating her, breaking the charge instantly.

Sean raced forward, with the second barrel ready to fire, but it wasn't necessary. The lioness had recoiled, rearing back violently, clawing at her sand-clotted eyes, toppling over and then bounding up again, and careering back into the reed-bed, barging blindly into the sheer bank, rolling and falling, and struggling up again. The sound of her wild run and agonized roars dwindled.

Sean reached Claudia and with an arm around her, jerked her to her feet. Her legs were unable to support her, and he had to half carry, half drag her to the Toyota and bundle her into the front seat.

At the same time, Riccardo scrambled into the back seat of the Toyota, and Sean leapt up onto the running board and with his free hand held the rifle like a pistol, pointed out into the darkness, ready for another charge.

'Go!' he shouted at Job, and the Matabele driver let out the clutch and they flew down the riverbed, lurching and jolting over the heavy going.

Nobody spoke for almost a minute, until they had climbed out of the riverbed onto the smoother track and then Claudia said in a small strangled voice, 'If I can't pee right now, I'm going to burst.'

'We could always point you at Snarly Sue like a fire extinguisher and wash her away,' Sean suggested coldly, and in the back seat, Riccardo let out a delighted guffaw. Even though Claudia recognized the nervous relief and tension in her father's laugh, she resented it bitterly. It aggravated the total humiliation she had suffered.

It was an hour's drive back to camp and when they arrived, Moses, Claudia's camp servant, had the shower filled with piping hot water. The shower was a twenty-gallon oil drum suspended in the branches of a mopane tree, a thatched grass screen, open to the stars, and a cement floor.

She stood under the rush of steaming water and as her body turned bright pink, she felt the humiliation and the nausea of the adrenalin over-dose fade away, to be replaced by that buoyant sense of well-being that comes only from having survived extreme danger.

While she soaped herself, working up a rich lather, she listened to Sean. He was fifty yards away at his makeshift gymnasium at the back of his own tent, but his regular hissing breathing carried clearly as he worked with the iron weights. He had not missed a session in the four days she had been in camp, no matter how long and hard the day's hunting had been.

'Rambo!' She smiled contemptuously at his masculine conceit and yet more than once, during the last few days, she had caught herself surreptitiously contemplating his muscled arms, or his flat greyhound belly or even his buttocks, round and hard as a pair of ostrich eggs in his khaki shorts.

Moses carried the lantern ahead of her, escorting her back from the shower in her silk dressing-gown, with a towel tied like a turban around her hair. He had laid out her mess kit for her, khaki slacks and a Gucci tee-shirt, ostrich-skin mosquito boots, exactly what she would have chosen herself.

Moses washed her soiled clothes every day, and his ironing was crisp perfection. Her slacks crackled softly as she pulled them on. They added to her sense of well-being.

She took her time drying her hair and brushing it out. She used an artistic trace of make-up and lipstick, and when she looked in the small mirror, she felt even better.

'Who's the vain one now?' she smiled at herself, and went out to where the men were already at the camp-fire, gratified when they stopped talking, and watched her make her entrance. Sean rose from his camp chair to greet her with those silly limey manners that disconcerted her.

'Sit down!' She tried to sound brusque. 'You don't have to keep jumping up and down.'

Sean smiled easily. 'Don't let her see how she is succeeding in getting up your nose,' he warned himself, and he held the canvas camp chair for her while she sat down with the soles of her mosquito boots to the camp-fire.

'Get the Donna a peg,' Sean ordered the mess waiter. 'You know the way she likes it.'

The waiter brought it to her on a silver tray. It was perfect. A dash of Chivas whisky in a crystal glass, barely enough to colour the Perrier water, and filled right up with ice. The waiter was dressed in a snowy white kanza robe, the hem well below his knee, a scarlet sash over his shoulder to denote that he was the head waiter, and a scarlet pillbox fez on his head. His two assistant waiters stood respectfully in the background, also in scarlet fez and flowing white robes. For Claudia it was mildly embarrassing, there were twenty servants to care for three of them, all so sybaritic and colonial and exploitative. This was 1987, for God's sake, and the empire was long gone – but the whisky was delicious.

'I suppose you expect me to thank you for saving my life,' she said, as she sipped it.

'Not at all, ducky.' Sean had learned almost immediately that she hated that form of address. 'I wouldn't even expect you to apologize for your crass stupidity. To be quite frank with you, I was worrying more about having to kill the lioness. Now that would have been tragic.'

They fenced lightly, skilfully, and Claudia found herself enjoying it. Every thrust that went through his guard gave her a satisfied glow, better even than a good day in court. She was disappointed when the head waiter announced in sepulchral tones, 'Chef say dinner she is ready, Mambo,' and Sean led them into the dining tent that was lit by candles in a many-branched Meissen porcelain candelabra. The cutlery was solid silver, Claudia had furtively checked the hallmarks, and the Waterford crystal wine-glasses sparkled on the table-cloth of Madeira lace-work and a robed waiter stood behind each of their folding canvas safari chairs, ready to serve.

'What do you fancy tonight, Capo?' Sean asked.

'A touch of Wolfgang Amadeus,' Riccardo suggested, and Sean pressed the 'play' button on the tape-deck before going to his seat, and the limpid strains of Mozart's piano concerto number seventeen shimmered in the candlelight.

The soup was made with green peas and pearl barley and buffalo marrow bones, spiced with a fearsome chili sauce that Sean called *Peli Peli Ho Ho*.

Claudia had inherited her father's taste for chili and garlic and red wine, but even she could not face the second course, buffalo tripes in a white sauce. Both men liked their tripes green, which was simply a euphemism for improperly cleaned of the original contents.

'It's only chewed grass,' her father had pointed out, which made her feel squeamish until she turned and caught a whiff of the special dish that chef had prepared for her alone. Beneath a golden pie crust steamed a savoury stew of antelope fillets and kidneys. Chef had shaken his tall white cap when she had suggested the addition of ten cloves of garlic.

'Cook book say no garlic, Donna.'

'My book say plenty garlic, it say very loud ten cloves garlic, okay, chefie?' And the chef had grinned in capitulation.

23

Claudia had almost instantly overwhelmed the entire camp staff with her easy manner and relaxed charm.

The wine was a rich and robust South African Cabernet, every bit as good as her favourite Chianti, and she gave both wine and pie her full attention. The day's rigours and the sun and fresh air had honed her appetite. Like her papa, she could eat and drink freely without adding an ounce of flesh or fat to her waistline. Only the conversation was a disappointment. As on every other evening the men were talking about rifles and hunting and the killing of wild animals. The gun talk was mostly unintelligible gibberish to her.

Her father said things like 'The .300 Weatherby can move a 180-grain bullet at 3200 foot per second, that gives you over 4000 foot/lb of muzzle energy and stupendous hydro-static shock.'

And Sean would respond. 'You Yanks are obsessed with velocity. Roy Weatherby has blown up more bullets on African game than you have eaten spaghetti, Capo. Give me high sectional density, Nosler construction and moderate velocity . . .'

No normally intelligent person could keep that up for hour after hour, she told herself, and yet every night of the safari so far she had gone to bed and left the two of them at the camp-fire still at it over their cognac and cigars.

When they spoke of the animals, however, she could take more interest and even participate, usually to vent her disapproval. They talked mostly of particular individual animals, legendary old males for which Sean had pet names, which annoyed Claudia, just the way it irritated her when he called Papa 'Capo', as though he were a mafia don. One such animal he referred to as 'Frederick the Great', or simply 'Fred'. This was the lion they were hunting now, the lion for which they had hung the buffalo carcass.

'I've seen him twice so far this season, one client even had a shot at him. Mind you, he was shaking so much with nerves he missed him by a football field.'

'Tell me about him,' Riccardo leaned forward eagerly.

'Papa, he told you about him last night,' Claudia reminded him sweetly. 'And the night before, and the night before that. . . .'

'Little girls should be seen and not heard,' Riccardo chuckled. 'Didn't I ever teach you anything? Tell me about Fred, again.'

'He's got to be well over eleven foot, and not just length. He's got a head on him like a hippo, and a mane like a black haystack. When he walks, it ripples and tosses like the wind in a msasa tree,' Sean rhapsodized. 'Cunning? Sly? Fred knows it all, he's been shot at at least three times that I know of. Wounded once by a Spanish hunter over in Ian Piercy's concession three seasons ago, but he recovered. He didn't get that big by being stupid.'

'How are we going to get him?' Riccardo demanded.

'I think the two of you are disgusting,' Claudia cut in before Sean could reply. 'After seeing those glorious creatures today, those beautiful little cubs. How can you bring yourself to kill them?'

'I didn't see any cubs shot today,' Riccardo remarked as he nodded to the waiter offering him another helping of tripe. 'In fact, we went to a great deal of trouble and risk to ensure their survival.'

'You are devoting forty-five days of your life to the sole purpose of killing lions and elephants!' Claudia shot back. 'So don't get all righteous with me, Riccardo Monterro.'

'I am always fascinated by the confused thought processes of your average shrieking liberal,' Sean intervened and Claudia turned on him gleefully, lusting for battle.

'There is no confusion in my mind. You are here to kill animals.'

'The same way that a farmer kills animals,' Sean agreed. 'To ensure a healthy flourishing herd, and a place for that herd to survive.'

'You are not a farmer.'

'Oh yes, I am,' Sean contradicted. 'The only difference is that I slaughter them on the range, not in an abattoir, but like any farmer, my chief concern is the survival of my breeding-stock.'

'They are not domestic animals,' Claudia contested. 'Those are beautiful wild animals.'

'Beautiful? Wild? What the hell has that got to do with it? Like anything else in this modern world, the wild game of Africa has to pay its way if it's going to survive. Capo, here, is paying tens of thousands of dollars to hunt a lion and an elephant. He is giving those animals a monetary value far above goats and cattle, so that the newly independent government of Zimbabwe is willing to set aside concessions of millions of acres in which the game can persist. I hire one of those concessions, and I have the strongest incentive in the world for protecting it from the grazers and poachers and making certain I have plenty of game to offer my hunters. No, ducky, legal safari hunting is one of the most effective arms of conservation in Africa today.'

'So you are going to save the animals by shooting them with high-powered rifles?' Claudia demanded scornfully.

'High-powered rifles?' Sean laughed softly. 'Another emotive liberal parrot cry. Would you prefer us to use low-powered rifles? Won't that be rather like demanding that the butcher uses only blunt knives to cut throats? You are an intelligent woman, think with your head, not your heart. The individual animal is unimportant. His life span is limited to a few short years. In the case of this lion we are hunting, probably twelve years at the very most. What is beyond price is the continued existence of the species as a whole. Not the individual, but his entire kind. Our lion is an old male at the very end of his useful life span during which he has protected his females and his young and already added his genes to the pool of his race. He will die naturally within the next year or two. Much better that his death produce ten thousand dollars in cash which will be spent on providing a safe place for his cubs to live, than having this wilderness encroached upon by swarming black humanity and their scrawny herds of goats.'

'My God, listen to you.' Claudia shook her head sadly. '"Swarming black humanity", those are the words of a racist and a bigot. It's their land, why can't they be free to live where they choose?'

'And that is the logic of woolly-headed liberalism,' Sean laughed. 'Make up your mind whose side you are on, the beautiful wild animals or the beautiful wild blacks. You can't have it both ways; when the two come into competition for living space, the wild animals always come off losers, unless we hunters can pay the bill for them.'

He wasn't an easy man to argue with, she conceded, and she was relieved when her father cut in and gave her a moment to gather her wits.

'There can be no doubt on which side my darling daughter stands. After all, Sean, you are talking to a senior member of the commission for the reinstatement of the Inuit people to their traditional lands.'

She smiled at him sweetly. 'Not Inuit, Papa. People will think you are going soft. Not even Eskimos – your usual description is gooks, isn't it?'

Riccardo smoothed back the thick waves of silver at his temples. 'Shall I tell you how my daughter and her commission go about determining how much of Alaska belongs to the Inuits?' he asked.

'He's going to tell you anyway.' Claudia leaned across to stroke her father's hand. 'It's one of his party routines. It's very funny, you'll love it.'

Riccardo went on as though she had not spoken. 'They go down Fourth Street, in Anchorage, that's where all the bars are, and they grab a couple of Eskimos that are still on their feet. They put them in an airplane and fly them down the peninsula, and they say to them: "Now, tell us where

27

your people used to live. Show us your traditional tribal hunting grounds. How about that lake over there, did your people fish there once upon a time?"' Riccardo changed his voice, he was an excellent mimic. '"Sure!!" says the Eskimo in the back seat, squinting out the window, his eyes full of Jack Daniels. "That's where my gran-pappy fished."'

He changed voices, imitating Claudia. '"And what about those mountains over there, the one which we wicked white folk who stole it away from you call Brooks Range, did your gran-pappy ever hunt there?"' He changed to his Eskimo intonation. '"Sure did, man. He shot a whole mess of bears there. I remember my gran-mommy telling me about it."'

'Go on, Papa. You've got a marvellous audience tonight. Mr Courtney is enjoying your wit hugely,' Claudia encouraged him.

'You know something?' Riccardo asked, 'Claudia has never yet had an Eskimo turn down a lake or a mountain she has offered him, isn't that something else? My little girl has got a perfect score, never a single refusal.'

'You are just plain lucky, Capo,' Sean told him. 'At least they might leave you something, here they took the lot.'

Claudia woke to the clink of crockery outside the flap of her tent and Moses' polite cough. Nobody had ever brought her tea in bed before. It was a luxury that made her feel marvellously decadent. It was still pitch dark and icy cold in the tent. She could hear the crackle of frost on the canvas as Moses opened the flap. She had never expected it to be so cold in Africa.

She sat up in the camp-bed with a quilt over her shoulders, cupping her hands around the tea mug and watched Moses fussing about the tent. He poured a bucket of hot water into her wash basin and set a clean white towel beside it. He filled the tooth mug with boiled drinking water and squeezed toothpaste onto her brush for her. Then he brought a brazier of burning charcoal and placed it in the centre of the tent.

'Too cold today, Donna.'

'And too damned early,' Claudia agreed sleepily.

'Did you hear the lions roaring last night, Donna?'

'I didn't hear a thing.' She yawned. They could have had a brass band playing 'America, the Beautiful' beside her bed without waking her.

Moses finished laying out her clothes on the spare bed. He had polished her boots until they shone.

'You want something, Donna, you call me,' he told her as he backed out of the tent flap.

She shot out of the warm bed and stood over the brazier shivering while she held her panties over the coals to warm them before pulling them on.

The stars were still shining when she left the tent. She paused to look up, still amazed by the jewelled treasure chest of the southern sky. She picked out the great cross with a sense of achievement and then went to the camp-fire where the men were, and held her hands out gratefully to the flames.

'You haven't changed since you were little.' Her father smiled at her. 'Do you remember how I used to battle to get you out of bed to go to school every morning?' And a waiter brought her a second cup of tea.

Sean whistled and she heard Job start the Toyota and drive it around to the front gate of the stockade, and they began pulling on their heavy gear. Jerseys and anoraks, caps and woollen scarves.

When they trooped out to the hunting car, they found the rifles in the racks and Job and Shadrach, the two Matabeles, standing in the back with the little Ndorobo tracker between them. The tracker was a childlike figure who came only to Claudia's armpit, but he had an endearing wrinkled grin and bright mischievous eyes. She had been predisposed to like all the black camp staff, but Matatu was already her favourite. He reminded her of one of the dwarfs from *Snow White*. The three blacks were bundled up against the cold in army-surplus greatcoats and knitted Balaclava caps, and they answered Claudia's greeting with white grins in the darkness. All of them had fallen under her spell.

Sean took the wheel and Claudia sat on the front seat between him and her father. She crouched down behind the windscreen and cuddled against Papa for warmth. In the short time she had been on safari, she had come to love this start to the day's adventure.

They drove slowly over the winding bumpy track and as the night retreated before the advance of dawn, Sean switched off the headlights.

Claudia peered into the combretum forest and down the grassy glades that intersected it that Sean called 'vleis', trying to be the first to spot some elusive and lovely creature, but always Sean or her father murmured first, 'Kudu on the left' or 'That's a reed-buck', or Matatu leaned over from the back to tap her shoulder and point out a rarer sight with his tiny pink-palmed hand.

The dusty track was pocked with the spoor of the animals that had crossed in the night. Once they came across the fresh droppings of an elephant, still steaming in the chill of dawn, a knee-high pile which everybody climbed out of the Toyota to examine closely. At first, Claudia had been disconcerted by this avid interest in dung, but now she was accustomed to it.

'Old beggar,' Sean said. 'On his last set of teeth.'

'How do you know that?' she demanded.

'Can't chew his food,' he replied. 'Look at the twigs and leaves in the dung, almost whole.'

Matatu was crouched by the spoor, examining the great round footprints, the size of dustbin-lids.

'See how smooth the pads of his feet are,' Sean told her. 'Worn down like an old set of car tyres. Old and big.'

'Is it him?' Riccardo asked eagerly, and glanced at the .416 Rigby rifle in the gun-rack behind his seat.

'Matatu will tell us,' Sean shrugged, and the little Ndorobo spat in the dust, and shook his head mournfully as he stood up. Then he spoke to Sean in piping falsetto Swahili.

'It's not the one we want. Matatu knows this bull,' Sean translated. 'We saw this one last year down near the river. He has one tusk broken off at the lip, and the other is worn down to a stump. He might once have had a magnificent pair, but he's far over the other side of the hill now.'

'You mean Matatu can recognize a particular elephant by his footprints?' Claudia looked incredulous.

'Matatu can recognize a particular buffalo out of a herd of five hundred, and he'll know that animal again two years later just by a glance at the spoor.' Sean exaggerated a little for her. 'Matatu isn't a tracker, he's a magician.'

They drove on with small wonders occurring all around them: a kudu bull, grey as a ghost, striped with chalky lines, maned and hump-backed, his long corkscrew horns glinting in the gloom, slipped away into the forest; a genet cat caught out from his nocturnal prowling, spotted and golden as a miniature leopard, peering at them with astonishment from the brown grass of the verge. A kangaroo rat hopped ahead of the Toyota. Troops of chittering guinea fowl with waxen yellow helmets on their heads ran through the grass beside the track and Claudia no longer had to ask, 'What is that bird?' or 'What animal is that?' She was beginning to recognize them and this added to her pleasure.

Just before the sunrise, Sean parked the Toyota at the foot of a rocky hill that rose abruptly out of the forest and they climbed out stiffly and took off their heavy outer clothing. They climbed the side of the kopje, three hundred feet of steep uneven pathway, without a pause, and Claudia tried to disguise her ragged breathing as they came out on the summit. Sean had timed the ascent perfectly, and as

31

they reached the top, the sun burst out of the distant forest and lit it all with dramatic colour and brilliance.

They looked out over a panorama of forest and glade that glowed with golden grass to other high sheer kopjes standing like fairy castles, all turreted and towered in the dawn. Other hills were great dumps of black rock, like the rubble left over from the Creation.

They shed their sweaters, for the climb had warmed them and even the first rays of the sun held the promise of the noonday heat and they sat on the front edge of the hill and played their binoculars over the forest below. Behind them, Job laid out the food box that he had carried up and in minutes, he had a fire going. It had been too early to eat breakfast before they left camp, but now at the odour of frying bacon and eggs, Claudia felt her saliva flooding.

While they waited for their breakfast, Sean pointed out the terrain. 'That is the Mozambique border over there, just beyond the second kopje, only seven or eight miles from here.'

'Mozambique,' Claudia murmured, peering through her binoculars. 'The name has such a romantic ring to it.'

'Not so romantic. It's just another triumph of African socialism and the carefully thought-out economic policy of chaos and ruination,' Sean grunted.

'I can't take racism before breakfast,' Claudia told him icily.

'All right,' Sean grinned. 'Suffice it to say that just across the border there you have twelve years of Marxism, corruption, greed and incompetence, just beginning to bear fruit. You have a civil war raging out of control, famine that will probably starve a million people, and epidemic disease, including Aids, that will kill another million in the next five years.'

'Sounds like a fun place for a vacation,' Riccardo said. 'How about breakfast. Job?'

Job brought them plates of eggs and bacon and fried

French bread followed by mugs of strong aromatic coffee. They ate off their laps, glassing the forest through their binoculars between mouthfuls.

'You are a pretty good cook, Job,' Claudia told him.

'Thank you, ma'am,' Job answered quietly. He spoke English with only a slight accent. He was a man in his late thirties, with a tall and powerful physique and wide-spaced intelligent eyes in the handsome moon face typical of the Matabele and their Zulu origins.

'When did you learn?' Claudia asked, and the Matabele hesitated and glanced at Sean before he said in his deep soft voice, 'In the army, ma'am.'

'Job was a captain in the Ballantyne Scouts with me,' Sean explained.

'A captain!' Claudia exclaimed, 'I didn't realize that . . .' she broke off quickly, looking embarrassed.

'You didn't realize there were black officers in the Rhodesian army,' Sean finished for her. 'There is a lot more to know about Africa than what they show you on CBS television.'

Shadrach, the second gunbearer, was sitting fifty yards farther along the crest, where he had a better view towards the north, and now he whistled softly and pointed up that way. Sean wiped the last of the egg yolk off his plate with the toast and stuffed it in his mouth. He passed the plate to Job. 'Thanks, Job, that was great.' And went to join Shadrach. The two of them peered down into the forest.

'What is it?' Riccardo called impatiently.

'Elephant,' Sean replied, and both Riccardo and Claudia sprang up and hurried to join them.

'Where? Where?' she demanded.

'Big one?' Riccardo asked. 'Can you see his tusks? Is it him?'

'Too far to be sure, a couple of miles.' Sean pointed out the indistinct grey blur amongst the trees and Claudia was amazed that such a huge animal was so difficult to see. It took some minutes before it moved slightly and she was able to pick it out.

'What do you think?' Riccardo asked. 'Could it be Tukutela?'

'It could be,' Sean nodded. 'But it's a thousand to one against it.'

Tukutela. Claudia had listened to them discussing this elephant at the camp-fire. Tukutela, the angry one, was one of those legendary animals of which there were only a handful left in the whole length and breadth of Africa. A bull elephant with tusks that weighed over a hundred pounds each. Tukutela was the main reason that her father had come back to Africa for the last time. For he had once seen Tukutela. Three years before, he had been on safari with Sean Courtney, and the two of them had followed the great elephant for five days. Matatu had led them over a hundred miles on the spoor before they had come up with him. They had stalked to within twenty paces of the enormous and ancient beast as he fed on the fruits of a marula tree. They had studied every wrinkle and crease in his riven grey hide. They were so close that they could have counted the remaining few hairs in his tail, the rest worn away over the years, and they had gazed in silent awe upon his ivory.

Riccardo Monterro would have willingly paid any price to possess those tusks as his own trophy. He had asked Sean in a whisper, 'Isn't there any way I can have him?' And he had seen Sean hesitate before he shook his head.

'No, Capo. We can't touch him. More than my licence and my concession are worth.' For around his neck, Tukutela wore a collar, a sturdy thing of nylon, tough as a heavy-duty truck tyre, and suspended from it was a radio transmitter.

Some years previously, the old bull had been darted from a helicopter by members of the government elephant research project, and while he was unconscious, they had riveted the radio collar around his neck. This made Tukutela a 'designated research animal' and placed him beyond the reach of legal safari hunters. Of course, he was still at risk from ivory poachers, but no licensed hunter could legally hunt him.

While the elephant was under the drug, Dr Glynn Jones, the government veterinarian in charge of the project, had measured his tusks. His report was not for general publication, but his secretary was a nubile blonde who thought that Sean Courtney was the most awe-inspiring thing she had ever seen in her young life. She had duplicated a copy of the report for Sean.

'From Jonesy's measurements, one tusk will weigh 130 pounds and the other a few pounds lighter,' Sean had whispered to Riccardo as they studied the old bull, and they had stared at the tusks hungrily.

At the lip, they were as thick as Sean's thigh and there was no taper to them. They were stained almost black with vegetable juice. The tips were rounded off bluntly, according to Doctor Jones, the left tusk was eight foot four and a half inches, the right tusk eight foot six and a quarter, from lip to tip.

In the end, they had walked away and left the old bull to his solitary wandering, and then only six months ago, the blonde secretary had been making breakfast for Sean in her tiny bachelor flat in the Avenues in Harare, when she mentioned quite casually, 'Did you know that Tukutela has thrown his collar?'

Sean was lying naked on her bed, but he sat up quickly. 'What did you say?'

'Jonesy was in an awful pet. They put the radio direction finder on Tukutela and all they got was his collar. He had managed to tear it off at last and had hurled it into the top of a msasa tree.'

'You clever little beauty,' Sean said happily. 'Come here and get your prize.' And the girl had dropped her dressing-gown on the floor and rushed across the room.

So Tukutela had thrown his collar, and was no longer a

'designated research animal'. Once again, he was legal game. That same day, Sean had sent a cable to Riccardo in Alaska, and received the reply the following afternoon.

'I'M COMING STOP BOOK ME FULL SAFARI 1ST JULY TO AUGUST 15TH STOP I WANT THAT JUMBO STOP CAPO'

And now, as Riccardo stood on the crest of the kopje, studying that far-off smudge of elephant grey in the forest below, he was shaking with excitement.

Claudia studied him with open amazement. This was her father, the coolest cat in the business, the master of *savoir faire*. She had seen him negotiating a ten-million-dollar contract and betting a prince's ransom across the tables at Vegas, without any visible emotion, but here he was shivering with excitement like a schoolboy on his first date, and she felt a rush of affection for him.

'I haven't understood just how much this means to him,' she thought. 'Perhaps I am being too hard. This is the last thing in his life that he truly wants.' And she wanted to put her arms around him and hug him and tell him, 'I'm sorry, Papa. I'm sorry that I have been trying to deprive you of this last pleasure.'

Riccardo was not even aware of her existence. 'It could be Tukutela,' he repeated softly, speaking almost to himself, as though he was trying to will it to be so, but Sean shook his head.

'I've got four good trackers watching the river. Tukutela couldn't cross without them knowing, besides it's still too early. I wouldn't expect him to leave the valley until the last waterholes along the escarpment dry up, another week or ten days at the earliest.'

'He could have slipped through.' Riccardo ignored his explanation. 'It's just possible that it is him down there.'

'We'll go down and take a look, of course,' Sean nodded in agreement. Riccardo's passion did not amaze him as it had his daughter. He understood it totally, had seen it in fifty other men like Riccardo, the powerful, aggressive, successful men, who made up his clientele, men who did not try to conceal or check their instincts. The hunting imperative was part of every man's soul; some denied or suppressed it, others diverted it into less blatantly violent avenues of expression, wielding clubs on the golf course or racquets on the court, substituting a little white ball for the prey of flesh and blood, but men like Riccardo Monterro gave their passions full rein and would settle for nothing less than the ultimate thrill of the chase and the kill.

'Shadrach, bring the *Bwana's* .416 *banduki*,' Sean called. 'Job, don't forget the water-bottles. Matatu, *akwendi*, let's go!'

They went directly down the steep front slope of the kopje, leaping lightly from boulder to boulder, and at the bottom, they dropped naturally into their running formation with Matatu leading to pick up the spoor, followed by Job and Sean with their almost supernatural eyesight to sweep the forest ahead, the clients in the middle, and Shadrach in the drag to hand Riccardo the Rigby when he needed it. They went swiftly, but it was almost an hour through the forest before Matatu picked up the huge dished spoor in the soft earth, and the litter of stripped twigs and branches that the elephant had strewed behind him as he fed. Matatu stopped on it, turning back to roll his eyes, and give shrill piping cries of disgust.

'It's not Tukutela. It's the old one-tusk bull,' Sean told them. 'The same one whose spoor we saw on the road this morning. He has circled back this way.'

Claudia watched her father's face and saw the intensity of his disappointment, and felt her heart squeeze for him.

Nobody spoke on the march back to the Toyota, but when they reached it, Sean said softly, 'You knew it wasn't going to be that easy, didn't you, Capo.' And they grinned at each other.

'You're right, of course. The chase is everything. Once you kill, it's only dead meat.'

'Tukutela will come,' Sean promised him. 'This is his

regular beat. He'll be here before the new moon, that's my promise to you, but in the meantime there is the lion. We will go check bait to see if Frederick the Great is going to oblige us.'

It was only another twenty minutes' driving to the dry riverbed below the hide and the buffalo bait. They left the Toyota parked on the white sand, and Claudia felt a tremor of last night's terror as they climbed the path up the far bank and saw the pad marks of the lioness in the earth behind the hide. Then Sean and his gunbearers were talking excitedly and Matatu was chittering like an agitated guinea fowl.

'What is it?' Claudia demanded, but nobody answered her and she had to trot to keep up with them as they hurried down the open tunnel through the bush to where the remains of the carcass hung in the wild fig.

'Somebody tell me what's happening,' Claudia begged them, but she stayed well back from the bait. The stench was just too much for her to bear. The men showed no distaste at all as they prodded and peered at the reeking remains, and even Claudia could see the difference from the previous evening.

Yesterday, the carcass had been virtually untouched, now more than half of it had been devoured. Only the head and forequarters remained, and Sean had to stretch up above his head to reach it. The bones of spine and ribs had been chewed to splinters, and the thick black skin ripped by claw and fang, so that it hung in tatters like a funeral flag.

While Sean and the gunbearers examined the carcass, Matatu searched the earth around the base of the fig tree, giving excited little yaps like a hound questing for the scent. Sean picked something off the jagged white ribs of the carcass and showed it to Riccardo, and both of them laughed excitedly, passing whatever it was from hand to hand.

'Won't somebody talk to me, please?' Claudia insisted, and Sean called to her.

'Come on then, don't stand so far away.'

Reluctantly, holding her nose theatrically, she approached and Sean held out his right hand to her, palm up. On it lay a single hair, almost as long and black as one from her own head.

'What is it?'

Riccardo took the hair from Sean's hand, holding it between thumb and forefinger, and Claudia saw that the back of her father's arms were goose-bumped with excitement, and his dark Italian eyes glowed as he replied.

'Mane hair.'

Then he seized her hand and pulled her across to the base of the fig tree.

'Take a look at that. Look what Matatu has found for us.'

The little tracker was grinning with proprietorial pride as he indicated the churned earth. Five cubs and two lionesses had trampled the soft footing into talcum dust, but one perfect print stood out in the confusion. It was double the size of the other smudged prints, as big as a soup plate, and, looking at it, Claudia felt again the stirring of terror. Whatever animal had left that pad mark must be monstrous.

'Last night, after the lionesses had seen us off, he came. He waited until the moon had set and he came in the darkest hours of the night,' Sean explained. 'And he left again before dawn. He ate damned nigh half a buffalo, and then he took off again before first light. I told you that he is a cunning old devil.'

'A lion?' Claudia asked.

'Not just any old lion.' Riccardo shook his head. 'Frederick the Great has come at last.'

Sean turned away and beckoned his men to come to him. The three of them, Job and Shadrach and Matatu, squatted around him in a circle and Claudia and Riccardo were forgotten as they planned the hunt, working out their tactics, discussing in detail every aspect, every eventuality. Their concentration was absolute, and it was an hour before

39

Sean stood up and came to where Riccardo and Claudia sat in the shade.

'The trick is going to be getting him to come in before nightfall,' he told them. 'And we all agree that the only way to do that is to set up a fresh bait for him and build a new hide. The lionesses have rumbled this one, and old Fred is going to be as suspicious as all hell. He's going to lurk out there until well after dark or until we can entice him in somehow.'

Sean sat down between them, and was silent for a moment.

'You know, Capo, sometimes for a good friend, someone I can trust, I am prepared to bend the rules a little.' He spoke deliberately, drawing with a twig in the dirt between his feet, and not looking at Riccardo.

'I'm listening,' Riccardo nodded.

'There may be only one way that we will get this lion,' Sean said softly. 'Jack-light him.'

They were silent for a long time, and though Claudia did not know what 'Jack-light' meant, she realized that Sean was suggesting something beyond law or decency, and that her father was tempted. She was angry with Sean for putting temptation in her father's way, but she knew better than to intervene. She kept silent and willed her father to refuse to give in to temptation.

Riccardo shook his head. 'No, let's do it right.'

'We can try,' Sean shrugged. 'But he has been shot at over a bait, and wounded once. It won't be easy.'

They were silent again for almost a full minute, then Sean went on, 'The lion is a nocturnal animal. The night is his time. If you truly want this lion, I think you'll have to take him in darkness.'

Riccardo sighed, and shook his head. 'I want him very badly, but not badly enough to kill him without respect.'

Sean stood up. 'It's your safari, Capo,' he agreed quietly. 'I just want you to know that there are not many men I'd make that offer to. As a matter of fact, offhand I can't think of anyone else I'd do it for.'

'I know,' Capo said. 'Thank you, Sean.' And Sean walked back to the fig tree to help his men to lower the remains of the carcass so the pride could reach it.

As soon as he was out of earshot, Claudia asked her father, 'Jack-light? What is that?'

'Putting a spotlight on an animal after dark, and shooting it in the beam. It's illegal, highly illegal.'

'The bastard,' she said bitterly.

Riccardo did not react to her denunciation, but went on softly, 'He was prepared to put his career on the line for me. That's one of the best things anyone has ever done for me.'

'I'm proud that you refused him, Papa, but he is a bastard.'

'You don't understand,' he said, 'You can't possibly understand.' He stood up and walked away, and immediately she felt a throb of guilt. She did understand. She understood that this was his last lion, and that she was spoiling the pleasure of it for him. She was torn between her love for him, and her protective instinct for that marvellous animal and her sense of right and justice.

'It should be easy to do the right thing,' she thought. 'But it so seldom is.'

So over the days that followed, they hunted the old lion with ethical tactics. They had to provide fresh baits for him and the lionesses, and Riccardo shot the buffalo Sean pointed out to him, another barren cow, and then two days later, a decrepit bull with horns worn down to stumps and his ribs showing through his bald mud-caked hide.

Each day Sean moved the bait or repositioned the thatched hide, trying to find a location which the black-maned male would feel sufficiently confident to approach in broad daylight. Evening after evening, they sat in the hide until an hour after darkness had fallen and then drove back to camp dejected and discouraged. When they visited the bait again the following morning they found that the lion had fed, leaving his mane hairs and his huge pad-marks to tantalize them, and had departed again before dawn.

Cursing the beast bitterly. Sean changed tactics. He lowered the remains of the rotten bait on its chain so that lionesses and cubs could reach it readily. By this stage, it was mostly dried skin and gnawed bone. Five hundred metres up the river, he hung a fresh carcass, at a height that only the big lion could reach in a tree that stood alone in a glade of shoulder-high dry winter grass. He hoped that without the harassment of the females and cubs the lion might come earlier to the bait.

To make him feel even more secure, he placed the hide across the dry riverbed in the fork of a teak tree. It was a machan platform fifteen feet above ground level. From the machan, they had a view across the white sand of the dry riverbed.

Sean did not clear all the grass around the bait tree. He wanted the lion to feel protected by good cover. He merely opened a keyhole in the grass, barely as wide as the body of the lion, through which they could see the carcass.

'If he comes, you'll have to wait until he rears up to feed, Capo,' he explained as they went into the machan an hour after noon, to wait out the long drowsy hot afternoon.

Sean allowed Claudia to bring a paperback copy of Karen Blixen's *Out of Africa* to read.

'Just as long as you don't rustle the pages,' he warned her.

The lionesses and their cubs came early. They were so conditioned to feeding from a bait by now, that they showed not the least trepidation at approaching. First they came to the new bait in the grassy glade, and inspected it wistfully. Both lionesses made attempts to feed from it, but it was just out of their reach.

For the last few days, the eyes of the young lioness, Growly Gertie, had been irritated and infected by the river sand that Sean had fired into them. Tears ran down her cheeks and her eyelids were swollen and inflamed, but now they were healing and clearing, the swelling was abating and there were only smears of yellow mucus in the corners of her eyes.

After a while, they gave up trying to reach the carcass, and led their cubs down the riverbank to the old stinking bait.

From the machan, they could hear the pride growling and ripping at the bait five hundred metres downstream, but as the afternoon passed, so the sounds of feeding dwindled into silence as the lionesses satiated themselves and went to lie up in the shade.

Half an hour before sunset, the small hot breeze that had been blowing all afternoon, dropped abruptly and that peculiar hush of an African evening descended on the veld. The sparse winter growth of leaves on the trees was still, not a blade of yellow grass stirred in the glade across the riverbed, and the fluffy papyrus reeds below the bank ceased their perpetual nodding and bowing and stood as though listening intently. It was so quiet that Claudia looked up from her book, and then closed it softly and sat listening to the absolute silence.

Then suddenly a bush-buck barked on the far bank, an alarm call so clear and loud in the hush that Claudia jumped involuntarily. Immediately, she felt Sean's light firm touch on her hip, a warning, and she heard her father's breathing, quick and deep as though he had just finished a hard rally on the court.

The silence had an ominous weight to it now, as though the world held its breath. Then she heard her father exhale softly, and she glanced sideways at him. His expression was rapt as that of a communicant kneeling for the Sacrament. God, he was a handsome man, she thought. Except for the silver wings at his temples, he looked so much younger than his years, so tanned and lean and fit. As yet, there was no external sign of the treachery of his own body that was destroying itself from within.

His excitement was infectious and she felt her own blood course more swiftly, driven by the quickening of her pulse, and she turned her head slowly to follow the direction of her father's gaze. He was looking off to the right, out across the river, to where the trees of the forest met the tall pale grass at the edge of the glade.

The only living creature out there was a grey parrot-like bird perched on the top branch of a bush willow. Sean had told her it was a grey lourie, the notorious 'go away bird' that plagued the hunter with its raucous warning cry. The bird squawked now, 'G'way! G'way!' But as it fluttered on the high branch, it was twisting its neck, craning to peer down into the long grass below the bush willow.

'Here he comes. The bird can see him,' Sean whispered only inches behind her ear, and Claudia strained her eyes looking for she knew not what.

'Watch the grass,' Sean guided her, and she saw the movement. The tips of the grass trembled and pushed, a stealthy furtive movement that passed slowly down the glade towards the river-bank, and then the grass behind it was still again. It was like the movement of a large trout in a still pool, the creature unseen, just the surface bulging and stirring to mark its passing.

All movement ceased for long minutes at a time.

'He's listening and checking the scent,' Sean explained. She had never expected him to show emotion such as excitement, but his whisper was tight and scratchy.

The movement of the grass tips began again, coming on towards the bait tree, and suddenly her father gave a small breathy gasp, and at the same moment, Sean warned her again. Perhaps he had meant to touch her hip once more, but his fingers closed on her upper thigh instead.

His touch was a shock, made more intense by her first sight of the beast. The lion passed through a gap in the grass, which the lionesses had trampled, and she glimpsed the top of his head, the dense bush of his mane, dark and curling, swaying and rippling to his slow imperial stride, and for an instant she caught the flash of yellow eyes below the mane.

She had never seen any creature so menacing, and yet so majestic. It was the briefest glimpse, before the grass covered him again, but it left her shaken and breathless, and Sean's hand was still on her thigh.

Suddenly, she realized that she was sexually aroused, the tension in her lower belly, the hardening thrust of her nipples against the cotton shirt and the warm flooding of her loins surprised her. She felt an almost irresistible urge to let her thighs relax and fall open under Sean's fingers, even though the folly of it would be monumental. If she had been asked to describe a human being who most offended and angered her, the description would have fitted him perfectly. She knew that if she showed the slightest vulnerability, he would exploit it ruthlessly. 'And I don't even like him,' she told herself desperately. Yet her legs were trembling, he must feel it, and she couldn't move.

Then he took his hand off her leg, but the way he did it was offensive. He did not simply lift it away, he turned it into a caress, drawing his fingers lingeringly over her thigh and hip, a disconcerting sensation for which she was unprepared. She felt her cheeks and her throat turn hot with resentment, but she stared out across the riverbed to that stealthy movement that stopped at last below the bait tree.

The silence drew out while Claudia tried to bring her emotions under control.

'It wasn't him,' she told herself. 'I wasn't reacting to him. He has nothing for me. It was the tension and excitement of the moment, nothing to do with him. He's not the least bit attractive to me. I like sensitivity and subtlety, and he is obvious and overpowering and brutal.'

Across the river, there was an abrupt disturbance in the grass and the sound of a heavy body flopping to earth.

Behind her, she felt Sean shake with soft and silent laughter, and for an incredulous moment, she thought he was laughing at her, then he whispered, 'He's lain down. Can you believe it, he's taking a rest right under the bait. The cocky son-of-a-bitch.'

Sean was thinking about the girl as much as about the lion. The unconcealed antipathy she bore him he returned in full measure, which made it more amusing to tease and plague her. Of course, the lion-hide was always a good place to catch a woman off-balance. He had begun many a memorable affair here. When they were in the hide they were psychologically under his control, like children in a classroom. He was the master and they were conditioned to obey his will, and the tension and nervous excitement made them receptive and compliant, the promise of danger and bloodshed heightened awareness, physical and sexual. It had been fun to find out that this bumptious, spoilt, self-righteous American bitch was no different from any of the others.

She was probably hating herself and him at this moment for that momentary lapse. He smiled thinly as he sat up close behind her. He had judged it with the fine instinct of the gifted philanderer, for it was, of course, a gift. He had read with attention Casanova's memoirs and there the old rogue had described it precisely. When she is receptive, every woman gives out subtle little signs, breathing, flush of skin, change of poise, tiny body movements, even odour, that very few men can even recognize, let alone interpret. It was a gift that only the great lovers possessed. Knowing when to act, and how far to push each stage, that was the trick, he told himself.

From where he sat, he could see her right cheek and the long dark lashes of the eye above, even though she was deliberately keeping her head turned away from him now.

She had bound her jet hair into a thick braid that hung down between her shoulder-blades, so her neck was exposed, an elegant column that supported the small neat head. Her neck and cheek were still flushed with angry arousal beneath skin that was already darkened by the African sun to the tone where she could have modelled for an expensive sun cream in one of the glossy women's magazines.

As he studied her, the flush abated and she regained her composure, but under her thin cotton tee-shirt, the nipple on the one pert, almost girlish, breast that he could see, was in silhouette. It was still standing out, the size and colour of a ripe mulberry, a dark wine colour through the thin material, then it began to shrink and subside; the phenomenon intrigued him and he laughed again soundlessly.

'You've given yourself a blinding hard-on,' he chuckled. 'And you can't even stand the little witch.' He switched his attention from her back to the unseen cat in the grass across the river.

It was almost fully dark before they saw the lion again, there was just a fading memory of the sunset on the western horizon but Sean had positioned the bait and blind so that it back-lit the scene for them. They heard the grass rustle and stir as the lion stood up, and they leaned forward eagerly. Riccardo lifted the buttstock of the rifle to his shoulder and peered into the long tube of the telescopic sight.

Abruptly, the lion reared out of the grass, a great dark, shapeless mass, just visible against the pale sky, and they heard the creak of the chain that held the bait as he swung upon it with all his weight, tearing at the carcass as he began to feed.

'Can you see your sights?' Sean asked Riccardo. The lion was making so much noise that he raised his voice to an almost conversational pitch, but Riccardo did not reply. He was moving the long barrel of the rifle in slow circles, trying desperately to pick up the cross hairs of the sight against the last fading glimmer of the sunset.

'No!' he admitted defeat at last. 'It's too dark.'

Claudia felt a lift of relief that she wouldn't have to

witness the slaughter, but Sean said quietly, 'All right, we'll just have to sit it out and try and get a crack at him in the dawn.'

'All night!' Despite his injunctions to silence, Claudia was so startled by the prospect of spending the night in the hide that she protested plaintively.

'You signed on to be tough, didn't you?' Sean smiled at her alarm.

'But, but . . . won't Job bring the truck?' She sounded desperate.

'Not unless he hears a shot.' And she subsided miserably in her chair.

The night was interminable and cold, and the mosquitos came from the stagnant green pool in the riverbed and whined around their heads, ignoring the repellent that Claudia smeared on her exposed skin.

Across the river, the lion fed at intervals, and then rested. A little after midnight, he began to roar, crashing bursts of sound that brought Claudia out of an uncomfortable doze, and made her heart jump against her ribs. The terrible sound ended in a diminishing series of throaty grunts.

'Why does he do that?' Claudia asked breathlessly.

'To let the world know who is boss around here.'

Then the hyena came, shrieking and hooting like a pack of ghouls, gibbering with excitement at the smell of the kill, and the lion drove them off, rushing heavily in the grass, snarling and roaring, but they came edging back as soon as he returned to feed, and they tittered and whooped at him, forming a restless circle around the bait tree.

An hour before dawn, Claudia at last fell into a fitful sleep, hunched down in the chair with her neck twisted at an awkward angle, and she awoke with a start, to find it was light enough to make out the links of the chain that held the buffalo carcass.

In the forest close by, a pair of ground hornbills, grotesque black birds as big as a wild turkey with the same bald red heads, were booming their dawn chorus in a ritual duet. Beside her, Riccardo was stretching and yawning and Sean stood up, rocking the machan.

'What's happened?' Claudia mumbled. 'Where's the lion?'

'He took off an hour ago,' her father told her. 'Long before shooting light.'

'Only one way you are going to get this cat, Capo, and that's with a jack-light, or with a hell of a lot of luck.'

'I'm a lucky guy,' Riccardo grinned and they heard the distant beat of the Toyota's engine growing louder as Job came in to pick them up.

They stayed in camp all that day, catching up on sleep lost the previous night, but when they went into the hide again that evening to wait for the lion, he had disappeared. He did not come to the bait the following night either, and the safari came upon a period of hiatus. Sean and his team worked diligently but fruitlessly to find the lion. There was no report from the scouts whom Sean had placed to watch the elephant crossings on the Chiwewe river which was the northern boundary of Sean's concession. Riccardo Monterro was not interested in hunting lesser plains game, such as sable antelope, or kudu, or eland. These activities would have filled the days of another safari.

Only the two lionesses and their cubs stayed on the banks of the riverbed taking up permanent domicile.

'Courtney's five-star hotel,' Sean complained. 'Gourmet meals delivered daily.'

The pride became so accustomed to their visits, that the lionesses retreated only a hundred yards or so into the forest with a few perfunctory low-key growls and watched with interest as a fresh carcass was hauled into the tree. They barely contained their impatience until the Toyota pulled away, and it was still in full view when they came loping back to inspect the latest offering.

However, Frederick the Great did not return. They saw no sign of his huge distinctive pugmarks around the baits or upon the dirt tracks that Sean patrolled each day, searching the area for forty miles around the camp.

'But why would he just vanish like that?' Riccardo protested.

'Because he is a cat – and who knows how a cat thinks!'

Since that brief but torrid episode in the lion hide, the relationship between Sean and Claudia had altered subtly. Their bickering had become more vindictive and bitter, their overt resentment more intense, and their efforts to discomfort each more spirited.

When she called him a racist, he smiled at her. 'In America that word is dreaded as the ultimate insult that can end a man's political career, or ruin his business or ostracize him from society. You are all so terrified of it, and the blacks know it and exploit it to the full. Even the toughest hard-headed businessman or politician rolls over like a puppy dog and whines if you call him that,' Sean told her gleefully. 'This isn't America, ducky, and here we aren't terrified of that word. Here racism is the same as tribalism, and we are all blatant tribalists, especially the blacks. If you want to experience true dedicated tribalism and racism, then come and live in one of the newly independent African states. If you call your average black politician a racist, he would take it as a compliment, it would be the same as calling him a patriot.'

Her wounded protestations were ample reward for his efforts as he looked for new ways to provoke her.

'Did you know I am a South African?' he asked, and she looked appalled.

'I thought you were a Brit.' He shook his head and smiled in that infuriating way of his.

'I imagine you support your government's sanctions against my country.'

'Of course, every decent person does.'

'Even if it means that a million blacks starve as a direct consequence?' He did not wait for her to reply. 'What about disinvestment of American business from my country, you are all for that too?'

'I campaigned for it on campus,' she told him proudly. 'I never missed a rally or a march.'

'So your plan is to convert a country by withdrawing all your missionaries and burning down the cathedral, that's brilliant!'

'You are twisting it.'

'We should be grateful to you for the success of your efforts, you forced your own citizens to sell our assets back to us at five cents in the dollar. Overnight you created two hundred multi-millionaires in South Africa, and every one of them had a white face. Congratulations and our sincere thanks, ducky.'

But while they argued, they were avidly aware of each other, and that physical contact they had shared lay between them like a poisonous serpent, dangerous, but intriguing.

Claudia had been celibate for almost two years now, ever since she had split from the physician whom she had lived with for a short while until his demands for marriage became intolerable. Celibacy did not suit her affectionate Latin nature, but she was fastidious. She found herself lying awake in her tent at night listening to Sean's voice from the camp-fire as he talked to her father, the soft masculine rumble, just low enough for her to be unable to catch the words. Once she thought she heard her name, and she sat up and strained her hearing, disappointed that she could not hear what he said about her.

Then, when at last he called goodnight to Riccardo and went to his own tent, he had to pass close to hers. She lay rigid in bed, listening to his footsteps and watching the beam of his flashlight through the canvas, preparing an icy dismissal in the most insulting terms, and then experiencing the tiniest prick of disappointment as his footsteps passed on without a check.

On the ninth morning of the safari when they drove out to check the bait on the riverbank, the younger lioness, her eyes now completely healed, was once again violently aggressive, snarling at Sean and mock-charging him from a hundred yards with her tail lashing as soon as he dismounted from the Toyota to inspect the bait. When she backed off and turned to retreat, they saw the pink stain of blood on the soft, pale beige fur beneath her tail.

'Growly Gertie has come into season,' Sean exulted. 'Now we have the one bait that Frederick the Great won't be able to resist. You said you were a lucky guy, Capo, now let's find out just how lucky.'

Sean wanted to get this lion before this extraordinary opportunity passed, there was no time to track down one of the huge buffalo herds along the Chiwewe river for a fresh bait, so Riccardo shot a young kudu bull from a herd of bachelors near the camp. They hung the carcass on the bait tree in the glade where they had last seen the big male lion; this time, low enough for the lionesses to reach it easily; and they climbed into the machan in the early afternoon. Within an hour the lionesses had picked up the scent of fresh blood and came trotting down the dry riverbed, followed by the straggling, squabbling bunch of cubs. While the older lioness fed heartily from the fresh kudu carcass, the younger female ate only lightly and sporadically. In between she prowled restlessly around the area of trampled grass beneath the tree, snarling at her cubs, or rolling on her back, or sitting up to lick at the blood smear beneath her own tail. At intervals, she stood staring into the forest and then held her head low to the ground and let out a long, melancholy moan. It was a sound so full of agonized longing that Claudia felt herself empathizing with the sleek and beautiful creature.

'That's right, Gertie,' Sean whispered behind Claudia's

shoulder. 'Call to Big Daddy, tell him what sweets you've got for him here.'

'It's not fair,' Claudia thought fiercely. 'It's not fair to use her like this.'

Suddenly both lionesses leapt up to face into the forest, and the older female snarled softly. Alarmed, the cubs ceased their endless play and huddled behind their dams. Then the young lioness went forward through the grass, slinking and undulating her whole body in a blatantly sexual display, and she emitted a series of low welcoming moans.

'Steady, Capo.' Sean's hand was on Riccardo's arm, preventing him from raising the rifle. 'Take your time.'

Then out of the forest came the lion. At first they saw only the tip of his mane above the grass, as he came forward at an eager trot to meet the lioness. She rushed forward shamelessly, and in a trampled clearing they came together.

'Wait, Capo,' Sean whispered. He wanted the girl to watch it.

The lioness brushed her body against the male, back and forth she stroked him with the full length of her silken flanks, and the lion fluffed out his mane, so that he seemed to double in size, responding to her advances, licking her face as she cuddled into the dense dark bush of his mane.

Then deliberately she turned and presented him with her hind quarters, cocking her tail high, sending a spurt of pink-stained urine out under his nose. The lion groaned and curled his upper lip, exposing his great, yellow fangs in a rictus of passion; his back arched reflexively and Claudia wriggled in her seat as the lion stretched out his neck and licked the female under the tail with a long, curling, pink tongue.

The lioness submitted to his caress for a minute, then whirled flirtatiously and, from across the river, they heard her low purrs of invitation. Sean placed his hand lightly on Claudia's thigh. The gesture was concealed from her father by the side of the chair. She made no attempt to pull away.

The lioness turned from the male, ran a few light mincing paces and then flattened her body against the earth, looking back over her shoulder. The lion came to where she lay, moving with a stiff-legged gait, and he covered her body with his own, standing astride her, and as he lowered his haunches over hers, his penis unsheathed from its pouch, glistening pinkly, and the lioness laid her tail forward along her back.

Sean ran the tips of his fingers up to the juncture of Claudia's thighs, and he could feel the springing mattress of her pubic hair through the cloth of her breeches. Her thighs opened slightly under his hand.

The lion humped his back over the female in a series of convulsive, regular spasms, and then he threw back his huge, maned head and roared and the lioness roared with him and he reached down and bit her lightly in the back of the neck, a fond possessive gesture.

For long moments, they were frozen together like that and then the lion leaped off her, and at the same moment, Claudia reached down and placed her hand over Sean's. She took his little finger and twisted it back against the joint so viciously that she almost dislocated it, and agony shot up his arm to the shoulder.

He almost cried out in protest, but Riccardo was sitting close and though his view of his daughter's lower body was obscured by the canvas side of the chair, he would certainly guess at Sean's advances. With an effort, Sean kept silent, and drew his hand back, surreptitiously massaging the damaged finger, and he could see the corner of Claudia's mouth was curled in a vindictive little smile.

Across the river the lioness stood up and shook herself. Then she walked out with a slow satisfied air on to the open riverbank. There she paused and looked back at the lion where he was sitting on his haunches still half hidden in the long grass.

'Get ready, Capo.' Sean was still massaging his finger.

It was five o'clock in the afternoon, and the sun was at a perfect angle, lighting the far bank as though it were a stage. The range was a measured ninety-six yards from the machan to the bait tree. Riccardo Monterro was the finest rifleman that Sean had ever guided on safari. At that range, he could place three bullets through the same hole.

The lioness mewled seductively and the lion stood up and followed her out onto the open riverbank. He stood behind her, broadside on to the machan across the river, lit by the golden sunlight.

'He's a gift from heaven, Capo,' Sean whispered, and tapped Riccardo's shoulder. 'Take him!'

Slowly Riccardo lifted the buttstock of the rifle to his shoulder. It was a .300 Weatherby Magnum. The massive cartridge under the firing-pin was loaded with eighty grains of powder and a 180-grain Nosler partitioned bullet. It would cross the open riverbed at over three thousand feet per second. When it entered living flesh, it would drive a shock wave ahead of it that would turn the internal organs, lungs and heart, to jelly and suck that jelly out of a massive exit hole, blowing them in a red spray over the grass beyond where the animal stood.

'Take him!' Sean said, and Riccardo Monterro looked through the telescopic sight; the lion's body filled most of the magnified field of the lens.

He could see the individual hairs in the dense curling bush of mane, and the detail of each sculptured muscle beneath the skin. One inch behind the lion's shoulder, on the lateral centre line of its body, was a tiny scar on the sleek hide. It was shaped like a horseshoe, a lucky horseshoe, and it made a perfect aiming point. He aligned the cross-hairs of the sight on the scar, and they bounced slightly to the elevated beat of his own heart. He took up the slack in the trigger, feeling the final resistance under his finger before the sear released and the rifle fired.

Beside her father, Claudia sat rigid with horror. The lion

turned his head and looked across the riverbed at her. The mating had touched and moved her deeply.

'He's too glorious to die,' she thought, and almost without conscious effort, she opened her mouth and screamed with all the strength of her lungs.

'Run, damn you! Run!'

The result stunned even her. She had not believed a living creature could react so swiftly. From lazy immobility, all three animals exploded into flight. They dissolved into golden blurs of movement.

The oldest lioness disappeared almost instantaneously into the long grass, with all the cubs rushing after her. The younger lioness raced along the edge of the bank. So swift was her run that she did not seem to touch the earth; like a swallow drinking in flight she skimmed the surface, and the lion followed her. For all his bulk and the dark mass of his mane, he moved as lightly as she did, reaching out those massively muscled legs in full stride.

Riccardo Monterro swivelled in his chair, the rifle to his shoulder, staring into the brilliant glass lens, swinging with the cat's run. The lioness swerved into the grass and was gone. The lion followed her but the instant before he disappeared, the report of the Weatherby rifle drove in on their eardrums, painful and deafening, and even in full sunlight, a long tongue of flame flashed out across the riverbed.

The lion stumbled in his run and with a single, loud cough vanished into the grass. In the silence, their ears sang with the memory of gunfire, and they stared out at the empty clearing, subdued and appalled.

'Nice work, ducky!' Sean said softly.

'I'm not sorry,' she said defiantly, and her father reloaded the rifle with a savage movement that sent the empty brass case spinning and sparkling away in the sunlight. He stood up, rocking the flimsy machan and without a glance at his daughter, climbed down the makeshift ladder.

Sean picked up his .577 double rifle and followed him

down. They stood at the bottom of the tree and Riccardo unbuttoned the flap of his breast pocket and offered Sean a Havana from his pigskin cigar-case. Neither of them usually smoked during the day, but now Sean accepted one and bit off the tip.

They lit their cigars and smoked for a while in silence. Then Sean said quietly. 'Call your shot, Capo.'

Riccardo was a marksman of such expertise that he could tell precisely where his bullet had gone the moment after he fired it. Now he hesitated, and then said grudgingly. 'That cat was motoring. I was too quick. I didn't lead him enough.'

'Gutshot?' Sean asked.

'Yeah,' Riccardo nodded. 'Gutshot.'

'Shit,' said Sean. 'Shit, and shit again.'

They both looked across at the dense stand of long grass and tangled thorny patches of undergrowth on the far bank.

It was ten minutes before the Toyota arrived, summoned by that single gunshot. Job and Shadrach and Matatu were grinning with expectation, they had hunted six safaris with Riccardo Monterro and they had never known him to miss. They jumped out of the Toyota, peered across the river, and their grins faded slowly, and were replaced by expressions of deepest gloom as Sean said, '*Intumbu!* In the guts!'

The three of them went back to the Toyota and began to prepare for the follow-up in silence.

Sean squinted up at the sun. 'Dark in an hour,' he said. 'We haven't got time to let the wound stiffen.'

'We could leave him until the morning,' Riccardo suggested. 'He'll be sick by then.'

Sean shook his head. 'If he dies in there, the hyena will get him. No trophy. Besides which, we can't leave the poor beggar to suffer all night.'

They fell silent as Claudia climbed down the ladder from the machan. When she reached ground level, she would not look at them, but tossed back the plait of dark hair over her shoulder defiantly and marched across to the Toyota. She climbed into the front seat and folded her arms across her small breasts, staring ahead grimly.

'I'm sorry,' Riccardo said. 'I've known her for twenty-six years. I should have guessed she'd pull one like that.'

'You don't have to come, Capo,' Sean did not answer him directly. 'Stay with Claudia. I'll go across and get the job done. That's what you pay me for.'

It was Riccardo's turn to ignore the remark.

'I'll carry the Rigby,' he said.

'Make sure that you are loaded with soft-nosed bullets,' Sean advised.

'Of course.' They walked side by side to the Toyota, and Riccardo changed the lighter Weatherby for the big Rigby. He opened the breech to check that there were soft-nosed mushrooming bullets in the magazine, then filled the loops on his cartridge belt from a fresh packet.

Sean leaned against the side of the Toyota, and changed the cartridges in his big double rifle for others from the loops on the breast of his bush jacket.

'Poor bloody animal,' he said. Although he was looking at Riccardo, he was speaking to Claudia. 'It would have been a good clean kill, but now he's in the grass there, still alive with half his guts shot away. It's the most painful wound there is.' He saw the girl wince and her cheek pale. She would not look at him.

'We'll be lucky if someone doesn't get killed,' Sean went on with ghoulish relish. 'It will probably be Matatu. He has to go ahead on the spoor, and the little beggar always refuses to run. If it's anybody, it will be Matatu that gets it today.'

Despite herself, Claudia glanced piteously at the little Ndorobo.

'Cut it out, Sean,' Riccardo ordered. 'She knows how stupid she has been.'

'Does she?' Sean asked. 'I wonder.' He snapped the rifle

closed. 'Okay, Capo, wear your leather jacket. If the lion gets you down, it may protect you a little, not much, but a little.'

The three blacks were waiting on the edge of the bank. Job carried the eight-bore shotgun loaded with buckshot, but the other two were unarmed. It took a peculiar kind of courage to follow a wounded lion into thick cover without carrying a weapon.

Even in her agitation, Claudia noticed the trust with which they looked at Sean Courtney. She sensed that they had shared mortal danger so many times before that a peculiar bond united their small exclusive group. The four of them were closer than brothers, or lovers, and she felt a sting of envy. She had never been that close to another human being in her life.

In turn Sean touched each of them on the shoulder, a light unsentimental gesture of affirmation, and then he spoke softly to Job. A shadow passed over the Matabele's handsome features, and for a moment it seemed that he might protest, but then he nodded acceptance and crossed to the Toyota, standing guard beside Claudia with the shotgun.

Sean held the double-barrelled rifle across the crook of his arm as he combed his thick glossy hair back from his forehead with his fingers and then bound it up out of his eyes with a strip of plaited leather around his forehead.

Even though she loathed him, she found herself admiring the heroic figure he cut as he made these last preparations to face the terrible danger and gruesome death that she had, in a large measure, prepared for him. The sleeves had been cut out of his bush jacket and he wore short, khaki pants, so that his limbs were bare and tanned. He was even taller than her father, but his waist was slimmer and his shoulders wider, and he carried the squat heavy rifle easily in one hand.

He glanced across at her, and his gaze was level and

green and contemptuous. She was possessed suddenly, by a premonition of impending disaster, and she wanted to plead with him not to cross the river, but before she could speak he had turned away.

'Ready, Capo?' he asked, and Riccardo nodded, holding the Rigby at high port across his chest. His expression was solemn. 'All right, let's move out.' Sean nodded at Matatu and the little man led them down the bank.

In the riverbed, they fell into hunting formation with the tracker leading. Sean followed close behind him watching the reed bed ahead. Riccardo came next, leaving a gap of ten paces between them to reduce the confusion in a close-quarter *mêlée*, and Shadrach followed him in the drag position.

As they crossed, they filled their pockets with smooth water-worn pebbles from the riverbed. Below the far bank, they paused to listen, then Sean passed Matatu and went up first. He stood alone in the trampled clearing below the bait tree for almost five minutes, listening and staring intently into the tall grass beyond.

Then he began to lob pebbles into the grass, systematically working the area where the lion had disappeared. The pebbles clattered against other stones or bounced off the stems of shrubs, but there was no challenging growl. Sean whistled softly and the others scrambled up the bank and fell into their positions, and Sean nodded at Matatu.

They went forward slowly. There are many grave-stones in Africa marking the resting places of men who hurried after a wounded lion. Matatu concentrated all his attention on the ground at his feet. He never looked up at the wall of grass ahead. He placed his complete trust in Sean. At the edge of the grass, he hissed softly and with his hand behind his back made a secretive gesture.

'Blood,' Sean told Riccardo softly without looking back at him. 'And belly hair. You were right, Capo. It's a gutshot.'

He could see the wet gleam of blood on the stems of the grass.

'*Akwendi!*' he told Matatu, and drew breath like a diver poised on a cliff above a deep and icy pool. He held that breath as he stepped forward and the tall grass closed around him, limiting his vision like the sinister and murky waters of the pool.

The impact of the bullet had been a mighty blow in the lion's flank, that slewed him round and numbed his entire body behind his rib-cage.

Then the grass closed about him as he raced forward, and immediately he felt secure and confident. Within twenty strides he stopped and stood looking back over his shoulder, listening and drawing the scent into his flared nostrils, lashing his tail from side to side.

There was no sensation of pain, just a numbness and weight in his entrails as though he had swallowed an iron-stone boulder. He smelled his own blood, and turned to sniff at his side. The exit wound the bullet had left was the size of an egg cup and from it oozed blood that was almost tarry black. Mingled with the blood, were the liquid contents of his own bowels. They made a tiny pattering sound as they dribbled onto the dry earth beneath him. He licked at the wound and blood glutted his jaws.

Then he lifted his head and listened again. He heard human voices in the distance, beyond the river and he growled softly, feeling his anger begin to mount, associating the blood and heaviness in his belly with the presence of man.

Then the lioness called him, a low gasping moan, and he turned and followed her. He did not run now for the weight in his belly hampered him and his back legs felt numb and heavy. The lioness was waiting for him a little farther on. Eagerly she rubbed herself against him, and then tried to lead him away, trotting off ahead of him. He moved heavily after her, stopping to listen and lick the running wound, and she turned back impatiently and moaned at him and nuzzled his face, sniffing and licking at his wound, puzzled and distressed by his behaviour.

His legs were heavy as tree-trunks now, and ahead of him was a thicket of wild ebony. He turned aside and pushed his way into the dense and tangled undergrowth, and he sighed as he lowered his body, curling the black tuft of his tail under him as he lay down.

The lioness fretted and worried at the edge of the thicket, calling to him with small mewling entreaties. Then when he did not respond, she followed him into the thicket and lay down beside him. She licked at his wound and the lion closed his eyes, and began to pant softly as the pain began.

The pain swelled in his body becoming a vast, suffocating weight that grew and grew within him, seeming to distend his belly until it was on the point of bursting. The lion groaned softly and bit at his own flank, trying to kill this thing within him, this living agony that was feeding on his entrails.

The lioness attempted to distract him. She was confused and worried, and she wriggled around and pressed her hind-quarters into his face, offering him her swollen and weeping genitalia, but the lion closed his eyes and turned his head away, and each breath rasped like a wood saw in his throat.

Then he heard voices again, the whispered voices of men, and he raised his head and his eyes burned yellow and fierce as he found a focus for his suffering, and hatred grew out of the agony of his belly, and his rage was dark and all-engulfing.

Something crashed into the branches of the wild ebony thicket above his head and he growled, a rattling exhalation of air through his tortured throat.

*

They went forward slowly into the grass, and it reached above their heads, and enclosed them so closely that they could see no more than two or three paces ahead. The lion's blood was painted on the grass and the stems were pushed over by the passage of his body so the trail was easy to follow. The blood on the grass gave Sean and Matatu the exact height of the wound, and the faeces mixed with the blood told them that the bowels had been penetrated. It was a mortal wound, but death would be slow and agonizing.

Within twenty yards of entering the grass, Matatu paused, and indicated the puddle of dark, tarry blood.

'He stopped here,' he whispered, and Sean nodded.

'He won't have gone far,' Sean guessed. 'He's waiting for us, Matatu, and when he comes, you run back behind me. Do you hear me?'

Matatu grinned at him. They both knew he would not obey. Matatu had never run, he would stand the charge as he always did.

'All right, you stupid little bugger.' Sean was tense. 'Get on with it.'

'Stupid little bugger,' Matatu repeated happily. He knew that Sean only called him that when particularly proud of him, or pleased with him.

They moved along the blood spoor, pausing every three or four paces while Sean lobbed pebbles into the grass ahead of them, and when there was no response, moving forward again cautiously.

Behind him, Sean could hear the click, click of the safety-catch on the Rigby. Riccardo was snapping it on and off as they advanced, a nervous gesture that betrayed his agitation. Although the sound irritated him, Sean felt a stir of admiration for the man. This was probably one of the most dangerous activities in which a man could engage. They don't come much worse than a gut-shot lion in close cover. This was Sean's job, but for Riccardo, it was a once in a lifetime test, and he had not failed it yet.

Sean tossed another pebble into the grass ahead, and listened to it rattle on the branch of a low tree.

As they went on, Sean thought about fear. For some men, fear was a crippling and destroying emotion, but for those like Sean, it was an addiction. He loved the sensation of fear, it was like a drug flowing through his veins, heightening all his senses, so he could feel the chequering on the polished walnut stock of the rifle under his fingers and the brush of each individual blade of grass against his bare legs; his vision was so enhanced that he saw it all through a crystal lens that magnified and dramatized each image, he could taste the very air he breathed and smell the crushed grass under his feet and the blood of the lion they were following. He was vividly, vibrantly alive, and he gave himself up to fear, as an addict would to a syringeful of heroin.

He tossed another pebble into the ebony thicket that stood like an island in the sea of grass just ahead of them, and it fell through the branches, rattling and crackling, and the lion growled from the depths of the thicket.

The fear of death was so pleasurable as to be almost unbearable, an emotional orgasm, stronger than any woman had ever given him, and Sean slid the safety-catch off the rifle and said, 'He's coming, Matatu. Run!' And exultation was in his voice, and time slowed down, another phenomenon produced by fear.

From the corner of his eye, he saw Riccardo Monterro step up beside him, taking his place in the firing line, and he knew what it was costing him.

'Good man!' he said loudly, and at the sound of his voice, the branches of the ebony thicket shook, as a heavy body rushed through them and there was a terrifying, growling, grunting uproar, coming straight at them.

Matatu stood perfectly still, like a guardsman on parade. Matatu had never run. Sean stepped up on one side of him and Riccardo, on the other, and they lifted their rifles and aimed into the wall of grass as that thing rushed in upon them, flattening the tall stems with its charge, roaring now, blasts of sound that were like a physical assault on their senses.

The grass opened in their faces and a huge, tawny body hurled itself upon them.

They fired together and the crash of gunfire drowned the enraged roaring. Sean fired the second barrel, the two shots sounding as one, and the huge 750-grain bullet tore into the charging animal, stopping it as though it had run into a cliff. Riccardo was working the bolt of the Rigby and a rolling echo of gunfire filled all the air about them.

The dead animal fell at their feet, and they stood with rifles raised, staring down at the bleeding carcass, dazed by the swiftness and the savagery and the beat of gunfire in their heads.

In the silence, Shadrach stepped forward. Like Matatu he had stood his ground, and now he stooped to the carcass, and then jerked back and shouted aloud what they had not yet fully realized.

'It's not the lion!'

As he said it, the lion charged. He came straight at them out of the thicket as his mate had done, but even more swiftly, driven by the agony in his belly and the black rage that filled him. He came grunting like a locomotive at full throttle, and they were unprepared, their rifles unloaded, bunched up too closely around the carcass of the lioness, and Shadrach was between them and the lion.

The lion came bursting out of the tall grass in full charge and it seized Shadrach in its jaws, biting into his hip, and the momentum of its charge carried it into the tight knot of men standing close up behind Shadrach.

It knocked them all off their feet, Sean went over backwards, crashing into the earth on his shoulder-blades and the back of his neck with stunning force. He was holding the rifle in front of his chest, instinctively trying to protect it from damage as he went down, and the engraved barrels slammed into his sternum as he hit the earth. Pain shot through his chest but he held on to the weapon and rolled on to his side.

Ten feet away the lion was savaging Shadrach. It had him pinned under its massive paws as it mauled his hip and upper leg.

'Thank God, it's not a leopard,' Sean thought as he broke open the rifle to reload. A leopard will not fix on one man if it attacks a group of hunters. It will bound from one to the other, in rapid succession, maiming and killing all of them with dazzling speed. Furthermore a leopard's main prey is the baboon, so it knows precisely how to despatch a primate. It goes instinctively for the head, taking off the scalp and top of the skull, while its back legs kick down the belly, stripping out the intestines with hooked yellow claws, very quickly, very efficiently.

'Thank God, it's not a leopard.' The great beast was fixed on Shadrach, pinning him with its claws, worrying the leg, and with each growl a scarlet spray of blood puffed out of its jaws. The Matabele gunbearer was screaming and beating ineffectually at the huge maned head with both clenched fists.

Sean saw Riccardo in the grass beyond them scrambling to his knees, crawling towards where the Rigby rifle had been thrown.

'Don't shoot, Capo,' Sean yelled at him. In a *mêlée* like this one, an inexperienced man with a loaded rifle was many times more dangerous than the attacking animal. The bullets of the Rigby would crack through the lion's body and smash into anybody beyond.

Sean had two spare cartridges held between the fingers of his left hand. It was the old hunter's trick for the fast reload, and he slid the two cartridges into the empty breeches and snapped the action shut.

The lion was chewing on Shadrach's lower body. Sean could hear the bone crunch and crackle like dry toast under those dreadful fangs. His nostrils were full of the fetid, gamey smell of the lion, of dust and the reek of blood of man and beast.

Beyond them he saw Riccardo had the rifle. He was on his knees, his face ashen with shock, cramming cartridges into the breech of the Rigby.

'Don't shoot!' Sean yelled again. The lion was directly between them. A bullet that hit the animal would come straight on into him.

It takes a special technique to shoot an attacking animal off a prostrate man without killing them both. It was deadly dangerous to run up to them and shoot down into the animal's body with the man lying under it.

Sean made no effort to rise to his feet. He rolled like a log, cushioning the rifle, flipping over three times, the manoeuvre that was second nature from his Scouts' training. Now he was lying alongside the lion, almost touching it, and he thrust the rifle into its lower ribs, aiming upwards, and he fired. It only needed one of those 750-grain bullets.

The shot lifted the lion clear of Shadrach's body, tossing it lightly aside, and the bullet tore out of its back between the shoulders, and went straight on up into the sky.

Sean dropped the rifle and knelt over Shadrach, taking him in his arms, and looked down on the leg. The fangs had inflicted penetrating stiletto wounds. From hip to knee the black flesh was riddled.

'Matatu!' Sean snapped. 'In the Toyota. The medicine box. Get it.' And the tracker vanished into the grass.

Riccardo crawled to Sean's side and looked at the leg.

'Sweet Mother Mary,' he said softly. 'It's the femoral.' Bright arterial blood was pumping up in a regular jet out of the deepest wound, and Sean reached into it, thrusting his fingers into the hot flesh.

He got a grip on the slippery, rubbery, pulsing worm with thumb and forefinger and pinched with all his strength.

'Hurry, Matatu! Run, you little bugger, run!' he bellowed.

It was less than three hundred yards to the Toyota, and Matatu ran like a frightened fawn. He was back within minutes. Job was with him carrying the white chest with the red cross on its lid, and he opened it.

'In the instrument roll,' Sean told Job brusquely. 'Haemostats.'

Job passed him the stainless-steel clamps, and Sean fastened them on the ruptured artery and taped them against the thigh. His hands were wet and bright with blood, but he and Job had done this work fifty times during the bush war, and his movements were swift and confident.

'Rig up a drip set,' he ordered Job. 'We'll give him a bag of Ringers lactate to start with. Rig it.'

As he spoke he was screwing the nozzle on a tube of Betadyne and now he slid the nozzle as deeply as it would go into one of the puncture wounds in Shadrach's thigh and squeezed the thick iodine paste into it until it forced itself out of the mouth of the wound like tobacco-yellow toothpaste. Shadrach lay without protest or any sign of pain, watching them as they worked, replying to Job in monosyllables when he spoke to him in Sindebele.

'Drip set is ready,' Job said.

Without a word, Sean took the canula out of his hands. Shadrach was his man, his responsibility. He would allow no one else to do this, not even Job. He twisted Shadrach's arm, exposing the inside of the elbow and worked up a vein with a skilled milking motion, and he hit it with the needle at the first attempt, and nodded to Job to let the plasma flow.

'Hey, Shadrach!' Sean's grin was remarkably convincing as he laid a blood-smeared palm briefly against the Matabele's cheek. 'I think you poisoned that old lion good. He eats your leg and he's dead – poof! Like that!' Shadrach chuckled. It amazed Riccardo to hear it, even though he had fought and worked with tough men before. 'Give Shadrach one of your cigars, Capo,' Sean suggested, and he began to strap the leg with clean white tape from the chest to stop the residual bleeding.

Once he had strapped the leg, he went over the rest of Shadrach's body quickly. He smeared Betadyne into all the rents and tears left by the lion's claws.

'We can't afford to overlook the merest scratch,' he grunted. 'That old lion has been feeding on putrid carcasses. His teeth and mouth are a reeking pit of infection, and there is rotten meat packed in the grooves of his claws. Gangrene kills most of the victims of a mauling.'

Still not satisfied, Sean injected a full ampoule of penicillin into the transfusion bag. That would swamp the body with antibiotic. Sean nodded and stood up. It had taken him less than thirty minutes, and studying the bandages and the drip set that Job was holding over Shadrach's supine form, Riccardo doubted that a trained doctor could have worked more swiftly or efficiently.

'I'm going to fetch the Toyota,' Sean told them. 'But I'll have to bring it around by way of the ford. That will take a little time, it will be dark by the time I get back.' He could have sent Job to fetch the truck, but he wanted to get the girl to himself. 'There are spare blankets in the chest, keep him wrapped and warm.' He looked down at Shadrach. 'Little scratch like that. I want you back at work pretty damn quick, otherwise I'll dock it off your wages.'

He picked up the .577 and he strode back through the grass to the riverbank. As he trudged through the sandy water-course, his anger at last came upon him, more powerful for being so long delayed.

Claudia was sitting alone in the front of the Toyota as he came up the bank. She looked forlorn and abandoned, but he felt no twinge of pity. She stared aghast at his blood-caked hands.

Sean placed the .577 in the gun-rack without looking at her, and then spilled water from the jerry can over his hands and scrubbed them together, washing off most of the blood. He climbed into the driver's seat and started the Toyota, swung it in a tight circle and sent it back along the track that followed the river downstream.

'Aren't you going to tell me what happened?' Claudia asked at last. She had meant to sound unrepentant and full of bravado, but it came out in a small subdued voice.

'All right,' Sean agreed. 'I'll tell you. Instead of a quick merciful kill there was total chaos and confusion. The lioness charged us first. We shot her by mistake in the long grass. Not that we would have had much option anyway. She was coming all the way.' Sean switched on the headlights, for the sun was gone and the forest darkening. 'Okay, so now the lioness is dead. Her cubs are still unweaned, they are goners, all three of them. They'll starve to death inside a week.'

'Oh no!' Claudia whispered.

'Then the lion charged after his mate. He caught us all ends up. We weren't ready for him, and he got Shadrach down, He almost chewed his leg off. The bone is shattered from hip to knee. He may lose the whole leg, I don't know, perhaps he'll get lucky and just end up with a permanent limp. Anyway you look at it, he's not going to be a tracker any more. I'll find him a job as a skinner or camp servant, but he's a Matabele warrior and menial work is going to break his heart.'

'I'm so sorry.'

'You are sorry?' Sean asked. His voice low and furious. 'Shadrach is my friend and my companion. He has saved my life more times than I can count and I've done the same for him. We have fought a war together, we have slept under the same blanket, eaten from the same plate, trekked ten thousand miles together in the heat and the dust and the rain. He is more than a friend. I have two brothers, same mother and father, but Shadrach means more to me than either of them. Now you tell me you're sorry. Well, thanks a lot, ducky. That's a great comfort.'

'You have every right to be angry. I understand!'

'You understand?' he asked. 'You understand nothing. You are an arrogant ignoramus from a different hemisphere. You are a citizen of the land of the quick fix, and you come and try your simplistic naïve solutions here in Africa. You try to save a single animal from his destiny, and you end up by killing a female and sending her three cubs to lingering death and condemning one of the finest men you'll ever meet to the life of a cripple.'

'What more can I say?' she asked. 'I was wrong.'

'At this late hour your new-found humility is most touching.' His low voice lashed her. 'Sure, you were wrong. Just as you and your people are wrong to try and starve an African nation of thirty million souls into acceptance of another one of your naïve solutions. When the damage you have inflicted is beyond repair, will you again say "I'm sorry, I was wrong," and walk away and leave my land and my people to bleed and suffer?'

'What can I do?'

'We have thirty days of safari remaining,' he said bitterly. 'I want you to keep out of my hair for that time. The only reason I don't cancel the show right now, and send you packing back to your Eskimos and your human rights, is that I just happen to think your father is a pretty fine man. From now on, you are under sufferance. Just one more peep out of you and you are on the next plane back to Anchorage. Do I make myself clear?'

'Abundantly.' And there was a trace of spirit in her tone once more. Neither of them spoke again during the rough ride down to the ford and back up the far bank to the glade in which the bait tree stood.

By that time Job and Matatu had a fire going. The glow of the flames guided Sean to where Shadrach lay, and he climbed out of the Toyota and went to him immediately.

'How is the pain?' He squatted beside him.

'It is a little thing,' Shadrach replied, but Sean saw the lie in the grey tone of his skin and the sunken eyeballs, and he filled a disposable syringe from a glass ampoule of morphine. He waited for the drug to take effect before they lifted Shadrach between them and laid him in the back of the truck.

Job and Matatu had skinned out both lions while they waited, and they loaded the bundle of green salted skins onto the bonnet where it would cool in the night wind.

'It's a hell of a lion,' Sean told Riccardo. 'You've got yourself a magnificent trophy!'

Riccardo shook his head and said, 'Let's get Shadrach back to camp.'

Sean drove with care, rolling the truck gently over the rougher spots, trying to protect Shadrach from the worst jolting.

Claudia insisted on sitting in the back with Shadrach, cushioning his head on her lap. Riccardo sat up in front with Sean and he asked quietly, 'What happens now?'

'I'll radio Harare as soon as we get into camp. They will have a private ambulance at the airport to meet him. I'll be gone a couple of days. I'll see Shadrach well taken care of and, of course, I'll have to put in a report to the government game department and try and square it.'

'I hadn't gotten around to thinking about that,' Riccardo said. 'We killed a lioness with cubs and had a man mauled. What will the government do?'

Sean shrugged in the darkness. 'There is a better than even chance they'll pull my licence and take the concession away from me.'

'Hell. Sean. I didn't realize. Is there anything I can do?'

'Not a thing, Capo, but thanks for the offer. You are out of it. It's between me and the department.'

'I could take full blame for the lioness, say I shot her.'

'No good.' Sean shook his head. 'No blame on the clients. That's departmental doctrine. Whatever you do, I am fully responsible.'

'If they pull your licence . . .' Riccardo hesitated, and Sean shook his head again.

'No, Capo, they won't cancel the safari. That's also departmental doctrine. Finish the safari. Don't offend the paying client. Government needs the hard currency you bring. Only after you have left, they'll bring out the axe for me. You are out of it. I'll be back in two days, and we'll hunt that big elephant together. You don't have to worry.'

'You make me sound like a selfish bastard. I'm worrying about you and your licence, not about enjoying myself.'

'We'll both enjoy ourselves, Capo. After all, if I do lose my licence, it will be the last time that you and I ever hunt together, Capo.'

Claudia could overhear the conversation from where she sat in the back of the truck and she knew why her father did not reply. He knew that it was his last hunt, licence or no licence. Claudia had taken an emotional battering during the last few hours, and thinking about Papa now, she felt the tears well up and scald her eyelids. She fought them back and then it was no longer worth the effort and she wept for all of them, for her father and the lioness and the cubs, for that beautiful male lion, and for Shadrach and his shattered leg.

One of her tears fell on to Shadrach's upturned face, and he stared up at her in perturbation. She wiped the droplet from his cheek with her thumb and her voice was thick and muffled with grief as she whispered to him, 'It's going to be all right, Shadrach.' Even she realized what a crass and fatuous lie that was.

Sean had a scheduled radio contact with his office in Harare at ten o'clock every evening. The journey home was so slow that they reached camp with only minutes to rig the aerial and connect the radio to the Toyota's twelve-volt battery before the schedule.

The contact was good; one of the reasons for the late schedule was the better radio reception in the cool of the evening. Reema's voice with its Gujurati intonation came through clearly. She was a pretty Hindu girl who ran Sean's Harare office with ruthless efficiency.

'We have a casevac.' Sean used the terminology of the bush war for casualty evacuation. 'I want an ambulance standing by to meet me.'

'Okay fine, Sean.'

'Set up a person-to-person telephone call with my brother, Garrick, in Johannesburg for ten a.m. tomorrow.'

'Will do, Sean.'

'Make an appointment for me to see the director of the game department tomorrow afternoon.'

'Director is in New York for the Wildlife Conference, Sean. The deputy director is in charge.'

Sean switched off the hand microphone while he swore bitterly, he had forgotten about the Wildlife Conference. Then he pressed the transmit button again.

'Okay, Reema my love, get me an appointment with Geoffrey Manguza then.'

'Sounds serious, Sean.'

'We just invented the word.'

'What is your ETA? 'I'll have to file an emergency flight plan for you.'

The security authority was always so jittery about South African hot pursuit of terrorists into Zimbabwe or pre-emptive South African raids on terrorist facilities in Harare itself that they usually required flight plans to be filed forty-eight' hours in advance.

'Take off here in fifty minutes. ETA Harare 2300 hours. Pilot and two pax,' Sean told her.

It was half an hour's drive from the camp to the airstrip. Riccardo and Claudia were in the Toyota when they drove out.

Sean took the back seats out of the Beechcraft and placed

a mattress on the floor for Shadrach. By this time, Shadrach was feverish and restive. His temperature was 101 and the glands in his groin, hard and lumpy as walnuts. Sean didn't want to look under the dressings on the leg, afraid of what he might find, but one of the minor claw wounds on Shadrach's belly was definitely infected already, weeping watery pus and emitting the first faint odour of putrescence.

Sean administered another dose of penicillin through the canula of the drip set and then he and Job and two of the camp skinners very gently lifted Shadrach into the aircraft and settled him on the mattress.

Shadrach's wife was a sturdy Matabele woman with an infant strapped to her back with a length of trade cloth: They loaded her considerable baggage and then she clambered up and sat beside Shadrach on the mattress, placed the infant on her lap, opened her blouse and gave the child her milk-engorged breast to suckle. The aircraft's empty luggage compartments Job filled with sacks of dried game meat, a valuable commodity in Africa. Then Job drove the Toyota to the far end of the runway to give Sean the headlights for take-off.

'Job will look after you while I am away, Capo. Why don't you take the shotgun and go for dove and sand grouse down at the pools? Best wing shooting you'll ever have, better than white winged dove in Mexico,' Sean suggested.

'Don't worry about us. We'll be just fine.'

'I'll be back as soon as I possibly can. Tukutela won't be crossing before the new moon. I'll be back before then. It's a promise, Capo.'

Sean held out his hand and as Riccardo took it, he said, 'You did good work with the lions, Capo, but then you were never short of bottom.'

'What kind of limey word is that?' Riccardo asked. "Bottom"?'

'How about a good Yankee word then? "Cojones"?'

'That will do,' Riccardo grinned at him.

Claudia was standing beside her father and now she smiled hesitantly, almost shyly, and took a step forward as if to offer her hand.

She had released her hair from its plait and brushed it out into a dense, dark mane around her head. Her expression was soft and her eyes big and dark and lustrous. In the Toyota headlights her classical Latin features went beyond the merely handsome, and Sean realized for the first time that she was truly beautiful. Despite her beauty and her penitent attitude, he kept his own expression cold and forbidding, nodded at her curtly, ignored the tentative offer to shake his hand, climbed up onto the wing of the Beechcraft and ducked into the cockpit.

Sean had cut the airstrip out of the brush himself and levelled it by dragging a bundle of old truck tyres up and down it behind the Toyota. It was narrow, rough and short, with a gradient falling towards the river. He lined up with the Beechcraft's tail-plane backed into the bushes, and stood on the brakes facing down the slope. He aimed at the lights of the Toyota at the far end of the strip while he ran up to full power on both engines and then let the brakes off. Just short of the trees at the end of the strip he pulled on the flaps and bounced the Beechcraft into the air. As always he crossed himself blasphemously with mock relief as he cleared the tree-tops and turned on course for Harare.

During the flight, he tried to plan his strategy. The director of the game department was an old friend, and Sean had successfully dealt with him in equally serious circumstances. However the deputy, Geoffrey Manguza, was a horse of literally another colour. The director was one of the few white civil servants still in charge of a department of government. Manguza would succeed him soon, the first black head of the game department.

He and Sean had fought on opposite sides during the bush war, and Manguza had been an astute guerrilla leader and political commissar. The rumour was that he did not like the safari concession owners, most of whom were white. The concept of private exploitation of State assets offended his Marxist principles, and he had shot too many white men during the war to have any great deal of liking or respect for them.

It was going to be a difficult meeting, Sean sighed.

Reema was waiting for him as he taxied in. As a modern Indian woman, she had abandoned the sari in favour of a neat slacks suit. She was not so modern, however, that she wished to choose her own husband. Her father and her uncles were working on that at the moment, and had already come up with a likely candidate in Canada. A professor of Oriental religions at Toronto University. Sean hated them for it. Reema was an ornament to Courtney Safaris, and he knew that he would never be able to replace her.

She had the ambulance waiting on the tarmac beside the light aircraft hangars. Regularly, Reema bribed the guards on the main gate with dried game meat from the concession. In Africa, meat or the promise of meat opens all gates.

They followed the ambulance to the hospital in the Kombi. While Sean sat in the passenger seat glancing through the most urgent mail she had brought for his attention, Reema recited a list of the important developments during his absence.

'Carter, the surgeon from Atlanta, cancelled . . .' That was a twenty-one-day safari, and Sean glanced up sharply, but Reema soothed him. 'I phoned the German soap manufacturer in Munich, Herr Buchner, the one we turned down in December. He jumped at it. So we are full, back to back, for the rest of the season.'

'How about my brother?' Sean interrupted. He didn't tell her that it was touch and go that there was going to be an end to the season.

'Your brother is expecting your call and as at six o'clock this morning the telephone was still working.' In Zimbabwe

77

that was something that couldn't be taken for granted.

At the hospital, there were at least fifty seriously ill patients awaiting admission ahead of them. The long benches were full of huddled, miserable humanity and the stretchers were blocking the aisles and doorways. The admission clerks were in no great hurry and waved Shadrach's stretcher to a far corner.

'Leave it to me,' said Reema, and she took the senior admissions clerk by the elbow and led him aside with an angelic smile, talking to him sweetly.

Five minutes later, Shadrach's admission papers were processed and he was being examined by an East German doctor.

'How much did that cost?' Sean asked.

'Cheap,' Reema answered. 'A bag of dried meat.'

Sean had picked up sufficient of the German language from his safari clients to be able to discuss Shadrach's case with the doctor. The man was reassuring. Sean said goodbye to Shadrach.

'Reema has your money. She will come to see you each day. If you need anything tell her.'

'I will be with you in spirit when you hunt Tukutela,' Shadrach said softly, and Sean had to clear his throat before he could answer.

'We will hunt many more elephant together, old friend.' And he walked away quickly.

The next morning when at last he got through to Johannesburg, the telephone line was crackling with static.

'Mr Garrick Courtney is in a board meeting,' the girl on the switchboard at Centaine House, the Courtney Group headquarters, told him. 'But he gave orders to put your call through directly.'

In his mind's eye, Sean saw once again the boardroom, panelled in figured walnut, the huge Pierneef canvases framed by the elaborate panels, and his brother, Garry, sitting at the head of the long table, beneath the crystal chandelier that his grandmother had imported from Murano in Italy, in the chairman's high-backed throne.

'Sean!' Garry's voice cut through the static, bold and assured. How he had changed from the puny little runt who used to pee his bed.

The job could have been Sean's if he had wanted it and had been prepared to work for it. Sean was the eldest son, but he did not want the job. Still he always experienced a twinge of resentment when he thought of Garry's Rolls and Lear jet and holiday home in the south of France.

'Hello Garry. How's it going?'

'All well here,' Garry told him. 'What's the problem?' It was typical of their relationship that any contact meant there was a problem to solve.

'I might need to put a bit of honey with the cheese,' Sean told him diplomatically. It was their private code for money to Switzerland, and Garry would understand that Sean would be bribing somebody for something. It happened often enough.

'Okay, Sean. Just give me the amount and the account number.' Garry was Sean's partner in the safari company, and held forty per cent of the shares.

'Thanks, Garry, I'll call you some time tomorrow. How's the rest of the family?' They chatted for a few minutes longer, and when he hung up Reema came through from the outer office.

'I managed to get through to the game department at last.' Reema had been trying all morning. 'Comrade Manguza will see you at four-thirty this afternoon.'

Geoffrey Manguza was a tall Shona with a very black complexion and close-cropped hair. He wore silver-framed eye glasses, and a dark blue suit. However, his neck-tie was Hermes, Sean recognized the horse carriage logo, and his wristwatch was a Patek Philippe with a black crocodile-skin strap. They were not your run-of-the-mill Marxist accessories and Sean found that encouraging. However, the deputy director did not rise from behind his desk to welcome him.

'Colonel Courtney,' he greeted him unsmilingly, using Sean's previous rank to let him know that he knew that Sean had commanded the Ballantyne Scouts, one of the elite Rhodesian groups, after Ballantyne, the founder of the regiment, had been killed in action. It was also a reminder that they had been enemies, and might still be so.

'I prefer plain mister.' Sean smiled engagingly. 'That other business is behind us now, Comrade Manguza.'

The deputy director inclined his head, neither agreeing nor disagreeing. 'What can I do for you?'

'Unfortunately, I have to report an unintentional transgression of the game regulations . . .' And Geoffrey Manguza's expression hardened, and remained like that while Sean described the accidental shooting of the lioness and Shadrach's subsequent mauling. When Sean finished by submitting the written report that Reema had typed for him, Geoffrey Manguza let the document lie untouched on his desk top while he asked a few pertinent and unsympathetic questions.

'You do realize, Colonel Courtney,' he used the rank again deliberately, 'that I am obliged to take a most serious view of this entire business. It seems to me that there has been negligence and serious disregard for the safety of your clients and your own staff. Zimbabwe is no longer a colony, and you cannot treat our people the way you did before.'

'Before you make your recommendation to the director, I would like to clarify a few points for you,' Sean told him.

'You are free to speak, Colonel.'

'It's almost five o'clock now.' Sean checked his watch. 'Won't you allow me to buy you a drink at the golf club, and we can discuss it in more relaxed surroundings?'

Manguza's expression was inscrutable but after a few moments' thought he nodded. 'As you wish. I have a few small matters to attend to before I leave here, but I will meet you at the club in half an hour.'

He kept Sean sitting on the veranda of the golf club for forty minutes before he put in an appearance. It had once been the Royal Salisbury Golf Club. However, the first two words had been dropped from the title lest they perpetuate the colonial past. Nevertheless, the first remark Geoffrey Manguza made after he had taken the chair opposite Sean and ordered a gin and tonic was, 'Strange isn't it, a few years ago, the only way a black man could have got in here was as a waiter, and now I am on the committee and my handicap is five.' Sean let it pass, and changed the subject to that of rhino poaching across the border with Zambia. Manguza made no effort to pursue that topic. He watched Sean through the silver-rimmed spectacles and as soon as he stopped speaking, cut in immediately.

'You wished to clarify a few points for me,' he said. 'We are both busy men, Colonel.'

This directness was disconcerting. Sean was preparing for a typically round-about African approach, but he adapted his pitch.

'First of all, Mr Manguza, I wanted to tell you what a high price I and my associates place on the Chiwewe concession.' Sean used the word 'price' deliberately. 'I telephoned them this morning and explained this unfortunate incident and they are anxious to have it resolved at any price.' Again he used the word, and paused significantly.

There was a certain etiquette to be observed in negotiations such as these. To the western mind it was bribery, but in Africa it was simply the Dash System, a universal and acceptable means of getting things done. Government might put up posters in all public buildings depicting a booted foot crushing a venomous serpent under the slogan 'Stamp out Corruption' but nobody took that very seriously. In fact, in a bizarre fashion, the posters themselves constituted official recognition of the practice.

At this stage, Geoffrey Manguza should have agreed that recompense was due, or given some other indication of his willingness to listen to reason. He said nothing, merely stared at Sean from behind those glinting lens until Sean was forced to speak again.

'If you've finished your drink, why don't we take a stroll down the eighteenth fairway?' The club veranda was crowded and the happy hour in full swing with too many listening ears. Manguza swallowed the last of his gin and tonic, and without a word led the way down the steps to the lawn.

The last four-ball was coming down the eighteenth, but Sean kept to the edge of the rough, and as the players and their caddies straggled past, Sean said softly, 'I told my associates that you are the most powerful man in the department, and that the white director is merely your rubber stamp. I told them that you had it in your power to sidetrack an official enquiry, and dismiss any charges arising from this most unfortunate incident. I was so certain that I laid a bet of ten thousand US dollars with them. If I win my bet, those winnings are yours, Mr Manguza, paid into any account you nominate anywhere in the world.'

Manguza stopped and turned to face him and Sean was taken aback when he saw his expression. Manguza's voice quivered with fury as he said, 'Your assumption that I am open to a bribe is an insult to me personally. That I could tolerate, but it is also an insult to the revolution and the revolutionary heroes who died in the struggle to free this country of the imperial and colonial yoke, it is an insult to the party and our leaders, to the Marxist spirit and ultimately to the African people as a whole.'

'I only suggested a lousy ten grand, not the return of the monarchy, for the love of Allah.'

'You may smile your supercilious white smile, Colonel Courtney, but we know you well. We know about your South African connections, and about the bunch of Matabele hooligans you have gathered about you. We know that all of them fought with you against the forces of revolutionary democracy. They are counter-revolutionaries and capitalist-roaders and you are their leader.'

'I shot a lioness by mistake, and one of my capitalist-roaders got bitten, that's the full extent of my counter-revolutionary activities.'

'We are watching you, Colonel,' Manguza told him ominously. 'You can be certain that I will make the correct recommendation in your case, and that the insult to me and my people will not be forgotten.'

Manguza turned and strode back towards the club-house and Sean shook his head.

'So we say farewell to the beautiful Chiwewe concession,' he murmured. 'I really blew that one!' Despite his levity, he felt a sliding sensation of disaster in the pit of his stomach.

The office of Courtney Safaris was in the Avenues, between Government House and the golf club and Reema was waiting for him in the outer office, its walls decorated with colour posters of wildlife and photographic enlargements of satisfied clients with their trophies.

She jumped up from her desk the moment Sean came in.

'The hospital called an hour ago, Sean. They have amputated Shadrach's leg.'

For long moments, Sean could neither speak nor move, then he crossed slowly to the filing cabinet and took a glass and a half-empty bottle of Chivas from the top drawer. He sagged onto the sofa and poured a three-finger jolt of whisky.

'The ending to a perfect day,' he said, and tossed back the whisky.

Reema left him sitting on the sofa. There were only two more drinks left in the bottle, and when they were gone, Sean went down to the Monomatapa Hotel. The hotel was full of tourists, and amongst them was a blond teutonic

Valkyrie in full *Out of Africa* costume. She caught his eye across the lounge the moment that Sean walked in and smiled.

'What the hell!' Sean said to himself. 'It's cheaper than whisky, and no hangover either.'

The German Fräulein laughed delightedly at Sean's rudimentary German, and not long afterwards it transpired that she had the presidential suite on the fourteenth floor all to herself. She ordered a bottle of Mumm from room service and they drank it in bed.

I n the morning, while Reema filed a flight plan for him, taking a bag of dried meat down to air traffic control, Sean returned to the hospital.

They had taken Shadrach's leg off only inches below the hip. The East German doctor showed Sean the X-ray plates. 'Hopeless!' He pointed out the bone fragments. 'Like confetti!'

There was no place to sit in the crowded surgical ward, so Sean stood beside Shadrach's bed for a while and they talked about the battles and the hunts they had shared. They did not mention the leg, and when they had run out of reminiscences, Sean gave the ward sister a hundred dollars to look after him and went out to the airport.

Reema had the flight plan for him and the Beechcraft was refuelled and loaded with everything from fresh fruit and vegetables to toilet paper for the camp.

'You are a heroine, Reema,' he said, and then standing beside the aircraft, he described the meeting with Geoffrey Manguza.

'It doesn't look very cheerful,' he ended. 'You had better begin looking for another job.'

'I'm sorry for you, Sean,' she said. 'But don't worry about me. I was wondering how to break the news to you. I'm leaving for Canada on September 16th. It's all arranged, I'm going to be the wife of a professor.'

'You be happy,' Sean ordered, and for the first time kissed her, and she blushed under her nut-brown skin which made her prettier than ever.

Sean made three low-level passes over the camp and on the third he saw the Toyota pull out towards the airstrip with Job driving and Matatu standing in the back. He landed and taxied the Beechcraft into its cage of galvanized diamond-mesh wire which was designed to discourage the elephant from pulling the wings off and the lions from chewing the tyres.

When Job and Matatu arrived in the Toyota, they transferred the cargo to it, and then Sean told them about Shadrach's leg.

They had fought all through the bush war together and were hardened to casualties, but Sean saw the pain and grief in his eyes as Job murmured, 'We will need a new number two gunbearer. Pumula, the skinner, is a good man.'

'Yes, we will use him,' Sean agreed.

For a while they stood silently, paying tribute to their maimed companion. Then, still without speaking, they climbed into the Toyota and drove back to camp.

Rather than slacks, Claudia Monterro wore a dress for dinner that evening, a floating silk chiffon in pure white with silver and turquoise Seminole jewellery. Against her tanned skin and jet black hair the effect was stunning. However, Sean made certain not to show his admiration and he directed all his conversation at her father.

After he had told Riccardo about Shadrach and his meeting with Manguza, the evening was gloomy and cheerless. Claudia left the men at the camp-fire but they did not sit there long before Riccardo said goodnight and went off to his tent. Sean took a bottle of whisky from the dining tent and went down towards the servants' village.

Job's tent and those of his two wives were set apart from the others, on the bank of the river overlooking a deep pool where hippo lay like dark rock islands in mid-stream. When Sean seated himself on the carved native stool across the fire from Job, one of the wives brought two glasses and knelt beside him while he poured a large peg for each of them. The pretty young Matabele girl with Job's infant strapped on her back took the glass to her husband, and Job saluted Sean across the flickering flames.

They drank in silence and Sean watched Job's face in the firelight as he stared out across the river. The silence was companionable and comforting and Sean let his thoughts wander back down the years as he rolled the smoky taste of whisky over his tongue.

He remembered the day he had first met Job Bhekani. It had been on a hill with only a number. Hill 31, a rocky hill, thick with stands of dense wild ebony and Jesse bush where the enemy waited. Job had been on the hill for two days, and his eyes were wild and bloodshot. Sean had parachuted in that morning with five sticks of his own scouts. They fought side by side the rest of that day, and in the dusk when the hill was cleared and those of the enemy still alive had fled down the rocky slopes and disappeared into the forest, Sean and Job had helped each other to where the helicopter waited to take them out. They had gone down the hill slowly, wearily, dragging their weapons, arms around each other's shoulders and their blood mingling when it oozed from under the field dressings.

'Blood brothers whether you like it or not,' Sean had croaked, grinning at Job from under the camouflage cream and soot and dust, and a week later when Job was released from base hospital, Sean had been waiting for him personally with his transfer papers.

'You've been seconded to Ballantyne Scouts, Captain.'

And Job had smiled that rare wide smile and said, 'Let's go, Colonel.'

From his file, Sean knew that Job had been born on the Gwai river and attended the local mission school where he had obtained a bursary to the University College of Rhodesia and Nyasaland from where he had graduated with a first in Politics, History and Social Anthropology. From there he had gone on with another bursary to Brown College in Chicago and got his masters the same year that Ian Smith declared unilateral independence.

Only much later when they had tried and tested their friendship, did Sean learn how Job had herded his father's cattle along the Gwai river and come, even as a child, to know and love the wilds. Job's father was one of the grandsons of King Lobengula, son of great Mzilikazi, so Job was a direct descendant of the royal Zulu line, and this was apparent in his carriage and his features. The powerful jaw and deep forehead, the dark intelligent eyes and domed skull beneath the thick close-cropped curls.

During his studies and his sojourn in America, Job had come to abhor the Communist doctrine and all its works, so it was natural that on his return to Africa, he had enlisted in the Rhodesian African Rifles and within a year had earned his commission.

After the war when the Lancaster House Agreement had given the country over to Robert Mugabe and his people's democracy, Job had sat and passed with honours, the civil service entrance exam, for government and politics was the swift high-road to power and wealth.

However, he was branded a 'sell-out' who had fought the war on the wrong side, the losing side, and he was a Matabele when the power was in the hands of the Shona tribe. Every door to advancement was barred against him. Angry and disillusioned he had come back to Sean.

'Damn it, Job, you are miles too good for any job I could offer you in a safari company.'

'Tracker, skinner, gunbearer, whatever you have, I'll take it,' Job had insisted.

So they had hunted together as they had fought, side by side, and within a year, Sean had made him one of the directors of Courtney Safaris. They always referred to these quiet evenings, drinking whisky around the camp-fire, as directors' meetings.

It amused Job to adopt various roles for different circumstances. In front of safari clients he shifted to what he called, 'Plantation Nigger Mode' when he called Sean *Bwana* and *Nkosi* and acted out the charade of the by-gone colonial era.

'Don't be a prick, Job. You demean yourself,' Sean protested at first.

'It's what the clients expect,' Job had reasoned. 'We are selling them an illusion, man. They are playing eagle scouts and Ernest Hemingway. If they guessed I had a master's in history and politics, it would frighten the hell out of them.' And reluctantly, Sean had gone along with the act.

When they were alone, as they were now, Job changed into what he called his 'Homo Sapiens Mode' and became the thoughtful intelligent educated man he truly was. As they talked, they switched easily from Sindebele to English, each of them as perfectly at ease and comfortable in each other's language as they were in each other's company.

'Look, Sean, don't worry too much about losing this concession. It hasn't happened yet, and even if it does, we'll find a way around it.'

'Give me some comfort. I could do with it.'

'We could apply for another concession, somewhere in Matabeleland where my family still has pull. Down Matetsi way or even on the Gwai river, that's my home turf.'

'No good.' Sean shook his head. 'After this fiasco, I'll have the mark of the beast on me.'

'We'd apply in my name,' Job suggested, and smiled wickedly. 'I'd make you one of my directors and you can call me *Bwana!*'

They laughed together, the mood lightening, and when Sean left Job at his fire and walked back to the main camp in the darkness, he felt cheerful and optimistic for the first time in days. Job had the power to effect that transformation in him.

As he approached his own tent, something pale moved in the moon shadow beneath the trees and he stopped abruptly. Then he heard the tinkle of silver jewellery, and realized that she must have been waiting for him.

'May I speak with you?' Claudia said softly.

'Go ahead,' he invited. Why did that Americanism 'speak with', rather than 'speak to' irritate him so, he wondered.

'I'm not very good at this,' she admitted and he gave her no encouragement. 'I wanted to apologize.'

'You are apologizing to the wrong person, I've still got both my legs.'

She flinched and her voice trembled. 'You are without mercy, aren't you?' Then she lifted her chin. 'All right, I guess I deserved that, I've been an idiot. I thought I knew it all, but it turns out I knew very little, and in my ignorance I've done immense damage. I know it doesn't help much, but I'm desperately sorry.'

'You and I are from different worlds, we have not a single thought or feeling in common. We could never hope to understand each other, let alone be friends, but I do know what it took for you to say that.'

'A truce, then?' she asked.

'All right, a truce.' He held out his hand and she took it. Her skin was smooth as the petal of a rose, her hand slim and cool, but her grip was firm as a man's.

'Good-night,' she said, and released his hand and turned away.

He watched her walk back towards her own tent. The moon was two days from full and the white dress was ethereal and misty. Beneath it her body was slim and her limbs long and elegant.

In that moment, he admired her spirit and liked her more than he had ever done in all the time he had known her.

Sean slept as lightly as a hunter and a soldier. The natural sounds of the bush did not disturb him, not even the shrieks of the hyena pack around the fortified trophy shed, where the lionskins were curing.

However at the light scratch on the canvas of his tent, he was instantly awake and reaching for his flashlight and the .577 propped at the head of his bed.

'Who is it?' he asked quietly.

'It's me, Job.'

Sean glanced at his Rolex wristwatch, the luminous hands pointed to three o'clock.

'Come in, what is it?'

'One of the trackers who we left on the river has come into camp. He has run twenty miles.'

Sean felt the back of his neck prickle and he swung both legs out of bed.

'Yes?' he said eagerly.

'At sunset this evening Tukutela crossed the river out of the National Park.'

'Is it certain?'

'It is certain. They saw him close by. It is Tukutela, the Angry One, and he has no collar around his neck.'

'Where is Matatu?' Sean stood up and reached for his pants, and the little Ndorobo piped at the entrance. 'I am ready, *Bwana*.'

'Good. We leave in twenty minutes. Marching packs and water-bottles. We'll take Pumula in Shadrach's place. I want to be on Tukutela's spoor before it is light enough to see it.'

Bare-chested, Sean strode across to Riccardo's tent, and heard his even snores as he paused at the flap.

'Capo!' The snores cut off abruptly. 'Are you awake? I've got an elephant for you. Get your arse out of the sack. Tukutela has crossed. We leave in twenty minutes.'

'Hot damn!' He could hear Riccardo was still half asleep. He stumbled about in the dark tent. 'Where the hell are my pants? Hey, Sean, wake Claudia, will you?'

There was a lantern burning in Claudia's tent. She must have heard the excitement.

'Are you awake?' Sean asked at the flap, and she opened it and stood with the lantern light behind her. Her night-dress reached almost to her ankles, there was lace at her throat and cuffs, but the cloth was so fine that the light struck through it, and her naked body was in silhouette.

'I heard you telling Papa,' she said. 'I'll be ready. Will we be walking? Should I wear my hiking boots or moccasins?'

He was certain that she was putting on this show delib-erately, and he felt a prudish outrage that was totally alien to his nature. 'Today you'll walk further and faster than you ever have in your life before,' he told her harshly. 'She's showing herself off like a tramp,' he thought, ignoring the proven fact that his taste usually ran strongly towards tramps, 'just when I was starting to respect her,' and a reprimand rose to his lips. He bit it off and tried not to look at the flowing shape of her hips, as graceful as the lines of a celadon porcelain vase thrown by a master craftsman of the T'ang dynasty. He wanted to turn away to show his indifference and his contradictory disapproval, but he was still standing there when she let the tent flap drop.

'Truce, be damned,' he muttered furiously as he strode back to his tent. 'She's still in the ring throwing punches.' But his anger puzzled him. With any other woman, even one half as lovely, he would have been delighted by the exhibition.

'She's got more class than that,' he explained to himself, and then remembered how much he despised and disliked her. 'This bimbo is getting you all up a gum-tree,' he warned himself, and then burst out laughing. The dreadful gloom of Shadrach's amputation and the imminent loss of his licence were dispelled.

He was going to hunt one of Africa's legendary beasts, and the presence of this woman, in some unaccountable manner, added spice to his mood of high anticipation.

There was frost on the grass in the low vleis they crossed. It sparkled in the headlights, and the game they saw was lethargic with the cold, barely moving out of the road to let the Toyota pass in the night. They reached the ford on the Chiwewe river an hour before dawn. The waters were black and shining as anthracite in the last beams of the moon, and the tall trees along either bank were a silvered host, like two opposing armies of mythical giants.

Sean parked the Toyota well off the track, and left one of the skinners to guard it. They fell naturally into established hunting formation, with the clients in the centre. Pumula took up Shadrach's old position in the drag; a muscular taciturn man with a thick woolly bush of a black beard, he carried Riccardo's Rigby on its sling.

All the men, including Riccardo, were under field packs, even Claudia carried her own water-bottles. Job had Riccardo's second rifle, the Weatherby, over his shoulder, and as always Sean lugged the .577 Nitro Express. Once the hunt had begun he never let it out of his hands. They moved out, heading upstream, and within a mile they had warmed up and were pushing harder. Sean noticed that Claudia moved well on those long legs of hers, and was keeping up without difficulty. She gave him a saucy grin as she noticed his appraisal.

The dawn light was hardening when the tracker who had come in with the news of Tukutela's crossing, exclaimed and pointed ahead. It was light enough to make out a fresh blaze on the trunk of a pod mahogany tree which guarded a low place on the riverbank. 'There!' said the tracker. 'I marked the spoor.'

At a glance, Sean saw that this was a natural crossing place for large animals. Troops of hippo had pioneered a pathway through the reed-beds, and down the ten-foot riverbank. Herds of buffalo and elephant passing over it had consolidated it and improved the gradient.

The African veld is criss-crossed with a network of game trails, and a dozen or so of these came in through the forest, like the spokes of a wheel, to concentrate on this river crossing. Everyone in the party quickened step at the tracker's exclamation, but Matatu reached the main pathway ahead of them and darted down it, turning his head to use the light of dawn most effectively, dabbing lightly at the earth with the tip of the peeled wild willow wand he carried.

He had not gone five paces before he straightened and looked back at Sean, his features wreathed in wrinkles of happiness and excitement.

'It is him!' he chirped. 'These are the feet of the father of all elephants. It is Tukutela! It is the Angry One!'

Sean looked down at the great dished spoor in the fine dust of the game path and he felt as though a spring tide had begun to flow in his life.

His excitement was replaced by a sense of destiny, an almost religious gravity.

'Matatu,' he said. 'Take the spoor!' Formally, he announced the start of the hunt.

The spoor was clear as a highway, following the game trail directly into the forest away from the river.

The old bull was striding out briskly as though he knew that the crossing was the danger point. Perhaps that was why he had chosen to cross at sunset, so that darkness would cover him until he was clear.

For five miles he had gone without a check, and then suddenly he had turned aside from the game trail into a thicket of rambling thorn which had come into blossom and new shoot. He had moved back and forth, feeding on the blooms and succulent shoots, and his spoor was confused, the thicket trampled and torn.

Matatu and Job went into the thorn thicket to unravel it, while the rest of the party hung back to let them work unhindered.

'I'm thirsty!' Claudia unhooked one of the water-bottles from her belt.

'No!' Sean stopped her. 'If you drink on your first thirst, you'll want to drink all day, and we have only just begun.'

She hesitated a moment, considering defying him, but then she hooked the bottle back on her belt.

'You are a hard taskmaster,' she said.

Matatu whistled softly on the far side of the thicket.

'He has worked the spoor out,' Sean told them, and let them through the thorn.

'How much have we gained?' he asked Matatu. They had started almost ten hours behind the bull, but every time he had paused to feed, they cut that lead.

'He did not feed long,' Matatu shrugged. 'And now he is going hard again.'

The bull had turned off the game trail and was following a stony ridge, almost as if he was deliberately obscuring his own spoor. He left no indications for the average human eye to follow, but Matatu went after him with complete authority.

'Are you sure he is still on it?' Riccardo asked anxiously.

'Capo, you've hunted with Matatu too often to ask that question,' Sean told him.

'But what can he see?' Claudia wanted to know. 'It's just rocks and gravel.'

'The elephant's pads leave a scuff on the rock, they bruise the lichen, leave smears of dust. There is fine grass growing between the stones, he has disturbed it, bending the stems in the direction of his passing. The disturbed grass catches the light differently.'

'Could you follow it?' Claudia wanted to know, and Sean shook his head.

'No, I'm not a magician.' They had been speaking in barely audible whispers, but Sean said, 'That's enough chatter, let's keep it down to a bellow from now on.'

So they went on in silence, and the forest about them was a perpetually changing show.

There were forty different varieties of the combretum family of trees, and this was not exclusively combretum forest, as many other varieties were mingled with them, each with a distinctive shape of trunk differing in the colour and texture of bark, some with branches denuded by winter, others with dense foliage of a myriad shades of green and gold and orange and cinnabar.

At times, the forest enclosed them like a palisade, then only moments later opened vistas of far hills and weirdly shaped kopjes, of open glades, and vleis from some of which the tall grass had been burned and the tender shoots laid a carpet of green over the black ash.

The new growth of grass had attracted herds of antelope into the vleis. They stood out in the open, sable antelope with long horns curved like scimitars, the proud necks of blood arabs, upper bodies sooty black as the ash of the vlei and their bellies snowy white.

Reed-buck with horns pricked forward inquisitively and tails like white powder puffs, zebra at a distance seeming not striped but a uniform grey colour, and wildebeest with roman noses and scraggly beards chasing each other like clowns in mindless circles, stirring the black ash in a cloud about themselves.

When the lion is not hunting, the animals that are his

natural prey are amazingly trusting and will stand and stare at him as he slouches past within fifty yards of them. In the same way they seemed to sense that this file of humans was not a threat, and they let them approach closely before moving off at a leisurely trot, and Claudia's delight buoyed her so she felt no fatigue even after four hours of hard walking.

In a gorge between two hills, water had been trapped in a narrow rock-pool. It was stagnant and green and bubbling with the gas of rotting vegetation, but the old bull had drunk from it and left a pile of his spongy yellow dung beside it.

'We'll take ten minutes' rest here,' Sean told them. 'You can have a drink now.' He looked at Claudia. 'But try to limit it to two mouthfuls, unless you'd like to try some of that.' He indicated the foul pool, and she grimaced.

He left her sitting beside her father and went to where Matatu stood alone at the head of the pool.

'What is it?' he asked. After twenty years, he could read the little man's moods. Matatu shook his head and his wrinkles sagged lugubriously.

'Something is not right here,' Matatu told him. 'The bull is unhappy. He goes one way and then the other. He travels swiftly, but without purpose. He does not feed, and he walks as though the ground burns his feet.'

'Why is that, Matatu?'

'I do not know,' he admitted. 'But I do not like it, *Bwana*.'

Sean left him and went back to where Claudia sat. 'Let's take a look at your feet.' He had spotted the slight limp she had developed in the last hour.

'Are you serious?'

She began to smile, but he took one of her feet in his lap, untied the laces, and pulled off her boot and sock. Her feet were long and narrow like her hands, but the skin was delicate and there was a bright pink spot on her heel and another on the ball of her big toe. Sean cleaned the tender spots with cotton wool and surgical spirit. It gave him an intimate and sensuous pleasure to handle those finely formed feet, but he told her severely, 'These must have been hurting you. Don't try and be brave, another few miles and you would have had blisters like a bunch of grapes, and we would have had a cripple on our hands.'

He taped the tender spots. 'Change socks,' he ordered. 'And the next time tell me as soon as it hurts.'

She obeyed him meekly, and they went on.

A little before noon, the spoor changed direction again and ran due east. 'We have gained an hour or two on him,' Sean whispered to Capo. 'But Matatu doesn't like it and neither do I. He's spooky and tense and he's heading straight for the Mozambique border now.'

'Do you think he has sensed us?' Capo was worried, but Sean shook his head.

'Impossible, we are still hours behind him.'

They stopped again briefly at noon to eat and rest, and when they went on again, they had not gone more than a mile before they entered a grove of marula trees. The ripe yellow fruit lay thickly on the ground beneath them and the old bull had not been able to resist that. He had fed heartily, spending at least three hours in the grove, shaking the trees to bring down more fruit, then at last setting off again eastwards as though suddenly remembering a rendezvous.

'At least, we have gained three hours on him,' Sean told them, but he was frowning. 'We are only ten miles from the Mozambique border. If he crosses, we have lost him.'

Sean considered running the spoor. In the old days of the bush war, he and Job and Shadrach never walked in pursuit of the enemy. Running, they had been able to cover sixty or seventy miles in a single day. He glanced back at Claudia; she might surprise him for she moved like an athlete and despite the incipient blisters there was still spring and snap in her step. Then he looked back at Riccardo and abandoned the idea. Capo was wilting in the ninety-five-degree heat of the valley. Sean tended to forget sometimes that Riccardo was only a year or two short of sixty. He had always been so fit, but now he was showing signs of distress, his eyes sunken in plum-coloured hollows and a greyish cast to his skin.

'Old beggar is looking sick,' Sean thought. 'I can't push him harder.'

He had let his attention wander, and now he almost ran into Matatu as the tracker stopped suddenly, still hunched over the spoor.

'What is it?' he demanded. The little man's agitation was obvious. He was shaking his head, and muttering in that obscure Ndorobo dialect that even Sean could not understand.

'What . . . ?' Sean broke off as he saw it. 'Oh shit!' he blurted. Two separate pairs of human tracks had come in from the side and now overlaid the elephant trail's pad marks. Here the earth was sandy and friable, the tracks clear.

Two men, wearing rubber-soled shoes. Sean recognized the distinctive pattern of the soles. Those ubiquitous Bata tennis shoes, locally manufactured, and sold for a few dollars in every street market and general dealer's store.

Even Riccardo picked out the alien human prints. 'Who the hell is that?' he demanded, but Sean ignored him and drew aside with Job to watch Matatu work.

Matatu scurried back and forth picking over the spoor like an old hen, and then came back to them. They squatted down, Job on one side of Sean, Matatu on the other – the council of war, from which only Shadrach was missing.

'Two men. One young and tall and thin, he walks on his toes. The other older, shorter, fatter. Both are carrying packs and *banduki*.' Sean knew he had deduced all this from the length of stride, the different way the two men heeled and toed under packs, and the unbalancing of a heavy weapon carried in one hand. 'They are foreigners. The men of the valley do not wear shoes, and these men came in from the north.'

'Zambian poachers,' Job grunted. 'They are after rhino horn, but they stumbled on the elephant and he is too big to let pass.'

'Bastards!' said Sean bitterly. In 1970 there had been an estimated twelve thousand black rhinoceros left in Zambia across the Zambezi river. Now there were none, not a single animal left. A Yemeni nobleman would pay fifty thousand dollars for a dagger with a rhinoceros-horn handle, and the poachers organized themselves like military expeditions. There were still a few hundred rhinoceros left on the southern side of the Zambezi valley, and from the Zambian side the poachers crossed the river in the night, slipping past the game department patrols. Many of the poachers had been bush fighters in the guerrilla war. They were hard men and killers of men as well as of the great animals on which they preyed.

'They will be carrying AKs.' Job looked at him. 'And there are probably more than two men, they will have out-flankers. We are outnumbered and outgunned, Sean. What do you want to do?'

'This is my concession,' Sean said. 'And Tukutela is my elephant.'

'Then you might have to fight them for both.' Job's noble Matabele features were solemn, but his eyes sparkled; he could not conceal the battle lust in them.

Sean stood up. 'Damned right, Job. If we catch them, we are going to fight them.'

'Then we must hurry.' Matatu stood up beside him. 'They are two hours ahead of us, and Tukutela must stop soon to feed. They will have him before we get there.'

Sean strode across to where Riccardo and Claudia were resting in the shade.

'Poachers!' he told them. 'Probably armed with automatic

weapons. Two at least, possibly more, all of them ruthless killers.'

They stared at him wordlessly, and Sean went on. 'We will have to move fast to prevent them getting to Tukutela before we do. I'll leave you and Claudia to follow with Pumula at your own speed. Job and Matatu and I are going to run the spoor, and try to drive them off before they get to the elephant. You keep the Rigby, Capo, and Job will take the Weatherby.'

As he began to turn away, Riccardo caught his arm. 'Sean, I want this elephant. More than anything left in my life, I want this elephant.'

'I will try and save him for you,' Sean nodded. He understood entirely. He felt the same way.

'Thank you.' Riccardo let his hand fall to his side and Sean went to where Job and Matatu were waiting. They had handed over their field packs to Pumula and carried only their water-bottles. Sean glanced at his stainless-steel Rolex. Four minutes since they picked up the poachers' spoor, four minutes wasted.

'Hot pursuit!' Sean ordered. 'And expect ambush!'

Job smiled at him. 'Old times,' he said. 'It makes me feel young again.'

Matatu pulled his loin-cloth up between his legs and tucked the skirt under his belt, then whirled and went away on the spoor at a loping trot. Sean had seen him keep up that pace from sun up to sun down. He went out onto the right flank, and Job who was left-handed took his natural side. Sean changed the cartridges in the .577 and began to run. Within seconds, Riccardo's group was out of sight in the forest behind them, and Sean concentrated all his attention ahead.

It required special skills and vast experience to keep the formation intact in this type of broken country. The flankers had to keep slightly ahead of the tracker, anticipating the line of the spoor, sweeping the terrain for ambush, covering and protecting Matatu, and yet keeping fifty paces out on each side, breaking their own trail, and still maintaining contact with the opposite flanker, all this while on the run and mostly out of sight of each other, with Matatu setting a furious pace in the centre.

When the spoor turned, the man on the outer flank had to wheel on the centre, covering twice the distance of his opposite number, and when the spoor crossed open ground, they had to increase the angle on the flank, forming an inverted spearhead formation, always protecting the centre, keeping contact with subtle bird-calls, the flute of a wood dove, the whistle of a bul-bul, the warble of a shrike, the pipe of a black kite, each had meaning, each a command or a warning.

All this and two other essentials, silence and speed. Job and Sean ran like a pair of kudu bulls, lightly and soundlessly, ducking and weaving under branches through thickets and thorns, quick and vigilant.

After the first hour, Matatu flashed a hand signal down a break in the forest, and Sean understood it readily. 'Two more,' the signal said.

Another pair of poachers had joined the first two, and they also were closing swiftly with the elephant.

They ran for another hour, never slackening for a moment, and Matatu signalled again from the centre.

'Very close.' An eloquent flash of his pink palm. 'Beware. Danger.' And Sean whistled like a sand grouse, checking the pace, the signal for imminent contact and they came down to a wary trot.

The trail had led them up the side of a low tableland, along an ancient elephant trail that was well trodden into the iron-hard earth. When they came out on top of the flat plateau they felt the stir of the evening breeze, cool and blessed out of the east, and Sean held his sweaty face up to it.

The plateau was less than a mile wide, and they crossed

it quickly and reached the far rim, dropping to their bellies and sliding over the sky line without showing a silhouette against the blue and then crouching below the crest and sweeping the ground below them, a shallow valley with another forested tableland beyond. A riverbed meandered down the centre of the valley, its course marked with a narrow ribbon of dark green riverine bush, and the rest of the valley fairly open: pale, winter grass shining in the sunlight, dotted ant-hills, each the size of a cottage, widely separated umbrella acacia with flat tops, and lemon-yellow trunks. Sean surveyed it all swiftly.

Out on the left. Job gave the penny-whistle snort of a reed-buck, one of the most urgent alarm calls in their repertoire. He was pointing down into the valley, half left from their front. Sean followed the gesture. For a moment he saw nothing, and then suddenly Tukutela, the Angry One, stepped into view.

He had been hidden from Sean by one of the huge ant-hills, but now he strode out into the open meadow, and Sean gasped aloud. Even from almost a mile away, Sean realized that he had only poorly remembered the magnificence of this animal.

Tukutela was the dark grey of volcanic rock, tall and gaunt; even at this distance Sean could make out the folds and tucks of his ancient riven hide, and the knotted outline of his spine beneath it. His ears fanned gently with each stride, and their edges were tattered and eroded, like a pair of battle ensigns torn with shot and blackened with the smoke of cannon.

Tukutela's tusks were black also, stained with age and the sap of the tall trees he had destroyed with them. From his gaping lower lip the tusks flared outwards, and then curved in again towards each other so the tips almost met nine feet from his lip. They were without taper, solid columns of ivory, hanging so low that in the centre they drooped below the level of the winter grass, and they seemed to over-burden even that massive frame. There would probably never be another pair of tusks like that ever again. This elephant was legend and history.

Sean felt a hot flare of guilt. No matter the legality of it, the killing of this beast would be a crime against Africa, an affront to the gods of the wilderness and the very soul of man, yet he knew he would not hesitate to do it, and that knowledge added poignancy to his sense of guilt. As a hunter, the nobler the quarry, the greater the compulsion to take the trophy. Job whistled again, pointing, diverting Sean's attention from the elephant, and only then Sean saw the poachers.

They were already closing in on the bull. He could see all four of them. They had just left the trees at the bottom of the slope, and were moving in single file into the grass meadow. The grass reached to their armpits, and their heads and shoulders bobbed like the cork line of a fishing-net in the pale sea of grass. Each of them carried an AK 47 assault rifle slung over his shoulder.

The light swift bullets those weapons fired were not at all suitable for hunting massive-bodied species, but Sean knew the technique. They would get in close and all four would open fire together, blazing hundreds of rounds into the bull, riddling his lungs with copper-jacketed bullets, bringing him down under the sheer weight of automatic fire power.

The line of poachers was swinging out to flank the elephant, not heading directly towards him, but keeping well below the wind, so that a fluke of the breeze would not carry their scent to him. Despite this detour, they were running hard and gaining on him swiftly. The bull was still totally unaware of their existence, heading with long swaying strides down towards the riverbed, but at this rate, Sean realized that they would intercept him and open fire before he reached it.

The government directive from the game department to the concessionaires was in plain language. Unauthorized armed men in a hunting concession, if apprehended in what was clearly a hunting operation, were presumed to be poachers. Four game department rangers and one concessionaire had been murdered by poachers during the past four years, and the directive was that fire could be opened on poachers without warning. The prime minister, Robert Mugabe, had made it even plainer. 'Shoot to kill,' were his exact words.

The .577 Nitro Express was a devastating weapon at close quarters, but over a hundred yards the heavy bullet dropped away rapidly. The group of poachers was six hundred yards away across the valley floor and Sean jumped up, and crouching low, slipped across the face of the slope to where Job was lying behind a fallen tree-trunk.

He dropped down beside him. 'Give me the Weatherby,' he ordered, and took the lighter weapon from his hands. Job was an excellent shot, but this called for Bisley-standard marksmanship.

Sean jerked the bolt open and checked that there was a cartridge in the chamber. It was a 180-grain Nosler, and Sean tried to estimate how much the bullet would drop over the range of six hundred yards, firing downhill, with a light breeze on his left shoulder. He remembered from the ballistic table that the bullet drop at three hundred and fifty yards would be six inches, at six hundred yards it would probably be four foot or more.

While he worked it out, he stripped off his shirt, rolled it into a bundle and placed it on the fallen tree-trunk behind which he and Job were crouched.

'Back me with the big *banduki*. Shoot very high with it,' he told Job, and settled behind the tree-trunk, resting the fore-end of the Weatherby on the pad of the shirt. He screwed the variable telescopic lens to full power and gazed through it.

He picked up the heads of the file of poachers. With this magnification, he could recognize two of the men as

Matatu had described them from their spoor. The tall lean one was leading, and he wore a blue denim jacket, traditional guerrilla uniform from the days of the bush war. Behind him came the shorter heavier man. He had a tiger-striped camouflage cap on his head and wore a plain khaki shirt.

Beyond them Sean could see the elephant. The magnification of the lens foreshortened the range so that the poachers seemed very close to their quarry. Even as he watched them, the leader of the column unslung the automatic rifle from his shoulder and made a gesture with his other hand. Behind him, the other three poachers fanned out into a skirmishing line and slipped their rifles off their shoulders, holding them at high port.

Sean snuggled down behind the Weatherby, digging in his heels, regulating his breathing, his forefinger resting lightly on the trigger. He picked out the tall leader in the denim jacket, and let the cross-hairs of the telescopic sights drift over the man's head.

The image wavered and quivered in the heat, and Sean watched the watery lines of mirage, for they were indicators of the strength and direction of the breeze; when they leaned over, the breeze was gusting, but they rose straight upwards like smoke in the lulls between gusts.

He drew a long breath, let half of it out and held the rest. The mirage steadied in a lull, and he took his aim a full body-length above the poacher's head. The image looked good but he did not pull the trigger. He squeezed the grip of the rifle with his whole hand as though he were modelling clay.

The butt plate slammed back into his shoulder as the barrel jumped high in the typically vicious Weatherby recoil, and he lost sight of the target.

Before he could collect himself, Job exulted, 'Shayile! A hit!' And when Sean brought the lens back there were only three heads showing above the grass.

All three poachers had turned and were firing their

weapons back towards the slope where Sean and Job were hidden, blazing wildly on fully automatic, their AKs beating like the rattle of kettledrums.

Beyond them, Sean saw the old bull elephant in full flight. His ears streaming back and his great black tusks lifted high above the grass, he crashed into the narrow ribbon of dark bush and out the other side.

'Run, my beauty,' Sean breathed. 'If I can't have you, nobody else will.' And he turned his full attention back to the band of poachers.

They were a crack unit, that was immediately obvious, two of them were throwing covering fire at the kopje, while the third had run to where the leader had gone down in the grass, and dragged him to his feet. The blue denim-clad leader had lost his rifle, and he was doubled up and clutching his side.

'Nicked him!' Sean muttered, and fired again. He saw dust fly above the grass, as his bullet fell close beside them. The poachers began to pull out, dragging their leader with them, placing an ant-hill between them and the kopje. Both Sean and Job were firing deliberately, but the range was increasing every second, and although Sean saw dust fly very close to the scurrying figures, they could not claim another hit before the band disappeared into the grass and scrub, and the clatter of automatic fire dwindled into silence.

Sean and Job waited fifteen minutes peering down into the valley, but they did not get another glimpse of them before Sean stood up.

'We'll go and take a look.'

'Careful,' Job warned. 'They could have doubled back to lay an ambush.' That was another old guerrilla trick, and they went down the slope cautiously.

Matatu led them to where the poacher had fallen. It was an area of flattened grass. The man's weapon had disappeared, one of the other poachers must have retrieved it. Matatu picked one of the grass stems and held it out to

Sean. The blood on it was almost dry. However, the bleeding had not been profuse and they found less than a dozen droplets on the grass or balled on the dry earth.

'Flesh wound,' Sean grunted. The drift of the breeze must have pushed the bullet off the vital areas of the man's body.

'Who do we follow, Tukutela or the poachers?' Job wanted to know.

'The poachers will be halfway back to Lusaka by now,' Sean grinned. 'Follow the elephant!' he ordered Matatu.

They tracked Tukutela across the riverbed and up the farther side of the valley. After his first panicked rush, the old bull settled down into that swinging stride that ate up the ground at a prodigious rate, and which he could keep up for days. He was boring away towards the east, towards the Mozambique border, only deviating slightly from his course to take a gap in a line of hills, or to climb the easier gradient when there was no pass.

They ran hard on his spoor. Not having to take precaution against ambush, they could push themselves to the limits, but the elephant was pulling away from them, and the day was wasting. The sun was casting their own long shadows ahead of them.

There was no defined border with Mozambique, no fence or cut line through the forest, but a sixth sense warned Sean that they had crossed.

He was about to give orders to halt when Job whistled softly and made a cut-out signal with his left hand. Matatu pulled up and shook his head in agreement, and the three of them bunched up and stood looking along the faint spoor which ran ahead of them into the darkening, eastern forest.

'Mozambique,' Job said. 'He has gone away.' And the others did not deny it.

'He still goes fast.' Matatu spat on the spoor. 'Faster than any man can run. We will not see Tukutela again this year.'

'Yes, but there will be another season,' Sean said. 'Next year, he will range back into the National Park and come again in the new moon across the Chiwewe river. We will be waiting for him.'

'Perhaps.' Matatu took a pinch of snuff from the duiker-horn container that hung around his neck. 'Or perhaps the poachers will find him again, or he will walk onto a land-mine in an old battlefield in Mozambique, or perhaps he will die of his own great age.'

The thought filled Sean with melancholy. Tukutela was a part of the old Africa. Sean had been born too late fully to experience that era. He had only been able to glimpse vestiges of it, yet he had a deep, nostalgic reverence for the history and past of his continent. It was all going so fast, trodden under the greedy rush for power by the thoughtless hordes of the emerging nations, by the unbridled tribal rivalries and the lawlessness of this new age. Once again, Africa was becoming the dark continent, but this time without the glory of its natural treasures, the wild game decimated, the forests hacked down for fuel, the very earth abused by primitive agriculture and animal husbandry, and the Saharan deserts each year marching southwards. Tukutela was one of the very few remaining treasures.

Sean turned back. He had wanted that elephant. He had wanted him with the utmost parts of his being. Now as he turned back into the west, the disappointment weighed down his legs and his heart, and he went heavily.

A little before midnight, they found Riccardo and Claudia sleeping on a mattress of cut grass, under a lean-to shelter beside a fire that had burned down to coals, while Pumula sat guard at the second fire close by.

Riccardo came awake the instant Sean touched his shoulder, and he scrambled up eagerly.

'Did you find him? What happened? What about the poachers?'

'He's gone, Capo. Across the border. We chased off the poachers, but Tukutela got clear away,' Sean told him, and Riccardo sagged back on the grass mattress and listened in silence while Sean described the chase and the contact with the poachers.

Claudia sat close to her father, and when Sean told them how Tukutela had crossed into Mozambique, she slipped her arm around his shoulders in a gesture of comfort.

'All right.' Sean stood up. 'There is one of my hunting tracks that cuts through about five miles south of here. Matatu and I will go back to fetch the truck, and Job will lead you to the track. I'll meet you there. Should take us four or five hours.'

By the light of the stars alone, Matatu led Sean for four hours through forest and dense bush, bringing him at last unerringly to where the truck was parked.

It was another hour's drive to the rendezvous where they found Claudia and Riccardo and the others sitting beside a fire on the verge of the rough track. They climbed wearily into the truck and Sean turned back and headed towards camp. It was four o'clock in the morning, over twenty-four hours since they had set out with such high hopes on the hunt.

They drove in silence for a while with Claudia asleep on her father's shoulder. Then Riccardo asked thoughtfully, 'Do you know where Tukutela has gone?'

'Beyond our reach, Capo,' Sean told him grimly.

'Seriously.' Riccardo was impatient. 'Is there one of his regular haunts where he will be headed?'

'That's rough country in there,' Sean murmured. 'Chaos and confusion. Villages burned and deserted, two armies fighting each other, with Mugabe's lads joining in.'

'Where has that elephant gone?' Riccardo insisted. 'He must have an established range.'

Sean nodded. 'We have worked it out, Job, Matatu and I. We reckon that he holes up from July to September in the swamps below the Cabora Bassa dam. Then in late September or the beginning of October, he crosses the Zambezi and heads north into Malawi, into the dense rain forest around Mlanje. He hides there until after the rains break and then comes south again, crosses the Zambezi near Tete and goes back into the Chiwewe National Park again.'

'So he will be heading for the swamps now?' Riccardo asked.

'More than likely,' Sean nodded. 'We'll get another crack at him next season, Capo.'

They reached camp at dawn, and there were steaming hot showers and freshly ironed clothes ready for them, and a huge breakfast spread in the dining tent. Sean loaded crispy bacon and fried eggs onto their plates.

'When we have finished breakfast, we'll catch up on some of the sleep we missed last night, sack out until lunch time.'

'Suits me,' Claudia agreed readily.

'Then we'll have a conference. We must work out our plans for the rest of the safari, we still have almost three weeks. We can try for another bull elephant, I can't offer you anything like Tukutela, but we might be able to find a sixty-pounder for you, Capo.'

'I don't want a sixty-pounder,' Riccardo said. 'I want Tukutela.'

'Don't we all, but let's drop it now.' Sean's irritation was undisguised. 'We can't do anything about it, let's just drop the subject.'

'What if we crossed the border and followed him into the swamps?' Riccardo did not look up from his eggs and bacon, and Sean studied his face before he laughed mirth-lessly.

'For a moment, you had me worried. I thought you meant it. We'll get Tukutela next season.'

'There isn't going to be another season,' Riccardo told him. 'You know damn well that Geoffrey Manguza is going to pull your licence and take Chiwewe away from you.'

'Thanks, Capo, you certainly know how to make me feel good.'

'No sense fooling ourselves. This is our last chance at that elephant.'

'Correction.' Sean shook his head. 'It's over for this season. We had our chance and we blew it.'

'Not if we follow him into Mozambique,' Riccardo said. 'Follow him into the swamps.'

Sean stared at him. 'My God, you are serious!'

'I told you. There is nothing that I want more in this life than that elephant.'

'So you expect Job and Matatu and me to commit suicide for a whim of yours.'

'No, I don't expect it for a whim – let's say for half a million dollars rather.'

Sean shook his head, but no words came out, and Riccardo went on.

'I feel responsible for you losing your licence. With half a million you could buy a good concession in Zambia or Botswana, or fifty thousand acres of game ranch in South Africa. Half a million. Think about it.'

Sean jumped up from the breakfast table so violently that he knocked his plate to the ground. He strode away without looking back.

He stood alone at the edge of the camp staring down towards the river where a small herd of impala were drinking, and a white-headed fish eagle sat on a dead tree above the green water. He did not see them.

He thought about what it would be like next year without his own concession. He owed his brother Garry almost fifty thousand dollars and his overdraft at the bank in Harare was touching ten thousand. Reema had told him that the bank manager was anxious to speak to him. Sean had avoided the appointment on his last visit to Harare.

He was over forty and he had accumulated nothing. His father might be delighted to welcome him back to the family company, bur his brother Garry was the chairman now and he would be less enthusiastic.

He thought about air-conditioned offices, neckties and dark business suits, interminable meetings with lawyers and engineers, rush-hour traffic and the smell of the city.

He thought about his father's philosophy, heartily endorsed by his brother, that a man had to start at the bottom of the company and 'work his way up'. Garry had more than twenty years' start on him. Garry loved it and he hated it.

He thought about half a million dollars. With that amount of money in his back pocket, he could thumb his nose at his bank manager, at Geoffrey Manguza, and at Garry Courtney, and at the rest of the world, and tell them all to go and get stuffed.

He turned away from the river, and started down the path to Job's tent. Job was eating alone at his own campfire, served by his youngest wife. He gave her a quiet order to leave when he saw Sean coming, then he took the coffee pot off the coals and poured a second mug and dribbled condensed milk from the can into it.

Sean sat on the carved native stool beside him and took the mug from him. He spoke in Sindebele.

'What would you think of a man who followed a great elephant like Tukutela to his secret place in the swamps along the Zambezi?'

'A man of such stupidity does not bear thinking of.' Job blew on his coffee to cool it, and they were silent for a long while.

Matatu, who had been sleeping in his hut nearby, sensed the presence of his master, and came out, blinking and yawning in the early sunlight, to squat at Sean's feet. Sean let his hand rest on the little man's shoulder for a moment. He felt him wriggle with pleasure under the touch. He did not even have to ask Matatu. He would go where Sean went, without question, without a moment's hesitation, so Sean spoke directly to Job.

112

'Job, old friend of many years, I give you something else to think on. Monterro wants to follow the elephant, he is offering half a million dollars. What do you think of half a million dollars?'

Job sighed. 'I do not have to think too long on that. When do we leave?'

Sean squeezed his arm hard, and stood up.

Riccardo was seated at the breakfast table with a cup of coffee and a cigar. Claudia was beside him, and they had been arguing. The girl's face was still flushed and her eyes asparkle, but she lapsed into silence as Sean entered the tent.

'Capo,' Sean said. 'You have no idea what it will be like across there. It will be Vietnam all over again, but this time without the back-up of the US army. Do you understand that?'

'I want to go,' Capo nodded.

'All right. Here are my terms. You will sign an indemnity, for whatever happens to you. I am not responsible.'

'Agreed.'

'Then I want a written acknowledgement of debt for the full amount, binding on your estate in the event of your death.'

'Give me the paper.'

'You are crazy, Capo, do you know that?'

'Sure,' Riccardo grinned. 'But what about you?'

'Oh, I was born crazy,' Sean laughed with him as they shook hands, and then he sobered. 'I want to fly a reconnaissance along the border to make sure there are no surprises waiting for us. If all is clear, we'll cross tonight. It will mean forced marches and travelling light. I want to be in and out in under ten days.'

Riccardo nodded and Sean told him, 'Get some rest now. You are going to need it.'

He was about to turn away when he caught Claudia's furious gaze. 'I'll radio Reema to send down another charter flight to pick you up tomorrow. She'll wangle you on the first commercial flight back to Anchorage.'

Claudia seemed about to reply when Riccardo laid his hand over hers. 'Okay,' he said. 'She'll go. I'll see to it.'

'Damn right, she'll go,' Sean said. 'She certainly isn't coming into Mozambique with us.'

Sean taped over the identification markings on the Beechcraft's wings and fuselage, obliterating them from the scrutiny of a ground observer. He made certain that the tape was so firmly adhering to the metalwork that the slipstream could not strip it away. While he worked, Job checked the emergency stores aboard the aircraft, in case they were forced down. Rather than the heavy double-barrelled rifle, he loaded Sean's lightweight 30/06 with the black glass-fibre stock.

They took off and Sean banked onto an easterly heading, keeping barely fifty feet above the treetops. He flew with the map on his lap, checking each landmark as it appeared ahead of them. Job sat beside him in the right-hand seat, while Matatu was in the seat behind Job. Even after all these years, Matatu was terrified of flying, and still occasionally suffered from air-sickness. Sean refused to allow him to sit in the seat behind him.

'Silly little bugger will puke down the back of my neck again.' So Job had to run that risk.

They reached the border and turned northwards along it, searching for troop movements or for any evidence of human presence. They found nothing, until thirty minutes later they saw the sheen of water on the horizon, an inland sea formed by the man-made dam on the Zambezi River. 'Cabora Bassa,' Sean grunted. The hydro-electric scheme, one of the biggest and most expensive in Africa, had been built by the Portuguese before they relinquished the colony to self-government.

Although the South Africans would have taken all the power that the project could supply, transporting it southwards across the grids to their great mines at Palabora in the Transvaal, and the revenue would have gone a long way to alleviating Mozambique's desperate economic plight, Cabora Bassa no longer sold a single kilowatt of electricity. The southbound power lines were continually sabotaged by the rebel forces, and the government troops were so demoralized that they made little attempt to protect the repair crews from attack. Thus it was years since a repair had even been attempted.

'By now the turbines are probably just piles of rust. Score another sweeping triumph for African Marxism,' Sean chuckled, and dropped a wing to turn 180 degrees and head back southwards. On this leg he flew deeper into Mozambique, setting a zigzag course to cover more ground, once again searching for occupied villages or mobile military units.

They found only the patterns of old cultivated lands, now gone back to weed and bush, and burned-out deserted villages, with no sign of human life around the shells of roofless huts.

Sean intersected the road running between Vila de Manica and Cabora Bassa, and flew along it for ten miles. He was so low that he could see the ruts and potholes in the surface and weeds growing in the wheel tracks. No vehicle had used it for months, perhaps years. The culverts and bridges had been destroyed by explosives and the bodies of mined vehicles, burned out and rusted, littered the verges.

He turned back towards the west and the border now, searching for a place that all three of them remembered so well. As they came up ahead, Sean recognized the symmetrical hillocks they called Inhlozane, 'The Maiden's Breasts', and south of them the confluence of two minor rivers, now reduced to strings of green pools in wide sand beds.

Job pointed ahead. 'There it is.' And in the back seat, Matatu forgot his fear and discomfort to cackle with laughter and clutch Sean's shoulder.

'Inhlozane. Do you remember, *Bwana*?'

Sean banked steeply over the junction of the two rivers, circling them, all three of them peering down. They could make out no traces of the old guerrilla camp. The last time they had been here was in the spring of 1976 and they had come as the scouts, Ballantyne's Scouts.

Under interrogation, a prisoner had revealed the existence of a major guerrilla training camp in this area, and the Rhodesian high command had sent one of the Vampire jets over on a high photographic run. The camp had been cunningly concealed, and every artifice of camouflage employed. However, the Rhodesian evaluators were highly skilled, most of them ex-RAF personnel. It is possible to camouflage the dugouts and hutments used by hundreds of men and women, but the pathways between them are the tell-tales. Thousands of feet moving daily between barracks and lecture huts, between mess halls and latrines, going out to forage for firewood or carrying water from the river, beat pathways that from the air look like the veins in a dead leaf.

'Between two and two and a half thousand,' the airforce photographic reconnaissance squadron leader had told the briefing. 'They have been there for approximately six months, so training is almost complete. They are probably just waiting for the rains to break before beginning a major offensive.'

A simultaneous incursion by two thousand trained terrorists would have strained the Rhodesian security forces' capabilities to breaking point.

'Preemptive strike,' General Peter Walls, the Rhodesian Commander-in-Chief, had ordered. 'I want a battle plan prepared within twenty-four hours.' The code name chosen for the attack was 'Popeye'.

Rivalry between the Selous Scouts and the Ballantyne Scouts was fierce, and Sean had been jubilant when he had been given the ground attack role of 'Popeye' in preference to the Selous lads.

They had gone in with the slow and ancient Dakotas, crowded on the benches along the fuselage, fifty men and their equipment to an aircraft, sitting on their parachutes. Almost equal numbers of black and white troopers, but homogeneous in their camouflage paint, they had jumped from three hundred feet, just enough height for the parachutes to flare before they hit the ground. From that height they jokingly referred to themselves as 'meat bombs'.

The jump area was twelve miles from the guerrilla training camp, and ninety-six miles inside the Mozambique border. They were on the ground an hour before sunset. All three hundred Scouts were assembled and ready to move out by nightfall.

They had made the approach march by moonlight, each man carrying a pack that weighed almost a hundred pounds, most of that weight made up of ammunition for the RPD machine-guns. They had reached the fork of the river after midnight and prepared their ambush position along the south bank, overlooking the dry riverbed and its shallow green pools, facing the training camp on the far bank.

Sean, with Job beside him, crept along the bank checking every position personally, speaking to his men in whispers, calling them by name. They had lain for the rest of the night behind their machine-guns, and the small sounds and the smells of the wood-smoke and cooking food had drifted across to them on the night breeze.

At dawn, a bugle had sounded reveille in the dark forest that hid the camps, and they had seen the obscure movement of many persons in the gloom beneath the trees.

Twenty minutes later, precisely at the moment of good shooting light, the Vampires had come whistling in from the west and dropped their napalm canisters. Towering balls of orange flame shot through with evil black smoke had erupted into the sky palling the sunrise; the heat and the chemical stink of the napalm came rolling down to where the Scouts lay in ambush. The Vampires had deliberately dropped their loads of napalm along the northern perimeter of the camp, sealing off that escape route with a wall of fire.

The Canberra bombers came in twenty seconds behind the Vampires, and their bomb loads were fragmentation and high-explosive. They fell into the camp with jarring crumping detonations, sending up fountains of dirt and debris, and the trainee guerrillas who survived came out of the forest, screaming and howling in a panic-stricken mob.

The napalm had cut them off from the north, and they poured into the riverbed, and came running directly at the waiting machine-guns. Sean let them come, studying them with a detached interest. There were almost as many women as men, but it was difficult to differentiate between the sexes. They wore no uniform, some were in khaki shorts and tee-shirts with portraits of guerrilla leaders or political slogans printed on the chests. Others wore blue denim or bush jackets and some were bare-chested and in their underwear. Nearly all of them were young, in their middle or late teens, all of them terrified and running blindly to escape the conflagration of napalm and high-explosive.

They splashed into the pools, and the sand held their feet, slowing them. As they ran, they looked back over their shoulders at the flames and dust of the camp, so none of them saw the gunners that waited for them on the south bank.

The riverbed was filled with struggling humanity, like a pit full of rats, and as the first of them reached the bank on which Sean lay and began to clamber up the steep earthen side, he blew a piercing blast on his whistle. The last note of the whistle was drowned out by gunfire, three hundred automatic weapons opening up together.

Sean had been hardened by years of brutal warfare, but even he found the carnage stunning. At close range, the volleys of machine-gun fire tore a human body to shreds, and went on to destroy the next rank and the next. Shot boiled the white sand of the riverbed, so it rose in a fog waist-high, and turned the running figures to ghostly silhouettes in the dust, and then hid them as they collapsed or were flung carelessly aside by point-blank bursts of fire.

The din lasted for four minutes, and then there were no more targets and the guns fell silent. Between them they had fired fifty thousand bullets into the riverbed and the barrels of the guns were so hot that, like the plate of a stove, they ticked and pinkled as they cooled. Though their ears were dulled and numbed by the roar of gunfire, they could hear the moans and cries of those who still lived in the riverbed.

Sean blew another blast on his whistle and they leaped down the bank, and went forward in a skirmishing line.

Sean's orders were that the only prisoners to be taken were to be officers or political commissars. As they crossed the river, they shot those who showed any signs of life, holding the muzzles against their heads, a single bullet for each, making certain that they would never recover from their wounds to attack another Rhodesian farm house or hack the arms and legs off the black villagers who refused to supply them with food and women. They left nobody alive in the riverbed and then went on to sweep through the camp, tossing grenades into the dugouts, searching the huts for survivors, and more importantly for maps and documents. Like all good Marxists, the guerrillas were obsessed with record-keeping. The capture of the camp archives was one of the major priorities of 'Popeye'.

Racing at the head of his men, Sean was the first to reach the headquarters hut in the centre of the camp. He recognized it by the gaudy flag drooping on its flagpole in front of it.

The doorway was dangerous. He fired a burst through the grass wall and then dived in head first through the window. There was a tall black man in the front office. He was dressed in blue denims, and he was scooping armfuls of documents out of the paraffin boxes that served as filing cabinets and dumping them in the centre of the floor. Clearly he was going to attempt to burn them, but now he dropped his armful of paper and reached for the pistol in the holster on his belt.

Sean kicked his legs out from under him and as he dropped, he slammed the butt of his weapon into the side of his neck just below the ear. As Sean rolled to his feet, Matatu appeared beside him like a grinning gnome and stooped to slit the unconscious guerrilla's throat with his skinning knife.

'No.' Sean stopped him. 'We want that one.' Job was seconds behind him, bursting into the room with the heavy RPD machine-gun held ready across his hip.

'Okay, Captain,' Sean ordered him. 'Get a detail to recover all this bumf.' He glanced at his watch. 'The choppers will be here in twenty minutes.'

The Rhodesian air force was desperately short of helicopters. They were under sanction by every nation in the world except South Africa, and a British warship was blockading the Mozambique channel to deny those ports to them.

They could risk only two helicopters for this operation and one of those was loaded with captured documents, almost five tons of them: lists of the trainees, and their organization, target priorities and supply sheets, equipment dossiers, training manuals, field evaluations of Rhodesian counter measures, communist propaganda, maps of the attack routes and safe corridors, the entire order of battle of the guerrilla army. It was a treasure trove, its acquisition a greater blow to the enemy than the hundreds of bodies lying in the riverbed, but it filled one of the precious helicopters.

The second Alouette helicopter Sean used for 'Casevac'

and for ferrying out the prisoners. However, the Scouts had taken more casualties than he had anticipated: three troopers had been injured in the parachute drop, torn cartilages and sprained ligaments, and five others had been wounded by the desultory and quickly suppressed counterfire of the more plucky of the guerrillas. Then one of the guerrillas had feigned dead in the riverbed and thrown a grenade when the Scouts came forward, killing a black trooper and wounding two others. The Scouts always took their dead out for decent burial and the trooper's corpse was already in its green plastic body bag.

In addition to his own casualties, Sean's men had captured eight suspected officers and commissars. The guerrilla leaders wore no insignia of rank but could usually be identified by the superior quality of their clothing, by their sunglasses, wrist-watches and by the rows of ballpoint pens in their breast pockets.

They had too many passengers for the helicopters, and Sean was forced to keep five of his prisoners with him for the outward march. He picked those who looked fit enough to survive a forced march with the Scouts, and one of these was the man they had captured in the command hut.

Forty-five minutes after the attack had begun, the last helicopter took off and the Scouts were ready to move out. They could expect the Frelimo counter-attack to be dilatory and unenthusiastic, but Sean was taking no chances. He was on the riverbank surveying the carnage of the killing ground. They couldn't afford the time to make a body count, but the air force would run another reconnaissance later this morning and they would get a fair estimate from the photographs.

'Must be at least fifteen hundred,' Sean decided. They were lying in heaps and windrows like newly cut wheat and already the flies were hanging over them in a grey mist.

Sean turned away from the scene. 'All right,' he called. 'Move them out!'

The first section of fifty men set off at a trot. The troop trucks would race across the border and come in as far as they could to meet them, but the men would still have to run thirty miles or more before they could ride, a full marathon under arms, but most of the ammunition had been shot away and the packs were almost empty.

Job hurried across to where Sean stood on the bank. 'The prisoner you took, Colonel. I have recognized him. It's Comrade China himself.'

'Are you sure?' Sean did not wait for Job to reply. 'Damn, if I had known I would have sent him out on the chopper.'

Comrade China was high on the wanted list of the Rhodesians. He was the area commander of the entire north-eastern sector, the equivalent of a major-general, and one of their most successful commanders, a man with a lot of interesting stories to tell to military intelligence.

'Make sure he gets out safely. Captain,' Sean ordered brusquely. 'Treat him like your new wife.'

'China refuses to march,' Job said. 'We can't shoot him, and we can't carry him. He knows that.'

Sean strode across to where the prisoner was held under guard. He squatted sullenly with his hands behind his head.

'On your feet and march,' Sean ordered, and Comrade China spat on Sean's boots. Sean unbuckled his holster and drew the .357 Magnum revolver. He laid it against the side of the man's head.

'On your feet,' he repeated. 'Your last chance.'

'You won't shoot,' the man sneered. 'You daren't shoot.' And Sean fired. The muzzle was aimed over Comrade China's shoulder, but the barrel was pressed hard against his ear.

Comrade China screamed and clutched at his ear with both hands. A thin trickle of blood from his ruptured eardrum ran out between his fingers. 'On your feet!' Sean said and, still holding his damaged ear, Comrade China spat at him again. Sean laid the revolver barrel against his other ear. 'After your ears, we will take out your eyes, with a sharp stick.' Comrade China stood up.

'At the double, move out.' Job took over. He placed his hand between China's shoulder-blades, and sent him tottering down the riverbank.

Sean took one more look around the battlefield. It had been done swiftly and thoroughly, what the Scouts called 'a good kill'.

'All right, Matatu,' Sean said softly. 'Let's go home.' And the little Ndorobo ran ahead of him.

When Comrade China faltered and his knees went rubbery and he collapsed from the agony of his burst eardrum, Sean gave him a subcutaneous shot of morphine from a disposable syringe and a drink from his water-bottle.

'For a soldier of the revolution who shoots babies and chops the feet off old women, this is a stroll in the park,' Sean told him. 'Brace up, China, or I'll blow your other ear out.' And he took one of his elbows and Job the other. Between them, they hoisted him to his feet and half carried him until the morphine had a chance to work, but they kept up the pace of the running column of Scouts through the forest and over the rolling rocky hills.

'You may have killed some of our people today.' After a mile or so the morphine was working and China became loquacious. 'Today you have won a single little battle, Colonel Courtney, but tomorrow we will have won the war.' China's voice was harsh with bitter self-righteousness.

'How do you know my name?' Sean asked with amusement.

'You are famous, Colonel, or should I say infamous. Under you, this pack of killer dogs is even more dangerous than when the murderous Ballantyne himself was leading it.'

'Thank you for the pretty compliment, my old China, but aren't you claiming victory a little prematurely?'

'The side which controls the countryside by night wins the war.'

'Mao Tse-tung,' Sean smiled. 'A most appropriate quotation for one of your name.'

'We control the countryside at last, we have you bottled up in your villages and towns. Your white farmers are losing heart, their women are sick of war. The black peasants are openly sympathetic to our cause. Britain and the world are against you. Even South Africa, your only ally, is growing disenchanted with the struggle. Soon, very soon . . .'

They argued as they ran, and despite himself, Sean could not suppress a grudging admiration for his prisoner. He was quick-witted, his command of English impressive and his grasp of politics and military tactics even more so. He was physically strong and fit. Sean could feel the wiry muscle in his arm as he supported him, and few other men with a burst eardrum could have sustained the pace of the march.

'He would make a superb Scout,' Sean thought. 'If we could turn him . . .' Many of his most valuable men were former guerrillas, captured and skilfully turned by Rhodesian intelligence.

So as they ran on he studied Comrade China with renewed interest. He was probably a few years younger than Sean. He had refined Nilotic features, more Ethiopian than Shona, a narrow high-bridged nose and chiselled lips rather than the broadly negroid. Even the morphine could not dim the intelligence of his large dark eyes. He was a handsome man, and of course, he would be tough and utterly ruthless. He would not have reached his rank were he not.

'I want him,' Sean decided. 'My God, he would be worth another full regiment to us.' And he tightened his grip on the man's arm, a proprietorial gesture. 'This little darling is going to get the full treatment.'

The vanguard ran into a Frelimo patrol in the middle of the morning and brushed them aside, hardly slackening their pace to do so. The corpses in their blotched Frelimo camouflage lay beside the track as they trotted past.

They came up with the troop convoy a little after midday. The trucks were guarded by the Eland armoured cars, and they had cans of ice-cold Castle beer in the cool boxes. The Scouts had covered forty-two miles in just over seven hours, and the beer tasted like nectar.

Sean gave a can to Comrade China. 'Sorry about your ear,' he told him, and saluted him with the beer can.

'I would have done the same to you,' China smiled, but his eyes were inscrutable. 'To our next meeting?' he suggested the toast.

'Until we meet again,' Sean agreed, and handed him over to a guard detail under a white sergeant. Then he climbed into the command armoured car to lead the final stage of withdrawal.

Sean extricated his column and had them back across the border ten and a half hours after the attack began. Ian Smith, the prime minister, came on the radio net in person to congratulate him and inform him of his decoration, a bar to his silver cross.

Sean didn't learn about Comrade China's escape until the column went into laager that evening. Apparently, China had slit the canvas hood of the troop truck and slipped through it while his guard was dozing. Undeterred by his manacles, he had dropped off the speeding truck, screened by the dust boiling out from the back wheels, and rolled into the head-high elephant grass along the verge.

Two months later, Sean had seen an intelligence report that placed China in command of the successful attack that had wiped out a supply convoy on the Mount Darwin road.

'Yes, Matatu, I remember it all very well,' Sean answered his question, and made one more steep turn above the site of the old terrorist base before he returned the Beechcraft to straight and level flight on a southerly heading.

He did not, however, fly as far southwards as the railway line that linked the port of Beira to the land-locked Zimbabwe border. This was a focus for all the military and rebel activity in the area, and the countryside would be swarming with Frelimo and Zimbabwean troops, all armed with RPG rockets and eager to get a shot at an unmarked low-flying aircraft with no flight authorization.

'At least', Sean told Job, 'it looks like a possibility.'

Job agreed. 'The border opposite our camp seems unde-fended and deserted.'

'Worth a try for half a million?' Sean asked, and Job just grinned at him.

'One more little chore before we go home,' Sean told them.

It required precise navigation and an eye for the terrain, but Sean crossed back into the Zimbabwean side and flying low they were able to pick out the spot where the previous day they had first come across the poachers' tracks; from that point, with Matatu craning his head to see down and calling directions, they found the tableland and valley where they had come up with the band of poachers and taken them under fire. From the air the distances seemed much shorter than they had on foot.

Matatu directed Sean along the trail the old bull had made towards the border. It seemed that his gift for direc-tion and terrain was not impaired by height above the ground, and Sean was following their course on the map he held in his lap.

'We are crossing back into Mozambique now.' Sean was scribbling notes on the map.

'That way.' Matatu leaned over the back of the seat and pointed out a more northerly track. Sean knew better than to argue with him, and turned a few degrees left.

Minutes later Matatu demanded he turn slightly south again.

'Little bugger is actually sensing the old bull's trail, he is thinking like the elephant,' Sean marvelled and at that moment, Matatu gave a squeak of triumph and pointed urgently out of the side window.

As they flashed across another dry riverbed, Sean glimpsed the tracks trodden in the soft sand. They were so deep that they were filled with shadow, a string of dark beads on the white background. Even Sean, who for twenty years had watched Matatu work, was amazed. On instinct alone, Matatu had followed the bull to this river-crossing. It was a supernatural feat.

Sean circled the tracks, his port wing-tip pointing directly at them, so steep was his turn.

'Which way now?' he called to the back seat, and Matatu tapped his shoulder and pointed downstream. Without demur, Sean followed the gnarled black finger.

'There he is!' Job shouted suddenly, and Matatu shrieked with laughter and clapped his hands, bouncing in his seat like a child at the pantomime.

A mile ahead the river ran into a wide vlei that still held water from the last rains. The elephant's humped back showed above the tops of the tall reeds that surrounded the pool, like a grey whale in a sea of green.

As they raced low towards him, the elephant heard the Beechcraft's engine. He lifted his head and spread his ears wide, turning to face them, and they saw his tusks, those legendary shafts of black ivory raised to the sky. The beauty of their curved symmetry struck Sean all over again.

There was just a glimpse of them as they flashed overhead, but the image was printed vividly on his mind's eye. Half a million dollars and those tusks, he had risked his life a hundred times for much lesser prizes.

'Going back for another look?' Job asked, twisting his head to try and see back over the tail-plane.

'No,' Sean shook his head. 'We don't want to disturb him more than necessary. We know where to find him, let's go home.'

*

'It's my half-million dollars that you are so gaily throwing around,' Claudia told her father.

'How do you work that out?' Riccardo asked. He was lying on his camp-bed dressed in a pair of silk pyjama bottoms, his chest and his feet bare. Claudia noticed that most of his body hair was still crisp, curly and black, with only a patch of fuzzy grey in the centre of his chest.

'My inheritance,' she explained sweetly. 'You are blowing my inheritance, Papa.'

Riccardo chuckled. She had the sass of a divorce lawyer, coming bursting into his tent to renew the argument which he thought he had finalized in the mess tent over breakfast.

'If I'm not going to get it in your will, the very least you can do is let me enjoy it with you now.'

'According to the last audit, young lady, you will have a little over thirty-six million coming to you after taxes, and after I have allowed myself this small extravagance. I hasten to add that every cent is tied up in a trust fund that not the most crafty lawyers will ever break. I don't want you handing my hard-earned loot out to one of your bleeding-heart charities.'

'Papa, you know the money has never interested me. What interests me is coming with you on this crazy jaunt after the elephant. I came to Africa with you on the understanding that I was to be included in everything. That was our bargain.'

'I'll say it one more time, *tesoro*, my treasure.' He only called her by that baby name when he was feeling very affectionate or very exasperated. 'You are not coming into Mozambique with us.'

'You'd go back on your solemn promise?' she accused.

'Without a qualm,' he assured her. 'If your safety or happiness was involved.'

She jumped up from the canvas camp-chair and began to prowl around the tent. He watched her with secret pleasure. Her arms were folded over those pert little breasts, and she was frowning heavily, but the frown left no lines on her smooth plastic skin. In looks she reminded him of the young Sophia Loren, his favourite actress. Now she stopped beside the camp-bed and glared down at him.

'You know I always get my way,' she said. 'Why don't you make it easier for both of us, and just say I can come.'

'I'm sorry, *tesoro*. You aren't coming.'

'All right.' She drew a deep breath 'I don't want to do this, Papa, but you leave me no choice. I have begun to understand what this means to you, why you are prepared to pay such a vast sum for a chance to do it, but if I can't go with you, as is my right and my duty, then I will prevent you from going.'

He chuckled again, easily and unconcernedly.

'I am serious, deadly serious, Papa. Please don't make me do it.'

'How can you stop me, little girl?' he asked.

'I can tell Sean Courtney what Doctor Andrews told me.'

Riccardo Monterro came to his feet in one lithe swift movement and seized her arms.

'What did Andrews tell you?' he asked in a voice as thin and cutting as a razor blade.

'He told me that last November you had a little black spot on your right arm,' she said. Instinctively, he put his right arm behind his back, but she went on. 'It had a pretty name, melanoma, like a girl's name, but it wasn't pretty at all, and you left it too late. He cut it out, but the pathologist graded it Clark 5. That's six months to a year. Papa. That's what he told me.'

Riccardo Monterro sat down on the bed and his voice was suddenly very weary.

'When did he tell you?'

'Six weeks ago.' She sat down beside him. 'That is why I agreed to come to Africa with you. I didn't want to be apart from you for one day of the time we have left. That is why I am coming with you into Mozambique.'

'No.' He shook his head, 'I can't let you.'

'Then I will tell Sean that at any moment it may reach your brain.'

She did not have to elaborate. Andrews had been most graphic as he described the many possible directions the disease could take. If it went to the lungs, it would be death by suffocation, but if it affected the brain or nervous system, it would be either general paralysis or total derangement.

'You wouldn't,' he said, shaking his head. 'The last thing in my life that I really want. You wouldn't deny it to me?'

'Without a qualm,' she repeated his own words. 'If you refuse me my right to be with you for every one of these last days, and to be with you at the end as is the duty of a loving daughter.'

'I can't let you.' He let his face sink into the cup of his hands, a gesture of defeat that hurt her, and it required all her resolve to keep her tone firm.

'And I can't let you die alone,' she replied.

'You don't understand how much I want this thing, it's the last thing in my life. The old bull and I will go together. You don't understand, if you did you wouldn't prevent me.'

'I'm not preventing you,' she said gently. 'I want you to have it, if you will let me come with you.' As she said it, they both became aware of a faint vibration in the air, and they looked up together.

'The Beechcraft,' Riccardo murmured, 'Sean is on his way back to the airstrip.' He glanced at his wristwatch. 'He'll be here within the hour.'

'And what will you tell him?' Claudia asked. 'Will you tell him that I am coming with you?'

'No!' Sean let out a bellow. 'No bloody fear! Forget the idea, Capo. She can't come and that's absolutely bloody final!'

'For half a big M, I get to call the shots,' Riccardo told him quietly. 'I say she's coming, so she's coming.'

They were standing beside the Toyota. Riccardo and Claudia had met Sean as he drove into camp. Sean drew a breath and glared at father and daughter as they stood side by side confronting him. He saw that both their expressions were set and determined.

Sean had been on the point of bellowing again, but with an effort he checked himself. 'Be reasonable, Capo.' He moderated his tone. 'You know it's impossible.'

They stared at him grimly, closed against argument or reason.

'It's war out there. I can't take her.'

'Claudia comes with us.'

'The hell she does.'

'What are you making a fuss about, is it because I am a woman?' Claudia spoke for the first time. 'There is nothing a man can do that I can't.'

'Can you pee standing up?' He wanted to disconcert her, make her lose her temper, but she ignored the crude jibe and went on as though he had not spoken.

'You've seen me hike, I can stand the heat and the tsetse fly, I'm as good as my father.'

He turned from her deliberately and spoke to Riccardo.

'As her father you can't allow it. Can you imagine what would happen to her if she were caught by a gang of Renamo cutthroats?'

He saw Riccardo flinch, but Claudia had seen it also and before he could weaken, she took his hand and spoke up firmly.

'Either I go, or nobody goes, and you can kiss your half a million good-bye, Colonel Sean Courtney.'

That was the key, the half-million dollars. She had him, and they both knew it. He couldn't afford to pass it by, but he made one last effort.

'Is she in charge around here, Capo? Do I take my orders from you or from her?'

'That won't work either.' Claudia tried to keep her tone placatory, although she longed to tear into him with tooth and nail. That crude sally of his rankled. 'My father and I are agreed on this. Both of us go, or we call the deal off. Isn't that right, Papa?'

'I'm afraid that's it, Sean.' Riccardo looked tired and discouraged. 'It's not negotiable. If you want your money, you take Claudia along with us.'

Sean turned on his heel and strode away towards his own tent, but after a few paces, he stopped and stood with his hands on his hips.

Sean's shouts had attracted the camp servants, and they hovered around the mess tent and peered out of the doorway and windows of the kitchen hutments, apprehension mingled with curiosity.

'What the hell are you all gawking at?' Sean roared. 'Have you got no work to do around here?' And they disappeared with alacrity.

Sean turned and walked slowly back to where the two of them stood beside the Toyota.

'Okay,' he agreed, staring coldly at Claudia. 'Cut your own throat, but don't come to me for a bandage.'

'I won't, that's a promise.' Her voice was honey dripping, more irksome to him than straightforward gloating would have been, and they both knew that their declared truce was at an end.

'We've got some paperwork to do, Capo.' Sean led the way to the mess tent without looking back at them.

With two fingers, Sean typed out the indemnity statements on his old portable Remington, one for Riccardo and one for his daughter. Each began; 'I acknowledge that I am fully aware of the danger and the illegality . . .' Then he typed an acknowledgement of debt for Riccardo to sign and called Job and the chef to witness the signature. He sealed all the copies in an envelope addressed to Reema at the Harare office and locked it in the small steel safe at the back of the mess tent.

'Let's do it, then,' he said.

The poaching expedition would consist of the three whites, Job, Matatu, Pumula and the stocky, bearded tracker who had picked up Tukutela's spoor at the river-crossing. His name was Dedan.

'It's too many, but each of those tusks weighs 130 pounds,' Sean explained. 'Matatu is too small to act as a porter. We need four big men to bring them back.'

Before the equipment was loaded into the Toyota, Sean ordered it laid out, and he opened and checked each pack. Claudia protested when he opened her personal pack. 'That is an invasion of my privacy!'

'So take me to the supreme court, ducky,' he challenged as he went through it remorselessly, throwing out most of the tubes and bottles of cosmetics, allowing her only three tubes of moisturizer and sunscreen.

'One change of underwear,' he ordered, discarding half a dozen pairs of panties. 'But you'll need two more pairs of thick socks. Get them.'

He pulled out her box of Tampax. 'Everything a man can do, and then some,' he remarked coldly. 'You don't need the box, it takes up too much space. Pack them loose.' Her poorly suppressed fury gave him a sour pleasure.

By the time he had finished, they were down to the barest essentials, and the packs were carefully weighed and apportioned depending on the strength and physical condition of each bearer. Sean, Job, Pumula and Dedan carried sixty pounds each, Riccardo and Matatu forty, while Claudia was down to twenty-five pounds.

'I can carry more,' she protested. 'Give me forty, the same as Matatu,' Sean did not bother to answer her.

'And what's more, I eat half as much as any of you!' But he had already turned away to supervise the loading of the Toyota.

There were still four hours of daylight remaining when they left Chiwewe camp, but Sean drove the first section very fast, jouncing them around in their seats. It was partly an expression of his objection to Claudia's presence but mostly an urgent desire to be at the jump-off point before nightfall.

As he drove, he spoke in a tightly controlled voice. 'Before we commence this guided tour of the Mozambiquan paradise of the proletariat, this shining gem of African socialism, will you bear with me while I give you a few facts and figures.' Nobody protested, so he went on. 'Until 1975 Mozambique was a Portuguese colony. For almost five hundred years it had been under Portuguese control and had been a reasonably happy and prosperous community of some fifteen million souls. The Portuguese, unlike the British or German colonists, had a relaxed attitude towards miscegenation and the result was a large mulatto population, and an official policy of "Assimilado" under which any person of colour, if he attained certain civilized standards, was considered to be white and enjoyed Portuguese nationality. It all worked very well, as indeed did most colonial administrations, especially those of the British.'

'Bullshit,' said Claudia demurely. 'That's limey propaganda.'

'Limey?' Sean smiled thinly. 'Careful, your prejudice is showing, nonetheless your average Indian or African living today in a former British colony is a damned sight worse off now than he was then. Certainly that goes one hundred times more for your average black man living in Mozambique.'

134

'At least they are free,' Claudia cut in, and Sean laughed.

'This is freedom? An economy managed under the well-known socialist principles of chaos and ruination which has resulted in a negative growth rate of up to ten per cent per annum for every year since the Portuguese withdrawal, a foreign debt amounting to double the gross national product, a total breakdown in the educational system, only five percent of children regularly attending a recognized school, one doctor per forty-five thousand persons, only one person in ten with access to purified drinking water, infant mortality at 340 per 1000 births. The only worse countries in the world are Afghanistan and Angola, but as you say, at least they are free. In America, where everybody eats three huge meals a day, freedom may be a big deal, but in Africa a full belly counts for a hell of a lot more.'

'It can't be as bad as that,' she protested.

'No,' he agreed, 'It's a lot worse. I haven't mentioned two other factors, the civil war and Aids. When the Portuguese were pushed out, they handed over to a dictator named Samora Machel and his Frelimo party. Machel was an avowed Marxist. He didn't believe in the nonsense of elections, and his rule was directly responsible for the present condition of the country, and for the emergence of the National Mozambiquan Resistance or as it is known to its friends and admirers, Renamo. Nobody knows much about it, what its objectives are, who its leaders are, all we know is that it controls most of the country, especially the north, and that it is made up of a pretty ruthless bunch of characters.'

'Renamo is a South African front organization, directed, supplied and controlled from Pretoria,' Claudia helped him out. 'Committed to the overthrow of sovereign government and the destabilization of the southern continent.'

'Well done, ducky,' Sean nodded approval. 'You've been studying the wisdom and erudition of the Organization of African Unity and the non-aligned nations. You have even

135

mastered their jargon. If only South Africa had the military and technological capability to commit half the skulduggery it is accused of, it would not be simply the most powerful country in Africa, it would be running the entire world.'

'I keep forgetting you are one of them, which is silly of me. You don't attempt to conceal your bigotry. The simple fact is that your government and apartheid are the scourge and the curse of Africa.'

'Of course, we are responsible for everything, the Aids epidemic, the famines of Ethiopia and Angola and Mozambique, the breakdown of government in Uganda and Zambia, the corruption in Nigeria and Zaire, it's all a dirty South African plot. We even killed Samora Machel, we fed vodka to the Russian crew of his Tupolev jet and with our incredibly sophisticated technology, lured them over the border. Machel hit one of our racist mountains with such force that his brains and major organs were instantly expelled from his body, nevertheless our apartheid doctors kept him alive long enough to torture state secrets out of him. That is the truth as determined by UNO and OAU.'

'Shut up,' said Riccardo Monterro. 'I've had enough. Shut up, both of you.'

'Sorry,' Sean grinned at him. 'I get carried away. I just wanted to let you know what to expect when we cross the border. We can just hope that we aren't going to meet any of the lads from either Frelimo or Renamo, there is not a lot to choose between them. They both shoot the same bullets.'

The thought made the back of his own neck prickle, and he felt his mood lighten. He was going into mortal danger again, and the thrill of it began. Somehow having the girl with him no longer irked but rather heightened that anticipation, and he felt his resentment of her begin to fade. He was glad she was here rather than jetting back to Alaska. Sean drove on in a silence that gripped them all, even the men standing braced against the roll-bar in the back of the Toyota. The closer they came to the border, the deeper the silence became.

At last Sean turned and looked over his shoulder, and Job nodded in agreement.

'This is it, ladies and gentlemen,' Sean said quietly. 'All change!' He let the Toyota trundle to a halt where the track crossed a stony ridge.

'Where are we?' Riccardo asked.

'As close as we can safely get to the border, about three miles. From here, it's shanks' pony.'

Riccardo swung one leg out of the truck, but Sean said sharply, 'Hold it, Capo, step onto that slab of rock, leave no tracks.'

One at a time, each carrying their own pack, they alighted from the truck, at Sean's instruction stepping precisely in the footsteps of the person in front. Matatu was the last off, and he came backwards brushing over the sign with a switch of dried grass, wiping out every trace of their departure from the truck.

The chef had come with them to drive the truck back to the camp.

'Go in peace, *Mambo*!' he called to Sean as he pulled away.

'Fat hope,' Sean laughed, and sent him off with a wave. Then to Job, 'Anti-tracking, let's go!'

Neither Riccardo nor Claudia had ever watched anti-tracking procedure, for while hunting they had always run free in pursuit. The formation for anti-tracking was Indian file, Job leading and everyone else stepping in his footprints. Behind them all, Matatu, the old maestro, was covering the sign, replacing a pebble lichen-side up, stroking a blade of grass into its original position, flicking at the earth with his grass switch, picking up a leaf dislodged from a low-hanging branch or the bruised blade of grass on which a foot had trodden.

Job avoided the game paths and soft ground, choosing

always the line of march which was most obscure and yet moving surprisingly fast, so that within half an hour, Claudia felt the chill of fresh sweat between her shoulder-blades and at the cleavage of her shirt-front.

Job led them to the top of a low kopje, and Sean motioned them to conceal themselves below the skyline with the sunset behind them.

Watching them work, Riccardo remarked softly, 'Pumula and Dedan seem to know what they are doing.' The two of them had moved out to guard the flanks without being ordered to do so.

'Yes,' Sean settled down between him and Claudia, using the same low bush for cover. 'They were both non-coms in the Scouts, they've done this before.'

'Why are we stopping here?' Claudia asked.

'We are sitting on the border,' Sean explained, 'and we'll spend the last of the daylight studying the ground ahead. As soon as the moon comes up, we'll move in. You can relax until then.'

He lifted his Zeiss binoculars and stared through them; a few yards away Job lay on his belly and focused his own pair of binoculars in the same direction. They lowered the binoculars from time to time to blink their vision clear or polish an imaginary speck from the lens. Claudia had noticed how they protected and looked after these most essential tools of their craft, but apart from that, their concentration on the terrain ahead was absolute, and ended only when the last gleam of the sunset faded. Then Sean buttoned the binoculars into his top pocket and turned to her.

'Time for your make-up,' he said. For a moment she did not understand and then she felt the greasy touch of camouflage cream on her cheek and instinctively pulled away.

'Hold still,' he snapped. 'Your white face shines like a mirror. It's good for insects and sunburn also.'

He daubed her face and the backs of her hands.

'Here comes the moon.' Sean finished working on his own camouflage and screwed the top back on the tube of cream. 'We can go in now.'

Sean changed the formation once again, putting out flankers. Job and Pumula, while he led the centre and, once again, Matatu brought up the rear, diligently sweeping their tracks.

Once Sean stopped and checked Claudia's equipment. A loose buckle on her pack had been tapping regularly in time with her stride, a noise so small that she had not noticed it.

'You sound like the charge of the Light Brigade,' he breathed in her ear, as he adjusted it.

'Arrogant bastard,' she thought, and they went on in silence, an hour and then another hour without pausing. She never knew the exact moment when she crossed the border. The moonlight through the forest was silvery, and the shadows of the trees flickered over Sean's broad shoulders ahead of her.

Gradually the silence and the moonlight gave the march a dream-like unreality, and she found herself mesmerized by it, her movements were like those of a sleep-walker, so that when Sean stopped abruptly she bumped into him and might have fallen had he not whipped a hard muscular arm Around her and held her.

They stood frozen, listening, staring into the dark forest. After almost five minutes Claudia moved slightly to free herself from his arm, but instantly his grip tightened and she submitted to it. Out on the right flank. Job gave a bird call, and noiselessly Sean sank to the ground drawing her down with him, and her nerves strained tighter as she realized that there must be real danger out there. Now his arm no longer annoyed her. Instinctively she relaxed and pressed a little closer to him. It felt good.

Another soft bird call from the darkness, and Sean put his lips to her ear.

'Stay!' he breathed, and she felt lonely and exposed as he released her, and she watched him disappear like a ghost into the forest.

Sean moved in a low crouch, rifle in one hand, reaching forward to touch the earth with the fingers of his left hand, brushing away the dry twigs and leaves that might crackle under his foot before stepping forward. He sank down ten feet from where Job lay and glanced across at his dark shape. The pale palm of Job's hand flashed a signal, and Sean concentrated on the left front that Job had indicated.

For long minutes, he neither saw nor sensed anything untoward, but he trusted Job completely and he waited with the hunter's patience. Suddenly he caught a taint on the night air and he lifted his nose and sniffed at it. Both his confidence and his patience were repaid. It was the acrid stink of burning tobacco, one of those cheap black Portuguese cigarillos. He remembered them so well, they had been issued to the guerrillas in the days of the bush war, and were probably Frelimo issue still.

He signalled Job and they went forward, leopard-crawling, absolutely silently, forty paces, and Sean picked out the glow of the cigarette as a man drew upon it. Then the man coughed, a soft phlegmy sound, and spat. He was at the base of one of the large trees directly ahead; now Sean could make out his shape. He was sitting with his back to the trunk.

'Who is he? Local tribesman? Poacher? Bee hunter? Refugee?' None of those seemed likely. This one was awake and alert, almost certainly a sentry. As Sean reached that conclusion, he sensed other movement farther out, and he flattened against the earth.

Another man emerged from the forest, and came directly to where the sentry was rising to his feet to meet him. As soon as he stood, Sean could make out the AK 47 rifle slung over his shoulder, muzzle down. The two men talked softly together.

'Changing the guard,' Sean thought as the new sentry leaned against the tree and the other man sauntered back into the forest.

'That is where the camp is,' Sean guessed.

Still on his belly, he leopard-crawled forward, passing well wide of the sentry who would be fresh and vigilant. Once he was within the perimeter, Sean rose into a crouch and went forward swiftly.

He found the camp in a fold of ground up against the hills. It was a fly-camp, no huts nor shelters, only two small fires that had burned down to coals. He counted eleven men lying around the fires, all of them with a blanket pulled completely over their heads in typical African fashion. There might be five or six others on guard duty, but it was a small band.

Even lacking automatic weapons Sean and his men could have dealt with them. All of Sean's men still carried their piano-wire nooses and Matatu his skinning knife with the blade so sharp that it was honed down to half its original width. Nobody in the camp would have even woken up.

Sean shook his head with regret, he was certain now that these were either Frelimo regular troops or Renamo guerrillas. He had no quarrel with them, whoever they were. Just as long as they did not interfere with his elephant hunt. Sean backed away and Job was waiting for him at the perimeter.

'Eleven of them at the fires,' Sean breathed.

'I found two more sentries,' Job agreed.

'Frelimo?'

'Who knows?' Job shrugged, and Sean touched his arm and they crept away, farther out of earshot of the camp so they could speak more freely.

'What do you think, Job?'

'A small group, they mean little. We can go around them.'

'They could be the advance guard for a bigger party,' Sean suggested.

141

'These are not crack troops,' Job muttered contemptuously. 'Smoking on guard duty, sleeping next to a fire, they aren't soldiers, they are tourists.' Sean smiled at the term of derision. He knew that Job's determination was more Anglo-Saxon than African. Once he had decided, it was difficult to dissuade him.

'You want to go on?' he asked.

'For five hundred thousand dollars,' Job whispered, 'you're damned right I want to go on!'

Claudia was afraid. The African night was so charged with mystery, with uncertainty and menace. The wait aggravated her feeling of apprehension. Sean had been gone for almost an hour, and though her father was close beside her, she felt alone and very vulnerable.

Then suddenly, Sean was back, and she experienced a rush of relief. She wanted to reach out for him and cling to him, and was ashamed of herself for the weakness. Sean was whispering to her father, and she drew close to listen. Her arm touched Sean's bare arm, but he did not seem to notice, so she left it there for the feeling of security and comfort it gave her.

'Small party of armed men camped up ahead,' Sean was explaining. 'Not more than twenty of them. We don't know who the hell they are, but we can circle around them and keep going, or we can turn back. It's up to you, Capo.'

'I want that elephant!'

'This is probably your last chance to pull out,' Sean warned him.

'You are wasting time,' Riccardo said. Claudia was torn by her father's decision. It would have been such an anticlimax to turn back now, and yet her first taste of the real flavour of Africa had been disconcerting. She realized as the march resumed and she fell in behind Sean, that this was the first time in her life that she had been beyond the trappings and buttresses of civilization, the first time that there was no police force to protect her, no recourse to law or justice or mercy. Here she was as vulnerable as an antelope to the leopard, in a forest full of predators.

She quickened her step, closing up behind Sean, and found to her surprise that in some bizarre fashion she was more alive and aware than she had ever been before. For the first time in her life, she was on the bottom rung of existence, the level of survival. It was a novel and quite overwhelming sensation. She was glad that her father had not decided to turn back.

Claudia had long lost all sense of direction for Sean led unpredictably. They turned and twisted through the forest, sometimes moving swiftly and at others, creeping forward a stealthy pace at a time and then freezing into absolute stillness at a signal from the flank which often she had not even heard. She noticed Sean look up at the night sky every few minutes and guessed that he was navigating by the stars, but to her their whorls and blazes and fields were as confused as the lights of a foreign city.

Then after a while, she realized that they had not turned nor paused for a long while, and were once again heading in a straight line. Obviously, they were clear of danger for the moment. With the excitement over, she soon felt the weight of her legs and the weariness in the small of her back. The pack between her shoulders seemed to have quadrupled in weight, and she glanced at her wristwatch. The luminous dial showed her that they had been going for almost five hours since circling around that hidden camp.

'When will we rest?' she wondered, but made it a point of honour to keep close behind Sean, and not to lag by a single pace. Almost as though a refrigerator door had opened, the temperature plunged and when they crossed another open glade, the dew on the long grass soaked the legs of her trousers, and her boots squelched. She shivered, for the first time in real discomfort.

'When will he rest?' She stared at Sean's back, resenting him, willing him to stop. On he went and still on, and she had the feeling that he was deliberately trying to humiliate her, to break her down, to force her to squeal for mercy.

'I'll show you.' She did not slacken her pace as she reached back and unstrapped her Gortex ski jacket from the top of her pack. It was really cold now, the frost crackled underfoot, and her feet were numb but she kept her station in the line and quite suddenly she realized that she could see clearly each thick glossy tress of hair down the back of Sean's neck.

'Dawn, I thought it would never come.' And as she thought it, Sean stopped at last, and she pulled up beside him with the nerves in her legs jumping and trembling with fatigue.

'Sorry, Capo,' Sean spoke softly past her. 'I had to push a little. We had to get well clear of that bunch before light. How are you making out?'

'No problem,' Riccardo muttered, but in the grey dawn light, his face looked pale and drawn. He was suffering as she was, and she hoped she didn't look as bad. He went to find a place to sit, and lowered himself stiffly.

Sean glanced at Claudia still standing beside him. Neither of them spoke, but he had a faint enigmatic smile on his lips.

'Don't ask me how I feel,' she thought. 'I'd rather drink Drain-o than tell you the truth.'

He inclined his head slightly, condescension or respect, she wasn't sure.

'First day and the third are always the worst,' he said.

'I feel fine,' she said. 'I can go on quite happily.'

'Sure,' he grinned openly. 'But you'd better go and look after Papa rather.'

Sean brought mugs of tea to where she sat beside her

father, wrapped in her lightweight down-filled sleeping-bag against the dawn chill. Job had brewed on a tiny smokeless fire which he extinguished immediately the billy boiled. The tea was strong and sweet and scalding, she had never tasted anything more welcome. With it, he handed her a stack of maize cakes and cold cuts of venison. She tried not to wolf them.

'We'll move on in a few minutes,' he warned her, and when he saw the dismay in her eyes, he explained.

'We never sleep next to a cooking-fire, it can attract the uglies.'

They went on five miles and in the middle of the morning, on higher ground in a place secure and easily defended, Sean showed her how to scoop a hollow for her hip and use her pack as a pillow. She fell asleep as though she had been sandbagged.

She could not believe it when he shook her awake only a minute later. 'It's four o'clock.' He handed her a mug and another stack of maize cakes. 'You've slept six hours straight, we are moving out in five minutes.'

Hastily she rolled her sleeping-bag and then peered at herself in the metal hand-mirror which she had surreptitiously retrieved after Sean had thrown it out of her pack.

'Oh God,' she whispered. The camouflage cream had caked and striped with her sweat. 'I look like Al Jolson in drag.' She tidied her hair, dragging her comb through the tangles, and then tied a scarf around it.

With short breaks every two hours, they kept going all that night. At first, Claudia's legs felt as though they were in plaster casts, but soon she walked the stiffness out of them and she kept her place in the line without lagging, though the pace Sean set was every bit as hard as the previous night.

In the dawn, they drank tea. Claudia had begun to depend on the brew. She had always been a coffee-drinker, but now on the march, she found herself fantasizing over her next scalding mug of tea.

'It's the only thing keeping me going,' she confided to her father, only half joking.

'They say the limeys conquered their empire on the stuff,' Riccardo nodded agreement, as Sean came across from where he had been in deep discussion with Matatu and Job.

'We are only a few hours' march from the reed-beds where we saw Tukutela from the air.' He looked pointedly at Claudia. 'I'd like to try and get there before we sleep, but, of course, some of us are a little bushed . . .' He let it hang between them, a dare and an accusation.

'I need a little stroll to settle my breakfast,' she said amiably, but she wished her face was not coated with black cream. She hated conceding even the slightest advantage to him.

As Sean walked away, her father swilled the tea leaves in his mug and flicked them out.

'Don't fall for him, *tesoro*. He'd be too big a handful even for you.'

She stared at him, outraged and appalled. 'Fall for him? Are you out of your skull, Papa? I can't stand the sight of him.'

'That's what I mean,' he chuckled.

She jumped up and threw her pack onto her back with unnecessary strength, and then told her father with disdain, 'I could cope with him and five others like him, with my eyes closed and one hand tied behind my back, but I've got better taste than that.'

'Which is fortunate for you,' he murmured just low enough so she was uncertain what he had said.

A little before noon that day, Matatu led them into the papyrus beds which surrounded the green pool which they had seen from the air. He led them directly to the great dished spoor, printed in the mud, and they gathered round to inspect it.

'See!' Matatu told them. 'This is where Tukutela stood when he heard the *indeki* coming. Here and there he turned to look up in the sky and challenge us.' Matatu imitated the old bull, holding his head at the same angle, humping his back and cupping his hands at each side of his head. It was such a faithful impression, that for a moment, he seemed to become the old bull, and they all laughed. Claudia forgot her fatigue and clapped in applause.

'Then what did the old bull do?' Sean demanded, and Matatu spun and pointed along the run of the spoor.

'He went away with all his speed, he went fast and very far.'

'Well,' Sean said. 'That puts us almost exactly forty-eight hours behind him and we have to sleep now, we'll be fifty-five hours behind him when we march again.'

Tukutela's dam had been the matriarch of a herd of over one hundred beasts. She had come into her last period of oestrus in her fifty-second year, and over the days that it lasted, she had been mounted and serviced by six of the herd bulls, all young animals, vigorous and at the height of their powers.

It was the ideal formula for the conception of an extraordinary calf, old cow and young bull. Although it was uncertain which seed had taken root in her, the old cow had carried the genes of great elephants, big in body and tusk, in natural intelligence and the urge to dominate. These same genes had made her the leader of her herd, and now she transferred them to the foetus she carried in her womb.

She carried him twenty-two months and then in the year when the German askaris under General von Lettow-Vorbeck were ravaging eastern Africa, the year 1915, she had left the herd and accompanied only by another old female past calf-bearing, her companion of forty years, she had gone deep into the fastnesses of the swamps that lie on the south bank of the Zambezi river and there on an islet fringed with ivory nut palms, surrounded by miles of papyrus beds, and with the white-headed fish eagles chanting overhead, she had cleared an area of sandy earth for her couch. When her time came, she had spread her back legs and squatted over the open area, squealing in the agony of her labour, her trunk rolled up on her chest.

Her eyes had no tear ducts to drain them so the tears poured freely down her withered cheeks as though she wept, and the spasms racked her huge gaunt frame.

The other old cow stood close beside her like a midwife, caressing her with her trunk, stroking her back and rumbling with sympathy. She had forced out the calf's head, and then rested for a minute, before the last violent effort expelled the purple-pink foetal sac and the calf had fallen to the earth, rupturing the umbilical cord. Tukutela had begun to struggle immediately, still trapped in the glistening mucus-coated membrane and the old cow, her companion, had stood over him and, with the prehensile tip of her trunk, delicately stripped it away.

Then with her trunk his dam had gently and lovingly lifted him to his feet, and placed him between her front legs, making the deep purring rumble of elephant content-ment. Still wet and smooth and shining pinkly from his birthing, covered in copious gingery hair, almost blind, Tukutela had rolled his little trunk back onto his forehead and reached up instinctively to the twin breasts on his mother's chest.

While he tasted for the very first time the rich creamy milk, his dam picked up the foetal sac and afterbirth and stuffed them into her mouth, chewing and swallowing and, at the same time, using her trunk to cover the damp and blood-stained spot upon the earth with sand.

The three of them, his mother, her companion and Tukutela, had remained on the island for almost two weeks while the calf had mastered the use of his legs and trunk, the pigment of his skin had darkened and his eyes adjusted to the harsh African sunlight. Then, when she considered him strong enough, she had taken him to find the herd, pushing him ahead of her and lifting him over the steep and difficult places.

The din of a hundred elephant feeding had carried to them from afar, the crack and crash of breaking branches and the pig-like squeals of the calves at play. Tukutela's dam trumpeted her return and the herd had come rushing up to greet her. Then, discovering the new calf, they had crowded around to touch him with their trunks, puffing his scent into their mouths, so that they would recognize it always thereafter.

Tukutela cowered between his mother's front legs, overwhelmed by the huge bodies that surrounded him, making little baby noises of terror, but his mother draped her trunk over him and rumbled to reassure him. Within hours rather than days, he ventured out from her protection to join the other calves, and to begin carving for himself a niche in the hierarchy of the breeding herd.

The herd was a close-knit group, almost all its members blood relatives, mutually reliant upon each other so that the education and discipline of the young was a concern of all.

The calves were always kept in the centre of the herd, and their antics were strictly supervised by the old barren cows who were their self-appointed nursemaids. Their care and protection was intense but any infringement of the herd law was punished instantly: a tree branch wielded with gusto across the recalcitrant's back and hind-quarters would ensure terrified squeals and instant obedience.

Tukutela learned his place in every situation; at the centre when the herd was relaxed and feeding; between his mother's front legs when they were on the march, or in flight from danger. He learned to react instantly to the alarm signal, learned to recognize it even when given by an animal on the further outskirts of the group.

At the signal, the instantaneous silence, in contrast to the preceding happy uproar of the herd, was an eerie phenomenon of elephant behaviour.

Tukutela's development was closely parallel to the ages of a human being: his infancy lasted two years during which time he shed the tiny milk tusks with which he had been born and then entered on his juvenile years when his true tusks emerged beyond his lips. At first, these were covered by a cap of smooth enamel, but as soon as he was weaned and began to use his tusks to feed with and in mock combat with his peers, this was worn away and the true ivory beneath exposed.

His tusks would continue to grow in length and girth throughout his entire life even into his extreme old age, but the genes which dictated their extraordinary development came down from his dam along with all her other gifts of strength and bulk and intelligence.

By the age of three, Tukutela had learned the attitudes of threat and submission towards others, and his play was boisterous with much ear-flapping and threatening and barging which further developed his unusually robust frame.

Once his dam weaned him, her care became less intensive and he was allowed more range and freedom, though he still came under her fierce protection at the first threat, and on the march his place was close beside her in the lead, so very early on he learned the herd's territory.

This was a vast area, from the shores of Lake Nyasa in the north to the rain forests of the Chimanimani mountains in the south, west to the deep gorge where the Zambezi river forces itself between narrow rock cliffs with the roar of perpetual thunder and east five hundred miles to where the same mighty river spread out across wide flood plains and swampy littoral before debouching through multiple mouths into the Indian Ocean.

He learned the mountain passes and the ancient elephant roads, he learned the groves where succulent fruits grew and the seasons when they ripened. She led him to burned-out savannahs just as the first tender green shoots pushed through the ashes and to the salt licks where for thousands of years the elephants had come to prise out lumps of mineral-rich earth with their tusks and eat it with all the relish of small boys with sticks of candy, over the centuries quarrying deep excavations in the red African earth.

The herd was on the Mavuradonha mountains in the south when the msasa forests put out new leaf and their sap began to flow; they were in the dense rain forests on Mount Mlanje when the rest of the range baked in the long African droughts. Always the old cow led them to water, for the herd was totally dependent upon that precious fluid. They must drink each day or experience terrible hardship, they needed copious quantities to nurture their great bodies, to cleanse their hides and, more simply, for the luxurious pleasure of the wallow. The watering hole was an important gathering place for the herd, a place where their bonds were reaffirmed and where many of the rituals of their social behaviour were played out. Even the act of procreation usually took place in the water, and when the cows chose the place for their birthing, it was nearly always near water.

Sometimes there was abundant water, the great green African rivers, the mountains upon which the perpetual drizzling rains fell, and the wide swamplands where they waded belly deep through papyrus beds to reach the islands. At other times, they had to dig for it in the dry riverbeds, or patiently wait their turn at the seeps to thrust their trunks into the deep eye of the secret well and suck up a bitter brackish mouthful at a time.

Their range was wide, and their contact with human beings infrequent. There was a great war raging in a far-off land and it had sucked most of the white men to its centre. The men that the herd encountered were usually half-naked and primitive tribesmen who fled before them. Yet Tukutela learned very early that a special aura of dread surrounded these strange hairless baboon-like beings. At five years of age he could identify their peculiar acrid odour on a light breeze from many miles away, and even the faintest taint of it made him and the entire herd uneasy.

Yet Tukutela was eleven years of age before he had his first memorable encounter with human beings. One night while following their time-honoured route along the south bank of the Zambezi, his dam had stopped abruptly at the front of the herd and lifted her trunk at full stretch above her head to scent the air. Tukutela had imitated her and become aware of a tantalizing odour. He had puffed the taste of it into his mouth and his saliva poured down and dribbled from his lower lip. The rest of the herd bunched up behind them and were almost immediately consumed by the same appetite. None of them had ever smelled sugar cane before.

The old matriarch led them upwind and within a few miles they came out on an area of the riverbank that had been recently cleared and irrigated and planted with cane. The long sword-shaped leaves glistened in the moonlight, and the aroma was rich and sweet and irresistible. The herd rushed into the new fields, pulling up the plants and stuffing them down their throats in a greedy passion.

The destruction was immense, and in the midst of it suddenly the herd was surrounded by lights and the shouts of men's voices and the beating of drums and metal cans. Panic and pandemonium overtook the herd and as they charged out of the field there was a shocking series of loud reports and the bright flash of gunfire in the night. It was the first time Tukutela had ever smelled burned cordite smoke. He would remember it always and associate it with the squeals of those elephants who had been mortally hit.

The herd ran hard at first and then settled into the long stride that covered the ground at the speed of a cantering horse. By morning, one of the young cows, her first calf under her belly, could no longer keep up with the herd and slumped down on her front knees, bright blood trickling from the bullet wound in her flank.

The matriarch turned back to assist her, calling and encouraging her, but the cow could not rise, and the matriarch moved up beside her. Using tusks and trunk, she lifted the fallen animal to her feet and attempted to lead her away. It was in vain, for the dying animal slumped down and lay with her legs folded up under her, and the smell of her blood upset the herd and they milled about her, swinging their trunks and flapping their ears.

One of the herd bulls, in a desperate effort to revive the fallen cow, mounted her in a stylized attempt at copulation, but a gout of arterial blood spurted from her wound and with a groan she toppled over on her side.

Unlike most animals, the elephant recognizes death, especially in one of its own group, and even the immature Tukutela was affected by the strange melancholy that followed the cow's death. Some members of the herd approached the carcass and touched it with their trunks, almost a gesture of farewell, before they wandered away into the grey thorn scrub.

The matriarch stayed on when the others had left, and Tukutela stayed with her. He watched as his dam began to strip the surrounding trees of their branches and pile them over the carcass of the dead cow. Only when it was completely hidden under a great mound of vegetation, was she satisfied.

The dead cow's unweaned calf had stayed beside its mother's corpse, and now the matriarch shooed it ahead of her as she followed the herd. Twice the calf tried to double back to where its mother lay, but the matriarch blocked it, turning it with her trunk and pushed it along.

A mile away, the rest of the herd was waiting in a grove of yellow-stemmed fever trees. Many of the younger calves were suckling, and the matriarch pushed the orphan calf towards where one of the older calves, one almost due to be weaned, was showing only perfunctory interest in his mother's dugs. She shoved the orphan between the cow's front legs and instinctively the little animal rolled its trunk onto its forehead and reached up for the teat. The cow made no objection, accepting the role of foster mother with equanimity. The matriarch stood beside the pair rumbling to them encouragingly, and when she led the herd on, the orphan calf had displaced the older calf between the cow's front legs.

It seemed that from then on the herd's contact with men bearing firearms became every season more frequent, especially when the bulls were with the breeding herd.

The mature bulls kept a loose liaison with the breeding herd. They found the noisy and boisterous behaviour of the young animals annoying, and the competition for food demanding. No sooner would one of the bulls shake down a rain of ripe pods from the top branches of a tail thorn tree but a dozen youngsters would rush over to gobble them, or he would push over a msasa tree to get at the new leaf, leaning with his forehead against the trunk, and snapping the three-foot diameter of hard wood with a report like a cannon shot. Immediately four or five greedy young cows would push themselves in front of him before he could sample the juicy pink leaves.

So the bulls would wander away from the herd, singly or in bachelor groups of three or four. Perhaps also they realized instinctively that the herd was likely to attract the hunters, and they would be safer away from it. Sometimes they were only a few miles away, sometimes as far as thirty or forty, but they seemed always to be aware of the herd's location and would return when the cows were in season.

When the bulls were with the herd, was the time that there was most likely to be that sudden crash of gunfire, and the squeal of wounded animals and the headlong rush of huge panic-stricken bodies through the brush.

When Tukutela was a juvenile, under ten years of age,

154

there had been six huge bulls associated with the herd, animals carrying thick shafts of ivory, but over the years that he grew towards maturity these were gradually whittled down. Each dry season one or more of them fell to the sound of riflefire, and only the mediocre bulls, or those with worn or damaged ivory, remained.

By this time, Tukutela had grown into an unusually large young bull, and his tusks were beginning to develop, clean and white and sharp-pointed, already showing promise of what they would one day become. As he grew, so the matriarch, his dam, declined. Slowly the outline of her bones appeared through the folds and hangs of her wrinkled grey hide, so she became a gaunt and skeletal figure. Her sixth and last molar was already chipped and half worn away, she ate with difficulty, and the slow starvation of age had begun. She relinquished her place at the head of the herd to a younger more robust cow, and shambled along behind. On the steep places where the elephant road climbed the mountain passes Tukutela would wait for her at the crest, rumbling to bring her up over the difficult places, and he stood close to her in the night as he had as a calf.

It had been a dry season and the waterholes were less than half full. The approaches to the water had been churned by the elephant herds and rhinoceros and buffalo to glutinous black mud, in some places deep as an elephant's belly, and it was here that the old matriarch stuck.

Lunging in an attempt to free herself, she fell over sideways and the mud sucked her down until only part of her head was clear.

She struggled for two days. Tukutela tried to help her, but even his enormous strength was of no avail. The mud held her fast, and gave him no footing nor purchase. The old cow's struggles became weaker, her wild screams more feeble, until at last she was still and silent except for the hiss of her breathing.

It took two more days, and Tukutela stood beside her all that time. The herd had long ago departed, but he remained. She gave no outward sign of passing from life to death, other than the cessation of her harsh breathing, but Tukutela knew it instantly and he lifted his trunk high and bugled out his grief in a cry that startled the wild fowl from the waterhole in a cloud of noisy wings.

He went to the edge of the forest and plucked the leafy boughs and he brought them to the waterhole and he covered his dam's muddy carcass with them, building for her a high green funeral bier. Then he left her and went into the veld.

He did not rejoin the herd for almost two years. By that time, he was sexually mature and he could no longer resist the scent of oestrus that the breeze brought down to him.

When he found them, the herd was gathered on the bank of the Kafue river, ten miles upstream from where it makes its confluence with the great Zambezi. Some of the herd members came out to meet him as he approached, and they entwined their trunks with his and pushed their foreheads together in greeting, and then allowed him to join the main body.

There were two cows in season and one of them was an animal of similar age to Tukutela. She was prime, fat with good grazing and browsing that the rains had raised. Her ivory was thin and very white, as straight and sharp as knitting needles, and her ears had not yet been torn or tattered by thorn and sharp twigs. She spread them now as she recognized Tukutela as her peer, and came to twine her trunk with his.

They stood with their heads together rumbling gently at each other, and then disentangled their trunks and began to caress each other lightly with the tips, moving down the length of each other's bodies until they stood head to tail.

The tips of the trunk are as sensitive and dextrous as the fingers of the human hand and Tukutela reached down between her back legs and groped for her vaginal opening. She began to sway from side to side, rocking her whole body, an expression of extreme pleasure. As he manipulated her, so her oestrus discharge flowed down freely drenching his trunk and the aroma of it filled his head. His penis emerged from its fleshy sheath, as long as a man is tall and as thick as one of his legs; the tip of it brushed the earth below his belly. Its length was variegated with blotches of pink and black but the skin was smooth and shining and the head flared like the mouth of a trumpet. Elephants belong to the testiconda group, and his testicles were contained deep in the body cavity so there was no external evidence of them.

When both of them were fully aroused Tukutela nudged her gently down the bank and into the river. The green waters closed over them, intensifying their pleasure in each other, supporting their great bodies, buoying them up so they were light and nimble.

They submerged until only their trunks were above the surface, sporting together, breaking out again like blowing whales, and the water poured off them in sheets, cleansing their grey hides of dust and dirt, darkening them to the colour of coal.

Tukutela reared over her, and placed his forelegs on each side of her back. In the water, she supported him easily. Her vagina was placed far forward between her back legs, and he needed all of his length to reach it. His penis took on a life of its own, pulsing and jerking and twisting as it flared upwards to conform to the angle of her opening. Only the first third of its length was able to bury itself in her. His whole body shuddered and convulsed and both creatures trumpeted together and thrashed the waters to white foam.

He stayed with the herd three days, and then the female's oestrus ended and Tukutela became restless. He had inherited his dam's instinct for survival, and he sensed danger with the herd. On the third day, he ghosted away into the grey thorn scrub. He went alone, with no other bull for company.

Each season, when he returned to the herd he was stronger, his tusks longer and thicker, darkening to the colour of alabaster with vegetable juices. On occasion there were other bulls competing to service the females, and he had to fight for his right.

At first, he was driven off by older more experienced males, but each season his tusks and his cunning grew, until none of the other herd bulls stood up against him, and he had his pick of the cows. However, he never stayed more than a few days with the herd, and always he departed alone and sought out fastnesses which his dam had showed to him, the swamps inaccessible to man, the thickest forests, the tallest beds of elephant grass. It was as though he realized the danger that those tusks would bring upon him.

In his thirty-fifth year, he was a huge animal, weighing seven tons and standing over twelve feet at the shoulder. His tusks, though not anywhere as heavy as they would one day be, were perfectly symmetrical and long and pointed.

For days after leaving the herd that season he had been unaccountably nervous. He moved restlessly, testing the air often, raising his trunk high and then puffing it into his mouth. Once or twice he detected it, but the acrid scent was faint, just a tiny shadow on his consciousness.

However, he could not keep moving endlessly. His huge frame each day required over a ton of grass and leaves and fruit and bark to sustain it. He had to stop to feed. In the early morning, he stood in a dense grove of combretum trees, stripping bark. He used the point of a tusk to prise a gash in the bark, then he gripped the tag end in his trunk and with an upward jerk ripped loose a strip of bark fifteen feet up the bole of the tree. He rolled the bark into a ball and stuffed it into his mouth.

Intent on his task, he relaxed his vigilance. An elephant has poor eyesight, he cannot distinguish stationary objects only a few yards distant, although he can instantly delect movement. Furthermore, his eyes are placed well back in the skull, impeding his forward view and the spread of his ears tends to block his peripheral vision to the rear.

Using the small morning wind to negate the bull's marvellous sense of smell, moving with extreme stealth so that his fine hearing was frustrated, the hunters approached him from behind, staying in his blind spot. There were two of them and they had followed him ever since he had left the herd. Now they crept up very close to him.

The bull turned broadside to the hunters, ready to move on to the next tree and he showed them the long curved gleam of his tusks.

'Take him!' said one man to the other, and the Spanish maker of fine sherries lifted his double-barrelled rifle which was engraved and inlaid with gold and he aimed for Tukutela's brain.

Over his sights, he picked out the dark vertical cleft in the front of the ear and followed it down to its lowest point. That was where the actual opening of the eardrum was situated. Having found it he moved his aim forward three inches along an imaginary line from the aperture of the ear towards the elephant's eye.

The Spanish sherry-maker was on his first African safari. He had shot chamois and moufflon and red deer in the Pyrenees, but a wild African elephant is none of these timid creatures, and the Spaniard's heart was thudding into his ribs and his spectacles were fogged with his sweat and his hands shook. The professional hunter with him had patiently instructed him how and where to place his shot, but now he could not hold his aim upon it, and every second his breathing became more laboured, his aim more erratic. In desperation he jerked the trigger.

The bullet hit Tukutela a foot above his left eye and fifteen inches from the frontal lobe of the brain, but the honeycombed bony sponge of his skull cushioned the shock.

He reeled back on his haunches and flung his trunk straight up above his head and gave a deep roaring growl in his throat.

The Spanish hunter turned and ran, and Tukutela whirled to face the movement, launching himself off his haunches. The professional hunter was directly under his outstretched trunk, and he flung up his rifle and aimed into Tukutela's head, into the roof of his open mouth between the bases of the long curved tusks.

The firing-pin fell on a dud primer with a click, the rifle misfired and Tukutela swung his trunk down like the executioner's axe, crushing the man to the earth.

The Spaniard was still running and Tukutela went after him, overhauling him effortlessly. He reached out his trunk and curled it around his waist. The man screamed and Tukutela tossed him thirty feet straight up into the air. He screamed all the way down until he hit the earth and the air was driven from his lungs. Tukutela seized him by one ankle and swung his body against the trunk of the nearest tree with a force that burst the man's internal organs, spleen and liver and lungs.

Tukutela raged through the forest with the corpse held in his trunk, beating it against the trees, lifting it high and slamming it down upon the earth, until it disintegrated and he was left with only the stump of the leg in his grip. He flung that aside and went back to where he had left the professional hunter.

The blow from the trunk had shattered his collar-bone, broken both his arms and crushed in his ribs but the hunter was still alive and conscious. He saw Tukutela coming back for him, the long trunk dangling, the huge ears extended and blood from his wound dribbling down to mingle with the blood of the Spaniard that splattered his chest and front legs.

The hunter tried to drag his mangled body away. Tukutela placed one great foot in the centre of his back, pinning him down, then with his trunk, he plucked off his limbs, one at a time, legs and arms, tearing them away from the joints of hip and shoulder, and throwing them aside. Finally he wrapped his trunk around the man's head and pulled it away from the shoulders. It rolled like a ball bouncing across the ground as Tukutela hurled it from him. His rage abated, overtaken by the pain in his head, and Tukutela stood over the bodies that he had destroyed, rocking from one foot to the other, rumbling in his throat as first the pain and then the melancholy of death came over him.

Despite the pain in his head and the slow drip of blood into his eye from the wound above it, he began the ritual of death that he had learned from his dam so many years previously. He gathered the parts of his victims, the squashed trunks and mutilated limbs, and piled them in a heap. He picked their accoutrements out of the grass – rifles, hats, water-bottles – and added them to the bloody pile. Then he began to strip the trees of leafy branches and to cover it all with a mound of green.

The bullet wound healed cleanly, but soon there were other scars to add to the little white star that it left above his eye. A weighted spear from a dead-fall trap opened his thick grey hide from shoulder to knee, and he almost died from the infection that followed. The spread of his ears caught on thorn and hooked twigs, the edges became tattered and eroded. He fought for the cows when he joined the breeding herd, and although none of the other bulls could prevail against him, their tusks slashed and cut and marked him. Then there were other encounters with men.

Despite the dire danger associated with it, that first taste of the sweet juice of the sugar cane so long ago had been addictive. Tukutela became a compulsive garden raider. Sometimes he would lurk for days in the vicinity of a patch of cultivation, getting up his courage. Then when there was no moon, in the deepest hours of the night, he would go in stepping soundlessly as a cat on his big padded feet.

Millet, maize, papaya, yams, he loved them all, but sugar cane he could never resist.

At first, he allowed himself to be driven off by the flaming torches and the shouting and the drums, but then he learned to answer the shouts with his own wild screams and to charge at the guardians of the forbidden gardens.

On separate occasions over the next ten years, he killed eight human beings in the course of his raids, pulling their bodies to pieces like a glutton dismembering a chicken carcass. He grew reckless in his greed for the sweet cane. Whereas after previous raids, he would travel a hundred miles in a single non-stop march to distance himself from retribution, this season he began to return to the same field on consecutive nights.

The villagers had sent a message to the *Boma* of the colonial district commissioner, begging for assistance. The D.C. had sent one of his askari armed with a .404 rifle and the askari was waiting for Tukutela. The askari was a policeman and neither a great hunter nor marksman. He hid himself in a pit in the middle of the field, quite happy in his own mind that the elephant would not return to the field that night; for Tukutela had already made a reputation for himself across his vast range and his habits were known: he was notorious as the garden raider who had killed so many villagers, and who never returned to the scene of his crime.

The askari awoke from a deep sleep in the bottom of his pit to find Tukutela blotting out the stars over his head, munching on the standing cane. The askari snatched up his .404 and fired a bullet upwards into Tukutela's belly. It was not a mortal wound and Tukutela hunted the askari remorselessly, quartering downwind until he picked up the scent and following it to the pit where the man crouched paralysed with terror. Tukutela put his trunk down into the pit and plucked him out.

The wound took many weeks to heal. The pain gnawed at his guts and Tukutela's hatred of man grew upon it.

Though Tukutela did not understand the reason for it, his contact with man became ever more frequent. His old range was being whittled down; every season there were more tracks and roads cutting through his secret places. Motor vehicles, noisy and stinking, buzzed through the silent places of the veld. The great forests were being hacked down and the earth turned to the plough. Lights burned in the night, and human voices carried to him wherever he wandered. Tukutela's world was shrinking in upon him.

His tusks were growing all this time, longer and thicker, until in his sixtieth year, they were great dark columns.

He killed another man in 1976, a black man who tried to defend his few wretched acres of millet with a throwing spear, but the head of the spear lodged in Tukutela's neck and formed a chronic source of infection, a constantly suppurating abscess.

Tukutela had long ago ceased to seek out the breeding herd. The scent of oestrus on the wind awakened in him only a sweet fleeting nostalgia, but the driving force of the procreative urge had dulled and he pursued his solitary ways through the shrinking forests.

There were some areas of his old range that remained untouched, and from experience Tukutela came to recognize them and to realize that they formed a sanctuary where he was safe from man's harassment. He did not understand that these were the national parks, where he was protected by law, but he spent more and more of his time in these areas, and over the years learned their precise boundaries, and became reluctant to venture across them into the dangerous world beyond.

Even in these sanctuaries he was wary, driven always by his hatred and fear of them to attack men wherever he found them, or to fly from the first acrid taint of them on the breeze. His faith in the safety of the sanctuary was tested when the hunters found him even there. He heard the report of a firearm and felt the sting of the missile, not differentiating between the sound of a rifle and a dart gun, but when he tried to locate and destroy his attackers, a strange lethargy overtook him, a terrible weakness in his thick columnar legs and he slumped unconscious to the earth. He awoke to the terrifying stench of men all around him, thick and repulsive on the air, even on his own skin where they had touched him. When he lumbered unsteadily to his feet, he found a strange serpentine device suspended around his neck and the chronic abscess on his neck caused by the spear wound was burning with the fires of antiseptics. He tried to wrench off the radio collar, but it defied even his might and so, in frustration, he devastated the forest around him, smashing down the tall trees and ripping out the bushes.

The men who watched his rage from afar laughed and one of them said, 'Tukutela, the Angry One.'

It took Tukutela many long seasons before he at last succeeded in ripping that hateful collar from around his neck, and hurling it into the top branches of a tree.

Although he recognized the sanctuary of the parks in which he now spent most of his days. Tukutela could not deny his deepest instincts and at certain seasons of the year, he became restless. The wanderlust came upon him, the urge to follow once again the long migratory road that his dam had first taken him over as an infant. He would be drawn to the boundary of the park by this irresistible longing and he would feed along it for days gathering his courage until he could no longer contain himself and he would set out fearfully and nervously, but with high anticipation for the far-off fastnesses to the east.

Of these, the vast Zambezi swampland was his favourite. He did not recognize it as his birthplace, he only knew that here the waters seemed cooler and sweeter, the grazing more luxuriant and his sense of peace deeper than any other place in his world. This season as he crossed the Chiwewe river and headed east, the urge to return to that place seemed even greater.

He was old now, long past his seventieth year and he was weary. His joints ached so he walked with a stiff exaggerated gait. His old wounds pained him, especially the bullet which had driven through his bony skull and lodged beneath the skin above his right eye. It had formed a hard encysted lump of gristle which he touched occasionally with the tip of his trunk when the pain was bad.

His craggy old head was weighed down by those huge ivory shafts; each day their burden was less supportable. Those tusks alone were a monument to his former glory. For the old bull was going back rapidly now. The sixth set of molars, the last and largest of his teeth, were all but worn away and the starvation of age was upon him. Every day, he was a little weaker, slowly his food was limited more and more to the softer more readily masticated grasses and shoots, but he could not take enough of them.

His huge frame was gaunt and his skin hung in bags at his knees and around his neck. There was a sense of melancholy in him, such as he had experienced only seldom in his life, the same feeling that had encompassed him as he waited for his dam to die beside the waterhole. He did not recognize that feeling as the premonition of his own impending death.

It seemed to Tukutela that as soon as he crossed out of the park, the pursuit began. He sensed that it was more determined, more persistent than ever before. It seemed to him that the forest was full of the human creatures, following him, waiting for him at each turn, and he could not head directly eastwards but must jink and twist to avoid the imaginary and real dangers that beset him.

However, when the sudden cacophony of gunfire roared out close behind him, Tukutela fled directly eastward at last, instead of doubling back towards the sanctuary of the park. It was a hundred miles and more to where the swamps began and the route was perilous, but he could not deny the deep instinct that drove him on.

Ten hours later, he stopped to bathe and drink and feed in an isolated marshy place, still a great distance from the true swamps. This was one of the way-stations on the old migratory road.

He had not been there for more than a few hours before the aircraft had rushed low overhead, filling the air with its buzzing roar, startling and angering Tukutela. In some vague way, he associated this machine with the deadly danger of the hunters. It left the same foul stench upon the air as the hunting vehicles which he had encountered so often before, and he knew he could rest no longer in this place, the hunters were closing in.

The great swamps were his refuge and he fled towards them.

'He won't stop now until he is into the swamps.' Sean Courtney was squatting beside the spoor. 'He's thoroughly alarmed, and we can't hope to catch him before he gets into them.'

'How far?' Riccardo asked, and Sean stood up and studied him as he replied.

'Eighty or ninety miles, Capo. Just a stroll.' Riccardo wasn't looking well. There were dark sweat patches soaking through his shirt and he seemed to have aged ten years in the last four days.

'What will we do if the old bugger keels over on us?' Sean wondered, and then thrust that thought aside. 'Okay, gang, we'll eat and sleep here. Move on again at four.'

He led them to the edge of the marsh, onto firm dry ground. Fatigue and heat had dulled their appetites. They needed sleep more than food and soon they were sprawled out in the shade like dead men.

Sean woke with the feeling that something was amiss;

he sat up quickly, his hand already on the rifle, and swept a glance around him.

'Claudia.' He jumped to his feet. She was gone. Her pack lay ten paces away where she had slept. He wanted to shout for her, flouting his own security rules, and that was a measure of his concern.

He strode out of the perimeter, and whistled for the sentry. Pumula came in immediately.

'The donna,' Sean demanded in Sindebele. 'Where is she?'

'That way.' Pumula pointed towards the river.

'You let her go?' Sean demanded.

'I thought she was going to the bush . . .' Pumula excused himself, '. . . to relieve herself. I could not stop her.'

Sean had already started to run down the hippo path into the reeds that surrounded the largest and deepest of the pools, when he heard the splash of water ahead.

'This dilly bitch is going to drive me crazy,' he told himself as he burst out on the edge of the pool.

The pool was a hundred yards across, deep and green and still. For all its comical appearance the hippopotamus is the most dangerous animal in Africa. It has probably killed more human beings than all the other dangerous species put together. The old bulls are cantankerous and aggressive, a cow with a new calf will attack without provocation and a bite from those gaping jaws whose tusks are adapted to shearing coarse river reeds will cut a man in two. The crocodile is a sly and efficient killer. This pool was the ideal haunt of both hippo and crocodile and Claudia Monterro was in it up to her waist.

Her wet clothing, shirt and panties and socks, all freshly washed, were draped over the reeds at the edge, and Claudia was facing away from him leaning forward and with both hands working up a lather of soap in her hair.

The skin of her back was lightly tanned and flawless except for the paler line left by the strap of a bikini top across her shoulder-blades. Her flanks were lean but elegantly shaped into the waist, and the knuckles of her spine just showed between the ridges of fine athletic muscle on each side of it.

'What the hell do you think you're doing?' Sean snarled, and she turned to face him, hands still in her soapy hair, eyes screwed up against the suds.

'Is this how you get your jollies?' she demanded, but making not the slightest effort to cover her bosom. 'You pervert, creeping and peeping?'

'Get your arse out of there, before you get it bitten off by a croc.' Her jibe had stung him, but even in his anger he saw that her breasts were better than he had guessed. The cold water made the points stick out at him.

'Stop gawking,' she yelled back at him. 'And get lost.' She ducked her head under and then stood erect once again with soap lather streaming down her body, her hair shining and slick as a sheet of black silk over her shoulders.

'Get out of there, damn you, I'm not going to stand here arguing,' he ordered.

'I'll get out when I'm good and ready.'

Sean plunged straight into the pool, and reached her before she could avoid him. He seized her arm, and though it was slippery with soap, he dragged her towards the bank; kicking and lashing at him with her free hand, spitting with fury.

'You bastard, I hate you. Leave me alone.'

He controlled her easily with one hand. In the other, he still held his big double-barrelled rifle. His khaki shorts ran water and his velskoen boots squelched as he dragged her out. He snatched up her wet shirt and threw it at her.

'Get dressed!'

'You've got no right, I'm not going to accept this, you brutal ham-handed . . . you've hurt my arm.' She proffered her upper arm, exhibiting his red fingermarks on the skin, holding the wet shirt loosely at her side, shaking and pale with rage.

Strangely it was her navel that drew his eyes. It stared accusingly at him from the flat plain of her midriff, like a cyclopean eye, a perfect dimple at that moment more erotic than even the dense triangular bush of sodden hair beneath it. He dragged his eyes away, and she was so angry that she seemed totally oblivious of her nudity. He thought she might actually attack him, and he stepped back. As he did so he looked beyond her and saw a tiny arrow-head of ripples slipping silently across the still green surface of the pool towards them. At the apex of the vee-shaped ripple were two black lumps; gnarled and no bigger than a pair of large walnuts, they came at surprising speed.

Sean grabbed her arm, the same arm about whose injuries she was complaining, and jerked her back past him, away from the water's edge so viciously that she sprawled on her hands and knees in the mud.

He swung up the .577 Express rifle and aimed between the black eye lumps of the approaching crocodile. The eyes were at least nine inches apart, he calculated as he rode the pip of the foresight between them, a big old mugger.

The thunder of the rifle was stunning in the silence of the reeds and the bullet flicked an ostrich feather of spray from the surface, dead centre between the eye protuberances. The crocodile rolled sluggishly onto its back, its tiny brain mangled by the shot.

Claudia scrambled to her feet and stared over his shoulder as the reptile flashed its butter-yellow saurian belly. Sixteen feet from chin to the tip of its long crested tail, its jaws clicked as its nerves spasmed from the brain shot. The fangs as long and thick as a human forefinger overlapped the grinning scaly lips. It sank slowly back into the pool, the creamy belly fading into the green depths.

Claudia's fury had evaporated. She was staring into the pool, shivering uncontrollably, shaking her wet hair.

'Oh God, I didn't realize . . . how horrible.' She swayed towards him, shattered and vulnerable. 'I didn't know.' Her body was cold from the pool, long and sleek and wet as she pressed against him.

'What is it?' Riccardo Monterro shouted from the edge of the reed-bed. 'Sean, are you all right? What happened? Where's Claudia?'

At the sound of her father's voice, she jumped back from him guiltily and for the first time tried to cover her breasts and crotch.

'It's all right, Capo,' Sean yelled back. 'She's safe.'

Claudia snatched up her panties and pulled them on hastily, hopping on one foot in the mud, turning her back to him as she picked up her shirt and thrust her arms into the sleeves. When she turned back to him she had recovered her anger.

'I got a fright,' she told him. 'I didn't mean to grab you like that. Don't make any big deal out of it, buster.'

She zipped up the fly of her jeans and lifted her chin. 'I would have grabbed the garbageman if he'd been handy.'

'Okay, ducky, next time I'm going to let them bite you, lion or croc, what the hell.'

'You shouldn't have any complaints,' she said over her shoulder as she marched back up the path. 'You got yourself a big eyeful and I noticed you made a meal of it, Colonel.'

'You're right. You gave me a good peep. Not bad, a bit skinny perhaps – but not bad.'

And his grin expanded as he saw the back of her neck turn angry red.

Riccardo ran down the path to meet them, frantic with worry, and he seized Claudia and hugged her with relief.

'What happened, *tesoro*? Are you all right?'

'She tried to feed the crocs,' Sean told him. 'We are moving out in exactly thirty seconds from now, that shot will have alerted every ugly within ten miles.'

*

'At least I got that filthy black muck off my face,' Claudia told herself as they struck out away from the marshes. Her damp clothing felt cool and clean on her skin, and she was invigorated by her perilous bathe.

'No harm done,' she thought. 'Except I got ogled.' Even that no longer troubled her. His eyes on her naked body had not been altogether offensive, and in retrospect there was a satisfaction in having tantalized him.

'Eat your heart out, lover boy.' She watched his back as he strode out ahead of her. 'That was the best you are ever likely to lay eyes on.'

Within a mile her clothes had dried and there was no energy for any extraneous activity. The whole of her existence became the act of picking up one foot and swinging it forward after the other.

The heat was fierce and became fiercer still as they reached the rim of the escarpment of the Zambezi valley and started down. The air changed its character. It lay on the earth in silvery streams like water, it quivered and shimmered like curtains of crystal beads and changed the form and shape of things at a distance so that they squirmed and wriggled, doubled in size, assuming monstrous shapes in the mirage, or disappeared from view, swallowed up by the cascades of heated air.

Farther off the air was blue, so when she looked back, the escarpment down which they were climbing was washed with pale blue, misty and ethereal. The sky was a different blue, deep and vigorous, and the clouds stood upon the firmament in towering ranges the colours of lead and silver, their bottoms cut cleanly horizontal to the earth, their heads shaped like full-rigged ships, mainsail and topsail, royal and skysail piled up into the blue heavens. Under the cloud ranges the air was trapped and lay upon the earth so that it felt as heavy as hot syrup. They trudged along beneath its weight.

From the forest around them the minute black mopane

171

flies came swarming and gathered at the corners of their eyes and mouths, crawled up into their nostrils and into their ears to drink the moisture from their bodies. Their insistence was exquisite torture.

As each long mile fell behind them, so vistas of the valley floor opened ahead and on the horizon they could at last make out the dark belt of riverine vegetation which marked the course of the great Zambezi. Always Matatu danced along ahead of them like a wraith, following a trail that no other eye than his could discern, tireless and unaffected by the heat, so that Sean had to call him back for the regular periods of rest with which he interrupted the march.

'There is no sign of game,' Riccardo remarked, peering ahead through his binoculars. 'We haven't seen so much as a rabbit since we crossed into Mozambique.'

It was the first time he had spoken in hours and Sean was encouraged. He had begun seriously worrying about his client. Now he responded quickly.

'This was once a paradise of big game. I hunted here before the Portuguese pulled out and the buffalo were running in herds ten thousand strong.'

'What happened to them?'

'Frelimo fed the army with them. They even offered me the contract for the slaughter, they couldn't understand why I refused. In the end they did it themselves.'

'How did they do it?'

'From helicopters, they flew low over the herds and machine-gunned them. They killed almost fifty thousand buffalo in three months. For all that time the sky was black with vultures and you could smell the killing fields from twenty miles off. When the buffalo were finished they started on the other game, the wildebeest and the zebra.'

'What a cruel and savage land this is,' Claudia said quietly.

'Surely you don't disapprove?' Sean asked. 'It was done

172

by black men, not whites. It couldn't possibly be wrong.' He glanced at his Rolex wristwatch. 'Time to move on.'

He put out his hand to help Riccardo to his feet, but the older man shrugged the hand away. Nevertheless, Sean fell in beside him as the march resumed and let Claudia move up directly behind Matatu, while he chatted quietly to her father, jollying him along, trying to distract him from his weariness.

He recounted anecdotes from the bush war. He pointed out the site of the guerrilla training camp as they passed a few miles north of it and described the raid by the Ballantyne Scouts. Riccardo was interested enough to ask questions.

'This Comrade China sounds like a good field commander,' he commented. 'Did you ever find out what happened to him, after he escaped?'

'He was active right up to the end of the war. A tough cookie, all right. His men had to back-pack all their munitions into Rhodesia and a Russian T.5 anti-tank landmine weighs almost seventy pounds. The story goes that Comrade China brought in one of them at enormous cost in sweat and blood and laid it on the main Mount Darwin road for one of our regular armoured patrols. However, the local blacks had hired a bus that same weekend to go into town to watch the football match and they touched off the landmine. There were sixty-five of them on the bus and twenty-three of them survived the explosion. Comrade China was so incensed by the waste of his precious T.5 that he sent for all the next-of-kin of the victims, and the survivors who were still able to walk, and fined them each ten dollars to cover the cost of another landmine.'

Riccardo had to stop and double over with laughter and Claudia turned on them furiously.

'How can you laugh? That is the most outrageous story I have ever heard.'

'Oh, I don't know,' Sean replied evenly, 'I don't think

ten dollars was so outrageous. I think old China was being fairly lenient.'

She tossed her head and lengthened her stride to catch up with Matatu, and Riccardo asked still chuckling, 'After the war, what happened to this character?'

Sean shrugged. 'He was in the new government in Harare for a while but then he disappeared in one of the political purges. He might have been liquidated, the old revolutionaries are always looked on with distrust when the regime they fought for comes to power. Nobody likes sharing a bed with a trained killer and toppler of other rulers.'

Sean called a halt an hour before dark for a brew of tea and their frugal evening meal. While Job cooked it over his small smokeless fire, Sean took Matatu aside and talked to him quietly. The tracker watched Sean's face as he spoke, nodding eagerly, and as soon as he finished Matatu slipped away, heading back the way they had come.

Riccardo looked a question as Sean came back to join them and he explained.

'I sent Matatu to back-track us. Make sure we aren't being followed. I'm worried about that shot. It could have called up those uglies we found near the border.'

Riccardo nodded and then asked, 'Have you got a couple of aspirin, Sean?'

Sean opened the side flap of his pack and shook three Anadin tablets from their bottle.

'Headache?' he asked as he passed them to Riccardo, and he nodded as he popped them into his mouth and washed them down with a swallow of hot tea.

'The dust and sun glare,' he explained, but both Sean and Claudia were studying him and Riccardo bridled.

'Damn it, don't look at me like that. I'm fine.'

'Sure,' Sean agreed smoothly. 'Let's eat and move on to find a place to sleep.' He went across to the cooking-fire and squatted beside Job. They talked softly.

'Papa,' Claudia moved a little closer to her father and touched his arm, 'how are you feeling, honestly?'

'Don't worry about me, *tesoro*.'

'It has started, hasn't it?'

'No,' he replied too swiftly.

'Doc Andrews said there might be headaches.'

'It's the sun.'

'I love you, Papa,' she said.

'I know, baby, and I love you too.'

'An ocean and a mountain?' she asked.

'The stars and the moon,' he confirmed, and put his arm round her shoulders. She leaned against him.

As soon as they had eaten, Job doused the fire and Sean got them up and moving again. Tukutela's spoor was easy to follow in the soft earth and he and Job had no need of Matatu for this stage. However, at dark they were forced to stop for the night.

'We'll reach the swamps tomorrow afternoon,' Sean promised Riccardo as they stretched out on top of their sleeping-bags.

Claudia lay awake worrying about her father long after the others were asleep. Riccardo snored softly, lying on his back with arms extended like a crucifix. When she raised herself on one elbow to look at him in the starlight, she heard Sean's light breathing alter subtly and sensed that he was awakened by her movement. He slept as lightly as a cat, sometimes he frightened her.

Even her concern for her father was at last overcome and she fell into that dark drugged sleep of exhaustion. Waking was like coming back from a faraway place.

'Wake up, come on, wake up.' Sean was slapping her face lightly, and she pushed his hand away and sat up groggily.

'What?' she mumbled. 'God, it's still dark.'

He had left her and gone to her father. 'Come on, Capo, wake up, man, wake up.'

'What the hell, what is it?' Riccardo's voice was slurred and grumpy.

'Matatu has just come into camp,' Sean told them quietly. 'We are being followed.'

Claudia felt the icy wind of dread blow across her skin.

'Followed? By whom?'

'We don't know,' Sean said.

'The same bunch that were camped at the border?' Riccardo asked. His voice was still slurred.

'Possibly,' Sean said.

'What are you going to do?' Claudia asked, and was annoyed that her tone sounded afraid and confused.

'We are going to give them the slip,' Sean said. 'Get up on your hind legs.'

They had slept with their boots on. They had simply to roll their sleeping-bags and they were ready to move out.

'Matatu is going to lead you away and cover your spoor,' Sean explained. 'Job and I are going to lay a false trail for them in the original direction. As soon as it's light we'll break away and circle back to join you.'

'You aren't going to leave us alone?' Claudia blurted fearfully, and then bit it off.

'No, you won't be alone, Matatu and Pumula and Dedan will be with you,' Sean told her disdainfully.

'What about the elephant?' Riccardo demanded. His voice had firmed. 'Are you breaking off the hunt? You going to let my elephant get away?'

'For a few lousy gooks armed with a couple of lousy AK 47s?' Sean chuckled. 'Don't be ridiculous, Capo. We will shake them off and be after Tukutela again before you know it.'

*

176

Sean and Job waited while Matatu assembled his group and then shepherded them away. By now Riccardo and Claudia had learned the basics of anti-tracking and went swiftly under Matatu's direction, while the tracker brushed and covered the sign behind them.

Once they were clear, Sean and Job trampled the area around the camp, back and forth and round in circles until they had confused any remaining spoor and then they fell into single file, Sean leading, and went away at a run. They did not make it too apparent that they were laying a false trail, but adopted all the usual precautions, which would not fool a good tracker.

It was the old Scouts' pursuit pace that Sean set, seven miles an hour, and gradually he began to veer off in a southerly direction. Matatu was heading northwards towards the river and Sean would lead the pursuit directly away from them.

While he ran, Sean puzzled over the identity of his pursuers – government soldiers or rebels, poachers or simply armed bandits looking for plunder – it was impossible to guess. However, Matatu had been worried when he came into camp.

'They are good, *Bwana*,' he had told Sean. 'They have done well to follow the spoor we left, and they were coming on fast. They move in formation like bush fighters, with flankers out.'

'Didn't you get a good look?' Sean had asked, and the little Ndorobo shook his head.

'It was getting dark, and I wanted to get back to warn you. They were closing in swiftly.'

'Even the best tracker won't be able to follow us in darkness, we've got the rest of the night to get clear of them.'

It was a strange reversal of roles, Sean thought grimly, as he and Job trotted through the dark bush. They, the hunters, were now being hunted just as remorselessly.

At first he had considered breaking off the chase after the elephant and doubling back for the border. Riccardo Monterro's condition was causing him real concern, and so was Matatu's warning that their pursuers were skilled and appeared dangerous. However, he had swiftly rejected the idea; they were beyond the point of no return.

'No turning back,' Sean said aloud, and grinned as he admitted to himself the true reasons for his determination, two ivory tusks and half a million dollars in cash. By now he was honestly not certain which of those were the most compelling. Those tusks were beginning to loom large in his imagination. They represented the old Africa, a symbol of a better world that had vanished. He wanted them more than he had ever wanted anything in his life, except perhaps half a million dollars, and he grinned again.

In the first light of dawn, they were running directly southwards and they had covered twenty miles since splitting off from the rest of the party.

'Time to disappear, Job,' he grunted, without breaking stride. There must be no indication to the trackers following them that they were about to split again.

'Good place just ahead,' Job agreed. He was running exactly in Sean's footprints.

'Do it,' Sean said, and as they ran under the low branches of a grevia tree Job reached up and swung himself off the ground. Sean did not look back, did not alter his stride. Job would work himself through the branches of the closely growing grevia until he found a good place to drop off and anti-track away.

Sean ran on for twenty minutes, once again curving away into the south-west, heading for a low ridge that just showed in the dawn ahead of him. He crossed the ridge and as he had anticipated from the lie of the terrain found a small river in the valley beyond. He drank at the edge of the pool, and milled around, splashing water onto the bank as though he were bathing.

A tracker would expect him to choose this as a breakaway point, wading either upstream or downstream before leaving the river again. They would send scouts along both banks to search for sign. Sean waded downstream supporting himself on overhanging branches to give them a trail to confirm their suspicions. Then without leaving the water he returned to the exact spot where he had entered the stream, and on the bank he carefully dried his feet and legs, replaced his dry velskoen shoes that he had hung around his neck on their laces, and back-tracked on his incoming spoor.

He retraced his footsteps to the crest of the ridge, walking backwards, stepping precisely on his original footprints and at the top of the ridge he employed the same trick that Job had. He swung himself into the air from a branch and over-handed himself well clear of the spoor before lowering himself to the edge of a rock slab and anti-tracking away.

'Even Matatu wouldn't be able to unravel that,' he thought with satisfaction, as he struck off back towards the north at a run.

Two hours later he joined up with Job at the rendezvous, and in the early afternoon they came up with the other party waiting for them five miles north of the point where they had split up.

'Good to see you, Sean. We were beginning to worry,' Riccardo told him as they shook hands, and even Claudia smiled as he flopped down beside her and said, 'My kingdom for a cup of tea.'

As he sipped at the mug which Matatu brought him, he listened attentively to the little tracker. Matatu squatted beside Sean and chattered in his excited falsetto.

'Matatu went back and kept an eye on the camp we left,' Sean translated for Riccardo and Claudia's benefit. 'He didn't dare approach too closely but he saw the gang that was following us arrive. This time he counted twelve of them. They searched the area of the camp, and then

179

took the bait and followed the false trail that Job and I had laid for them.'

'So we are clear then?' Riccardo asked.

Looks like it,' Sean agreed. 'And if we push along we should be able to reach the beginning of the swamps either this evening or early tomorrow.'

'What about Tukutela?' Riccardo asked.

'Well, we know from his tracks approximately where he would have reached the swamps. We'll just cast along the edge until we find where he went in, but we've lost a lot of ground on him. We'll have to go hard if we don't want him to get away from us. Do you feel up to it, Capo?'

'Never better,' Riccardo said. 'Lead on, man.'

Before they set off again, Sean went quickly over their packs. They had consumed a great deal of the provisions and he redistributed the remainder. By giving both Job and himself an extra ten pounds or so, he was able to reduce Riccardo's pack to twenty pounds and Claudia's to a mere ten pounds, just her sleeping-bag and personal items.

They both responded well to their reduced burdens but Sean once again marched beside Riccardo to encourage him and watch over him. Claudia was still going surprisingly well, he needn't have worried about her at all. Under her light pack she was stepping out lithely. He took pleasure in watching her long legs driving and her hard little buttocks oscillating in those tight blue jeans. They reminded him of the cheeks of a chipmunk chewing a nut.

They were on the valley floor now, and there were open vleis and baobabs, those trees with bloated trunks, bark like a reptile's skin, and crooked bare branches from which a few late cream of tartar pods still hung. It was easy to see why the Zulus said that the gods had accidentally planted the baobab upside down with its roots in the air.

Far ahead of them a slow standing cloud of evaporation marked the position of the swamps, and the alluvial soil was sandy and yielding under foot.

'Just think of this, Capo.' Sean was trying to divert him. 'You are probably one of the last men who will ever hunt a great elephant in the classical tradition of the long chase. This is the way it should be done, man. Not grinding around in a Land-Rover and then leaning out of the window to kill him. This is how Selous and "Karamojo" Bell and "Samaki" Salmon hunted their elephant.'

He saw Riccardo's expression light up at the idea of being compared to those grand masters of the chase, men from another age when all elephant had been fair game. 'Samaki' Salmon had hunted and killed four thousand elephant in his lifetime. There had been a different morality in those days. Today a man with a bag of those dimensions would be accounted a villain and a criminal but in his day, 'Samaki' Salmon had been respected and honoured. He had even hunted with Edward, Prince of Wales, as his client.

Sean knew that Riccardo had an avid interest in the old-time elephant hunters, so he enlarged on their careers.

'If you want to do it the way "Karamojo" Bell did it, Capo, you have to walk like this. Bell wore out twenty-four pairs of boots a year and had to replace his porters and gunbearers every few weeks. They just couldn't keep up with him.'

'That was the golden age.' Riccardo extended his stride a little as he thought about it. 'You and I should have lived then, Sean. We were born after our time.'

'A true hunter should kill a great elephant with his legs. He should walk him down. That's the respectful and proper way and that is what you are doing now, Capo. Enjoy every step you take, for you are treading in old Bell's footprints.'

Unfortunately the effects of Sean's encouragement were not enduring; within an hour Riccardo was flagging again and Sean noticed a new disconcerting unsteadiness in his gait. He stumbled and would have fallen had not Sean caught his arm.

'We all need a five-minute break and a cup of tea.' Sean led him to the shade.

When Job brought the tea mugs, Riccardo mumbled, 'Have you got a couple more aspirins for me?'

'You all right, Capo?' he asked, as he handed him the tablets.

'Damned headache again, that's all.' But he would not meet Sean's eyes.

Sean looked across at Claudia who was sitting close beside her father, but she also avoided his gaze.

'Do you two know something I don't?' Sean demanded. 'You both look guilty as hell.' He didn't wait for an answer but stood up and went to join Job at the small fire where he was baking a fresh batch of maize cakes for their evening meal.

'The aspirin will make you feel better,' Claudia told her father softly.

'Of course, aspirin is a sure-fire cure for cancer once it reaches the brain,' he agreed, and then as he saw her agonized expression be blurted, 'I'm sorry, I don't know why I said that. Self-pity isn't my usual style.'

'Is it bad, Papa?'

'I can tolerate the headache, but I'm getting a little double vision that worries me,' he admitted. 'Damn it, I was feeling so well a few days ago, it's all happened so quickly.'

'The exertion,' she said, pitying him. 'Perhaps that is what has aggravated it. We should turn back.'

'No,' he said with utter finality. 'Don't èven talk about that again.' She inclined her head in aquiescence.

'The swamps are not far ahead. Perhaps we'll have a chance to rest,' she said.

'I don't want to rest,' he said. 'I realize just how little time I have left. I don't want to waste a moment of it.'

Sean came back to them. 'Are you ready to go on?'

Claudia glanced at her wristwatch. They had rested for

less than half an hour. It was too short and she would have protested but her father pushed himself to his feet.

'All set,' he said, and she could see that even that short break had refreshed him.

They had been going only a few minutes when Riccardo said quite cheerfully, 'Those hamburgers that Job has cooked smell just great. Makes me feel hungry.'

'Those hamburgers are maize cakes,' Sean chuckled. 'Sorry to disappoint you.'

'You can't bullshit me,' Riccardo chuckled with him. 'I can smell the fried onions and beef.'

'Papa.' Claudia looked back over her shoulder and frowned sharply, and Riccardo stopped chuckling and looked distraught.

'There might be hallucinations,' Doc Andrews had warned Claudia. 'He may begin to see things, or imagine various odours. I can't give you an exact progress of the disease, of course, and there may be periods of swift deterioration followed by longer periods of remission. Just remember, Claudia, that his fantasies will be very real to him, and episodes of hallucination can be followed by periods of complete lucidity.'

That evening Sean would not stop to brew tea. 'We have to try and make up the ground we've lost,' he told them, and they ate the cold maize cakes and biltong – slivers of salted, air-dried venison – on the march.

'One large hamburger with fried onions and all the trimmings coming up, Capo,' Sean teased him. Claudia glared at him, but Riccardo laughed uneasily and munched on the unappetizing fare as he walked.

They no longer had a spoor to follow, so Sean kept going long after night had fallen. The long tortuous miles fell slowly behind them and the brilliant southern stars burned over their heads. It was almost midnight before they stopped and unrolled their sleeping-bags.

Sean let them sleep until the dawn light was strong

enough to make out the way ahead. The landscape had changed. During the night they had entered the region that was held in thrall by the great Zambezi. These were ancient flood plains that were inundated when the river broke its banks during the torrential rainy season. They were dry now, although almost devoid of trees; a few long-dead mopane and acacia thorn trees drowned by the floods still held up twisted bare branches to the hazy blue sky, standing out on the empty plains like lonely sentinels.

As they moved out into the open, the dried mud had cracked into bricklets beneath their feet, the edges curling up, and the clumps of swamp grass were brown and matted and dead from drought. When the breeze switched fitfully they could smell the swamps still out of view ahead, the odour of mud and rotting vegetation.

The mirage shimmered across the plains, so there was no clear horizon; land and sky merged into each other like water. When they looked back the tree-line crawled like a long black serpent below the milky sky, undulating and vibrating softly in the mirage, and the dust devils spun upon themselves twisting and swaying like belly-dancers.

Out on the plain Sean felt exposed and vulnerable. There was just the scant chance of a Frelimo patrol plane passing this way searching for Renamo bands and they were as obvious as fleas on a white sheet. He wanted to hurry but then glanced back at Riccardo and knew that they would have to rest again soon.

Ahead of Sean, Matatu gave a cry that made his nerves jump. Sean knew what it meant and he ran forward, passing Claudia, and stopped beside Matatu.

'Well, all right!' He clapped Matatu's shoulder and then went down on one knee to examine the earth.

'What is it?' Riccardo sounded alarmed, but Sean lifted his head and grinned at him.

'It's him. Tukutela. We've cut his spoor again just where Matatu predicted that we would.' And he touched the marks of the huge pads whose weight had crushed the bricklets of dried mud to talcum powder. The spoor was so clear that the difference between the bull's rounded front feet and the more oval hind feet was immediately apparent, and the forward edges of each footprint were nicked by his toe-nails.

'Still heading straight for the swamps.' Sean stood and shaded his eyes against the glare as he followed the direction of the spoor. Not far ahead another line of trees was drawn like a pencil along the horizon where a narrow curved finger of higher ground reached out across the plains.

'In a way we are fortunate,' Sean remarked. 'A few years ago there were so many herds of buffalo and game on these flats that Tukutela's spoor would have been wiped out in a few hours by their hooves. Now, since the Frelimo government converted them all to army rations, Tukutela is the only living thing for miles around.'

'How far behind him are we?'

'We've made up a bit of ground.' Sean lowered his hand from his eyes and turned to him. 'But not enough, and if the uglies catch us out here in the open . . . Luckily Tukutela's spoor is headed straight for the line of trees ahead. They will give us some cover.' He gestured to Matatu to take the spoor once again.

Now the expanse of the wide plain was dimpled with old ant-hills, mounds of clay thrown up by colonies of termites, some of them the size of a large cottage. Tukutela's spoor meandered between them. However, the line of growth was by now so close that they could make out the individual trees. The finger of high ground formed a natural causeway from the edge of the forest across the wide plains to the beginning of the true swamps. There were ivory nut palms, bottle-stemmed palms, and the low ilala palms with their fan-shaped leaves, mixed with wild fig and on the highest ridge of the long causeway grew a few massive baobab, with trunks of elephantine grey bark.

With relief Sean followed the spoor of the old bull off

the plain and into the trees of the isthmus. Here the elephant had stopped to dig out the juicy roots of an ilala palm, and drop a pile of spongy yellow dung.

'The elephant rested here,' Matatu explained, lowering his voice to a whisper. 'He is an old man now and he tires easily. Here he stood to sleep, see how he shuffled his feet in the dust, and when he awoke he dusted his body. See where he scooped it up with his trunk and threw it over his back.'

'How long did he stay here?' Sean asked, and Matatu put his head on one side as he considered the question.

'He rested here until late yesterday afternoon when the sun was there.' Matatu pointed ten degrees above the western horizon. 'But when he went on he went more slowly. He feels safer now that he is close to the swamps. We have gained on him.'

Sean exaggerated Matatu's estimate as he passed it on to Riccardo and Claudia. He wanted to encourage them. 'We are making really good gains on him now.' He put on a cheerful and confident air. 'We might even catch up with him before he gets into the deep swamps, if we don't waste any time.'

The spoor headed down the isthmus and the old bull had fed quietly as he moved along it, keeping up on top of the low ridge where the bush was thickest. Directly ahead of them stood another gigantic baobab tree. Its bark was grey and folded and riven as the old bull's hide.

For the moment Sean had left Riccardo's side and moved up to his original position behind Matatu. He wanted to caution the tracker not to set too fast a pace, but before he could speak he heard a strange guttural cry behind him and he whirled around.

Riccardo's face was swollen and congested with blood, his eyes blazed and seemed to start from their sockets. Sean thought he was suffering from some kind of seizure, but Riccardo was pointing ahead, his hand shaking with violent emotion.

'There he is,' he croaked, in a thick unnatural voice. 'For God's sake, can't you see him?'

Sean whirled and followed the direction of his outstretched arm.

'What is it, man?'

He was looking ahead, and he did not see Riccardo turn to Pumula and snatch the Rigby rifle off his shoulder, but he heard the metallic clash of the bolt as Riccardo chambered a cartridge.

'Capo, what the hell are you doing?' He reached out to restrain him, but Riccardo shoved him backwards. Sean was unprepared and off balance, and he staggered and almost fell.

Riccardo ran forward to the head of the line and then he stopped and threw up the rifle.

'Capo, don't do it.' Sean was sprinting to catch him, but the Rigby crashed out and the barrel jumped high, driving Capo back a pace with the heavy recoil.

'Have you gone crazy?' Sean could not reach him before he fired again, and the heavy bullet tore a flurry of white wet bark from the trunk of the baobab. The echoes of the shot rolled across the plains.

'Capo.' Sean reached him and seized the rifle, forcing the muzzle up towards the sky just as Capo fired the Rigby for the third time.

Sean wrested the weapon out of his grip.

'In the name of all that's holy, man, what on earth do you think you're doing?'

All their eardrums were numbed by the thunder of gunfire, and Sean's angry outraged voice sounded small and hollow after it.

'Tukutela,' Riccardo mouthed. 'Don't you see? Why did you stop me?' His face was still flushed and he was shaking like a man with malarial fever. He reached once more for the Rigby in Sean's grasp, but Sean jerked it away from him.

187

'Pull yourself together,' he shouted angrily and tossed the empty rifle to Job. 'Don't let him get it again.' And turned back to Riccardo.

'Are you out of your mind?' He seized him by the shoulders. 'The sound of those shots will carry for miles.'

'Leave me!' Riccardo struggled. 'Don't you see him?' And Sean shook him viciously.

'Snap out of it, you're shooting at a tree. You've blown your lid!'

'Give me the rifle.' Riccardo was pleading, and Sean shook him again and roughly turned him to face the baobab.

'Look at it, you bloody madman! There's your elephant!' He shoved him towards it. 'Take a good look!'

Claudia ran forward and tried to restrain Sean. 'Leave him alone, can't you see he's sick?'

'He's gone crazy!' Sean pushed her aside. 'He's calling up every Frelimo and Renamo thug within fifty miles, and he's chased any elephant . . .'

'Leave him,' Claudia came back at him, and Sean let go of her father and stepped back.

'All right, ducky, he's all yours.'

Claudia rushed to her father and embraced him. 'It's all right, Papa! It's going to be all right!'

Riccardo was staring uncomprehendingly at the deep raw wounds in the bark of the baobab from which sap was oozing.

'I thought it was . . .' he shook his head weakly. 'Why did I do that? I don't . . . I thought it looked like an elephant.'

'Yes, Papa, yes.' Claudia was hugging him. 'Don't upset yourself.'

Job and the rest of the hunting team were quiet and unhappy, watching this strange episode that none of them could fathom. Sean turned away in disgust. It took him a few seconds to get full control of himself, then he asked Matatu, 'Do you think we are close enough for Tukutela to have heard the shooting?'

188

'The swamps are close, and the sound carries over this flat earth as it does over water,' Matatu shrugged. 'Perhaps the elephant heard, who knows?'

Sean looked back the way they had come. From the ridge they could see out across the flood plain into the dusty distances.

'Job, what chance that the terrs heard?'

'We'll find out the hard way, Sean. It depends how close behind us they are.'

Sean shook himself, trying to rid himself of his anger the way a spaniel shakes off water.

'We'll have to rest here. The *mambo* is sick. Brew a billy of tea, and we'll decide what to do,' he ordered.

He walked back to where Claudia was still holding her father. She faced Sean defiantly, turning her body to shield Riccardo from him.

'Sorry I pushed you around, Capo,' Sean said mildly. 'You gave me a hell of a fright.'

'I don't understand,' Riccardo mumbled. 'I could have sworn it was him. I saw him so clearly.'

'We will break for a cup of tea,' Sean told him. 'I think you've got a touch of the sun. It can turn a man's brain to jelly.'

'He'll be fine in a few minutes,' Claudia said confidently, and Sean nodded coldly at her.

'Let's get him into the shade.'

Riccardo leaned back against the bole of the baobab and closed his eyes. He looked pale and bewildered, a rash of sweat droplets sparkled on his chin and upper lip. Claudia knelt beside him and dabbed them away with the corner of her scarf, but when she looked up at Sean he jerked his head in a peremptory gesture and she stood up and followed him.

'This doesn't come as any surprise to you, does it?' he accused, as soon as they were beyond earshot. She did not reply and he went on, 'Just what kind of daughter are you anyway? You knew he was sick and you let him come out on this jaunt.'

Her lips were trembling and as he stared into them he saw that her honey-coloured eyes were swimming, he had not expected tears from her. They took him by surprise. He felt his fury slipping away and he had to make an effort to bolster it.

'It's too late to start blubbering now, ducky. We've got to find a way to get him home. He's a sick man.'

'He's not going home,' she murmured, so low that he barely caught the words. Her tears were hanging on thick dark lashes and he stared at her in silence. She swallowed hard and then said, 'He's not a sick man, Sean. He's dying. Cancer. It was diagnosed by a specialist before we left home. He predicted that it could attack the brain like this.'

Sean's fury crumpled.

'No,' he said. 'Not Capo.'

'Why do you think I agreed to let him come and insisted on coming with him? I knew that this was his last hunt – and I wanted to be with him.'

They were silent, staring at each other, then she said, 'You care. I can see that you truly care for him. I didn't expect that.'

'He's my friend,' Sean said, puzzled himself by the depth of his own sadness.

'I didn't think you were capable of gentleness,' she went on softly. 'I may have misjudged you.'

'Perhaps we misjudged each other,' he said, and she nodded.

'Perhaps we did,' she said. 'But thank you anyway. Thank you for caring about my father.'

She began to turn away to go back to Riccardo but Sean stopped her.

'We still haven't settled anything,' he said. 'We haven't decided what we are going to do.'

'We go on, of course,' she answered. 'Right to the bitter end. That's what I promised him.'

'You've got guts,' he told her softly.

'If I have, then I got them from him,' she replied, and went to her father.

The mug of tea and a half dozen Anadin tablets revived Riccardo. He was acting and talking completely rationally again, and none of them made any further reference to his wild behaviour, although quite naturally it had thrown a pall over all of them.

'We must move on, Capo,' Sean told him. 'Tukutela is walking away from us every minute we sit here.'

They followed the ridge of high ground, and now the odour of the swamps was stronger, brought to them by the fitful inconstant wind.

'That's one of the many reasons the elephant like the swamps,' Sean explained to Riccardo. 'There the wind is always shifting, turning and switching. It makes it much more difficult to get close to them.'

There was a gap in the trees ahead, and Sean stopped and they gazed out through it.

'There they are,' he said. 'The Zambezi swamplands.'

The ridge on which they stood was like the back of a sea serpent, swimming across the open flood plains. Now just ahead of them it ducked below the surface and disappeared at the point where the open plains gave way to endless expanses of papyrus and reeds.

Sean raised his binoculars and surveyed the swamps ahead. The reed-beds seemed limitless, but he had flown over them and he knew that they were interspersed with shallow lagoons of open water and narrow winding channels. Farther out, almost on the horizon, he could see the loom of small islets, dark patches of almost impenetrable bush-crowned islands and through the lens of the binoculars he could just make out the curved palm stems with their high fluffy heads.

The past season had been particularly dry and the water level would be low, in most places not more than waist deep, but the mudbanks would be black and glutinous and the channels much deeper. The going would be arduous, and apart from the mud and water, reeds and water plants would impede each step they took, winding themselves around their legs as they tried to move.

For them each mile through the swamps would be the equivalent of five on dry land, while the elephant would be in his element. He loved mud and water. It supported his great bulk and his foot pads were designed by nature to expand as he put his weight upon them, forcing a wide opening, and then they would shrink in diameter as he lifted them, freeing themselves readily from the clinging mud.

Tukutela could gorge on reeds and soft water plants and swamp grass, and the dense bushy islets would afford variety to his diet. The suck of mud and the splash of water would warn him of an approaching enemy and the fitfully turning wind would protect him, bringing the scent of a pursuer down to him from every quarter. In all Tukutela's wide range, this was the most difficult place to hunt him.

'It's going to be a Sunday-school picnic, Capo,' Sean lowered the binoculars. 'Those tusks are as good as hanging over the fireplace in your den already.'

The old bull's spoor went out to the very end of the land bridge, and then down into the papyrus beds, where the undulating sea of green fronds swallowed the trail and left not a sign.

'Nobody can follow a trail in there.' Riccardo stood at the line where dry friable earth ended and damp swamp mud began. 'Nobody can find Tukutela in there,' he repeated, staring at the wall of swamp growth higher than his head. 'Surely they can't?'

'You are right, nobody can find him in there,' Sean agreed. 'That is, nobody except Matatu.'

They were standing in the remains of a village that had

been built on the end of the isthmus. Clearly the previous occupants had been fishermen, members of one of the small tribes who live along the banks of the Zambezi and make their livelihood from her abundant green waters. Only the racks on which they had dried their catches of tilapia bream and barbeled catfish still stood, but their huts had been burned to the ground.

Job was searching the outskirts of the village and he whistled for Sean. When Sean went to join him he was standing over an object which lay in the short grass. At first glance Sean thought it was a bundle of rags and then he saw the bones protruding from it. They were still partially covered by shreds of dried skin and flesh.

'When?' Sean asked.

'Six months ago, perhaps.'

'How did he die?'

Job squatted beside the human skeleton and when he turned the skull it snapped off the vertebrae of the neck like a ripe fruit. Job cupped it in his hands, and it grinned at him with empty eye-sockets.

'Bullet through the back of the head,' Job said. 'Exit-hole this side.' It was like a third eye in the bone of the forehead.

Job replaced the skull and walked deeper into the grass. 'Here's another,' he called.

'Renamo has been through here,' Sean gave his opinion. 'Either looking for recruits or dried fish or both.'

'Or else it was Frelimo looking for Renamo rebels, and they decided to question them, with an AK.'

'Poor buggers,' Sean said. 'They get it from both sides. There will be plenty more of them lying around, they are the ones who escaped from the huts before they burned.'

They started back towards the village and Sean said. 'They were fishermen, they would have had their canoes here. They will probably be hidden, but we could certainly use one. Go through the edge of the papyrus beds and then search the bush behind the village.'

Sean crossed to where Riccardo and Claudia were sitting together. As he came up, he looked at her enquiringly and she nodded and smiled optimistically.

'Papa's doing fine, what is this place?'

He explained their reasoning as to the fate of the village.

'Why would they kill these innocent people?' Claudia was appalled.

'In Africa these days you don't have to have a reason for killing somebody, other than a loaded gun in your hands, and a fancy to fire it off.'

'But what harm could they have done?' she insisted.

Sean shrugged. 'Harbouring rebels, withholding information, hiding food, refusing the services of their women, any one of those crimes, or none of them.'

The sun was a red ball through the swamp haze, so low above the tops of the papyrus that Sean could look directly at it without screwing up his eyes.

'It'll be dark before we can leave,' he decided. 'We'll have to sleep here tonight and start again at first light tomorrow. One consolation is that now Tukutela has reached the swamps, he will slow down. He's probably not more than a couple of miles ahead of us right now.' But as he said it he thought about those shots that Riccardo had fired. If the bull had heard them, he would still be running. There was, however, no point in telling that to Riccardo. He looked shaken and despondent, and he had been almost silent since the incident.

'He is just a husk of the Capo I knew, poor old devil. The last thing I can do for him is to get him that elephant.' Sean's sympathy was genuine and unaffected and he sat down beside him, and began to draw him out, describing what lay ahead, and how they would hunt for the old bull in the papyrus beds.

The hunt was all that now seemed to interest Riccardo, and for the first time that day he became animated and once he even laughed.

Claudia flashed a grateful smile at Sean, and then stood up and said, 'I've got a little private business to attend to.'

'Where are you off to?' Sean demanded immediately.

'The little girls' room,' she told him. 'And you are definitely not invited.'

'Don't go wandering off too far, and no swimming this time,' he ordered. 'You'll get enough of that tomorrow.'

'I hear and obey, O great white *Bwana*.' She gave him a sarcastic curtsy and set off out of the perimeter of the burned village. Sean watched her go uneasily and was about to call another warning after her when there was a shout from the papyrus bed and his attention was diverted from Claudia.

He jumped up.

'What is it, Job?' he yelled, and went down to the water's edge.

There were more confused shouts and splashing from the depths of the papyrus, and then Job and Matatu emerged, dragging something long and black and waterlogged between them.

'Our first bit of luck.' Sean grinned at Riccardo and slapped him on the shoulder.

It was a traditional *mokorro* dugout canoe, about seventeen foot long, hewn from a single log of the sausage tree, *Kigelia africana*. The body of the dugout was just wide enough for a person to sit in it, but it was usually propelled by a man standing in the stern and wielding a long punt pole.

Job tipped the water out of the craft and they examined it carefully. The hull had been repaired and caulked in a few places, but seemed reasonably sound.

'Search the village,' Sean ordered. 'They must have had caulking material here. See if you can find it, and then send Dedan and Pumula to cut a couple of punt poles.'

Claudia screamed, and they all spun to face the sound. She screamed again, the sound was strangely muffled and far off, and Sean began to run, snatching up his rifle from where he had left it beside the nearest burnt-out hut.

'Claudia!' he yelled. 'Where are you?' Only his echo mocked him from the forest. 'Where are you? . . . are you?'

When Claudia stood up and rebuckled her belt, she found that it came in easily a full two notches shorter around her waist. She smiled down at her own belly with approval. Now it was no longer flat but definitely concave. The long march and frugal rations had stripped every last ounce of fat from her frame.

'Strange how in an age of plenty we set out to starve ourselves.' She smiled again. 'I'm going to enjoy putting on those lost pounds, plenty of pasta and red wine when I get home.'

She started back towards the village, and then realized that in her search for privacy she had gone further than she had intended and that a thicket of wiry thorn brush blocked her way back. She turned aside to circumvent it and came upon a broad pathway running directly down through the bush towards the edge of the swamp. She followed it thankfully.

Claudia did not realize that she was following a hippo road, one of the wide thoroughfares that the great amphibians followed on their nightly forays into the forest. However, the road had not been used for many months. The hippopotamus in the area had been decimated along with the other game. She was in a hurry to get back to her father, and she was feeling slightly uneasy at her isolation from the rest of the party. She strode down the pathway, just short of a run.

Ahead of her an old mat of dried papyrus stems was spread across the road from side to side. It had obviously been placed there by the previous occupants of the village, and although it served no purpose that Claudia could imagine, it was no obstacle to her progress and she stepped on to it without slackening her pace.

The pitfall had been dug for the express purpose of trapping a hippopotamus. It was ten feet deep with funnel-shaped sides, that would tumble one of the huge beasts down into its depth and wedge it securely between the earthen walls. The opening was covered by branches strong enough to carry the weight of a man or a lesser animal, but not that of a hippo. Over these branches the builders had spread the papyrus stems.

However, the pitfall had been built a long time previously and both branches and mat had rotted and weakened. They collapsed under Claudia's weight, and she screamed as she dropped through into the pit beneath, and screamed again as she hit the sloping side and bounced off it. The bottom of the pit was covered with a few inches of stagnant water that had seeped into it. Claudia landed awkwardly with one leg twisted up under her and then rolled on to her back in the mud.

The breath had been driven from her lungs and there was a fierce pain in her left knee. For a few minutes she could not respond to the faint shouts she heard from above. She sat up, clutching her injured knee to her chest and gasping wildly to fill her agonized lungs. At last she managed a strangled shout.

'Here! I'm here.'

'Are you all right?' Sean's head appeared above her, peering down anxiously.

'I think so!' she gasped, and tried to stand up, but the pain shot through her knee and she fell back. 'My knee,' she said.

'Hold on. I'm coming down.' Sean's head withdrew. She heard voices. Job and Matatu and her father. Then a coil of nylon rope dropped down towards her, unfurling as it fell. Sean lowered himself swiftly down the rope and dropped the last few feet to land with a splash in the mud beside her.

'I'm sorry,' she said contritely. 'I guess I've done it again.'

'Don't apologize,' he grinned. 'I'm not conditioned to it. For once, it's not your fault. Let's take a look at your leg.'

He squatted beside her. 'Move your foot. Capital! Can you bend your knee? Splendid! At least no bones broken. That's a relief. Let's get you out of this hole.' He tied a loop in the end of the rope and slipped it over her head and shoulders and settled it under her armpits.

'Okay, Job,' he called up. 'Take her up. Gently, man, gently.'

As soon as they reached ground level, Sean made a more thorough examination of her knee.

He rolled up the leg of her jeans and said, 'Shit!'

As a Scout commander he had extensive experience of the type of injury that a paratrooper is prone to, broken bones, torn cartilage, sprained ligaments in ankle and knee. Already Claudia's knee was ballooning and the first tinge of bruising coloured the smooth tanned skin.

'This might hurt a little,' he warned, and manipulated her leg gently.

'Ouch!' she said. 'That's damned sore.'

'Okay,' he nodded. 'It's the medial ligament. I don't think you've torn it, it would be more painful if you had. Probably just sprained it.'

'What does that mean?' she asked.

'Three days,' he replied. 'You won't be walking on it for at least three days.'

He put his arm around her shoulders. 'Can you stand up?' he asked, and when she nodded he helped her to her feet. She leaned against him, standing on her good leg.

'Try putting a little weight on it,' he said, and immediately she exclaimed with pain.

'No, I can't use it.'

He stopped and picked her up in his arms as though she

were a child and carried her back to the village. She was surprised by his strength and then, although her knee was beginning to throb, she relaxed in his arms. It was a good feeling. Papa had carried her like this when she was a little girl, and she had to resist the urge to lay her head against Sean's shoulder.

When they reached the village he set her down in the clearing, and Matatu ran to fetch his pack. Her injury had diverted Riccardo's attention from his own troubles, and he came to fuss over his little girl in a way which ordinarily would have annoyed her. Now she submitted to it, thankful for his revived animation and attention.

Sean strapped the knee with an elastic bandage from his first-aid kit and then gave her an anti-inflammatory tablet to swallow with hot tea.

'That's about all we can do for it,' he told her, and sat back. 'Only thing that will fix it is time.'

'Why did you say three days?'

'It takes that long. I've seen a hundred knees just like yours, except that they were usually a lot more hairy and not nearly as pretty.'

'That's a compliment.' She raised an eyebrow. 'You are getting soft, Colonel.'

'Part of the treatment, and of course, totally insincere,' he assured with a grin. 'The only question now, ducky, is what on earth are we going to do with you?'

'Leave me here,' she said promptly.

'Are you out of your mind?' he asked, and Riccardo backed him up immediately.

'That's out of the question.'

'Look at it this way,' she reasoned calmly. 'I cannot move for three days, by which time your elephant will be long gone, Papa.' She held up her hand to forestall his argument. 'We cannot go back. You can't carry me. I can't walk. We would have to sit here anyway.'

'We cannot leave you alone, don't be ridiculous.'

'No,' she agreed. 'But you can leave someone to look after me while you go on after Tukutela.'

'No.' Riccardo shook his head.

'Sean,' she appealed to him. 'Make him see that it is the sensible thing to do.'

He stared at her and the admiration she saw in his gaze gave her a full warm feeling in her chest.

'Damn it,' he said softly. 'You're all right.'

'Tell him it will only be for a few days, Sean. We all know how much that elephant means to Papa. I want to give it to him as my . . .' she almost said 'last gift', but then she changed it, 'as my special gift to him.'

'I can't accept it, *tesoro*.' Riccardo's voice was gruff but blurred and he lowered his head to hide his feelings.

'Make him go, Sean,' Claudia insisted, and gripped his forearm firmly. 'Tell him I'll be as safe here with Job to look after me as I would be in the swamp with the two of you.'

'She just may have a point, Capo,' Sean said. 'But, hell, it's not my business. It's between the two of you.'

'Will you leave us alone, Sean?' Claudia asked, and then without waiting for a reply, she turned to her father. 'Come and sit here next to me, Papa.' She patted the ground beside her. Sean stood up and walked away, leaving them together in the gathering darkness.

He went to sit beside Job. They sat in the companionable silence of old friends, drinking tea and smoking one of Sean's last cheroots, passing it back and forth between them.

An hour passed. It was entirely dark before Riccardo came to where the two of them sat. He stood over them and his voice was rough and drawn with sadness.

'All right, Sean,' he said. 'She has convinced me to do as she wants. Will you make the arrangements to go on with the hunt first thing tomorrow morning? And, Job, will you stay here and look after my little girl for me?'

'I'll look after her for you, sir,' he agreed. 'You just go kill that elephant. We'll be here when you come back.'

Working in the moonlight they moved out of the burned-out village and built a fly camp a few hundred metres back in the forest.

They made a lean-to shelter for Claudia and under it placed a mattress of cut grass. Sean left the medical kit and most of their remaining provisions in the shelter with her. He detailed both Job and Dedan to remain with Claudia. Job would keep the light 30/06 rifle with the fibreglass stock, and Dedan had his axe and skinning knife.

'Send Dedan back to keep an eye on the isthmus. Any Frelimo or Renamo patrols will come that way. At the first sign of trouble, get the girl into the swamp and hide out on one of the islands.' Sean gave Job his final orders, and then sauntered across to where Riccardo was taking leave of his daughter.

'Are you ready, Capo?'

Riccardo stood up quickly and walked away from Claudia without looking back.

'Don't get into any more trouble,' Sean told her.

'You neither.' She looked up at him. 'And Sean, take care of Papa for me.'

He squatted down in front of her and offered her his hand as he would have if she had been a man, and he tried to think of something witty to say, but he could not.

'Okay, then?' he asked instead.

'Okay, then,' she agreed, and he stood up and walked down to the edge of the swamp where Matatu and Pumula and Riccardo were waiting for him beside the dugout canoe.

Matatu took up his position in the bows of the frail craft, Sean and Riccardo were amidships, sitting on their depleted packs and holding their rifles across their laps. Pumula stood in the stern with one of the freshly cut punt poles and propelled the dugout in response to Matatu's hand signals.

Within seconds of pushing off from the bank, they were surrounded by a high palisade of papyrus, and their view was restricted to the wall of reeds and the small patch of lemon-yellow dawn sky overhead. As they passed, the sharp pointed leaves of the reeds were dashed into their faces, threatening their eyes, and the webs that the tiny swamp spiders had spun between the stems of the reeds wrapped over their faces, sticky and irritating. The night's clammy chill hung over the swamp and when they came out suddenly into an open lagoon, there was a heavy mist lying over the surface and a flock of whistling duck alarmed the dawn with the clatter of their wings.

The dugout was heavily overloaded with the four men aboard. There was only an inch or so of freeboard and if any one of them moved suddenly, water slopped on board and they were forced to use the tea billy to bail almost continually, but Matatu signalled them on.

The sun rose above the papyrus and immediately the mist twisted into rising tendrils and then was gone. The water lilies opened their cerulean blossoms and turned them to face the sunrise. Twice they saw large crocodiles lying with just their eye-knuckles exposed. They sank below the surface as the dugout slid towards them.

The swamps were alive with birds. Bitterns and secretive night herons lurked in the reed-beds, little chocolate-brown jacanas danced over the lily pads on their long legs, while goliath herons as tall as a man fished the back waters of the lagoons. Overhead winged formations of pelicans and white egrets, cormorants and darters with serpentine necks, and huge flocks of wild duck of a dozen different species.

The heat built up swiftly and was reflected from the surface of the water into their faces so that the two white men were soon sweating through their shirts. At places the water was only a few inches deep and they were forced to climb out and drag the dugout through to the next channel or lagoon. Under the matted reeds the mud was black and foul-smelling and reached to their knees.

In the shallower places the elephant's pads had left deep circular water-filled craters in the mudbanks. The spoor of the old bull led them deeper and ever deeper into the swamplands, but there was consolation in the swift progress that the dugout made across the lagoons and channels, thrust on by the long punt pole. For a while, Sean spelled Pumula in the stern but soon Pumula could no longer abide his clumsy strokes and took the pole away from him.

There was only room for one man to stretch out in the bottom of the dugout. Riccardo slept in it that night, while the others sat waist-deep in the mud, leaning against the hull of the canoe and took what rest the clouds of mosquitoes allowed them.

Early the following morning, when Sean stood up out of the mud, he found that his bare legs were swarming with black leeches. The repulsive worms were attached to his skin, bloated with the blood they had sucked from him. Sean used a little of their precious supply of salt to rid himself of them. To pull them loose would leave a wound into which the leech had injected anti-coagulants and which would continue to bleed profusely and probably become infected. However, a dab of salt on each leech made them twist and contort with agony and fall off leaving only a sealed wound on the skin.

When he opened his trousers, Sean found that they had crawled up into the cleft between his buttocks and were hanging like black grapes from his genitalia. He shuddered with horror as he worked on them, while safely in the dugout Riccardo watched with interest and made facetious comment:

'Hey, Sean, this must be the first time you've ever objected to a bit of head!'

*

S ean set the end of the punt pole in the mud and steadied it while Matatu shinned up it like a monkey and peered ahead. When he came down he told Sean, 'I can see the islands. We are very close. We will be there before noon, and unless Tukutela has heard us, he will be on one of the islands.'

Sean knew from flights over the area and from study of his large-scale map that the islands formed a chain between the swamplands and the main channel of the Zambezi. They dragged the dugout through the shallows, Sean hauling on the nylon rope tied to the bows, and Pumula and Matatu shoving in the stern. When Riccardo offered to assist, Sean told him, 'Take a free ride, Capo. I want you nicely rested so that you don't have any excuses if you mess up your shot at Tukutela.'

At last Sean saw the fronds of the palm trees rising above the screen of papyrus ahead, and abruptly the water deepened, and he went under to his chin. He dragged himself out and they all clambered back on board. Pumula poled them through to the first island. The vegetation was so dense that it overhung the water, and they had to push their way through to reach the shore.

The earth was grey and sandy, leached by a million floods, but it was good to have dry land under foot. Sean spread out their wet clothing and equipment to dry while Matatu slipped away to make a circuit of the island. The water had just boiled in the billy when Matatu was back.

'Yes,' he nodded at Sean. 'He passed here yesterday early, while we were leaving the village, but he has settled down now. The peace of the river is upon him, and he feeds quietly. He left this island at sunrise this morning.'

'Which way did he go?' Sean asked, and Matatu pointed. 'There is another larger island close by.'

'Let's take a look.'

Sean poured a mug of tea for Riccardo and left him with Pumula, while he and Matatu skirted the northern shore, forcing their way through the dense growth until they reached the base of the tallest tree on the island and climbed into its top branches.

Sean settled into a high crotch of the tree, snapped off the few leafy twigs that obscured his view and gazed out on a scene of magnificent desolation.

He was sixty feet above the island and could see to the misty horizon. The Zambezi flowed past the island. Its waters were an opaque glassy green so wide that distance had reduced the great trees that lined the far bank to a dark band that separated green water from the high alps of cumulus cloud that soared anvil-headed into the blue African sky.

The Zambezi flowed so swiftly that its surface was ruffled by eddies and whirlpools and wayward counter currents. Floating carpets of swamp grass had been torn loose by the current and sailed past, seeming as substantial as the island beneath him. Sean thought about crossing that forbidding river in the frail dugout. It would take more than one trip to get them all across and he abandoned the idea. There was only one way out, and that was back the way they had come.

He transferred all his attention to the chain of islands which stood like sentinels between the mother river and her spreading swamps. The nearest island in the chain was three hundred metres away; the channel between was clogged with reeds and water hyacinth and lily pads. The blooms of the water lilies were spots of electric blue against the green water and even in the tree-top Sean could catch wafts of their perfume.

Sean raised his binoculars and meticulously swept the channel and the nearest shore of the island, for even a great elephant could be swallowed up by the sweep and magnitude of this land- and waterscape.

Suddenly his nerves jumped as he saw movement weighty and ponderous in the reeds and the gleam of wet hide in the sunlight. His excitement was stillborn, followed by the pull of disappointment in his guts, as he recognized the broad misshapen head of a hippopotamus emerging from the swamps.

In the lens of his binoculars he could see the pink-shot piggy eyes and the bristles in the disproportionately tiny ears. The hippo fluttered them like the wings of a bird, shaking off the droplets that sparkled like diamond chips, forming a halo above its huge head. It plodded through the mud, crossing from one lagoon to another, pausing only to loose an explosive jet of liquid dung that it splattered with a violent stirring motion of its stubby tail. The force of this discharge flattened the reeds behind the obese animal.

With relief, Sean watched it move on and submerge itself in the further lagoon. The rotten hull of the dugout would have offered no protection from those heavy curved tusks in the gape of huge jaws.

At last Sean glanced across at Matatu in the fork beside him, and the little Ndorobo shook his head.

'He has moved on, so must we.'

They scrambled down to the ground and went back to where they had left Riccardo. The voyage in the *mokorro* and a good night's sleep had invigorated him. He was on his feet, impatient and eager for the hunt, the way Sean had known him before.

'Anything?' he demanded.

'No.' Sean shook his head. 'But Matatu reckons we are close. Absolute silence from now on.'

While they loaded the dugout, Sean gulped a mug of the scalding tea and kicked sand over the fire.

They punted and pushed the canoe across the channel to the next island, and once again Sean climbed into a tree-top while Matatu scurried into the dense undergrowth to pick up the elephant's spoor again. He was back within fifteen minutes and Sean slid out of the tree to meet him.

'He has moved on,' Matatu whispered. 'But the wind is

bad.' He looked grave, and took the ash bag from his loin-cloth and shook out a puff of powdery white ash to demonstrate. 'See how it turns and changes like the fancy of a Shangane whore.'

Sean nodded and before they crossed to the next island he stripped off his sleeveless bush shirt. Naked from the waist up he could feel instantly the slightest vagary of the breeze on the sensitive skin of his upper body.

On the next island they found where Tukutela had left the water to go ashore, and the mud he had smeared on the brush as he passed was still slightly damp. Matatu shivered with excitement like a good dog getting his first whiff of the bird.

They left the canoe and crept forward, feeling their way through the heavy bush, thankful for the breeze that clattered the palm fronds overhead to cover the small sounds of their footfalls in the dead leaves and dry twigs. They found where the old elephant had shaken down the nuts from one of the palms and stuffed them down his throat without chewing them with his last worn set of molars, but he had moved on again.

'Run?' Sean whispered, fearful that the bull might have sensed their presence, but Matatu reassured him with a quick shake of his head and pointed to the green twigs that the elephant had stripped of bark and left scattered along his tracks. The raw twigs had not completely dried out, but the spoor led them on a meandering beat across the island and then once more plunged into the channel on the far side. They sent Pumula back to bring the dugout around to where they waited and when he arrived piled Riccardo into it and pushed him across, wading waist-deep beside him, moving stealthily and silently until they reached the next island.

Here they found a pile of dung, spongy and soft with reeds and hyacinth that the bull had eaten, and beside it the splash mark of his urine as though a garden hose had been played upon the earth. It was still so wet that Sean scooped a handful of the dirt and moulded it into a ball like a child's mud cake. The pile of dung had a dry crust but when Matatu thrust his foot into it, it was moist as porridge and he exclaimed with delight at the body heat still trapped within.

'Close, very close!' he whispered excitedly.

Instinctively Sean reached for the cartridges looped on his belt and he changed them for those in the double-barrelled rifle, careful to mute the click of the rifle's sidelock as he closed it. Riccardo recognized the gesture, he had seen it so often before and he grinned with excitement and clicked the Rigby's safety-catch on and off, on and off. They crept forward in single file, but disappointment dragged them down again as the spoor led them across the island, and then on the far side once more entered the papyrus beds.

They stood facing the wall of reeds, staring at the point where Tukutela had pushed down the stems as he went through. One of the flattened stems quivered and began slowly to rise into its original position. The elephant must have passed only minutes ahead of them. They stood in a frozen group, straining to listen beyond the susurration of the wind in the papyrus.

Then they heard it, the low rumble like summer thunder heard at a great distance, the sound that an elephant makes in his throat when he is content and at peace. It is a sound that carries much farther than its volume would suggest, but nevertheless Sean knew that the bull was not more than a hundred yards ahead of them and he laid his hand on Riccardo's arm and drew him gently up alongside him.

'We have to be careful of the wind,' he began in a whisper, and then they heard the swish and rush of water sucked up in the bull's trunk and squirted back over his own shoulders to cool himself, and they caught a brief glimpse of the black tip of his trunk as he lifted it high above the tops of the papyrus ahead of them.

Their excitement was so intense that Sean felt his throat closed and dry, and his whisper was rough.

'Back off!'

He made a cut-out hand signal which Matatu obeyed instantly, and they backed away, a stealthy pace at a time, Sean leading Riccardo by the arm. As soon as they were into the undergrowth Riccardo demanded in a furious whisper, 'What the hell, we were so close.'

'Too close,' Sean told him grimly. 'Without any chance of a shot in the papyrus. If the wind had swung just a few degrees it would have been over before it began. We have to let him get across to the next island before we can close in.'

He led Riccardo back faster, and then stopped below the outspread branches of a tall strangler fig.

'Let's take a look,' he ordered. They propped their rifles at the base of the trunk, and Sean helped Riccardo to reach the first branch and then followed him as he climbed upwards from branch to branch.

Near the top of the fig they found a secure stance and Sean steadied Riccardo with a hand on his shoulder, and they stared down into the papyrus beds.

They saw him immediately. Tukutela's back rose above the reeds. It was wet and charcoal-black from the spray of his trunk, the spine was curved and prominent beneath the rough wrinkled hide. He was faced away from them, his huge ears flapping lazily, the edges torn and tattered, the thick veins twisted and knotted like a nest of serpents beneath the smoother skin behind their wide spread.

A row of four egrets rode upon his back, perched along his spine, brilliant white in the sunlight with yellow bills, sitting hunched up but attentive, bright-eyed sentinels who would warn the old bull at the first approach of danger.

While he was in the water, there was no way that they could come at him and he was well over three hundred yards away, far beyond effective rifle shot. So they watched him from the tree-top as he made his slow majestic way across the channel towards the next island.

When Tukutela reached the deepest stretch of open water he submerged completely; only his trunk rose above the surface, waving and coiling in the air like the head of a sea-serpent. He emerged on the far side of the channel with water streaming down his darkly mountainous sides.

Standing together on the branch of the fig, Riccardo and Sean were savouring this high point in both their hunting experience. Never again would there be another elephant like this. No other man would ever gaze upon such a beast. He was theirs. It seemed that they had waited their lifetimes for this moment. The hunter's passion eclipsed all other emotion, at that moment rendering everything else in their lives effete and tasteless. Here was something primeval, sprung from the very wells of the soul and it affected them as great music might affect others.

The old bull lifted his head and turned aside for a moment, affording them just a brief glimpse of his dark-stained ivory, and they stirred unconsciously, affected by the sight of those long perfectly curved shafts as by the creation of a Michelangelo or the body of a beautiful woman. At that moment, there was nothing else in their universe. They were perfectly in tune, a bond of companionship and shared endeavour welded them.

'He's beautiful!' Riccardo whispered.

Sean did not reply, for there was nothing to add.

They watched the old bull reach the far island and heave his body from the water, climb the low bank and stand for a moment, tall and gaunt and shining wet in the sun, before he pushed his way into the undergrowth and it swallowed up even his bulk. The egrets were brushed from his back and rose up like snowy scraps of paper in a whirlwind. Sean tapped Riccardo on the shoulder and he shook himself as though awaking from a dream.

'We'll cross in the canoe,' Sean whispered, and sent Pumula to bring the craft around the islet.

They sat flat in the bottom of the *mokorro* so that their heads would not show above the tops of the reeds and they propelled themselves across the narrow neck of swamp by pulling on the stems of the papyrus. Soundlessly they slid through the reed-beds, and the light breeze held true and steady. Sean felt every light touch of it on his bare shoulders.

They reached the shore and Sean helped Riccardo out of the canoe, and they pulled it up onto the bank, careful not to make the faintest sound.

'Check your load,' Sean whispered, and Riccardo turned the bolt of the Rigby and drew it back just far enough to expose the shining brass cartridge in the chamber. Sean nodded approval and Riccardo closed the bolt silently. They went forward.

They were forced to move in single file, following the path that the bull had opened through the otherwise impenetrable growth. Matatu led them a few paces at a time, and then they all froze to listen.

Suddenly there was a loud crackling uproar in the bushes just ahead of them, and they saw the branches sway and toss and shake. Riccardo swung up the Rigby, but Sean restrained him, grabbing his forearm and pushing the muzzle of the rifle down.

They stood stonily, staring ahead, hearts pounding, and listened to the old bull feeding. Only thirty paces from them he was ripping down branches, swinging his ears back and forth to a leisurely rhythm, rumbling contentedly, and they could not catch even the barest glimpse of grey hide.

Sean still had hold of Riccardo's arm and now he drew him onwards. Step by step they edged through the green press of leaves and vines and drooping branches. Ten paces, and then Sean halted. He eased Riccardo forward, pushing him ahead, and Sean pointed over his shoulder.

For long seconds Riccardo could make out no details in

the jumbled growth and confused shadows. Then the bull flapped his ears again, and Riccardo saw his eye through a hole in the vegetation. It was a small rheumy eye, with the slightly opaque blue cast of age, and the tears oozed down the wrinkled cheek below it, giving it a look of great wisdom and infinite sorrow.

That sorrow was contagious, it engulfed Riccardo in a black wave, it weighed down his soul, transforming his ardent predatory passion to a devastating sadness and mourning for this life that was about to end. He did not lift the rifle.

The elephant blinked its eye, the lashes surrounding it were thick and long, and the eye looked deep into Riccardo's own, seemed to pierce his very soul, seemed to mourn for him as he mourned for the old bull. Riccardo did not realize that the evil thing in his brain was once more bending and reshaping reality, he knew only that the sorrow in him was as insupportable as the black oblivion of death.

He felt Sean lightly tap him between the shoulder-blades, screening even that tiny movement from the bull. It was the urgent command to fire, but it was as though Riccardo had left his own body and hovered just above it, looking down upon himself, watching both the man and the beast with death in them and death all about them, and the tragedy engrossed him and robbed him of his will and power of movement.

Once again Sean tapped him. The elephant was fifteen paces away, standing perfectly still, a looming grey shadow in the undergrowth. Sean knew that Tukutela's sudden stillness was the old bull's response to the premonition of danger. He would stand only for a few seconds longer, and then plunge away into the dense undergrowth.

He wanted to seize Riccardo's shoulder and shake him, he wanted to cry out, 'Shoot, man, shoot!' But he was helpless, the slightest movement, the faintest sound would trigger the old bull into flight.

Then it happened as Sean had known and feared it would. It seemed that Tukutela had been snatched away, had disappeared in a puff of grey smoke. It was impossible that such a huge beast could move so quickly and so silently in such dense bush, but he was gone.

Sean seized Riccardo's arm and pulled him along with him, dragging him after the vanished bull. Sean's face was contorted with anger and dark rage filled his chest and made it difficult for him to breathe. He wanted to vent that rage on Riccardo. He had risked his very life to put him in the position to take this animal, and the man had not even raised his rifle.

Sean ran forward, his grip upon Riccardo's arm was savage, and he dragged him through dense scrub and thorn, oblivious to his discomfort. He was certain that Tukutela would try to reach the next island in the chain, and he hoped for another chance at him as he crossed the open channel. He would force Riccardo to take even a long shot, hoping to cripple and slow the bull, so that Sean could follow and finish him off.

Behind him Matatu screamed something that was unintelligible, a warning, a cry for help perhaps, and Sean came up short, and stood listening. Something was happening that was totally unexpected, for which he was unprepared.

He heard the sudden crash and crackle in the undergrowth, and then the wild trumpeting squeal of an enraged elephant, but the sound was from behind him, not the direction in which Tukutela had vanished. For an instant Sean did not understand, and then the reality dawned upon him and he felt the goose bumps rise upon his naked back.

Tukutela had done something that no elephant he knew of had ever done before. The old bull had not fled, but instead had circled downwind of them to get their scent. Even as he stood now, Sean felt the wind touch his naked back, like the caress of a treacherous lover bearing his scent down to where the great bull was rushing through the dense bush, hunting for him.

'Matatu,' Sean yelled. 'Run! Run across the wind!' He shoved Riccardo roughly against the trunk of a towering teak tree.

'Get up there,' he snarled at him. The lower branches were easy to climb, and Sean left him and raced back to protect Matatu.

He charged headlong through the bush, jumping over fallen logs, his rifle held across his chest, and the forest rang to the elephant's wild and angry squeals.

He was closing swiftly, like an avalanche of grey rock. Tukutela rolled through the forest, splitting and dashing the smaller trees that stood in his way, seeking out the evil acrid smell of humanity, following it down so that once again he could wreak upon them the accumulated hatred of his long lifetime.

Suddenly Matatu darted out of the bush just a few paces ahead of Sean. He would stand to meet any odds with Sean beside him, and now instead of running across the wind as Pumula had done, his instinct had led him directly back to his master's side.

As he saw him, Sean changed direction in mid-stride, signalling urgently for Matatu to follow him. He ran a hundred swift paces out to one side, across the wind, trying to deny their scent to Tukutela.

He stopped and crouched with Matatu beside him. His tactic had been successful, Pumula also must have got out of Tukutela's wind. For the moment Tukutela had lost their scent. The forest was absolutely still, the silence so intense that Sean could hear his pulse beating in his own head.

He sensed that the old bull was very close to them, standing as still as they were, listening with ears spread wide, only that long trunk questing for the smell of them. There had never been an elephant like this, he thought, a bull who actively hunted his persecutors. How many times has he been hunted, Sean wondered, how many times has man inflicted hurt upon him that he attacks so fiercely at the first hint of human presence?

'Tukutela, the Angry One, now I know why they named you.'

Then there was a sound in the forest, one that Sean had not expected, a human voice, raised loudly, and it took him a moment to realize that it was Riccardo Monterro.

'Tukutela, we are brothers!' he was calling to the elephant. 'We are all that is left from another age. Our destiny is linked. I cannot kill you!'

The bull heard him and squealed again, a sound so loud and pitched so high that it was like an auger driven into their eardrums. Tukutela charged the sound of the human voice, like a grey battle-tank. He crashed through the undergrowth, going straight for it, and within fifty yards the scent of man, loathsome and infuriating, filled his head once again and he followed it down to its source.

Riccardo Monterro had made no effort to climb the teak tree where Sean had left him, he simply leaned against the trunk and closed his eyes. The pain in his head came upon him as suddenly as the blow of an axe, and it blinded him, filling his vision with bursting stars of light, but through the pain he heard the old bull elephant squeal and the sound filled him with remorse and bitter despair.

He let the Rigby slip from his hands and fall into the leafy trash at his feet and he reached out his empty hands and staggered blindly to meet the elephant, wanting in some desperate way to placate and make recompense to the great beast, calling to it. 'I mean you no harm, we are brothers.' And ahead of him the bush crackled and burst open and Tukutela bore down on him like a collapsing cliff of granite.

Sean raced back to where he had left Riccardo, ducking under branches and bounding over obstacles in his path, and he heard the terrifying rush of the bull and the voice of the man just ahead of him.

'Here!' he screamed. 'Here, Tukutela! Come! Come this way!' trying to pull the elephant off Riccardo and onto himself, but he knew it was of no avail. Tukutela had fixed on his victim, and nothing would deter him. He would carry his charge through to the death.

The centre of Riccardo's vision cleared, and he looked through an aperture in his head that was surrounded by shooting white lights and Catherine wheels of spinning fire. He saw Tukutela's vast grey head burst out of the green forest wall above him, and the long stained tusks came over him like the cross-ties of a roof about to fall.

In that moment, the elephant came to embody all the thousands of animals and birds that Riccardo had slaughtered in his lifetime as a hunter. He had a confused notion that the tusks and long trunk poised above him were the symbols of some semi-religious benediction that would absolve him and redeem the blood that he had spilled and all the life he had destroyed. He reached up both hands to them, joyfully and thankfully, and he remembered a phrase from his early religious instruction.

'Forgive me. Father, for I have sinned,' he cried.

Sean saw the bull's head rear out of the thicket ahead of him. It was facing almost directly away from him with ears cocked and rolled along the top edge. He heard Riccardo's voice though he could not understand the words, and he realized that Riccardo must be almost directly beneath the bull's out-thrust tusks and reaching trunk.

Sean plunged from his headlong run to a dead stop in a single pace and threw up the .577 Express rifle. It was the most difficult angle for the brain shot, with the elephant positioned away from him, and the bulk of its shoulder covering the spinal column.

The target was no bigger than a ripe apple and there was no indication of where exactly it lay buried in the huge bony casket of the skull. He had to trust his experience and his instinct. For a moment, it seemed as he looked over the open Express sights of the rifle that he could see into the skull, where the brain seemed to glow in the bony depths like a firefly.

Without conscious effort his trigger finger tightened as the pip of the foresight covered that glowing spot. The bullet bored through the sponge of bone as though it were air, it cleaved the old bull's brain, and he felt nothing. His passage from full enraged life to death was a fleeting instant and his legs collapsed and folded under him. He dropped on his chest with an impact that jarred the earth and shook loose the dead leaves from the branches above him. A cloud of pale dust swirled around his massive carcass and his head dropped forward.

His right tusk drove into Riccardo Monterro's body, entering his belly a hand's-breadth below the sternum of his rib cage, and it passed through him at the level of his kidneys and came out through his spine just at the point where it merged with his pelvis.

The shaft of ivory which Riccardo had coveted and risked both fortune and life to obtain, now pinned him to the earth, skewered him as cleanly as a whaler's harpoon. He looked down at the tusk in surprise. There was no pain, no sensation in his lower body which was twisted up under the bull's coiled trunk, no pain even in his head.

For a moment his vision was clear and bright as though everything he looked at was lit by brilliant floodlights, and then it began to fade and darkness closed in upon him. Just before the darkness engulfed him completely, he saw Sean Courtney's face floating before him, and heard his voice fading as though he were sinking away into an abyss.

'Capo, Capo,' it echoed in his ears, and Riccardo Monterro made a huge effort and said, 'She loves you. Look after my little girl.' And then the darkness swallowed him and he saw and heard nothing more, ever again.

*

S ean's first impulse was to free Riccardo Monterro's body. He tugged at the tusk which impaled him, but it was so thick that he could not get a fair grip upon it, and Riccardo's blood was oozing from the terrible wound. It coated Sean's hands so that he left sticky red prints upon the ivory as he strained at it.

Then he realized the futility of his efforts, and stepped back. The full weight of Tukutela's huge head and body was resting on those tusks. After piercing Riccardo's torso the ivory point had gone on to bury itself deep in the soft sandy earth. It would take half a day's work to free the body.

In death, the man and the beast were locked together, and suddenly Sean realized how appropriate that was. He would leave them like that.

First Matatu and then Pumula appeared from out of the forest and stood beside Sean staring in awe at the grim spectacle.

'Go!' Sean ordered. 'Wait for me at the canoe.'

'The ivory?' Pumula asked diffidently.

'Go!' Sean repeated, and at the tone of his voice, they crept quietly away.

Riccardo's eyes were wide open. Sean closed them with a gentle stroke of his thumb and then unknotted the cotton scarf from around Riccardo's neck and bound up his jaw to prevent it sagging into an expression of idiocy. Even in death, Riccardo Monterro was still a handsome man. Sean leaned against the elephant's head and studied Riccardo's face.

'It happened at just the right time, Capo. Before the disease turned you into a vegetable. While you still had most of your zest and vigour, and it was a fitting end for a man like you. I'm glad you didn't die between soiled sheets. I only pray that I will be as fortunate.'

Sean laid his hand upon one of the tusks and stroked it. It had the texture of precious jade beneath his fingertips.

'We'll leave them for you, Capo,' he said. 'These tusks

will be your headstone. God knows, you paid for them in full.'

Sean straightened up and followed Riccardo's tracks back into the forest until he found the Rigby lying in the dead leaves. He brought it back and placed it in the crook of Riccardo's right arm.

'A warrior should be buried with his weapons,' he murmured, but there was still something missing. He could not go and leave Riccardo like this. He could not leave him lying exposed to an uncaring sky. He must cover him decently.

Then Sean remembered the legend of this elephant and how he disposed of the dead. He drew the heavy knife from the sheath on his belt and turned to the nearest green bush. He slashed off a leafy branch and covered Riccardo's face with it.

'Yes,' he murmured. 'That's right, that's proper.'

Working swiftly, he hacked down the branches and covered Riccardo's corpse and the head of the old bull under a mound of green leaves.

At last he stood back and picked up the .577. He tucked it under his arm and he was ready to leave.

'No regrets, Capo,' he said. 'For you, it was a good life right up to the very end. Go in peace, old friend.'

He turned away and went down to where the canoe was moored.

The reeds scraped softly along the hull of the canoe as Pumula poled it along. None of them spoke.

Sean sat amidships, hunched forward with his chin in the cup of one hand. He felt numbed, emptied of all emotion except sadness. It was like coming back from a raid in the days of the bush war with every man silent and sad.

He looked at his right hand in his lap and saw the little half moons of dark red under his fingernails. 'Capo's blood,' he thought, and trailed his hand over the side of the canoe, letting the warm swamp waters wash away the stain.

He let the hunt replay itself through his mind, as though it were a silent recording. He saw it all again very vividly from their first sighting of the old bull to the moment that he rushed forward to find Riccardo Monterro impaled beneath the huge grey head.

Then for the first time, he heard sound. Riccardo's voice echoed in his head, faint and breathless, fading swiftly.

'She loves you,' he had said, and the rest trailed away unintelligibly. 'She loves you.' The meaningless words of a dying man, the wanderings of a diseased brain. Riccardo could have been harking back to any one of the hundreds of women who had filled his life.

Sean lifted his hand out of the water. It was clean, the blood washed away.

'She loves you.' He could have been trying to tell Sean of one particular woman.

Sean looked up from his wet hand and stared ahead. Her memory had been with him these last few days, always there in the recesses of his conscience yet coming to the fore at unexpected moments. Often while thinking of the great elephant, he had suddenly smiled at something she had said. This morning during the final stages of the hunt he had reached outboard from the canoe, and picked the bloom of a water lily. He had held it to his face and smelled the perfume, felt the silky touch of the petals on his lip and thought of Claudia Monterro.

Now he stared ahead and for the first time admitted to himself how much he looked forward to seeing her again. It seemed that she was all that could cancel out his grief for her father. He thought about the sound of her voice and the way she held her head when she was about to challenge him. He smiled at the bright specks of anger he could so readily kindle in her eyes, and the way she pursed her lips when she was trying to prevent herself laughing at one of his own digs.

He thought about the way she walked, and the way she felt when he had carried her in his arms, and he remembered the texture of her skin like the petals of the water lily when he touched her under pretext of helping or guiding her.

'We are absolutely and completely wrong for each other,' he smiled, and the melancholy of a few moments previously loosened its grip. 'If Capo was talking about her, then he had definitely gone completely round the bend.' But his anticipation was honed to a sharper edge.

He looked up at the sky. The sun had set. It would be dark in a short while. Even as he watched, Venus as the evening star appeared with a miraculous suddenness and twinkled low down in the west. One after another, the fixed stars followed her entrance, popping through the darkening canopy of night in strict order of their magnitude.

Sean looked up at the stars and he thought of Claudia, and he wondered why she evoked such contrary feelings in him. He compared her to some of the other women he had known, and realized how shallow and fleeting those experiences had been. Even his marriage had been inconsequential, a wild impulse based on simple-minded lust. It had been swiftly consummated, satiated and terminated, a disastrous mistake which he had never repeated. He could only vaguely remember what the woman who had been his wife looked like now.

He thought about Claudia and realized with a small shock that her image was so clear in his mind that he could almost count the individual lashes around those big honey-brown eyes, and the tiny laughter lines at the corners of her mouth. Suddenly he very much wanted to be with her again, and as he acknowledged that fact he began to worry.

'I must have been crazy to leave her alone,' he thought, and as he stared ahead into the dark swamps a multitude of horrid chances that might have befallen her began to plague him.

'Job is with her,' he tried to console himself. 'But I should have stayed to care for her and sent Job with Capo.' Even though he realized that had been impossible, still he fretted.

He felt the canoe check under him as Pumula rested on his pole, hinting at permission to stop for the night.

'I'll take her for a while,' Sean said. 'We'll keep going until we get back to the village.'

While Pumula and Matatu curled up in the bilges, Sean stood in the stern and swayed to the monotonous thrust and reach of the punt pole. He steered by the cross and the pointers, reckoning true south at the intersection of their extended centre lines.

The papyrus stems hissed softly against the hull in strict rhythm to his thrusts, and soon the work became so repetitive and automatic that he could let his mind wander, and all those wanderings seemed to return in the end to Claudia Monterro at the centre.

He thought about her bereavement, how although she had been expecting it, yet it would still devastate her. He composed the words he would use to tell her and then to comfort her. She knew of his own feelings for her father, and the companionship that they had shared in the hunting veld. She knew of their mutual regard for each other.

'I am the right person to help her through the first sorrow. I knew him so well. I will help her to remember all that was good about him.'

He should have dreaded bearing the sad tidings, but instead he found himself looking forward to taking the role of her comforter and protector.

'Perhaps we will be able to drop the postures of antagonism that we have both forced upon ourselves. Instead of accentuating our differences, perhaps we'll be able to explore what we have in common.' He found himself lengthening

222

and quickening his stroke with the punt pole and he had to force himself to slow down.

'You won't last the night at that pace,' he thought, but his eagerness to be with her kept him going long after fatigue demanded a halt.

Hour after hour he kept it up, until Pumula woke of his own accord and came to spell him, but Sean slept fitfully and was back in the stern as the coming of day turned the eastern sky to a murky ruby and then to pale lemon, and the water fowl flighted overhead, their wings whistling softly as they stabbed at the dawn.

Two hours later, Sean sent Matatu up the punt pole and he had not reached the top before he pointed gleefully ahead. However, it was early afternoon before the prow of the canoe knifed through the last dense stand of papyrus and ran ashore on the sand below the burnt village.

Sean leapt onto dry land and strode through the ruins of the village, trying not to break into a run.

'Job should have kept a better watch,' he thought angrily. 'If we can arrive unseen . . .' he did not finish the thought. Just ahead was the thicket in which they had built Claudia's shelter, and Sean stopped abruptly.

It was too quiet. His sixth sense of danger warned him. Something was wrong. He went down fast and hard, falling flat and rolling quickly into cover with the .577 held in front of him.

He lay and listened. The silence was a physical weight. He wet his lips and imitated the clucking sound of a francolin, one of the Scouts' assembly calls that Job would recognize. There was no reply. He went forward at a leopard crawl, and then stopped again. Something sparkled in the short grass just in front of his face. He picked it up and felt his stomach chill.

It was the empty brass case of a 7.62mm cartridge, and it was head-stamped in Cyrillic script, Soviet military issue for firing in the AK assault rifle. Sean held it to his nose, and smelt the burnt powder. It had been fired very recently. He glanced around him quickly and saw other empty shells lying in the grass, evidence of a fierce fire-fight.

He rolled to his feet and was running, jinking and twisting as he sprinted towards the thicket to throw off the aim of a hidden gunman.

As he reached the edge of the thicket, he dropped to earth again, flicking over as he hit the ground. Immediately, he saw the corpse, it lay face down under a low thorn bush only a few yards ahead. It was a black man. The body had been stripped of clothing and boots.

'Job!' The name ripped from his throat. He crawled forward, until he lay side by side with the body. A single bullet had ploughed out of the man's back, and the flies crawled over the wound. The blood had dried to a black crust and he smelt the whiff of corruption.

'Dead twenty-four hours,' he estimated, and rose to his knees. No further need for caution now. Gently he lifted the dead head. The corpse's neck was stiff with *rigor mortis* and he grunted with vast relief and let the head drop with a thud. The man was a stranger.

'Job!' he called. 'Claudia!' It was a despairing cry, and he ran forward to the lean-to in which he had left her. It was deserted.

'Job!' He looked around him wildly. 'Claudia!'

There was another naked black body lying at the edge of the clearing, and he ran to it. It was another stranger, a skinny little runt of a man with the top shot off his skull. He was also starting to stink, his belly blowing up like a shiny black balloon.

'Two of the bastards,' Sean said bitterly. 'Nice shooting, Job.'

Matatu had followed Sean and was checking the lean-to. He left it and began to work out in circles, darting back and forth like a gun dog quartering for a sitting grouse.

Sean and Pumula stood and watched him, not joining his search so that they would not trample the sign.

Within minutes Matatu scurried back.

'They are the same *shifta* who followed us before. There are fifteen of them, they surrounded the hut and came in at a rush. Job shot these two with the 30/06 *banduki*.' He offered Sean the empty cartridge cases. 'There was much struggling, but they took them.'

'The memsahib?' Sean dreaded the reply.

'*Ndio*,' Matatu replied in Swahili. 'Yes, they took her also. She is still limping, but they led her away, one on each side. She was fighting them all the way. Job was hurt, and so was Dedan. Perhaps they were beaten, and I think their arms are bound. They walk unsteadily.' Matatu pointed towards the corpses. 'They stripped their dead of uniforms and boots and *banduki* and then went back.' He pointed along the isthmus.

'When?' Sean asked.

'Yesterday, early. Perhaps they rushed the camp at dawn.'

Sean nodded grimly, but inside he cried, 'Claudia, oh God, if they touch you, I'll rip their guts out.'

'Hot pursuit,' he said aloud. 'Let's go!'

Pumula ran back to grab the equipment and water-bottles from the canoe, and Sean was still shrugging into the shoulder-straps of his pack when he started to run. The near exhaustion of the long night of poling the canoe faded away. He felt strong and angry and indefatigable.

Within the first mile, they settled into the pursuit pace of a Scout raiding party. The spoor was still cold and Sean dispensed with any precautions against ambush. He relied entirely on Matatu to pick up any sign of a booby trap or anti-personnel mine that might have been laid on the tracks to hinder pursuit, but apart from that they went in single file at a speed not much below that of an Olympic marathon.

Claudia's image seemed to dance ahead of Sean and winged his feet.

Fifteen of them, Matatu had said, and they would be tempted by Claudia's sweet white body. There were no signs yet that they had stopped to have sport with her. He accepted without reservation Matatu's interpretation that they had crept up on the camp in the dawn, and taken it at a rush, willing to accept casualties without inflicting them. It seemed that they had wanted prisoners rather than kills. Other than a few blows with a rifle butt, it looked as though both Dedan and Job had come through it unscathed, but it was Claudia who had his full concern.

They were forcing her to march on her injured leg. That would only aggravate the knee, and perhaps cause permanent damage. If she slowed them down too much, they would start to become impatient and threatening. It all depended on just how much they needed a white prisoner as a hostage, probably as a bargaining chip with western governments. It depended on who they were, Frelimo or Renamo or free-lance bandits, it depended on how much control there was over them, on who commanded them, and how strong was his authority, but any way he considered it, Sean knew that Claudia was in terrible danger.

Did they realize that there was a pursuit? They must have read the sign going into the village and known that three men – no, four with Capo – were missing from the original party. The answer was, yes. They probably anticipated a pursuit by this group. That would make them nervous and excitable.

Claudia would be no great advocate for her own safety. He could just imagine her arguing with them, demanding her human and legal rights, refusing to follow their orders. Despite his concern, he grinned without humour, as he thought about it. They probably believed they had caught a pussy-cat, but they would soon realize that they had instead a full-grown female tiger on their hands.

His grin faded. He was certain she would deal with them in precisely the fashion best designed to antagonize them and jeopardize her chances of survival. If the leader of the group was a weak man, she would push him to the point where he had to demonstrate his authority to his own men. African society was patriarchal and he would resent a woman who refused to bow to his will. If they were the same group that had wiped out the village they had amply demonstrated their brutality.

'Just for once, ducky, button those lovely lips of yours,' he pleaded with her silently.

Ahead of him, Matatu checked his run and made a sweeping gesture, and Sean pulled up.

'Here they rested.' Matatu pointed to where the group had sat in the shade of a grove of young mopane.

There were the crushed butts of black cigarettes in the dust, and Matatu pointed to the raw white slashes on the mopane from which branches had been chopped. The smaller twigs had been trimmed from them and discarded. The leaves on these were already wilted, confirming Matatu's estimate of time, yesterday morning.

The cutting of branches puzzled Sean for a moment and then Matatu explained. 'They have built a *mushela* for the mem.' And Sean nodded with relief. Claudia on her injured leg had been holding up the march, but rather than ridding themselves of her through the simple expedient of a bullet in the back of the head, they had built a litter of mopane poles on which to carry her. That was a welcome development, and it changed Sean's estimate of Claudia's chance of survival. They had placed a higher value on her than Sean had dreaded they might.

However, the most crucial period would have come yesterday evening when they decided to camp for the night. Her captors would have had a full day to study her, to ogle her body and puff up their imagination and their courage. Sean found he could not bear to face the possibility of what might have happened to her if the leader had lost control of his men.

'Come on, Matatu,' he growled. 'You are wasting time.' If it had happened at all, it would have happened last night. He was already too late but still every second of delay galled him.

The spoor led them back up the isthmus retracing their own route across the dry flood plains heading towards the south. The trail was broad and easy to follow, fifteen men and their captives making no attempt at anti-tracking. Matatu read the spoor and reported that they were forcing Dedan and Job to carry the litter with Claudia on it, and Sean was happy that the two of them were able to do so. Whatever injuries they had sustained in the attack must have been superficial, and he could be certain that Job would employ every ruse to slow down the march, and allow them to catch up.

Even as he thought it, Matatu exclaimed and pointed to the marks in the soft earth where Job had dropped his end of the litter and sprawled theatrically on his hands and knees, only crawling up after he had been surrounded and hectored by his captors.

'Good man,' Sean grunted without checking his stride. 'But don't push them too far.' It was a delicate game Job was playing.

At pursuit speed they were overhauling the clumsy and slow-moving group so rapidly that Sean was beginning to hope they might catch up with them before nightfall.

'That's going to be interesting,' he decided. 'Three of us with only the .577 against fifteen thugs armed with AKs.'

So far they had found no booby traps set for them. It was usually terr tactics to mine their own spoor and Sean pondered their failure to do so. These could be untrained bandits, or they might lack the light plastic anti-personnel mines, or they could be unaware of the pursuit or, worst thought, they could be planning some surprises later.

'We'll deal with that one also when we come to it.'

Matatu pulled up again. 'They cooked here last night.'

He pointed to the remains of a camp-fire, and there were the marks where they had sat while they rested and ate. A few black safari ants were scurrying about the site foraging for the scraps of food that they had spilled and there were more cigarette butts.

'Search,' Sean ordered. 'Job will have tried to get a message to us.' While Matatu and Pumula went over the area carefully but quickly, Sean glanced at his watch: 1600 hours, they had been going just over three hours, they still had plenty of daylight and a good chance to catch them before dark.

'Here is where they put the mem's litter.' Matatu pointed out the marks in the earth. 'Here she stood.'

Sean studied her footprints, smaller, neater and narrower than the boot prints of her captors. When she walked she had favoured her leg, dragging the toe.

'Did you find anything?' he demanded roughly. 'Did Job leave a message?'

'Nothing.' Matatu shook his head.

'All right. We'll drink now,' he ordered, and handed out salt tablets from his pack. He didn't have to caution them to self-control. Three swallows each from the bottles, and then they screwed the stoppers tightly closed. They had paused for less than five minutes.

'Let's go,' said Sean.

An hour later, they found where the raiders had slept that night. The fact that they had moved on after eating and not slept beside their cooking-fire told Sean that they were trained troops.

'Search again,' Sean ordered. Any information that Job could have left for them would be valuable.

'Nothing,' Matatu reported back a few minutes later, and Sean felt a prick of disappointment.

'All right. Keep going,' he ordered, and was about to turn away when something made him pause and he glanced around the camp-site.

'Where did the memsahib sleep?' he demanded.

'There.' Matatu pointed. Somebody, probably Job, had cut an armful of leaves and grass for her mattress. Her body had flattened the pile. Sean squatted beside it, and carefully sifted through it, searching for any clues.

There was nothing. He lifted away the last few leaves and was beginning to rise to his feet. He was disappointed, the feeling that she had left something for him had been very powerful.

'So much for ESP,' he grunted, and then noticed the button, half buried in the dust under the mattress of straw.

He picked it out and stood up. It was a brass button from the waistband of her denim jeans, engraved 'Ralph Hutton'.

'Designer jeans, that's my ducky.' He slipped it into his pocket. 'But it doesn't tell me anything,' he broke off, 'unless . . .' He knelt again and gently brushed aside the dust under where the button had lain. He was right, she had used the button as a marker and beneath it had buried a scrap of cardboard, the flap torn from the lid of a packet of cheap Portuguese cigarillos. It was not more than two inches long and half as wide, very little space for the message she had written with a charcoal stick scavenged from the fire.

'Fifteen Renamo.' That was invaluable intelligence, confirming Matatu's estimate of numbers, and now at least he knew who they were dealing with, Renamo.

'Cave.' The next word puzzled him. 'Cave?' Then suddenly he realized it was the old public schoolboy warning from the Latin 'caveat' – beware.

He smiled despite himself. 'Where did she ever learn a limey expression like that?' Then he remembered she was a lawyer and read on.

'Cave. They expect you.' She and Job would have overheard them discussing the pursuit. That information was just as valuable.

'All OK.' And she had signed it, 'C.'

He stared at the scrap of cardboard, holding it in the palm of his hand as though it were a relic of the true cross.

'You little beauty, you,' he whispered. 'You've got to be the brightest, gutsiest . . .' He shook his head in wonder, a choking sensation in his throat. For the very first time, he admitted his longing for her and then suppressed it firmly as he came to his feet. There was no time nor opportunity for such self-indulgence now.

'Renamo,' he told Matatu and Pumula. 'You were right, there are fifteen of them. They know we are following. We can expect an ambush.'

They both looked grave, and Sean glanced at his wrist-watch. 'We can catch them before dark.'

Within an hour they came upon the first ambush that the Renamo had set for them. Four men had lain beside the trail at the point where the causeway across the flood plains joined the main forest on the higher ground. The ambush had been cunningly sited on the far edge of a narrow vlei, across open ground with a good field of fire. It had been abandoned only a short time before they came up to it.

'They are putting down a rolling rearguard.' Sean felt queasy at the risk he had taken with such a reckless pursuit.

In the dust were the distinctive double marks left by the bipod of an RPD light machine-gun, one of the simplest and yet the most deadly effective of all guerrilla weapons. If he had led his men into the vlei while that gun was still in position, it would have all been over in a few hellish seconds. He had been pushing too hard, not taking even elementary precautions. His concern for Claudia had unbalanced his judgement.

Renamo had pulled out just before they reached the vlei, they had judged the time of his arrival with disconcerting accuracy, the margin had been far too narrow. The crew of the RPD would have moved back, and resited the ambush farther along the trail in order not to fall too far behind their main party.

'Flankers out,' Sean ordered reluctantly. 'Ambush precautions.' It would slow them to half their previous speed. Now it would be impossible to catch up with Renamo before nightfall.

Three men were too few. It left only Matatu on the spoor, and Sean and Pumula on the flanks. They had a single weapon between them, the big-bore, slow-firing double. They were going in against trained bush fighters armed with automatic weapons, and they were expected.

'Just another name for suicide,' Sean told himself, but despite the odds he had to restrain himself from quickening the pace.

In the centre, Matatu whistled. At that moment, he was out of Sean's line of sight. Even though it was not a warning signal. Sean fell flat and carefully checked his front and both flanks before he stood up again and went to join him.

Matatu was squatting beside the trail with his loin-cloth drawn up modestly between his legs, but his expression was worried. He stabbed a finger at the spoor without speaking, and Sean saw immediately what was troubling him.

'Where the hell did they come from?' It was a protest more than a question. The odds against them had just been multiplied many times, and for the first time, Sean felt the lead weight of despair on his shoulders.

The original band of Renamo had been reinforced by an even larger group; at a glance it looked like a full company of infantry.

'How many?' he demanded of Matatu, and this time, even he could not give an exact figure. The tracks were overlapped and confused.

Matatu took a little snuff, using the ritual to disguise his uncertainty. He sneezed, and his eyes ran with tears which he wiped away with his thumbs. Then he held up the spread fingers of both hands and shut them four times.

'Forty?'

Matatu grimaced apologetically and showed another set of fingers.

'Between forty and fifty.' Sean unscrewed his water-bottle and took a mouthful. The water was hot as soup, but he gargled with it before he swallowed.

'I will count them later,' Matatu promised, 'when I have learned them all, but now . . .' He spat on the trampled earth, mortified by his failure.

'How far behind are we?' Sean demanded, and Matatu used his forefinger like the hour hand of a clock to indicate a segment of the sky.

'Three hours,' Sean translated. 'We'll never catch them before nightfall.'

When it was dark Sean said, 'We'll eat while we wait for the moon.' But when it rose, it was only a sliver of silver, soon blotted out by cloud, and there was not enough light to follow even that broad clear spoor. Sean thought of keeping going blindly through the night, trying to get ahead of them and then shadowing them hoping for some fortuitous opportunity to reach Claudia and Job and release them.

'That's dreaming in Technicolor,' he told himself.

They had been going hard for days now and were all of them tottering on the edge of exhaustion. Blundering around in the dark, they would either run on top of the Renamo night guards or would miss them completely.

'We'll sleep now.' He was forced to give up at last. As Renamo knew they were being followed they might send a detachment back to try and surprise them.

Sean went into laager for the night well off the trail, in a thicket of thorn that would snag an attacker attempting to sneak up on them. They all desperately needed rest and he would rely on the thorn rather than posting sentries. The night was icy cold and they lay in a huddle sharing each other's body warmth. Sean was already sliding into the black hole of exhaustion when Matatu's whisper called him back.

'There is one of them,' Matatu began, then broke off and Sean opened his eyes with resignation.

'Tell me,' he invited drowsily.

'There is one of these Renamo I have seen before.'

'You know one of them?' Sean came fully awake.

'I think so, but it was long ago, and I cannot remember where.'

Sean was silent as he considered that simple statement, and what it really entailed; Sean would have had difficulty remembering the faces of every person he had met in, say, the last ten years. Here was Matatu bemoaning the fact that he could not instantly recognize a single set of footprints, which he had last seen years previously out of a jumble of other tracks.

Though he had seen Matatu perform similar feats so many times before, even he felt a creep of doubt at Matatu's claim.

'Go to sleep, you silly little bugger.' He smiled in the darkness, and took him by the scruff of the neck and shook the little man's woolly head with rough affection. 'Perhaps you'll dream his name in your sleep.'

Sean dreamed of Claudia. She was running naked through a dark forest. The trees were black and leafless with crooked limbs. A pack of wolves pursued her. They also were black as night but with glistening white fangs and red lolling tongues. Claudia called his name as she ran and her skin was pale and luminous as the moon. He tried to go to her but his legs dragged as though he waded through a pool of treacle. He tried to call her name, but his tongue was lead in his mouth and no sound came from his throat.

He awoke with a hand roughly shaking his shoulder, and he tried to shout again but it came out in a garbled slur.

'Wake up!' Matatu shook him. 'You were crying and moaning. Renamo will hear you!'

He sat up quickly. The cold seemed to have frozen the muscles in his legs, and the terror of the dream was still upon him. It took him seconds to focus on reality and remember where he was.

'You're getting past it, boyo.' He was humiliated. A Scout slept soundlessly and awoke to immediate awareness or had his throat cut while he was grunting and snoring.

'It will be light enough soon,' Matatu whispered. Already the dawn chorus of bird calls tinkled and chirruped through the forest and he could make out the lattice-work of thorn branches against the sky.

'Let's go.' Sean stood up.

While the sun was still low and the dew was on the grass, they came up to the dry riverbed in which Renamo had bivouacked for the night. The band had moved on again at first light but could not be far ahead.

Matatu picked Claudia's footprints out of the rack in the soft sand of the riverbed. 'She moves with less pain,' he told Sean, 'The leg is healing but Job and Dedan are still carrying her. Here she climbed into the litter.'

Matatu left the distinctive feminine prints and hovered over another set of larger male tracks that to Sean were indistinguishable from all the others, except that whoever had made them wore boots with a double herring-bone pattern on the sole.

'I know him,' Matatu whispered. 'I know the way this one walks . . .' He shook his head in frustration and turned away.

They went forward with extreme caution now. The trail led them directly towards the higher ground along the escarpment of the valley, and soon they entered the foothills. Whoever commanded the Renamo column knew exactly where he was headed.

Sean was expecting at any moment to make contact with the rearguard of the column. He dreaded the thought that the first warning they might receive could be the wicked crackle of an RPD light machine-gun, firing at a cyclic rate of six hundred rounds a minute.

Here in the hills every boulder, every fold of ground was a possible enemy redoubt and had to be minutely inspected before they could move on. Sean fretted with impatience but forced himself to gear his advance to the difficult terrain.

They turned the corner of another low hill and through a frieze of graceful msasa trees an open vista stretched ahead to where the massif of the central escarpment rose above its foothills.

'There it is,' Sean murmured. 'That's where they'll be laying for us.'

The spoor was pointed directly at a pass through the escarpment. The entrance was guarded by cliffs of red stone, and the gut of the pass was almost devoid of trees or cover and yet the sides were heavily bushed. It was a natural trap, a perfect killing ground.

Matatu whistled in the centre, and Sean doubled over, keeping off the crest as he ran down to join him. From the centre, there was an unimpeded view up the gut of the valley and Sean saw movement against the scree and yellow grass. He lifted the binoculars to his eyes and the line of dark moving specks resolved through the lens into a column of men.

They were toiling up the incline in single file. Most of them wore tiger-striped camouflage and jungle hats, although a few were dressed in a motley of denim and khaki. The front of the column was already into the bush at the head of the valley at least three miles distant, but through his binoculars, Sean counted twelve men.

The litter was in the centre, four of them were carrying it. Two men on the front poles and two on the back. Sean tried to pick out Claudia's form but before he could refocus his binoculars, the litter and the bearers had reached the tree line and disappeared.

Sean lowered his binoculars and polished the lens with his handkerchief. Pumula had come in from the other flank, and now he and Matatu crouched in the jumble of rock and coarse bush and studied the lie of the land in gloomy silence. Again Sean raised the glasses and studied the steep bushy sides. It was a perfect site for an ambush, they could catch Sean's party in enfilade and crossfire as they tried to climb the valley.

'How many did you see?' Sean asked without lowering his binoculars. 'Have they all gone into the trees at the head of the valley?'

'I saw only a few,' Pumula murmured.

'*Masesh*,' Matatu spat unhappily. He was referring to the lees of the millet beer that after fermentation the Batonka fishermen use as a ground bait to lure the shoals of bream into Lake Kariba's shallows.

He spat again. 'That valley is the mouth of the crocodile. They want us to put our heads into it.'

Sean studied the sides of the valley, taking his time, every few minutes lowering the binoculars to rest his eyes and then lifting them again. He began at the top of the slope and swept gradually downwards. When he reached the bottom, he began at the top again, going over the same ground time and again. He tried not to think of that sighting of the litter, or the tiny figure he thought he had seen upon it. He concentrated entirely on his search and, ten minutes later, he was rewarded.

It was a single flash of sunlight reflected from the lens of a wristwatch or the lens of a pair of field-glasses.

'There they are.' He lowered his own glasses. 'Yes, Matatu, you are right. They have put out the bait, now they are waiting for us.'

He sat down behind the boulder and tried to think it through logically, but Claudia's memory kept intruding and deflecting his reasoning. There was only one certain conclusion, and that was that it was hopeless to continue the pursuit. He looked up. Matatu and Pumula were watching him with expressions of blind faith. In almost twenty years, they had never seen him at a loss. They waited patiently for him to perform the miracle yet again.

Sean found it infuriating. He jumped up and went back down the hill to think without those trusting eyes upon him. He found a spot that was well concealed and yet had a good all-round view so that nobody could sneak up on him and he settled down with the .577 across his lap to consider his options.

The first one he crossed from his mental list was an attack on the Renamo column. Even leaving aside the puny forces he had available, he had to consider the hostages that Renamo had in their hands. Even with a company of fully armed Scouts, he would still have been unable to attack.

'So what can I hope to achieve by following them?' he asked himself. 'Apart from gratifying this new and mawkish desire to be as close as possible to Claudia Monterro.'

Probably the best chance of release of the captives from Renamo clutches was not his own intervention but diplomatic negotiations through Renamo's reputed allies, the South African government in Pretoria. However, even the South Africans would not be able to achieve anything if they were unaware that an American citizen had been captured by Renamo.

'Okay.' Sean made his first firm decision. 'I have to get a message back to the American embassy in Harare.' Immediately he realized that this took care of his other major worry. Matatu and Pumula were his responsibility. Up to now he had been leading them into a suicidal situation. They had been more and more on his conscience the closer they drew to the Renamo column. This was the excuse he had been looking for.

'I'll send both of them back to Chiwewe with a message for Reema.' He opened the flap of his back-pack and found his small leather-covered notepad. He began to compose the message.

Reema had all Riccardo's and Claudia's personal details on the safari files, everything from their physical descriptions to their passport numbers. Riccardo was an important and influential man. Sean would not tell her that he was dead, but implied in his message that both father and daughter were captives of Renamo. The US embassy could be relied on to react swiftly and he would be in contact with Pretoria within hours of receiving the news.

Of course, since the imposition of US sanctions on that country the relations between Washington and Pretoria were at a historically low ebb, and the influence of the US in southern Africa was no longer the overriding factor that it had once been. Nonetheless, the South Africans could be relied on to intercede with Renamo on the simplest humanitarian grounds.

'Okay, that takes care of Matatu and Pumula.' Sean signed the message, tore the pages out of his notepad and folded them. Then as an afterthought he filled another page of instructions for Reema covering the $500,000 that Riccardo's estate owed them. She was to pass these on to Sean's lawyer.

Then, at last, he had to make his own decision. He could run back across the border, carrying the message himself, and within two or three days he could be drinking Castle lager in the Meikles Hotel and working out how to spend Capo's half-million bucks. That was the sensible and logical thing to do but he had already dismissed the idea before he considered it.

'So I'll follow the column and wait for an opportunity.' He grinned at the absurdity of his decision. 'What opportunity?' he wondered at himself. 'A chance to shoot my way into an encampment of fifty-plus terrs with the old .577, free the three prisoners, and with one mighty bound whip them a hundred miles to the border, carrying Claudia with her injured leg on my back!'

He stood up and resettled his pack between his shoulders,

and crept back up to the slope where Matatu and Pumula were lying watching the escarpment. He dropped down beside Matatu.

'Anything?' he asked, and Matatu shook his head. They were silent for many minutes while Sean plucked up his courage to tell the little man he was sending him back.

While he did so, he scowled through the binoculars at the spot up the long valley where he knew Renamo had set their ambush. Matatu seemed to sense that something unpleasant was brewing. He kept glancing at Sean with a troubled expression, but when Sean finally turned to him, he burst into a sunny ingratiating grin and wriggled his entire body in his eagerness to please and to stave off whatever was coming.

'I remember,' he said eagerly. 'I remember who he is.'

Side-tracked for the moment, Sean frowned at him in puzzlement. 'Who? Who are you talking about?'

'The leader of the Renamo,' Matatu told him happily. 'I told you yesterday I knew his footprints. Now I remember who he is.'

'Who is he then?' Sean asked suspiciously, ready to reject the information.

'Do you remember when we jumped from the *indeki* to attack the training camp at the fork of the rivers?' Matatu twinkled at him and Sean nodded guardedly. 'Do you remember how we killed them in the riverbed?' Matatu chuckled with the delightful memory of it. 'Do you remember the one we caught while he was trying to burn the books. The one who refused to march, and you blew his ear in?' Now he giggled at that fine joke. 'The blood came out of his earhole and he squeaked like a virgin.'

'Comrade China?'

'China.' Matatu had a little difficulty with the pronunciation. 'Yes, that is the one.'

'No!' Sean shook his head. 'It isn't China. That's not possible!'

Now, Matatu had to cover his mouth to muffle his delighted squeals of laughter. He loved it when he was able to confound and astound his master. There was no better joke than that.

'China!' He spluttered with mirth and stuck his forefinger in his own ear. 'Pow!' he said, and it was so funny he almost choked. 'Comrade China.'

Sean stared at him unseeingly, while he adjusted his mind to this extraordinary intelligence. All his instincts were to reject it out of hand, but Matatu didn't make mistakes of that nature.

'Comrade China!' Sean breathed softly. 'That changes the odds a little.'

He cast his mind back to that distant day. The man had made such an impression upon him that even from the crowded and confused events of that bloody little war, he retrieved a clear image of Comrade China. He remembered his fine Nilotic head and the dark intelligent eyes, but his physical features were hazy compared to Sean's memory of the sense of confidence and purpose that the man exuded. He had been a dangerous man then, and Sean expected that now he would be even more experienced and formidable.

Sean shook his head. At one time his nickname in the Scouts had been Lucky Courtney'; it looked as though he had used up his ration of that commodity. He couldn't have chosen anybody he would have wanted less to command the column of Renamo than Comrade China.

Matatu had almost exhausted his mirth, and was now battling with the hiccoughs that followed, clutching at his naked belly and throat to hold them down, while occasional spasms of laughter interspersed the loud hiccoughs.

'I'm sending you back to Chiwewe,' Sean told him harshly, and the laughter and hiccoughs were instantly extinguished. Matatu stared at him in disbelief and utter despair. Sean could not face those eyes, and their tragic accusation.

He turned to Pumula and brusquely called him across to where he lay. 'This note is for the chef at camp. Tell him to radio the message to Miss Reema in Harare. Matatu will guide you back. Don't stop to pick your nose on the way, do you understand me?'

'*Mambo*.' Pumula was an old Scout. He would obey without argument or question.

'All right, go,' Sean ordered. 'Go now.' And Pumula held out his right hand. They shook hands the African way, gripping palms and then thumbs and then palms again. Pumula crawled down off the ridge, and once he was clear, jumped to his feet and trotted away. He did not look back.

At last Sean forced himself to look at Matatu. He crouched low to the ground, trying to make his small frame smaller still to escape Sean's notice.

'Go!' Sean ordered brusquely. 'Show Pumula the way back to Chiwewe.'

Matatu hung his head and shivered like a whipped puppy.

'Get the hell out of here!' Sean growled at him. 'Before I kick your black butt!'

Matatu lifted his head and his eyes were tragic, his expression abject. Sean wanted to pick him up and hug him.

'Get out of here, you stupid little bugger!' Sean made a face of terrifying ferocity, and Matatu crept away a few paces and then paused and looked back imploringly.

'Go!' Sean lifted his right hand threateningly. At last the little man accepted the inevitable and slunk away down the slope. Just before he disappeared into the coarse scrub at the foot of the slope, he paused and looked back one more time, seeking just the faintest sign of encouragement or weakness. He was the epitome of dejection.

Deliberately, Sean turned his back on him and raised the binoculars to study the terrain ahead, but after a few seconds the image blurred and he blinked his eyes to clear them and despite himself, glanced quickly over his shoulder.

Matatu had vanished. It was a strange feeling not to have him there. After a few minutes, Sean lifted the binoculars again and resumed his study of the escarpment line, pushing Matatu out of his mind.

On either side of the mouth of the long valley, the red rock cliffs stretched away unbroken for as far as Sean could see. They were not particularly high; at the lowest points they were only a few hundred feet, but they were vertical and some stretches were even overhanging where softer strata of rock had been eroded from under the harder super-imposed upper layers, and formed a shallow horizontal cave.

The entrance of the valley was as inviting as the mouth of a carnivorous plant to an insect, and the cliffs were forbidding and inaccessible, but Sean concentrated upon them. He swept them with the binoculars, in both direc-tions as far as he could see. Of course, it might be necessary to move some miles along the cliff to find a route that was scalable, but that would burn up precious time. He kept swinging the binoculars back to the same point.

A quarter of a mile to the right-hand side of the nearest rock portal of the valley, there was a route that looked as though it might just go, but it wouldn't be easy without a companion and lacking even basic rock-climbing equip-ment. He would be burdened by the rifle and his pack, and he would have to make the attempt in the dark. To go out on that exposed cliff in daylight would be to invite a little AK target practice.

Through the binocular lens, he picked out a rocky buttress which was faulted like a fire escape. It seemed to offer a way round the overhanging section of cliff, and above that it led to a narrow horizontal ledge running several hundred feet in either direction. From that ledge there appeared to be two possible routes to the top of the cliff, one was a narrow crack or chimney and the other an open face down which grew the exposed serpentine roots of a huge ficus tree that stood tall and massive on the skyline.

The roots crawled and twined against the sheer red rock, like a nest of mating pythons, that formed a ladder to the top of the cliff.

Sean glanced at his wristwatch. He had three hours to rest before it was dark enough to make the attempt and suddenly, he felt exhausted. He realized that it was not only the physical exertion of the chase, but also the emotional drain of having glimpsed Claudia and Job in the Renamo column, and the parting with Matatu.

He anti-tracked meticulously back off the ridge and searched for a secure place to hole-up during what was left of daylight. When he found a hidy-hole amongst rock and scrub with a safe line of retreat, he loosened his bootlaces to rest his feet, but kept the rifle in his lap and slumped down over it. He munched a maize cake and protein bar from his emergency pack and drank a few careful mouthfuls from his water-bottle.

He knew he would wake when the sun touched the horizon. He closed his eyes and fell almost instantly asleep.

On the journey back to Chiwewe camp, Matatu led Pumula at a steady trot. They kept going through the night and the next afternoon stopped to refill their water-bottles in the marsh where they had spotted Tukutela from the air.

Pumula wanted to rest. Matatu did not bother to argue with him. He faced towards the west and went away at that swaying trot on his skinny knob-kneed legs and Pumula was forced to follow. They crossed the border between Mozambique and Zimbabwe during the dark hours of the night, and ran into the safari camp in the middle of the following afternoon.

The consternation caused by their arrival was tremendous. In his agitation, the chef even forgot to don his tall cap and snowy apron before rushing out of his hut to greet them and demand the news of the *mambo*.

Matatu left Pumula to hand over Sean's written message and answer the barrage of questions. He went to his own hut and curled up like a puppy on his bed, an ancient iron frame with a lumpy coir mattress, a gift from Sean and his most treasured possession. He slept through all the subsequent excitement, even chef bellowing into the microphone of the VHF radio, attempting by volume alone to reach Reema in Harare almost three hundred miles distant.

When Matatu awoke, he had slept five hours. The camp was dark and silent. He repacked the small leather pouch that was his only luggage, retrieved his remaining store of precious snuff from under his mattress and refilled the horn that hung around his neck.

He crept quietly from the sleeping camp. When he was well clear, he straightened up and faced towards the east.

'Silly little bugger,' he said happily, and began to run, going back to his rightful place beside the man he loved more than a father.

Sean woke with the first chill of evening in the air. Ahead the cliffs of the escarpment were fading into the smoky purple dusk. Sean stretched and looked around for Matatu. When he remembered he was gone, it gave him a physical jolt in the pit of his stomach. He tied his bootlaces and drank again. When he stoppered the water-bottle, he held it to his ear and shook it. Still half full.

He opened the breech of the .577, slipped the cartridges out of the twin chambers and exchanged them for two others from the loops on his bush-jacket. He squeezed an inch of black camouflage cream from the crumpled tube and rubbed it over his face and the backs of his hands. That completed his preparation and he stood up and moved quietly up the slope.

He spent the last twenty minutes of daylight glassing the entrance to the valley and the top of the cliffs through his binoculars. As far as he could see, nothing had changed. Then he studied and memorized the route up the cliff face.

As the night spread its cloak over the escarpment, he slipped quietly over the ridge and crept up towards the base of the cliff. The bush grew dense and tangled there and it took him much longer than he had anticipated to reach the rocky wall.

It was almost completely dark by then, but he was able to identify the starting point of the climb by a small bush growing in a crack of the cliff which he had marked through the binoculars.

Sean had never used a carrying sling on his rifle. It could be mortally dangerous in thick bush when the sling caught on a branch just as the buffalo or wounded elephant began its charge. He lashed the short-barrelled weapon under the flap of his back-pack with his sleeping-bag. The butt stuck out on one side of his shoulders and the muzzles on the other, making an awkward unbalanced load. He went to the cliff face and laid his hands on it, getting the feel of it. The stone was still hot from the sun and the texture was smooth, almost soapy under his fingers.

Before the war, rock-climbing had been one of his passions. He loved the risk, the terror of the open face and drop sucking at his heels. He had climbed in South America and Europe, as well as on the Drakensberg and Mount Kenya. He had the requisite sense of balance and the strength in his fingers and arms. He could have been one of the top international climbers but for the intervention of the bush war. However, he had never attempted a climb like this before.

His boots were soft velskoen without reinforced toes. He had no ropes, no anchorman, no pitons nor karabiner, and

246

he would be opening this route in darkness, barely able to see the next hold above, following a pitch which he had studied from a mile distant, going blind on red sandstone, the most treacherous of rock.

He stepped up on the face and began to climb. He used his toes, and his fingers, leaning back from the rock, keeping in fine balance, never stopping, never jerking or fighting the holds, smoothly as molten chocolate, flowing upwards.

At first the holds were solid, the kind he called 'jug handles', then the face leaned out slowly and the holds were mere flakes and indentations. He used them lightly and briefly, a touch of his fingers, a nudge of his toes and he was past, putting the minimum of weight on each but even then feeling the frailer flakes of stone grate and creak threateningly under his fingers – but he was gone before the hold could fail.

In places, he could not see above his head and he climbed by instinct, reaching up in the darkness, his fingertips as sensitive as those of a pianist as they brushed the rock and then locked into it. Without check or pause, he covered the first pitch and reached the ledge a hundred feet up from the base.

The ledge was narrower than it had appeared through the binoculars, no more than nine inches wide. With the pack strapped on his back and the rifle protruding on each side of his shoulders, it was impossible for him to turn his back to the rock and use the ledge as a bench to sit upon.

He was forced to stand facing the cliff, with his heels hanging over the edge, and the weight of pack and rifle pulling on his shoulders, trying to drag him backwards. He was less comfortable on the ledge than he had been on the face. He began to shuffle along it, spreading his arms like a crucifix to steady himself, his fingers groping for irregularities in the rock face, the sandstone an inch from the tip of his nose.

He went left along the ledge, seeking the vertical crack

that he had spotted through the binoculars. It had been his first choice of the two possible routes. Sean had the rock-climber's instinctive distrust of roots and branches and tufts of grass. They were always unreliable, too treacherous to risk life upon.

He counted his shuffling crablike paces along the ledge, and by the time he reached a hundred the ledge under his toes had narrowed dangerously and the muscles in his thighs were burning and quivering from the unnatural strain of counter-balancing the rifle and pack.

Twenty paces more and the cliff face was beginning to bulge out towards him, forcing him further backwards and he had to thrust his hips forward to keep himself from toppling out over the sheer drop. It was only a hundred feet to the bottom, but it would crush and kill just as surely as a fall from the top of Eiger north face.

The strain on his legs was intolerable now. He thought of going back and trying the roots of the ficus but he doubted that he still had that choice. He wanted to stop, just to rest his legs a moment and gather himself but he knew that would be the end of it. To stop on a pitch like this was defeat and certain death.

He made himself take another pace and then another, now he was forced backwards so his back was arched and his legs were numb to the ankles; he could feel them juddering under him, he knew they were going. Then suddenly the fingers of his left hand touched the crack, and it was as though a syringeful of adrenalin had been squirted into one of his arteries.

His legs steadied under him, and he managed another pace. His fingers danced over the crack, exploring it swiftly. It was not wide enough to get his shoulder into it, and it narrowed quickly.

Sean thrust his hand into it as deep as it would go and then bunched his fist, jamming it securely into the crack. Now he could hang back on his arm and rest his back and his aching legs. His breathing hissed and sawed in his chest and the sweat was streaming down his body, soaking his shirt. Sweat melted the camouflage cream from his face and burned his eyes, blurring his vision.

He blinked rapidly and lifted his head. He was surprised to see that the cliff face above him was visible against the night sky, and that he could make out the crack running vertically up its side.

He turned his head and saw that while he climbed the moon had cleared the horizon in the east and its beams turned the forest below to a frosty silver.

He could not wait any longer. He had to keep moving. He reached up with his free hand and thrust it into the rock crack above the other and made another jam-hold. Then he twisted his foot and pressed the toe into the crack three feet up from the ledge; he straightened his foot and it wedged securely. He put his weight on it and, with the other foot, stepped up and repeated the action. Hand over hand, foot over foot, he walked up the crack, hanging back from the rock face, once more in balance, the strain removed from his legs and back and his weight evenly distributed.

He could see the top of the cliff now, only a hundred feet above his head, and then he felt the crack begin to open wider; his fists and feet were no longer finding secure jams. One of his feet slipped under him, rasping harshly over the rock until it caught again.

He turned his body, trying to wedge his shoulder into the crack, but the barrel of the rifle clanged against the face, blocking his turn. He hung there for a few seconds before he could force himself back into balance on his legs and then groped above his head searching the depth of the crack for another secure hold. He found only smooth sandstone, and he knew he was stuck.

He had about fifteen seconds before his legs gave in under him. He understood clearly what he had to do, but it went contrary to all his instincts.

'Do it,' his voice grated in his own ears. 'Do it, or die.'

He reached down and opened the quick release buckle on the waistband of his back-pack. Then he straightened one arm and reached backwards and downwards; the carrying strap slid off his shoulder and down his arm, catching in the crook of his elbow. The altered weight of the pack and the rifle slewed his whole body around and he had to fight to stay on the cliff face.

He thrust his head into the crack, trying to hook onto the rock with his chin and the back of his head, the strap of the back-pack locking his arm behind him. He gathered all his strength, braced his neck muscles, his head jammed in the crack and let go. Now he was held only by his head and feet, he straightened both arms behind him. For an aching moment, the strap caught on a fold of his bush jacket, and then it slipped down over his arm.

The pack dropped off his back and fell away into the darkness. Relieved of the weight, Sean tottered and swayed and then with both arms free, he grabbed wildly at the edges of the rock crack and managed to hold himself from plunging after his pack into the abyss.

He clung to the rock and listened to the pack striking the cliff as it fell, the steel of his rifle barrel ringing like a bronze bell off the rock, waking the echoes and sending them bounding from kopje to cliff, a terrifying sound in the night. Long after the pack and rifle had come to rest at the base of the cliff, the echoes still reverberated against the hills.

Sean swung himself sideways and was able at last to wedge his shoulder into the crack. He rested like that, panting wildly, the terror of death for the moment unnerving him. Then slowly his breathing eased and his terror was replaced by the familiar glow of adrenalin in his blood. Suddenly, it felt very good still to be alive.

'Right to the very edge,' he whispered hoarsely. 'You have been there again, boyo.' The greater the terror, the more intense the thrill. He no longer amazed himself, but here he was again gloating at just how close he could get without going over the edge.

The thrill was too fleeting, within seconds it began to fade, to be replaced by realization of his position. His pack was gone. The rifle, his water-bottles, sleeping-bag, food, all gone. All that remained were the contents of his pockets, and the tiny emergency pack and hunting-knife looped to his belt.

He whispered, 'We'll worry about that when we get to the top.' And he began to climb again. With one shoulder wedged into the crack, he was able to push and drag himself upwards an inch at a time, paying for it with skin from his knuckles and bare knees.

Gradually the crack continued to open wider, until it became a full chimney, and he could get his whole body into it and double one leg under him to propel himself upwards more swiftly. At the top the chimney had eroded and crumbled. One side wall of the chimney had broken away, but it had left a narrow buttress with a flat top. Sean was able to transfer his weight across the chimney until he was standing on this precarious pinnacle.

The top of the cliff was still ten feet above his head. When he reached up to the full stretch of his arms standing on the tips of his toes the ledge was still just out of reach. The chimney wall had broken away clearly leaving a smooth almost polished surface, without even the minutest hold or purchase. A good safe climber moved from hold to hold, with never a single moment when he was totally insecure. In a situation such as this that hypothetical climber would have driven an iron piton into the rock to give him the hold he needed.

'Look Mummy, no pitons,' Sean said grimly. 'We'll have to jump for it.' He would only have one chance at it. If he missed his hold on the ledge once he had launched himself, then the next stop would be the base of the cliff.

He set both feet firmly and sank down at the knees, but

he was so cramped on the tip of the buttress that he could not get low enough before his face touched the rock and his backside stuck far out over the drop.

He took a breath and used both arms and legs to propel himself straight upwards. It was an awkward hampered jump but he got high enough to hook both his hands over the edge. For a moment, they began to slide back and then his fingers gripped and held.

He kicked both legs and drew himself upwards by the main strength of his arms. His chin came level with the ledge, and in the moonlight he saw in front of him a false crest, simply another ledge below the true top of the cliff.

The ledge was obviously occupied by a colony of rock hyrax. The stink of their droppings, sharp and ammoniacal, filled Sean's lungs as he gasped from the effort of holding himself. The hyrax is a plump fluffy animal. Although it is only the size of a rabbit, it is a remote relative of the elephant, and as endearing in appearance as an infant's soft toy. These hyrax were deep in their rocky burrows now and the ledge seemed deserted. Sean hoisted himself up smoothly and hooked one elbow over the edge; he kicked again, gathering himself for the final effort and then froze.

The silence of the night was cut by a loud high-pitched hiss, like the leaking valve of a truck tyre. In the moonlight what he had taken for a pile of rock lying directly in front of his face, altered shape, seeming to melt and flow.

In an instant, Sean realized that it was a snake. Only one of the adders would hiss as loudly, and only one adder was that large.

It was coiled upon itself, loop after loop of its thick scaly body glistening softly, and as it cocked its neck into the menacing 'S' shape, its eye caught the light of the moon and winked at him sardonically. The huge flat head was the distinctive spade shape of the gaboon adder, the largest of all the adders and one of the deadliest of all Africa's venomous snakes.

Sean could drop back and try to regain his stance on the narrow pinnacle of rock, but that was a slim chance and if he missed it, he would plunge down the cliff face. A much better chance would be to try and brave it out.

He hung with legs free, trying to control his breathing, staring in horror at the loathsome creature. It was cocked to strike, less than two feet from his face, and he knew it could lunge out almost its full body length, seven feet or more. The slightest movement would trigger it.

He hung on his arms, every muscle of his body rigid, staring at the adder, trying to dominate it by the force of his will. The seconds drew out slowly as spilled molasses, and he thought he detected the first relaxation in the taut 'S' of its neck.

At that moment, his left hand slipped, his fingernails rasped on the rock and the adder struck with the force of a blacksmith's hammer.

Sean rolled his head to the side, like a boxer avoiding a punch. The adder's cold scaly nose jarred against his jawbone and there was a fierce tug against his neck and shoulder, so powerful that it jerked one hand loose from its hold on the rock, and spun him half around. He was sideways to the ledge, holding on with only his left arm.

He knew that the adder had hooked its fangs into his shoulder or the side of his throat and he expected the exquisite fire of its venom to kindle in his flesh. The serpent was locked onto him, dangling down the front of his body, thick as a salami sausage; it squirmed and thrashed, hissing explosively in his ear. The cold loathsome touch of its slippery scales brushed against his bare flesh.

Sean almost screamed with the sheer horror of it. The adder's weight threw him about as it lashed from side to side, and its loud hisses deafened him. He felt his single-handed grip on the ledge slipping, but the prospect of the drop below him was suddenly insignificant when compared to this foul creature fastened to his neck.

He felt an icy spray of liquid on the side of his throat and his jaw; it dribbled down the opening of his bush jacket, and with a rush of relief he knew that the adder had missed his throat and had fastened into the collar of his jacket. Its fangs were fully two inches long and viciously recurved, designed to penetrate and hang on to its prey. Hooked into the khaki cotton material of his collar, its violent struggles were forcing the venom out of the hollow bony needles, squirting onto his throat and bare skin.

The realization that the fangs had not penetrated his flesh rallied him, firmed his grip on the ledge and arrested his slow slide into the drop. His right hand was still free. He reached up and seized the adder's neck just at the back of its flat diamond-shaped head. His fingers could barely span the massive body, and he felt the enormous power of its muscles beneath the glassy scales.

He tried to pull it free, but the fangs were like fish hooks in the heavy cloth, and the serpent hissed more viciously and its grotesque body, patterned like a patchwork quilt, coiled around his forearm. He used all his strength, holding onto the ledge with his left arm, heaving at the adder with his right, and he tore the fangs from the roof of its gaping mouth so that its dark blood mingled with the copious flow of its venom, and he flung the twisting coiling body far out over the drop. Then he swung back and grabbed with his right hand at the rock of the ledge.

He was sobbing softly with horror and exertion, and it was fully half a minute before he could gather himself sufficiently to pull himself up and crawl onto the ledge.

He knelt on the rock floor and shrugged out of his bush jacket. The front of it was wet with venom, and one of the adder's fangs was broken off and still buried in the cloth of the collar. He worked it loose and, careful to avoid the needle point, flicked it out over the cliff. Then with his handkerchief he wiped his skin dry.

He considered the danger of wearing the jacket again.

The venom might be absorbed through the pores of the sensitive skin under his jaw, it could cause ulcers or worse, but to discard the jacket would expose his body to tomorrow's tropical sun. He hesitated and rolled the jacket and fastened it onto his belt. He would wash it out at the first opportunity.

The thought of water made him aware of his thirst. The climb had dehydrated him, and his water-bottle was with his pack at the bottom of the cliff. He had to find water before tomorrow's noon, but now his first concern must be to get off the exposed face of the cliff and into cover.

He stood up, and felt the night breeze cold on the sweat of his bare upper body. From the ledge on which he stood, it was an easy pitch to the crest, more a scramble than a climb. However, he took it carefully and when he reached the top he lay for a few minutes with just his head peering over the crest.

A haze of light cloud had veiled the moon and Sean could see very little. The bush that grew so densely up the sides of the valley had spread across the tops of the cliff and formed a dark wall just ahead. There were probably forty yards of rocky ground, open except for coarse knee-high grass, and then he would be into the cover of the bush.

He rose to his feet, and ran forward crouching as low as possible as he crossed the skyline, and he was halfway to the edge of the bush when the light hit him.

It stopped him dead as though he had run into the rock cliff, and he flung up his hands instinctively to protect his eyes for his vision had been shattered and starred by the brilliance of the light beamed full into his face. Then he flung himself face forward into the grass and flattened his body against the stony earth.

The beam of light threw long black shadows behind each boulder and cast a bright reflective glow from the pale winter grass. Sean dared not raise his head. He pressed his face to the earth, exposed and vulnerable and helpless in that fierce white beam.

He waited for something to happen but the silence was unbroken. Even the usual night sounds of nocturnal birds and insects were quenched, so that the voice when at last it boomed out of the trees, magnified and distorted by an electronic bullhorn, was as shocking as a blow in the face.

'Good evening, Colonel Courtney.' It was spoken in good English, barely touched by an African accent. 'You made excellent time. Twenty-seven minutes fifteen seconds from the base of the cliff to the top.'

Sean did not move, but he lay and absorbed the bitter humiliation of it. They had been toying with him.

'But I cannot give you high marks for stealth. What was it you threw down the rock? It sounded like a bunch of old tin pots.' The speaker chuckled sardonically and then went on, 'And now, Colonel, if you are sufficiently rested, would you be gracious enough to stand up and raise both hands above your head?'

Sean did not move.

'I beg of you, sir. Don't waste your time and mine.'

Sean lay still, considering wildly the possibility of dashing back over the crest behind him.

'Very well, I see you have to be convinced.' There was a brief pause and Sean heard a soft order given in dialect.

The burst of automatic fire tore into the earth three paces from where he lay. He saw the fiery blur of the muzzle flashes amongst the dark trees and heard the distinctive rush of the RPD light machine-gun, like a strip of heavy-duty canvas being ripped through. The stream of bullets scythed the grass and raised a mist of yellow dust in the bright light.

Sean came slowly to his feet. The beam of light fastened on his face but he refused to turn his head away or shield his eyes.

'Hands at full stretch above the head please, Colonel.'

256

He obeyed. His naked upper body was very white in the light.

'I am delighted to see you have kept yourself in good shape, Colonel.'

Two dark figures detached themselves from the tree line. Keeping well clear of the light beam, they circled out on either side of him and came up in Sean's rear. From the corner of his eyes, Sean saw they wore tiger-striped battle dress and that their AK rifles were aimed at him. He ignored them until suddenly the steel butt plate of one of the rifles crashed into his spine between the shoulder-blades and he fell to his knees.

The voice on the bull-horn gave a sharp order in dialect to prevent them striking him again and they closed on either side of him and forced him to his feet. One of them searched him swiftly, stripping him of knife, belt and emergency pack and patting his pockets. Then they backed off, leaving him naked except for his khaki shorts and velskoen, but they kept their AKs aimed at his belly.

The light bobbed as the man carrying it advanced out of the wall of bush. Sean saw that it was one of those portable battle lights powered by a heavy rechargeable battery pack that the man carried on his back. Slightly behind him, keeping back in the shadow, came the man with the bull-horn.

Even through the dazzling beam of the battle light Sean saw that he was tall and lean, and that he moved with a cat-like grace.

'It's been a long time, Colonel Courtney.' He was close enough not to have to use the bull-horn and Sean recognized his voice.

'Many years,' Sean agreed.

'You'll have to speak up.' The man stopped a few paces in front of Sean and jokingly cupped one hand to the side of his head. 'I am deaf in one ear, you know,' he said, and Sean grinned sardonically at him through his black camouflage cream.

'I should have done a better job, and blown your other ear out while I was about it, Comrade China.'

'Yes,' China agreed. 'We really must discuss old times together.' He smiled and he was even more handsome than Sean remembered, relaxed and charming and debonair. 'However, I'm afraid you have delayed me a little, Colonel. Pleasant though it is to renew acquaintance, I cannot afford more time away from my headquarters. There will be an opportunity to talk later, but now I must leave you. My men will take good care of you.'

He turned and disappeared into the darkness beyond the beam of light. Sean wanted to call after him, 'My men, the girl, are they safe?' but he restrained himself. With a man like this, it was best to show no weakness, to give him nothing he could use to his advantage later. Sean forced himself to remain silent when the guards urged him forward with practised use of their gun butts.

'We'll join the main column soon,' Sean comforted himself, 'and I'll see for myself how Claudia and Job are doing.'

The thought of Claudia was a refreshing draught that he craved even more than sweet cool water.

There were ten men in his guard detail under the command of a sergeant.

Obviously they were picked troops, powerful and lean as the pack of wolves of his nightmare. Soon they intercepted a well-beaten footpath and they closed up around him and urged him to a jog-trot, heading southwards into the night.

None of his captors spoke. It was an eerie experience, just the sound of their light footfalls and quick shallow breathing, the creak of equipment and the hot feral smell of their bodies close around him in the night.

After an hour, the sergeant signalled a pause, and they stopped beside the track. Sean reached across to the nearest guerrilla and tapped the water-bottle on his belt.

The man spoke to the sergeant. The first words since they had started and Sean understood him. He was speaking Shangane. The Shanganes were the remnants of one of the tiny Zulu tribes that had been defeated by King Chaka's impis at the battle of Mhlatuze River in 1818. Unlike so many of the other lesser chieftains, Soshangane had resisted incorporation into Chaka's empire and fled northwards with his shattered impis to found his own kingdom along the borders of present day Zimbabwe and Mozambique.

So the Shangane language was Zulu-based, and over the years many of Sean's camp staff had been Shangane for, like their Zulu ancestors, they were a fine and noble people. Sean spoke their language fluently for it contained many similarities to Sindebele.

He did not, however, make the mistake of letting his captors know this and gave no indication of having understood as the trooper said, 'The *mabunu* wants to drink.'

'Give it to him,' the sergeant replied. 'You know the *inkosi* wants him alive.'

The man handed Sean the bottle and though the water was brackish and was tainted by swamp mud, to Sean it tasted like chilled Veuve Clicquot served in a crystal glass.

'The *inkosi* wants him alive,' the sergeant had said. Sean pondered that as he handed the bottle back. The *inkosi*, or chief, was obviously Comrade China, and they had orders to care for him. That gave him a little comfort, but he did not have long to savour it. After only a few minutes, the sergeant gave the order and they resumed that mile-eating jog-trot towards the south.

They ran up the dawn and at any moment Sean expected them to overhaul the main column which was holding Claudia and Job captive, but mile succeeded mile without any sign of them. Now that it was light, Sean could look

259

for the tracks of the column on the footpath ahead but there were none. They must have taken a different route.

The sergeant in charge was a veteran. He had flankers out sweeping the verges of the footpath ahead for an ambush by Frelimo, but what seemed to concern him more than attack from the forest was the menace from the sky. At all times they attempted to keep under the canopy of the forest, and whenever they were forced to cross open ground, they stopped and searched the sky, listened for the sound of engines, before venturing out, and then they crossed to the next line of trees at a full run.

Once during the first morning they heard the sound of a turbo-aircraft engine, faint and very far off, but instantly the sergeant gave an order and they all dived into cover. A trooper lay on each side of Sean and forced him to keep his head down and his face to the ground until the last murmur of the aircraft engine faded.

This preoccupation with aerial attack puzzled Sean; all he had heard and read indicated that Frelimo's air force was so weak and scattered as to be almost non-existent. The types of aircraft they possessed were obsolete and unsuited to ground attack, and a shortage of skilled technicians and spares only compounded their ineffectuality. These men, however, were taking the threat very seriously indeed.

At midday the sergeant ordered a halt. One of the troopers prepared food on a small fire, which he doused as soon as it was cooked. They moved on a few miles before stopping once more to eat the meal. Sean was given an equal share. The maize meal was cooked stiff and fluffy and was well salted, but the meat was rancid and on the point of putrefying. In the average white man it would have caused an immediate attack of enteritis, but Sean's stomach was as conditioned as any African's. He ate it without relish, but without trepidation either.

'The food is good,' the sergeant told Sean in Shangane as he sat beside him. 'Do you want more?' Sean made a pantomine of incomprehension and said in English, 'I'm sorry I don't know what you are saying.' The sergeant shrugged and went on eating. A few minutes later he turned back to Sean and said sharply, 'Look behind you, there's a snake!' Sean resisted the natural impulse to jump to his feet and instead grinned ingratiatingly and repeated, 'I'm sorry I don't understand.'

The sergeant relaxed and one of his men remarked, 'He does not understand Shangane. It is all right to speak in front of him.'

They ignored him for the remainder of the meal and chatted amongst themselves, but as soon as they had finished, the sergeant produced a pair of light manacles from his pack and locked one side on to Sean's wrist and the other onto his own. He delegated sentry duty to two of his men and the rest of them settled down to sleep.

Despite Sean's exhaustion, he had been going for days now on only brief snatches of sleep, he lay awake and pondered all he had learned, and the missing pieces of the puzzle. He was still not certain that he was in Renamo hands, he had only Claudia's brief note to suggest that. On the other hand, Comrade China had been a commissar in Robert Mugabe's Marxist ZANLA army, but Renamo was a rabidly anti-communist organization committed to the overthrow of the Marxist Frelimo government. That didn't add up correctly.

Furthermore, China had fought the Rhodesian army of Ian Smith. What was he doing here across the border, involved in another struggle in a foreign country? Was China a soldier of fortune, a turncoat, or an independent warlord taking advantage of the Mozambiquan chaos for his own private ends? It would be interesting to find out.

With all this to think about, still his last thought before sleep finally overcame him, was of Claudia Monterro. If China wanted him alive, then it was highly probable that

261

he wanted the girl alive as well. With that thought, he fell into a deep, dark sleep with a faint smile on his lips.

He woke to the ache of abused muscles and the bruises left by gun butts, but the sergeant had him up and running immediately southwards again into the cool shades of evening. Within a mile, his muscles warmed and the stiffness evaporated. He settled into the run, matching his escorts easily. Always he looked ahead, hoping at any moment to see the tail of the main column emerge from the darkness, and to see Job and Dedan carrying Claudia's litter.

They ran through the night and when they stopped again to eat, his captors began to discuss him through their mouthfuls of maize and high-smelling meat.

'They say that in the other war, he was a lion, an eater of men,' the sergeant told them. 'It was he that led the attack at Inhlozane, the training camp at the Hills of the Maiden's Breasts.'

The troopers looked at him with interest and dawning respect.

'They say that it was veritably he, in person, who destroyed one ear of General China.'

They chuckled and shook their heads, that was a fine joke.

'He has the body of a warrior,' said one of them, and they considered him frankly, discussing his physique as though he were an inanimate object.

'Why has General China ordered this?' another asked, and the sergeant grinned and picked a shred of meat from his back teeth with a fingernail.

'We must run the pride and the anger out of him,' he grinned. 'General China wants us to change him from a lion into a dog who will wag his tail and do his bidding.'

'He has the body of a warrior,' the first man repeated. 'Now we must discover if he has the heart of a warrior.' And they all laughed again.

'So it's a contest, then.' Sean kept his face impassive. 'All right, you bastards, let's see which dog wags its tail first.'

In a perverse fashion, Sean began to enjoy himself. The challenge was much to his taste. There were ten of them, all in their twenties. He was just over forty years of age, but that handicap made it even sweeter and helped him to endure the monotony and hardship of the days that followed.

He was careful not to let them know that he understood that this was a contest. He knew it was dangerous to antagonize or humiliate them. Their goodwill and respect would be more valuable than their hatred and resentment.

Sean had spent his entire adult life in the close company of black men. He knew them as servants and as equals, as hunters and soldiers, as good and loyal friends and as bitter cruel enemies. He knew their strengths and weaknesses and how to exploit them. He understood their tribal customs, their social etiquette, he knew how to flatter and please and impress them, how to gain their respect and make himself agreeable to them.

He showed them just the right degree of respect, but not enough to make them contemptuous. He took especial care not to challenge the sergeant's authority or force him to lose face in front of his men. He made the most of their sense of humour and of fun. With sign language and a little clowning he made them laugh, and once they had laughed with him their whole relationship altered subtly. He became more a companion than a captive and they no longer used the steel-edged gun butts as instruments of casual persuasion. Most importantly, he was every day picking up little snippets of information.

Twice they passed burned-out villages. The cultivated lands around them had gone back to weeds, the black ashes blowing in the wind.

Sean pointed at the ruins. 'Renamo?' he asked, and his captors were outraged.

'No! No!' the sergeant told him. 'Frelimo! Frelimo!' And then he tapped his own chest.

'Me Renamo,' he boasted, and pointed at his men. 'Renamo! Renamo!'

'Renamo!' they agreed proudly.

'Well, that settles that,' Sean laughed.

'Frelimo. Bang! Bang!' He made the gesture of shooting a Frelimo and they were delighted, joining in the pantomime of slaughter enthusiastically. Their attitude towards him improved even further and at their next meal the sergeant handed him an extra-large cut of rotten meat. While he ate it, openly they discussed his performance to date, agreeing that he was acquitting himself admirably.

'But,' the sergeant asked, 'he can run and we know he can kill men, but can he kill a *henshaw*?'

Henshaw was the Shangane word for a falcon, and Sean had heard them use it many times over the last five days of their trek, and each time as they said the word, they looked up at the sky with a troubled expression. Now, once again at the mention of that bird, they looked unhappy and as a reflex glanced upwards.

'General China thinks so,' the sergeant went on. 'But who knows, who knows?'

By now, Sean was confident that his position was fairly secure, his relationship with the band would allow him to take the first liberty, and force a resolution of this trial by attrition.

On the next stage, he began to force the pace. Instead of keeping his station in the file of trotting men two paces behind the Shangane sergeant who led the column, he closed up until he was running on his heels, not quite touching him with each stride, and exaggerating his breathing so that the sergeant could feel it on the back of his thick sweaty back. Instinctively the sergeant lengthened his own stride and Sean matched him, keeping close, too close and pushing him.

The sergeant glanced over his shoulder irritably and Sean grinned at him, breathing into his face. The sergeant's eyes narrowed slightly as he realized what was happening, then he grinned back at Sean and extended his stride into a full run.

'That's it, my friend,' Sean said in English. 'Now let's see whose tail wags.'

The rest of the column had fallen behind. The sergeant called a sharp order to them to close up, and they went away at a killing pace. Within an hour, there were only three of them left, the others were straggled back over a mile of the forest floor and ahead of them the path climbed a steep incline to the crest of another tableland.

Sean moved up slightly until he was running shoulder to shoulder with the tall sergeant, but when he tried to pull ahead the man kept with him. The hillside was so steep that the path went up it in a series of hairpins, and the sergeant forged ahead of Sean at the first bend, but Sean caught him and passed him on the straight.

They ran at the top of their speed now, the lead changing back and forth between them and the third man dropped out before they were halfway up the hillside. They ran grimly, in a wash of sweat, their breathing harsh as the exhaust of a steam engine.

Suddenly Sean darted off the path, scrambling straight upwards, cutting across the bend and coming out fifty feet ahead of the Shangane. The sergeant shouted angrily at this ruse and cut the next bend himself. Now both of them abandoned the pathway and ran straight at the steep slope, jumping over boulders and roots, like a pair of blue kudu bulls in flight.

Sean came out on the crest three feet in front of the sergeant, and threw himself down on the hard earth and rolled onto his back moaning for breath. The sergeant dropped beside him with his breath sobbing in his chest.

After a minute, Sean sat up uncertainly and they stared at each other in awe.

Then Sean began to laugh; it was a harsh painful cackle, but after a few seconds the Shangane laughed with him, though clearly each gust of laughter was an agony. Their laughter grew stronger as their lungs regained function, and when the rest of the party struggled to the crest of the hill, they found them still sitting in the grass beside the track, roaring at each other like a pair of lunatics.

When the march resumed an hour later, the sergeant left the endless footpath and struck off across country towards the west and there was at last direction and purpose in the way he led the column.

Sean realized that the trial was over.

B efore dark they ran into a Renamo line of permanent defences.

They were entrenched along the bank of a wide but sluggish river that flowed green between sand bars and round water-polished boulders. The dugouts and trenches were revetted with logs and sandbags and meticulously camouflaged against aerial discovery. There were mortars and heavy machine-guns dug in, with commanding fields of fire across the river and sweeping the northern bank.

Sean had the impression that these fortifications were extensive and he guessed that this was the perimeter of a large military area, certainly battalion and possibly even division strength. Once they had crossed the river and been passed through the defences, Sean's appearance in the ranks of his escort created a stir of interest. Off-duty troopers turned out of their dugouts and crowded around them and his captors were clearly enjoying the elevated status that a white prisoner bestowed upon them.

The crowd of interested and jocular onlookers abruptly

thinned and parted as a tubby bespectacled officer strode through them. His escort saluted him with theatrical flourishes which he returned by touching the rim of his maroon beret with the tip of his swaggerstick.

'Colonel Courtney,' he greeted Sean in passable English. 'We have been warned to expect you.'

For Sean, it was refreshing to notice that Renamo wore conventional badges of rank, based on the Portuguese army conventions. This man had red field officer flashes and the single crowns of a major on his epaulettes. During the bush war the terrs had eschewed the capitalist imperialist traditions, and dispensed with the symbols of an elitist officer class.

'You will spend the night with us,' the major told him. 'And I look forward to having you as our guest in mess tonight.'

This was extraordinary treatment, and even Sean's captors were impressed and in a strange way rather proud of him. The sergeant himself escorted Sean down to the river and even produced a fragment of green soap for him to wash out his bush jacket and shorts.

While they dried on a sun-heated rock, Sean wallowed naked in the pool and then used the last of the soap to wash his hair and rid his face of camouflage cream and ingrained dirt. He had not shaved since he had left Chiwewe camp almost two weeks previously and his beard felt thick and substantial.

He worked up a lather of suds in his armpits and crotch and looked down at his own body. There was not a vestige of fat on him, each individual muscle was outlined clearly beneath the sun-darkened skin. He had not been in this extreme condition since the closing days of the war. He was like a thoroughbred racehorse brought up to its peak by a skilful trainer on the eve of a major race.

The sergeant lent him a steel comb and he brushed his hair out. It fell almost to his shoulders, thick and wavy and sparkling from the wash. He put on his damp clothes and let them dry on his body. He felt good, that charged restless feeling of being at the very pinnacle of physical fitness.

The officers' mess was an underground dugout devoid of ornament or decoration. The furniture was crude and hand-hewn. His hosts were the major, a captain and two young subalterns.

The food made up for its lack of artistic presentation by its abundance. A huge steaming bowl of stew made with sun-dried fish and chillis, the fiery *peri-peri* that was a relic of the Portuguese colonialists, and great mounds of the ubiquitous maize-meal porridge.'

It was the best meal Sean had eaten since leaving Chiwewe, but the highlight of the evening was the drink that the major provided, unlimited quantities of real civilized beer in metal cans. The labels read 'Castle Lager' and in small print at the bottom, 'Verwaardig in Suid Afrika, Made in South Africa'. It was an indication as to which country was Renamo's good friend.

As the guest in mess, Sean proposed the first toast. He stood and raised his beer can.

'Renamo,' he said. 'And the people of Mozambique.'

The major replied, 'President Botha, and the people of South Africa,' which settled it conclusively. They knew Sean was from the south and was, therefore, an honoured guest.

He felt so secure in their company that he could relax and for the first time in months allow himself to get moderately drunk.

The major had fought for the Rhodesians during the bush war. He told Sean that like Job Bhekani he had been a subaltern in the Rhodesian African Rifles, the elite black regiment which had fought so effectively and inflicted such slaughter amongst the ZANLA guerrillas. They soon established the camaraderie of old brothers-in-arms. Without obviously pumping him, Sean was able to nudge the conversation along and pick up the crumbs of information that the major let fall more freely as the cans of beer were consumed.

Sean's estimation had been correct. This was part of the northern perimeter of a Renamo army group. The fortifications were deep and dispersed as a precaution against aerial bombardment. From this base, they marauded southwards, hitting the Frelimo garrisons and strafing and raiding the railway line between Beira on the coast and Harare, the capital of Zimbabwe.

While they were still working on the first case of beer, Sean and the major discussed with seriousness the significance of that rail link. Zimbabwe was a completely land-locked nation. Its only arteries to the outside world were the two railway lines. The major one was southwards, into South Africa, via Johannesburg to the major ports of Durban and Cape Town.

Mugabe's Marxist government bitterly resented being reliant on the nation which, for them, epitomized all that was evil in Africa, the bastion of capitalism and the free-market system, the nation which had for the eleven long years of the bush war propped up the white regime of Ian Smith. Mugabe's hysterical rhetoric against his southern neighbour was incessant and yet the foul hand of apartheid was curled around his jugular vein. His instinct was to look eastward into Mozambique for salvation. During his struggle for independence Mugabe had been nobly assisted by the Frelimo President of Mozambique, Samora Machel, whose own struggle against the Portuguese had only just culminated in freedom from the colonial yoke.

Frelimo, his brother Marxists, had provided Mugabe with recruits and arms and full support for his guerrillas. Without reservation, they had offered him the use of bases within their territory from which to launch his attacks on Rhodesia. It was only natural now that he turned once more to Mozambique to provide an escape from this awful humiliation of being seen by the rest of Africa, by his brothers in the Organization of African Unity, to be dealing with the monster of the south, not only dealing with, but totally dependent upon it for every litre of gasoline, for every ounce of the daily stuff of survival.

The railway line to the port of Beira on the Mozambique channel was the natural solution to his predicament. Of course, the port facilities and the main-line system under the African socialist management had been allowed to fall into almost total disrepair. The solution to that was simple and well-tried: massive aid from the developed nations of the West. As every good African Marxist knew, they were fully entitled to this, and any attempt to withhold it could be countered by the equally simple and well-tried expedient of dubbing it blatant racism. That dread accusation would force immediate compliance. The estimate of the costs of work needed to restore the port and main line to full efficiency was four billion American dollars. However, as actual costs in Africa usually exceeded estimates by a hundred per cent, the sum of eight billion dollars was more realistic. A mere bagatelle, nothing more than their due, a fair price for the West to pay for the pleasure and prestige that Mugabe would derive from being able to thumb his nose at the monster of the south.

There was only one small obstacle in his way, the army of Renamo. It sat astride that vital rail link, attacking it almost daily, blowing up bridges and culverts, ripping out the tracks and shooting up rolling stock.

The actual damage they caused was minor compared to the fact that their depredations gave the Western governments a fine excuse for withholding the funds needed to restore the main line to the condition in which it would be able to carry all of Zimbabwe's imports and exports.

The Frelimo government's efforts to protect the line were so fumbling and inept that the Zimbabweans themselves were forced to assist them. Over ten thousand of Mugabe's own troops were tied up in trying to fend off Renamo attacks on the line. Sean had heard estimates of the cost of these operations to Zimbabwe's economy, already one of the shakiest in sub-Saharan Africa, as high as a million dollars a day.

It was ironic that Mugabe, once the guerrilla, was now forced into the role of passive defender of fixed hardware and permanent positions. He was experiencing the stings of the flea, that he had once so merrily dispensed.

Sean and the Renamo major laughed at the joke, and began on the second case of good apartheid lager. This marked the passing of the time for serious conversation.

Now they reminisced happily about the days of the bush war and they soon discovered that they had both been at the same contact in the Mavuradonhas on the day when they had killed forty-six guerrillas, 'a good kill', as a successful action was always referred to. Sean's Scouts had lain in wait in the gulleys and re-entrances to the hills, acting in the role of stop group, while the RAR had dropped by parachute on the far side and formed the sweep line to drive the terrorists onto the Scouts.

'You drove out as many bush-buck as gooks,' Sean remembered. 'I didn't know which to shoot first.' And they laughed and talked of other dangerous sorties, of crazy ops and of wild chases and 'good kills'.

They drank to Ian Smith, the Ballantyne Scouts and the Rhodesian African Rifles. There was still plenty of beer remaining so they drank to Ronald Reagan and Margaret Thatcher. When they ran out of conservative leaders to toast, Sean suggested, 'Damnation to Gorbachev!'

This was enthusiastically adopted, and the major countered immediately with, 'Damnation to Frelimo and Chissano.' The list of left-wingers was longer than that of conservatives, but they worked their way steadily down it, damning them all from Neil Kinnock to Teddy Kennedy and Jesse Jackson.

When they finally parted, Sean and the major embraced like brothers. Sean had filled all his pockets with cans of beer, so that when he returned to his Shangane guards they too greeted him affectionately as he distributed the cans amongst them.

In the morning, the Shangane sergeant shook him awake while it was still dark. Sean's headache was terrifying and his mouth tasted as though a hyena had slept in it. It was one of the penances of being superbly physically fit. The body's reaction to the abuse of alcohol was proportionately violent, the hangovers more fierce, and he had not a single aspirin for solace.

However, by the middle of the morning Sean had sweated out the last drops of stale beer. Their route was still south and west, and as they ran they saw many more fortifications and strong points. As the major had told him, they were cunningly dispersed and hidden. He saw light field artillery in sandbagged emplacements, together with mortars in their redoubts, and detachments armed with RPG rockets, the mobile hand-held stalwarts of the guerrilla arsenal. All the troops he saw seemed to be cheerful and of high morale, well-fed and equipped. Nearly all of them wore the tiger-striped camouflage and combat boots with rubber soles and canvas uppers.

His escort had replenished their packs from the garrison stores. When they stopped to eat, the maize meal was in two-kilo paper sacks marked 'Premier Mills', and the matches with which they lit the fire were 'Lion Matches' and the new bars of soap 'Sunlight', all with the familiar double legend beneath the name, 'Verwaardig in Suid Afrika, Made in South Africa'.

'It's almost like being home again,' Sean chuckled.

*

272

The Renamo defensive lines were in concentric rings like the ripples on a pond, and soon Sean realized they were approaching the centre. They passed what were obviously training areas, where fresh-faced black recruits, both male and female, some of them in their early teens, sat in rows under thatched sun shelters like school-children in a classroom studying the makeshift blackboard so attentively that they barely glanced up as Sean's detachment trotted by.

From the blackboards, Sean saw that the subjects they were being taught ranged from the infantry field manual to political theory.

Beyond the rear training areas they entered what appeared to be a series of low sparsely manned kopjes. It was only when they were within a few metres of the side of one of these hills, that Sean spotted the entrances to the dugouts.

They were more elaborately constructed and cunningly concealed than the others that they had been passing all day. These would be invisible from the air and impervious to aerial bombardment, and Sean could tell, by the changed deportment of his guards and their more severe posture towards him, that they had reached the headquarters area of the Renamo army group.

Still, he was taken by surprise when without ceremony they turned aside and drew up at the entrance to one of the underground bunkers. There was a brief exchange while the Shangane sergeant handed Sean over to the guards at the entrance, before Sean was hustled down the steps into the subterranean maze of corridors and caverns hacked out of the earth. The bunker was lit by bare electric bulbs and somewhere far-off, he heard the hum of a generator. The side walls were revetted with sandbags that had been dressed neatly and the roof was reinforced with hewn logs.

They entered a communications room. Sean saw at a glance that the radio equipment was sophisticated and well maintained. A large-scale map of the whole northern and central Mozambique provinces of Zambezia and Manica covered one wall.

Sean studied the map surreptitiously. He saw at once that the broken mountainous ground in which this Renamo army group was ensconced was the Serra da Gorongosa, the mountains of Gorongosa, and that the river they had crossed which formed the Renamo defensive line was the Pungwe river. The main railway line ran only thirty or forty miles further south of this position, but before he could glean more information from the map, he was hurried down another short passageway at the end of which there was a curtained-off doorway.

His escort called a respectful request to enter and the reply was sharp and authoritative. One of them prodded Sean and he pushed the curtain aside and stepped into the room beyond.

'Comrade China,' Sean smiled. 'What a pleasant surprise.'

'That form of address is no longer appropriate, Colonel Courtney. In future, please address me as General China, or simply as "Sir".'

He sat at a desk in the centre of the dugout. He was dressed in the ubiquitous tiger-striped battledress, but it was adorned with silver paratrooper wings and four rows of gaudy ribbons across his left breast. A yellow silk scarf was knotted at his throat and his maroon beret and webbing belt hung on a peg behind him. The butt of the automatic pistol in the webbing holster was ivory-handled. General China was obviously taking his conversion from Marxism to capitalism very seriously.

'I understand that you have acquitted yourself well during the last few days and that you are sympathetic towards Renamo, its allies and its objectives.' His attitude towards Sean was benign, and it made him uneasy.

'How do you know that?' he demanded.

'We do have radio, you know, Colonel. We aren't total

274

barbarians.' China indicated the VHF set on the bench along the side wall of the dugout. 'You passed a pleasant evening with Major Takawira, at my suggestion.'

'Now would you like to tell me what the hell this is all about, General. You have abducted the citizens of two friendly and powerful nations, South Africa and America.'

General China held up his hands to stop him. 'Please spare me your outrage, Colonel. Our people in Lisbon and elsewhere have already received complaints from both the Americans and the South Africans. Of course, we have denied abducting anybody, and adopted an attitude of injured innocence.' He paused and studied Sean for a moment. 'Very enterprising of you to have got a message to the American embassy so soon, but then I wouldn't have expected anything less of you.'

Before Sean could reply, he lifted the hand-set of the field telephone on his desk and spoke quietly in a language that Sean recognized as Portuguese but could not understand. He hung up and glanced expectantly towards the screen doorway, and instinctively Sean did the same.

The canvas curtain was drawn aside and three persons ducked through the dugout. There were two uniformed black women carrying sidearms and AK rifles and between them, escorted closely, dressed in sun-bleached but freshly laundered khaki shirt and loose-fitting shorts, the same clothes she had worn when last he saw her, was Claudia Monterro.

She was thin. That was the first thing that struck Sean. Her hair was drawn back and tied in a plait at the back of her head, and she was tanned to the colour of melba toast.

Her eyes were huge in her thin face and he had never before truly noticed the fine structure of her cheek and jaw bones. At the sight of her his heart seemed to stop and swell against his ribs, and then race away again.

'Claudia!' he said, and her head jerked towards him. The blood drained from her face, leaving a *café-au-lait* colour beneath her tan.

'Oh my God,' she whispered, 'I was so afraid . . .' she broke off, and they stared at each other, neither of them moving for a dozen beats of his heart, then she said his name. 'Sean.' And it sounded like a sob. She swayed towards him and lifted her hands, palms upward in a gesture of supplication, and her eyes were filled with all the suffering and hardship and longing of these last days. With two long strides, he reached her and she threw herself against him and closed her eyes and pressed her face against him. She had both arms locked around his chest, the strength of her grip hampered his breathing.

'Darling,' he whispered, and stroked her hair; it felt thick and springing under his fingers. 'My darling, it's all right now.'

She lifted her face to him and her lips quivered and parted. Blood had flowed back under the smooth brown skin. She seemed to glow and the light in her eyes had changed to the sparkle of dark yellow topaz.

'You called me darling,' she whispered.

He lowered his head over her and kissed her. Her lips opened under his and the inside of her mouth was hot and lubricious. He probed it deeply with his tongue and it tasted like the sap of sweet young grass.

From the desk, General China said quietly in Shangane, 'Very well, now take the woman away.'

Her guards seized Claudia and plucked her out of his embrace. She gave a small despairing wail and tried to resist, but they were powerful heavily built women, and between them they lifted her feet off the ground and hustled her back through the screen doorway.

Sean shouted, 'Leave her,' and started after them, but one of the guards drew the pistol from her webbing holster and pointed it at his belly. The canvas screen dropped between them and Claudia's cries of protest dwindled as she was dragged away. In the silence, Sean turned slowly back to the man at the desk.

'You bastard,' he whispered furiously. 'You set that up.'

'It went better than I could possibly have hoped for,' General China agreed, 'although some previous conversation that I had with Miss Monterro concerning you gave me the idea that she was more interested in you as a man than as a professional hunter.'

'I'd like to twist your head off your shoulders. If you hurt her . . .'

'Come, come, Colonel Courtney. I'm not going to hurt her. She is far too valuable. She is a bargaining chip, surely you realize that.'

Slowly Sean's fury abated and he nodded stiffly.

'Okay, China, what do you want?'

'Good.' General China nodded. 'I was waiting for you to ask that question. Sit down.' He indicated one of the stools facing his desk. 'I'll order a pot of tea and we can talk.'

While they waited for the tea, General China busied himself with the papers on his desk, reading and signing a batch of orders. It gave Sean a chance to recover himself. When an orderly brought the tea, General China gestured for him to clear the papers from the desk.

When they were alone again, China sipped at his mug and regarded Sean over the rim. 'You ask what it is that I want. Well, I must confess that at first, it was nothing more complicated than simple retribution. After all, Colonel, it was you that destroyed my command that day at the camp at Inhlozane. You put the only blemish on my professional career, and you inflicted permanent physical damage on my person.' He touched his ear. 'Reason enough for me to want revenge. I'm sure you will agree.'

Sean remained silent. Although he had not tasted tea in days and craved it, he had not touched the mug which stood on the edge of the desk in front of him.

'Of course, I knew that you were operating the Chiwewe hunting concession. In fact, as a junior minister of Mugabe's government, I was one of those who gave approval to the grant. I thought, even then, that it might be useful to have you so close to the border.'

Sean forced himself to relax. He realized that he might learn more, achieve more by a show of co-operation rather than defiance. It was difficult to do, for he could still taste Claudia's mouth. He picked up the tea mug and took a mouthful.

'You certainly get around,' he smiled. 'Comrade one day, general the next. Marxist government minister one day, Renamo warlord the next.'

China waved a hand deprecatingly. 'The dialectics of Marxism never truly interested me. Looking back now, I realize that I enlisted in the guerrilla army for a very good capitalistic reason. At the time it was the best way to get on in life – does that make any sense to you, Colonel?'

'Perfect sense,' Sean agreed. This time his smile was genuine. 'It's a well-known fact that the only way communism can be made to work is if you have capitalists to pay the bill and manage the show.'

'You phrased that very well.' China nodded his appreciation. 'I only found that out later, once ZANLA had ousted Smith and taken over the government in Harare. I discovered that as a former guerrilla I was feared and mistrusted by the soft fat cats who had avoided the actual fighting but now had taken control of the show. I saw that far from receiving my just rewards, I was more likely to end up in Chikarubi prison so I allowed my capitalistic instinct to guide me. With a few other like-minded citizens, we were arranging another change of government, and we were able to convince some of my old comrades-in-arms, who occupied senior positions in the Zimbabwe army, that I would make a suitable replacement for Robert Mugabe.'

'The good old African game of coup and counter-coup,' Sean suggested.

'It is refreshing to talk to someone who follows the

reasoning so readily,' China nodded approval. 'But then you are an African, albeit of the less fashionable hue.'

'I'm flattered to be recognized as one,' Sean told him. But to return to your altruistic desire to put the best man in charge . . .'

'Ah, yes . . . well, somebody boasted to a woman, and she told her other lover who just happened to be Mugabe's Chief of Intelligence, and I was forced to cross the border in some haste, and here I fell in with yet others of my former comrades who now had joined Renamo.'

'But why Renamo?' Sean asked.

'It is my natural political home. I am good at what I do and Renamo welcomed me. You see, I am part Shangane. As you know our tribe sprawls over both sides of the artificial line imposed by surveyors of the colonial era, who took no consideration of demographic realities when they agreed on borders.'

'If you are now a capitalist, General China, as you claim to be, then there must be more in it than that. Some future reward in store for you?'

'You do not disappoint me,' China said: 'You are as perceptive and devious as any African. Naturally, there is something in it for me. When I have assisted Renamo to form the new government of Mozambique with South Africa as its ally, between them they will be able to apply irresistible pressure on Zimbabwe. They will be able to force a change of government in Harare . . . a new president to replace Mugabe.'

'From General China to President China in one mighty bound,' Sean cut in. 'I'll give you one thing, General, you don't think small.'

'I'm touched by your appreciation of my aspirations.'

'But where does all this leave me? You talked earlier of revenge for your impaired hearing – what made you so forgiving?'

China frowned and touched his ear. 'To tell the truth I

would have enjoyed that. In fact, I had already planned a nocturnal raid on your camp at Chiwewe. I had moved up a unit of my men to the border opposite your concession, and was awaiting only an opportunity to escape from my duties here for a few days personally to pay you a visit, when a change of plan was forced upon me.'

Sean raised an eyebrow to signal his interest and attention.

'Very recently there has been a drastic alteration in the balance of power here in the central province. We of Renamo had fought ourselves into a dominant position. In fact, we control all the country except the major towns, we have reduced food production to the point where Frelimo must rely almost entirely on foreign aid, we have virtually strangled their transport system. We raid the roads and railways at will, and our forces move freely about the countryside recruiting from the villages. We have, in fact, set up our own alternative administration. However, all that changed very recently.'

'What happened?'

China did not answer immediately, but stood up from the desk and went to stand in front of the wall map. 'As a distinguished counter-guerrilla fighter, Colonel Courtney, I do not have to explain our strategy to you nor do I have to lecture you on the weapons that we employ in the "war of the flea". We don't fear nuclear bombs, heavy artillery or modern pursuit planes. We chuckled when Robert Mugabe purchased two squadrons of fighters from his Soviet friends, obsolete MIG 23. Floggers that the Russians were pleased to be rid of and which Mugabe cannot afford to keep in the air. There are few, very few modern weapons that we fear except . . .' China paused and turned to face Sean again, 'but you are the expert, Colonel. You know as much as any man alive about anti-guerrilla operations. What do we fear most?'

Sean did not hesitate. 'Helicopter gunships,' he said.

China sat down heavily in his seat again. 'Three weeks ago the Soviets delivered a full squadron of Hind helicopters to the Frelimo air force.'

Sean whistled softly. 'Hinds!' he said. 'In Afghanistan they call them the Flying Death.'

'Here we call them *henshaw* – the falcons.'

'There is no air force in Africa that could keep a squadron of Hinds in the air for more than a few days, they simply don't have the back-up,' Sean shook his head, but China contradicted him quietly.

'The Russians have supplied technicians and munitions and spares, as well as pilots. They aim to smash Renamo in six months.'

'Will they succeed? Can they succeed?'

'Yes,' China said firmly. 'Already they have severely limited our mobility. Without mobility, a guerrilla army is defeated.' He made a gesture that took in the dugout. 'Here we cower underground like moles, not warriors. Our morale, which was so high just a month ago is crumbling away. Instead of looking proudly ahead, my men cringe and look to the skies.'

'It's not an easy life, General,' Sean commiserated with him. 'I'm sure you'll come up with something.'

'I already have,' China nodded. 'You.'

'Me against a squadron of Hinds?' Sean chuckled. 'I am flattered, but include me out.'

'That is not possible, Colonel. As the Americans say, you owe me one.' He touched his ear. 'And I owe you one, Miss Monterro.'

'All right,' Sean nodded with resignation. 'Spell it out for me.'

'The plan that I have in mind requires a white face and a trained officer who understands black troops and speaks their language.'

'Surely, General China, you don't subscribe to old General von Lettow-Vorbeck's theory that the best bush troops in the world are black soldiers with white officers. Why the hell don't you do whatever this is yourself?'

'I know my own limitations,' China said. 'I am a better administrator than a soldier. Besides, I have explained, I need a white face.' He held up one hand to prevent Sean interrupting again. 'Initially you'll be working with a small group. Ten men.'

'My Shangane escort,' Sean got ahead of him. 'That's the real reason you sent me off on that little jaunt with them.'

'Perceptive, Colonel. Yes, your reputation seems to be well founded. In just a few days you have gained their respect and, dare I say it, loyalty. I think that they'll follow you on the most hazardous assignment.'

'I'll need more than ten Shanganes, there are two others I want with me.'

'Of course, your Matabeles,' China agreed readily. 'They are definitely part of my calculations.'

This was the opportunity to enquire about Job and Dedan for which Sean had been waiting.

'Are they both safe?' he demanded.

'Quite safe and well, I assure you.'

'I won't even discuss anything further until I have seen them and spoken to them,' he said flatly, and China's eyes narrowed.

'I beg you not to adopt that attitude, Colonel. It will only make our future relationship difficult and unpleasant.'

'I mean it,' Sean repeated stubbornly. 'I want to speak to my men.'

General China glanced at his wristwatch and then sighed theatrically.

'Very well.' He lifted the hand-set of the telephone and spoke into it again, then looked up at Sean. 'The two of them will be required to work with you, you can explain that to them. There is an excellent chance that, with all your co-operation, I will be persuaded to give you your freedom. Of course that offer of freedom includes the nubile Miss Monterro.'

'You are very generous,' Sean was ironic.

'Wait until you hear my full terms. You might think I drive a hard bargain.' General China turned to the lieutenant who came through the doorway in response to his summons and said in Shangane, 'Take this man to visit the two Matabele prisoners,' he ordered. 'You may allow them to talk for –' again he glanced at his wristwatch – 'ten minutes. Then bring him back here.'

There were three men in the escort that marched Sean down the underground passages and out into the dazzling sunshine.

The prison barracks consisted of a single hut of mud daub and thatch surrounded by a stockade of poles and barbed wire, the whole covered by a spread of camouflage net. A warder unlocked the gate to the stockade and Sean went in. He walked to the door of the hut.

Over an open fireplace in the centre of the floor stood a black three-legged pot. Two thin mattresses of split reeds on each side of it were the only other furnishings. Dedan was asleep on the one mattress, while on the other Job sat cross-legged and stared into the smouldering coals.

'I see you, old friend,' Sean said softly in Sindebele, and Job came slowly to his feet, and just as slowly began to smile.

'I see you also,' he said, and then they laughed and embraced, clapping each other on the back. Dedan jumped up from the other mattress, grinning with delight, and seized Sean's hand, pumping it brutally.

'What took you so long, Sean?' Job asked. 'Did you find Tukutela? Where is the American? How did they catch you?'

'I'll tell you all that later,' Sean cut him off, 'there are more important things now. Have you spoken to China, did you recognize him as the one we caught at Inhlozane?'

'Yes, the one with the ear. What are our chances with him, Sean?'

'Too early to be sure,' Sean warned. 'But he is talking about some sort of deal.'

'What?' Job broke off, and they both spun to face the door of the hut.

Outside there was the abrupt shrilling of alarm whistles and wild shouts.

'What's going on?' Sean demanded, and strode to the doorway. The gate to the stockade was still wide open, but the guards were scattering, unslinging their weapons and peering up at the sky. The lieutenant was blowing shrill hysterical blasts on his whistle as he ran.

'Air raid,' said Job at Sean's shoulder. 'Frelimo gunships, there was one two days ago.'

Sean heard the engines now, very faint and distant, and the whistling whine of the rotors, growing swiftly shriller and more penetrating.

'Job!' Sean grabbed his arm. 'Do you know where they are holding Claudia?'

'Over there,' Job pointed through the doorway. 'A stockade like this one.'

'How far?'

'Five hundred metres.'

'The gates are open, and the guards are gone. We are going to make a bolt for it.'

'We are in the middle of an army, and what about the gunships?' Job protested. 'Where can we go?'

'Don't argue, let's go.'

Sean raced through the doorway and out of the stockade gates. Job and Dedan were close behind him.

'Which way?' Sean grunted.

'Over there, beyond that clump of trees.'

The three of them ran in a bunch. The camp was almost deserted as Renamo took to their dugouts and bunkers, but Sean saw that there were crews manning the light anti-

284

aircraft guns in the fixed emplacements, and they passed a small detachment armed with the portable RPG rocket-launchers heading for the nearest kopje. Elevation would give them a good field of fire from which to launch. However, the RPG was not an infra-red seeker and had very limited surface-to-air capability.

The Renamo were so preoccupied that not one of them even glanced at Sean's white face as they scurried to take up their positions. Now the whistle of approaching rotors was punctuated by the crackle and rap of ground fire.

Sean did not even look round. Ahead, he saw the glint of barbed wire. The women's stockade was also well camouflaged under brush and netting, and it too seemed deserted by the female wardens.

'Claudia!' he shouted, as he came up to the fence and gripped the wire. 'Where are you?'

'Here, Sean, here!' she yelled back. There were two huts inside the stockade wire. The doors were locked and there were no windows. Claudia's voice came from the nearest building, and was almost drowned out by the thunder of engines, the shriek of rotors, and the roar of ground fire.

'Give me a boost,' Sean ordered, and backed away from the wire. The fence was seven feet high, he judged. Job and Dedan ran forward and crouched below it. Sean sprinted straight at them and as he leapt up, he drove his feet into the cupped hands they had formed for him with interlocking fingers. In unison, they bobbed up and flung their arms high, flipping Sean forward and over. He cleared the wire easily, somersaulted in the air and landed on his feet. He cushioned the shock, tumbling like a paratrooper, and rolled smoothly back onto his feet, using his momentum to hurl himself forward.

'Clear the door!' he yelled at Claudia, as he built up speed and crashed into the crude hand-hewn panel.

It was too solid and heavy to shatter under the drive of his shoulder, but the hinges ripped clean out of the daubed wall, and crashed inwards in a cloud of dust and flying fragments of dried mud.

Claudia was crouched against the far wall, but as he burst into the hut behind the falling door panel, she rushed forward to meet him. He caught her in his arms, but when she tried to kiss him, he whirled her round by one arm, and ran with her to the door.

'What's happening?' she gasped.

'We are making a break.' As they ran out into the sunlight again he saw that Job and Dedan had a hold on the bottom strand of the fence. With all the strength of their arms and legs, they were dragging it upwards, opening a narrow gap between the wire and the sun-baked earth. Sean stooped to the same strand from the inside, settling his grip between the clusters of spikes and he heaved upwards. Under the combined strength of the three of them the ground at the foot of the nearest fence pole cracked and gave, the pole was lifted a few inches out of the hole in which it was planted, and the strand of wire came up in their hands.

'Down on your belly!' Sean grunted at Claudia. 'Get under it!'

She was lean and nimble as a ferret, and the barbs cleared her back with inches to spare as she wriggled through.

'Hold it!' Sean barked at Job, and they strained up, black muscles knotting, faces contorted with the effort.

Sean dropped flat and pushed himself under the wire. Halfway through he felt one of the steel spikes snag in his flesh and stop him dead.

'Pull me through,' he ordered, and while Dedan continued to hold up the wire, Job stooped and they linked hands in a fireman's grip.

'Pull!' Sean ordered, and Job heaved. Sean felt his flesh tear and the blood spurt down his back, then he was free.

As he rolled to his feet Claudia gasped, 'Your back!' But he seized her arm again and demanded of Job, 'Which way?' He knew that Job would have studied the camp during the days he had been imprisoned here. He could rely on his judgement.

'The river,' Job responded immediately. 'If we can float down, clear of the camp.'

'Lead the way,' Sean ordered, and he had to shout to make himself heard. All around them rose the stutter of automatic small arms fire. The deeper clatter of heavy machine-guns, sounding like a stick drawn sharply across a sheet of corrugated iron, and then even that din was drowned out by a thunder like the Victoria Falls in flood. Sean knew exactly what it was, although he had never heard it before. The sound of the Gatling-type, multi-barrelled cannon mounted in the nose of a Hind helicopter, firing 12.7mm bullets like the jet of a fire hose.

He felt Claudia falter beside him at the gut-melting terror of that sound, and he jerked her arm.

'Come on!' he snarled at her. 'Run!' She was still limping slightly from her injured knee ligament, as they followed Job and Dedan down towards the river. Though they were still under the spread branches of the forest, just ahead of them was open ground.

A small party of Renamo were doubling across this opening, coming up the track towards them, eight or nine men in Indian file and each of them carried an RPG mobile rocket-launcher. As they ran, their faces were turned up towards the sky, seeking a target for their rockets.

The detachment of rocketeers was still two hundred metres from them when suddenly the earth around them erupted. Sean had never in all his war experience seen anything like it. The ground dissolved, seemed to turn to a liquid that boiled into a fog of dust under the jet of 12.7mm cannon shells.

Along a wide swathe of cannon fire all was destroyed, even the trees disappeared in a whirlwind of wood fragments and shredded leaves; only the shattered stumps still stood as the storm of fire passed on. The ground was left like the furrows of a freshly ploughed field and on it was scattered the remains of the party of RPG rocket men. They were hacked and minced as though they had been fed through the cogs of some fearsome machinery.

Sean still had a grip on Claudia's arm and he pulled her down into the grass beside the track just as a shadow swept over them. However, the canopy of branches overhead must have screened them from the eyes of the gunner in the helicopter. Job and Dedan had also dived for cover in the grass verge beside the path and avoided detection.

The Hind cruised overhead, barely fifty feet above the tops of the trees, and abruptly they had a full view of the machine as it crossed over the open ground where the torn corpses of the rocket men lay scattered.

Sean felt a physical shock at the sight of it. He had not expected it to be so large and so grotesquely ugly. It was fifty feet long.

The Russians themselves called it 'Sturmovich', the humpback. It was a deformed monster: aberrant and ungainly, the green and brown splotches of tropical camouflage gave it the appearance of disease and leprous decay. The bulging double canopies of armoured glass looked like malevolent eyes and so fierce was their gaze that Sean instinctively flattened himself in the grass and flung a protective arm over Claudia's back.

Below the gross body of the gunship hung an assembly of rocket pods, and as they stared at it in awe the machine hovered and rotated on its own axis, lowered its blunt unlovely nose and fired a spread of rockets.

They launched with fiery sibilance on plumes of white smoke, streaking across the river and bursting on the ant's nests of sandbagged bunkers in fountains of flame and smoke and dust.

The noise was deafening and the shrill whine of the gunship's rotors was like an awl screwing into their eardrums. Claudia covered both her ears and sobbed.

'Oh God! Oh God!'

The Hind revolved slowly, seeking fresh targets, and again they cowered away from it. It moved away from them, hunting along the bank of the river. The Gatling-cannon in its remotely controlled turret in the nose fired blasts of solid metal into the forest, destroying all in its path.

'Let's go!' Sean shouted above the uproar and dragged Claudia to her feet. Job and Dedan ran ahead of them, and the earth ploughed by the gunship's cannons was soft and spongy under their feet.

As they passed the dead men, Job stooped without breaking his run and snatched up one of the undamaged RPG launchers. At the next stride he stooped again and grabbed a fibreglass back-pack that contained three of the finned projectiles for the RPG, and then went bounding away, on towards the riverbank. With her injured knee, Claudia could not match that pace, and even with Sean pulling her along they fell almost a hundred yards behind.

Job and Dedan reached the riverbank. It was steep and rocky, fractured cliffs of water-polished black stone. A gallery of tall riverine trees spread their branches out over the swiftly flowing apple-green waters.

Job looked back at them anxiously, for they were still out in the open. His face contorted as he screamed a warning and dropped the fibreglass pack at his feet and swung the short squat barrel of the RPG up to his shoulder, pointing it at the sky above Sean's head.

Sean did not look up, he knew there was no time for that. He had not isolated the shrieking rotors of the second incoming Hind from the deafening uproar caused by the first machine, but now the din was escalating to the point of pain.

Running beside them was a narrow donga, eroded by the storm waters of the rainy season, but now dry and sheer-sided. Sean swept Claudia off her feet and jumped with her in his arms. The earthen gulley was six feet deep and they hit the bottom with an impact that clashed Sean's teeth together in his jaws just as the lip of the gulley dissolved under a jet of cannon fire.

The earth on which they lay shuddered like a live thing beneath them, as though they were insects being shaken from the flanks of a gigantic horse. Earth, ripped from the lip of the gulley by the sheets of cannon fire, fell on them in clouds, heavy clods raining on their backs, knocking the breath out of them, dust choking them, burying them alive.

Claudia screamed and tried to fight herself out from under the layer of dust and dry earth, but Sean held her down.

'Lie still,' he hissed at her. 'Don't move, you dilly bird.' The Hind swivelled and cruised back, now directly over the gulley, searching for them, the gunner traversing the thick stack of multi-barrels of the Gatling-cannon in its remote turret.

Sean turned his head slightly, looking up from the corner of one eye. His vision was obscured by dust, but as it cleared, he saw the great splotched nose of the Hind hanging in the air only fifty feet directly overhead. The gunner must have picked out their white skins, which made them targets of preference. Only the thin layer of fresh earth protected them from his scrutiny through the gunsight of his cannon.

'Hit him, Job,' Sean pleaded aloud. 'Hit the bastard.'

On the cliff above the river, Job dropped on one knee. The RPG 7 was one of his favourite weapons. The huge gunship was hovering over the gulley only fifty yards away.

He aimed twelve inches below the edge of the pilot's canopy. The RPG was highly inaccurate, and even at point-blank range he gave himself latitude should the missile fly off track. He held the cross-wire steady for a beat of his pumping heart and then pressed the trigger. The exhaust of white smoke blew back over his shoulder and the rocket streaked away, flying fair and true, to strike only inches higher than he had aimed on the rim where the armoured glass canopy joined the camouflaged metal fuselage.

The rocket burst with the force which would blow the engine block out of a Mac truck, or burst the boiler of a railway locomotive. For an instant, the front of the Hind was obliterated by flame and smoke, and Job whooped triumphantly, jumping to his feet, expecting the hideous monster to crash out of the sky in a sheet of its own smoke and fire.

Instead the huge helicopter jumped higher, as though the pilot had flinched at the rocket-burst close beside him, but when the smoke blew away, Job realized with disbelief that the fuselage was unscathed. There was only a sooty black smear on the painted metal to mark the spot where the rocket had struck.

As he stared the ugly nose of the Hind swivelled towards him, and the many-eyed muzzles of the cannon sought him out. Job hurled the RPG launcher away, and jumped out from the cliff top, dropping twenty feet to hit the water, just as the cannon tore the great branches from the tree under which he had stood. Cannon fire chewed through the trunk as cleanly as a lumberjack's cross-saw and the whole tree leaned outwards and then toppled down the cliff and hit the surface of the river in a cloud of spray.

The Hind pulled away, lifting and banking, cruising on down the riverbank. Unharmed by the rocket hit and as deadly as before, it sought its next target.

Sean crawled to his knees, coughing and gasping.

'Are you all right?' he croaked, but for a moment Claudia could not answer him. Her eyes were blinded with sand, and her tears cut wet runnels through the dust that caked her cheeks.

'We've got to get into the water.' Sean pulled her to her feet, and half-pushed half-pulled her up the side of the gully.

They ran together to the top of the cliff and looked down. The felled tree was floating away on the current, a huge raft of leafy branches.

'Jump!' Sean ordered, and Claudia did not hesitate. She threw herself far out, and dropped away to strike the water feet first. Sean followed while she was still in the air.

He surfaced with Claudia's head bobbing beside him. The dust was washed off her face, and her hair was slicked over her eyes, shiny with streaming water.

Together they struck out for the floating mass of branches and leaves. She was a strong swimmer, and even with boots on her feet and fully dressed, she kicked out powerfully and dragged herself through the water with a full over-arm crawl.

As she reached the floating tree trunk, Job stretched out a long arm and drew her in beneath the branches. Dedan was already there and Sean ducked in a second later. They each clung to a branch and the leaves formed a low green bower over their heads.

'I hit him,' Job complained angrily. 'I hit him right on the nose with a rocket. It was like hitting a bull buffalo with a slingshot. He just turned and came straight at me.'

Sean wiped the water from his eyes and face with the palm of his hand. 'Titanium armour plate,' he explained quietly. 'They are almost invulnerable to conventional fire, both pilot's cockpit and the engine compartment are tight and solid. The only thing you can do when one of those bastards comes at you is run and hide.'

He flicked his sodden hair back out of his eyes. 'Anyway, you pulled him off us. He was just about to blast us with that dirty great cannon.' Sean swam across to Claudia.

'You shouted at me,' she accused. 'You were quite rude. You called me a dilly bird.'

'Better abused than dead,' he grinned at her, and she smiled back.

'Is that an invitation, sir? I wouldn't mind a little abuse – from you.' Under water, he slipped an arm around her waist and hugged her.

'My God, how I have missed your cheek and sauce.'

She pressed herself against him. 'I only realized after you were gone . . .' she whispered.

'Me too,' he confessed. 'Up to then, I thought I couldn't stand you. Then I realized I just couldn't do without you.'

'I feel weak when you say that, tell me you really mean it.'

'Later,' he hugged her. 'First let's just try and get out of here alive.' He left her and paddled across to Job's side of the leafy cavern.

'Can you see the bank?'

Job nodded. 'Looks like the raid is over. They are coming out of the bunkers.'

Sean peered out from under the concealing branches. He saw troops moving cautiously about on the near bank.

'They'll be picking up the pieces for a while before they realize that we've scarpered, but keep an eye on them.'

He paddled across to Dedan who was watching the far bank.

'What do you see?'

'They are busy with themselves.' Dedan pointed. A stretcher party was working along the bank, picking up the dead and the wounded, while work details had already begun repairing the damaged fortifications and replacing destroyed camouflage. Nobody looked out across the river.

There was other debris floating downstream with them, severed branches and damaged equipment, empty oil drums, enough to draw attention away from their flimsy refuge.

'If we can avoid discovery until nightfall, we should have floated down beyond the army. Just keep both eyes wide open, Dedan.'

'*Mambo*,' he acknowledged, and concentrated his attention on the bank.

Sean swam quietly back to Claudia and hung on to the branch beside her. She reached out for him immediately.

'I don't like you to be away for even a moment,' she whispered. 'Did you really mean what you said?'

He kissed her and she kissed him back so fiercely that her teeth bruised his lower lip. He enjoyed the mild pain.

She broke the embrace at last and immediately demanded again, 'Did you mean it?'

'I can't do without you,' he answered.

'You can do better than that.'

'You are the most magnificent woman I've ever known.'

'That's not bad, but it's still not what I want to hear.'

'I love you,' he admitted.

'That's it, oh Sean, that's it. And I love you too.' She kissed him again, and they were oblivious to all else, their mouths blending and their bodies clinging wetly together below the surface.

Sean did not know how long it was until Job disturbed them. 'We are going ashore,' he called.

The push of the current had forced the floating tree to the outside of the next river bend and it was already dragging on the submerged sand bar. When Sean lowered his feet, he touched bottom.

'Walk it into deeper water,' Sean ordered, and still concealed beneath its leafy bulk, they heaved and pushed it out until they felt it come free of the sand bar and the current picked it up again and drifted it into the next stretch of the river.

Sean was panting from the effort as he hung on to a branch above him, only his head above the surface. Claudia paddled across to him and hung on to the same branch.

'Sean,' she said, and her mood had changed. 'I haven't been able to ask you, mostly because I don't want to hear the answer.' She broke off and drew a deep breath. 'My father?' she asked.

Sean was silent as he sought the words to tell her, but it was Claudia who spoke again.

'He didn't come back with you, did he?'

Sean shook his head and his sodden locks dangled into his face.

'Did he find his elephant?' she asked softly.

'Yes,' Sean answered simply.

'I'm glad,' she said. 'I wanted that to be my last gift to him.'

Now she let go of the branch and slipped both her arms around Sean's neck, laying her cheek against his so she did not have to watch his face as she asked the next question.

'Is my father dead, Sean? I must hear you say it before I will believe it.'

With his free arm he held her tightly and gathered himself to reply.

'Yes, my darling. Capo is dead, but he died a man's death – the kind he would have wanted, and Tukutela, his elephant, went with him. Do you want to hear the details?'

'No!' She shook her head, holding him tightly. 'Not now, perhaps not ever. He is dead, and a part of me and my life dies with him.'

He could find no word of comfort and he held her as she began to weep for her father. She wept silently, clinging to him, the grief shaking her. Her tears mingled with the droplets of river water on her face, but he tasted their diluted salt on his lips as he kissed her again and his heart went out to her.

So they floated down on the wide green river, with the smoke and the smell of battle drifting over them from the bombarded banks and the faint cries and groans of the wounded carrying to them across the water. Sean let her expend her silent grief, and slowly the sobs that rocked her abated and at last she whispered throatily:

'I don't know how I could have borne it without you to help me. You were so much alike, the two of you. I think that's what attracted me to you in the first place.'

'I take that as a compliment.'

'It was meant as one. He gave me a taste for men of power and strength.'

Floating beside them, almost within touching distance, was a corpse. Trapped air ballooned the tiger-striped camouflage battle jacket and the body floated on its back. The face was very young, a boy of fifteen years perhaps. His wounds were washed almost bloodless, just a faint pinky discharge like smoke in the green water drifted from them, but it was enough.

Sean saw the gnarled saurian heads, scaled like the bark of an ancient oak, coming swiftly down the current following the taint of blood. Ripples spreading from the hideous snouts, long tails fanning, two big crocodiles, racing each other for the prize.

One of the reptiles reached the corpse and reared out of the water; its jaws, lined with uneven rows of yellow fangs gaped wide, then closed over the corpse's arm. The fangs met through dead flesh with a grinding sound that carried clearly to them, and Claudia gasped and turned her head away.

Before the crocodile could pull the body below the surface the second reptile, even larger than the first, fastened its jaws into the dead belly, and began a gruesome tug-of-war.

The fangs of the crocodile are not designed to shear cleanly through meat and bone, so they held on with locked jaws and used their great combed tails to spin in the water, twisting viciously in a lather of white foam, rending the corpse between them, dismembering it, so they could hear the sinews tear and the joints of shoulder and groin separate.

In fascinated horror, Claudia looked back and gagged as one of the giant reptiles rose high out of the water with an arm in its jaws, and gulped at it convulsively. The creamy yellow scales of its throat bulged as the limb slid down and then it lunged back to tear another morsel from the body.

Tugging and fighting over the pathetic human fragments, they worked away from the floating tree and Sean, remembering the long tear in his back from the barbed wire, felt a lift of relief, for his own blood must be scenting the green waters.

'Oh God, it's all so horrible,' Claudia whispered. 'It's becoming a terrible nightmare.'

'This is Africa.' Sean held her, trying to give her courage. 'But I'm here with you now, it's going to be all right.'

'Will it, Sean? Do you think we will get out of this alive?'

'There is no money-back guarantee,' he admitted, 'if that's what you are asking for.'

She gave one last sob, and then leant back in his arms and looked steadily into his eyes.

'I'm sorry,' she said. 'I'm acting like a baby. I nearly let go there, but it won't happen again. I promise you that. At least I've found you, before it's too late.' She smiled at him with forced gaiety, bobbing with water up to her chin. 'We'll live for today, or what is left of it.'

'That's my girl.' He grinned back at her. 'Whatever happens, I'll be able to say I loved Claudia Monterro.'

'And was loved by her in turn,' she assured him, and she kissed him again, a long lingering kiss, warm and spiced with her tears, an expression not of lust but of longing, for both of them a pledge and an assurance, something true and certain in a world of dangerous uncertainty.

Sean was not even aware of his own pervading physical arousal, until she broke the kiss and demanded breathlessly, 'I want you now, this minute. I won't . . . I dare not wait. Oh God, Sean, my darling, now we are alive and in love, but by tonight we could both be dead. Take me now.'

He glanced quickly around their leafy arbour. Through the chinks he could see the banks. They seemed to have drifted below the Renamo fortifications. There was no further sign of life below the galleries of tall riverine trees, and the silence of the African noon was heavy and somnolent. Closer to them, just beyond arm's length, floated Job and Dedan, but only the backs of their bare heads were visible as they surveyed the riverbanks.

Sean looked back at Claudia, looked into her honey-gold eyes, and he wanted her. He knew that he had never wanted anything in his life so desperately.

'Just say it one more time,' she breathed huskily.

'I love you,' he said, and they kissed again, but a different type of kiss, hard where the first had been soft, hot where it had been warm, and savagely urgent where it had been gentle and lingering.

'Quickly,' she said into his mouth. 'Every second is precious.' And her hands below the surface of the water were tearing at their clothing. He had to use one hand to keep them from slipping under the green water, but with the other he helped her as best he could.

She opened the front of his bush jacket and then her own shirt to the waist and pressed herself to him. Her breasts were lubricated by the cool water. Her nipples were hard with wanting him, he could feel them distinctly sliding over his chest, they felt as big as ripe grapes.

He tugged the tongue of the leather belt that held her khaki shorts and she lifted herself to make it easier for him to un-zip the fly, and then kicked to free her legs as he worked the clinging wet cloth down over her buttocks. He slipped the garment over his arm to prevent it floating away and she was naked from the waist down. In frantic haste she opened the front of his trousers and thrust in both hands to scoop him out.

'Oh Sean,' she blurted. 'Oh God, my darling. You are so big, so hard. Oh please, quickly, quickly!'

In the water they were both weightless and as lithe as mating otters. Her long legs closed around his body wrapping him, her knees up under his armpits, her ankles locked across the small of his back as she searched for him blindly. He angled his hips to meet her thrusts and they almost succeeded but it slipped away harmlessly between their tense naked bellies.

She groaned softly with frustration and reached down and seized him again. Then with a lewd and beautiful arching of her back she took in just the tip of him. They strained against each other and suddenly her body went rigid and her golden eyes opened so wide they seemed to fill her face, as he went sliding full length into her. After the cold green water she was so hot that it was almost unbearable and he cried out involuntarily.

Both Job and Dedan glanced around in surprise, then looked away in embarrassment but Sean and Claudia were oblivious to all the world.

It was over very swiftly and she hung around his neck exhausted as a marathon runner at the end of a gruelling race.

Sean recovered his voice first. 'I'm sorry,' he said. 'It was so quick. I couldn't wait. Did you . . . ?'

'I was there long before you.' She grinned up at him, a lopsided and uncertain grin. 'It was like being in an auto accident, quick, but devastating!'

They remained locked together by the embrace of her legs and arms, for a long time, quiet and resting, until she felt him shrivel and slip away and only then she released the grip of her legs and reached up with her mouth to kiss him tenderly.

'Now you belong to me, and I to you. Even if I die today, it won't matter so much. I have had you in me.'

'Let's try for a little more than one day.' He smiled gently down at her. 'Get dressed now, my love.' He handed her back her clothing. 'While I check on what's happening in the real world out there.'

He swam away from her and went to Job. 'What do you see?' he asked.

'I think we are clear of the lines,' Job answered, avoiding

Sean's eyes tactfully. Strangely, it did not embarrass Sean that Job knew what had happened between Claudia and himself. He still felt elated and triumphant at the consummation of their love, and nothing could degrade it.

'As soon as it's dark enough, we'll swim the tree in towards the bank and get ashore.' Sean glanced at his Rolex. Not more than two hours to sunset. 'Keep your eyes open,' he said, and swam across to Dedan to repeat the warning.

He tried to estimate the rate of the current by watching the bank, and decided it was not more than two miles an hour. They would still be dangerously close to the Renamo lines when the sun set, and the river was flowing eastwards towards the sea, so they would have to work their way round or through General China's forces to reach the Zimbabwe border in the west. It was a formidable task but Sean still felt optimistic and invulnerable. He left Dedan's side and swam back to Claudia.

'You make me feel good,' he said.

'That's going to be my job in future,' she assured him. 'But what do we do now?'

'Nothing until dark, except steer this liner down the river.'

She cuddled against him under the water, and they held each other and watched the riverbanks drift slowly by.

After a while she said, 'I'm getting cold.'

They had been in the water for almost two hours, Sean realized, and though it was only a few degrees below their body temperature it was gradually chilling them through.

She slanted her eyes at him and gave him a naughty grin. 'Can't you think of something to prevent hypothermia?' she asked. 'Or do I have to make a suggestion?'

'Well,' he pretended to reflect, 'we can't light a fire.'

'Can't we?' she asked. 'Do you want a bet?' And she reached down and after a few seconds she whispered, 'See, nothing to it, and I didn't even use matches.'

'It's a miracle!' he agreed, and began to unbuckle her belt again.

'This time let's see if we can make the miracle last longer than ten seconds,' she suggested.

As the sun set, it turned the surface of the river to a luminous serpent with scales of furnace orange and glowing crimson.

'Now we can begin working in towards the bank,' Sean ordered, and they began to swim the floating tree across the current. It was heavy and ungainly, most of its bulk below the surface, and it resisted their efforts to move it closer to the bank. All four of them kept at it, kicking out strongly, and ponderously it began to swing across the wide waters.

The sun slipped below the horizon and the waters turned black as crude oil, the trees along them were dark cut-out silhouettes against the last glow of the sunset, but they were still thirty metres from the southern bank.

'We'll swim from here,' Sean decided. 'Keep close together. Don't get separated in the dark. Is everybody ready?'

They bunched up, clinging to the same branch. Sean reached for Claudia's hand and opened his mouth to give the order, and then closed it again, and cocked his head to listen.

He was surprised that he had not heard it before, perhaps the sound had been muffled by the high banks of the river and the tall trees that lined its winding course. However, it was suddenly loud and unmistakable, the sound of an outboard motor running at high speed.

'Oh shit,' he whispered bitterly, and looked towards the near bank. Only thirty metres away, it could just as well have been thirty miles.

The whine of the motor rose and fell as the acoustics of water and trees played tricks, but it was clearly coming downstream fast, running down from the direction of the Renamo lines. Sean ducked his head to gaze through a chink in the vegetation, and he saw a glow in the darkness, a beam of light that shafted briefly across the night sky and then bounced from the dark trees along the bank, glinted from the water, and swept boldly along the banks.

'Renamo patrol boat,' Sean said. 'And they are looking for us.'

Claudia tightened her grip on his hand, and no one else spoke.

'We'll try to hide in here,' Sean said, 'though I don't see how they can miss us. Get ready to duck under when the light hits us.'

The sound of the motor changed, slowing down, and then the craft swept round the upstream bend of the river a few hundred yards distant but coming down swiftly on the current towards them.

The beam of the spotlight played alternately along each bank, lighting them like day. It was an enormously powerful beam, probably one of the portable battle lights similar to the one which had trapped Sean at the top of the cliffs.

As the beam switched from bank to bank it briefly illuminated the craft and its crew. Sean recognized it as an eighteen-foot inflatable Zodiac driven by a fifty-five-horsepower Yamaha outboard, and though he could not count the occupants, there were at least eight or nine of them and they had a light machine-gun mounted in the bows. The man with the battle light was standing amidships.

The beam of light glanced over their refuge, dazzling them for an instant with its malevolent white eye, passing on and leaving them blinded by its brilliance, then coming back remorselessly and holding them captive. Sean heard someone give an indistinct order in the Shangane language, and the Zodiac altered course towards them, the beam of the battle light still fastened on them.

All four of them sank low in the water, until only their nostrils were exposed and they cowered behind the branch to which they were clinging.

The helmsman of the Zodiac throttled back, and slipped the engine into neutral. The black rubber craft drifted on the current, level with them but twenty feet off; the battle light darted and probed the leafy mass.

'Turn your face away,' Sean told Claudia in a tight whisper, and took her in his arms below the surface. Even their tanned faces would shine in the light and he screened her and turned the back of his head towards the Zodiac.

'There is nobody there,' somebody said in Shangane. Although spoken at conversational level the voice carried clearly across the water to where they were hiding.

'Go around!' another voice ordered in a tone of command, and Sean recognized the Shangane sergeant who had been his escort. A white wake spread out behind the Zodiac as it began to circle the floating tree.

The light beam cast stark black shadows from the tangled branches and struck dazzling reflections when it touched the water. As the Zodiac circled, they paddled quietly to the further side of their leafy refuge, and when the beam fastened on them, they slid softly below the surface, trying not to gasp for breath as they came up again.

The deadly game of hide and seek lasted all of eternity, before the voice in the Zodiac said again, 'There is nobody there. We are wasting time.'

'Keep circling,' the sergeant's voice answered, and then after another minute, 'Gunner, fire a burst into the tree.'

In the bows of the Zodiac, the muzzle flashes of the RPD light machine-gun twinkled like fairy lights, but a storm of shot tore into the floating tree with brutal and stunning savagery. It cracked in their eardrums, and thumped into the branches over their heads cutting loose a shower of leaves and twigs, it ripped away slabs of bark and kicked spray from the surface of the water, odd shots ricocheting into the night, wailing like demented spirits.

Sean pulled Claudia below the surface, but still could hear the bullets plunging into the water above them or striking the trunk of the tree. He kept down until his lungs burned as though they were filled with acid and only then pulled himself to the surface to catch another breath.

The gunner in the Zodiac was firing taps, not a single continuous burst. Like a Morse operator on the key, an expert gunner has his own distinctive style that others can recognize. This one fired double taps, five rounds each, it needed a concert pianist's touch on the trigger to achieve such precision.

As Sean and Claudia came back to the surface, straining for the sweet taste of air, Dedan also came up only three feet in front of them. The reflection of the battle light lit his head clearly. His short woolly beard streamed water, his eyes were like balls of ivory in his ebony face and his mouth was open, drinking in air.'

A bullet touched his temple, just above the ear. His head flinched to the shot, and it opened his scalp cleanly as a sabre cut. Involuntarily he cried out, a glottal bellow like that of a heart-shot bull buffalo, then his head fell forward and he sank face down into the dark waters.

Sean lunged out and caught his upper arm, pulling him back to the surface before he drifted away, but his head lolled and his eyes had rolled back in their sockets, exposing only the whites.

However, the men in the Zodiac had heard his cry and the Shangane sergeant shouted to one of his men, 'Get ready to throw in a grenade,' then to them, 'Come out of there. I'll give you ten seconds.'

'Job, answer him,' Sean ordered with resignation. 'Tell him we are coming out.'

Matabele and Shangane could understand each other, and Job shouted to them not to fire again.

Claudia helped Sean keep Dedan's head above the surface and between them they pulled him towards the Zodiac. The battle light dazzled them, but hands reached down from out of the glare and one at a time dragged them on board.

Shivering like half-drowned puppies, they huddled in the centre of the boat. They had Dedan's body stretched out between them and Sean lifted his head gently into his lap. He was unconscious, barely breathing, and gently Sean twisted his head to examine the bullet wound across his temple.

For a moment, he did not recognize what he was seeing. From the long shallow wound bulged something white and glistening in the lamp light.

Beside him, Claudia shuddered violently, and whispered, 'Sean, it's his, it's his . . .' She could not bring herself to say it, and only then Sean realized that Dedan's brain, still contained in the tough white membrane of the *dura mater*, was bulging out through the rent in his skull like an inner tube through a hole in an auto tyre.

The Shangane sergeant gave an order and the helmsman gunned the outboard motor and swung the Zodiac upstream. They ran at full throttle back towards the Renamo lines.

Sean sat on the floorboards with Dedan's head in his lap. There was nothing he could do, except clasp his wrist and feel Dedan's pulse grow weaker and more erratic, then finally fade away altogether.

'He's dead,' he said quietly. Job said nothing and Claudia turned her face away.

Sean held the dead head in his lap all the long return. Only when the helmsman cut the engine and coasted in to the bank did he look up. There were lighted lanterns and dark shapes awaiting them at the landing.

The Shangane sergeant gave a brusque order and two of his men lifted Dedan's corpse off Sean's lap and dumped him face down on the muddy bank. Another trooper grabbed Claudia's arm and dragged her to her feet. He shoved her roughly ashore and when she whirled on him furiously to protest, he lifted his AK butt to strike her in the centre of her chest.

Sean was close beside him and he caught the man's arm and stifled the blow.

'Do that again, you son of a syphilitic hyena,' he said softly in Shangane, 'and I'll hack off your *mtondo* with a blunt axe and make you eat it without salt.'

The trooper stared at him, amazed more by his perfect Shangane than the threat itself, and on the bank the Shangane sergeant let out a bellow of delighted laughter.

'Better do what he says,' he warned his trooper, 'unless you are very hungry. This one means what he says.' Then he grinned at Sean. 'So you talk Shangane like one of us, and you understood everything we said!' He shook his head ruefully. 'I won't let you fool me again!'

Wet, cold and dishevelled they were dragged unceremoniously into General China's bunker and paraded before his desk. One glance at his face and Sean recognized that the man was in a cold fury.

For almost a full minute he stared at Sean without rising from his seat, and then he said, 'The woman is being moved to another camp, well away from here. You will have no further opportunity to see her, until I order it.'

Sean kept his expression neutral but Claudia gave a little cry of protest, and seized Sean's arm as though she could prevent the threatened separation. General China nodded with satisfaction at her distress, and went on quietly, 'She no longer merits the special treatment which she has been given up until now, and I have ordered that she be placed in irons to prevent any further attempts at escape. She will also be kept in solitary confinement.'

The two female gaolers were standing against the wall beside his desk, and he glanced at them and nodded. The taller of the two wore sergeant's stripes on her sleeve. She gave an order to the squat toad-faced trooper beside her, and the woman came forward. The stainless-steel manacles dangled from her hand.

Claudia tightened her grip on Sean's arm and shrank away from her. The woman hesitated, and the tall sergeant gave another sharp command. The gaoler grabbed Claudia's wrist and without apparent effort plucked her away from Sean's side.

With the expertise of long practice, she spun Claudia around and thrust her face hard against the sandbagged wall of the bunker, snapping the manacles on one wrist as she did so, then pulling both Claudia's arms behind her back and locking the second cuff on her other wrist.

She stepped back and the tall female sergeant stepped up and took Claudia's hands and lifted them high between her shoulder-blades. Claudia gasped with pain as she was forced onto her toes. The sergeant inspected the manacles; they were closed snugly around Claudia's wrists, but she was not satisfied. Deliberately the sergeant tightened them two more notches and Claudia gasped again.

'That's too tight, they are cutting into me.'

'Tell that bitch to loosen them,' Sean snapped at General China, and he smiled for the first time that evening and leaned back in his chair.

'Colonel Courtney, I have given orders that the woman is not to be allowed another chance to escape. Sergeant Cara is only doing her duty.'

'She is cutting off the circulation. Miss Monterro could lose her hands to gangrene.'

'That would be unfortunate,' General China agreed. 'However, I will not interfere, unless . . .' he paused.

'Unless?' Sean demanded savagely.

'Unless I am assured of your complete co-operation and unless I have your parole that you will not attempt another escape.'

Sean looked down at Claudia's hands. Already they were beginning to swell and change colour, darkening to a leaden hue, the bright steel bands cutting into her wrists, the veins puffing up into dark blue cords below the manacles.

'Gangrene is a dangerous condition and unfortunately our facilities for amputation of limbs are very primitive,' General China remarked.

'All right,' Sean said heavily. 'I give you my parole.'

'And your co-operation,' he prompted.

'And I promise co-operation,' Sean agreed.

General China gave an order and the sergeant used the key on the manacles, letting them out two notches each and immediately the swelling of Claudia's hands dissipated and her skin colouring began to return to its normal creamy tan as the blood drained away.

'Take her away!' China ordered in English and the sergeant nodded to her assistant gaoler. They each seized one of Claudia's arms and dragged her to the door.

'Wait!' Sean shouted, but they ignored him and when he tried to follow her, the big Shangane sergeant seized his arms from behind in a hammer lock.

'Sean!' Claudia's voice had a note of hysteria. 'Don't let them take me!' But they pushed her out of the bunker and the canvas curtain fell between them.

'Sean!' Her voice came back to him.

'I love you!' he shouted after her, struggling against the sergeant's grip. 'It will be all right, darling. Just remember I love you. I'll do what I have to do to get you out of here.'

The promise rang hollowly in his own ears and her voice was a despairing wail. 'Sean!' And then again very faintly. 'Sean!' Then silence beyond the curtain.

Sean found he was panting with emotion but he forced himself to cease struggling and stand quietly. The sergeant relaxed his grip and Sean shrugged him away and turned to General China.

'You bastard!' he said. 'You rotten bastard!'

'I see that you are in no mood for sensible discussion,' China told him, and glanced at his wristwatch. 'And it's well after midnight. We'll let you cool off.' He looked at the sergeant and changed to Shangane. 'Take them,' he indicated Sean and Job, 'feed them, give them dry clothes and a blanket, let them sleep and bring them to me at dawn tomorrow.' The sergeant saluted and pushed them towards the door.

'I have work for them to do,' China warned him. 'Make sure they are in condition to do it.'

Sean and Job slept side by side on the floor of a dugout with a guard sitting over them. The floor was of hard-packed damp earth and the blankets were verminous, but neither the discomfort, nor the tickle of insects crawling over his skin, nor even thoughts of Claudia could keep Sean awake.

The sergeant woke him in the dark of pre-dawn from a profound and dreamless sleep by dumping an armful of clothing on his prostrate body.

'Get dressed,' he ordered.

Sean sat up and scratched the bite of a bed bug.

'What's your name?' It was a relief to be able to speak Shangane freely.

'Alphonso Henriques Mabasa,' the Shangane told him proudly, and Sean smiled at the unlikely combination. The name of a Portuguese emperor, and the Shangane name for one who strikes with a club.

'A war club on your enemies and a meat club on their wives?' Sean asked, and Alphonso guffawed.

Job sat up and grimaced at Sean's ribald sally.

'At five in the morning, before breakfast!' he protested, and shook his head sadly, but Sean heard Alphonso delight-edly repeating the joke to his men outside the dugout.

'With the Shangane, it doesn't take much to establish the reputation of being a wag,' Job remarked in Sindebele as they sorted through the bundle of clothing Alphonso had brought them. It was all secondhand but reasonably clean. Sean found a military-style cloth cap and a suit of tiger-striped battledress, and discarded his bush jacket and shorts which were by now in rags. He kept on his comfortable old velskoen.

Breakfast was a stew of kapenta, the fingerling dried fish he thought of as African whitebait, and a porridge of maize meal. 'What about tea?' Sean asked, and Alphonso laughed.

'You think this is the Polana Hotel in Maputo?'

Dawn was just breaking when Alfonso escorted them down to the riverbank where they found General China and his staff inspecting the damage done by the Hind gunships.

'We lost twenty-six men killed and wounded yesterday,' China greeted Sean. 'And almost as many deserters during the night. Morale is sinking fast.' He spoke in English and it was clear that none of his staff understood. Despite the circumstances, he looked dapper and competent in his beret and crisply ironed battledress, medal ribbons across his chest and general officer's stars on his epaulettes. The ivory-handled pistol hung on his webbing belt and he wore aviator-style mirrored sunglasses with thin gold frames.

'Unless we can stop those gunships, it will be over in three months, before the rains can save us.'

The rains were the time of the guerrilla when head-high grass, impassable roads and flooded rivers hamstringed the defender and afforded concealment and sanctuary to his tormentor.

'I watched those Hinds in action yesterday,' Sean told him cautiously. 'Captain Job here borrowed one of your RPG 7 rocket-launchers and scored a direct hit with an AP rocket.'

China looked at Job with new interest. 'Good,' he said. 'None of my own men have been able to do that yet. What happened?'

'Nothing,' Job answered simply.

'No damage,' Sean confirmed.

'The entire machine is encased in titanium armour plate,' China nodded, and looked up at the sky, a nervous gesture as though he were expecting one of the humpbacked monsters to appear miraculously. 'Our friends in the south have offered us one of their new Darter missile systems, but there is the difficulty of bringing in the launch vehicles, heavy trucks over these roads and through Frelimo-controlled territory.' He shook his head. 'We need an infantry weapon, one that can be carried and used by foot soldiers.'

'As far as I know there is only one effective weapon of that kind. The Americans developed a technique in Afghanistan. They adapted the original Stinger missile and worked out a way of getting through the armour. I haven't any idea of the details,' Sean added hastily. He knew it was unwise to set himself up as an expert, but the problem was intriguing and he had allowed himself to be carried away.

'You are quite correct, Colonel. The modified Stinger is the only weapon that has proved effective against the Hind. That's your task, the price of your freedom. I want you to procure a shipment of Stingers for me.'

Sean stopped dead on the riverbank and stared at him, and then he began to smile. 'Certainly,' he said. 'A piece of cake. Do you have a preference for colour and flavour, how about baboon-ball blue and kiwi fruit?'

For the first time that morning China smiled back at him. 'The Stingers are here already, it's simply a matter of picking them up.'

Sean's grin faded. 'I hope, most fervently, that this is a joke. I know that Savimbi has been given Stingers by the Yanks, but Angola is on the other side of the continent.'

'Our Stingers are much closer than that,' China assured him. 'Do you remember the old Rhodesian Fire Force base at Grand Reef?'

'I should,' Sean nodded. 'The Scouts operated out of there for almost a year.'

'Of course, I remember.' China touched the lobe of his ear beneath the gaudy beret. 'It was from there you launched the attack on my camp at Inhlozane.' His expression was suddenly bleak.

'That was in another war,' Sean reminded him.

China's expression relaxed. 'As I was saying, the Stingers we want are at Grand Reef.'

'I don't understand.' Sean shook his head. 'The Yanks would never give Stingers to Mugabe. He is a Marxist and there is no deep love between Zimbabwe and the US. It doesn't make sense.'

'Oh yes, it does,' China assured him. 'In a roundabout African way, it makes good sense.' He glanced at his watch. 'Tea time,' he said. 'I believe you were asking for a brew this morning. No matter what side we were on, the war made us all tea addicts.'

China led them back to his command bunker and an orderly brought in the smoke-blackened kettle immediately.

'The Americans dislike Mugabe, but they dislike the South Africans more,' China explained. 'Mugabe is harbouring and assisting ANC guerrillas operating across his borders into South Africa.'

Sean nodded grimly. He had seen photographs of the carnage created by a limpet mine detonated in a South African supermarket; it had happened on the last Friday of the month, payday for monthly workers, when the store was crowded with housewives and their offspring both black and white.

'The South Africans have vowed to pursue the guerrillas wherever they run. They have already repeatedly made good that threat, hot pursuit across the borders of all their neighbours. The ANC have announced their intention of stepping up their bombing of soft civilian targets. Mugabe knows what the consequences will be, so he wants a weapon to deal with the South African Puma gunships when they cross his border to cull the ANC.'

'I still don't believe the Yanks would supply him with Stingers,' Sean said flatly.

'Not directly,' China agreed. 'But the British are training Mugabe's army for him. They are the middle men. They have got the Stingers from the Americans and they are training Mugabe's crack Third Brigade to use them at Grand Reef.'

'How the hell do you know all this?'

'You must remember that I was once a minister, albeit a junior one, in Mugabe's cabinet. I still have good friends in high places.'

Sean thought about it. 'You are right,' he nodded. 'It is all typically African. So the Stingers are at Grand Reef.'

'They were delivered by a Royal Air Force Hercules fourteen days ago, and are scheduled to be deployed along; the South African and Zimbabwe border by the beginning of next month. They will be aimed at your countrymen, Colonel Courtney.'

Sean felt a stirring of patriotic outrage, but he kept his expression neutral.

'The training is being conducted by Royal Artillery personnel, a captain and two NCOs, so you will begin to understand why I require a white face for my plans.'

'It certainly begins to sound ominous,' Sean muttered. 'Tell me what it is exactly that you require.'

'I want you to go back to Zimbabwe and bring me those Stinger missiles.'

Sean showed no emotion as he asked, 'In exchange?'

'Once the missiles are delivered to me, I will remove the manacles from Miss Monterro and transfer her to quarters where you will be able to visit her regularly,' he paused and allowed himself a knowing smile, 'and spend some time with her each day or evening in private.'

'What about our release?'

'Yes,' China agreed. 'All three of you will be released after you have performed one additional service for me – after first obtaining the Stingers.'

'And what is that service?'

China held up both hands. 'One thing at a time, Colonel Courtney. The missiles first. Once you have delivered them, we will discuss the final part of our bargain.'

Sean scowled into his tea mug as he turned it over in his mind, trying to find some vantage point to adopt, but China interrupted him.

'Colonel, every minute you waste merely prolongs Miss Monterro's –' he searched for the correct word – 'her discomfort. Until I have those missiles, she will wear her manacles night and day, waking or sleeping, eating or performing all the other essential functions of life. I suggest you begin immediately laying out your plans to procure them for me.'

Sean stood up and went to the large-scale wall map behind China's desk. He didn't really need to study it. He could have closed his eyes and visualized every valley and peak, every wrinkle of land along the border between Mozambique and Zimbabwe. The railway line crossed the border near the little town of Umtali, and twenty kilometres beyond it on the Zimbabwe side a tiny red aircraft symbol marked the position of the Grand Reef airfield and base.

Sean touched the stylized aircraft symbol with his forefinger, and Job came to stand beside him. They both stared at it thoughtfully. How many times had they sortied from that field, shambling out to the rumbling Dakota transports under the burden of parachute and battle packs and weapons. Each of them could picture clearly the position of every building, the hangars and barracks and perimeter defence.

'Twenty Ks from the border post,' Job said softly, 'fifteen minutes by truck, but we'll never get there on foot.'

'You spoke of a plan, General China. What do you have in mind? Can you provide us with vehicles?' Sean asked without looking round.

'Some time ago my men captured three Unimog trucks,

with authentic Zimbabwe army paintwork and papers. We have them hidden,' China answered, and Sean breathed a sigh of relief.

'My plan is for you to cross the border disguised as Zimbabwean troops.'

'I'll bet there is a huge volume of military traffic through the border post.'

'There is,' China affirmed.

'We'll need Zimbabwe army uniforms for all the black troops and something for me.' Sean tapped his finger on the map. 'We will have to wheedle our way into the base without firing a shot.'

'I have a British field officer's uniform for you,' China said softly. 'It's genuine and I have the papers to go with it.'

'How the hell did you get that?'

'Three months ago we attacked a Zimbabwe column near Vila de Manica. There was a British observer with the column and he got caught in the crossfire. He was a major in one of the guards regiments, seconded to the high commissioner in Harare as a military attaché, according to his papers.

'The uniform has been cleaned of blood and the tears made by fragmentation grenade have been patched most expertly. The tailor who did the work made my own uniform.' China smoothed the fit of his tunic over his lean flanks and looked pleased with it. 'He will alter the captured uniform to fit you, Colonel. The British major was about your height, but a great deal larger around the waist and backside.'

'A guards regiment,' Sean smiled. 'I don't know about my accent, any Englishman would pick me out as a colonial the instant I open my mouth.'

'You will have to deal only with the Third Brigade guards at the base gates. I assure you they will not have such discerning ears.'

315

'Okay,' Sean said. 'So we may be able to get in, but how the hell do we get out?' He was beginning to enjoy himself, becoming absorbed with the problem.

'Not so fast, Sean.' Job was studying the map. 'We can't just pitch up at the gates without an invitation and demand entry. With the Stingers there the security will be at a maximum.'

'That is correct,' China concurred. 'However, I have more good news for you. I actually have a man inside the base. He is a nephew of mine, we are a large family.' He looked complacent as he went on. 'He is in signals, a warrant officer, second in command of the Grand Reef communications centre. He will be able to fake a signal from the Zimbabwe high command authorizing an inspection of the Stinger programme by the military attaché. So the guards at the base will be expecting you. They won't scrutinize your pass too closely.'

'If you have a man inside the base, he'll know exactly where the Stingers are stored,' Job suggested eagerly.

'Right,' China nodded. 'They are in number three hangar. That's second from the left.'

'We know exactly where number three hangar is,' Sean assured him, and frowned as he tried to anticipate the other problems they would encounter.

'I will want to know the packaging of the missiles, sizes and weights.' China scribbled a note on his pad. 'And there must be instruction manuals covering their operation. Those will certainly be in the office of the Royal Artillery captain. I must know exactly where that is.' He ticked off each item on his fingers as it occurred to him, and Job added his own ideas.

'We'll need a diversion,' he suggested. 'A second unit to stage an attack on the base perimeter furthest from the hangar and training centre, plenty of tracer and RPG rocks and white phosphorus grenades – we will need another squad for that.'

It was like old times, how often had they worked together like this, each stimulating the other, their excitement kept under tight rein, but sparkling in their eyes.

Once Job remarked, 'I'm glad it's the Third Brigade we'll be going against, that bunch of nun-killers and child-rapers, they led the purge in Matabeleland.' The slaughter and atrocity that had accompanied the brigade's sweep through the tribal areas from which the Matabele political dissidents had been operating was fresh in both their memories.

'Two of my brothers, my grandfather . . .' Job's voice dropped to a deathly whisper. 'The Third Brigade threw their bodies down the old shaft at Antelope Mine.'

'This isn't personal vengeance,' Sean warned him. 'All we want is those Stingers, Job.' The intertribal hatred in Africa was as fierce as any Corsican vendetta, and Job had physically to shake himself to break the spell of it.

'You're right, but a few Third Brigade scalps would be a nice little fringe benefit.'

Sean grinned. Despite his admonition, the thought of taking on ZANLA again gave him equal satisfaction. How many good men, and women, how many dear friends had he lost to them over the eleven long years of the bush war, and how complex were the lines of hatred and loyalty that held together the very fabric of Africa. Only an African could ever understand it.

'Okay.' Sean brought them back to hard reality. 'We have got in. We have the Stingers, say two loaded Unimogs. I have found the manuals. We are ready to pull out. The diversion has lured most of the guards to the southern perimeter of the base, on the far side of the airfield. Now we have to get out. They aren't going to be so happy about letting us go.'

'We charge the gates,' Job said, 'Use one truck to break down the barricades.'

'Yes,' Sean nodded. 'And then? We aren't going to be able to get out of the country through the border post at

317

Umtali. By that time the whole Zimbabwe army and Frelimo will all be after us.'

They both turned back to the wall map again. Sean reached up and traced the road that branched northwards, just before it reached the town of Umtali, and then ran parallel with the border as it traversed the rugged eastern highlands towards Inyanga National Park, an area of misty peaks and wet densely forested valleys. He touched one of the valleys, a green wedge driven deeply into the barrier of mountains.

'Honde Valley,' he read the legend. The road crossed the head of it and the valley itself was a funnel that led down to the border and the Mozambique uplands. It formed a natural re-entrance to the highlands, a gateway which had been one of the major infiltration routes of the ZANLA guerrillas from their training bases in Mozambique. The hard way, Sean and Job had learned all its secrets, the hidden trails and strong points, the false ports and the concealed passes.

'The track down to St Mary's mission,' Sean said and they stared at it. 'That's as far as we can take the trucks.'

'From there is only six Ks to the border,' Job murmured.

'Six hard Ks,' Sean qualified. 'And we won't be clear just because we have crossed into Mozambique. We will still have them after us until we get into Renamo-held ground.'

Sean turned back to General China. 'I'll want porters waiting for us at St Mary's mission. How far does your control of territory extend?'

'The porters will present no problem.' China came to stand between them and pointed to a speck on the map marked Mavonela. 'And I can have trucks waiting at this village. Once you reach Mavonela, I will consider that you have made good delivery of the missiles.'

'I suggest we don't try and bring out forty Stingers with one column of porters,' Job cut in. 'It will make a perfect target for Mugabe's MIGs. One load of napalm is all it would take.'

'And of course, Frelimo can call in their Hinds,' Sean added. 'You are right, Job. Once it is light enough for air-attack, we will bombshell.' He was referring to the old guerrilla trick of splintering the column and offering numerous small elusive targets, rather than a single large ungainly one. 'Can you arrange for a series of RZs rather than a single RZ at Mavonela village?' He used the old Scouts' abbreviation for a rendezvous.

'Yes,' China nodded. 'We will disperse the transport along the Mavonela road.' He traced it out. 'One truck every kilometre, hidden under camouflage netting, and we'll move the Stingers out on the last stage under cover of darkness.'

'All right, let's draw up a timetable,' Sean said. 'Let's get it all down on paper. I'll need writing material.'

China opened a drawer of his desk and brought out a cheap notebook and ballpoint pen. While they worked, China sent for his quartermaster, a chubby little man who had run a men's outfitters in Beira before economic necessity rather than ideological commitment had forced him to leave the town and seek employment in the deep bush with China's guerrillas.

He arrived carrying the uniform for a staff officer of the Irish Guards in the field, complete with insignia, headgear, webbing and boots in his arms. Sean donned the uniform for a fitting without interrupting their planning session. The tunic and trousers had to be taken in, and the boots were a size too large.

'Better too big than too small,' Sean decided. 'I'll wear a couple of pairs of socks.'

The tailor tucked and pinned and crawled around Sean's feet as he let the trouser bottoms down an inch.

'Fine.' Sean examined the guards major's papers that China laid out on the desk top. From the photograph, Sean saw that the major had been a fleshy fair-haired individual in his late forties.

'Gavin Duffy,' Sean read the dead man's name aloud. 'You'll have to alter the ID photograph.'

'My propaganda officer will take care of that,' China told him.

The propaganda officer was a mulatto, half Portuguese, half Shangane, and he was armed with a polaroid camera. He took four mug shots of Sean and then spirited away the deceased guards major's ID card to doctor the photograph.

'All right.' Sean turned back to China. 'Now I want to take command of the men who will make up the raiding party and see them properly kitted out. You'll have to explain to them that they are to take their orders from me in future.'

China smiled and stood up. 'Follow me, Colonel. I'll take you to meet your new command.'

He led the way out of the bunker, but once they were on the path through the forest that led down to the river, Sean fell in beside him and they continued to discuss the raid.

'Obviously I am going to need more than the original ten men in Sergeant Alphonso's squad, at least another detachment to make the diversionary attack on the base,' Sean broke off as the mournful wail of the hand-operated sirens rose from the camp, and instantly all around them was turmoil and confusion.

'The Hinds!' shouted China. 'Take cover!' And he sprinted for a sandbagged emplacement amongst the trees nearby. There was a twin-barrelled 12.7mm anti-aircraft weapon mounted in the emplacement. It would be a prime target for the Hind gunners and Sean looked around quickly for alternative cover.

In the long grass on the opposite side of the track, he spotted a less conspicuous shell-scrape and ran for it. As he tumbled into it, he heard the oncoming roar of the Hind gunships and the cacophony of ground fire built up swiftly. Job jumped down into the fox-hole and squatted beside him, and then another smaller figure appeared above them and as nimble as a hare leapt into the hole.

For a moment, Sean did not realize who it was, not until the wrinkled face creased like a used napkin into a wide black smile and the man said happily, 'I see you, *Bwana*.'

'You! You silly little bugger!' Sean stared at him in disbelief. 'I sent you back to Chiwewe. What the hell are you doing back here?'

'I went back to Chiwewe, as you commanded,' Matatu said virtuously. 'Then I came back to look for you.'

Sean still stared at Matatu in awe as he considered what that statement entailed. Then he shook his head and began to smile, immediately the little man's answering grin seemed to split his face in two.

'Nobody saw you?' Sean demanded in Swahili. 'You came through the lines into the headquarters of an army, and nobody saw you?'

'Nobody sees Matatu, when Matatu does not want to be seen.'

The earth trembled under them, and the sound of rockets and gunfire forced them to put their heads close together and shout into each other's faces.

'How long have you been here?'

'Since yesterday.' Matatu looked apologetic. He pointed to the sky where the Hinds were circling. 'Since those machines attacked yesterday. I was watching when you jumped into the river. I followed you along the bank when you used the tree as a boat. I wanted to come to you then, but I saw crocodiles. Then in the night the bad men, the *shifta*, came in the boat and brought you back here. I waited and watched.'

'Did you see where they took the white woman?' Sean demanded.

'I saw them take her away last night.' Matatu showed little interest in Claudia. 'But I waited for you.'

'Can you find out where they took her?' Sean asked.

'Of course.' Matatu's grin faded and he looked indignant. 'I can follow them anywhere they took her.'

Sean unbuttoned his tunic pocket and pulled out his new notebook. Crouched in the bottom of the shell-scrape with an air-raid thundering overhead, he composed the first love letter he had written in years. Filling the single tiny sheet of cheap notepaper with all the assurances and comfort and cheer that he could muster, he ended it, 'Be strong, it won't be for much longer and remember I love you. Whatever happens, I love you.'

He ripped the page out of the notebook and folded it carefully. 'Take this to her.' He handed it to Matatu. 'See that she gets it and then come back to me.'

Matatu tucked the scrap of paper into his loin-cloth and waited expectantly.

'Did you see the hole in which I slept last night?' Sean asked.

'I saw you come from there this morning,' Matatu nodded.

'That will be our meeting-place,' Sean told him. 'Come to me there, when the *shifta* are asleep.' Sean looked up at the sky. The raid had been fierce but short-lived. The sound of engines and gunfire was dwindling, but dust and smoke drifted over their shelter.

'Go now,' Sean ordered, and Matatu jumped to his feet eager to obey, but Sean took his arm. It was thin as a child's and Sean shook it affectionately. 'Don't let them catch you, old friend,' he said in Swahili.

Matatu shook his head and twinkled with amusement at the absurdity of that thought and then, like a puff of smoke from the genie's lamp, he was gone.

They waited a few minutes to let Matatu get clear and then climbed out of the shelter. The trees around them were torn and shattered with shell and rocket fire; across the river an ammunition store was burning and RPG rockets and phosphorus grenades were exploding, sending dense white smoke towering into the sky.

General China came striding down the path to meet them. There was a sooty stain on the sleeve of his uniform and dust on his knees and elbows. His expression was furious.

'Our position here is totally compromised,' he fumed. 'They raid us at will and we have no response.'

'You'll have to pull your main force back out of range of the Hinds,' Sean shrugged.

'I can't do that.' China shook his head. 'It will mean that we can no longer maintain our stranglehold on the railway. It will mean conceding control of the main road system to Frelimo, and inviting them to come on the offensive.'

'Well then,' Sean shrugged again, 'you are going to take a hammering if you remain here.'

'Get me those Stingers,' China hissed. 'Get them, and get them quickly!' And he strode away down the path.

Sean and Job followed him to the bunker complex on the riverbank where a company of guerrillas, forty men, obviously forewarned of the general's approach, were drawn up in a makeshift parade ground of beaten earth the size of a tennis court. They seemed oblivious of the air-raid damage, the smoke and debris, and the scurrying first-aid parties and damage control teams around them.

Sean recognized Sergeant Alphonso and his Shanganes in the first rank. He came forward and saluted General China, then wheeled and gave the order for the detachment to stand easy. General China wasted few words and little time. He raised his voice and addressed them brusquely in Shangane.

'You men are being given a special task. You will, in future, take your orders from this white officer.' He indicated Sean beside him. 'You will follow those orders strictly. You all know the consequences of failing to do so.' He turned to Sean. 'Carry on, Colonel Courtney,' he said, then strode away back up the path towards the command bunker. Instinctively Sean almost saluted him and then checked himself.

'Screw you, China,' he muttered under his breath, and then gave his full attention to his new command.

Of course, he already knew Sergeant Alphonso's squad well, but the additional men that China had found for him were as likely a looking bunch as he had seen in the Renamo ranks. China had given him his very best. Sean moved slowly down the front rank, inspecting each of them. They were all equipped with AKM assault rifles, the more modern version of the venerable AK 47. In places the blueing was worn from the metal with long usage, however the weapons were meticulously clean and well maintained. Their webbing was in first-class order, and their uniforms, although again well worn, were neatly patched and repaired.

'Always judge a workman by the state of his tools,' Sean thought. These were top soldiers, proud and hard. He stared into each of their eyes as he came level with them and saw it there. Of all the people of Africa, Sean felt the greatest rapport with the Zulu-originated tribes, the Angoni and Matabele and Shangane. If he had been given his choice these were exactly the type of men he would have chosen for this assignment.

Once he had finished the inspection, he went back to the front and addressed them for the first time in Shangane. 'You and I together are going to burst the balls of the dung-eating Frelimo,' he said quietly, and in the front rank Sergeant Alphonso grinned wolfishly.

With her hands still manacled behind her back, the two female wardresses and an escort of five troopers marched Claudia Monterro through the darkness over a rough track. Often she stumbled and when she fell and sprawled full length, she was unable to use her hands to protect herself from the rocky surface. Soon her knees were raw and bleeding, and the march became a torturous nightmare.

It seemed without end, hour after hour it went on and every time she fell the tall sergeant harangued her in a language she could not understand. Each time it required more of an effort to regain her feet, for she was unable to use her hands and arms to balance herself.

She was so thirsty that her saliva had turned to a sticky paste in her mouth, her legs ached and her hands and arms held so long in such an unnatural position were numb and cold. Sometimes, she heard voices in the darkness around her and once or twice smelled smoke and saw the glow of a camp-fire or a feeble paraffin lantern so she knew that she was still within the Renamo lines.

The march ended abruptly. She guessed that they were still near the river, she could feel the chill of its waters in the air and see the taller riverine trees silhouetted against the stars and she could smell humanity around her: stale ash of the cooking-fires and woodsmoke, human sweat in unwashed clothing, and human body wastes and the sour odours of garbage. At last, they led her through a barbed wire gate into another prison compound, and dragged her towards one of a row of dugouts.

The two wardresses took her arms and hustled her down a set of earthen steps and pushed her into the darkness so she tripped and fell once more on her injured knees. Behind her, she heard a door being closed and barred, and the darkness was absolute.

After a short struggle she regained her feet, but when she tried to stand full height, the top of her head bumped on the low roof. It felt like a roof of undressed wooden poles still in their bark. She shuffled backwards, stretching out her fingers behind her until she touched the door. It

325

was of hand-sawn planks, rough and sharp with splinters. She pressed her weight upon it but it was solid and unmoving.

Bent over to protect her head, she shuffled around her prison. The walls were damp earth. Her cell was tiny, about six feet square, and in the far corner she stumbled over the only furnishing it contained. It was metal and she explored it with her foot and found that it was an iron bucket. The ripe stench from it left no doubt of its purpose. She completed the circuit of her cell and came back to the door.

Her thirst was an agony now, and she called through the door.

'Please I need water.' Her voice was a harsh croak and her lips felt tight and dry, ready to split. 'Water!' she called, and then remembered the Spanish word and hoped it was the same in Portuguese. 'Agua!'

It was futile. The earthen walls seemed to swallow and deaden the sound of her voice. She shuffled to the far corner and sank down to the dark floor. Only then she realized just how physically exhausted she was, yet the manacles on her wrists prevented her lying on her back or side. She tried to find a position in which she could rest comfortably and at last by wedging herself upright in a corner of the cell she succeeded.

The cold and something else woke her, and she was confused and disorientated. For a moment she believed she was back in her father's home in Anchorage and she cried out for him.

'Papa! Are you there?'

Then she smelled the damp and the sewage bucket, and felt the cold in her joints and her pinioned arms, and she remembered. Despair swept over her like a black wave and she felt herself drowning in it. Then she heard again the sound that had awakened her, and she went rigid and felt the cold sweat burst out on her neck and forehead.

She knew what it was instantly. Claudia had none of

the more usual feminine phobias, she had no terror of spiders or snakes, there was just one unnatural terror which afflicted her. She sat rigid and listened to the scampering sounds of a creature moving about her cell. That sound was the stuff of her nightmares, and she stared into the darkness trying to will it away from herself.

Then suddenly she felt it on her. The sharp little claws pricking her skin, the cold touch of paws on her flesh. It was a rat and by the weight of it on her, it must have been huge, as big as a rabbit, and she screamed wildly and lunged to her feet and kicked out blindly at it. When she stopped screaming at last, she shrank into the corner and found she was trembling in wild spasms.

'Stop it!' she told herself. 'Pull yourself together!' And by an enormous effort of will, she regained control. There was complete silence in the darkness, her screams had frightened the creature away for the time being but she still could not bring herself to sit on the dirt floor again, for she was terrified that it would return.

Despite her exhaustion she stood propped in the corner and waited out the rest of the night. She dozed, almost fell asleep on her feet, then jerked awake again. That sequence happened many times, and then as she came awake for the last time, she realized that the darkness was no longer total and she could see.

Light was filtering into the cell and she blinked and found the source of it. There were slits and gaps between the poles of the low roof. These had been daubed with clay and grass, but in one or two places the dried clay had fallen out of the cracks allowing chinks of light through. Stems of coarse elephant grass hung down untidily from the cracks.

Fearfully she looked around the cell, but the rat had disappeared, it must have squeezed through one of the gaps between the poles.

Claudia stumbled across to the reeking galvanized sewage bucket, and only as she stood over it did she realize her predicament. Her hands were locked behind her back and with that realization her need became irresistible.

Her fingers were almost devoid of feeling, but in desperate haste she was able to grip her leather belt and gradually work it through the loops of her trousers until the buckle was in the small of her back. She was whimpering with the effort of self-control needed to delay her bodily functions while she clumsily unclasped the belt.

She had lost so much weight that as soon as her belt was loosened her trousers fell around her ankles and she was able to hook a thumb under the elastic of her panties and drag them down as far as her knees.

Always fastidious, Claudia experienced the worst hardship of her captivity when her efforts to cleanse herself properly failed. She found herself sobbing with humiliation as she finally managed to dress again. Her wrists were rubbed raw and her arms ached from the strenuous efforts needed to perform this simple task. She huddled in the corner of her cell and the stench of the bucket seemed to permeate the very depth of her soul.

A single ray of sunlight shot through a chink in the roof poles and pinned a brilliant silver coin on the far wall. She watched it move infinitely slowly down the earthen wall, and somehow it seemed to warm and cheer her enough to dull the cutting edge of her despair.

Before the coin of light reached the floor of the cell, she heard a scraping at the door as the bars were drawn and the door forced open against its primitive hinges. The tall sergeant stooped into the cell and Claudia scrambled to her feet.

'Please,' she whispered. 'You must let me wash,' she said in her schoolgirl Spanish, but the wardress showed no sign of having understood. In one hand she carried a metal billy-can of water and in the other a bowl of stiff maize cake. She placed the billy-can on the floor and then tipped the lump of maize cake into the dirt beside it.

Claudia's thirst, which she had managed temporarily to

subdue, returned in even greater agony, and she almost whimpered at the sight of the billy. It contained almost two litres of clear water.

She sank down on her knees before it like a worshipper and looked up at the wardress.

'Please,' she said in Spanish. 'I must use my hands, please.' The wardress chuckled, the first animation she had shown, and she nudged the billy dangerously with the toe of her boot; a little water slopped over the rim.

'No,' Claudia croaked. 'Don't spill it.'

On her knees she bent over and tried to reach the water with her tongue, thrusting it out as far as it would reach, and felt the blessed wetness on the very tip, but the rim of the metal billy was cutting into her face.

She looked up again. 'Please, help me.'

The wardress laughed again and leaned against the wall watching her efforts with amusement.

Claudia stooped again and gripped the rim of the billy between her teeth. Carefully she tilted it and a few drops trickled between her lips. The pleasure was so intense that her vision clouded. She drank a sip at a time until the level in the billy had fallen to where the liquid could no longer flow into her mouth. However, the vessel was still more than half full and her thirst seemed only to have been aggravated by what she had managed to drink.

Still holding the rim between her teeth, she carefully raised her head, and tilted it backwards. It was too quick. She choked as the water flooded into her mouth, and the billy slipped from between her teeth, water splashed down her chest and puddled on the floor to be quickly absorbed into the dirt.

The wardress let out a shrill shriek of laughter, and Claudia felt the tears of despair fill her eyes. She only just managed to smother the sob that came up her throat.

The wardress deliberately stepped onto the white maize cake, smearing it into the dirt, then with another snort of laughter snatched up the empty billy and left the cell. Claudia heard her still giggling as she rebarred the door of the cell.

She could judge the passage of time by the angle of the sunlight through the chinks in the roof. The first day seemed interminable. Despite the discomfort of the manacles, she was able to sleep fitfully but while she was awake she occupied herself by planning to increase her chances of survival.

Water was her most pressing need. The little she had drunk might just see her through this day, but she knew that she was already suffering from dehydration.

'I have to find some method of drinking from that billy,' she told herself, and spent most of that afternoon wrestling with the problem. When the solution came to her, she lurched to her feet so hastily that she bumped the back of her head on the log roof. She ignored the hurt and examined the untidy tufts of elephant grass that hung down from between the chinks of the roof. She selected one of the grass stems and took it carefully between her teeth, worried it loose and let it drop to the floor. She knelt over it and by straining backwards managed to get a hand to it. Fortunately it was dry and brittle and snapped readily between her fingers. She broke it into four equal lengths each about nine inches long and, once again by backward contortions, planted them upright in the loose earth of the floor. She turned round, knelt and picked up the first of them between her lips. She tried to blow through it, but it was blocked with pith and dirt. She discarded it and went on to the next.

When she blew through this one, a tiny cork of dirt flew out of the end like a blow-pipe and then it was hollow and clear. She flopped onto her backside and sat in the middle of the dirt floor with the straw still stuck in her mouth, laughing around it with triumph. Her sense of elation and achievement dispelled the corroding sense of despair which had almost destroyed her will to keep on living.

She crawled to the corner and carefully hid the precious

straw, and then for the rest of that day planned how she would use it.

The rays of sun no longer penetrated to her cell, and the heavy gloom of evening was on her before she heard the wardress at the door. She huddled in her corner when the sergeant stooped into the cell and carelessly dumped the stodgy lump of boiled maize meal into the dirt and stood the metal billy beside it.

She leaned back expectantly against the door jamb and waited for Claudia to scramble for the food and drink like an animal on all fours. Claudia crouched motionlessly in the furthest corner of the cell and tried to show no expression, but her throat contracted in an involuntary swallowing reflex and her thirst was a raging beast within her.

After she had not moved for a few minutes, the sergeant said something irritable in Portuguese and gestured to the billy. With an immense effort Claudia prevented herself from looking down at it and the woman shrugged and once again stepped onto the maize cake and ground it into the dirt. She gave a snort of unconvincing laughter and backed out through the door, dragging it shut behind her, but the billy-can was left standing at the threshold.

Claudia forced herself to wait until she was certain that the wardress had truly left and was not watching her through a spy hole. Once she was sure she was not observed, Claudia crawled in frantic haste to the corner where she had hidden the straw and picked it up between her lips. Still on her knees she crossed to the billy-can and stooped over it.

She drew the first mouthful through the straw and let it trickle down her throat, closing her eyes with pleasure. It was as though she were drinking down a magic potion. She felt new strength and resolve flow through her veins.

She drank most of the contents of the billy-can, drawing out the pleasure of it until it was almost totally dark in the cell, but she could not bring herself to eat the sticky mess of maize cake smeared into the dirt.

She hoarded the remains of the water, taking the wire handle of the billy-can between her teeth and carefully moving it to the far corner of the cell where she could ration herself to small sips during the long hours ahead. She settled down for the night feeling almost cheerful and a little light-headed as though she had drunk champagne rather than plain unboiled river water.

'I can endure anything they do to me,' she whispered to herself. 'They aren't going to break me. I won't let them, I won't.'

Her mood did not last. Almost as soon as it was fully dark in the cell, she realized her terrible mistake in leaving the uneaten maize cake on the floor.

Last night there had been only one rat, and it had fled when she screamed at it. This night the odour of food brought them pouring through the gaps in the roof. To her frenzied imagination, it seemed that the floor of the cell was swarming with furry bodies. The smell of them clogged her nostrils, the nauseating ratty smell like boiling horns and hooves in a glue pot. She cowered in her corner, shivering with cold and horror, and they brushed against her legs and scurried over her feet, squeaking and squealing as they fought for the scraps of spilled porridge.

At last, Claudia succumbed to panic. Screaming, on the edge of hysteria, she kicked out at them wildly; one of them whipped round and bit her naked ankle, the sharp little teeth were like a razor cut. She screamed again and kicked, trying to dislodge it, but for a few dreadful seconds its curved teeth were buried in her flesh, and then at last she sent it flying into the darkness.

The rat hit the billy-can containing her treasured water and she heard the metal clank against the wall and the liquid splash onto the earthen floor. She crawled to the overturned container and wept with despair.

After long hours of horror and dark terror, the rats consumed the last of the maize and disappeared back through the roof. Claudia sank to her knees, exhausted both physically and emotionally.

'Please God, let it end. I can't go on.'

She toppled over on her side and lay in the dirt, shivering and sobbing softly to herself, and at last dropped into the dark void of oblivion.

She woke with something tugging at her hair, and a strange grinding sound very close to her ear. Still groggy with sleep it took her long seconds to realize what was happening to her. She had slumped over sideways and one cheek was pressed to the dirt floor. She lay for a moment, enduring the sharp pulls on her hair and the grinding crunching in her uppermost ear and then the terror came back to her in full force.

A rat was chewing off her hair, cutting it with those sharp curved incisors, gathering it for nesting material. So great was her horror that it paralysed her. She could not move. Her whole body tingled, her stomach knotted with cramps and her toes and fingers curled with the strength of revulsion.

Suddenly she was no longer terrified. Her fear changed to anger. In one lithe movement she rolled to her feet and began to hunt the loathsome creature.

Relentlessly she pursued it around the cell, following it only by sound, the tiny scratch and patter of its feet. She no longer kicked out wildly, but deliberately aimed each blow at the sound. Twice the creature tried to climb to safety, but each time Claudia heard it and used her whole body to sweep it from the wall and knock it back to the floor.

This killing anger was an emotion she had never experienced before. It heightened all her senses, it rendered her hearing so acute that she could visualize each movement of her prey; it quickened her physical responses so her kicks were fast and powerful and when one of them landed on the warm furry body, the shrill squeal of pain and fear from the rat inflamed her.

She cornered it against the door of the cell and again stamped on it. She felt the small bones break under her heel, and she stamped again and again, sobbing with the effort, keeping it up until the carcass was soft and mushy under her feet.

When, at last, she backed away and sank down in her corner, she was still trembling, but no longer with terror.

'I've never killed anything before,' she thought, amazed at herself and this secret savage side to her nature which she had never suspected existed.

She waited for the familiar feeling of guilt and disgust to overwhelm her. Instead she felt as strong as though she had come through some ordeal which had armed her and equipped her to overcome whatever dangers and hardships lay ahead.

'I'm not going to give in, not ever again,' she whispered. 'I'm going to fight and to kill if I have to. I shall survive.'

I n the morning when the wardress came for the billy-can, Claudia confronted her resolutely, thrusting her face only inches from the black woman's, and keeping her voice measured but firm.

'Take this out.' She indicated the rat's carcass with her foot. The woman hesitated and Claudia said, 'Do it, now!' And the wardress picked up the mangled carcass by the tip of the tail, and glanced back at Claudia with a measure of respect in her dark eyes.

Carrying the empty billy and the dead rat she left the cell. When she returned a few minutes later with the billy-can refilled and the bowl of maize meal, Claudia subdued her thirst and maintained her new attitude of calm authority as she indicated the sewage bucket.

'That has to be cleaned,' she said, and the woman snapped a retort in Portuguese.

'I'll do it.' Claudia did not waver, holding the woman's gaze until she broke the eye contact. Only then did she turn her back and offer her manacled hands to the wardress.

'Undo these,' she ordered, and obediently the wardress unclipped the key from her webbing belt.

Claudia almost cried out as the handcuffs came away. The blood rushed back to her hands and Claudia held them to her chest and massaged them tenderly, biting her lips against the pain, horrified by the condition of her swollen hands and torn bruised wrists.

The wardress prodded her in the small of the back and gave an order in Portuguese. Claudia took up the handle of the sewage bucket and, brushing past the woman, climbed the stairs. The sunlight and warmth and clean dry air were like a benediction.

Claudia looked around the stockade quickly. It was obviously a women's prison, for a few dispirited feminine figures lolled in the dust beneath the single ebony tree in the centre. They were in ragged loin-cloths, their naked upper bodies so painfully thin that the ribs stood out clearly beneath the dusty dark skin and their breasts, even those of the younger women, were empty and dangled loosely as the ears of a spaniel. Claudia wondered what their crimes had been, or if their mere existence had caused their captors offence.

She saw that her own bunker was only one of a row of a dozen or so. It was obvious that these were reserved for the more important or dangerous prisoners.

The gates of the stockade were guarded by a pair of burly black females dressed in the usual tiger stripes and toting AK assault rifles. They peered curiously at Claudia and discussed her with animation. Beyond the gates, Claudia had a glimpse of the broad green flow of the Pungwe river, and for a moment entertained fanciful visions of plunging into it to bathe her battered body and wash her filthy clothes, but the wardress prodded her painfully in the back and urged her towards the screened latrines at the rear of the stockade.

When they reached them the wardress made hand signals for Claudia to empty her bucket into the communal pit, and then turned away to chat with one of the other wardresses who had sauntered across to join them with her AK 47 rifle over her shoulder.

The back wall of the latrine was also the rear wall of the stockade. However, it offered no avenue of escape. The poles were as thick as her leg, lashed securely together with bark rope, and their tops were several feet higher than she could reach.

She abandoned the idea of escape before it was fully formed and tipped the contents of the bucket into the deep pit. Immediately a humming cloud of flies rose from the depths and circled her head.

Wrinkling her nose with disgust, Claudia was backing towards the exit when a soft whistle stopped her dead. It was a low-pitched mournful note, so unobtrusive that she would have ignored it completely if she had not heard it so often before. It was one of the clandestine signals that Sean and his trackers used. Sean had told her once that it was the call of a bird called a bou-bou shrike, and because of its associations rather than its pitch, it electrified her.

She glanced quickly towards the screened entrance to the latrine, but it was safe. She heard the voices of the wardress and her colleague still chatting outside, and she pursed her lips and tried a soft unconvincing imitation of the whistle.

Instantly it was repeated from just beyond the back wall of the latrine and Claudia's hopes soared. She dropped the bucket and ran to the wall of poles, putting her eye to one of the larger chinks. She almost screamed when an eye looked back at her from only the thickness of the poles and then a voice, a well-remembered voice, whispered, 'Jambo, memsahib.'

'Matatu,' she gasped.

'Silly little bugger.' Matatu gave her the only words of English he knew, and she had to fight to prevent herself bursting out with the laughter of relief and hope and amusement at the incongruity of that greeting.

'Oh Matatu, I love you,' she blurted, and a folded scrap of paper was thrust through the chink into her face. The instant her fingers closed on it, Matatu's eye was snatched away from the peep-hole as though on a fishing line.

'Matatu,' she whispered desperately, but he was gone. She had spoken too loudly and she heard the wardress call out, and her footsteps at the entrance.

Claudia spun round and with the same movement crouched over the reeking pit. The wardress looked round the thatched screen and Claudia snapped at her furiously, 'Get out, can't you see I'm busy.'

And the woman involuntarily jerked her head back. Claudia was trembling with excitement as she unfolded the note and recognized the handwriting, and at the same time she was stricken with terror that it would be taken from her before she could read it. She refolded it quickly and slipped it deeply into the back pocket of her trousers, where she would be able to retrieve it even with her hands cuffed behind her.

Now she was eager to return to the privacy of her cell. The wardress pushed her down the stairs, but without the viciousness of before.

Claudia replaced the sewage bucket in the corner and then when the wardress pointed at her wrists, she held them out obediently. The touch of the metal on her abraded and bruised skin seemed even more galling than it had been before. The muscles and tendons of her upper arms and shoulders knotted in protest.

Once Claudia was manacled the wardress seemed to recapture her harsh mood of authority. She tipped the contents of the maize bowl onto the floor and lifted her boot to grind it into the dirt.

Claudia flew at her. 'Don't you dare!' she hissed, thrusting her face close to the woman's, glaring into her eyes so viciously that she recoiled involuntarily.

'Get out!' Claudia told her. '*Allez*! Vamoose!' And the wardress backed out of the cell with a muttered but unconvincing show of defiance, and dragged the door closed behind her.

Claudia was amazed at her own courage. She leaned against the door trembling with the effort that the contest of wills had cost her, only then realizing the risk that she had taken – she could have been brutally beaten or deprived altogether of her precious supply of water.

It was Sean's letter that had given her the strength and bravado to defy the wardress. Leaning against the door, she reached back into her pocket and touched the scrap of folded notepaper, merely to reassure herself that it was safe. She would not read it yet. She wanted to delay and savour that pleasure. Instead, she retrieved her drinking straw from its hiding-place.

After she had drunk from the billy, she ate the maize cake, delicately picking it out of the dirt with her teeth and trying to shake loose the earth and dirt that clung to the sticky lumps of porridge. She was determined not to leave a scrap of it, not only because she was hungry but because she knew she would have need of all her strength in the days ahead, and because she had learned that food scraps attracted the rats. Only when she had eaten and drunk, did she allow herself the luxurious pleasure of reading Sean's note.

She took it out of her pocket and carefully smoothed it between her swollen fingers. Then she squatted and placed it in the beam of sunlight that fell in a corner of the cell, and at last turned and knelt over it.

She read slowly, moving her lips like a semi-literate, forming every word that he had written as though she could taste it on her tongue.

'Be strong, it won't be for much longer and remember,

I love you. Whatever happens, I love you.' Her vision swam with tears as she read his last words, and then she sat back and whispered softly, 'I'll be strong. I promise you that I'll be strong for you, and I love you too, with my very existence, I love you.'

'They may fight like women,' said Sergeant Alphonso, as he surveyed the piles of captured Zimbabwean army equipment. 'But at least they dress like warriors.'

The uniforms had been supplied by Britain as part of their aid commitment to Mugabe after the capitulation of Ian Smith's white regime. They were the finest quality, and Alphonso and his men stripped off their old faded and patched tiger-striped battledress with alacrity. In particular they were delighted with the gleaming black leather paratrooper boots with which they replaced their eclectic collection of tattered joggers and grubby tennis shoes.

Once they had decked themselves out in this captured finery and fallen in on the beaten-earth parade ground, Sean and Job went down their ranks checking and instructing them on the correct way to wear each item of uniform. The quartermaster tailor followed behind them, correcting any gross discrepancy in size and fit.

'They don't have to be perfect,' Sean said. 'They won't be on parade, just good enough to pass a casual glance. We haven't got time to waste on the niceties of dress.'

After the men were fully kitted out, Sean and Job worked on their plan of Grand Reef base for the rest of that day and most of the night. First they sat on opposite sides of a desk in the headquarters communications room and brainstormed for every detail of the base lay-out that they could dredge from their memories. By nightfall, they were satisfied that they had the most accurate picture that they could hope for. However, Sean had learned from experience that it was difficult for an illiterate to visualize physical reality from a two-dimensional drawing, and discreet enquiry had revealed that almost all his new command, although battle-tried warriors, could neither read nor write.

Most of the rest of that night, they worked on building a scale model of the base, setting it out on the beaten surface of the parade ground, working by lantern light. Job had an artistic flair and whittled model buildings from the soft balsa-like wood of the baobab tree, and used water-washed pebbles of various colours from the sandbanks of the river to lay out the airstrip and roads and perimeter fences of the base.

The following morning the raiding party was paraded and inspected by Captain Job and Sergeant Alphonso and then seated around the model in a ring. The model proved to be a major success, provoking lively comment and query.

First Sean described the raid, moving matchboxes down the pebble roadways to represent the column of Unimogs, illustrating the diversionary attack on the perimeter, the withdrawal of the loaded trucks and the rendezvous on the Umtali road. Once he had finished he handed his pointer to Sergeant Alphonso.

'All right, Sergeant, explain it to us again.' The ring of attentive troopers delighted in correcting the occasional mistakes and omissions that Alphonso made. When he was finished he handed the pointer to his senior corporal to repeat the lecture. After five repetitions, they all had it perfectly memorized and even General China was impressed.

'It only remains to see if you can do it as well as you explain it,' he told Sean.

'Just give me the trucks,' Sean promised.

'Sergeant Alphonso was with the unit that originally captured them. He knows where they are hidden. Incidentally the guards major whose uniform you will use was killed in the same action.'

'How long ago was that?' Sean asked.

'About two months ago.'

'Beauty!' said Sean bitterly. 'That means that those trucks have been lying in the bush all that time. What makes you think they are still there, or that they are still in running order?'

'Colonel,' China gave that thin cold smile that Sean was coming to know and loathe so well, 'for Miss Monterro's sake you had better pray they are.' The smile vanished. 'Now, while the men draw their rations and ammunition, you and I will have a final discussion. Come with me, Colonel.'

Once they were in the communications room of the command bunker, China turned to Sean with his expression bleak. 'During the night, I received a radio message from my agent in Grand Reef base. He only transmits in an emergency, otherwise the risk is too high. This is an emergency. Training on the Stinger systems is complete. They have orders to move the missiles out of Grand Reef within the next seventy-two hours, depending on availability of transport aircraft.'

Sean whistled softly. 'Seventy-two hours – in that case we won't make it.'

'Colonel, all I can tell you is that you had better make it. If you don't, you will have no further value to me and I will begin thinking of old times.' He touched his damaged ear significantly. Sean stared him out silently until China went on, 'However, not all the news is bad, Colonel. My agent will meet you in Umtali and give you full intelligence on the buildings where the Stingers are being held, the room used as a lecture theatre, and the training manuals. He will accompany you to the base. He is well-known to the guards at the gates. He will assist your entry and guide you to the training centre.'

'That's something,' Sean growled. 'Where will I meet him?'

'There is a night club in Umtali. The Stardust, a gathering place for pimps and whores. He will be there every evening from eight until midnight. Alphonso knows the Club. He will take you to it.'

'How will I recognize your agent?'

'He will wear a tee-shirt with a large portrait of the comic book hero, Superman, on the chest,' China said, and Sean closed his eyes as though in pain while China went on. 'The man's name is Cuthbert.'

Sean shook his head and whispered, 'I don't believe this is happening to me. Superman and Cuthbert!' He shook his head again as if to clear it. 'What about the RZ with the porters at St Mary's mission?'

'That is arranged,' China assured him. 'The porters will cross the border tomorrow night as soon as it is dark and conceal themselves in the caves in the mountains above the mission station to await your arrival.'

Sean nodded and changed the thread of the discussion.

'If we leave now, how long will it take for us to reach the spot where the Unimogs are hidden?'

'You should be there before noon tomorrow.'

'Is there anything else we should discuss?' Sean asked, and when China shook his head, Sean stood up, slung his AKM assault rifle on one shoulder and with his free hand lifted the small canvas duffel bag that contained the dead guards major's uniform and his personal kit.

'Until we meet again, General China.'

'Until we meet again, I will take good care of Miss Monterro. Never fear, Colonel.'

The column was heavily laden. Each man carried food and water for two days together with ammunition, the extra belts for the RPD machine-guns, grenades and rockets for the RPG 7 launchers.

Though they could not run under that weight, Sergeant Alphonso in the van set a cracking pace. Before nightfall they passed through the Renamo lines into the 'Destruction area', a free-fire zone where there was a possibility of encountering Frelimo patrols, and Sean ordered a change of formation. They opened up to intervals of ten metres between the men in the single file of the main column and he posted flankers at the head and tail to guard against surprise attack.

They kept going hard during the night with ten-minute breaks every two hours, and by dawn they had covered almost forty miles. During the dawn break, Sean moved up to the head of the column and squatted between Alphonso and Job.

'How much further to the trucks?' Sean demanded.

'We have done well,' Alphonso replied, and pointed ahead. 'The trucks are there in that valley.'

They were on the foreslope of another area of hilly forested ground and below them the terrain was broken and bad. Sean appreciated why General China had chosen this area of the Serra da Gorongosa to defend. There were no roads in this wilderness and an attacking army would have to fight its way past an endless series of natural strong points and fortresses.

The valley that Alphonso pointed out was some miles ahead of them and beyond it the country changed from its savage mood and flattened into a broad gentle plain. Down there the dark forest was broken up and blotched with paler grasslands.

Alphonso pointed to the horizon. 'Over there are the railway line and the road to the coast . . .' He was about to speak again when Sean caught his arm to silence him and cocked his head in a listening attitude.

It was some seconds before the sound separated itself from the gentle susurration of the dawn wind in the forest below them and hardened into the whine of turbo engines and spinning rotors.

'There!' Job's eyesight was phenomenal and he picked out the approaching specks even against the dark background of hills and forests.

'Hinds.' Sean spotted them and Alphonso shouted a warning. 'Take cover.' The column scattered into cover and they watched the gunships come on, rising and dropping as they kept low over the hills, sailing northwards towards the Renamo lines in an extended formation.

Sean watched them through the Russian-made binoculars he had acquired from the Renamo stores. It was the first opportunity he had had to study a Hind at leisure. There were four of them and Sean surmised that there would be three flights of four machines to a full squadron of twelve.

'My God, they are grotesque,' he murmured. It seemed impossible that anything so heavy and misshapen could ever break the ties of gravity. The engines were housed in the top of the fuselage below the main rotor and formed the humpback that gave the machine its nickname. The air intakes to the turbos were situated above the cockpit canopy. The belly drooped like that of a pregnant sow. The nose was deformed by the hanging turret which housed the Gatling-cannon and from the stubby wings and bloated belly were suspended an untidy array of rocket systems and ordnance stations and radar aerials.

At the rear of the engine mountings the ungainly lines of the machine were further disturbed by another extraneous structure which seemed to have been tacked onto it as an afterthought.

'Exhaust suppressor boxes.' Sean remembered an article he had read in one of the flying magazines to which he subscribed. These structures masked the exhaust emissions of the twin turbo engines and shielded them from the infra-red sensors of hostile missiles. The author of the article had lauded their efficacy, but although they made the machines almost invulnerable to heat-seekers, the weight of the devices combined with that of the titanium armour to reduce severely the Hind's speed and range. Sean wished he had read the article with more attention; for he could not recall the figures for airspeed and range that the author had quoted.

The flight of gunships passed a mile or so to the east of them boring steadily northwards.

'General China is in for a breakfast show,' Job remarked as he rose from cover to reassemble the column and continue the march.

Although they had been going all night the pace never slackened and even Sean was impressed by the condition and training of Alphonso's company. 'Almost as good as the Scouts,' he decided, and then grinned to himself. 'Nobody could be that good.'

More than once, Sean dropped back to check that the men he had in the drag were anti-tracking and covering spoor. For now there was real danger that a Frelimo patrol might find them. He had fallen only a few hundred metres behind the rear of the column and was down on one knee studying the earth intently, when suddenly he knew that he was not alone, that he was being watched.

Instantly Sean threw himself forward, the rifle coming off his shoulder as he rolled over twice into the cover of a fallen log beside the path and froze, his finger on the trigger, his gaze raking the bush where he thought he had seen the flirt of movement.

It was closer than he had imagined. From the clump of grass right beside him came a mischievous giggle and Sean raised his head and whispered furiously, 'I've warned you not to sneak up on me like that.'

Matatu's head popped out of the grass and he grinned merrily.

'You are getting old, my *Bwana*. I could have stolen your socks and boots without you knowing.'

'And I could have shot your brown backside full of holes. Did you find the mem?'

Matatu nodded and his smile slipped.

'Where is she?'

'Half a day's march upstream, in a stockade with many other women.'

Is she well?'

Matatu hesitated, torn between telling the truth and telling Sean what would please him. Then he sighed and shook his head.

'They keep her in a hole in the ground, and there are marks on her arms and legs. They force her to work with the shit-buckets . . .' He broke off as he saw Sean's expression and went on hurriedly, 'but she laughed when she saw me.'

'Did you give her the paper?'

'*Ndio*. She hid it in her clothing.'

'Nobody saw you?'

The reply was beneath Matatu's dignity and Sean smiled. 'I know, nobody sees Matatu unless Matatu wants them to . . .' Sean broke off and both of them looked upwards.

Faintly, from far away, came the now familiar whistle of turbo engines and rotors.

'The Hinds, returning from clobbering the Renamo lines,' Sean murmured. The machines were out of sight beyond the canopy of the forest trees, but the sound passed swiftly southwards.

'With their limited range, their base can't be too far,' Sean thought and looked at Matatu thoughtfully. 'Matatu, those *indeki*, could you find the place where they come from, and where they return to?'

Matatu's gaze flickered with a moment's doubt, and then he grinned, once again brimming with bravado.

'Matatu can follow anything, man or animal or *indeki*, anywhere it goes,' he boasted confidently.

'Go!' Sean ordered. 'Find the place. There will be trucks and many white men. It will be well guarded. Don't let them catch you.'

346

Matatu looked affronted and Sean clasped his shoulder with affection. 'When you have found the place, come back to General China's camp at the Pungwe river. I will meet you there.'

As unquestioningly as a gun dog sent to retrieve a downed pheasant, Matatu bounded to his feet and tucked up the folds of his loin-cloth.

'Until we meet again, go in peace, my *Bwana*.'

'Go in peace, Matatu,' Sean called softly after him as the little man trotted away into the south. Sean watched him out of sight and then hurried to catch up with Alphonso's column

'They keep her in a hole in the ground, and there are marks on her arms and her legs.' Matatu's words echoed in his head, fuelling his imagination and his anger and his determination.

'Hold on, my love. Stick it out. 'I'll come to get you . . . soon,' he promised her, and himself.

They crossed the rim of another line of rocky kopjes, using a screen of jesse bush to conceal their movements against the skyline, and from good cover on the foreslope Alphonso pointed down into the valley below.

'That is how we brought the trucks in,' he explained, and Sean saw that the dry river-course would be the only access for a vehicle into this bad country. Even then it must have been a laborious task negotiating the rocky chutes and barriers that broke up the stretches of smooth river sand in the depths of the gorge.

'Where did you hide the trucks?' Sean asked without lowering his binoculars, and Alphonso chuckled.

'Unless Frelimo is cleverer than I think they are, I will show you.'

They left sentries posted along the ridge, to warn of the

approach of an enemy patrol, then Alphonso led the rest of the column down into the gorge. The lower they descended, the steeper became the sides, until there were sheer cliffs on each side and they were forced to traverse along a narrow game trail to reach the river bottom. It was suffocatingly hot in the narrow gorge, no breeze reached down here, and the rock absorbed the sun's heat and threw it back at them.

'The trucks?' Sean demanded impatiently, and Alphonso pointed to the cliffs opposite.

'In there,' he said, and Sean was about to snarl irritably at him when he realized that the cliffs had been carved by wind and flood water over the ages.

'Caves?' he asked, and Alphonso led him through the ankle-deep river sand to the cliff face.

Some of the cave entrances were merely scooped shallowly into the red rock, others had collapsed or were clogged with debris brought down by the summer floods. Alphonso indicated one of these and gave an order to his men. They stacked their weapons and began to clear the debris from the mouth of the cavern.

Within an hour they had opened it sufficiently for Alphonso and Sean to scramble through into the cave. Deep in the gloomy gut, Sean made out the shape of the first truck. His eyes accustomed themselves to the poor light as he moved towards it and he saw others parked beyond it.

'How the hell did you get them in here?' he asked incredulously.

'We pushed and carried them,' Alphonso explained.

'I hope to hell we'll be able to get them out again,' Sean muttered, and climbed onto the running board of the nearest vehicle.

It was coated with a thick layer of red dust. He yanked open the door on the driver's side and sneezed in the dust, but saw with relief that the key was still in the ignition.

He reached in and turned it. Nothing happened. The

ignition light stayed dark and the needles on the dashboard instruments never flickered.

'I disconnected the batteries,' Alphonso told him, and Sean grunted.

'Bright lad, but how the hell did you know to do that?'

'Before the war, I was a bus-driver in Vila de Manica,' Alphonso explained. It was odd to think that he had ever had such a prosaic occupation.

'All right,' Sean said. 'Then you can help me get this one started. Is there a tool box?'

Each of the trucks was equipped with two spare tyres, hand pump, tool box, tarpaulin and long-range fuel tank. Once Sean had reconnected the battery of the first truck, there was sufficient charge to produce a dull red glow in the ignition lamp on the dashboard and to raise the needle of the fuel gauge to the 'half' position but insufficient to kick the engine over.

'Find the crank handle,' Sean ordered. It was secured behind the passenger seat in the cab. Two hefty Shanganes swung the engine over with such gusto that it fired and stuttered and then burst into a steady roar. Thick blue exhaust smoke filled the cavern and Sean lifted his foot off the accelerator pedal. Two of the tyres were flat and had to be pumped by hand. While this was being done, the troopers cleared the last of the rocks and tree trunks from the mouth of the cave and with the transmission in four-wheel drive, Sean reversed sharply down the incline and bounced and jolted over the rough ground.

When the truck hung up on the boulders of the river bank and the wheels spun without purchase, twenty men flung their combined weight on it, and by brute force shoved it through. The Unimog crashed over the lip of the bank and into the riverbed. Sean drove it clear and parked under the opposite cliffs. He left the engine running to charge the depleted battery and they climbed back to the cavern and started work on the second truck.

Apart from flat tyres and batteries, they found no serious defects in any of the vehicles. One after the other, they coaxed the engines to life and then manhandled them down into the riverbed. It was the middle of the afternoon by the time all three trucks were lined up on the white river sand.

'Get the men to change uniforms now,' Sean ordered. 'Leave their other gear in the cave.'

Joking and laughing, they stripped off their Renamo tiger stripes and donned the British-pattern battledress of the Zimbabwean army. While they were busy, Sean went over the vehicles again. He found the army registration papers in a plastic wallet in the cubby-holes of each of the Unimogs.

'Hope we never have to show them,' he grumbled to Job. 'They are probably listed as stolen or destroyed.'

He opened the caps on the fuel tanks and physically checked the contents of each.

'Enough to get us to Grand Reef and back to St Mary's,' he estimated. 'With not much to spare.'

He ordered the windscreen and side windows of the cabs to be cleaned, but the bodywork to be left as it was, caked with mud and dust. It gave them the appearance of a patrol returning from a sortie into the deep bush and, more importantly, partially obscured the military markings and registration numbers.

Once the men had changed into their disguise and cached their Renamo uniforms, Sean and Job inspected each man and his equipment minutely, before allowing him to board one of the Unimogs.

It was almost five o'clock before they were ready to leave. Both Job and Alphonso had heavy-vehicle driver's licences and one of the Renamo troopers who gloried in the name of Ferdinand da Costa claimed driving experience. Sean took the passenger seat beside him to check his performance.

Job drove the leading truck, Alphonso in the middle and Sean and the learner driver in the rear. Apart from a heavy foot on the accelerator pedal, Ferdinand da Costa proved himself an adequate driver, but Sean took the wheel from him at the difficult places.

In line astern, they churned through the heavy sand, following in the wheel ruts of Job's Unimog, winding up the river-course for half a mile before they reached the first obstacle.

It required the combined efforts of all forty men to heave and shove the trucks up the first rocky chute in the riverbed, and even then they had to cut twenty-foot-long mopane poles and use them as levers to prise the wheels up over the larger boulders.

The powerful truck motors bellowed in high revolutions, blue diesel smoke billowed from the exhausts and Sean remarked to Job, 'An open invitation to every Frelimo within twenty miles to join the party.' Then he checked his wrist watch. 'We are falling behind our schedule.'

They tried to make up time along the easier stretches of the river-course, but the sunset and darkness caught them still almost twenty kilometres from the main east-to-west road between the sea and the border post at Umtali.

Nightfall made the journey more arduous. Sean dared not use the trucks' headlights, and they had to proceed in darkness alleviated only by starlight and a moon in its last quarter.

It was after midnight before they could at last leave the riverbed by negotiating a low spot in the bank. With four men walking ahead of the lead truck to guide it around ant-bear holes and other concealed obstacles, they struck out directly southwards and within two hours had intersected the overgrown disused track that Alphonso had told Sean about.

Sean called a halt and they spread the field map on the bonnet of the lead truck and by flashlight studied it anxiously.

'We are here,' Alphonso told him. 'This track runs up

to an old asbestos mine, it was abandoned by the Portuguese in 1963 at the start of the Frelimo war.'

'We'll rest up here,' Sean decided. 'Get the trucks off the road and covered with branches. We must expect the Hinds to over-fly us sometime tomorrow. No cooking-fires, no smoking.'

At four o'clock that afternoon, they woke those still asleep and ate a hasty meal of cold rations. Sean ordered the journey to be resumed and they stripped the camouflage from the trucks. They boarded the entire raiding party except for the four men who walked ahead of the leading truck, examining the ancient overgrown wheel-ruts of the track for Frelimo anti-vehicle landmines, probing any suspicious lump or hollow with a bayonet before waving the column forward.

The sun was just setting when they at last came in sight of the main road, its macadamized surface snaking through the open forest and winding around the scattered kopjes. Sean halted the column well back out of sight of the road and went forward with Job, leaving Alphonso in command.

From the top of a commanding hillock they kept the road under observation until it was fully dark. During that time two patrols passed, both heading eastwards, each comprised of three or four battered and dusty Unimogs packed with armed men in Zimbabwean combat gear, and with an RPD light machine-gun mounted above the cab.

They rumbled along with strict intervals of a hundred metres between vehicles and watching them through the binoculars Sean remarked, 'Well, at least we look like the real thing.'

'Except for your pale face,' Job pointed out.

'A birth defect,' Sean apologized. 'But I'll keep it out of sight until it's needed.'

They scrambled down from the hilltop and trudged back along the track to the hidden trucks.

'From here you are on your own,' Sean told Ferdinand,

the driver. 'Do try to remember to put the clutch in before you change into bottom gear, you'll find it a great help.'

Dressed in the uniform of the deceased guards major, Sean climbed into the back of the cab, behind Job's driving seat. The space was barely sufficient to contain him, he had to twist his shoulders at an angle from his hips and sit flat on the metal floorboards. It was uncomfortable to begin with, but Sean knew that within a few hours it would become agony. However, he was out of sight and yet able to communicate with Job merely by raising his voice.

Without headlights, the column drove the last mile to the juncture with the main road. The scouts they had sent ahead whistled that the road was clear and they raced forward and swung onto the macadamized surface, heading westwards towards the border.

As soon as they were safely onto the highway, they switched on the headlights and dropped their speed to fifty kilometres an hour, and adjusted their spacing to the regulation hundred-metre intervals. To an observer they were just another Zimbabwean mechanized patrol.

'So far, so good,' Job called over the back of the seat to where Sean was hiding.

'What's the time?'

'Seven minutes past eight.'

'Perfect, we'll hit the border post just after ten, when the guards are thinking of going off duty.'

The hundred kilometres to the border seemed much further. The metal floorboards of the cab were corrugated and cut into Sean's buttocks, transferring the impact of every pothole in the neglected highway up his spine into his skull.

'Get under the tarp! Border post ahead!' Job called at last.

'Not too bloody soon,' Sean assured him as the truck slowed and the overhead floodlights flooded the cab. Sean pulled the tarpaulin over his head and sank down as low as he could below the seatback.

He felt the truck brake and trundle to a halt. Job switched off the engine and opened the door of the cab.

'Wish me luck,' he muttered, as he stepped down from the cab.

Neither of them knew what to expect. The border formalities must surely be relaxed to accommodate the interchange of troops guarding the railway line. Job was dressed for the part and in possession of a genuine army pay book and ID. The truck's registration papers were likewise genuine and yet they could be compromised by some small unforeseen detail or by an alert border guard.

If anything went wrong, Job would give a single long blast on his whistle and they would shoot their way out. All the rifles and rocket-launchers were loaded, and the RPD machine-guns on the cabs were manned.

As the minutes drew out so Sean's nerves stretched tighter. He expected at any moment the shrilling of Job's whistle and the shouting and the gunfire.

Then at last there was the crunch of footsteps in gravel and the voices of Job and a stranger approaching the truck. Both doors of the cab opened and Sean tried to shrink himself as the truck tipped slightly under the weight of more than one man climbing aboard.

'Where do you want me to drop you off?' Job asked casually in Shona, and a voice Sean had never heard before replied, 'At the edge of town. I'll tell you where.'

Sean turned his head a stealthy inch and through the gap between the seats saw the blue serge cloth of a customs inspector's uniform. With horror, he realized that Job was giving an off-duty inspector a lift into Umtali.

The truck pulled forward and the inspector lowered the side window and shouted to the guards on the barrier.

'It's all right, open!' And as they accelerated ahead, Sean had a glimpse of the raised barrier through the window. He had to cover his mouth to prevent himself laughing aloud with relief and triumph.

On the back of the Unimog, the troopers seemed infected by the same reckless spirit of abandon. They were singing as the column wound down the hill to the town of Umtali. Job was casually discussing with the customs inspector the merits of the Stardust Night Club, and the price of a short time with one of the bar girls.

'Tell Bodo, the barman at the Stardust, that you are a friend of mine,' the inspector advised Job when they dropped him off on the outskirts of the town. 'He'll get a special price for you, and tell you which of the girls have the clap and which ones are clean.'

As they pulled away, Sean could at last crawl out from behind the seat and slump gratefully into the passenger seat.

'What the hell kind of trick was that?' he complained. 'You damn nearly gave me a hernia.'

'What better way to get VIP treatment,' Job chuckled, 'than to have the head of the customs service as a pal. You should have seen the guards at the border saluting us!'

'Where is this night club?'

'Not far, we'll be there before eleven.'

They drove in silence for a few minutes while Sean rehearsed the next order he had to give. He waited until Job turned the truck into a dimly lit side street and switched off the engine. In the side mirror, Sean watched the other two Unimogs pull in behind them, cut their engines and switch off their headlights.

'Back home again,' Job chuckled. 'Nothing to it.'

'Back home,' Sean agreed. 'And back home is where you are going to stay.'

There was a long silence and then Job turned his head and looked at Sean thoughtfully.

'What do you mean by that?'

'This is the end of the road for us, Job. You aren't coming to Grand Reef, you aren't high-jacking any Stingers, and you sure as hell aren't coming back to Mozambique with me.'

'You're firing me?' Job asked.

'That's it, pal. I've got no more use for you.'

Sean took a small wad of Zimbabwe dollars, part of the expense money General China had provided, and offered it to Job. 'Get rid of that uniform as soon as you can. If they catch you in it, they'll shoot you. Take the next train back to Harare and go see Reema at the office. She's holding about four thousand dollars in back pay and bonus for you. That will be enough to tide you over until Capo Monterro's estate pays out the money it owes us. My lawyers will handle that. You will be entitled to half of it . . .'

Job ignored the proffered money. 'You remember that day on Hill 31?' he asked quietly.

'Shit, Job, don't pull that sob stuff on me.'

'You came back for me,' Job said.

'Because sometimes I'm just a bloody fool.'

'Me too,' Job smiled. 'Sometimes I'm just a bloody fool.'

'Listen, Job, this is not your shauri any more. There is nothing in it for you. Get out. Go back to your village, buy yourself another couple of pretty young wives with Capo's dollars. Sit in the sun and drink a few pots of beer.'

'Nice try, Sean. Pity it didn't work. I'm coming back with you.'

'I'm giving you a direct order.'

'I'm refusing to obey it, so convene a court-martial.'

Sean laughed and shook his head. 'She's my woman, so it's okay for me to risk my life.'

'I've been nursemaiding you for almost twenty years and I'm not giving up now,' Job said, and opened the cab door. 'Let's go and find Cuthbert in his Superman suit.'

Sean left his cap and tunic on the seat, the insignia of a famous regiment would be out of place in a cheap night club. The Stardust was at the end of the lane in a converted furniture factory, a barn-like building with all its windows blacked out. They could hear the music from a hundred paces out, the hypnotic repetitive beat of the new wave African jazz.

Women clustered around the entrance. In the overhead light their dresses were as colourful as butterfly wings. Their hairstyles were flocculant afros, or the intricate beaded dreadlocks of the Rastafarians, their faces painted into death masks of rouge and purple lipsticks with iridescent green eyelids like iguana lizards.

They swarmed around Sean and Job, rubbing themselves against them like cats.

'Hey man, get me in!' they pleaded. 'Give me five dollars to get in, darling, I'll dance with you and jig-jig, man. Everything.'

'Come on, whitey.' A child with a tender immature body in a shiny dress of cheap nylon, the face of a black Madonna and ancient weary eyes, seized Sean's arm. 'Take me with you and I'll give you something you've never had before.' She reached down the front of Sean's body and cupped her hand to fondle him. Sean took her wrist and restrained her.

'What have you got that I've never had before, sweetheart? Aids?'

They pushed their way through the rustling nylon skirts and clouds of cheap perfume and at the door paid their five dollars. The doorman stamped their wrists with an indelible dye in lieu of an entrance ticket and they ducked through the black curtain.

The music was a stunning, painful assault, the lights were revolving strobes and ultra-violet. The dance floor pulsated with humanity transformed into a single primitive organism, like some gigantic amoeba.

'Where is the bar?' Sean bellowed into Job's ear.

'I'm a stranger here myself.' Job seized his arm and they struggled through the engulfing sea of light and sound and gyrating bodies.

The faces around them were transported as in religious

357

fervour, eyeballs rolled glaring white in the rays of the ultra-violet lamps, sweat glistened on upraised arms and streamed in rivulets down jet-black cheeks.

They reached the bar. 'Don't risk the whisky!' Job yelled. 'And make them open the beer in front of you.'

They drank directly from the cans, besieged in a corner of the bar with the ocean of humanity pressing hard against them.

There were a few white faces, all male, tourists and peace corps and military advisors, but most of the clientele were black soldiers still in uniform so that Sean and Job blended into their surroundings.

'Where are you, Cuthbert, in your Superman shirt?' Sean pushed away one of the more persistent bar girls, and peered over the heads of the dancers. 'We'll never find him in here.'

'Ask one of the barmen,' Job suggested.

'Good thinking.' Sean reached across and grabbed the front of the barman's shirt to get his attention, and then stuck a five-dollar bank note into his top pocket and shouted the question in his ear.

The barman grinned and yelled back, 'Wait! I find him.'

Ten minutes later, they saw Cuthbert working his way down the bar towards them, a skinny little man and the Superman tee-shirt was at least two sizes too large for him.

'Hey, Cuthbert, anybody ever tell you that you look like Sammy Davis Junior?' Sean greeted him.

'All the time man, man.' Cuthbert looked pleased, Sean had obviously picked out his pet vanity.

'Your uncle sends his love, can we go somewhere to talk?' Sean suggested as they shook hands.

'Best place to talk is here,' Cuthbert answered. 'Nobody else going to hear a thing you say. Get me a beer, can't talk with a dry throat.'

Cuthbert downed half his beer at a draught and then

asked, breathless from the effort, 'You were supposed to be here last night. Where you been, man?'

'We were delayed.'

'You should have been here last night. Would have been easy, man. Tonight, well, tonight is different.'

'What has changed?' Sean asked with a sink of dread in his chest.

'Everything changed,' Cuthbert said. 'The Hercules arrived 1700 hours. Come to pick up the goods.'

'Has it left yet?' Sean demanded anxiously.

'Don't know for sure. She was still there when I left the base at 2000 hours. Sitting out there in front of number three hangar. Perhaps she still there now, perhaps she long gone. Who knows?'

'Thanks a lot,' Sean said. 'That's a great help.'

'That's not all, man.' Cuthbert clearly enjoyed being the bearer of evil tidings.

'Hit us with it, Cuthbert.'

He finished the beer in another long swallow and held up the empty can. Sean ordered another and Cuthbert waited for it, drawing out the suspense masterfully.

'Two full para-commandos of the Fifth Brigade came down from Harare in the Hercules. They real cool, those Fifth Brigade cats,' Cuthbert said with relish. 'They real mean dudes, no shit.'

'Cuthbert, you've been watching too much "Miami Vice" on television,' Sean accused, but he was worried. The Fifth Brigade were the elite of the Zimbabwean army, converted by their North Korean instructors into ruthlessly efficient killing machines. Two full para-commandos of a hundred men each, added to the standing garrison of Third Brigade troops, almost a thousand crack veterans on base.

'Your uncle says you are going to take us in, Cuthbert. Pass us through the gates.'

'No way, man!' Cuthbert was vehement. 'Not with those Fifth Brigade cats in there.'

'Your uncle will be pissed off with you, Cuthbert. He's a pretty cool cat himself, man, Uncle China is.' Sean imitated Cuthbert's hip jargon.

Cuthbert looked worried. 'Man, I've fixed your pass,' he explained hurriedly. 'You'll have no trouble getting in. The guards are expecting you. You don't need me, man. No sense I should compromise myself, no sense at all.'

'You've got the pass here?'

'Right on. The password too. You'll have no trouble.'

'Let's go.' Sean took Job's arm and steered him towards the door. 'That Hercules could take off any time.'

Cuthbert hurried between them down the lane to where the three Unimogs were parked.

'Here's the pass.' He handed the plastic-covered card to Sean, it was slashed with a scarlet 'Top Priority' cross.

'The password is a number, "fifty-seven", and your reply is "Samora Machel". Then you show the pass and sign the book. Simple as a pimple, man. You in like Flynn.'

'I'll tell your uncle that you couldn't bring yourself to come with us.'

'Hey, give me a break, will you? No sense me getting culled, man. I'm more use to my uncle alive and kicking than dead meat.'

'Cuthbert, you are wasted in signals, you definitely should be on television.' Sean shook hands with him and watched him scurry back into the Stardust Club.

There were clusters of women around the back of each of the three trucks, giggling and joking with the troopers who hung out over the tail-gates. One of the girls was climbing aboard, boosted by eager hands, her mini-skirt rucked up high on her long thin black legs.

'Get those whores out of there, Sergeant,' Job snapped at Alphonso, and the women around the tail-gates scattered and three or four others descended hastily from the backs of the Unimogs with their skimpy clothing in varying stages of disarray.

Sean and Job climbed into the cab of the lead truck and as they drove off Sean buttoned on his tunic and tipped his cap at a rakish angle over one eye.

'What are we going to do?' Job asked.

'Number three hangar at Grand Reef is in full view of the main road. We will drive up the highway. If the Hercules is still there, we go in. If not, well, we'll go back the way we came.'

'What about the Fifth Brigade?'

'They're just a bunch of ex-gooks,' said Sean. 'You weren't afraid of them before, so what's changed?'

'Just asking to pass the time,' Job grinned at him sideways. 'You want to tell Alphonso about them?'

'What Alphonso doesn't know, won't hurt him,' Sean said. 'Just keep going.'

The column of three trucks drove sedately through the sleeping town of Umtali. The streets were deserted but Job obeyed the traffic lights punctiliously and then they were out on the open highway.

'Twelve minutes past eleven.' Sean checked his watch, and then read the road sign in the beam of the headlights.

'Grand Reef Military Base, fifteen kilometres.'

He felt the familiar tightness in his stomach muscles, the shortness in his breath and consciously slowed and regulated his breathing. It was always like this before a scene.

'There she is,' Job said softly as they topped a rise in the highway.

The airfield was fully lit, the beacon lights glowing orange and the blue and green dotted lines of the taxi-ways and runway beyond them.

In the stark white light of the floods, even at a distance of almost two miles, the Hercules looked gigantic. Its forty-foot-high tail-fin towered above the roof of number three hangar.

Sean recognized immediately that it was one of the

Marshall stretched-out conversions of Lockheed's Hercules original C MK3 transports for the Royal Air Force.

The RAF roundels were painted on the monstrous silver fuselage and on the high tail-fin.

'Pull over,' Sean ordered, and Job flicked his tail-light indicators and pulled into the side of the road. He switched off his headlights and one after the other the following Unimogs did the same.

In the silence Sean said softly, 'So the Hercules is still here. We are going in.'

'Let's do it,' Job agreed.

Sean jumped down from the cab and ran back to the second truck just as Alphonso climbed down to the roadside.

'Sergeant, you know what to do. I'll give you forty-five minutes to get into position. Then I want exactly ten minutes of diversionary fire, everything you've got.'

'The first plan was twenty minutes of diversion.'

'That's changed,' Sean told him. 'We expect a much stronger response than we first thought possible. Ten minutes and then pull out fast. Head straight back for St Mary's mission, we are abandoning the RZ on the Umtali pass. Hit them hard and then get out. Understood?'

'Yehbo.'

'Go!' Sean said, and Alphonso jumped up into the cab. Through the open window he saluted Sean and gave him a cheery grin.

'Break a leg,' Sean said softly, and the Unimog pulled out and headed down the highway towards the brightly lit base.

Sean watched the headlights turn off the main highway onto the secondary road that by-passed the perimeter fence of the airfield, then he lost them amongst the trees. Sean marked the time with the bevel ring on his Rolex and walked back to join Job in the leading truck.

He lay back in the passenger seat, pushed his cap to the back of his head and focused his binoculars through the open window at the huge aircraft that squatted on the tarmac under the floodlights.

The tail ramp at the rear of the fuselage was lowered like a drawbridge. He could see into the cavernous cargo hold.

There were four or five human figures moving about inside the hold and two more at the foot of the ramp. As he watched, a forklift truck trundled out of the open doors of number three hangar. Its fork arms were loaded with a stack of long wooden cases, four of them, one on top of the other. The cases were of raw white wood, and stencilled on them in black paint were letters and numerals which he could not decipher. He did not need to, the shape and size of the crates were unmistakable.

'They are loading the Stingers,' Sean said, and Job sat up straight in the driver's seat.

The forklift truck wheeled around the stern of the Hercules, and then climbed the open ramp and disappeared into the cargo hold. Minutes later it reappeared, drove down the ramp and wheeled into the hangar. Sean glanced at his watch, only five minutes had passed since Alphonso had driven ahead to set up the mock attack.

'Come on,' Sean muttered, and shook the Rolex on his wrist as if to speed up the mechanism.

Twice more, they watched the loaded forklift truck make the journey from out of the hangar, up into the belly of the Hercules and return empty.

Then it turned aside and parked at the far end of the hangar. The driver in blaze orange overalls climbed down from his seat and sauntered back to stand with the two other stevedores at the tail ramp.

'Loading completed,' Sean whispered again, and checked his watch. 'Seven minutes to go.'

Job unbuttoned the flap of his holster and drew the Tokarev 7.62 pistol. He withdrew the magazine and checked the load, then slapped the magazine back into its recess in the pistol grip and returned the pistol to its holster.

Through the binoculars, Sean saw the men who had been working in the cargo hold come down the ramp in a group. Three of them were white men, two of those in flying overalls and the other in British regulation battledress. Two pilots and one of the Royal Artillery instructors, Sean guessed.

'Start up!' he said, and Job kicked the engine to life.

'We should try to knock out those floodlights,' Sean muttered. 'We can't load the truck in the full glare, not with the Fifth Brigade breathing down our necks.'

He was looking at his watch, tilting the dial to catch the glow of the instrument panel.

'Okay, Job. Here we go!' he said, and the Unimog pulled forward. In the rear-view mirror, Sean watched the second truck driven by Ferdinand fall in behind them.

As they drove parallel to the main runway of the airfield Sean was assailed with a thousand memories. It all seemed exactly as it had been ten years before. No hangars or buildings had been added. He picked out the windows of his old office in the main admin block beyond the control tower, and as Job slowed the truck and turned onto the short driveway that led from the highway to the base gates, Sean almost expected to see the insignia of the Ballantyne Scouts between that of the Rhodesian Light Infantry and the Rhodesian African Rifles on the arch above the gates.

Job halted the truck under the lights facing the wire-mesh gates and two guards came to each of the side windows of the cab. They carried their AK rifles at the trail and peered in at Job and Sean.

Job lowered the side window and exchanged the pass-words with the commander of the guard and handed him the plastic-covered pass. The man took it to the guard house and made an entry in the register, then two of his men opened the main gates and he waved the convoy through.

Casually Sean returned the salute that the guards threw him as he passed, and he told Job quietly, 'Just like Cuthbert said, simple as a pimple. Now head straight down towards the admin block, but turn behind the control tower as you reach it.'

Job drove slowly, obeying the on-base fifteen mph speed limit and Sean unbuttoned the flap of his webbing holster and drew his pistol. He withdrew the magazine, pressed two cartridges out into the palm of his hand and then reloaded them in reverse order and slapped the magazine back into its recess in the pistol grip.

'Why do you always do that?' Job asked.

'Just for luck,' he said, as he saw Job watching.

'Does it work?' Job wanted to know.

'Well, I'm still alive, aren't I?' Sean grinned tightly. He pulled back the slide, pumping a round into the chamber of the pistol, engaged the safety and slipped the weapon back into its holster.

'Pull in behind the number three hangar,' he told Job, and he swung the truck across the hard stand in the full glare of the overhead floodlights into the shadowy area at the back of the hangar where they were screened from the control tower and the admin block.

As the truck stopped Sean jumped down and glanced around him quickly. The second Unimog pulled in beside the first, and armed men in battledress swarmed out over the tail-gates of both. With three quick strides Sean reached the back door in the corrugated metal wall of the hangar. It was unlocked and he stepped through. Job followed him immediately.

The hangar was empty except for a single light aircraft parked in the far corner. The bleak concrete floor half the size of a football field was stained with old oil spills, and the steel girders of the roof arched high overhead. It was brightly lit.

The forklift driver and the stevedores in their blaze

orange overalls were halfway across the floor, coming directly towards Sean in a group, chatting and smoking cigarettes in direct defiance of the huge prohibition notices in red letters on the hangar walls. They stopped in confusion as they saw Sean come through the door with the armed men behind him.

'Secure them,' Sean ordered. As Job rounded them up swiftly, Sean looked beyond them.

Along the opposite wall of the hangar were a line of office cubicles with side walls of painted chipboard and glass windows. Through a lighted window, Sean saw the head and shoulders of one of the pilots in his blue RAF overalls. He had his back towards Sean, and he was gesticulating as he spoke to somebody out of sight.

By now the stevedores were lying spread-eagled on the concrete floor, each with a man standing over him and the muzzle of an AKM pressed into the back of each of their necks. It had been done swiftly and silently.

With the pistol in his hand, Sean ran to the door of the office cubicle and jerked it open. Two men, one of the pilots and the Royal Artillery captain, were lolling in a pair of dilapidated armchairs under a wall which was covered with a collection of ancient girlie pin-ups which Sean guessed were relics of the bush war. The senior pilot sat on a cluttered desk in front of the lit window. All three of them stared at Sean in amazement.

'This is a commando raid,' Sean told them quietly. 'Stay exactly where you are.'

On the floor between the Royal Artillery captain's feet stood a square black bag with substantial locks and a Royal Artillery decal stuck on the side.

The gunner dropped a hand on it protectively, and Sean knew immediately what the bag contained. The gunner was in his mid-twenties, well built and competent-looking. The name tag on his breast read 'Carlyle'. He had blue eyes and thick sandy-coloured hair.

The senior pilot was a flight lieutenant, but he was middle-aged and over-weight. His flight engineer was balding and nondescript, with real fear in his eyes as he stared at the pistol in Sean's hand. Sean anticipated no trouble from either of them, and transferred his attention back to the gunner. He knew instinctively that this was the main man. He had the shoulders of a boxer, and he hunched them aggressively and scowled at Sean. He was young enough to be foolhardy and Sean held his gaze and warned him.

'Forget it, Carlyle. Heroes are out of fashion.'

'You are a South African,' Carlyle growled as he recognized the accent. 'Whose side are you on?'

'My own,' Sean told him. 'Strictly self-employed.' He glanced down at the black bag and Carlyle pulled it an inch closer to him.

'Captain Carlyle, you are guilty of gross dereliction of duty,' Sean told him coldly, and the gunner reacted to the accusation with the indignation of a professional soldier.

'What do you mean?'

'You should have posted guards while you were loading the missiles. You let us swan in here . . .' It distracted Carlyle as Sean had intended and gave Job the few seconds he needed to get his men into the office.

'Stand up,' he ordered the airmen, and they obeyed quickly, raising their hands and Job hustled them out of the office.

Carlyle remained in the armchair with the bag between his legs.

'Stand up!' Sean repeated the order.

'Screw you, Boer.'

Sean stepped up to him and seized the handle of the bag. Carlyle grabbed at it to prevent him and Sean brought the barrel of the pistol down across his knuckles. The skin split and Sean heard one of his fingers snap. He had misjudged it, he had not intended to inflict that kind of injury, but he kept his expression fierce.

'You have had your warning,' he said. 'My next offer is a bullet in the head.'

Carlyle was holding his injured hand to his chest, but his face was set and dark with fury as he watched Sean place the bag on the desk.

'Keys!' Sean said.

'Get stuffed,' said Carlyle. His voice was tight and hoarse with pain and Sean saw that his broken finger was standing out at an odd angle and swelling like a purple balloon.

Job reappeared in the door of the office cubicle. 'All secure,' he said, and glanced at his wristwatch. 'Four minutes to diversion.'

'Give me your knife,' Sean told him, and Job slid the trench knife from its sheath and passed it to Sean, hilt first.

Sean slashed the leather along the edge of the bag's steel frame and then pulled open the concertina hinge. There were half a dozen large loose-leaf folders filling the interior of the bag and Sean selected one. The file was covered in War Office red plastic and marked 'Top Secret'; he glanced at the title page:

FIELD MANUAL FOR INFANTRY USE OF THE
'STINGER' MODEL G4X
SURFACE-TO-AIR MISSILE

'Jackpot.' Sean turned the file so that Job could read it. It was a stupid thing to do. They were both distracted, turned towards the desk, studying the file.

Carlyle launched himself out of the chair. He was young and fast. The injury to his hand did not hamper him in the least, and he was across the narrow floor space before either of them could move to stop him and he dived head first into the frosted window in the middle of the far wall. It exploded in a sparkling shower of glass and Carlyle flipped over in mid-air like an acrobat.

Sean leapt to the empty window. Outside on the brightly

lit tarmac of the hardstanding, Carlyle rolled to his feet and ran. Job pushed Sean aside and stepped up to the window; lifting his AKM and taking deliberate care, he aimed at Carlyle's broad back as he sprinted across open ground towards the base of the control tower.

Sean grabbed the rifle and jerked the barrel down before Job could fire.

'What the hell are you doing?' Job snarled at him.

'You can't shoot him!'

'Why not?'

'He's an Englishman,' Sean explained lamely, and for a moment Job stared at him uncomprehendingly and Carlyle covered the last few yards and dived into the doorway at the base of the control tower.

'Englishman or Eskimo, we are going to have the whole Fifth Brigade down our throats in about ten seconds from now.' Job was obviously trying to control his anger. 'So what do we do now?'

'How long to diversion?' Sean asked to buy time. He had no answer to Job's question.

'Still four minutes,' Job answered. 'And it might as well be four hours.'

As he said it, the sirens began to howl like wolves, bringing the base to full alert. Obviously Carlyle had reached the ops room in the control tower. Sean stuck his head out of the shattered window and saw the guard turning out of the main gate-house on the far side of the runway. They, were dragging the spike boards across the approaches to the gates, to cut the tyres of an escaping vehicle to ribbons, and Sean saw the barrels of the 12.7mm heavy machine-guns depressing and traversing to cover the approaches. They were never going to get the trucks out that way.

'You should have let me sort him out,' Job fumed. How could Sean explain it to him? Carlyle had been a brave man doing his duty, and although the lines of loyalty to the old country had become blurred, Sean had the same blood in his veins; it would have been worse than murder to allow Job to shoot him down. It would have been a kind of fratricide.

Outside the hangar, the perimeter lights went on abruptly flooding the high security fence around the runway and taxi-way. The entire base area was lit like daylight.

If the commandos of the Fifth Brigade were in barracks and asleep when the alarm sounded, how long would it take them to come into action? Sean tried to make an estimate and then with self-disgust, realized that he was simply avoiding facing up to his own indecision and lack of any plan. He had lost control, and it was all blowing up in his face.

In a few minutes from now, he and Job and the twenty Shanganes of his commando were going to be overwhelmed. The lucky ones amongst them would be killed outright and so avoid interrogation by the Zimbabwe central intelligence organization.

'Think,' he told himself desperately, and Job was expectantly watching his face, waiting for orders. He had never seen Sean at a loss before. His unquestioning trust irritated Sean and made it even more difficult for him to reach any decision.

'What shall I tell the men?' Job prodded him.

'Get them . . .' Sean broke off as heavy gunfire broke out on the southern perimeter of the base on the opposite side to the hangar and out of their field of vision. Alphonso had been bright enough to realize that the plan had been derailed and he had started his attack a few minutes early.

They heard the whoosh-boom of RPG 7 rockets coming in through the perimeter wire and the duller thud-thud of mortar shells dropping in the base area. The 12.7mm machine-gun at the gates opened up, sluicing green tracer in pretty parabolas high into the darkness.

'How are we going to get out of here?' Job demanded.

Sean stared at him stupidly. He felt confused and

uncertain. Panic welled up from deep inside him, he had never suspected such a source existed. He didn't know what order to give next.

'Forget the bloody Stingers, just get us out of here.' Job grabbed his arm and shook it. 'Come on, Sean, snap out of it! Tell me what to do!'

'Forget the Stingers!' The words were like a slap with an open hand across his face. Sean blinked and shook his head. Forget the Stingers and forget Claudia Monterro. Without the missiles, Claudia would stay in the hole in the ground where Matatu had last seen her.

Sean glanced out of the open window again. He could see the gigantic tail-plane of the Hercules and part of the fuselage, the rest of the aircraft was obscured by the angle of the hangar wall. The metallic silver skin of the Hercules glittered in the arc lights.

Sean clamped down hard on the hot effervescence of panic that threatened to swamp him, and felt it subside.

'The lights,' he said, and glanced around him quickly. He spotted the fuse box on the office wall beside the door and he reached it in two strides and jerked open the cover.

The hangar had been built during Hitler's war when the RAF had used Rhodesia as one of its overseas training centres. The electrical wiring dated from that era and utilized the old-fashioned ceramic type fuse-holders.

'Give me an AK round,' Sean snapped at Job. His voice was crisp and decisive and Job obeyed instantly. He flicked one of the brass 7.62mm cartridges from the spare magazine in the pouch on his webbing.

Sean identified the main phase in the fuse box. The in-coming current would be distributed directly from the transformer at the gates, if he could over-load that he would blow the flying fuse on the transformer box.

He pulled out the ceramic fuse-holder and the hangar was plunged into darkness, but the light of the floods through the open window gave him sufficient light to see what he was doing. He jammed the AK cartridge into the lugs of the ceramic fuse-holder and snapped at Job.

'Stand back!'

The last vestiges of his panic were gone. He felt cold and resilient as a knife-blade. His mind was clear and he knew exactly what he was going to do.

He thrust the loaded fuse-holder back into its slot, and a blinding blue explosion of light like a photographer's flash bulb lit the darkened room, and Sean was sent flying backwards. He crashed against the office wall, half stunned, shaking his head, his vision starred with memories of the blue flash.

It took him a few moments to realize that the floodlights beyond the windows were extinguished and except for fiery bead necklaces of tracer flying across the dark sky and the brief glare of exploding grenades and rockets, the base was in darkness.

'Get the men into the Hercules,' he shouted.

Job was just a dark shadow behind the whirling Catherine wheels of fire that still disturbed his vision.

'What? I don't understand?' Job stammered.

'We are getting out in the aircraft.' Sean grabbed his shoulder and thrust him towards the door. 'Get Ferdinand and his boys on board and move your arse.'

Job ran, and Sean blundered blindly after him. His vision was returning swiftly. He turned towards the paler square of light that was the hangar doors.

'What about the prisoners?' Job called from the dark depths of the hangar.

Turn them loose,' Sean yelled back, and ran for the doors.

Although he did not have the Hercules conversion endorsed on his licence, Sean had flown the type before. In fact, he had accumulated almost 200 hours in the right-hand seat when he had flown with the South African air force in Angola and Namibia on anti-terrorist ops. It all came back to him now. He had enjoyed flying the Hercules and he remembered the remark a senior pilot had made.

'She's a lamb. I wish my wife was so docile.'

At the hangar door, Sean stopped suddenly.

'Matatu is right, you're getting old, Courtney,' he castigated himself and spun around. He charged back into the dark hangar and almost collided with Job.

'Where you going?'

'I forgot the bag,' Sean yelled. 'Get the men on board.'

He found the gunner's bag on the desk where he had left it and stuffed it under his arm. Job was waiting for him at the foot of the Hercules' loading ramp.

'All the men are on board,' he greeted Sean. 'You should have let me keep the pilot.'

'We didn't have time to convince him to co-operate,' Sean snapped. 'The poor bastard was in a blue funk.'

'Are you going to fly?'

'Sure, unless you want a shot at it.'

'Hey, Sean, have you ever flown one of these things?'

'There is a first time for everything.' Sean pointed forward. 'Come on, help me clear the chocks.'

They ran forward and dragged the wheel chocks clear, then Sean led the way up the steep angle of the ramp and stopped at the top.

'Here is the control for the ramp.' He showed Job the rocker switch in the side wall of the fuselage. 'Move it to the "up" position when I have got the first engine started and the red light goes on in that panel. It will switch to green when the ramp is up and locked.'

Sean left him and ran down the length of the Hercules' body. The Shanganes were milling about uncertainly in the darkness.

'Ferdinand!' Sean shouted. 'Get them to sit in the side benches and show them how to strap in.'

Sean groped his way towards the flight deck. He found the wooden missile cases loaded over the Hercules' centre of gravity between the wings. They were piled against the fuselage on wooden pallets and covered with heavy cargo netting. He eased past them and reached the door to the flight deck. It was unlocked and he burst through it and dumped the heavy gunner's bag into the map bin under the flight engineer's steel table. Through the cockpit windows, he saw that the mock attack on the south perimeter was still in full swing, but that the volume of fire from within the base was now much heavier than from the raiders out in the bush beyond the wire.

'The Fifth Brigade has woken up,' Sean muttered, and climbed into the left-hand seat and switched on the lights of the Hercules instrument panel. The vast array of glowing dials and switches was intimidating and confusing, but Sean would not allow himself to be daunted.

It was a lot simpler than starting the old Baron. He merely switched on and ran a finger along the rows of circuit breakers to ensure that they were all in.

'The hell with start-up checks.' He said and hit the start switch for the No. 1 engine. The starter motor whined and he watched the needle creep around the rev counter.

'Come on!' He pleaded. As revolutions touched 10% she automatically primed her combustion chamber with fuel and the engine ignited. He wound her up to 70% of power while he adjusted the earphones of the radio set on his head.

'Job, do you read?'

'Loud and clear, man.'

'Get the ramp up.'

'It's on its way.'

Sean waited impatiently for the ramp warning lamp on the panel to switch from red to green, and the moment it did so, he kicked off the wheel brakes and the Hercules rolled ponderously forward.

He was taxiing on one engine, and had to use gross opposite rudder to meet the asymmetrical thrust. However,

374

as he followed the pale strip of the taxi-way, he worked on the other three engines, and one after the other coaxed them to life, adjusting the controls as the power thrust altered.

'No wind,' he muttered. 'Makes no difference which direction for take-off.'

The main runway had been extended to accommodate the excessive take-off and landing requirements of modern jet fighters. However, the Hercules was STOL – short take-off and landing. It required only a fraction of the available distance and Sean steered her for the main intersection directly in front of the control tower.

So far the Hercules had drawn no fire. The heavy machine-guns at the gates were still firing wildly into the night sky. Poor fire control was always one of the problems with African troops who in all other respects made excellent soldiers.

On the other hand, at the southern perimeter the crack veterans of the Fifth and Third Brigades were showing what well-trained African troops were capable of. Their fire was going in deadly professional sheets, and already they had almost entirely extinguished Alphonso's initial onslaught. Apart from a few desultory mortar shells there was no longer any return fire from the dark sea of bush and forest beyond the base security fence.

It was only a short time before Carlyle managed to alert fully the garrison to the enemy within, and the flight controllers in the blacked-out tower realized that there was an unauthorized take-off in progress.

Sean was taxiing the Hercules at a reckless speed, so fast that she was already developing lift and wanting to fly. He knew that if he came off the concrete taxi-way onto the grass, there was a chance of bellying her or getting her stuck, but not as good a chance as having her shot up by the 12.7mm if he delayed the take-off a moment longer than was necessary.

'Job,' he spoke over the tannoy again, 'I'm going to give you cabin lights so you can make sure the lads are seated and strapped in. Take-off in forty seconds.'

He switched on the cabin lights to prevent chaos in the dark belly of the fuselage and then flicked his headset to the control tower frequency 118.6.

They were calling him stridently. 'Air Force Hercules Victor Sierra Whisky. State your intentions. I say again, Air Force Hercules.'

'This is Air Force Hercules Victor Sierra Whisky,' Sean replied. 'Request taxi clearance to avoid hostile ground fire.'

'Sierra Whisky, say again. What are your intentions?'

'Tower, this is Sierra Whisky. Request . . .' Sean mumbled and slurred his transmission deliberately, forcing the tower to ask for a further repetition. He was watching his engine temperature gauges anxiously as the needles crept up infinitely slowly towards the green.

'Tower, I am having difficulty reading your transmission,' he stalled them. 'Please repeat your clearance.'

Behind him Job barged open the door to the flight deck. 'The men are strapped in ready for take-off,' he called.

'Get into the right-hand seat and strap in,' Sean ordered without looking round. The engine temperature gauge needles were touching the bottom of the green. The main runway was coming up fast. Sean toed the wheel brakes, slowing for the turn and line up.

'Air Force Hercules. You are not cleared to taxi or line up. Repeat you have no clearance from tower. Discontinue immediately and take first left. Return to your holding area. I repeat return to your holding area.'

'Up yours, mate!' Sean muttered, as he pulled on ten degrees of flap and revolved the trim wheel to slightly tail heavy.

'Air Force Hercules. Stop immediately or we will fire upon you.'

Sean switched on the landing lights and swung the

376

monstrous aircraft onto the main runway. She handled as lightly as his little twin Beechcraft.

'You are a pussy cat, darling.' He knew that like a woman an aircraft always responded to loving flattery. He advanced the bank of throttle controls smoothly, and at that moment the heavy machine-gun beyond the tower opened up on them.

However, the Hercules was accelerating strongly and the gunner had not learned the art of forward allowance. He was shooting at the place that the aircraft had been seconds before and perhaps his nerves were still rattling for his fire was high as well as behind. The first long burst of tracer curved away over the high tail-fin.

'That cat needs shooting lessons,' Job remarked calmly. Sean always wondered if Job's cool and phlegmatic behaviour under fire was put on.

The next burst was low and ahead, the tracer splashed across the concrete runway just under the Hercules' nose.

'But he learns fast,' Job grunted a reluctant admission.

Sean was leaning forward slightly in the seat, with his right hand holding the bank of quadruple throttles fully open, with his left feeling the control wheel for signs of life, watching the airspeed needle revolve sedately around the dial.

'Here comes your friend,' Job said, and pointed out of the side panel of the canopy. Sean glanced around swiftly.

An open Land-Rover was tearing wildly across the grass verge alongside the main runway, its headlights cutting crazy patterns in the darkness as it bounced over the uneven ground. It was attempting to cut them off, and Sean could just make out the features of the man who stood in the back of the speeding vehicle.

'He doesn't give up easily, does he?' Sean remarked, and gave his attention back to the Hercules.

Carlyle must have commandeered one of the guard Land-Rovers and its black driver. He was standing in the open back, clinging to the mounting of the RPD machine-gun and his face was pale and contorted in the reflection of the Hercules' landing lights as he egged on the driver to greater speed.

'He's really taking it to heart.' Job leaned forward to watch with interest as Carlyle swung the machine-gun in its mountings, aiming up at the cockpit of the Hercules.

The driver swung the Land-Rover over on two wheels, until it was tearing along beside the huge rolling aircraft, only fifty yards away, almost level with the wing-tip.

'Hey, man,' Job shook his head, 'he's aiming at us personally.'

Carlyle braced himself behind the gun and the muzzle flashes blinked rapidly at them. Bullets raked the perspex canopy starring it with silver dollars, and both of them ducked instinctively as shot flew past their heads.

'He's a better shot than the other cat,' Job murmured and with the tip of his finger touched the drop of blood on his cheek where a splinter had cut him.

Sean felt the controls come to life in his hand as the Hercules approached flying speed and the wings developed lift.

'Come on, pussy cat,' he murmured, and Carlyle fired another burst at the same moment the Land-Rover hit a concrete culvert and bounced wildly, throwing his fire high and wild. He steadied himself and lined up to fire again.

'He's fast becoming my least favourite cartoon character.' Without flinching Job watched him take aim. 'Okay, here it comes!'

From the off-side the heavy machine-gun at the gates fired again and a stream of 12.7mm bullets skimmed the belly of the Hercules and flew on to pour into the racing Land-Rover beyond. They tore the front wheels off her and she somersaulted forward rolling end over end in a cloud of dust. From the corner of his eye, Sean saw Carlyle's body thrown high and clear.

'And so we say farewell to one of the last authentic heroes,' he intoned gravely, and eased back the control column of the Hercules. The great aircraft responded willingly, pointing her nose upwards.

Sean switched off the landing lights and cabin lights, plunging the machine into darkness so she no longer offered a target to the ground gunners. He hit the toggle to raise the landing gear and dump the flaps. Immediately the airspeed mounted and he put down one wing and went into a tight climbing turn.

Another burst of tracer followed them, floating up slowly and then accelerating as it approached until it sped past their wing-tip. Sean met the turn and banked the opposite way, weaving out of range.

'You want to make me sea-sick?' Job asked, and Sean ignored him as he checked the engine dials for possible damage.

It seemed impossible that the enormous target offered by the Hercules had received only a single burst of fire out of all the hundreds of rounds fired at it, but the needles on the dials all registered normal and responded instantly as he eased back on the boost and set revolutions for climb at five hundred feet a minute. However, the slipstream was whistling through the bullet holes in the canopy, ruffling Sean's hair and making conversation difficult, so that he had to raise his voice as he told Job, 'Go back and see if anyone was hit, then do a visual check for damage in the hold.'

The lights of Umtali town were off to the south and beyond them Sean could just make out the loom of mountains. He knew that the highest peak in the chain was 8,500 feet above sea level so he allowed a wide separation and levelled out at 10,000, then checked his heading.

Up until now, he had not thought about his navigation and was unsure of the bearings for a return to the Sierra da Gorongosa lines.

'Won't find them marked on any map,' he grinned. 'But we'll try 030 magnetic.' And he banked the Hercules onto that heading.

The adrenalin was still thick in his blood, the rapture of fear swirling him aloft on eagles' wings and he laughed again, just a little shakily and savoured the glorious thrill of it while it lasted.

The dark mountain tops slid away beneath him, just visible in the starlight like the shape of whales deep in an Arctic sea. He picked out the occasional pin-prick of light in the valleys, an isolated farm or mission station or peasant hut, and then as he crossed the frontier into Mozambique, there was nothing but darkness ahead.

'Nothing but darkness,' he repeated, and it seemed symbolic and prophetic. They were going back into the wasteland.

Sean eased back on power and began a gradual descent towards the lowland forests. Now that the mountain peaks were behind them, he didn't want to stay up high offering an easy target for the attack radar of a pursuing MIG fighter or an intercepting Hind gunship.

Job came back and locked the door of the flight deck.

'Any damage?' Sean asked, and Job chuckled.

'The floor of the cargo hold is ankle-deep in puke. Those Shanganes don't fancy your flying, man, they are up-chucking in all directions.'

'Charming.' Sean groped in the side pocket of the pilot's seat and came up with a packet of Dutch cigars, property of the RAF pilot.

'Well, look what we have here.' He tossed one to Job and they lit up and smoked contentedly for a few minutes before Job asked, 'How long before the MIGs catch up with us?'

Sean shook his head. 'They are based in Harare, I don't think they can catch us even if they scramble immediately. No. I'm not worried about the MIGs, but the Hinds are another story.'

They were silent again, watching the ripe celestial fruit of the stars that from the dark flightdeck seemed close enough to pluck.

'Are you ready to answer an embarrassing question?' Job broke the silence.

'Fire away.'

'You've got us up here, how the hell are you going to get us down again?'

Sean blew a smoke ring which was instantly obliterated by the slipstream through the bullet holes in the canopy.

'Interesting question,' he conceded. 'I'll let you know when I have an answer myself. In the meantime just worry about finding the Renamo lines in general and China's headquarters in particular.'

Five hundred feet above the tops of the forest trees, Sean levelled the Hercules, and reading the throttle and pitch settings from the instruction engraved on the instrument panel set her up for endurance flying.

'Another two hours before it will be light enough to even start looking for an emergency landing field,' he told Job. 'In the meantime, we can try to find the Pungwe river.'

An hour later, they spotted the gleam of water in the black carpet of forest ahead and seconds later the stars were reflected from a large body of dark water directly below them.

'I'm going back to check it,' Sean warned Job, and put the Hercules into an easy turn, watching the gyro compass on the panel in front of him rotate through 180 degrees before levelling out again.

'Landing lights on,' he murmured and flipped the switch. The tops of the trees below them were lit by the powerful lamps and they saw the river, a dark serpent winding away into the night. Sean threw the Hercules into a hard right-hand turn and then levelled out, flying directly along the course of the river.

'Looks like it,' he grunted, and switched off the landing

lights. 'But even if it is the right river, we won't be able to judge whether we are upstream or downstream of the lines until sunrise.'

'So what do we do?'

'We fly a holding pattern,' Sean explained, and banked the Hercules into the first of a monotonous series of figures of eight.

Around and around they cruised, five hundred feet above the tree-tops, crossing and recrossing the dark river at the same point, marking time, waiting for the dawn.

'Sitting duck for a Hind,' Job remarked once.

'Don't wish it on us,' Sean frowned at him. 'If you have nothing else useful to do, get the gunner's bag, it's in the map bin.'

Job lugged the bag to the front of the cabin and set it beside his seat, then settled himself comfortably.

'Read to me,' Sean instructed. 'Find something in there to amuse me and pass the time.'

Job brought out the red plastic-covered 'Top Secret' folders one at a time and thumbed through them, reading out the titles and chapter headings from each index page.

The first three files were all field manuals for the Stinger SAM Systems, covering their deployment in every conceivable situation from the decks of ships at sea to their use by infantry in every climatic zone on the globe, setting out in tables and graphs the missile's performance figures in all conditions from tropical jungle to high Arctic.

'All you ever wanted to know, but were afraid to ask,' Job observed, and picked out the fourth manual from the bag.

STINGER GUIDED MISSILE SYSTEM

Target Selection and Rules of Engagement

Operational Reports

Job read aloud, and then turned to the index and chapter headings.

1. Falklands Islands.

2. Arabian Gulf. 'Sea of Hormuz'

3. Grenada Landings.

4. Angola Unita.

5. Afghanistan.

Job read it out, and Sean exclaimed, 'Afghanistan! See if they give us anything about the Hind.'

Job set the bulky file on his lap and adjusted the beam of the reading lamp from its recess in the cabin roof above his head. He paged through the manual.

'Here we go! Afghanistan,' he read. 'HELICOPTER TYPES.'

'Find the Hind!' Sean ordered impatiently.

'SOVIET MIL DESIGN BUREAU TYPES
NATO DESIGNATION "H"'

'That's it,' Sean encouraged him. 'Look for the Hind.'

'Hare,' said Job. 'Hoplite. Hound. Hook. Hip. Haze. Havoc . . . here it is. Hind.'

'Give me the gen,' Sean ordered, and Job read aloud.

'This flying piece of artillery ordnance nicknamed by the Soviets, Sturmovich (or hunchback) known to Nato as Hind and to the Afghan rebels and many others who have encountered it in the field as 'The Flying Death', has gained a formidable reputation which is perhaps not fully justified.'

Sean interrupted fervently, 'Brother, I hope you know what you're talking about.'

Job went on,

'1. Impaired manoeuvrability, hovering and rate of climb characteristics as a consequence of the mass of its armour plating.

2. A limited range of 240 nautical miles fully loaded, again as a consequence of its armour weight.

3. A low max. speed of 157 knots and cruise speed of 147 knots.

4. Very high service and ground maintenance requirements.'

'That's interesting,' Sean cut in. 'Even this big baby,' he patted the Hercules' control column, 'is faster than a Hind. I'll remember that if we meet one.'

'Do you want me to read to you?' Job asked. 'If so, then shut up and listen.'

'My apologies, go ahead.'

'It is estimated that several hundred machines of this type have been employed in Afghanistan. Generally they have met with great success against the rebels although in excess of 150 have been destroyed by rebel troops armed with the Stinger SAM. These figures alone prove that the Hind can be effectively engaged by the Stinger SAM System employing the tactics set out in the following chapters.'

Job read on, giving the engine type and performance, the weapons and other statistics until, at last, Sean stopped him.

'Hold on, Job!' Sean pointed towards the east. 'It is getting light.'

The sky was pale enough to form a distinct horizon where it met the black land mass.

'Put the book away and go call Ferdinand up here. See if he can recognize where we are, and show us the way home.'

A strong odour of vomit surrounded Ferdinand as he stumbled onto the flight deck and the front of his tunic was stained. He leaned for support on the back of the pilot's seat, and Sean moved to put as much distance between them as possible.

'Look out there, Ferdinand.' Sean gesticulated through the bullet-punctured canopy. 'Do you see anything that you recognize?'

The Shangane peered dubiously around him muttering gloomily and then suddenly his expression cleared and lightened.

'Those hills.' He pointed out the side window. 'Yes, I

know them. The river comes out between them at a water-fall.'

'Which way is the camp?'

'That way, far that way.'

'How far?'

'Two full days' march.'

'Seventy nautical miles,' Sean translated time into distance. 'We aren't too far out. Thank you, Ferdinand.' Sean broke out of the monotonous figure-of-eight pattern and levelled the Hercules' gigantic wings.

Still low against the forest, he flew westwards, the direction Ferdinand had pointed, while behind them the dawn came on apace turning the eastern sky a hazy carmine. They chased the shades of night as they fled across the dark hills.

Sean aimed the nose of the Hercules at the gap that Ferdinand had pointed out and checked his wristwatch against the panel clock.

'Time for News Desk on the Africa Service of the BBC,' he said, and fiddled with the radio controls. He picked up the familiar signature tune on 15,400 megahertz.

'This is the BBC. Here again are the news headlines. In the United States, Governor Michael Dukakis has convincingly carried the State of New York against Senator Jesse Jackson in his bid for the democratic party presidential nomination. Israeli troops have shot dead two more protestors in the occupied Gaza Strip. One hundred and twenty passengers have died in an airline crash in the Philippines. Renamo rebels have highjacked an RAF Hercules transport from a Zimbabwe Air Force base near the town of Umtali. They have flown it into Mozambique where it is being pursued by aircraft of the Zimbabwe and Mozambiquan air forces. A spokesman said that both President Mugabe and President Chissano have given orders that the aircraft, which has no hostages on board but which contains sophisticated modern weapons intended for use against the rebels, is to be destroyed at all costs.'

Sean switched off the set and smiled across at Job.

'You never thought you'd make the news headlines, did you?'

'I can do without the fame,' Job admitted. 'Did you get the bit about being pursued and destroyed at all costs?'

The Hercules was fast approaching the gap in the line of hills. The light had strengthened so that Sean could make out the pearly gleam in the throat of the pass where the river tumbled down over wet black rock.

'Incoming!' Job yelled suddenly. 'One o'clock low!'

With his extraordinary eyesight, he had picked it up an instant before Sean did. The Hind had been lying in ambush, squatting like some monstrous insect in a hidden clearing in the forest, guarding the entrance to the river pass.

As Sean saw it, he understood clearly the tactics Frelimo had used to cut him off from the Renamo lines. They would have sent the full squadron of Hinds in during the night, as soon as they guessed where he was headed.

Operating at the limits of their range, the Hinds would have settled in a defensive line, landing to conserve fuel, hiding in the forest and sweeping with their pulse radars, listening in the silence for the sound of the Hercules' engines.

Almost certainly they had guessed that he would use the river as a navigational landmark. There would probably be other gunships waiting further upstream, forming an intercepting ring around the Renamo lines, but erring too far south, Sean had run headlong into this one.

It leapt out of the forest, rising vertically on the silver blur of its rotor, the deformed nose drooping, like a minotaur lowering its head to charge, blotched with leprous camouflage, obscenely ugly and deadly.

It was still below them but coming up swiftly, swelling in size as they converged. Within moments its Gatling-cannon would bear, already it was training upwards. Sean reacted without thought.

He rammed all four throttle controls fully open and the great turbos screeched as he thrust the nose down, diving straight at the helicopter.

He saw the rockets leaving the weapon pods under the Hind's wings, each one a black dot in the centre of a white wreath of smoke as it dropped clear. He remembered the statistics Job had read him only minutes before. The Hind carried two AT-2 Swatter missiles and four 57mm rocket pods.

He dived the Hercules through the barrage of rockets, they flashed past his head, a storm of smoke and death, and the Hind was only two hundred metres ahead, still rising to meet him, firing rockets at pointblank range but not allowing for his violent manoeuvre.

'Hold on!' Sean shouted at Job. 'I'm going to ram the bastard.'

The killing rage was on him, sweet and hot in his blood, there was no fear at all, just the marvellous urge to destroy.

At the last moment, the pilot of the Hind guessed his intention. They were so close that through the canopy, Sean could clearly make out his features below the helmet. The Russian's face was doughy white and his mouth a shocking red slash like an open wound.

He flicked the gunship over on its side, almost inverting it completely, closing down his collective so the Hind fell like a lead weight, trying to duck under the Hercules' outspread pinions.

'Got you, you son of a bitch!' Sean exulted, and the Hercules wing hit the tail of the gunship. The shock of impact threw Sean against his shoulder-straps, and the Hercules shuddered and lurched, the airspeed was knocked off her and she quivered on the edge of the stall only two hundred feet above the forest top.

'Come on, pussy cat,' Sean whispered like a lover.

He was babying the controls, coaxing her with gentle fingers.

Her damaged wing was down, tatters of torn metal hanging from it, whipping and banging in the slipstream, and the forest tops reached up like the talons of a predator to claw them out of the sky.

'Fly for me, darling,' Sean whispered, and the four engines, howling with the effort, held her up and then gradually lifted her clear.

The needle of the rate-of-climb indicator rose jerkily, they were climbing at two hundred feet a minute.

'Where's the Hind?' Sean yelled at Job.

'She must be down,' Job called back, both of them screaming at each other with terror and excitement and the triumph of it.

'Nothing could take a hit like that.' Then his voice changed. 'No, there she is, she's still flying. My God, will you look at that mother?'

The Hind was hard hit, skittering out to one side, the tail rotor and the rudder torn, almost completely gone. Obviously her pilot was fighting for her life as she lurched and rolled and wallowed about the sky.

'I don't believe it! She's still shooting at us!' Job cried, and a smoking rocket trail blazed across their nose.

'She's steadying.' Job was watching her through the side window. 'She's coming round, she's after us again.'

Sean met the Hercules' climb, and aimed for the pass through the hills. The rocky cliffs seemed to brush their wing-tips and the foaming white waterfall flashed beneath them.

'He has fired a missile.' As Job called the warning, the pass through the hills opened up ahead of them, and Sean lifted the Hercules' maimed wing high in a maximum-rate turn.

The huge aircraft hugged the cliff face, turning the corner just as the Swatter missile locked onto the infra-red emissions of her exhausts and sped down the gut of the pass. The Hercules cut the turn so finely that Sean had to use full power to hold the nose level, and looking upwards through the skylight of the canopy, he felt as though he could have reached out and touched the rockface as the Hercules stood on one wing-tip. The missile tried to follow her round but at the critical instant the Hercules disappeared from its line of sight, and the rocky corner blocked the infra-red emissions of her exhausts.

The missile crashed into the cliff face, gouging out a great fall of rock and filling the pass behind the Hercules with dust and smoke.

Sean brought the Hercules back on an even keel once again, gentling her, favouring her damaged wing.

'Any sign of the Hind?'

'No . . .' Job broke off as he saw the dread shape materialize through the dust and smoke. 'She's there, she's still coming!'

The entire rear section of the Hind's fuselage was twisted askew and half her rudder was missing. She staggered and lurched through the air, only barely under control and falling rapidly behind the fleeing Hercules. The pilot was a brave man, serving her, keeping her in action to the end.

'He's fired again!' Job cried, as he saw the missile drop from under the stubby wing roots and boost towards them on a tail of smoke.

'She's down!' Job watched the tail rotor of the gunship break away and spiral upwards while the body dropped like a spine-shot buffalo bull and hit the trees, breaking up in a tall burst of flame and smoke.

'Break right!' Job called desperately. Although the Hind was dead, her terrible offspring blazed across the sky, bearing down on them mercilessly.

Sean put the Hercules over as hard as she would go. The missile almost missed the turn and went skidding wide in overshoot, but it corrected itself and came around hard, spinning out a long billow of silver smoke behind it, and it fastened on the starboard number two motor.

For a moment, they were blinded as the smoke of the explosion swept over the canopy, and was as suddenly swept away. The Hercules convulsed as though in agony. The missile blast threw her wing up, miraculously knocking her back onto even keel and adroitly Sean held her there.

He looked across in horror at the damage. The number two engine was gone, blown out of its mountings, leaving a terrible gaping wound in the leading edge of the wing. It was a mortal blow. In her death throes, the Hercules careered across the sky, dragged around by the asymmetrical thrust of her live engines, the damaged wing flexing and beginning to fold backwards.

Sean eased back the throttles, trying to relieve the strain and balance the thrust. He looked ahead, and there was the river, wide and shallow and tranquil above the turmoil of the falls. The first rays of the sun were buttering the tops of the trees on either bank and the crocodiles lay black on the white sandbanks.

Sean flipped on the internal tannoy and spoke over the loudspeakers into the cargo hold. 'Hold on! We are going to hit hard!' he said in Shangane, and pulled his own harness adjustment in tighter.

The Hercules lumbered down heavily, both wings so badly damaged that Sean was amazed that she was still airborne.

'Too fast,' Sean muttered. She was dropping like an express elevator. They would hit the trees short of the river. He braced himself to lose a wing with disruption of air flow, and gingerly pulled on full flap to slow her down.

Far from destroying herself, the Hercules responded gratefully to the additional lift, and floated in with a semblance of her old elegance. She skimmed the tree-tops on the riverbank and Sean switched off the fuel pumps, mains and magnetos to prevent fire. He held the nose high, bleeding off speed and the needle on the airspeed indicator wound back sharply. The stall warning buzzer sounded, and then the deafening klaxon of the landing-gear chimed in, trying to warn him that his wheels were still up.

The controls went sloppy as the Hercules approached the stall, but they were out in the centre of the river, twenty feet up, dropping swiftly. The crocodiles slid off the sand-bar directly ahead, churning the green water in panic, and Sean kept feeling the control column back and back, fending her off until the last possible moment.

He felt the tail touch the water and the airspeed indicator was right down to forty knots. The Hercules stalled and belly-flopped into the river. A solid green wave broke over the nose and washed the canopy, spurting in through the bullet-holes.

Both Sean and Job were flung forward violently against their shoulder harnesses, and then the Hercules bobbed up and surfed on her belly, slowing down and turning to stop broadside to the current.

'Are you all right?' Sean barked at Job. For reply, Job unbuckled his harness and leapt out of the co-pilot's seat.

The deck was canted under Sean's feet as he stood up. Through the canopy he saw that the Hercules was floating down aimlessly on the current. Her empty fuel tanks and the air trapped in the fuselage were keeping her afloat.

'Come on!' He led Job back into the main hold and saw at a glance that the cases of missiles were still secured in their heavy cargo nets.

The Shanganes were in a panic, at least two of them injured, writhing and moaning in the puddles of drying vomit on the deck, one with the sharp jagged end of bone protruding through the flesh of his broken arm.

Sean spun the locking wheel on the emergency hatch and kicked it outwards. Immediately the nylon escape chute inflated and popped out like a drunkard's yellow tongue to flop onto the surface of the water below.

Sean leaned out of the open hatch. They were drifting towards another sand-bar and he judged that the water under their keel was only shoulder-deep for he could see the bottom clearly.

'Ferdinand.' Sean picked him out of the mob of milling Shanganes. 'This way, get them put!' He saw Ferdinand sober and lash out at the panic-stricken troopers around him, driving them towards the hatch.

'Show them how it's done,' Sean ordered Job. 'And once you are down, get them to haul the hull onto the sand-bar.'

Job folded his arms over his chest and jumped feet first onto the chute. He shot down into the water and then floundered to his feet. The water came up to his armpits and, immediately, he waded to the Hercules' side and threw his whole weight against it.

One at a time, the uninjured Shanganes followed him down the chute, and at the bottom, Job took charge of them. Sean shoved the last trooper through the hatch and then leapt out himself.

The water was just a few degrees below blood warm, and as soon as he surfaced he saw that all the men were straining against the Hercules' floating carcass and slowly moving her across the flow of the river. He added his own weight to theirs, and gradually the bottom shelved beneath their feet, and the water dropped to the level of their waists.

The belly of the Hercules ran aground, and she settled heavily as the fuselage flooded. The men dragged themselves onto the sand-bar and collapsed in sodden heaps, their expressions dull and bovine from the after-effects of terror and exertion.

Sean looked around him, trying to assess their position and plan his priorities. The Hercules was stranded high enough to ensure that only the lower part of the fuselage was flooded and that the missiles would not be submerged and have their delicate electronic circuitry ruined.

The current had swept them in under the sheer riverbank and the summer floods had piled dead trees and driftwood high against it. The sand-bar was merely a narrow strip below the bank.

'We must move fast,' Sean told Job. 'We can expect that the Hind was able to transmit a signal to the rest of the squadron, and they'll come looking for us.'

'What do you want to do first?'

'Unload the Stingers,' Sean answered promptly. 'Get them busy.'

Once Sean climbed aboard again he found that the hydraulic rams on the cargo door were still operating off the batteries and he lowered the ramp.

The weight of each wooden case was stencilled upon it. 152 lb.

'They are light, two men to a case,' Sean ordered, and he and Job lifted them onto the shoulders of each pair as they stepped forward. As soon as they received it, they trotted down the ramp onto the sand-bar, and up the bank into the trees. Ferdinand showed them where to stash them and cover them with driftwood.

It took less than twenty minutes to unload the cargo, and every minute Sean was in a ferment of impatience and anxiety. As the last case was carried ashore, he hurried out onto the ramp and peered up at the sky, expecting to hear the approaching whine of rotors and Isotov turbos.

'Our luck isn't going to last,' he told Job. 'We must get rid of the Hercules.'

'What are you going to do, swallow it or bury it?' Job asked sarcastically.

Against the forward bulkhead of the Hercules' hold was a 120-ton loading winch, used to drag cargo aboard. Under Sean's instruction, four Shanganes ran out the winch cable and used the Hercules' inflatable life raft to take the end of it across the river and shackle it to a tree on the far bank.

While they were doing this, Sean and Job searched the Hercules and stripped it of every item of useful equipment, from the first-aid kit to the stores of coffee and sugar in the tiny forward galley. With satisfaction, Sean saw that the tropical first-aid box was substantial and contained a good supply of malarial prophylactics and antibiotics. He sent it ashore with one of the Shanganes and ran back to the loading ramp.

The dinghy was returning and there was still no sound nor sight of marauding Hind gunships. It was too good to bear thinking about.

'Get everybody ashore,' Sean told Job, and went to the winch controls.

As he engaged the clutch, the steel cable came up taut and the Hercules' hull which was heavily beached on the sand-bar lurched and began to swing. He kept the winch running and the sand gritted and scraped under her belly as she was dragged by her own winch into deeper water.

As soon as she was afloat, Sean half closed the ramp to prevent her flooding too rapidly and winched her into the middle of the river, where the current was swiftest. As soon as she took the current and began to drift downstream, Sean grabbed the bolt cutters from their rack on the bulk-head and sheared the cable. The Hercules floated free.

On an impulse Sean cut a four-foot length from the end of the severed winch cable, and the stainless steel strands immediately began to unravel of their own accord. He rolled three of the separate strands into a tight loop and slipped the roll into his back pocket. Job would fit hardwood buttons to the strands. The garrotting wire was one of the Scouts' favourite clandestine weapons, and Sean had felt half-naked since he had lost his in the pack that he had dropped down the cliff. He transferred his full attention back to the Hercules.

'The fuel tanks are almost empty,' he murmured as he watched her progress downstream. 'She should float until she reaches the falls.' He stayed on board while at least two miles of riverbank went by.

In the meantime, he used the bolt cutters to sever the hydraulic pipes and fuel leads that ran along the roof of the cargo hold. A mixture of hydraulic fluid and Avtur dribbled and spurted and puddled onto the floor of the hold. Satisfied at last that he had done everything possible to throw off the pursuit, he balanced in the open escape hatch and pulled the pin from the phosphorus grenade that he had commandeered from Ferdinand.

'Thanks, old girl,' he spoke aloud to the Hercules. 'You have been a darling. The least I can offer you is a Viking's funeral.' He rolled the grenade down the deck of the hold and then leapt out of the hatch and hit the water. He came up swimming, reaching out in a full over-arm crawl with the image in his mind of those fat black crocodiles he had seen on the sand-bar.

Behind him, he heard the muffled bump of the exploding grenade but he never paused nor looked back until he felt the ground under his feet. By then, the Hercules was a quarter of a mile downstream, burning furiously but still afloat. Black oily smoke boiled up into the clear morning sky.

Sean waded the last few yards to the steep bank and crawled up it on hands and knees. While he sat there panting and gulping for breath, he heard the familiar and by now well-hated sound of rotors and Isotov turbo engines coming in fast. The smoke of the burning Hercules was a beacon that the Hinds would have spotted from fifty miles out.

Sean took a handful of mud from the bank on which he sat and smeared his bare arms and face. He crawled under a dense bush on the bank and watched the Hind come sweeping in over the treetops, banking in a wide circle around the burning hulk of the Hercules and then hovering like an evil vampire two hundred feet above it.

The flames reached one of the fuel tanks and the Hercules exploded in a dragon's breath, scattering pieces of itself across the river, the flames hissing into steam as they hit the water.

The Hind hung over the river for almost five minutes, perhaps searching for survivors, and then abruptly it rose high, turned its nose southwards and dwindled to a speck against the blue.

'Limited range and endurance, like the man said.' Sean stood up from his hiding place. 'Now go home like a good little Ruskie and report the target destroyed. Go tell Bobby Mugabe that he doesn't have to worry about his precious Stingers falling into the wrong hands.'

He reached into his top pocket and brought out the packet of Dutch cigars. The cardboard disintegrated in his hands and the leaf had dissolved into a soggy porridge. He tossed it into the river.

'Time I gave up anyway,' he sighed, and trudged along the bank, heading upstream.

Job was working on the two injured troopers.

'This one has got a nice set of cracked ribs and a broken collarbone.' Job finished the strapping and then indicated the other patient, 'I left this one for you.'

'Appreciate it,' Sean grunted, and examined the broken arm. 'It's a bloody mess.'

'Nice adjective,' Job agreed. Two inches of the shattered humerus protruded from dark bruises and blood clots. A buzzing swarm of metallic-blue flies were circling the clots, and Sean brushed them away.

'What have you done, so far?'

'Given him a handful of painkillers from the med box.'

'That should stun an ox,' Sean nodded. 'Get me a piece of nylon line and two of the strongest Shanganes.'

The arm had shortened dramatically and Sean had to get the ends of the broken bone to meet again. He looped the nylon rope around the trooper's wrist and gave the ends to the Shangane strong men.

'When I say pull, you pull, understand?' he ordered. 'Okay, Job, hold him.'

They had done this before, often. Job took up his

position sitting behind the patient and slipped his arms under his armpits and locked them around his chest.

'I'm going to hurt you,' Sean promised the patient, and the man stared back at him impassively.

'Ready?' Job nodded, and Sean glanced up at the rope. 'Pull!' They laid back with a will.

The injured man's eyes snapped wide open, and a rash of sweat droplets like blisters burst out on his skin.

'Pull harder!' Sean snarled at Ferdinand, and the arm began to elongate. The sharp point of protruding bone withdrew slowly into the flesh.

The Shangane ground his teeth together in the effort of restraining himself from screaming. The sound was like two pieces of glass being rubbed together forcibly, and it grated along Sean's nerve ends.

The point of bone popped back into the swollen purple wound and Sean heard the two ends rasp together deep in the flesh.

'That's it! Hold it!' he told Ferdinand, and deftly placed two splints from the first-aid box along each side of the arm. He strapped them in place with surgical tape, binding it up as firmly as he dared without cutting off the circulation, and then nodded at Ferdinand.

'Slowly. Let it go.' Ferdinand released pressure and the splints held the arm straight.

'Another breakthrough for medical science,' Job murmured. 'An elegant and sophisticated procedure, Doc.'

'Can you walk?' Sean asked. 'Or do we have to carry you home?'

'Of course, I can walk.' The trooper was indignant. 'Do you think I am a woman?'

'If you were, we would ask a top bridal price for you,' Sean grinned at him, and stood up.

'Let's inspect the loot,' he suggested to Job. It was their first opportunity to examine the crates from the Hercules.

There were thirty-five of them piled haphazardly under

397

the spreading branches of an African mahogany. With Ferdinand and four of his men assisting, they sorted through them, stacking them neatly after noting the lettering on each.

Thirty-three cases, each weighing 154 pounds were marked:

> STINGER GUIDED MISSILE SYSTEM
> 1 X GRIP STOCK AND ANTENNA
> 1 X INTERROGATOR
> 5 X LOADED LAUNCH TUBES

'That gives China 165 shots, and there are eleven Hinds left in the squadron after the one you knocked out of the sky,' Job calculated. 'Sounds good to me.'

'With the way some of these beauties shoot, they are going to need every one of them,' Sean grunted, and then his expression of deliberate pessimism lightened. 'Well, well! Here is one for the book!'

One of the two remaining odd-sized cases was stencilled:

> STINGER GUIDED MISSILE SYSTEM
> TRAINING SET M. 134
> TRACKING HEAD TRAINER

'That will make somebody's life a lot easier,' Job agreed. The captured manuals had discussed this training system which allowed an instructor to monitor a trainee's tracking technique during a simulated missile launch. It would be invaluable equipment for whoever was given the job of teaching the Renamo troops to use the system.

However, it was not until Sean examined the last and smallest case that the full value of the prize dawned on him.

The small wooden crate was stencilled:

> STINGER GUIDED MISSILE SYSTEM
> POST MODIFICATION SOFTWARE

'Sweet Trinity,' he whistled. 'It's a post, not a common or garden system, but a ruddy post that we have got ourselves here!'

'Let's take a look!' Job was as excited as he was.

Sean hesitated, like a child tempted to open his gift before the dawn of his birthday. He glanced up at the sky looking for Hinds, strange how he had picked up that nervous habit from his Shanganes.

'We daren't move until dark. Plenty of time to kill,' he capitulated, and leaned over to draw the bayonet from the sheath of Ferdinand's webbing.

Gently he prised open the lid of the crate and lifted away the slabs of white polyurethane packing. The software was contained in a heavy-duty plastic carry pack. He sprang the catches on the lid and opened the case. The dozens of software cassettes were each colour-coded, sealed in transparent glassine envelopes and fitted into tailored slots in the interior. This was what they had read about in the manuals they had borrowed from Carlyle, the British gunnery officer.

'Get the manuals,' Sean told Job. And when he brought them over they squatted beside the open case and pored through the heavy volume which described the post system.

'Here it is! Hind attack system. Colour code red. Numerical code S.42.A.'

Under the post system the Stinger missiles could be programmed to attack various targets by employing tactics and search frequencies specific to that type of aircraft. Simply by inserting one of the micro-cassettes into the console of the launcher, the missile could be instructed to alter its attack technique.

'"System software cassette. S.42.A.,"' Job followed the text with his forefinger as he read aloud from the manual, '"is targeted on the Hind helicopter gunship. The system employs a 'two-colour' seeker which registers both infra-red and ultra-violet emissions in two stages. The initial stage will lock to infra-red from the engine exhaust system.

'"The Hind's exhaust suppressors divert and emit those infrared rays through heavily armoured outlets below the main fuselage. Missile-strikes on this section of the Hind have proved ineffective.

'"The S.42.A. modification automatically switches the guidance system of the Stinger into ultra-violet seeker mode when range-to-target is reduced to a hundred metres. Ultra-violet is emitted principally from the air-intake ports of the Isotov TV3-117 turbo shaft engines. This area is the only section of the fuselage not encased in titanium armour plate and missile-strikes through the engine intake ports have resulted in hundred per cent kills.

'"To achieve effective ultra-violet acquisition, the initial launch of the missile must be made from below and dead ahead of the aircraft, at a range not exceeding 1000 metres nor less than 150 metres."'

Job closed the manual with a snap.

'Big casino!' he said. 'China is getting more than he ever hoped for.'

There were thirty heavy cases to carry and only twenty uninjured men, including Sean and Job. Sean cached the boxes that they were forced to leave. He would send a detail back to fetch them once they reached the Renamo lines.

Carrying what they could, including the trainer and the post modification equipment, they set out along the bank of the Pungwe river at nightfall, groping for a contact with the Renamo front line. They marched all that night.

The extended column, slowed down by the heavy cases of missiles, covered only twelve miles before sunrise. However, the weather had changed and the wind had backed into the east bringing in low cloud and a cold drizzle of rain that would hide them from the searching Hinds. They kept going all that day.

At dusk Sean let them rest for a few hours, and they huddled miserably in the rain until Sean roused them once again and they stumbled on, slipping and sliding in the mud, and cursing the loads upon their backs. An hour after sunrise the clouds rolled away and their sodden battledress steamed as it dried on their backs.

Two hours later they ran into the ambush.

They were moving through light savannah along the riverbank. The flat-topped acacia thorn trees were interspersed with clumps of coarse elephant grass.

Sean heard the metallic snap of the loading handle being jerked back to cock a machine-gun and before the sound had fully registered in his brain, he was diving forward, shouting a warning to his Shanganes. As he hit the sandy earth with his elbows and belly, he saw the muzzle flashes shimmering and dancing like fairy lights in the grass only thirty paces ahead and a blaze of shot passed over his head, making him blink and flinch.

He rolled left to throw the gunner's aim, holding the AKM with one hand as though it were a pistol, firing blindly to further confuse the attackers and groping for the grenade on his belt.

He was on the point of hurling the grenade when behind him Ferdinand shouted a challenge in Portuguese and the firing from the front shrivelled and died away. From the patch of elephant grass just ahead of Sean, a voice replied to the challenge and then Ferdinand was shouting urgently in Shangane, 'Cease fire! Cease fire! Renamo! Renamo!'

There was a long suspicious silence during which Sean kept his right arm cocked back ready to throw the grenade. He had seen too many good men called out to die in a false truce.

'Renamo!' A voice from the front reiterated. 'Friends!'

'All right!' Sean shouted back in Shangane. 'Stand up, Renamo. Let us see your beautiful friendly faces.'

Somebody laughed, and a grinning black face under a tiger-striped camouflage cap popped up out of the grass and ducked back immediately.

After a few seconds, when there was no more firing, another man stood up cautiously, and then another. Sean's Shanganes came to their feet and moved forward, slowly at first and with weapons cocked, and then they were meeting in the open ground, shaking hands and laughing and slapping each other's backs. They had run into the sector held by the battalion under the command of Major Takawira. He recognized Sean immediately and they shook hands with mutual pleasure.

'Colonel Courtney! What a relief to see you alive! We heard on the news from the BBC and Radio Zimbabwe that your aircraft had been shot down in flames with you and all your men wiped out.'

'I need your help, Major,' Sean told him. 'I've left twenty cases of missiles cached out there in the bush. I want you to send a detachment of a hundred men to fetch them in. One of my men will guide them to the cache.'

'I'll send my best men. I'll pick them out personally,' Takawira assured him.

'How far are we from General China's HQ?' Sean asked.

'The Frelimo helicopters have forced him to pull back. His new HO is only six miles upstream. I have just spoken to him on the radio and the general is most anxious to see you.'

Their progress was a triumphal march, for news of their success flashed through the Renamo lines ahead of them. Men in tiger stripes turned out to cheer them and shake their hands and thump their backs as they passed. The porters bore the cases of missiles aloft as though they were the ark of Jehovah and they, the priests of an arcane religion.

They sang the Renamo battle songs as they trotted along proudly under their burdens.

General China was waiting to greet them at the entrance to his newly constructed command bunker, resplendent in crisply laundered battledress and decorations, with the maroon beret cocked jauntily over one eye.

'I knew you would not fail me, Colonel.' For the first time in their acquaintance, Sean had the feeling that his smile was genuine.

'We lost almost thirty men under Sergeant Alphonso,' Sean told him brusquely. 'We were forced to abandon them.'

'No! No, Colonel!' General China clasped his shoulder in an unparalleled display of goodwill. 'Alphonso got out safely. He lost only three men in reaching the mission at St Mary's. I have just had radio contact with them. They will be in our lines by tomorrow evening at the latest. The entire operation was a brilliant success, Colonel.' He dropped his hand from Sean's shoulder. 'Now let us see what you have brought me.'

The porters laid the wooden cases at his feet. A black Caesar receiving the spoils of war, Sean thought ironically.

'Open them!' China beamed. Sean had never expected such childlike excitement from one usually so cold and contained. China was actually performing an ecstatic little jig, and rubbing his hands together as he watched the junior officers on his staff wielding jemmies and bayonet blades in an attempt to prise up the lid of the first crate. The steel strapping frustrated their efforts.

In the end China could no longer control himself and pushed his officers away, snatched a jemmy bar out of the hands of one of them and attacked the case himself. He was sweating profusely with excitement and exertion when at last the lid yielded and there were obsequious cries of congratulation from his staff as the contents were revealed.

The Stinger launcher was fully assembled with a missile tube loaded. The IFF interrogator was packed separately in a transparent glassine envelope ready to be plugged into the console head by its short coil of cable. The additional four disposal tubes, each containing a single missile, nestled in the moulded white polyurethane foam packaging. After firing the missile, the empty tube would be discarded and replaced by a fresh tube containing its own sixteen-pound missile.

The laughter and cheering gradually subsided and the general staff crowded forward to examine the contents of the case, albeit with a marked reserve as though they had discovered a nest of poisonous scorpions under a rock and expected that at any second a fanged tail would whip out at them.

General China slowly went down on one knee and reverently lifted the assembled launcher out of its foam nest.

His staff watched in awe as he settled the clumsy weapon on his shoulder. The missile tube extended behind him and the consol with its antenna, looking as mundane as a plastic milk crate, almost totally obscured General China's features. He peered studiously into the aiming screen of the console and gripped the triggered pistol stock.

He aimed the Stinger skyward and his staff uttered small sounds of encouragement and admiration.

'Let the Frelimo *henshaw* come now,' China boasted. 'We will see them burn.' And he began to make helicopter and machine-gun noises like a small boy at play, pointing the missile at flocks of imaginary Hind gunships that circled overhead.

'Pow! Pow!' he cried. 'Vroom! Swish! Boom!'

'Ka pow!' With a straight face, Sean joined in and the general's staff howled with delight and tried to out-do each other with the sounds of exploding and crashing helicopters.

Somebody began to sing and they all picked up the refrain, clapping their hands to the rhythm of the Renamo battle anthem, swaying and stamping their feet.

Now there were two hundred men singing, their voices

404

blending and rising into the beautiful melodious sound of Africa that made the goose-pimples rise on Sean's forearms and the hair on the back of his neck prickle. General China stood in the midst of them with the missile on his shoulders and led the chorus. His voice soared above the rest, amazing Sean with its range and clarity, a magnificent tenor which would not have disgraced any of the world's great opera houses.

The song ended with a shout of defiance, 'Renamo!' and their dark faces were lit by a fierce patriotic ardour.

'In this mood, they'll be hard men to beat,' Sean thought, and General China handed the launcher to one of his men and came to shake Sean's hand.

'Congratulations, Colonel.' He was earnest and happy at the same time, 'I think you have saved the cause. I am grateful.'

'That's fine, China,' Sean was ironical. 'But don't just tell me how grateful, show me.'

'Of course, forgive me.' China put on a little show of repentance. 'In the excitement I almost forgot, there is somebody very anxious to see you.'

Sean felt his breathing shorten and his chest constrict. 'Where is she?'

'In my bunker, Colonel.' General China indicated the carefully concealed entrance to the dugout amongst the trees.

Sean elbowed his way roughly through the ranks of excited soldiers, and as he reached the entrance to the bunker, he could restrain himself no longer and he went down the rough steps three at a time.

Claudia was in the radio dugout, sitting on a bench along the far wall with her two wardresses flanking her. He spoke her name when he saw her and she came to her feet slowly, staring at him, white-faced with disbelief. The bones of her cheeks threatened to burst through the almost translucent skin and her eyes were huge and dark as midnight.

As he crossed to her, Sean saw the marks on her wrists, livid weals crusted with fresh scab, and his anger matched his joy. He swept her into his arms and she was as thin and frail as a child. For a moment she stood quiescent in his embrace, and then fiercely she threw her arms around his neck and hugged him. He was surprised by her strength, and she shivered in convulsive spasms as she pressed her face into the hollow of his neck.

They stood locked together, not moving nor speaking for a long time until Sean felt the wetness soaking through his shirt front.

'Please don't cry, my darling.'

Gently he lifted her face between his hands, and with his thumbs wiped the tears away.

'It's just that I'm so happy now,' she smiled through the last of her tears. 'Nothing else matters any more, now that you are back.'

He took her hands and lifted them to his lips, kissing the broken scabbed skin on her wrists.

'They can't hurt me any more, not now,' she said, and Sean turned his head and looked at the two uniformed wardresses who still sat on the bench.

'Your mothers rutted with the stinking dung-eating hyena,' he said softly in Shangane, and they flinched at the insult. 'Get out! Go! Before I rip out your ovaries and feed them to the vultures!'

They glowered and hung their heads until Sean dropped his hand onto the butt of his pistol. Then they moved with alacrity, jumping up from the bench and sidling to the dugout steps.

Sean turned back to Claudia, and for the first time kissed her mouth. That kiss lasted a long time and when they drew unwillingy apart Claudia whispered, 'When they took off the handcuffs and let me wash, I knew you were coming back.'

Her words conjured up a picture of the degradation and brutality she had come through and Sean's reply was bitter.

'The bastard. Somehow I'm going to make him suffer for what he has done to you. I swear that to you.'

'No, Sean. It doesn't matter any more. It's over. We are together again. That is all that matters.'

They had only a few more minutes alone before General China came bustling into the radio dugout at the head of his staff, still smiling and elated.

He ushered Sean and Claudia through into his private office and seemed not to notice that they both treated his affable hospitality with icy reserve. They sat close together in front of his desk, quietly holding hands, not responding to his pleasantries.

'I have prepared quarters for you,' General China told them. 'In fact I have evicted one of my senior commanders and given you his dugout. I hope you will find it adequate for your needs.'

'We aren't planning on a long stay, General,' Sean told him. 'I want to be on my way back to the border, with Miss Monterro, tomorrow morning at the very latest.'

'Ah, Colonel, of course I want to accommodate you. From now on, you are an honoured and privileged guest. You have certainly earned your release. However, for operational reasons that happy moment must be delayed for a few days. Frelimo are moving in large concentrations of troops.'

Reluctantly Sean conceded. 'Fair enough, but in the meantime, we expect five-star treatment. Miss Monterro needs new clothes to replace these rags.'

'I shall have a selection of the best we have sent to your dugout from our stores. However, I cannot promise either Calvin Klein or Gucci.'

'While we are at it, we'll need a team of servants to do our laundry and cleaning and cooking.'

'I haven't forgotten your colonial origins, Colonel,'

China answered slyly. 'One of my men was an under-chef at the President Hotel in Johannesburg. He understands European tastes.'

Sean stood up. 'We'll inspect our quarters now.'

'One of my junior officers will escort you,' General China suggested. 'If there is anything further you need, please let him know. He has my personal orders to give you whatever he can to make you comfortable. As I have said before, you are honoured guests.'

'He gives me the creeps,' Claudia whispered, as the subaltern ushered them out of the dugout. 'I don't know when he frightens me more, when he is being charming or menacing.'

'It won't be for much longer.' Sean put his arm round her shoulders and led her into the open air, but somehow the sunlight lacked warmth and despite his assurances to Claudia, the chill of General China's presence persisted.

The dugout to which the subaltern led them was in the bush above the riverbank, not more than three hundred yards from the general's HQ. The entrance was screened with a piece of tattered camouflage net and the interior was freshly dug out of the hard red clay of the riverbank.

'It's so new that it probably hasn't yet acquired a permanent population of bed bugs and lice and other wild game,' Sean remarked.

The clay walls were damp and cool and there was ventilation through the spaces between the roof poles.

The only furnishings were a table and two stools of mopane poles against one wall, and opposite that a raised bedstead also of mopane poles and a mattress of combed elephant grass covered with a sheet of faded canvas. There was however, one extraordinary luxury, a mosquito net hung above the bed.

The subaltern who was escorting them summoned the domestic staff and the three of them lined up in front of Sean and Claudia. The two camp boys would take care of their laundry and cleaning under the supervision of the chef.

The chef was an elderly Shangane with a pleasant lined face and silver-frosted hair and beard. He reminded Claudia of a black Santa Claus. They both liked him immediately.

'My name is Joyful, sir.'

'So you speak English, Joyful?'

'And Afrikaans and Portuguese and Shona and . . .'

'Enough already.' Sean held up a hand to stop him. 'Can you cook?'

'I'm the best damned cook in Mozambique.'

'Joyful and modest,' Claudia laughed.

'Okay, Joyful, tonight we will have Chateaubriand,' Sean teased him, and Joyful looked doleful.

'Sorry, sir, no fillet steak.'

'All right, Joyful.' Sean relented. 'You just make us the best dinner you can.'

'I'll tell you when it's ready, sir and madam.'

'Don't hurry,' said Claudia, and lowered the netting across the doorway, summarily dismissing all of them.

They stood hand in hand and studied the bed thoughtfully. Claudia broke the silence.

'Are you thinking what I am thinking?'

'Before or after dinner?' Sean asked.

'Both,' she replied, and led him by the hand.

They undressed each other with aching deliberation, drawing out the pleasure of truly discovering each other's bodies.

Though they were already lovers, he had only had one fleeting glimpse of her, and she had never seen him naked. She studied him with big solemn eyes, not smiling, taking her time until he was forced to ask, 'Well, do I get the Monterro seal of approval?'

'Oh, boy!' she breathed, still deadly serious, and he lifted her on to the bed.

It was darkening outside the dugout when Joyful coughed politely beyond the screen doorway.

'Dinner is ready, sir and madam.'

They ate at the table of mopane poles by the light of a paraffin lantern that Joyful had scavenged from somewhere.

'Oh my God!' Claudia cried when she saw what Joyful had provided for them. 'I didn't realize how hungry I was.'

It was a casserole of plump green pigeons and wild mushrooms, with side dishes of steamed yellow yams and cassava cakes and banana fritters.

'General China sent this for you,' Joyful explained, and set cans of South African beer on the crowded table.

'Joyful, you are a paragon.'

They ate in dedicated silence, smiling across the table at each other between mouthfuls. At last Claudia groaned softly.

'I think I can just waddle as far as the bed, but definitely no further.'

'Suits me fine,' he said, and reached across to take her hand.

The mosquito net was a tent over them, creating an intimate and secret temple for their loving. The light from the lantern was soft and golden. It washed subtle tones and shadings across the planes of her face and the rounds and hollows of her body.

The texture of her skin fascinated him. It was so fine-pored as to seem glossed like warm wax. He stroked her shoulders and arms and belly, marvelling at the feel of her.

She rasped her fingernails through his short crisp beard, and pressed her face into the springing curls that covered his chest.

'You are as hairy and hard as a wild animal,' she whispered. 'And as dangerous. I should be terrified of you.'

'Aren't you?'

'A little, yes. That's what makes it such fun.'

She was starved to the point where her ribs showed clearly through her pale skin. Her limbs were slender and childlike, and the marks of her suffering upon them threatened to break his heart. Even her breasts seemed smaller, but it was as though their diminution had merely emphasized the sweet and tender shape. She watched him take the nipple of one between his lips and she stroked the thick curls at the back of his neck.

'That feels so good,' she whispered. 'But there are two.' And she took a handful of his hair to direct his mouth across to the other side.

Once while she sat astride him, he looked up at her and reached high to stroke the soft skin of her throat and shoulders and said, 'In this light, you look like a little girl.'

'And me trying so hard to prove to you what a big girl I am,' she pouted down at him, then leaned forward to kiss his mouth.

They slept so intricately entwined that their hearts beat against each other and their breath mingled and they woke to find that they had begun again while they still slept.

'He's so clever,' she murmured drowsily. 'Already he can find his way all on his own.'.

'Do you want to go back to sleep?'

'Do I, hell!'

Much later she asked him, 'Do you think we could make this last for ever?'

'We can try.'

But at last through the slats above them, the dawn sent orange-gold fingers of light, and Claudia cried softly, 'No. I don't want it to end. I want to keep you inside me for ever and ever.'

When Joyful brought the tea to the bedside, on the tray with the mugs was an invitation from General China to dine in the mess that evening.

General China's mess night was for Claudia and Sean less than an unqualified success, despite the general's continued efforts to charm them.

The buffalo meat he served was tough and rank and the beer made the officers of the general's staff loud and argumentative. The weather had changed and was close and sweltering even after dark and the bunker that served as a mess was thick with the smoke of cheap native tobacco and the odour of masculine sweat.

General China drank none of the beer, but sat at the head of the table ignoring the shouted conversation and hearty eating habits of his staff. Instead, he played the gallant to Claudia, engaging her in a discussion which she at first attempted to evade.

Claudia was unaccustomed to the table manners of Africa. She watched with an awful fascination as the stiff maize porridge was scooped from the communal pot in the centre of the table by many hands, moulded into balls between the fingers and then dipped into buffalo-meat gravy. Greasy gravy ran down their chins, and no attempt was made to moderate the conversation during mastication, so that small particles of food were sprayed across the table when one of them laughed or exclaimed loudly.

Despite the fact that she was still half starved Claudia had no appetite for the meal and it took an effort to concentrate on General China's dissertation.

'We have divided the entire country into three war zones,' he explained. 'General Takawira Dos Alves is the commander of the north. He commands the provinces of Niassa and Cabo Delgado. In the south, the commander is General

412

Tippoo Tip, and of course, I command the army of the central provinces of Manica and Sofala. Between us we control almost fifty per cent of the total ground area of Mozambique, and another forty per cent of the country is a destruction zone over which we are forced to maintain a scorched earth policy to prevent Frelimo growing either food for their troops or cash crops to finance their war effort against us.'

'So the reports of atrocities that we have received in the United States are true then.' He had engaged Claudia's interest at last. Her tone was sharp as she accused, 'Your troops are attacking and wiping out the civilian population in those destruction zones.'

'No, Miss Monterro.' China's smile was icy. 'The fact that we have moved the civilian population out of many of those destruction areas is unavoidably true, but all the atrocities, all the massacres and tortures, have been committed by Frelimo themselves.'

'They are the government of Mozambique, why would they massacre their own people?' Claudia protested.

'I agree with you, Miss Monterro, sometimes it is difficult to follow the devious working of the Marxist mind. The reality is that Frelimo is unable to govern. They are unable to provide even basic protection to the civilian population outside the cities, let alone give them services of health and education and transport and communications. To draw world attention away from the total failure of their economic policies and their lack of popular support, they have provided the international media with a Roman holiday of slaughter and torture which they blame upon Renamo and South Africa. It is easier to kill people than to feed and educate them, and the anti-Renamo propaganda is worth a million lives, to a Marxist that is.'

'You are suggesting that a Khmer Rouge style massacre is being conducted here in Mozambique by the government forces?' Claudia was aghast, pale and perspiring with the noise and fug of the subterranean mess, and with the horror of General China's explanations.

'I am not suggesting, Miss Monterro, I am simply stating the literal truth.'

'But, but, surely the world must do something?'

'The world is uncaring, Miss Monterro. It has been left for us, Renamo, to try to bring down the heinous Marxist regime.'

'Frelimo is the elected government,' Claudia pointed out, but General China shook his head.

'No, Miss Monterro, very few governments in Africa are elected. There has never been an election in Mozambique or Angola or Tanzania or any of the other gems of African Socialism. In Africa the trick is to seize power and hang onto to it at all costs. The typical African government plunges into the void left by the exodus of the colonial power and entrenches itself behind a barricade of AK 47 assault rifles. It then declares a one-party system of government which further precludes any form of opposition and it nominates a presidential dictator for life.'

'Tell me, General China,' Claudia raised her voice above the roar of conversation further down the mess table, 'if one day, your military efforts succeed and you and the other generals of Renamo vanquish Frelimo and become the new government of this country, will you then allow free elections and a truly democratic system to evolve?'

For a moment General China stared at her in astonishment and then he laughed delightedly.

'My very dear Miss Monterro, your childlike belief in the myth of the essential goodness of mankind is really rather touching. I certainly have not fought so hard and so long to gain power, simply to hand it over to a bunch of illiterate peasants. No, Miss Monterro, once we have the power it will remain safely in the right hands.' He extended his own elegantly shaped hands, pink palms uppermost, towards her. 'These,' he said.

414

'So you are every bit as bad as you say the others are.' There were hot red spots of anger on Claudia's cheeks. This was the man who had put chains on her wrists and incarcerated her in that vile pit. She hated him with all her strength.

'I think you are actually beginning to understand at last, even through the haze of your liberal emotions. In Africa there are no good guys and no bad guys, there are simply winners and losers.' He smiled again. 'And I assure you, Miss Monterro, that I intend to be one of the winners.'

General China turned away from her as one of his signals officers ducked through the low entrance to the bunker and hurried down to the head of the table. With an apologetic salute, he handed the general a yellow message flimsy. China read it without change of expression and then looked up at his guests.

'Please excuse me for a few minutes.' China placed his beret at the correct angle over one eye, then stood and followed the signaller out of the bunker.

The moment he was gone, Claudia leaned across the table to Sean. 'Can't we get out of here now? I don't think I can bear another moment of it. God, how I hate that man.'

'Mess tradition doesn't seem very strict,' Sean murmured. 'If we leave, I don't think anyone is going to take offence.'

As they crossed to the doorway, there was a drunken chorus of suggestive catcalls and whistles, and they went up the steps with relief.

The night air had cooled and Claudia breathed it in deeply and gratefully. 'I don't know which was more suffocating, the fug or the dialectic.' She breathed again, 'I never expected Africa to be like this. It's so confused, so illogical, it turns everything I know to be true upside down.'

'But it's interesting, isn't it?' Sean asked.

'Like a nightmare is interesting. Let's go to bed. At least that's something I can believe in completely.'

They turned towards their dugout shelter, but General China's voice halted them.

'You aren't leaving us so soon?' And his tall lithe form came striding towards them out of the darkness. 'I'm afraid I have disappointing news for both of you.'

'You aren't letting us go. You are reneging on our deal,' Sean said flatly. 'I knew this was coming.'

'Circumstances beyond my control,' China assured him smoothly. 'I have just had a radio report from Sergeant Alphonso. As you know I was expecting his return this evening and he and his men would have escorted you and Miss Monterro safely back to the border, however . . .'

'All right, let's hear it from you, China,' Sean snarled angrily. 'What new scheme have you cooked up?'

General China ignored the accusation and the tone in which it was delivered. 'Sergeant Alphonso reports that there is a massive build-up of enemy to the west of our lines. It seems that, emboldened by their gunships, Frelimo, backed by Zimbabwean contingents, are about to launch a full-scale offensive. We are probably already cut off from the Zimbabwe border. The territory that we once controlled seems certain to have been overrun by the enemy advance. Within hours it will become a battlefield, even now Sergeant Alphonso is fighting his way through and has taken some casualties. I am afraid you would not last long out there, Colonel. It would be suicide for you to try to reach the border now. You must remain under my personal protection.'

'What the hell do you want from us?' Sean demanded. 'You are up to something, I can smell the stink of it from here. What is it?'

'Your lack of confidence in my motives is very distressing,' China smiled coldly. 'However, the sooner the Hind gunships are destroyed, the sooner the Frelimo offensive will collapse and you and Miss Monterro will be returned to the civilized world.'

'I'm listening,' Sean told him.

416

'You are the only one, you and Captain Job, who understand the Stinger. In this our interests coincide. I want you to train a select contingent of my men to handle the Stingers.'

'That's all you want?' Sean stared into his face. 'We train your men to use the Stinger, then you let us go?'

'Exactly.'

'How do I know you won't move the goal posts again?'

'You pain me, Colonel.'

'Not nearly as much as I'd like to.'

'It's agreed then. You will train my men and in exchange I will have you escorted across the border at the very first opportunity.'

'What option do we have?'

'I'm so pleased that you are being reasonable, Colonel. It makes life much easier for all of us.' His voice became crisp and businesslike. 'We must begin immediately.'

'You'll have to let your staff sober up a little,' Sean told him. 'I'll begin first thing tomorrow, and I'll train the Shanganes under Alphonso and Ferdinand, if Alphonso makes it through the Frelimo offensive intact.'

'How long will it take you?' China wanted to know. 'From now on every hour will be vital to our survival.'

'They are bright lads and willing, I should be able to do something with them in a week.'

'You will not have that long.'

'I'll have the Stingers in action just as soon as I possibly can,' Sean retorted irritably. 'Please believe me, General, I don't want to hang around here a minute longer than I have to. Now we'll bid you good-night.' He took Claudia's arm as he turned away.

'Oh Sean,' she whispered. 'I have the terrible premonition that we are caught up in something from which we are never going to escape.' And Sean squeezed her upper arm to make her stop.

'Look up there,' he ordered softly, and she raised her face.

'The stars?' she asked. 'Is that what you want me to look at?'

'Yes, the stars.' They daubed the night as though a gigantic firefly had been crushed to death and its luminous essence smeared across the vault of heaven.

'They calm the soul,' Sean explained gently.

She breathed softly and deeply. 'Yes, you are right, my darling. Tonight we have our love, let's exploit it to the full and let tomorrow take care of itself.'

She felt safe and invulnerable under the tented mosquito netting. The lumpy grass-filled mattress had taken on the shape of their bodies and she did not notice the harsh touch of the canvas covering against her skin.

'If we made love ten thousand times, it would still not have taken the edge off my need for you,' she whispered, as she slipped over the edge of sleep.

She woke suddenly feeling the tension in his body against hers, and instantly he touched her lips to caution her to silence. She lay frozen in the darkness, not daring to move or breathe, and then she heard it. A soft scraping at the entrance of the dugout as the netting curtain was pushed aside and an animal passed through.

Her heart raced away and she bit her lip to stop herself gasping aloud as she heard the thing crossing the earth floor towards the bed. Its paws were almost soundless, just the faintest tick of grit compressed by the stealthy weight. Then she smelled it, the wild gamey smell of a meat-eating animal and she wanted to cry out.

Beside her, Sean moved suddenly, fast as a striking adder; he lunged through the mosquito net and there was a quick scuffle and squeal and she tried to crawl over Sean's back to escape whatever it was.

'Got you, you little bugger,' Sean said grimly. 'You don't sneak up on me twice and get away with it. Now tell me I'm getting old and I'll wring your neck!'

'You'll be young and beautiful for ever, my *Bwana*,' Matatu giggled, and wriggled like a puppy caught by the scruff of the neck.

'Where have you been, Matatu?' Sean demanded sternly. 'What took you so long, did you meet a pretty girl along the way?'

Matatu giggled again, he loved to be accused by Sean of dalliance and amatory exploits.

'I found the roosting place of the *henshaws*,' he boasted. 'The same way I find where the bees have their hive, I watched their flight against the sun and followed them to their secret place.'

Sean drew him closer to the bed and shook his arm gently. 'Tell me,' he ordered, and in the darkness Matatu squatted down and tucked his loin-cloth between his legs and made little self-important throat-clearing and humming sounds.

'There is a round hill, shaped like the head of a bald man,' Matatu began. 'On one side of the hill passes the *insimbi*, the railway, and on the other side the road.'

Sean propped himself on one elbow to listen and with his other arm, he encircled Claudia's naked waist and held her close. She snuggled against him, listening to Matatu's piping pixie voice in the darkness.

'There are many askari around the hill with big *banduki* hidden in holes in the ground.' Sean formed a vivid mental picture of the heavily garrisoned hilltop as Matatu described it to him. Beyond the outer defensive lines the gunships were laagered in separate sandbagged emplacements. Like battle tanks in hull-down fortifications, they would be impregnable, and yet they had only to rise and hover a few feet above ground level to bring into action their devasting Gatling-cannons and rocket pods.

'Inside the circle of roosting *henshaw*, there are many gharries parked and white men in green clothes who climb

419

on the *henshaw* and look inside them all the time.' Matatu described the mobile workshops and fuel tankers and the squads of Russian mechanics and technicians needed to keep the helicopters flying. The training manuals had pointed up the Hind's excessive requirements of service and maintenance, while those big Isotov turbo engines would guzzle Avgas.

'Matatu, did you see railway gharries on the line near the hill?' Sean asked.

'I saw them,' Matatu confirmed. 'Those big round gharries full of beer – the men who ride in the *henshaw* must be very thirsty.' Once many years ago, on one of his infrequent visits to the city with Sean, Matatu had seen a beer tanker disgorging its load at the main Harare beerhall. He had been so impressed that since that day he was utterly convinced that all tankers of whatever size or type contained only beer. Sean could not change his mind on this, Matatu would never accept that some of them actually carried less noble fluids such as gasoline and he always stared wistfully after any tanker they passed on the road.

Sean smiled now in the darkness at the little man's fixation. Fuel for the gunships was obviously being railed from Harare in bulk tankers, and transshipped into smaller road tankers. It was ironic that the fuel was almost certainly being originally supplied by the South Africans. However, if the helicopter squadron was storing its fuel within the laager itself they were taking a grave risk. It was something to bear in mind.

Matatu remained at the bedside for almost an hour while Sean patiently drew from him every possible detail he could of the gunship laager.

Matatu was certain that there were eleven helicopters in the emplacements, which tallied with his own estimate. Of the original twelve, one had been destroyed in the collision with the Hercules.

420

Matatu was equally certain that only nine of the gunships were actually flying. Hidden on a nearby kopje, he had watched the helicopters sortie from their laager at dawn, return for refuelling during the day and at nightfall come in to roost. Sean knew that Matatu could count accurately to twenty, but after that, he became vague and any greater number was described progressively as 'many' or 'a great deal' and finally as 'like grass on the Serengeti plains'.

So Sean was now fairly certain that two of the gunships had broken down and were probably awaiting spares, and he accepted Matatu's figure of nine operational gunships, still a formidable force, quite sufficient to turn the tide of the looming battle against Renamo unless they could swiftly be put out of the action.

When at last Matatu had finished his recitation he asked simply. 'Now, my *Bwana*, what do you want me to do?'

Sean considered in silence. There was really no reason why he should not bring Matatu in from wherever he was hiding up in the bush, allowing him openly to join the force of Shangane under his command as a tracker. However, he sensed that there might be some future advantage in keeping Matatu hidden from China's cold reptilian gaze.

'You are my wild card, Matatu,' he said in English and then in Swahili, 'I want you to keep out of sight. Do not let any of the men here see you, except Job and me.'

'I heard you, my *Bwana*.'

'Come to me each night as you have tonight. I will have food for you and I will tell you what to do. In the meantime, watch and tell me all you see.'

Matatu went so silently that they heard only the faint rustle of the netting at the entrance as he passed through.

'Will he be all right?' Claudia asked softly. 'I worry about him. He's so cute.'

'Of all of us, he is probably the most likely to survive.' In the dark, Sean smiled fondly after the little man.

'I'm not sleepy any more.' Claudia snuggled against him like a cat, and then much later she whispered, 'I'm so glad Matatu woke us up . . .'

I t was still dark when Sean turned Job out of his blanket the next morning. 'We've got work to do,' he told him, and while Job laced on his boots, he described his meeting with General China.

'You mean we are now instructors,' Job laughed softly. 'All we know about those Stingers is what we have read in the manuals.'

'That will have to change,' Sean told him. 'The sooner we get the Shanganes into action, the sooner we are going to get the hell out of here.'

'Is that what China told you?' Job raised an eyebrow at Sean.

'Let's get Ferdinand and his boys cracking,' Sean said brusquely to cover his own misgivings. 'We'll sort them into teams of two men, one to serve the launcher and the other to carry the extra missiles. Of course, the number two must be able to take over if the leader is put down.'

Sean pulled out his notebook and drew the candle stump closer, writing in its guttering yellow light.

'When do you expect Alphonso to get here?' Job stuffed his shirt into the top of his tiger-striped pants.

'Sometime today, if at all,' Sean replied.

'He's the best of the bunch,' Job grunted.

'Ferdinand is not bad,' Sean pointed out, and placed their names at the head of the page as his section leaders. 'Okay, we need thirty names for our number ones, give me some.'

It was like the old days, working together this way and Sean found he was beginning to enjoy himself.

As soon as it was light enough, they paraded the men

who had returned in the Hercules from the Grand Reef raid. With the two casualties missing there remained eighteen men under Ferdinand. Sean immediately gave Ferdinand a field promotion to full sergeant, and was rewarded with a huge grin and a flourishing salute that almost swept Ferdinand off his feet with his own vigour.

Sean had to find something to occupy them and keep them out of the way while he and Job gave themselves a crash course on the Stinger missile system.

'Sergeant.' Sean addressed Ferdinand by his rank for the first time. 'Do you see that hill over there?' It was just visible through the trees, shaded blue with distance. 'Take your men for a run around it and get them back here in two hours. Weapons and full field-packs.'

As they watched the column of men doubling away, Sean said, 'If Alphonso and his lads don't arrive by this evening, we'll have to recruit replacements. That's no problem, however, China will be keen to let us have his very best men. At the moment, we are right at the top of his list of favourite flavours.'

'In the meantime, let's hit those manuals,' Job suggested. 'I haven't swotted since varsity days. I'm not looking forward to it.'

Claudia joined them in the dugout, helping them sort through the thick loose-leaf red plastic-covered manuals, picking out the information relevant to their situation and discarding the vast body of technical data that they had no need of, and the operational reports and instructions that did not apply to deployment in this altitude and terrain. After two hours' work they had reduced the mass of information to one manageable slim volume.

'All right.' Sean stood up. 'Let's go find a training ground.'

They picked out a spot a few hundred metres downriver from the dugout where the side of a low kopje formed a natural lecture theatre. The tall riverine mahogany trees spread their branches overhead to provide cover from a surprise raid by the Hind gunships. When Ferdinand and his men returned bathed in sweat from their little outing Sean put them to work clearing the amphitheatre of thorn and scrub and digging shell scrapes conveniently close at hand for use when air raids interrupted classes.

'Right,' Sean told Job and Claudia. 'Now we can uncrate the trainer set and one of the launchers. From now on it's "look and learn", "show and tell" time.'

When they opened the first crate, Sean discovered that the battery power pack was discharged. However, each crate contained a small charger set with appropriate connections and transformers.

Ferdinand and his men under Job's supervision carried the power packs up to the headquarters' communications centre and at General China's order, they were given priority use of the portable 220 volt 15 kilowatt generator. Sean connected up the power packs in batches of five, but it would take twenty-four hours before they had power available for all the missile launchers.

With the batteries on charge they laid out the trainer set and one of the launchers on the makeshift table that Ferdinand had built on the floor of the open-air theatre under the trees. While Claudia read aloud from the instruction manual, Sean and Job stripped and reassembled the equipment until they were thoroughly familiar with all of it.

Sean was relieved and pleased to discover that with the exception of the IFF, the operation of the equipment was not a great deal more complicated than the conventional RPG 7 rocket-launchers. The RPG 7 was so much a part of the guerrilla arsenal that, as Job remarked, every single man in China's division could load and lock on a pitch-dark night in a thunderstorm.

'Anyway, we don't need the IFF,' Sean pointed out. 'Everything that flies in these skies, apart from the dicky birds, is a foe.' The IFF, 'Identification Friend or Foe', was a system that interrogated the target, determining from the aircraft's on-board transponder whether it was hostile or friendly, and preventing launch of missile against friendly aircraft.

Claudia found the section on the manual dealing with the IFF and under her tutelage, they disarmed the system, converting the Stinger into a free-fire weapon which would attack any aircraft at which it was aimed.

Without IFF fitted, the attack sequence for the missile is straightforward. The target is picked up in the small screen of the aiming sight, and the safety device above the pistol grip is disengaged with the right thumb. The actuator is engaged by depressing the button built into the reverse of the pistol grip. This starts the run up of the navigational gyro and releases a flow of freon gas to cool the infra-red seekers as they become active. With the sights held on the target, all incoming infra-red radiation is magnified and focused on the detector cell of the missile head. As soon as this radiation is of sufficient concentration to allow the missile to track to its source, the gyro stabilizer uncages, and the missile emits a high-pitched tone.

To fire the missile the operator depresses the trigger in the pistol grip with his forefinger which starts the electric ejector motor. The missile discharges from the launch tube through the frangible front seal and ejects to a safe distance, approximately eight metres from the operator, to protect him from rocket back-blast. At this point the solid fuel rocket motor fires and the blast of exhaust gas flares out the retractable tail-fins and the missile accelerates to four times the speed of sound. When an inertial force of twenty-eight times gravity is attained, the fuse shut-out is thrown open and the missile is armed. It tracks towards the target on a fire-and-forget trajectory, guided not by the operator but by its own proportional navigational system.

With the specialized 'Hind' attack cassette inserted in the launcher's RMP – reprogrammable micro processor – the system switches automatically into 'Two Colour' mode when it is a hundred metres from the infra-red source. At this point it abandons the infra-red radiations emitted by the engine exhaust suppressors and instead focuses on the much weaker ultra-violet emanations from the engine intakes. On this target the high-explosive warhead hits to kill.

'Even a Shangane could learn how to fire one of these,' Job said, and Sean grinned.

'Tut tut, your Matabele tribal racism is showing again.'

'It's like this, when you are genetically superior, there is simply no point in trying to conceal the fact.'

They both glanced expectantly at Claudia, but she did not even look up from the manual as she drawled, 'You are wasting your time, you two bigots. You aren't going to get a rise out of me this time.'

'Bigot,' Job savoured the word. 'It's the first time anybody has ever called me that. I love it.'

'That's enough fooling around.' Sean broke it up. 'Let's take a look at the trainer.'

After they had connected one of the freshly charged battery packs and assembled the trainer equipment, Sean gave his opinion.

'With this stuff, we can have the lads ready to go into action within days, not weeks.'

Once a micro cassette was inserted in the training monitor, the launcher screen simulated the image of a 'Hind' which the instructor was able to manipulate in various flight patterns, climbing, descending, side-slipping or hovering. While he did so he was able to watch the trainee's reactions as he attempted to acquire the ghost ship on his own screen and attack it with a phantom missile.

Sean and Job played with the trainer like a pair of teen-agers, flying the image in complicated manoeuvres. 'It's just like a Pac-man game,' Job enthused. 'But what we need is a dum-dum, a pseudo-Shangane to act as a trainee for us.'

Once more both the men looked at Claudia who was

still sitting cross-legged on the table studying the manual.

She looked up as she felt their eyes on her. 'A dum-dum?' she demanded. 'I'll show you dum-dum. Give me the launcher.'

She stood in the centre of the floor of the amphitheatre with the launcher balanced on her shoulder, and stared into the sighting screen. The bulky equipment seemed to dwarf her. She had reversed her camouflage cap so the peak stuck out behind her head, and it gave her the gamine air of a little league baseballer.

'Ready?' Sean asked.

'Pull!' she said, concentrating ferociously on the screen, and Sean and Job exchanged smug supercilious grins.

'Incoming!' Sean called sharply. 'Twelve o'clock high. Lock and load.'

He brought the ghost Hind in on a head-on attack at 150 knots.

'Locked and loaded,' Claudia affirmed, and in their screen, they watched the duplicate sight ring of her missile launcher swing up smoothly and centre on the approaching Hind.

'Actuator on,' she said calmly, and a second later, they heard the launcher sob and growl in her grip, and then settle into a steady insect whine, like an infuriated mosquito.

'Target acquired,' Claudia murmured. The Hind was six hundred metres out but coming in fast, swelling dramatically in the sights.

'Fire!' she said, and they saw the red light blink, and then change to green signalling that the rocket motor of the fictitious missile was running, and almost instantaneously the image of the Hind disappeared from the screen to be replaced by the flashing legend.

'Target destroyed! Target destroyed!'

There followed a profound silence. Job cleared his throat nervously.

'Flukes happen,' said Sean. 'Shall we try it again?'

427

'Pull!' said Claudia, and concentrated on her aiming screen.

'Incoming,' Sean called. 'Six o'clock high. Lock and load.'

He brought the next Hind in from behind her at tree-top level, attack speed. She had three seconds to react.

'Locked and loaded.' Claudia pirouetted like a ballerina and picked the Hind up in the sight ring. 'Actuator on.' As she said it, Sean flung the Hind into a climbing side-slip, giving her deflection in three planes. It would be like trying to hit a high bird in a gale of crosswind.

In their screen, they watched with disbelief as Claudia swung smoothly, keeping the image in the exact centre of her aiming ring and the missile sobbed and then settled into its high-pitched tone.

'Target acquired. Fire!'

'Target destroyed! Target destroyed!' The screen blinked at them, and they fidgeted uncomfortably.

Job murmured, 'Twice on the trot. That ain't no fluke, man.'

Claudia laid the launcher on the table, readjusted the peak of her cap over her eyes, and then placed her fists on her hips and smiled at them sweetly.

'I thought you said you didn't know how to shoot,' Sean accused her with righteous indignation.

'Would a daughter of Riccardo Enrico Monterro not know how to shoot?'

'But you are stridently opposed to blood sports.'

'Sure,' she agreed. 'I've never shot at a living creature. But I'm death to clay pigeons. Papa taught me.'

'I should have guessed when you said "Pull",' Sean groaned softly.

'As a matter of interest,' Claudia examined the fingernails of her right hand modestly, 'I was Alaska State women's skeet champion three years running, and runner-up at the national championships in '86.'

428

The two men exchanged embarrassed glances. 'She got you with a sucker punch.' Job shook his head. 'And you walked straight into it with both eyes closed.'

'All right, Miss Alaska,' Sean told her sternly. 'You are so damned clever, you've just landed yourself the job of instructor. From here on you are in charge of this equipment. Job and I will split the Shanganes into two classes and give them the basics. Then we'll pass them on to you for simulation. It'll speed up the whole works.'

General China interrupted them as he strode into the amphitheatre, beret cocked jauntily, slapping his swagger-stick against his thigh and taking in their preparations with quick inquisitive eyes.

'How soon can you begin training? I expected to be further along than this.'

Sean recognized the futility of trying to explain to him. 'We'll get along better without interference.'

'I came to warn you that Frelimo have launched their offensive. They are coming at us in force from the south and the west, a two-pronged drive, obviously trying to push us out of these hills, away from the river into more open terrain where they can deploy their armour and their heli-copters to better advantage.'

'So they are whipping the hell out of you,' Sean needled him with a thinly concealed sneer.

'We are falling back,' China acknowledged the jibe with just a glitter in his eyes. 'As soon as my men attempt to hold up their advance at a natural strong point, Frelimo simply calls in the Hinds. The Russian pilots are showing us the close-support skills they learned in the mountains of Afghanistan. They simply obliterate our defences. It is not a pleasant experience to listen helplessly on the radio while my field commanders plead for help. How soon can I send them the Stingers?'

'Two days,' Sean said.

'So long? Is there no way you can hurry it up?' Impatiently,

China slapped the swagger-stick into the palm of his hand. 'I want you to let me have at least one trained team immediately. Anything to be able to hit back at them.'

'That, General China, would be crass stupidity,' Sean told him. 'With all due respect,' Sean showed none in the tone of his voice, 'if you deploy the Stingers piecemeal, you'll be tipping your hand to the Hind crews.'

'What do you mean?' China's voice cracked like breaking floe-ice.

'Those Ruskie pilots have met the Stingers before, in Afghanistan, you can be pretty damn sure of that. They'll know every counter-measure in the book and then a few more. Right now they are blissfully convinced that they are the only things in the sky. Their guard is wide open, but you let one Stinger fly and all that will change. Okay, you might put one down, but the rest of the squadron will be ready for you.' China's frozen expression thawed and he looked thoughtful.

'So what do you suggest, Colonel?'

'Hit them all at once with everything you've got.'

'When? Where?'

'When they are least expecting it, a full-scale surprise attack on their laager – at dawn.'

'On their laager?' China shook his head irritably. 'We don't know where they laager at night.'

'Yes, we do,' Sean contradicted. 'I have already pinpointed the laager. I'll train Alphonso and Ferdinand and set up the raid for them. Give me two days, and they'll be ready to go.'

China thought for a moment, hands clasped behind his back, staring up at the blue African sky as though he expected at any moment to see those dread humpbacked shapes appear.

'Two days,' he agreed at last.

'Two days, and when I have your missile crews trained

and ready to leave on the raid, you let me and my party go. That is my condition.'

'There is a Frelimo column between here and the Zimbabwe border,' China reminded him.

'We'll take our chances,' Sean snapped. 'That is the bargain, do I have your word on it?'

'Very well, Colonel. I agree.'

'That's fine. Now when do you expect Alphonso and his detachment to arrive?'

'They have already reached our lines. I expect Alphonso and his men will be here in another hour or so, but they will be exhausted, they have been in action almost continuously for twenty-four hours.'

'They aren't on a Sunday school picnic.' Sean was callous. 'Send them to me as soon as they arrive.'

They came in at last, moving with the slack stumbling gait of a heavyweight boxer at the end of ten hard rounds. Their tiger-striped camouflage was encrusted with the filth of the battlefield, and their faces were grey with exhaustion.

While his men collapsed on the floor of the amphitheatre and slept where they fell, Alphonso described to Sean in flat prosaic terms the retreat from Grand Reef base and the flight to the mission station in the gut of the Honde Valley where they had abandoned the Unimog truck and crossed into Mozambique on foot.

'The bush is full of Frelimo, and the air is full of *henshaw*.' He paused and wiped his face wearily on a grubby tattered bandanna. 'It is witchcraft, but the *henshaw* can speak from the sky. They taunt us in the Shangane language. They tell us that they have magic that turns our bullets and rockets to water.'

Sean nodded grimly. The Russians must be using skyshout amplifiers to demoralize the Renamo defenders. That was another trick they had learned in Afghanistan.

'All along the line our men are being shot to pieces, or are running away. We cannot fight against the *henshaw*.'

431

'Yes, you bloody well can.' Sean seized the front of his tunic. 'I'll show you how. Get your men up. There'll be plenty of time to sleep later, when we have burned those Russian bastards out of the sky.'

Sean and Job had worked and fought with all these men and had come to know them by name and deed so they had formed a fairly accurate picture of their individual worth and capabilities.

They knew that there were no cowards nor shirkers amongst them. Alphonso had long ago sifted those out. However, there were those whom Job classified as 'oxen', the strong and stupid, the muscle and cannon fodder. The others were of varying degrees of intelligence and adaptability. At the top of the heap were Alphonso and Ferdinand.

Sean and Job sorted them into two groups and concentrated their efforts on the most promising in each group, quickly picking out those who had the image recognition to translate what they saw on the aiming screen of the launchers into finite terms in shape and space.

At the end of almost three hours, they had picked out twenty men who had the potential to assimilate swiftly the necessary training and to act as number ones in the missile teams, and as many again who might be able to fulfil the number two back-up role.

The others who showed no aptitude were allotted to the assault team which would be using conventional weapons in the attack Sean was planning. Of the missile trainees, Sean took one group and Job the other, and they began the monotonous task of familiarizing them with the actual weapons. Once again, they relied on the technique of repetition and reinforcement. Each trainee had his turn at stripping and reassembling, locking and loading, and aiming the launcher. While he did so, he explained to the class exactly what he was doing and Sean and Job corrected their mistakes while the rest of the class taunted them.

It was late afternoon before Sean sent the first group of five men, which included both Alphonso and Ferdinand, to Claudia for simulated attacks with the training equipment.

Alphonso scored three consecutive hits, and was immediately detailed to act as Claudia's assistant and translator. By nightfall, all five members of the first group had scored three consecutive hits which Claudia had arbitrarily decided was her passing standard, and Sean and Job had another ten men ready to begin simulator training as soon as it was sufficiently light the following morning. When it was too dark to continue, Sean dismissed them and Alphonso and his group staggered off wearily into the night, punch-drunk with fatigue and the effort of learning.

Joyful, the chef, had stolen the tripes from the buffalo carcass that had fed the officers' mess the previous evening. After the day's heat, they were a little ripe, but he had disguised that fact with a liberal addition of chopped wild onion tubers and peri-peri sauce. Claudia paled when Joyful proudly placed a steaming bowl of the tripes in front of her. In the end, hunger overcame her fastidiousness.

'Put hair on your chest,' Sean comforted her.

'That, my darling man, isn't high on my list of beauty aids.'

'Okay then,' he smiled at her. 'Put some weight on those skinny little buns of yours.'

'You don't like my buns?'

'I love your buns, that's why I want more of them, as much as I can get.'

When Matatu came creeping in out of the darkness, Sean fed him and he gorged on tripes until his naked belly bulged like a shiny black beach ball.

'All right, you greedy little bugger,' Sean told him. 'Now it's time for you to earn your keep.'

They led him up to the dark amphitheatre where they found that Job was waiting for them. He had already assembled the raw materials for building the scale model of the gunship laager. By the light of two paraffin lanterns, they started to lay it out. Matatu had been a party to these model constructions so many times during the bush war that he understood exactly what was required of him. Like so many who have never acquired the skills of reading and writing, Matatu had a photographic memory.

He strutted about importantly, giving Sean and Job instructions, showing them the topography of the countryside in and surrounding the laager, the shape of the hill on which it had been built, the relationship of it to the main road and the railway line.

Claudia showed a new talent which Sean had not suspected. Using the soft white wood of the baobab tree, she whittled eleven tiny scale models of the Hind gunships. They were fully recognizable as what they represented and when she sat them in their emplacements within the perimeter of the model laager, they added an authentic touch.

It was well after midnight before Claudia and Sean crept naked under the mosquito net in their dugout. They were both weary to their bones but even after they made slow languorous love neither of them could sleep, and they lay close in the darkness and talked. Mention of her father earlier in the day caused Claudia to hark back to her childhood. Listening to her, Sean was relieved that she was able to speak naturally and easily about her father. She had conquered the initial shock and sorrow and she remembered him now with only a nostalgic melancholy which was almost pleasure in comparison to the pain which had preceded it.

She described to Sean how at the age of fourteen, the very year that her womanhood had first flowered, the wonderfully secure cocoon of her life had burst asunder in the traumatic divorce of her parents. She painted a picture for him of the years that followed. The droughts of loneliness when she was separated from her father followed by the roaring floods of love and conflict when they came together again.

'You can see why I'm such a crazy mixed-up kid,' she told him. 'Why I have to strive to be the best at whatever I do, and why I'm always drawn to try and protect the underdog. Half the time, I'm still trying to win Papa's approval, while the other half of the time, I'm trying to flout and reject his elitist materialistic view of life.' She snuggled against Sean. 'I truly don't know how you are going to handle me.'

'Handling you will always be a pleasure,' he assured her. 'But keeping you in your place looks like a full-time job.'

'That's just the sort of thing that Papa would have said. You and I are in for some rip-roaring fights, mister.'

'Ah, but just think of the reconciliations, what fun they will be.'

In the end, they managed a few hours of sleep, and awoke surprisingly refreshed and clear-headed to take up the training where they had left off at nightfall the previous day.

While Claudia ran the last of the trainees through the attack sequences on the simulator, Sean and Job squatted beside the model of the gunship laager and Sean explained his plans for the attack. Job listened attentively and made the occasional suggestion, until at last they had it all clear in their own minds, the approach march, the attack and the withdrawl with the alternative actions to be taken if there were a hitch anywhere along the line.

'Okay.' Sean stood up. 'Let's give it to the lads.'

The Shangane troopers watched totally absorbed from their perches on the rock slopes of the amphitheatre while Sean and Job described the plans for the raid. They used river pebbles to denote the various units of the raiding party, moving them into place around the laager. When the attack began, Claudia manipulated her model Hinds and there were enthusiastic cheers from the watching Shanganes as one by one they were brought crashing to earth by volleys of Stinger missiles.

'Right, Sergeant Alphonso.' Sean replaced the counters in their original positions. 'Show us the attack again.'

Five times, they went over it. In turn, each of the section leaders described it to them, and the final cheers as the Hinds were destroyed lost none of their gusto for being so often repeated. At the end of the fifth show, Sergeant Alphonso stood up and addressed Sean on behalf of the entire unit.

'*Nkosi Kakulu*,' he began. He had never before used this form of address to Sean. Usually this was reserved for very high-ranking tribal chieftains. Sean was aware of the honour, and this proof that he had at last won the full respect and loyalty of these fiercely proud and hard-bitten warriors.

'Great Chief,' Alphonso said, 'your children are troubled.' There was a murmur of agreement and nodding of heads. 'In all that you have told us of the battle, you have not assured us that you will be there to lead us and to put fire in our bellies as you did at Grand Reef. Tell your children, *Nkosi Kakulu*, that you will be with us in the midst of the fighting and that we will hear you roaring like a lion as the *henshaw* fall burning from the sky, and Frelimo baboons run from us screaming like virgins feeling the prong for the very first time.'

Sean spread his hands. 'You are not my children,' he said. 'You are men of men, just as your fathers were men before you.' There was no higher compliment he could pay them. 'You do not need me to help you to do this thing. I have taught you all I know. The flames in your bellies burn with the same fury as the fire in the tall dry grass of winter. The time has come for me to leave you. This battle is yours alone. I must go, but I will always be proud that we were friends and that we fought side by side as brothers do.'

436

There was a low chorus of dissent, and they shook their heads and spoke together in low rumbling tones.

Sean turned away, and saw that while he had been speaking General China had come up and now stood quietly amongst the trees at the riverside, watching him. There were a dozen officers and men of his personal bodyguard behind him, all wearing the same maroon berets, but somehow, they seemed insignificant as China stepped forward and instantly commanded the attention of every person in the amphitheatre.

'I see your preparations are complete, Colonel Courtney,' he greeted Sean.

'Yes, they are ready, General.'

'Will you please go over the plans again, for my benefit.'

Sean singled out Sergeant Alphonso. 'Describe the raid for us again,' he ordered, and General China stood in front of the mock-up laager with the swagger-stick clasped behind his back and watched with quick bright eyes, interrupting sharply to ask his questions.

'Why are you using only half the available missiles?'

'The raiding column has to get through the Frelimo lines undetected. The missiles are bulky and heavy, a larger number would be superfluous and make discovery by Frelimo much more likely.'

China nodded, and Sean went on, 'You also have to take into account the possible failure of the raid. If that happens and you have bet all your Stingers on one throw of the dice . . .' Sean shrugged.

'Yes, of course, it's wise to keep half of the missiles in reserve. Even if the raid fails we will not be left entirely helpless. Carry on.'

Alphonso went through the plan step by step, illustrating with the coloured pebbles how the missile teams would move into position and lie in readiness five hundred metres from the perimeter of the gunship laager, two teams confronting each sandbagged emplacement.

437

At the signal of a red flare, the assault team would attack in full force from the south, hitting any fuel tankers that might be on the rail spur with RPG 7 rocket fire, sweeping the interior of the laager with mortar fire and then launching a frontal assault on the southern perimeter.

'The *henshaw* will take fright as soon as the shooting begins,' Alphonso explained. 'They will try to escape by flying away, but there will be a moment when they rise from the earth that they will still be low down, standing still in the air, the way a falcon hovers before it stoops. That is the moment we will kill them.'

Sean and China discussed every aspect of the plan until at last, China was satisfied.

'So when will you move out?'

'You keep saying "you".' Sean pulled him up. 'I'm not having anything more to do with it. Sergeant Alphonso will lead the attack. They'll move out this evening two hours before dark to penetrate the Frelimo lines during the night, lay up in cover tomorrow and launch the attack tomorrow night.'

'Very well,' China agreed. 'I'll address the men now.'

He was a compelling orator, Sean admitted, as he listened to China reminding them of the consequences of a Frelimo victory and exhorting them to deeds of valour and self-sacrifice. By the time he ceased speaking their faces were shining and their eyes sparkled with patriotic fervour. General China raised his voice. 'You are warriors so let me hear you sing the Renamo battle anthem.'

The forest echoed and rang to the haunting beauty of their massed voices, and Sean found his vision dissolving into a blur as his eyes filled with emotion. He had not realized how much these men had come to mean to him, until now that he was about to leave them.

'Colonel, I would like to speak to you in private,' General China broke into his sentimental reverie. 'Please come with me.'

With a word to Claudia and Job, Sean excused himself, 'Give them each one more run with the simulator.'

He fell in beside General China and as they set out for the headquarters bunker, Sean took no notice of the fact that China's bodyguard did not accompany them, but remained at the entrance of the amphitheatre in an arrogant manner.

When they reached the command bunker, General China led them through to his underground office. There was tea ready for them and Sean piled brown sugar into his mug and savoured the first steaming mouthful.

'So what did you want to tell me?' he asked.

China was standing with his back to him, studying the wall map of which he had marked the developing Frelimo offensive with coloured pins. He did not answer Sean's question and Sean would not pander to him by asking again. He sipped at the tea and waited.

A signaller came through from the radio-room and handed China a message flimsy. As he read it, the General exclaimed with disgust tinged with anxiety and reached up to move a group of coloured pins on the map. Frelimo had broken through in the west and were closing in remorselessly.

'We are not containing them,' China told Sean, without looking around. Another messenger ducked into the bunker. He was one of China's personal bodyguards, wearing the distinctive maroon beret. He whispered something to China and Sean thought he heard the word 'American'. It quickened his interest.

China smiled briefly and dismissed the man with a nod before he turned to Sean.

'It won't work,' he said.

'What won't work?'

'The attack as you have planned it.'

'Nothing is certain in war, as you should know, General. But I disagree. The plan has about a sixty per cent chance of total success. That's pretty good odds.'

'The odds would be considerably higher, perhaps eighty per cent, if you led the attack, Colonel Courtney.'

'I'm flattered by your estimate. However, it's hypothetical. I'm not leading it. I'm going home.'

'No, Colonel. You are leading the attack.'

'We had a bargain.'

'Bargain?' China smiled. 'Don't be naïve. I make bargains and break them as the need arises. The need has arisen I'm afraid.'

Sean sprang to his feet, his face pale as candle wax beneath the deep tan. 'I'm going,' he said. Despite his fury, he managed to keep his voice thin and tight. 'I'm taking my people and I'm leaving now. Right away. You'll have to kill me to stop me.'

China touched his deaf ear, and smiled again. 'That notion is not without its attractions, I assure you, Colonel. However, I don't think it will come to that.'

'We'll see.' Sean kicked back the stool on which he had been sitting and it hit the wall and crashed over on its side. He turned and ducked out of the low doorway.

'You'll be back,' China assured him softly, but Sean gave no sign of having heard him. He came out in the sunlight and strode down towards the river.

He had reached the amphitheatre before he realized that something was desperately amiss.

The Shanganes sat rigid at their places upon the slope, they seemed not to have moved since he had last seen them. Alphonso's features were graven in black ironstone, expressionless and dull, the shield of deliberate stupidity behind which the African distances himself from powers and forces against which he has no other defence.

Job was sprawled across the table in the centre of the amphitheatre. His tunic was floury with dust and his cap still lay in the dirt at his feet. He shook his head in a dazed uncertain fashion and droplets of blood dripped from his nose.

'What happened?' Sean ran to him, and Job stared at him, trying to focus his eyes. He had been brutally beaten. His lips were swollen into purple bruises, his mouth full of blood that stained his teeth like red wine. One eyebrow was cut through, a deep jagged split from which blood trickled down the side of his nose. Blood welled out of both nostrils, swelling into bright pink bubbles as he breathed through it. There were lumps on his forehead like overripe grapes, and the lobe of one ear was torn. Blood dripped onto the front of his dusty tunic.

'Job, what the hell . . . ?' Sean caught him by the shoulder. 'Who?'

'I tried to stop them!' Job blurted, his eyes fixed on Sean's face, 'I tried!'

'Take it easy.'

Sean tried to lead him to a seat, but he shook Sean's hands away and said, 'Claudia.'

A flash frost of dread chilled Sean's belly. 'Claudia!' he repeated, and looked around him wildly. 'Where is she, Job? What happened?'

'They took her,' Job repeated. 'China's goons. I tried to stop them.'

Sean reached for the pistol on his webbing belt. 'Where is she, Job?' The pistol grip filled his hand.

'I don't know.' Job wiped the palm of his hand down his face and looked at the blood. 'I was out cold, I don't know for how long.'

'China, you turd-munching bastard, you are going to die.' Sean whirled, ready to go charging back to the headquarters bunker.

'Sean, think first!' Job called urgently, and Sean checked. So often Job had saved him with those two words. 'Think first!'

It required an enormous effort of will, but for seconds, Sean managed to keep his head above the wave of his killing rage.

'The manuals, Job!' he gritted out. 'Burn them!'

Job blinked at him through the blood that spilled from the split eyebrow. 'Burn the manuals!' Sean repeated. 'Insurance, man. We are the only ones who know.'

Job's expression cleared. 'And the cassettes,' he exclaimed.

'Right!' Sean said. 'The cassettes. Give them to me.'

While Job hastily repacked the attack cassettes into their carrying case, Sean walked across to where Alphonso sat at the front of the amphitheatre and unhooked a phosphorus grenade from his belt.

Working swiftly, he used his pistol lanyard and the phosphorus grenade to rig a makeshift self-destruction device in the interior of the case of attack cassettes. He hooked the clip of his pistol lanyard through the pin of the grenade, and laid the grenade itself in the middle of the case. Using the point of a bayonet, he drilled a hole through the lid of the carrying case and threaded the end of the lanyard through it. When he locked the case, he looped the free end of the lanyard securely around his own wrist.

'Let China try and get them away from me now,' he said grimly. If the case were jerked out of his grip, or if he let it fall the lanyard would pull the pin of the grenade, destroying not only the contents but anybody standing nearby. He waited just long enough to watch Job set a match to the pile of instruction manuals.

Once they were fully ablaze he ordered Job, 'Stay here, make certain they are burned to ashes.'

Then lugging the case of cassettes, he started back to the headquarters bunker.

'I said that you would be back,' China greeted him, with that icy sardonic smile which faded swiftly as he saw the case that Sean carried and the lanyard looped around his wrist.

Sean lifted the case in front of him and flaunted it in China's face.

'There is the Hind Squadron, China,' he said, with an

effort keeping his voice level. 'Without this your Stingers are useless to you.'

China's eyes flicked towards the entrance of the dugout.

'Don't even think about it,' Sean warned him. 'There is a grenade inside the case, a phosphorus grenade. This lanyard is attached to the firing-pin. If I drop it, like if I was to die suddenly or someone were to pull it out of my hand, the whole lot goes up in a nice little bonfire, happy fifth of November.'

They stared at each other across the desk.

'So this is a pretty little stalemate, Colonel,' China's smile was reborn, even colder and more deadly than Sean had seen it before.

'Where is Claudia Monterro?' Sean asked, and China raised his voice, summoning an orderly from the radio room.

'Bring the woman!' he ordered, and they waited, both of them poised and alert, watching each other's eyes.

'I should have thought of the cassettes,' China said in conversational tones. 'That was good, Colonel. Very good. You can see why I want you to lead the attack.'

'While we are on the subject,' Sean replied, 'I have also burned the instruction manuals. There are only the three of us – Job, Claudia and me – who understand the Stingers.'

'What about the Shanganes, Alphonso, Ferdinand?' China challenged, and Sean grinned at him like a death's head.

'Not on, China. They know how to shoot them, but they don't have any idea how to program the micro processors. You need us. China. Without us the Hinds are coming after you, and there's not a damned thing you can do about it. So don't fool with me. I have your survival in my hands.'

There was a scuffle in the outer room, and both of them looked to the entrance as Claudia was pushed through from the radio room.

Her hands were once more manacled behind her back,

she had lost her cap and her hair tumbled into her face and down her neck.

'Sean!' she blurted when she saw him, and she pulled against the hands of the two bodyguards who held her, trying to reach him. They jerked her back and threw her against the side wall of the dugout.

'Tell your baboons to knock that off,' Sean snarled, and when they glowered at him, China restrained them with a sharp order.

'Put that woman in the chair!'

They forced her into the solid mahogany seat and at another order from China used the manacles to chain her wrists securely to the heavy arms of the chair.

'I have something of yours, Colonel, and you have something of mine. Shall we work out a deal?' General China suggested.

'Let us go,' Sean said promptly. 'At the border, I'll hand over the cassettes.' And China shook his head regretfully.

'Not acceptable. Here is my counter offer. You lead the attack on the Hind laager. When it is completed successfully, Alphonso will escort you to the border.'

Sean raised the booby-trapped case head high, and China smiled. In retaliation he drew the trench knife from its sheath on his belt. It was ivory-handled with a five-inch blade.

Still smiling he lifted a single hair from Claudia's scalp, and with a sharp jerk pulled it out. He held it up between thumb and forefinger and touched the hair with the blade. Half of the dark strand fell away and floated down to the earthen floor of the dugout.

'That is how sharp it is,' China said softly.

'If you kill her you haven't got anything to bargain with.' Sean's voice was harsh with strain and he was sweating.

'I have this to bargain with,' China replied, and he nodded to his guards at the doorway.

They led in someone whom Sean had never seen before. An apparition with an ancient skull-like head. The hair had fallen out in tufts, leaving shiny black patches on the scalp. The lips had shrunk and peeled back to expose teeth that were too large and white for that ruined head.

At a word from China the guards stripped away the single filthy ragged shift that covered the body, leaving it entirely naked, and for the first time, Sean realized that it was a woman.

Her body reminded him of the horror pictures he had seen of the survivors of Dachau and Belsen. She was a skeleton covered with baggy skin, her empty dugs dangled over the rack of her ribs, her stomach was drawn in so that her pelvic girdle was an empty bony basin. Her arms and legs were fleshless, the bony elbows and knees grotesquely enlarged.

Sean and Claudia stared at her with horror, unable to speak with the shock of it.

'Look at the lesions on her abdomen,' China invited in a pleasant voice, and numbly they obeyed.

They were blind boils, hard and shiny as ripe black grapes beneath the skin, covering her lower belly and disappearing into the wiry mop of her pubic hair.

While all their attention was on this pathetic figure, China reached down quickly with the knife and touched the back of Claudia's hand with the point of the blade. Claudia gasped and tried to jerk her hand away, but it came up short against the manacle chain and she stared down as a thin snake of bright blood trickled down her forefinger and dripped onto the floor.

'What did you do that for, you snot-gobbling bastard?' Sean demanded.

China smiled. 'It's only a scratch.'

Slowly he reached out towards the naked skeletal figure of the black woman, pointing with the knife at her shrunken belly.

'The extreme emaciation, and those characteristic lesions are diagnostic,' he explained. 'The woman is suffering from what we, in Africa, call the "Slim Sickness".'

'Aids,' Claudia whispered, and her voice was filled with the dread that single word conjured up.

Despite himself Sean took a step back from the dreadful figure before him.

'Yes, Miss Monterro,' China agreed. 'Aids in its terminal stage.'

He touched one of the marble-hard chancres on the woman's belly with the point of the blade, and she gave no reaction as it split open and a mixture of pus and dark tarry blood oozed from the wound and trickled down into the matted bush of her pubic hair.

'Blood,' whispered China, and gently scooped it up onto the bright silver blade. 'Warm living blood, swarming with the virus.'

He proffered the blade for Sean's inspection and involuntarily Sean pulled back further as blood dripped from the point.

'Yes,' China nodded. 'Something that even the bravest have reason to fear, the most certain, the most lingering, the most loathsome death of all the ages.'

With his free hand he took hold of Claudia's wrist.

'Consider this other blood. The sweet bright blood of a vibrant, beautiful, young woman.'

The scratch on the back of Claudia's hand was vivid, but the tiny flow of blood from it almost quenched it.

'Blood to blood,' China whispered. 'Sick blood to healthy blood.'

He brought the filthy blade closer to Claudia's hand and she stiffened in the chair, straining silently against the manacle, her face white with horror as she stared at the knife.

'Blood to blood,' China repeated. 'Shall we let them mingle?'

Sean found he could not speak, he shook his head dumbly, staring at the knife.

'Shall we do it, Colonel?' China asked. 'It's all up to you now.' He brought the blade closer to the open wound in Claudia's smooth creamily tanned skin.

'Just another inch, Colonel,' China whispered, and suddenly Claudia screamed; it was a wild ringing release of horror and terror, but China did not flinch. He did not look at her face and his knife hand was steady and tremorless.

'What shall we do, Colonel Courtney?' he asked.

He lowered the knife and touched her wrist with the flat of the blade, leaving a smear of diseased blood on the unblemished skin, only inches from the scratch on Claudia's hand, then slowly he moved the knife downwards.

'Speak quickly, Colonel. In seconds it will be too late.' The knife left a shiny track of blood like the slime trail of some disgusting snail across her skin. Inexorably it moved down towards the open wound.

'Stop it!' Sean screamed. 'Stop it!'

China lifted the blade away, and looked at him enquiringly. 'Does that mean we have reached an agreement?'

'Yes, damn you to hell! I'll do it!'

China tossed the contaminated knife into a corner of the dugout, and then opened one of the drawers in his desk and brought out a bottle of Dettol antiseptic. He soaked his handkerchief in the undiluted fluid, and then carefully wiped the smear of diseased blood from Claudia's skin.

The tension went out of her rigid body and she slumped in the chair. She was panting softly and trembling like a kitten left out in the rain.

'Turn her loose,' Sean croaked, but China shook his head.

'Not until we have made our terms of agreement clear.'

'All right,' Sean snarled. 'And the first of those terms is that my woman comes with me on the mission. No more dugouts filled with rats.'

China pretended to ponder that and then nodded. 'Very

well, but the second term is that if you fail me in any way, then Alphonso will kill her immediately.'

'Get Alphonso in here,' Sean demanded. The sweat had not yet dried on his forehead and his voice was still rough and unsteady. 'I want to hear you give him his orders.'

Alphonso stood to attention and listened expressionlessly as China told him, 'However, if the attack fails, if you are intercepted by Frelimo before you reach the laager, or if any of the *henshaw* are allowed to escape . . .'

Sean interrupted. 'No, General, a hundred per cent success is too high to hope for. Let us be reasonable and realistic. If I can destroy all but six of the Hinds, then it must be counted that I have fulfilled my part of the bargain.'

China frowned and shook his head. 'Even six Hinds will be sufficient to ensure our defeat. I'll allow you two. If more than two Hinds escape from the laager your mission will be a failure, and you must pay the price.' He turned back to Alphonso and went on with his instructions. 'And so, Sergeant, you will obey all orders from the Colonel, carrying out the attack exactly the way he has planned it, but if the raid fails, if more than two *henshaw* escape, then you are to take full command, and your very first duty will be to shoot the two whites, and their black servant – you will shoot them immediately.'

Alphonso blinked almost sleepily at the order. He did not turn his head to look at Sean, and Sean found himself wondering if, despite their relationship, the friendship that had grown up between them, despite the fact that Alphonso had called him *Nkosi Kakulu* and *Baba*, and had exhorted him to lead the mission, despite all of this, he would carry out the execution order.

Alphonso was an African Shangane and a warrior with a deep sense of tribal loyalty and a tradition of absolute obedience to his chief and tribal elders.

'Yes,' Sean thought. 'He'd probably have a few regrets, but without question or hesitation, he would do it.'

He raised his voice. 'All right, China, we all know exactly where we stand. Let Miss Monterro come to me now.'

The bodyguard removed her handcuffs and politely General China helped her out of the chair. 'I apologize for the unpleasantness, Miss Monterro, but I'm sure you will understand the necessity for it.'

Claudia was unsteady on her feet, and staggered before she reached Sean and clung to him.

'And so I'll wish you farewell and good hunting.' China gave them a small mocking salute. 'One way or the other, we will not meet again, I'm afraid.'

Sean did not deign to reply. With the case of cassettes in one hand and his other arm around Claudia's shoulders, Sean led her to the doorway.

They moved out two hours before darkness. It was an unwieldy column and the missile-launchers and the back-up missiles made awkward burdens; apart from their weight, the length of the packs made them cumbersome. They hooked up in thick bush when the path narrowed and slowed down the column's ability to react to threat and danger.

At first, Sean kept the column bunched up in a close cohesive whole. They were still some miles from the tenuous front line of the Renamo army, and would not be seriously menaced until much later in the march.

However, taking no chances, Sean kept the assault troops of the vanguard and rear vigilant and at the utmost degree of readiness to repel any attacks and to give the missile-bearers a chance to escape. To ensure this, Sean sent Job to the head of the column while he stayed in the centre where he could reach any trouble spot quickly and where he could be near to Claudia.

'Where is Matatu?' she asked Sean. 'We've just gone off and left him. I'm so worried about him.'

'Don't worry about leaving him behind. He's like one of those puppies which you can't send home. He'll follow me anywhere, in fact the little bugger is probably watching us out of the bush at this very moment.'

And so it proved, for as darkness descended on the column, a small shadow appeared miraculously at Sean's side.

'I see you, my *Bwana*,' Matatu twinkled.

'I see you also, little friend.' Sean touched his woolly head as he would his favourite gun dog. 'I've been waiting for you to find a way for us through the Frelimo lines, and so lead us to the roosting place of the ugly falcons.' And Matatu swelled with self-importance.

'Follow me, my *Bwana*,' he said.

Now with Matatu to guide them, Sean could rearrange the column into a more streamlined formation for passing through the Frelimo advance and getting into their rear.

To his advantage was the size of the battle being fought ahead of him. There were six thousand Frelimo and Zimbabwean troops advancing against less than half that number of Renamo defenders, and the area of the battlefield was tens of thousands of square miles in extent. The fighting ahead of them was taking place in small isolated pockets, while most of the ground was wild and rugged and deserted.

Sean sent Job and Matatu ahead with a small party of assault troops to find the wide gaps in the line and steer them through. The rest of the column followed at a discreet interval, protected by the conventionally armed assault division of Shanganes.

They kept going steadily through the night, runners coming back from Job and Matatu in the vanguard to guide them whenever it was necessary to make a detour or to change direction.

At intervals during the long cold march, they heard

distant gunfire and the sound of mortars and heavy machine-guns as elements of the Frelimo advance ran into the Renamo defence. Occasionally they saw the twinkle of signal flares soar above the dark forest, but there was no sound of Isotov turbos and helicopter rotors in the night. It was clear that the Hinds were limiting their depredations to the daylight hours when they could distinguish friend from foe and make their close-support operations more effective.

An hour before dawn Job came back down the column to find Sean.

'We aren't going to reach our first objective until an hour or so after first light,' he reported. 'The pace has been slower than we expected, what do you want us to do? Shall we take a chance on the Hinds finding us?'

Sean looked up at the sky before he replied. The first lemon-coloured flush of dawn was paling out the stars.

'The forest roof isn't dense enough to hide so many men and so much equipment,' he decided. 'We have to keep going and get them into hiding. Tell Matatu to quicken the pace.'

'What about the Hinds?'

'The main fighting is well behind us now, that is where they will be headed, we have to take the chance, but move fast.'

As the light strengthened so the faces of the men in the long column turned more frequently and fretfully to the sky. The pace was fast, almost a run. Although they had been going all night, still the Shanganes bore their heavy burdens with all the hardiness and fortitude of the African, burdens that would have broken the heart and the back of even a strong white man.

It was light enough to define the tree-tops against the orange blossom of dawn when Sean heard the dread whistle of turbos, faint and distant, passing to the east. The Hinds were flying their first sortie of the day, and the alarm was shouted down the length of the column. The porters dived off the path, seeking the nearest cover, and the section leaders crouched ready to wave the captured Frelimo colours that Sean had provided for each of them should the Hinds spot them and come in to strafe them.

The deception was not necessary for the pair of Hinds passed two miles east of their position. Sean saw their silhouettes, like deformed gnats, black against the oncoming dawn, and minutes later heard the thunder of their Gatling-cannons and the boom of their assault rockets as they pounded another Renamo stronghold amongst the ironstone hills far behind them.

Sean got the column moving again and the glimpse that they had been given of 'the flying death' sped their feet. An hour later, the tail end of the column clambered swiftly down the almost sheer side of the gorge at the bottom of which lay the dry riverbed and the caves where the captured Unimogs had been hidden.

It was almost a home-coming and the men crept thankfully into the gloom of the caverns and laid down the heavy packs.

'No fires,' Sean ordered. 'No smoking.'

They ate their rations of cold stodgy maize cakes and dried fish and then curled on the cavern floor and slept like a pack of hounds exhausted at the end of a day's hunting.

Sean found a private place for Claudia at the back of the cavern, behind a natural screen of tumbled sandstone blocks. He spread a blanket on the rocky floor and she sat cross-legged upon it and munched the unappetizing rations; but before she had half finished, she slumped sideways, asleep before her head touched the floor. Sean spread the other blanket over her for it was chilly in the depths of the cavern, and then he went back to the entrance.

Alphonso had rigged the antenna of the small portable two-way VHF radio. He was crouched beside the set with the volume turned low, listening to the situation reports of the Renamo field commanders as they reported in to General China's headquarters.

'It goes very badly,' he told Sean glumly. 'Frelimo will be on the riverbank by noon tomorrow, and unless the general pulls back, he will be overrun.' Alphonso broke off as he recognized their call sign in the jumbled static of the wave band.

'Banana Bush, this is Warthog,' he replied into the hand mike and then gave the 'primary objective established' code, 'Coca-Cola!' Sean smiled at this subtle commentary on modern Africa, and Banana Bush acknowledged and signed off. Their next report was scheduled for dawn tomorrow by which time the fate of the mission would be decided one way or the other.

Sean left Alphonso rolling up the antenna and packing the radio into its carrying case and from the entrance of the cavern watched the party of five men who under Job's supervision were sweeping the sandy riverbed with thorn branches to obliterate the last traces of their passing.

Job climbed back to the mouth of the cave and Sean asked, 'Sentries?'

'On each of the peaks.' Job pointed to the heights above them. 'I have covered every approach.'

'All right.' Sean led him back into the cavern. 'It's time to arm and program the Stingers.'

It took almost a full hour to assemble the launchers, connect the battery-packs and feed the cassettes into the micro computers in the consoles. Finally each of the launchers was fully armed and programmed for 'Two Colour' attack sequence on the Hind gunships, and they handed them back to the Shangane section leaders.

Sean glanced at his wristwatch, mildly surprised that it was still keeping time after all the abuse he had given it recently.

'We can grab a few hours' shut-eye,' he told Job, but neither of them made a move to do so.

Instead, as if by consent, they moved back to the entrance of the cavern, away from the others, and leaned against the rock wall with their shoulders almost touching, staring thoughtfully out into the riverbed where the early sunlight was sparkling the crystalline sand like powder snow.

'If you had taken my advice, you could be living high in the flesh pots of Harare now,' Sean murmured.

'And never have the chance to bag a Hind?' Job smiled carefully, his damaged lip was crusted with a fragile scab and a drop of blood like a tiny ruby appeared as it split open again. He dabbed at it with the corner of his bandanna, as he went on, 'We have hunted all the dangerous game together, Sean, in all the worst places. Buffalo in the jesse bush, elephant in the Kasagasaga. This will be another trophy, the best and biggest.'

Sean turned to study his face. It was typical of their friendship that their feelings should be so perfectly in tune. During the long night march, Sean's fury and hatred of General China had abated and given way to this emotion which Job had just articulated, the excitement of the hunter. They were both hunters, the chase was a fire and a passion in their blood which they had never attempted to suppress. They understood each other, recognized and accepted this bond between them which had grown stronger over the twenty years of their friendship. Yet they had seldom spoken of their feelings for each other, Sean realized.

'Perhaps now is the time to do so,' he thought, and said aloud, 'We are more than brothers, you and me.'

'Yes,' Job replied simply. 'We are beyond the love of brothers.'

They were silent then, not embarrassed by what had passed between them, but rather fulfilled and fortified by it.

'As a brother,' Sean broke the silence, 'may I ask a favour of you?'

Job nodded, and Sean went on softly, 'There will be hard

454

fighting at the laager. I would not want Claudia to fall into the hands of Frelimo if I were not there to prevent it. That is the favour I ask.'

A shadow passed behind Job's eyes. 'I do not like to think about that possibility.'

'If I am not there, will you do it for me?'

Job nodded, 'I give you my word.' if you have to do it, do not warn her, do not speak, do it unexpectedly.'

'She will not know it is coming,' Job promised. 'It will be quick.'

'Thank you,' Sean said, and clasped his shoulder. 'Now we must rest.'

Claudia was still asleep, her breathing was so gentle and silent that, for a moment, Sean was alarmed. He put his face close to hers and felt the warmth of her breath on his cheek. He kissed her and she murmured in her sleep and reached out, fumbling for him and sighing contentedly as he crept into the circle of her arms.

He seemed only to have closed his eyes for a moment, before a light touch on his cheek woke him again, and he looked up to see Job squatting over him.

'It's time,' Job's lips formed the words, and Sean gently disentangled Claudia's arms.

'Sleep sweetly, my love,' he murmured, and left her lying on the blanket.

The others were already waiting for him at the entrance of the cave, Matatu and Alphonso and the section leaders, only lightly armed so that they could move swiftly and steathily.

'Four o'clock,' Job told Sean, and he saw that the light in the riverbed had mellowed, the shadows were lengthening.

There was nothing more to say. They had both done this half a hundred times before.

'See you around,' Job said, and Sean nodded, as he strapped on his pack.

With Matatu dancing ahead of them like a forest sprite, they slipped out of the cavern and into the trees, turning immediately south and settling into their running formation.

Twice they heard the Hind gunships passing at a distance and once they were forced into cover as one of the helicopters came directly overhead.

However, it was high, over four thousand feet Sean estimated, flying at the top of its speed. Studying the aircraft through his binoculars, Sean guessed it had completed a mission and was racing back to the laager to refuel and rearm. To confirm this, he saw that the racks for the Swatter assault missiles below the fuselage were empty, and the nozzles of the rocket pods were scorched with the back blast of discharged rockets.

The Hind was heading on exactly the same bearing as Matatu was leading them, and even as Sean held it in the field of his binoculars, the Hind reduced power on its turbos and commenced its descent, homing in on its laager.

'Not more than five miles ahead,' Sean guessed, and glanced across at Matatu, who was waiting expectantly for Sean's approbation.

'Like a bee to its hive,' Matatu grinned.

'Your eyes are like those of the vulture,' Sean agreed. 'They see all.' And Matatu hugged himself with pleasure and rocked on his haunches. Sean's praise was all the reward he ever asked for.

Half an hour later they leopard-crawled up onto the crest of a low rocky kopje and slid over the skyline into the dead ground below before Sean raised his binoculars. He used his cap to shade the lens; a reflected ray of sunlight would telegraph their position like a heliograph.

He picked up the railway line immediately, less then two miles distant; the ballast was of blue granite and the single set of tracks gleamed dully in the late sunshine, polished by the steel wheels of rolling stock.

He followed the tracks for a mile and found the spur

onto which two railway tankers had been shunted. They were partially hidden by scraggly trees and rank bush, but minutes later a feather of dust rose out of the forest and a fuel bowser came down a dirt track and pulled in beside the leading tanker. Sean watched through the binoculars as overall-clad workers connected up the delivery hose and began pumping fuel between the two vehicles.

While this was happening, a Hind gunship rose with dramatic suddenness from the foreslope of the hill just beyond the railway spur, and at last, Sean had a positive fix on the laager.

The Hind rose to three hundred feet above the hill and then turned and bore away, humpbacked and nose-heavy, for one more mission over the battlefield in the north before the light failed, and the fighting was suspended for the night.

Now that he knew exactly where to look, Sean was able to make out other heavily camouflaged emplacements on the slopes of the hill. He counted six of them and said so to Matatu.

'There are two more,' Matatu grinned patronizingly as he pointed out the hidden emplacements that Sean had overlooked. 'And there are three more on the far side of the hill, you cannot see them from here.'

The wisdom of making this reconnaissance in daylight became clearer, as Sean was able to pick out the discrepancies between the model with which they had planned the raid and the actual topography of the laager and its surroundings.

Sean jotted the amendments in his notebook, making new estimates of the ranges and the fields of fire that his missiles could command. One by one, he called over each of the section leaders and pointed out exactly what positions he wanted them to occupy as soon as their teams arrived and darkness had fallen to cover them.

Satisfied that Matatu could supply no further information,

Sean despatched him. 'Go back to Job. As soon as it is dark, guide him and all the other soldiers up here.'

When Matatu was gone, Sean devoted the last hour of daylight to watching the gunships return out of the north. There were eleven of them, ample proof of the efficiency of the Russian maintenance crews who must have repaired the two Hinds that Matatu had reported were not flying. The entire squadron, less the single gunship that Sean had knocked out of the sky, was once again operational and doing dreadful execution amongst the Renamo guerrillas.

As each gunship hovered above the hillock and then settled into its emplacement, Sean pointed out the flying characteristics to his section leaders and urged them to mark well the exact position of each emplacement.

'That one is yours, Tendela.' He reinforced the target allocations. 'See how he stands in the sky. You will shoot from that clump of dark trees at the edge of the vlei. Have you marked it well?'

'I have marked it, *Nkosi Kakulu*,' they affirmed. The sky was washed by the blood of the dying day, and as he watched the red orb sink away beneath the trees, Sean wondered how much more blood the dawn would bring.

There was that short period of African twilight during which it was not yet dark enough to move off the ridge. There was nothing further to discuss and Sean and Alphonso sat close together. The feeling was so familiar. No matter how many times Sean waited like this, he would never be able to control or ignore the tension that pulled like rubber bands across his guts. It was the heady anticipation of the draught of terror which soon he would drink to its dregs. He longed for it as the addict does for the needle, and dreaded it to the limits of his soul.

'We will make a good kill,' Alphonso said quietly. 'It will be a fight for men who are truly men.'

Sean nodded. 'Yes, my friend, it will be a good fight, and

if we fail, then you must try to kill me. That also will be a good fight.'

'We will see,' Alphonso growled, his eyes reflecting the smoky red glare of the sunset. 'Yes, we will see.'

The crisp silhouette of the hill on which the Hinds were laagered dissolved with the onset of night. Then Venus appeared as the evening star and its cold unwavering light burned directly above the hilltop, seeming to single it out for them.

Within the first hour of darkness, the leading troopers of the raiding column emerged from the trees behind them. Job was at the head of the column with Matatu guiding him and Claudia beside him. Sean met them with a quiet word and immediately began to marshal the troopers into their various units. The section leaders took charge of their missile teams, and the Stinger launchers were unpacked and assembled; the spare missiles in their sealed frangible tubes were checked and readied.

Sean and Job and Claudia went from team to team, running the final checks on the missile launchers, making certain that the battery packs were fully charged and correctly connected, that the cylinders of freon gas were open-valved and that the sighting screens illuminated when the actuator was engaged.

At last, Sean was ready to deploy the missile teams, but before he did so, he called the section leaders together and, for the last time, made each repeat his orders. Satisfied at last, he began to despatch them to their attack positions. He allowed five-minute intervals between each team leaving the ridge.

Alphonso was in charge of the missile teams attacking the eastern perimeter of the laager and because he had farther to go to get into position, he left first.

When it was time for Job, who would lead the missile attack on the western perimeter, to go, he and Sean shook hands briefly. There was no exchange of good wishes, they were both superstitious about that. Instead Job asked face-tiously, 'Listen, Sean, about that four thousand dollars in bonus and back-pay, don't you want to pay me out now?'

'Will you take a cheque?' Sean grinned at him through the dark mask of his camouflage cream. Job answered his grin, punched his shoulder and moved away out of earshot so that Sean could speak to Claudia in private.

'I don't want to leave you,' she whispered, and Sean hugged her fiercely.

'Stay close to Job,' he ordered.

'Come back to me safely.'

'Yes.'

'Promise me.'

'I promise,' he said, and she pulled out of his embrace and turned away, disappearing into the darkness after Job.

Sean stared after her, he found that his hands were trembling. He thrust them into his pockets and clenched his fists.

'Love doesn't do much for one's fighting instincts,' he thought, and tried to dismiss her from his mind. 'She'll be all right with Job.'

The assault party was waiting for him patiently, squatting at the edge of the tree-line. Twenty-four men, the cannon fodder, the meat bombs, he thought ruefully, those who had failed the aptitude tests for operating the Stingers. While the missile crews would fire from stand-off positions five hundred metres outside the perimeter of the laager, the assault party would attack it head on and frontal, deliber-ately drawing fire while trying to flush the Hinds up into the air for the missile gunners to get a fair shot at them. It was this unit who would meet the 12.7mm cannons in their fortified positions, and all the other dangers and obstacles which certainly guarded the laager.

Theirs was the most dangerous task, and for that reason alone, Sean could not delegate the command of them to another. He would lead them in.

'Come on, Matatu,' he said quietly. When there was real danger at hand, wounded game in thick cover or an enemy position to attack, Matatu's self-chosen place was always at Sean's side. Nothing could dislodge him from it.

As a mark of his esteem Alphonso had presented Sean with an AKM assault rifle, the improved and up-dated version of the ubiquitous AK 47 which was much prized and sought after by the Renamo guerrillas. Sean carried this weapon now as he led the assault team down off the ridge, and, with Matatu guiding them through the night, circled out to get in between the main railway line and the laager, as close as was prudent to the spur of line on which the railway fuel tankers stood.

There was no urgency, they had all night in which to get into position, so they went with a stealth which increased the closer they came to the enemy positions.

It was after two o'clock in the morning and the small slice of the moon had set before Sean had them in their jump-off positions, spread out at precise intervals so that at his command, they could sweep forward in skirmishing formation.

He made one final inspection of their dispositions, crawling silently from man to man, personally sighting in the 60mm M4 commando mortars for them, by sense of touch alone checking their equipment, making absolutely certain that each of them clearly understood his objective and then leaving them with a whisper of encouragement and a brief but firm clasp of the shoulder. At last, with everything done that could be done, he settled down to wait.

This was always the worst and the best part of the hunt. As he lay in the silence, he wondered how much of his life he had spent like this, waiting for it to begin, waiting for shooting light, waiting in the blind for that breath-stopping moment when the leopard appeared with magical sudden-ness in the bait tree, an elegant silhouette against the pale backdrop of the dawn.

His mind went back over the years to those other adventures and wild endeavours, to the terrible risks and almost unbearable thrills, and suddenly it dawned upon him that this was probably the last time it would happen. He was over forty years of age and Claudia Monterro had entered his life, it was time for it to change. There was a sadness and, at the same time, a satisfaction in that thought.

'Let the last be the best of all the game,' he thought, and in the utter darkness of pre-dawn, he heard a sound at once both thrilling and terrifying, the shrill high whine of a mighty turbo engine, howling like a man-eating wolf in the night. It was joined almost at once by another and then another. The Hind squadron was starting engines, warming up for their first sortie in the dawn.

Sean checked his watch and the luminous dial showed eleven minutes before five. It was almost time. Without thinking, he unclipped the curved banana magazine from under the AKM rifle and replaced it with another from the pouch of spare magazines on his webbing. That habitual gesture gave him the comfort of long familiarity, and beside him, Matatu seeing him do it stirred expectantly. The dawn wind came softly as a lover and stroked Sean's cheek.

He turned his head towards the east and held up his hand with fingers spread. He could just make out the silhouette of his fingers against the coming dawn. It was what the Matabele called 'the time of the horns', when a herdsman could first see the horns of his cattle against the sky.

'Shooting light in ten minutes,' Sean reminded himself, and knew how long it would take those minutes to pass.

One after the other, the Hinds shut down their engines to an idle. The ground crews would be completing the refuelling and rearming, the flying crews would be going aboard.

Sean had to judge it exactly, the light must be just right. The Hinds would probably not use landing lights, and missile gunners must be able to see them clearly against the dawn.

The light bloomed swiftly. Sean closed his eyes and counted slowly to ten before he opened them again. Now he could make out the stark outline of the crest of the hill, like a cut-out in black cardboard, the lace-work of the msasa trees stood out against the purple sky, swaying gracefully to the dawn breeze.

'Shoot!' he said, and tapped the shoulder of the mortar man beside him. The trooper leaned forward holding the mortar bomb in both hands and dropped it into the mouth of the mortar tube. The charge in the tail ignited and with a polite pop hurled the signal bomb five hundred feet into the sky above the hilltop. It exploded in a twinkling red flare of lights.

Claudia Monterro followed Job down off the ridge, keeping so close behind him that she need only reach out her hand to touch him. Job carried one of the missile launchers across his shoulders, and behind Claudia the number two of their team was bowed beneath the weight of the spare rocket tubes.

The footing was loose and dangerous, while quartz pebbles as treacherous as ball-bearings rolled under foot. It pleased her that she was as steady and sure-footed as any of them over this difficult ground.

Nevertheless, she was sweating in the night chill as they reached the bottom of the slope and crept forward towards the perimeter of the laager. There was a time, only a few short weeks ago, when she would have felt inept and awkward in these circumstances, but now she orientated herself by the beacon of the evening star above the hilltop and responded instantly to Job's signals, picking her footfalls and anti-tracking almost instinctively.

They reached the dense copse of trees which was their attack position, and crept in amongst them. Claudia helped Job set up the Stinger ready for firing and then found herself a comfortable perch at the base of one of the trees to wait out the night.

Job left her there with just the Shangane number two loader for company, and he disappeared into the darkness like a hunting leopard. She was unhappy to see him go, but not long ago she would have been panic-stricken. She realized what a measure of self-reliance and fortitude she had been forced to learn in these last few weeks.

'Papa will be proud of me,' she smiled to herself, using the future tense as though her father still existed. 'Of course he does,' she assured herself. 'He's still out there somewhere looking out for me. How else would I have made it this far?' His memory was a comfort, and as she thought about him, he became confused in her mind with Sean, so that they seemed to merge into a single entity as though her father had somehow achieved a new existence in her lover. It was a good feeling that alleviated her loneliness, until suddenly Job returned as silently and abruptly as he had left.

'All the other sections are in position,' he whispered, as he settled down beside her. 'But it's going to be a long night. Try and get some sleep.'

'I'll never be able to sleep,' she answered, keeping her voice so low that he had to lean close to her to catch the words. 'Tell me about Sean Courtney, I want to know everything you know about him.'

'Sometimes he's a hero, and sometimes he's a complete bastard.' Job thought about it. 'But most of the time, he's something in between.'

'Then why have you stayed with him so long?'

'He's my friend,' Job answered simply, and then slowly, haltingly, he began to tell her about Sean, and they talked the night away.

Claudia listened avidly, encouraging him with quiet questions. 'He was married, wasn't he, Job?' Or, 'Why did he leave his home? I have heard that his family is enormously wealthy. Why did he choose this life?'

So the night passed, and in those hours they became friends, the first true friend she had found in Africa, and in the end he said to her in that beautiful deep African voice, 'I shall miss him, more than I can tell.'

'You speak as though the two of you are parting, and that isn't so. It will be the same.'

'No,' Job denied. 'It will never be the same. He will go with you now. Our time together has ended, yours is beginning.'

'Don't hate me for it, Job.' She reached out to touch his arm in appeal.

'You two will be good together,' he said. 'I think your journey with him will be as good as mine has been. My thoughts will go with you, and I wish you both great joy in each other.'

'Thank you, Job,' she whispered. 'You will always be our friend.'

Job lifted his arm and with fingers spread held his open hand against the dawn.

'The time of the horns,' he murmured softly. 'Soon now.' And as he said it, a flower of bright crimson fire burst open in the sky above the hill.

As the signal flare burst in the dawn sky, the battle was born. Sean always thought of it as the birth of a living thing, a monster which he could only try to direct but which had a life and a will of its own, a terrible thing which swept them all up and carried them along willy nilly.

He had placed the RPG 7 rocket-launchers in the hands

of his two best remaining gunners, but the expert marksmen had all gone to man the Stingers. The first rocket flew low, striking the earth twenty feet in front of the nearest fuel tanker; it burst in a vivid yellow flash and Sean saw one of the Frelimo sentries cartwheel bodily into the air. The second rocket was high, missing the tanker by six feet, reaching the top of its trajectory five hundred yards out and then dropping into the forest beyond, its detonation screened by trees and scrub.

'Aim, you Shangane oxen!' Sean bellowed at them, and he was up and running as he realized his mistake in not taking the first crucial shot himself.

The Frelimo sentries were screaming and scattering around the fuel tankers and from the perimeter of the laager a 12.7mm cannon opened up, sluicing gaudy strings of fiery tracer across the sky.

The rocketeer was fumbling to reload the RPG 7, but he was panicky and unsure in the dark. Sean snatched the launcher off his shoulder and with two deft movements had removed the protecting nose cap of the missile and cleared the safety-pin. He swung the launcher over his shoulder and dropped on one knee, aiming at the nearest tanker.

'All the time in the world,' he reminded himself, and waited for the puff of the morning breeze on his cheek to abate. The RPG 7 was wildly inaccurate in a crosswind for the push of the wind on its tail-fins would turn its nose into wind.

The breeze dropped and Sean centred the sights on the fuel tanker. The range was just on three hundred metres, the limit of the rocket's accuracy, and he fired. The missile sped true, and the side of the tanker erupted in a tall sheet of volatile Avgas. The sky filled with flames.

Sean snarled at the rocketeer beside him and the man fumbled another missile out of his pack, the cardboard propellant tube already attached to it.

Burning Avgas illuminated the southern slope of the hill

like noonday. Sean was kneeling in the open and the gunner on the 12.7mm swung his aim onto him.

The earth around Sean dissolved into billowing clouds of dust and flying clods, and the rocketeer ducked.

'Come on, you yellow bastard!' Sean completed the loading sequence unaided, making no effort to avoid the aim of the 12.7mm gunner.

He lifted the launcher on to his shoulder, and aimed at the second fuel tanker. It was lit up by the flames as though it were a stage effect, but as he was on the point of firing, the tanker was obscured by a dancing curtain of yellow dust and the volley of cannon fire passed so close to Sean's head that his eardrums creaked and popped as though he were in a decompression chamber.

He held his fire for three seconds and then as the curtains of dust blew open he fired through them, and the second tanker burst, blown clear of the railway lines by the explosion of its lethal cargo.

Burning Avgas flowed down the slope like the lava of a miniature Vesuvius, and Sean threw the launcher at the rocketeer's chest. 'Hit them on the head with the bloody thing!' he yelled at him. 'That's the only damage you are going to do with it!'

The mortar men were making better practice. Sean had sighted their weapons for them and they bobbed and weaved over the short mortar tubes as they dropped the finned projectiles into the open mouths. A steady stream of bombs lobbed high into the dawn sky and then rained down into the hilltop laager.

Sean watched the effect of the bursts with a dispassionate, professional eye.

'Good,' he murmured. 'Good.' But they had only been capable of carrying thirty bombs for each of the mortars; they weighed almost two kilos each and they would be expended in a few short minutes. They must rush the perimeter while the exploding bombs distracted the Frelimo gunners. He hefted the AKM rifle and slipped the safety-catch.

'Go!' Sean yelled, and blew a short series of blasts on his whistle. 'Go!'

The Shanganes came to their feet in a single cohesive movement, and swept down the hill, but there were only twenty of them, a puny line of running men, brightly lit by the flames. The 12.7mm gunners on the hill fastened on them, and the tracer flew in clouds about them, thick as a locust plague.

'Shit!' Sean laughed aloud in terror. 'What a way to go!'

One of the Frelimo guns had picked Sean out of the sweep line and was concentrating his fire on him, but Sean was plunging down hill with long flying strides and the gunner was shooting high and a little behind. Shot flashed past Sean so close he could feel the wind of it tugging at his tunic. Impossibly, he lengthened his stride, and beside him Matatu giggled shrilly, keeping pace with him down the hill.

'What's so goddamned funny, you silly little bugger!' Sean yelled at him furiously, and they hit the level ground beside the burning fuel tankers. The Frelimo gunner's field of fire was blanketed by the rolling screen of black smoke, and in the respite Sean marshalled his sweep line of racing Shanganes, pivoting them on the centre and directing them at the perimeter of the laager, pumping his right fist over-head to urge them on.

They used the smoke to cover themselves for the next two hundred metres of their charge. The dawn breeze was spreading it, sooty black and dense and low along the ground.

A Frelimo sentry staggered out of the smoke ahead of Sean. He wore faded and tattered denim jeans and grubby tennis shoes, he had lost his weapon and a rocket splinter must have hit him in the eye. The eye was dislodged from its socket and hung out on his cheek like a huge wet grape, dangling and bouncing on the thick cord of the optic nerve as the man jerked his head.

Without breaking his stride, Sean hit him in the belly with a tap of three from the AKM, firing from the hip. He jumped over the body as it hit the ground.

They came out of the smoke, still in sweep line. Sean glanced along the line and realized incredulously that they had not yet taken a single casualty, the twenty Shanganes were spread out and going hard, offering only fleeting targets through the smoke and flame to the disorientated Frelimo machine-guns.

At that moment, he saw the single strand of wire and the line of round metal discs on short steel droppers only a dozen paces ahead of him. The discs were each emblazoned with a stylized skull and crossbones in scarlet that caught the ruddy glow of the flames, and almost before he realized it, they were into the minefield that guarded the perimeter of the laager.

Two seconds later, the Shangane running on Sean's right-hand side triggered an anti-personnel mine. From the waist down his body was obscured by the dust and flash of the explosion and he dropped to the earth with both of his legs blown to bloody stumps below the knees.

'Keep going!' Sean screamed. 'We are nearly through!' And now his fear was a grotesque black beast upon his back that weighed him down and choked his breathing. To be maimed was a terror far beyond that of death, and the ground beneath his feet was sown with the steel capsules of terrible mutilation.

Matatu ducked in front of Sean, forcing him to check his stride. 'Follow me, my *Bwana*!' he piped in Swahili. 'Tread where I have trodden.' And Sean obeyed, shortening his stride to that of the little mannikin.

So Matatu ran him through the last fifty paces of the minefield, and Sean knew that he had never witnessed such a display of raw courage and devotion of one human being to another. Two more Shangane went down before they were through, their legs blown away beneath them. They left them lying in puddles of their own blood and minced flesh and jumped over the single strand of wire that marked the far side of the minefield.

Even in the terror and exhilaration of the moment, Sean felt his eyelids scalding with the strength of his gratitude and love for the little Ndorobo. He wanted to pick him up like a child's toy and hug him. Instead he gasped at him, 'You're so damned skinny it wouldn't have gone off even if you had stepped on one.' And Matatu twinkled with delight and ran at Sean's side as he charged the 12.7mm machine-gun in its sandbagged emplacement that lay dead ahead of them.

Sean was firing the AKM from the hip, short raking bursts, and he could see the head of the Frelimo gunner in the embrasure of the parapet of sandbags.

The gunner swivelled the barrel of the heavy machine-gun onto him, aiming for his belly and he was so close that Sean could see his eyes reflecting the red light of the fires as he sighted over it. The instant before he fired, Sean hurled himself forward, dropping under the shot like a runner sliding for the base plate; bullets whipped over his head and the muzzle blast beat in his eardrum, but he rolled forward and came up hard against the parapet, flattening himself against it, so close that he could have reached out and touched the muzzle of the machine-gun.

Sean unhooked the fragmentation grenade from his belt, drew the pin, and popped it into the embrasure beside him as though he were posting a letter.

He smiled as he heard the Frelimo gunner scream something unintelligible in Portuguese.

'Happy birthday!' he said, and the grenade exploded, blowing out through the opening in an exhalation of flame and fumes.

Sean jumped up and rolled over the top of the parapet.

There were two men in the emplacement, writhing and wriggling on the floor, and half a dozen others had abandoned the position and were sprinting away up the hill, unarmed and screaming with panic.

Sean left Matatu to finish the two wounded men on the floor with his skinning knife, while he seized the abandoned 12.7mm machine-gun and manhandled it to the rear wall of the emplacement. He aimed it up the hill at the fleeing Frelimo and fired a long traversing burst. Two of the runners dropped in their tracks and grinning happily, crooning to himself with the fun of it, Matatu dragged a steel box of spare ammunition belts across the bloody floor, and helped Sean reload.

With a fresh belt of 250 rounds loaded, Sean traversed the heavy machine-gun and his fire lashed the hillside above him, tracer swirling through the groups of running Frelimo and scattering them.

It seemed to Sean as though more than half the Shangane had survived the minefield and the bloody charge and assault. Roaring wildly with triumph, they were pursuing and harrying the routed defenders.

The barrel of the heavy machine-gun was so hot that it crackled like a horseshoe fresh from the blacksmith's forge.

'Come on!' Sean abandoned it and jumped onto the rear parapet, ready to follow his Shanganes deeper into the laager and to begin wrecking the Russian service installations.

As he stood poised on the parapet, backlit by the burning fuel tankers, a monstrous apparition appeared in the dawn sky ahead of him. Rising on its glittering rotor, turbos shrieking, a Hind gunship lifted out of its sandbagged emplacement not two hundred metres from where Sean stood. It looked like some prehistoric behemoth. Supernatural and other-worldly, it rotated ponderously until the mirrored eyes of the canopy stared at Sean and the multiple cannon barrel in the turret below its nose pointed at him like an accuser's finger.

Sean reached down and seized Matatu by the scruff of his neck and hurled him to the floor of the emplacement, and then threw himself full length on top of him, knocking the breath out of the little man just as a gale of cannon fire dissolved the parapet wall and turned it to clouds of driving dust and gravel.

The suddenness of it all was what shocked Claudia most. One moment the stillness and tranquil darkness of dawn and the next the glare and cacophony of battle, the sky lit by the brilliance of leaping flame and glittering floods of tracers, her ears pounded by bursting mortars, shells and grenades and the blasts of machine-gun fire.

It took long moments for her eyes to adjust to the intensity of light, and to orientate herself to the swift kaleidoscope of the battle. Job had pointed out to her the point on the perimeter of the laager through which Sean would lead the assault and she searched it anxiously. The tiny figures of running men on the exposed slope of the hill were lit by the flames of burning Avgas which cast dark spiderlike shadows that scampered ahead of each man. There were so many of them, little black ants scurrying about, and with a jolt of horror she watched some of them fall and lie very still in the confusion of movement and light and sound.

'Where is Sean?' she whispered anxiously. 'Can you see him?'

'On the left, at the edge of the smoke,' Job told her, and she picked him out by the tiny figure that ran ahead of him like a hunting dog.

'I see him, and Matatu.'

Just in front of the pair the earth seemed suddenly to bloom with dust and flame, and they were gone.

'Oh God. No!' she cried aloud, but as the dust blew aside on the morning breeze, she saw the two of them running on, tracer bullets flickering about them like hellish fireflies.

'Please, please protect him,' she breathed, and lost sight of him as he reached the first emplacement.

'Where is he?' She found that she had seized Job's arm and was shaking it wildly. 'Where is he, can you see him?'

Then suddenly Sean was there again, even at that distance he appeared an heroic figure balancing easily on the sandbagged parapet in the ruddy glow of the flames, and she cried aloud with relief.

Then she saw him cower and from out of the very earth, only a short distance ahead of him, the monstrous shape of a Hind gunship reared into the air and swung its monstrous head towards him, lowering it like a charging bull. She heard the roar of its cannon, and leaping fountains of dust and flying earth obscured Sean's distant figure as cannon shell raked across the hillside.

'Job!' she screamed. 'They have killed him!' She reached out for him again, but Job shook off her hand.

He was down on one knee, the launch tube of the Stinger across his right shoulder, his face in the reflected firelight fixed in a mask of concentration as he stared into the sight screen.

'Quickly!' Claudia whispered. 'Shoot quickly!'

The missile leapt from its long tube, and hot air and stinging particles of dust and dead grass were blown back into Claudia's face as the rocket motor ignited. She slitted her eyes and held her breath as she watched it dart away on its tail of smoke and flame leaving a trail of dazzling smoke behind it as it flew towards the crest of the hill where the Hind hovered against the dark sky.

She saw the slight kick in its trajectory, as the missile changed to the ultra-violet seeker, and lifted its nose fractionally, no longer aiming at the armoured exhaust ports but at the open mouth of the turbo intakes just below the humped gearbox of the rotor.

She thought she saw the missile actually fly squarely into

the intake, but the resulting explosion was deceptively mild, contained within the shell of titanium armour plate, so that none of its fury was dissipated. The Hind reeled wildly to the shot, throwing its nose high, falling backwards so that its tail rotor caught the rocky hillside and flipped it over sideways. It tumbled and bounced down the slope, rolling end over end, flames billowing from the throat of the air intake, its huge main rotor thrashing the earth and tearing itself to pieces, fragments hurtling into the night sky.

Claudia sought desperately for Sean, and gasped as she recognized him through the dust and the smoke, leaping back on to the parapet and then plunging on up the hillside with Matatu close behind him.

'Reload!' Job snapped at her, and with a guilty start she reached for the spare missile tube beside her and helped him clip it into the launcher.

The moment the Stinger was reloaded she glanced back at the laager. Sean was gone, but three more of the Hind gunships were airborne, soaring across the dawn, backlit by the flames. They were firing their cannon, some of them seeking targets within the laager where the attackers were in desperate hand-to-hand combat with the Frelimo garrison, others flailing the dark forest beyond the perimeter with their gales of tracer, trying to extinguish the hail of missiles that flew at them from out of the darkness.

Another Hind was hit and fell on its back, bursting into violent flame as it crashed into the rocky crest of the hill, and then another staggered in flight and curved down, mortally wounded, to hit the tree-tops and cartwheel through them to the earth.

As fast as they fell, others rose from their hidden emplacements with cannons blazing, sweeping down upon the attackers. Job leapt to his feet as a gunship tried to break away, climbing steeply up over their heads. He arched his back, pointing the missile almost vertically upwards, like a gun taking on a high-driven pheasant.

The Hind was a thousand feet up, climbing away, seeming to be safely beyond the Stinger's effective range, presenting a difficult angle and impossible trajectory, but the missile darted up, overhauling it effortlessly, and the great machine seemed to wince and tremble to the shot, standing for a moment stationary in the air, before it fell back with its damaged turbos screaming in mortal agony and dived into the valley, striking in a storm of breaking branches and torn tree-trunks.

'Reload.' Job did not even watch the Hind's death agony, and Claudia leaped to help him fit another missile tube to the launcher. She tapped his shoulder as she finished.

'Go!' she said.

Another Hind came out of the forest directly in front of them. The Russian pilot was flying so low that he seemed to be earth bound. He was dodging and ducking the huge machine behind the scattered trees, weaving like a boxer, the down-draught of the rotor flattening the tall elephant grass only a few feet below the Hind's belly.

Job turned to face the oncoming machine, standing out in the open, lit by the flames, and he braced himself, picking up the image of the Hind in the sight screen.

The Hind seemed to steady itself for an instant, and the blast of its Gatling-cannon swept around them like a hurricane wind. Standing beside Job, Claudia was blown off her feet by the force of it, and her ears buzzed with the supersonic shock of passing cannon shells.

Job was thrown on top of her, his weight driving the wind from her lungs, but they had fallen between two round boulders which deflected the rest of the volley of cannon fire, and the Hind passed over them, only feet above where they lay. The blast of its rotors slashed at them, whipping Claudia's hair into her face so that it stung her eyes like a scourge.

Then the Hind slid away like a cruising tiger shark, and Claudia was suffocating by Job's weight on top of her and half-blinded with dust and her own hair. She struggled to free herself and was suddenly aware that her hands were wet, and that hot liquid was spilling over her and soaking her shirt.

'Job!' she blurted. 'Get up! Get off me!' Only when he neither replied nor moved, but lay on her with a heavy loose weight, did she realize that the wetness that was dousing her was Job's blood. That knowledge gave her wild strength and she rolled his body aside, and dragged herself out from under him.

She crawled to her knees and looked down at him. A cannon shell had hit him high in the upper body, and the damage was horrific. It looked as though he had been savaged and mauled by some ferocious beast; his right arm was almost torn from the shoulder and was thrown above his head in a ghastly parody of surrender.

She stared at him numbly and tried to say his name. No sound came from her throat. She reached out and caressed his face, not daring to touch that terribly mutilated body. She felt a terrible sense of loss and opened her mouth again to give vent to her grief with a wail of despair. It came out in a wild shriek of rage. The force of her rage stunned her, and seemed to impel her out of her own body so that she watched herself from afar, amazed by the actions of this savage stranger who had usurped her body and who now lunged for the missile-launcher where it lay beside Job's body.

Then she found herself on her feet with the missile-launcher on her right shoulder, searching the sky for the Hind gunship. It was four hundred metres away, cruising the foot of the hill, sweeping over the forest, picking out its targets from amongst the trees and destroying them with short but terrible blasts of its forward cannon.

As she turned to face it, standing fully upright in the daylight glare of the fires, the pilot must have spotted her, for he swivelled the gunship on its own axis, bringing the cannon in the pod below his cockpit to bear upon her.

'Locked and loaded,' she said, and the voice was strange in her ears as she repeated the litany of death.

'Actuator on.' She saw the image of the Hind appear in the tiny screen before her eyes, and she centred it in the cross hair on the aiming ring and the missile sobbed and then steadied into its high-pitched electronic tone.

'Target acquired,' she whispered, and felt no fear as the silhouette of the Hind altered in her sight screen. Now it was facing her head-on, its cannon almost bearing, the gunner traversing fractionally to pick up her tiny figure in his own sights.

'Fire!' she said quietly, and squeezed the pistol grip. The shoulder pad jolted her as the Stinger launched, and she slitted her eyes against the back blast of the missile as it sped away at four times the speed of sound, running straight and true at the hovering machine.

The cannon in the Hind's nose blazed, but Claudia felt only the disrupted air of shot passing close over her head before the missile jerked almost imperceptibly and arrowed unerringly into the open throat of the machine's turbo intakes. The Hind had only a few feet to drop before it hit the earth and rolled over on to its side. In the moments before it was totally engulfed by burning fuel from the punctured belly tank, Claudia saw the panicky contortions of the pilot trapped under the armoured canopy and then even that was obliterated in a wall of flame.

'That was a human being,' she thought. 'A living and breathing person, and I destroyed him.' She expected a rush of guilt and remorse. How much a part of her was the belief that all life, especially human life, was sacred. The guilt did not come, instead she was borne aloft on a wave of savage triumph, the same berserk fury that had overtaken her so unexpectedly.

She looked around her swiftly, searching the sky for another target, something else to destroy, anything on which to wreak her vengeance. The dawn sky was empty. The burning carcasses of the Hind gunships lay strewn upon the slopes of the hill and amongst the trees of the valley forest.

'They are all down,' she thought. 'We got them all.'

From the forest, the Shanganes of the Stinger sections were swarming up the hill, breaking into the laager to support Sean's assault. She saw the Frelimo defenders throwing down their weapons, and cowering in their dugouts with hands raised pathetically, attempting to surrender, and watched dispassionately as the yelling Shanganes bayoneted and clubbed them like slaughtered chickens.

At her feet Job groaned, and instantly her rage was gone. She flung the empty missile-launcher aside and dropped down on her knees beside him.

'I thought you were dead!' she whispered, as she unwound the scarf from around her own neck with fingers which only now began to tremble. 'Don't die, Job. Please don't die.' The scarf was stained with sweat and dust, and its seams were unravelled and torn but she balled it up and stuffed it into the terrible wound, pressing down on it with her full weight to try and staunch the flood of his life's blood.

'Sean will be here soon,' she told him. 'Don't die, Job. Fight, please fight. I'll help you.'

Sean and Matatu crouched below the parapet, ducking lower as the storm of cannon fire flew only inches over their heads and filled their eyes and nostrils with dust from the ripped sandbags.

The instant the firing ceased, Sean bobbed up, just in time to see the stricken Hind fall tail-first against the rocky hillside and tear itself to pieces as it rolled down the slope.

'Well, blow me down, those damned Stingers actually work!' he laughed, still flying high on his own fear, and beside him Matatu giggled and clapped his hands.

'Like shooting sand grouse with the .577 *banduki*!' he

478

cried in Swahili, and then leapt to his feet to follow Sean over the parapet.

Three Frelimo troopers bolted out of their dugout as they saw them coming and Sean fired the AKM from the hip, a short tap that caught one of them low in the back and flung him face down. The other two threw down their rifles and fell to their knees, gibbering with terror, hands held high over their heads. Sean ran on past them and they collapsed with relief as he ignored them.

Sean was through the outer defences and into the laager proper with its service areas and hardened helicopter emplacements. The workshops and fuel dumps were heavily sandbagged and covered with camouflage netting. Stray mortar shells were still falling amongst them, kicking up geysers of dust and gusts of whistling shrapnel. One of the Hinds had fallen near the far perimeter of the laager and was burning fiercely, oily black smoke billowing back over the workshops.

In the confusion, human figures scurried about without apparent purpose, unarmed technicians in baggy grey overalls who flung up their arms when they saw Sean, most of them dropping onto their knees to emphasize their surrender. In full camouflage paint and with the blood lust and elation of battle contorting his features, Sean cut a ferocious and terrifying figure.

'Down!' Sean gestured at them with the barrel of the AKM and with transparent relief they fell face down in the dust and clasped their hands behind their heads.

Just ahead he made out the long drooping rotors of a Hind protruding above the sandbagged wall of its emplacement.

'One didn't even get up,' he thought as he raced towards it, and at that moment the rotors began to revolve slowly, building up speed swiftly. Somebody was attempting to start the machine.

Sean darted through the narrow entrance, and into the

deep circular emplacement. He checked his charge for a moment to survey the interior.

The Hind in its blotched camouflage towered over him, its rotors whirling over his head as they built up to start speed on the Isotov turbo engine. Three Russian ground crew were crowded around the front of the machine, and incongruously Sean noticed the crimson arrow emblem painted on the Hind's nose which designated them an 'Excellent Crew'. One of the cherished performance awards of the Soviet air force.

The ground crew turned their white faces towards Sean and gaped at him. He jerked the muzzle of the AKM at them and they fell back.

The canopy of the weapons cockpit of the helicopter was still open, and one of the flight crew was clambering up into it. Only his plump backside in grey flying overalls protruded. Sean reached up between his legs and seized a handful of the man's genitals. The Russian squealed shrilly as Sean used them as a handle to drag him backwards and threw him against the sandbagged side wall of the emplacement.

The spinning rotors whistled shrilly as the turbo engine caught, and Sean jumped up onto the boarding step of the helicopter. The pilot's canopy was also open, and Sean thrust his AKM forward.

The pilot at the controls was young and thin with pale blond hair cut very short. In his haste to get the Hind away he had not even donned his flying helmet. He turned his head to look at Sean. His complexion was marred by angry purple and red acne and his eyes were very pale blue. They widened dramatically as Sean touched the tip of his acne-scarred nose with the muzzle of the AKM and said, 'Party is over, Ivan. Let's go home.'

It was apparent that this helicopter had not been scheduled for the dawn sortie that morning and the pilot and his crew had only begun their attempt to get the machine airborne once the attack had begun. It was less than ten minutes since the first mortar shells had fallen into the laager, not sufficient time, although they had almost made it. .

'Kill the engine,' Sean told the pilot, and enforced the order by jamming the muzzle of the AKM into his nose with sufficient force to bring a smear of blood from one nostril and tears from both his pale eyes.

Reluctantly the pilot pushed the fuel mixture control to fully lean and cut both master switches. The whistle of the turbo died away.

'Out!' said Sean, and the pilot understood the gesture and tone, if not the word. He unclasped his safety-belt and climbed down into the laager.

Sean lined up the pilot, the flight engineer and the three members of the ground crew against the sandbagged wall.

'Welcome to the capitalist world, comrades,' he greeted them, and then looked back at the helicopter.

'Jackpot!' he grinned, still euphoric with the adrenalin in his blood. 'We've got ourselves a real live, working Hind, Matatu!'

Matatu was having a grand time. 'Let's kill them now,' he suggested merrily. 'Give me the *banduki*. Let me shoot them for you.'

Sean had only seen Matatu fire one shot in his entire life, when as a joke Sean had let him fire the double .577. It had lifted Matatu clear off his feet and deposited him ten feet away.

'You couldn't hit one of them, even at this range, you bloodthirsty little bugger.' Sean grinned down at him, and then once more concentrated all his attention on the Hind. The magnitude of the prize he had taken began to dawn upon him.

The Hind would be a magnificent escape vehicle. He and Claudia, Job and Matatu could get out of here with first-class tickets, and then with a drop of spirits, reality overtook him.

481

Sean had never flown a helicopter, did not even have the vaguest notion of how to do so. All he knew was that it required a delicate and expert touch on the controls and was entirely different from piloting a fixed-wing aircraft.

He looked back at the Russian pilot calculatingly. Despite the acne and his unprepossessing appearance, he thought he detected a stubborn and proud streak in the man's pale eyes and he knew that the air-force officers were amongst the elite of the Soviet armed forces. The Russian was almost certainly a fanatical patriot.

'Not much chance of getting you to act as ferry pilot,' he guessed, and then spoke aloud. 'All right, gentlemen, let's get out of here.' He indicated the exit from the emplacement, and under the barrel of the AKM, they trooped towards it obediently. As the Russian pilot passed, Sean stopped him and lifted the Tokarev pistol from the holster at his hip.

'You won't need that, Ivan,' he said, and tucked the pistol into his own belt.

There was a fortified workshop almost abutting the Hind's emplacement. It had been excavated into the hillside and roofed with poles and sandbags. Sean herded the Russians down into it and then looked around him.

The battle had fizzled out, although there were still a few desultory shots and the pop and bang of burning ammunition. Through the drifts of smoke and dust, he saw the Shanganes of the Renamo force rounding up the prisoners and searching for loot and booty. He recognized some of the missile crews. Once the Hinds had been destroyed, they must have abandoned their Stingers and rushed up the hill to join the sack of the laager.

He saw one of them bayoneting a Frelimo prisoner in the buttocks and legs and roaring with laughter as the man squirmed in the dirt, kicking and contorting his body in an attempt to avoid the point of the blade. Other Renamo were emerging from the dugouts, rifles slung over their shoulders and arms full of booty.

Sean was accustomed to the ethics of irregular troops in Africa, but still this blatant indiscipline annoyed him. He snarled at them, and it was a measure of the force of his personality and the authority that he wielded over them that even in the heady moments of victory, they obeyed him with alacrity. The Renamo who had been torturing his prisoner paused only to dispatch the maimed victim with a bullet in the back of the neck before hurrying to Sean's bidding.

'Guard these white prisoners,' Sean ordered them. 'If harm comes to them, General China will roast your testicles on a slow fire and make you eat them,' he warned.

Without looking back, he strode through the laager, reasserting his command, getting his triumphant howling shrieking Shanganes back to sanity. He saw Sergeant Alphonso ahead of him.

'We can't carry much loot away, let the men take their pick and then I want limpet mines in the store rooms after everything has been drenched with Avgas from the drums,' he ordered Sergeant Alphonso. Sean glanced at his wrist-watch. 'We can expect Frelimo to counter-attack the laager within the hour. I want to be gone by then.'

'No!' Alphonso shook his head. 'General China has moved three companies in between us to hold the Frelimo counterattack. He has ordered you to hold this position until he arrives.'

Sean pulled up short and stared at Alphonso. 'What the hell are you talking about? China is two days' march away on the river!'

Alphonso grinned and shook his head. 'General China will be here in an hour. He followed us with five companies of his best troops. He has never been more than an hour behind us, not since we left the river.'

'How do you know this?' Sean demanded, and Alphonso

grinned again and patted the radio on the back of the trooper who stood beside him.

'I spoke to the general ten minutes ago, as soon as we killed the last of the Russian *henshaw*.'

'Why didn't you tell me before this, you bastard?' Sean growled.

'The general ordered me not to. But now he has ordered me to tell you that he is very pleased with the killing of the *henshaw*, and he says that you are like a son to him. When he arrives he will reward you.'

'All right.' Sean changed his orders. 'If we have to hold the laager, get your men into the perimeter defences, we will use the 12.7mm heavy machine-guns.'

Sean broke off as a Shangane trooper came running up the hill towards him.

'*Nkosi!*' The man panted, and as soon as he saw his face, Sean knew it was bad news.

'The woman?' he demanded, seizing the messenger's arm. 'Is the white woman hurt?'

The Shangane shook his head. 'She is safe. She sent me to you. It's the Matabele, Captain Job. He is hit.'

'How bad?' Sean was already starting to run and he shouted the question over his shoulder.

'He's dying,' the Shangane called after him. 'The Matabele is dying.'

Sean knew where to look, he had himself selected the copse of knob-thorn acacia as Job's attack position. The first rays of the morning sun were turning the tops of the knob-thorns to gold as Sean ran down the hill. With the help of two Shanganes, Claudia had moved Job onto level soft ground beneath one of the trees. She had propped his head on one of the back-packs and had a field dressing over the wound.

She looked up and cried, 'Oh, Sean, thank God!' Her shirt was drenched with drying blood and she saw Sean's expression. 'Not my blood,' she assured him. 'I'm all right.'

Sean transferred all his attention to Job. His face was a sickly blue-grey colour and the flesh seemed to have melted like hot tar from his skull.

Sean touched his cheek and his skin was cold as death. Frantically he searched for a pulse in the wrist of Job's good arm and although it was faint and rapid, Sean's relief was intense.

'He's lost huge quantities of blood,' Claudia whispered. 'But, I have contained the bleeding now.'

'He's in shock,' Sean muttered. 'Let me have a look.'

'Don't lift that dressing,' Claudia warned him quickly. 'It's ghastly. He was hit on the point of the shoulder by a cannon shell. It's just mangled flesh and bone chips. His arm is hanging by a shred of muscle and sinew.'

'Take Matatu with you,' Sean cut in brusquely. 'Go up to the laager. Find where they had their first-aid post. The Russians will have a decent stock. Find it. I want plasma and a drip set. Dressings and bandages, those are the most urgent. But if you can find antiseptic and pain-killers . . .'

Claudia scrambled to her feet. 'Sean, I was so worried about you! I saw . . .'

'You don't get rid of me that easy.' He did not look up from Job's face. 'Now, off you go, and get back here as quick as you can. Matatu, go with Donna, look after her.'

The two of them went at a run. Until they returned with medical supplies, Sean was helpless. But for something to keep himself occupied he wet his bandanna from the water-bottle and began to sponge the blood and dirt from Job's face. Job's eyelids fluttered open and Sean saw that he was conscious.

'Okay, Job, I'm here. Don't try and talk.'

Job closed his eyes for a moment and when he opened them again, he swivelled them downwards, too weak to move his head, yet he was trying to look down at his body, trying to check the extent of his injuries. It was always the first reaction.

'Is it lung blood I'm losing? Are both my feet still here, both my hands . . . ?'

'Right arm and shoulder,' Sean told him. '12.7mm cannon nicked you. Just a little bitty scratch. You are going to make it, lad, written guarantee. Would I lie to you?'

A faint smile tugged up the corners of Job's mouth and he lowered one eyelid in a conspiratorial wink. Sean felt his heart begin to break. He knew he had lied. Job wasn't going to make it.

'Relax,' he ordered cheerfully. 'Lie back and enjoy it, as the bishop said to the actress. I'm in charge here now.'

And Job closed his eyes.

Claudia picked out the medical dugout by the red cross insignia at the entrance. There were two Shangane Renamo looting the interior, ransacking it for booty, but Claudia shrieked at them so violently that they slunk away guiltily.

The labels on the cartons of medical supplies were all in Russian Cyrillic script. Claudia had to rip the lids open and check the contents of each. She found boxes which contained a dozen plastic bags of clear plasma each, and gave two of them to Matatu. The drip sets were on the shelf below. Field dressings and bandages were easy, but she was flummoxed by the tubes of ointments and pill bottles. However, the contents of one tube were yellow brown and had the characteristic iodine aroma; she selected those and then she found that some of the labels had alternative notations in French and Arabic. She had a smattering of both languages, enough to identify which were antibiotics and pain-killers.

She found two field packs, obviously prepared for use by the Russian first-aid teams and included these in her selection; then she and Matatu, heavily laden, hurried out of the first-aid post.

486

Before she reached the perimeter of the laager again, a dreadfully familiar figure loomed out of the banks of drifting smoke ahead of her. This was the very last person she had expected to see here.

'Miss Monterro,' General China called. 'What a fortunate encounter. I need your assistance.' China was accompanied by half a dozen officers of his staff.

Claudia recovered swiftly from the shock of the unexpected meeting. 'I'm busy,' she snapped, trying to step around him. 'Job is badly wounded. I have to get back to him.'

'My need is greater than anybody else's, I'm afraid.' China put out an arm.

'Forget it,' Claudia flared at him. 'Job needs this stuff, or he'll die.'

'One of my men will take it to him,' China replied. 'You are coming with me, please. Or I'll have you carried. Not very dignified. Miss Monterro.'

Claudia was still protesting as one of the Renamo officers relieved her of her load of medical supplies, but at last she shrugged with resignation.

'Go with him, Matatu.' She pointed down the hill. The little man nodded brightly and Claudia allowed China to escort her back into the laager.

They picked their way through the shambles of the battle, and Claudia shuddered as she stepped over the charred corpse of one of the Frelimo garrison.

'Colonel Courtney's attack has succeeded beyond even my wildest expectations.' General China was affable and clearly delighted with what he saw around him. 'He even managed to capture a Hind gunship completely intact, together with the Russian air crew and ground crew.'

'I hope you won't keep me long. I have to get back.'

'Captain Job will live or die without you, Miss Monterro. I need your services as a translator in talking to the pilot.'

'I don't speak Russian,' Claudia told him flatly.

'Fortunately the pilot seems to speak Italian, how he

learned the language I cannot guess, but he keeps repeating, "*Italiano, Italiano*".' China took her arm and led her down the steps of the sandbagged and camouflaged dugout.

Claudia glanced round the dugout and saw instantly that it was an engineering workshop. A long work-bench ran down each wall. Set up on one of these were a metal lathe and drill press. A wide selection of hand tools was racked in cupboards above the benches and she recognized the electric and gas welding sets at the far end of the workshop. Her father had had his own workshop in the cellar of their home in Anchorage and she had spent so many evenings watching him pottering around down there.

The Russian prisoners, five of them, were at the far end of the underground room.

'Which one of you speaks Italian?' she asked.

A tall thin man stepped forward. He wore grey flying overalls and his face was scarred with acne. His pale blue eyes were shifty and nervous.

'I do, *Signora*.'

'Where did you learn?' Claudia asked.

'My wife is a graduate student from Milano. I met her while she was doing her doctorate at Patrice Lumumba University in Moscow.' His Italian was heavily accented and his grammar uncertain, but she understood him without difficulty.

'I am translating for General China,' she told him, 'but I must warn you that he is a savage and cruel man. I am neither his ally nor his friend. I cannot protect you.'

'Thank you, *Signora*. I understand, but I do not need protection. I am a prisoner-of-war under the Convention of Geneva. I have certain rights. So do my men.'

'What does he say?' China demanded.

'He says he is a prisoner-of-war, and he and his men are protected by the Geneva Convention.'

'Tell him that Geneva is far away. This is Africa and I was no signatory to any agreement in Switzerland. Here he

488

has only such rights as I decide he should have. Tell him he will fly the helicopter under my command and that his ground crew will service and maintain the machine in flying condition.'

As Claudia translated, she watched the pilot's jaw set and his pale blue eyes harden. He turned his head slightly and spoke to his men in Russian. Immediately they began to mutter and shake their heads.

'Tell this black monkey that we insist on our rights,' the pilot spoke scornfully. Claudia had heard that many Russians were racists, and the derogatory term the pilot used suggested that for him at least this was true. 'We refuse to fly or fight for him. That would be a traitorous act.'

His refusal was so obvious, that China did not wait for Claudia's translation.

'Tell him,' he cut in brusquely, 'that I have no time for argument, or for subtle persuasion. I ask once more for his co-operation and if he refuses, I will be forced to demonstrate my serious intentions.'

'*Signore*, this man is very dangerous,' Claudia told the Russian officer. 'I have seen him commit the most unspeakable atrocities. I have suffered torture by him, myself.'

'I am a Russian officer and a prisoner-of-war.' The pilot drew himself to attention, his tone stern. 'I know my duty.'

China was watching his face as the pilot replied. He smiled coldly as Claudia translated. 'Another brave man,' he murmured. 'We must now determine just how brave he is.'

Without looking at his staff officers, he gave them a quiet order in Shangane and while they trundled forward the chariot that held the oxyacetylene gas cylinders. China smiled steadily at the Russian officer. The man returned his regard with a cold pale stare as they matched wills.

China was the one who turned away. He went to the workbench and swiftly examined the tools and objects scattered upon it. He gave a grunt of approval as he selected

489

a thin steel rod and weighed it in his hand. It was the length and thickness of a rifle ramrod pierced at each end for a connecting screw, probably a control link from the Hind helicopter.

'This will do very nicely,' he spoke aloud, and then picked up a discarded woven asbestos welding glove. He pulled it onto his right hand, and then turned his attention to the gas welding set. Claudia, who had watched her father work, realized that China was well versed in the use of the apparatus. He lit the welding flame on the torch and swiftly adjusted the flow of oxygen and acetylene from their separate cylinders until the flame was a brilliant blue feather, hot and unwavering. Then he took up the metal rod in his gloved hand and began to heat the tip of it in the blue flame.

All the Russians watched him uneasily. Claudia saw the pilot's hard stare flicker uncertainly, as the shine of nervous sweat dewed on his upper lip.

'This man is an animal,' Claudia said softly in Italian. 'You must believe me when I tell you he is capable of the vilest acts. Please, *Signore*, I do not want to watch this.'

The pilot shook his head, dismissing her appeal, but he was staring at the tip of the metal rod as it began to glow cherry red.

'I will not be intimidated by brutish threats,' he said, but she detected the slightest catch and crack in his voice.

In China's gloved hand, the tip of the rod turned slowly to incandescent crimson and then to translucent white heat. China smiled and turned off the flame of the welding torch. He weaved the glowing tip of the rod in a gentle flourish, like a conductor's baton, and smiled at the pilot. It was the humourless reptilian smile of a cobra.

'I repeat my request. Ask him if he will fly for me.'

'*Nyet.*' Even though his voice cracked, the pilot's reply was decisive, and then he added in Russian, '*Obezyana*, black monkey!'

China stood in front of him and made a slow pass with the tip of the rod a few inches in front of the Russian's eyes.

'Tell him, *Signora*,' the pilot whispered, 'that without my eyes, I cannot fly.'

'Very true,' China nodded as Claudia translated, and he left the pilot and walked on down the line of white prisoners, waving the glowing tip of the rod in a slow mesmeric gesture in each of their faces, studying their reactions carefully. The plump mechanic in oil-stained overalls at the end of the line gave China his most satisfying response. He shrank away from the rod-until the wall of the dugout stopped him, and sweat ran down his fat rosy cheeks and dripped from the end of his chin. In a squeaky voice, he said something in Russian, and the pilot answered him with a sharp monosyllabic order.

'You don't like it, do you? My fat little white slug.' China smiled thinly at him and let him feel the radiated heat on his cheek. The back of the flight engineer's head was pressed against the wall, and he swivelled his eyes in their sockets to watch the rod.

The metal was cooling and with a small frown of annoyance, China left him and turned back to the work-bench and relit the welding torch. While he carefully reheated the tip of the rod, the mechanic sagged against the sandbags. He was sweating in dark patches through the cotton of his greasy overalls.

The pilot spoke softly to him in an encouraging tone, and the engineer nodded and straightened up. He glanced at his superior with an expression of patent gratitude and watching this brief exchange between the two men, China smiled again, this time with satisfaction.

When Claudia saw that smile, she realized suddenly that China had just run a selection test. He had chosen his victim. The mechanic was the least courageous of the five Russians, and the pilot had inadvertently disclosed his concern and friendship for the man.

'Please,' she whispered in Italian. 'Your friend is in terrible danger. You must do what this man asks if you wish to save him.'

The pilot looked at her, and from his expression Claudia saw he was beginning to waver.

'Please, for my sake. I cannot bear to watch.' But with despair, she saw the Russian's expression change as his resolve firmed once again. He shook his head and China saw that gesture.

He switched off the welding torch and blew softly on the white tip of the metal rod. He let the moment draw out agonizingly; every eye in the bunker was fixed on the point of glowing steel.

Then abruptly he gave an order in Portuguese and two of his men sprang forward and seized the mechanic by his arms. He gave a little squeal of protest, but they hustled him to the work-bench and threw him face down across its top. One of them jumped up and sat between his shoulder-blades pinning him down. He struggled ineffectually, kicking his legs. Swiftly and expertly, they strapped his ankles to the legs of the work-bench, and he lay helplessly sprawled face downwards with his backside sticking up in the air, stretching the cotton seat of his overalls.

The Russian pilot shouted a protest and stepped forward but one of the Renamo officers thrust a pistol into his belly and forced him back against the wall.

'I ask you again,' China told him. 'Will you fly for me?'

The pilot shouted at him in Russian. It was clearly an insult. His face was flushed now, the acne purple and shiny as buttons on his chin and cheeks.

China nodded at his men. One of them drew the trench knife from its sheath on his webbing belt and slit the waistband of the mechanic's overalls. Then he seized the severed edges of cotton and ripped them downwards, tearing the cloth loose so it hung in tatters around the pinioned man's knees. Under the overalls, the engineer wore a pair of elasticized blue underpants. The Renamo pulled these down as far as they would go.

Claudia stared in fascinated horror at the mechanic's exposed buttocks. They were very white and fat and round, covered with a scraggle of dark curly ginger hair. From between his thighs, his wrinkled hairy scrotum protruded backwards like that of a dog.

The pilot was shouting in Russian and Claudia found herself pleading weakly.

'Please, General China, please let me leave, I cannot bear this.' She tried to turn her head away and cover her eyes, but the dreadful fascination of it compelled her to watch through her fingers despite herself.

China ignored both the pilot's and Claudia's pleas, and spoke crisply to the officer who sat between the Russian's shoulder-blades. Still pinning him to the bench, the Renamo reached over and seized one of his buttocks in each of his hands and drew them sharply apart. Claudia's protests dried in her throat and she found herself staring dry-mouthed at the Russian's puckered rosey-brown anus as it nestled like a blind man's eye between his hairy cheeks.

China reached out towards it with the tip of the rod, then stopped three inches short of it. The mechanic felt the heat of it on his most intimate flesh, and began to struggle so violently that two more of the Renamo officers had to throw their combined weight on to his back to keep him pinned down.

'Yes?' China looked across at the Russian pilot. He was raving like a madman, his face contorted with outrage, shouting threats and accusations.

'I regret the necessity,' China said, and thrust the metal rod forward, his wrist cocked like that of a fencing master going on attack, a *flèche*.

As the glowing metal touched the sensitive skin the Russian screamed, a shattering high-pitched shriek that made Claudia cry out pitifully in sympathy.

The metal smoked and sizzled and spluttered, as China rotated his wrist, twisting the rod deeper and deeper into the Russian's body. Now his screams were great explosive gusts of sound, and Claudia clapped her hands over her ears to shut them out and turned away, running into the corner of the dugout and pressing her face against the rough sandbags.

The smoke filled her nostrils, her throat and her lungs, the obscene odour of burning flesh, of charring fat, coated her tongue and her gorge rose. She tried to contain it, but her vomit shot up her throat and in a projectile stream splashed onto the earthen floor between her feet.

Behind her the screams dropped gradually in volume, and became ghastly rattling groans. However, all the Russians were yelling their protest and fury, and the din was confusing.

Another whiff of burned flesh and spilled faeces made her retch again and then she wiped her mouth with the back of her hand and leaned her forehead against the sand-bagged wall. She was trembling wildly, and tears and sweat streamed down her cheeks.

Slowly the uproar behind her subsided, and the only sounds in the bunker were the mechanic's groans and gurgles. They were weaker now but nonetheless harrowing. Claudia could tell without looking at him that the Russian was dying.

'Miss Monterro.' China's voice was level and calm. 'Please get a grip on yourself, we still have work to do.'

'You are an animal!' she blurted. 'I hate you! Oh God, how I hate you!'

'Your feelings are not of the slightest interest to me,' China said. 'Now you will tell the pilot that I await his full co-operation.'

The flight engineer's groans distracted her. As she turned to face China, she saw that they had released the stricken man and allowed him to slump to the floor. China had made no effort to withdraw the metal rod from his body, and he was still transfixed. As he rolled weakly about on the earthen floor, he was plucking ineffectually at the protruding end of the rod. The heated metal had adhered to his bowels as it cooled, and was firmly rooted in his flesh. Every time he tugged at it a trickle of liquid faeces bubbled from the terrible wound.

'Speak to the pilot,' China commanded.

Claudia dragged her eyes from the dying man and addressed the pilot. 'Please do what he wants.'

'I cannot, my duty!' the pilot cried.

'The devil with your duty!' Claudia shouted back furiously. 'You and all your men will end up like this!' She gestured to the floor without looking down again. 'That's what will happen to you!' She turned to the other Russians who were shaken and appalled, pale with horror and terror.

'Look at him!' she screamed in English. 'Is that what you want?'

They did not understand the words but her meaning was clear to all of them. They turned their faces towards the pilot.

The pilot resisted their entreaties for a minute, and then at a word from China the Renamo officers seized another one of the ground crew and threw him screaming and kicking face down across the bench and the Russian pilot threw up both hands in a gesture of resignation.

'Tell him to stop,' he said wearily to Claudia. 'We will do as he orders.'

'Thank you, Miss Monterro.' China smiled at her charmingly. 'You are now free to rejoin Colonel Courtney.'

'How will you communicate with the pilot?' she asked uncertainly.

'Already he understands me.' China transferred the benevolence of his smile to the Russian. 'I assure you that he will learn to speak my language with the utmost fluency in a very short time indeed.' He turned back to Claudia. 'Please convey my respects to Colonel Courtney and ask him to join me at his earliest convenience. I would like to take my leave of him, to thank him and wish him *bon voyage*.' He gave her a mocking bow. 'So God speed, Miss Monterro. I hope that you will remember all of us, your friends in Africa, with affection.'

Claudia could find no words to reply, she turned to the door of the bunker and her legs were shaky and rubbery beneath her.

In a daze of horror, she stumbled down the hill. The sights around her which at another time might have sickened and appalled her, she hardly noticed.

At the foot of the hill, she paused and tried to get a grip on herself. She breathed deeply, trying to quell the intermittent sobs that still caught her unawares and she combed her hair back from her face with her fingers and retied the strip of cloth she was using as a headband. With the tail of her shirt, she wiped the tears and sweat from her face, and was shocked at the grimy smear they left on the cloth.

'I must look like hell,' she whispered, and clenched her hands to hide her broken fingernails, but she braced her shoulders and lifted her chin. 'Sean mustn't see me like this,' she told herself fiercely. 'Pull yourself together, woman.'

Sean looked up as she hurried to where he was still working over Job's blanket-wrapped body.

'What happened?' he demanded. 'What kept you?'

'General China is here. He made me go with him.'

'What did he want? What happened?'

'Nothing, not important. I'll tell you about it later. How is Job?'

'I've got a full litre of plasma into him,' Sean replied. He had suspended the drip set from a branch above them. 'His pulse is better. Job is as tough as an old buffalo bull. Help me dress the wound.'

'Is he conscious?'

'He comes and goes,' Sean warned her.

Beneath the field dressing was such a terrible injury that

neither of them could bring themselves to discuss it, especially as Job might be able to hear and understand them.

Sean smothered the entire area with iodine paste, and then bound it up again with pressure pads and clean white bandages from the medical pack. The blood and iodine soaked through the white even as he worked.

Between them they had to roll Job on to his side to pass the bandages over his back. Claudia held the half-severed arm in place, bending the elbow across his chest, and Sean strapped it securely. By the time they finished, Job's entire upper body was swathed in a cocoon of expertly applied bandage from which only his left arm protruded.

'His pulse is going again.' Sean looked up from his wrist. 'I'm going to give him another litre of plasma.'

There was a scattered outbreak of machine-gun and mortar fire from the forest beyond the hill laager, and Claudia looked up apprehensively. 'What's that?'

'Frelimo counter-attack.' Sean was still busy with the drip set. 'But China has three companies in there, and Frelimo are going to be less than enthusiastic now that they have lost their air support. China's lads should be able to hold them off with no trouble.'

'Sean, where did China come from? I thought . . .'

'Yes,' Sean cut in. 'I also thought he was back on the river. The crafty bastard was right on our heels, ready to rush in and grab the spoils.' He finished adjusting the plasma flow in the drip set, and squatted down beside Claudia, studying her face.

'All right,' he said. 'Tell me what happened.'

'Nothing.' She smiled brightly.

'Don't bullshit me, beautiful,' Sean said gently, and put an arm around her. Despite herself she choked on a sob.

'China,' she whispered. 'Right on top of what happened to Job. He made me translate for the Russian pilot. Oh God, I hate him. He's an animal. He made me watch . . .' she broke off.

'Rough stuff?' Sean asked, and she nodded.

'He killed one of the Russians, in the foulest possible way.'

'He's a lovely lad, our China, but try and put it out of your mind, we've got enough troubles of our own. Let the Ruskies worry about theirs.'

'He forced the Russian pilot to agree to fly the helicopter.'

Sean stood up, lifting her to her feet beside him. 'Don't think of China and the Russian any more. All we have to worry about is getting out of here.' He broke off as he saw Sergeant Alphonso and a half dozen of his Shanganes trotting down the hill towards them. All of them were laden with loot.

'Nkosi!' Alphonso's broad handsome face was wreathed in a beatific grin. 'What a fight, what a victory!'

'You fought like an impi of lions,' Sean agreed. 'The battle is won but now you must help us to get away to the border. Captain Job is badly hurt.'

Alphonso's smile faded; despite their natural tribal enmity, both men had developed a grudging respect for each other.

'How bad?' Alphonso came to stand beside Sean and looked down at Job.

'There was a fibreglass stretcher in the first-aid post,' Claudia said. 'We can carry Job on that.'

'It is two days' march to the border,' Alphonso murmured dubiously. 'Through Frelimo territory.'

'Frelimo are running like dogs with a hot coal under their tails.' Sean's tone was hard. 'Send two of your men to fetch the stretcher.'

'General China calls for you. He is leaving in the Russian *henshaw*. He wants to speak to you before he goes,' Alphonso said.

'All right, but I want that stretcher here when I get back,' Sean warned him, and glanced at his wristwatch. 'We will march for the border in one hour from now.'

'*Nkosi!*' Alphonso agreed cheerfully. 'We will be ready.'
Sean turned back to Claudia.

'I'm going to see China. I'm going to try to talk him into flying Job out in the helicopter, but I don't think my chances are particularly rosy. Please stay with Job and keep an eye on his pulse rate. I've found a disposable syringe of adrenalin in the medic pack, use it only as a last resort.'

'Please don't be long,' she whispered. 'I'm only brave when you're here.'

'Matatu will stay with you.'

Sean climbed the hill swiftly, passing the first string of Renamo porters. Obviously China was taking everything he could carry away, including boxes of helicopter spares and hundreds of jerry cans of Avgas. The lines of porters were heading back into the wilderness towards the river, and Sean paid them scant attention. His role was played. He was eager to get out, reach the border, get Job to where he could receive professional medical attention and get Claudia to safety. However, over all his urgency lay the nagging uncertainty, was China really going to stand by his word, and let them go? Was he not being just a trifle optimistic?

'We'll see,' he told himself grimly, and shouted at one of the Renamo officers who was supervising the loading of the porters. 'Where is General China?'

He found him with his staff and the captured Russians in the laager's command bunker, and China looked up from the map he was consulting and smiled affably as Sean entered.

'Colonel Courtney, my felicitations. You were magnificent. A famous victory.'

'And now you owe me a favour.'

'You and your party wish to leave,' China agreed. 'All debts between us have been paid in full. You are free to go.'

'No,' Sean shook his head. 'By my calculation, you still

owe me one. Captain Job has been badly wounded. His condition is critical. I want him flown out to Zimbabwe in the captured Hind.'

'You jest, of course,' China laughed lightly. 'I cannot risk sending such a valuable asset on a non-productive mission. No, Colonel, all debts are paid, please don't persist in extravagant demands. With my defective hearing, it only annoys me and I may be tempted to review my generous offer to allow you and yours to depart unhindered.' He smiled and held out his hand. 'Come now, Colonel. Let us part as friends. You have the services of Sergeant Alphonso and his men. You are a man of infinite resourcefulness. I am sure that you will contrive to get yourself and all your party to safety without any further assistance from me.'

Sean ignored the outstretched hand and China glanced at it and then lowered it to his side. 'So we part, Colonel. Me to my little war and, who knows, perhaps one day, a country of my very own. You to the tender embraces of your very rich, very beautiful young American.' His smile had a sly and foxy slant to it. 'I wish you joy and I am sure you do the same for me.' He turned back to his map, leaving Sean for an instant nonplussed and taken off balance. It was incomplete, it couldn't end like this. Sean knew there was more to come, but General China began dictating orders to one of his officers in Portuguese, leaving Sean standing uncertainly at the door of the bunker.

Sean waited a few moments longer, and then turned abruptly and ducked out through the entrance. Only after he was gone, China lifted his head and smiled after him, a gloating little smile which if Sean had seen it, would have answered his question.

*

500

lphonso's men had worked quickly. The litter was a fibreglass stretcher, one of those lightweight body-moulded types used by mountain rescue teams. Nonetheless it would still require four men to carry it over rough ground, and they had a long hard path to the border.

'Less than a hundred kilometres and not that hard,' Sean reassured himself. 'Two days, if we push it.'

Claudia greeted him with relief. 'Job seems stronger. He was conscious, asking for you, he said something about a hill, Hill 31?'

Sean flickered a smile. 'That's where we met. He's wandering a little, help me to get him onto the stretcher.'

Between them they lifted Job gently and settled him onto the fibreglass stretcher. Sean rigged the drip set on a wire frame above his head, and tucked looted grey woollen blankets around him.

'Matatu,' he said as he stood up. 'Take us home.' And he gestured to the first team of stretcher-bearers to take their positions.

It was less than two hours since sunrise, but they seemed to have lived an entire lifetime in that short period, Sean thought as he glanced back at the hilltop laager. Streamers of smoke drifted from its crest and the last column of General China's porters was disappearing into the forest below it, all heavily laden with booty.

The distant sounds of battle had finally dwindled into silence. The half-hearted Frelimo counter-attack had long ago fizzled out, and China was withdrawing his forces into the bad ground below the Pungwe river.

As Sean watched, the captured Hind helicopter rose slowly out of its emplacement and hung above the hill on its glistening rotor; then abruptly it dipped towards them, the sound of its engine crescendoed and suddenly Sean was staring into the multiple mouths of the Gatling-cannon in its nose.

As it raced towards him, he recognized China's face

behind the armoured glass canopy. He was perched in the flight engineer's seat, at the controls of the 12.7mm cannon. Sean saw the barrels of the cannon traverse slightly, coming on to aim. The Hind was only fifty feet above them, so close he could see China's teeth flash in his dark face as he smiled.

Their little column had not reached the edge of the forest. There was no cover, no protection from the blast of that terrible weapon, and instinctively Sean reached out and drew Claudia to him, trying to shield her with his own body.

Above them General China lifted his right hand in an ironic salute, and the Hind banked steeply away into the north-west, dwindled swiftly to a speck and was gone. They all stared after it silently, seized by a sense of anti-climax, until Sean broke the spell.

'Let's go, brethren!' And once again the stretcher-bearers started forward at an easy jog-trot, singing very softly one of the ancient marching songs.

Scouting ahead of them, Matatu came across a few scattered parties of Frelimo assault troops, but they were all in headlong retreat from the river wilderness. After the loss of their air support the Frelimo offensive seemed to have collapsed completely and the situation was fluid and confused. Although they were forced to detour further northwards than Sean had planned, Matatu steered them out of contact with any Frelimo and the stretcher-bearers were rotated regularly so they made swift progress.

At nightfall, they stopped to eat and rest. Alphonso made the scheduled radio contact with Renamo headquarters and gave them a position report. He received only a laconic acknowledgement without change of orders.

They feasted on tinned goods looted from the Russian stores, and smoked the perfumed Balkan tobacco in yellow cigarette paper with hollow cardboard filters.

Job was conscious again and complained in a husky whisper, 'There is a lion gnawing on my shoulder.'

Sean injected an ampoule of morphia into his drip set and it eased him, so that he was even able to eat a few mouthfuls of the bland-tasting tinned meat. However, his thirst was far greater than his hunger, and Sean held his head and helped him get down two full mugs of the surprisingly good Russian coffee.

Sean and Claudia sat beside the litter and waited for the moon to rise.'

'We are going in through the Honde Valley again.' Sean told Job. 'Once we get you to St Mary's Mission you'll be fine. One of the Catholic fathers is a doctor, and I'll be able to send a message to my brother, Garry, in Johannesburg. I'll ask him to send the company jet to Umtali. We'll fly you into Johannesburg General Hospital before you know what's hit you, mate. There you'll get the best medical attention in the world.'

When the moon rose they went on, and it was almost midnight before Sean called a halt for the night.

He made a mattress of cut grass beside Job's litter, and as Claudia drifted off to sleep in his arms, he whispered to her, 'Tomorrow night, I'll give you a hot bath and put you between clean sheets.'

'Promise?' she sighed.

'Cross my heart.'

From deeply ingrained habit, he woke an hour before first light and went to rouse the sentries for dawn stand-by.

Alphonso threw aside his blanket, stood up and fell in beside him. When they had made the sentry round, they paused on the edge of the camp and Alphonso offered him one of the Russian cigarettes. They smoked from cupped hands, shielding the glow of burning tobacco.

'What you told me about South Africa, is it true?' Alphonso asked unexpectedly.

'What did I tell you?'

'That men, even black men, eat meat every day?'

Sean smiled in the darkness, amused by Alphonso's

concept of paradise, a place where a man could eat meat every day.

'Sometimes they get so sick of eating beef', he teased, 'that they try chicken and lamb just for a change.'

Alphonso shook his head. That was beyond belief, no African could ever tire of beef.

'How much does a black man earn in South Africa?' he demanded.

'About five hundred rand a month if he is an ordinary unskilled labourer, but there are many black millionaires.' Five hundred rand was more than a man earned in Mozambique in a year, even if he were lucky enough to find employment. A million was a figure beyond Alphonso's powers of imagination.

'Five hundred?' He shook his head in wonder. 'And paid in rands, not paper escudos or Zimbabwe dollars?' he demanded earnestly.

'Rands,' Sean confirmed. Compared to other currencies in Africa the rand was as good as a gold sovereign.

'And there are things in the stores, things for a man to buy with his rands?' Alphonso demanded suspiciously. It was difficult for him to visualize shelves laden with goods for sale, other than a few pathetic bottles of locally produced carbonated soft drinks and packets of cheap cigarettes.

'Whatever you want,' Sean assured him. 'Soap and sugar, cooking oil and maize meal.' Half-forgotten luxuries in Alphonso's mind.

'As much as I want?' he asked. 'No rationing?'

'As much as you can pay for,' Sean assured him. 'And when your belly is full, you can buy shoes and suits and ties, transistor radios and dark glasses . . .'

'A bicycle?' Alphonso demanded eagerly.

'Only the very lowest men ride bicycles,' Sean grinned, enjoying himself. 'The others have their own motor cars.'

'Black men own their own motor cars?'

Alphonso thought about that for a long time.

'Would there be work for a man like me?' he asked with a diffidence that was completely out of character.

'You?' Sean pretended to consider it, and Alphonso waited apprehensively for his judgement. 'You?' Sean repeated. 'My brother owns a gold mine. You could be a supervisor on his mine within a year, a shift boss in two years. I could get you a job the same day you arrived at the mine.'

'How much does a supervisor earn?'

'A thousand, two thousand,' Sean assured him, and Alphonso was stunned. His Renamo pay was the equivalent of a rand a day, paid in Mozambique escudos.

'I would like to be a boss supervisor,' he murmured thoughtfully.

'Better than a Renamo sergeant?' Sean teased, and Alphonso chortled derisively.

'Of course, in South Africa you would not have the vote,' Sean ribbed him. 'Only pale faces get to vote.'

'Vote, what is a vote?' Alphonso demanded, and then answered himself. 'I don't have a vote in Mozambique. They don't have the vote in Zambia or Zimbabwe or Angola or Tanzania. Nobody has the vote in Africa, except perhaps once in a man's life to elect a president for life and a one-party government.' He shook his head and snorted. 'Vote? You can't eat a vote. You can't dress in a vote, or ride to work on it. For two thousand rand a month and a full belly you can have my vote.'

'Any time you come to South Africa, you come and see me.' Sean stretched and looked at the sky. He could see the trees against it. Dawn was only a short time away. He crushed out the butt of the cigarette and began to get to his feet.

'There is something I must tell you,' Alphonso whispered, and his altered tone caught Sean's full attention.

'Yes?' He squatted down again and leaned closer to the Shangane. Alphonso cleared his throat in embarrassment.

'We have travelled a long road together,' he murmured.

'A long hard road,' Sean agreed. 'But the end is in sight. This time tomorrow . . .' He did not have to go on and Alphonso did not reply immediately.

'We have fought side by side,' Alphonso said at last.

'Like lions,' Sean confirmed.

'I have called you *Baba* and *Nkosi Kakulu*.'

'You have honoured me thus,' Sean said formally. 'And I have called you friend.'

Alphonso nodded in the darkness. 'I cannot let you cross the Zimbabwe border,' he said with sudden decisiveness and Sean rocked back on his heels.

'Tell me why not.'

'You remember Cuthbert?' Alphonso asked, and it took Sean a moment to place the name.

'Cuthbert, you mean the one from Grand Reef air base. The one who helped us on the raid?' It all seemed so long ago.

'General China's nephew,' Alphonso nodded. 'That is the one I speak of.'

'Sammy Davis Junior.' Sean smiled. 'The cool laid-back cat. I remember him well.'

'General China spoke to him on the radio. This very morning from the laager of the *henshaw*, after our victory. I was in the outer room of the bunker. I heard everything he said.'

Sean felt a cold wind blow down his spine and the hair at the base of his skull prickled.

'What did China tell him?' he asked, dreading the reply.

'He ordered Cuthbert to let the Zimbabwean army know that it was you who led the raid on Grand Reef and stole the *indeki* full of missiles. He told Cuthbert to tell them that you would be crossing back into Zimbabwe through the Honde Valley at St Mary's Mission, and they must wait for you there.'

Sean's gut knotted with shock and for long moments he

was stunned by the enormity and cunning of the trap that China had prepared for him. The cruelty of it was diabolical. To allow them to believe that they were being set free, letting them taste the relief of crossing out of harm, when in fact, they were going to a fate even worse than China himself could have meted out to them.

The fury of the Zimbabwe high command would know no bounds. Sean was the holder of a Zimbabwe passport, a document of convenience but one which would make him a traitor and a murderer beyond any help from outside. He would be handed over to the notorious Zimbabwe Central Intelligence Organization and taken to the interrogation cells at Chikarubi prison, and he would never re-emerge from there alive. Job, despite his wounds, would share the same fate.

Even though Claudia was an American citizen, officially she no longer existed. It was weeks since she had been reported missing. By this time, interest in her case even at the United States embassies in Harare and Pretoria would have cooled. Along with her father, she was presumed dead and so she could expect no protection. She was as vulnerable as they were.

The trap was completely closed, there was no way out. The Renamo army behind them, Frelimo on either hand and the Zimbabwean CIO ahead of them. They were marooned in a devastated wasteland, doomed to be hunted down like wild animals or to slow starvation in the wilderness.

'Think!' Sean told himself. 'Find the way out.'

They could attempt to cross the Zimbabwe border at some other point than the Honde Valley, but the CIO would have the entire country alerted for them. There were permanent army blocks on every road. Without papers, they wouldn't get more than a few miles, and then there was Job, what would he do with Job? How could they transport a wounded man when every police and military post would be looking for somebody in a stretcher.

'We must go southwards,' Alphonso said. 'We must go to South Africa.'

'We?' Sean stared at him. 'You want to come with us?'

'I can't go back to General China,' he pointed out philosophically. 'Not after I have betrayed him. I will come with you to South Africa.'

'That's a trek of three hundred miles, through two opposed armies, Frelimo and the southern division of Renamo. And what about Job?'

'We will carry him,' Alphonso replied.

'Three hundred miles?'

'Then we will leave him behind.' Alphonso shrugged. 'He is only a Matabele and he is dying anyway, it will be no great loss.'

Sean caught the angry words that rose to his tongue and remained silent while he thought it out. Every way he twisted it and examined it he saw that Alphonso was right. To the north the dubious haven of Malawi was blocked by the waters of Cabora Bassa and by General China's division. To the east lay the Indian Ocean, and to the west the Zimbabwean CIO.

'All right,' Sean admitted reluctantly. 'South is the only way. Perhaps we can squeeze through between Frelimo and the southern division of Renamo. All we have to do is get across a heavily guarded railway line and the Limpopo river, and find enough to eat while we are doing it in a land that has been burned and devastated by ten years of civil war.'

'In South Africa, we will eat meat every day,' Alphonso pointed out cheerfully.

Sean stood up. 'Will your men follow you?'

'I will kill those that don't.' Alphonso was matter-of-fact. 'We can't let them go back to General China.'

'Right,' Sean agreed. 'And you will report on the radio schedule that I have crossed into Zimbabwe. We'll be able to string China along on the radio for four or five days. He won't realize that we have broken away southwards until we are well on our way and beyond his range. You had better talk to your men now. We'll have to turn south right away. Talk to them before they realize for themselves that we are up to something.'

Alphonso called in the sentries, and in the grey light of dawn the faces of the Shanganes were sober and intent as they squatted in a circle around him and listened to Alphonso describe to them the southern paradise to which he would lead them.

'We are all weary of fighting, of living like animals in the bush. It is time we learned to live like men, to find good wives to bear our sons.' He was filled with the fiery eloquence of the recent convert and before he had finished Sean saw the sparkle of anticipation in most of their eyes and he felt a lift of relief. For the first time, he began to believe that the journey ahead might just be possible, with a great deal of endeavour and an even greater deal of luck.

He went to tell Claudia and Job what lay ahead. Claudia was bathing Job's face with a damp rag. 'He's much better, a good night's rest.' Then she broke off as she saw his face. Claudia's spirits visibly plummeted as he explained to them what they had to do.

'It was too good to be true,' she whispered, 'I knew deep down that it wouldn't be that easy, that General China wasn't Santa Claus in disguise.'

Job lay so still on his stretcher that Sean thought he had once again slipped over the edge of consciousness and he reached out to check his pulse. At his touch. Job opened his eyes.

'Can you trust those Shanganes?' he whispered.

'We don't have much choice,' Sean pointed out, and then went on briskly. 'We . . .'

'Leave me here.' Job's whisper was barely audible, but Sean's expression hardened and his voice was brittle with anger.

'Cut out that sort of bullshit,' he warned Job.

'Without me you might have a chance,' Job insisted. 'If you have to drag this stretcher . . .'

'We've got twelve hefty Shanganes,' Sean pointed out.

'Better some of you get through than all of us die. Leave me, Sean. Save Claudia and yourself.'

'I'm getting angry.' Sean stood up and said to Claudia, 'We leave in ten minutes.'

They travelled cautiously southwards all that day. It was an intense relief not to have to watch the sky for the Hind gunships, although out of habit the Shanganes occasionally turned their faces upward. The closer they drew to the railway line, the slower their progress became and they spent much of their time hiding in the dense wild ebony thickets and clumps of jesse until Matatu came ghosting back to assure them that the coast was clear and to lead them onwards.

In the late afternoon, Sean left the main party hiding in a bushy ravine and went forward with Matatu. He was gone for almost two hours and the sun was setting when he reappeared silently and suddenly at Claudia's side.

'You startled me!' she gasped. 'You're like a cat.'

'The railway line is only a mile ahead. The Frelimo guards seem to be in a state of confusion still. There is a lot of military traffic on the line, and a great deal of panicky activity all around. The crossing is going to be a trifle tricky. As soon as the moon comes up, I'll go up and take another look.'

While they waited for the moon, Alphonso rigged the radio aerial and made his scheduled contact with General China's headquarters.

'The dove is in flight.' He gave the prearranged code so that China would believe that Sean and his party had crossed the border. After a brief pause, presumably while he relayed the message, the radio operator came back to Alphonso with the order to return to the main base on the river. Alphonso acknowledged and signed off.

'They won't expect me to arrive back for another two days.' Alphonso grinned as he packed up the radio. 'It will be that long before they start getting suspicious.'

As the moon pushed its bald silver pate above the trees, Sean and Matatu slipped away into the forest to make a final reconnaissance of the railway line.

A mile south of their position they found the place where the line crossed a narrow stream. Although the stream contained only a few shallow puddles, the banks were thick with riverine bush which would afford them good cover. Originally the bush must have been cleared for a hundred yards on each side of the line, but secondary growth had been allowed to spring up to waist height.

'Sloppy Frelimo bastards,' Sean muttered. 'That will give us some cover, and we'll stay in the riverbed.'

The main line crossed the stream over an embankment and culvert. There was a guard post on the approaches, fifty yards uptrack from the culvert. While Sean watched through his binoculars, a Frelimo sentry with his AK rifle slung on his back sauntered down to the bridge over the culvert. He leaned on the guard rail and lit a cigarette. The glow of the cigarette marked his progress as he ambled back to the guard post. He seemed to Sean to be a little unsteady on his feet, and when he reached the guard post, a faint ripple of feminine giggles carried to where Sean and Matatu lay.

'They are having a party,' Sean chuckled.

'Palm wine and jig-jig,' Matatu agreed enviously, and in the moonlight held up his right hand with his thumb trapped between his first two fingers, 'I would like some of that myself.'

'You randy little bugger.' Sean tweaked his ear. 'When we get to Johannesburg, I'll stand you to the biggest, fattest lady we can flush out.' Matatu's taste in amour ran to the mountainous. 'Like Sherpa Tensing on Everest,' Sean often remarked.

The distractions with which the railway guards had

provided themselves promised to make their crossing easier. Sean and Matatu withdrew quietly and started back to where they had left the rest of the party.

They had been gone for three hours and it was a few minutes before midnight, as they approached the camp. At the head of the ravine, Sean paused to give the recognition signal, the liquid warble of a fiery-necked nightjar. He didn't want to be shot by one of Alphonso's Shanganes. He waited a full minute for the reply, and when it did not come, he repeated the signal. Still there was silence and he felt the first tickle of alarm.

Instead of going straight in, they circled the ravine cautiously, and in the moonlight Matatu picked up unexpected spoor and squatted over it, frowning with alarm.

Sean whispered. 'Who? Which way?'

'Many men, our own Shanganes!' Matatu lifted his head and pointed to the north. 'They are going out, leaving camp.'

'Outgoing?' Sean was puzzled. 'Doesn't make sense, unless . . . ! Oh God! No!'

Swiftly, quietly, he closed in on the camp. The sentries he had set before he left were gone, their posts deserted. Sean felt panic rise in a wave that threatened to suffocate him.

'Claudia!' he whispered, suppressing the urge to shout her name aloud. He wanted to rush into the camp and find her, but he drew a series of deep breaths and fought back the panic.

He slipped the AKM on to fully automatic and went down on his belly, creeping in. The five Shanganes he had left asleep in the gut of the ravine were gone, all their equipment and their weapons had disappeared. He went on and made out the shape of Job's stretcher in the dappled moonlight; beside it, exactly as he had left her, Claudia's body wrapped in a blanket, but just beyond her another body lay sprawled. In the moonlight, he saw the sheen of wetness on the back of the man's head.

'Blood!'

Sean threw all caution aside and rushed to Claudia's body, dropping to his knees beside her and sweeping her into his arms.

She gasped and cried out, coming out of deep sleep, beginning to struggle in his arms, and then quieting as she realized who he was.

'Sean!' she blurted, still groggy with sleep. 'What is it? What happened?'

'Thank God,' he murmured fervently. 'I thought . . . !' He set her down gently, and reached across to where Job lay in the litter.

'Job, are you all right?' He shook him carefully, and Job stirred and murmured.

Sean jumped to his feet and went to where Alphonso lay. He touched his neck. The skin was warm, his pulse strong and even.

'Claudia!' he called. 'Bring the flashlight.'

In the beam of the flashlight, he examined the laceration in Alphonso's scalp.

'A nice little ding,' he grunted; although the bleeding had staunched spontaneously, he pressed a field dressing over it and bound it in place. 'Good thing they hit him on the head, or they might have done some serious damage.' He grinned wryly at his own joke.

'What happened, Sean?' Claudia demanded anxiously. 'I was fast asleep, I didn't hear a thing.'

'Lucky for you,' Sean tied the tag ends of the bandage, 'or you might have got the same treatment.'

'What happened, where are the others?'

'Gone,' he told her. 'Flown, deserted. They obviously didn't fancy the walk or the destination. They bashed Alphonso on the noggin and took off back to General China.'

She stared at him. 'You mean there are only the four of us now? All the Shanganes except Alphonso have gone?'

'That's right,' Sean agreed and Alphonso groaned and reached up to touch his bandaged head. Sean helped him sit up.

'Sean!' Claudia tugged at his arm and he turned back to her. 'What are we going to do?' Sean glanced across at Job's stretcher. 'What are we going to do with Job? How are we going to carry him? How are we going to get out of here now?'

'That, my love, is an extremely interesting question,' Sean agreed grimly. 'All I can tell you is that by this time tomorrow, our old pal General China is going to know that we are on the run, and he's going to know exactly where we are headed.'

She stared at him aghast. 'What are we going to do?'

'We don't seem to have much choice,' he said. 'There is only one road still open to us – we keep on the way we are going.'

He hauled Alphonso to his feet.

'That's impossible,' Claudia whispered anxiously. 'Two of you cannot carry the stretcher.'

'You're right, of course. We'll have to make some other arrangement.'

Between them, they lifted Job out of the stretcher and laid him on Claudia's blanket, then, while the others watched, Sean began to dismantle the fibreglass stretcher. Before he had finished, Matatu appeared silently out of the darkness and whispered a brief report to Sean.

Sean barely looked up as he told Alphonso, 'You taught them well. Your Shanganes have bomb-shelled, taken off in eleven different directions. If we followed we might catch one or two of them, but some of them are going to get back to China with the good news.'

Alphonso cursed the deserters bitterly, while Sean explained to Claudia and Job.

'I'm going to use the nylon webbing from the stretcher to improvise a sling seat.'

Claudia looked dubious. 'Job isn't strong enough to sit upright. The movement will reopen his wound, the bleeding . . .' She broke off as Sean glared at her.

'Can you think of a better way?' he snarled, and she shook her head.

Sean doubled the length of heavy green canvas and took the rifle slings from his AKM and Alphonso's AK to make carrying loops.

'We'll have to make adjustments as we go along,' he grunted, and then looked at Claudia. 'Instead of finding difficulties, make yourself useful by gathering all the equipment the Shanganes left. We'll have to make a selection.'

He picked out the equipment swiftly, discarding all but the most vital pieces. 'Alphonso and I will be carrying Job between us. On top of that we'll only be able to manage our basic weapons and a blanket each. Claudia and Matatu must lug the medical pack, the water bottles and a blanket each. Everything else will be left behind.'

'The canned food?' Claudia asked.

'Forget it,' Sean told her brusquely, and set about apportioning their loads. He cut everything down to the barest minimum, knowing that every pound of weight now would seem like ten after the first few miles. He even made Alphonso abandon his AK rifle and gave him the pistol that he had taken from the Russian pilot to replace it. He restricted himself to two spare clips of ammunition for his own AKM and he and Alphonso retained only a pair of grenades each, one fragmentation and the other phosphorus.

The abandoned equipment they piled in the bottom of the ravine and covered with loose earth and branches to conceal it from casual discovery by a Frelimo patrol.

'Okay, lad,' Sean told Job. 'Time to go.' He glanced at his wristwatch and found it was a little before three o'clock. They were well behind schedule and they only had a few hours of darkness left in which to make the crossing.

He knelt beside Job and eased him up into a sitting

position, then restrapped his injured arm firmly against his chest.

'This is the bad part,' he warned him, and between them he and Alphonso lifted Job to his feet. Job endured the movement in stoic silence, and stood supported between them.

Sean and Alphonso adjusted the nylon sling seat over their outer shoulders. They lifted Job into it, and he sat with his feet dangling, his good arm draped around Sean's shoulder while Sean and Alphonso linked their arms behind his back to support him.

'Ready?' Sean asked, and Job grunted softly, trying to conceal the pain that every movement caused him.

'If you think it's bad now . . .' Sean warned him cheerfully, 'just give it a couple of hours!'

They started down the ravine towards the railway line. They moved slowly, accustoming themselves to this awkward form of travel, trying to cushion Job between them, but they stumbled over the broken ground and Job swung on his seat and bumped against them. He made no sound, but Sean heard his ragged breathing close to his ear and when the pain stabbed him especially cruelly, he unconsciously dug his fingers into Sean's shoulder.

Slowly they moved down the shallow stream bed towards the culvert beneath the railway line. Matatu was a hundred yards ahead of them, just visible in the moonlight. Once he signalled them to halt and then after a few minutes beckoned them to come on. Claudia trailed fifty paces behind them so that she would have a start if they were discovered and forced to run back.

Carrying Job between them, it was not possible for Sean and Alphonso to move silently. Once they splashed into one of the muddy pools of the stream and they sounded like a herd of cavorting hippos in the silence.

Matatu had reached the culvert ahead of them and he signalled them frantically to hurry. They staggered forward under Job's weight and were in the open, when on the embankment above them, there was the sudden crunch of footsteps in the gravel ballast and the sound of voices.

Trying to keep low, they kept going at a clumsy run. They reached the culvert and carried Job into the dark concrete tunnel. Claudia was running doubled over only a few yards behind them and Sean reached back with his free hand and dragged her in out of the pale moonlight into the blessed darkness of the culvert.

They leaned against the concrete wall, stooped below the curved roof, trying to quiet their breathing, all of them panting wildly from that charge through the mud and sand of the stream bottom.

The footsteps and the voices above them grew louder and finally stopped almost directly overhead. It sounded like a man and a woman. The Frelimo garrison had either brought their own camp-followers with them, or had found lady friends in the refugee camps that had sprung up along the guarded railway line.

There was a spirited argument going on out there, the man's voice slurred with drink and the woman's shrill and shrewish as she protested and haggled. At last, they heard the man's voice raised in exasperation.

'Dollar *shumi*, ten dollars,' he said, and immediately the woman's voice softened and cooed agreement.

Then there was the sound of feet sliding in gravel and a few pebbles rattled down the embankment in the stream bed.

'They are coming down here!' Claudia breathed in horror, and they instinctively drew back deeper into the dark culvert.

'Quiet!' Sean whispered, and stooped to ease Job out of the canvas sling and prop him against the wall of the culvert.

As he drew the trench knife from the sheath on his webbing two figures appeared in the mouth of the culvert, silhouetted by the moonlight.

They were clinging together and laughing softly, the woman half supporting the man as they staggered forward. Sean gripped the knife underhand, the point of the blade belly high, ready to receive them, but they advanced only a few paces into the intimate darkness of the tunnel and then turned to face each other still giggling and whispering, both of them outlined against the moonlit exterior.

The Frelimo sentry pushed the woman against the wall and propped his rifle beside her while he fumbled to open his own clothing. The woman leaned back against the wall and with a practised gesture lifted the front of her skirt above her waist. Laughing and muttering drunkenly the sentry reeled against her and she used one hand to steady and guide him, the other still holding up her skirt.

If Claudia had reached out a hand she could have touched the couple, but they were locked together oblivious of all around them. The man began to push against her, his voice rising as he exhorted himself to greater effort, his movements becoming more frenzied. The woman clucked like a rider urging a mount forward and the Frelimo went from a canter to full gallop, pounding away with abandon.

Suddenly the man threw his head back, stiffening into rigidity, and crowed like an asthmatic rooster. Slowly he drooped and the woman laughed and pushed him away briskly. Still laughing, she smoothed down her skirt and seized the man's arm. The two of them staggered out into the sandy riverbed and disappeared round the corner of the culvert. The sounds of their scrambled ascent of the embankment dwindled and Sean slid the knife back into its sheath on his belt and said softly, 'That's what we call a tumble in the jungle!'

Claudia giggled with nervous relief. 'Two seconds flat, that just has to be a new world record,' she whispered, and Sean hugged her briefly.

'Shall we also be friends?' he whispered. 'Sorry I snarled at you.'

'I was being a dismal Jane, I deserved it. You won't have any more moaning and whining from me.'

'Stay close.' He turned back to grope for Job and found that he had slid weakly down the wall and was sitting on the sandy floor of the culvert.

As he stooped to help him to his feet, Sean's fingers touched his shoulder. The bandage was damp and his smile faded. The bleeding had started again.

'Nothing we can do about it now,' he thought, and gently eased Job to his feet.

'How are you doing, old son?'

'No worries.' Job's whisper was scratchy and faint.

Sean touched Matatu's shoulder and he obeyed the unspoken command, instantly creeping out the far side of the culvert and disappearing into the scrub on the stream bank.

A few minutes later the soft whistle of a night bird carried to them as Matatu gave the all clear. Sean sent Claudia ahead and gave her a full five minutes to get across the open ground of the cut line.

'Let's go.' Sean looked up from the luminous dial of his Rolex and they lifted Job into the sling seat and started forward into the moonlight.

The next hundred paces seemed like the slowest and longest Sean had ever covered, but at last they were into the forest beyond the cut line, and Claudia was waiting for them there.

'We've made it!' she whispered joyfully.

'We sure have, the first mile was a romp, only three hundred more to go,' he answered grimly, and they kept going.

Counting their paces against the second hand of his wristwatch, Sean estimated that they were averaging two miles an hour. Ahead of them, Matatu selected the easiest going. He was always out of sight in the forest ahead, only his soft bird calls guided them. At intervals Sean checked their heading against the stars, catching glimpses of the Southern Cross and its brilliant pair of pointers through the forest canopy ahead of them.

When the dawn paled out the stars, they stopped once again and Sean allowed them to drink for the first time, two swallows each from one of the water-bottles that Claudia carried. Then he turned his attention to Job's shoulder. The dressing was soaked with fresh blood and Job's face was grey as the ashes of a cold camp-fire. His eyes had sunk into dark sockets and his lips were dry and cracked, his breath whistling softly through them. The pain and loss of blood was taking a dreadful toll.

Gently Sean unwound the bandage and then he and Claudia exchanged a quick glance. The destruction of tissue was horrifying and the field dressing was caked into the wound cavity. Sean realized that if he tried to remove it, he would tear the flesh to which it had adhered and probably restart the bleeding. He leaned forward and sniffed the wound, while Job grinned at him, a skull-like twitching back of the lips.

'Steak tartare?' he asked weakly.

'All it needs is a little garlic,' Sean grinned back at him, but he had caught the first sickly whiff of corruption. He squeezed another half tube of iodine paste over the original field dressing and then stripped the plastic packaging from a fresh dressing and placed it over the wound.

Claudia held it in place as he rewrapped it with a new bandage from the medical pack. He rolled the blood-soaked bandage and stuffed it into a side pocket. He would wash it out at the first water that they came to.

'We must keep going,' he told Job. 'We've got to get well clear of the railway line. Are you up to it?'

Job nodded, but Sean could see the dread in his eyes. Every step they moved him was an agony.

'I'm going to give you another shot of antibiotic – I can give you a jolt of morphine at the same time?'

Job shook his head. 'Keep it for when it gets really bad.' He grinned again, a grimace that tugged at Sean's heart. He could not meet Job's eyes. 'Show us your best side,' he said, and made a performance of pulling down the trousers of Job's battledress and darting the hypodermic needle into one of his glossy black buttocks. Claudia averted her gaze modestly and Job whispered. 'It's okay, Claudia, you are allowed to look. Just don't touch, that's all.'

'You're as bad as Sean,' she said primly. 'Downright vulgar, both of you.'

They lifted Job back into the nylon sling seat and went on. By mid-morning the mirage shimmered and rose in glassy whirlpools from the rocky kopjes over which they were trekking, and the tiny mopane flies hovered in a fine mist around their heads, crawling into their nostrils and ears and eyes with infuriating persistence. With the heat came the thirst, and their sweat dried on their shirts and left irregular outlines in white salt on the cloth.

When they stopped at noon in the sparse dappled shade of an African teak, Sean knew they had all had enough and the worst heat of the day was still to come. They laid Job on a hastily cut mattress of dried grass and he lapsed almost immediately into a state that was more coma than sleep, and snored softly through his dry swollen lips.

The carrying sling had rubbed the skin from both Sean's shoulders, for he and Alphonso had changed sides at each of the hourly stops. The harsh nylon straps had galled Alphonso as badly and he muttered sullenly as he examined his injuries.

'Before this, I hated the Matabele simply because they are a flea-infested, thieving bunch of venereal apes. Now I have another reason to hate them.'

Sean tossed him the tube of iodine paste. 'Smear the *muti* on your grievous injuries, then stuff the empty tube in your garrulous mouth,' he advised, and Alphonso went off still muttering to find a place to lie down.

Sean and Claudia found a hollow screened by a low hook-thorn bush a short distance from where Job lay and Sean spread their blankets to make a nest for them.

He settled into it thankfully. 'I'm bushed.'

'How bushed?' Claudia asked, and knelt over him to nibble his ear.

'Not that bushed,' he qualified, and pulled her down beside him.

At sunset, Sean cooked a pot of maize-meal porridge on a tiny smokeless fire while Alphonso rigged the aerial and tuned the radio to the Renamo command frequency. There was a clutter of garbled broken-up traffic on their wavelength, probably Frelimo transmissions, but at last they heard their call sign through the jumble.

'*N'gulube*! Warthog! Come in, *N'gulube*! This is Banana Tree.'

Alphonso acknowledged and then made a fictitious position report that placed them still far north of the railway line, on a march back to the river area. Banana Tree acknowledged and signed off.

'They fell for it,' Sean gave his opinion. 'Looks like the Shangane deserters haven't reached base and blown the whistle on us, not yet anyway.'

In the last of the daylight, they ate the meal of maize porridge and Sean studied his field map and marked in his dead reckoning position. According to the map, the hilly ground seemed to extend for another thirty miles or so, and then descended gently to a more level plain on which a number of small villages and cultivated lands were marked; beyond that was the first natural barrier, another wide river that ran west to east directly across their route.

He called Alphonso across and asked him. 'The southern division of Renamo under General Tippoo Tip, do you know where his area begins, where his main forces are deployed?'

'Like us, they move all the time to confuse Frelimo. Sometimes they are here, other times down here near the

Rio Save.' He shrugged. Renamo is wherever the fighting is.'

'And Frelimo? Where are they?'

'They chase after Renamo, and then run like frightened rabbits when they catch them,' he guffawed. 'To us now, it doesn't matter who is who and where they are. Everybody we meet down here is going to try and kill us.'

'Great intelligence report,' Sean thanked him, and folded the map into its plastic wallet.

Quickly they finished the frugal meal and Sean stood up.

'All right, Alphonso. Let's get Job up and moving.'

Alphonso belched softly then grinned wickedly. 'He's your Matabele dog. If you want him, you carry him, I've had enough.'

Sean hid his dismay behind a neutral expression.

'You are wasting time,' he said softly. 'Get on your feet!' And Alphonso belched again and held his eyes, still grinning.

Slowly Sean reached down to the trench knife in its sheath and just as deliberately Alphonso reached and touched the Tokarev pistol tucked into his belt. They stared at each other.

'Sean, what is it?' Claudia asked anxiously. 'What is going on?' She had not understood the exchange in Shangane, but the tension was palpable.

'He's refusing to help me carry Job,' he replied.

'You can't carry him alone, can you?' Claudia said anxiously. 'Alphonso *will* help –'

'– or I'll kill him!' Sean replied in Shangane and Alphonso laughed out loud. He stood up and shook himself like a dog, turned his back on Sean, picked up his radio pack, Sean's AKM rifle and most of the water-bottles.

'I'll carry these,' he chuckled, shaking his head at the joke. 'You can carry your Matabele.' He ambled away southwards along the line of march.

Sean dropped his hand from the hilt of the knife and looked across at Job. He was watching quietly from his mattress of grass and Sean snarled at him, 'If you say it, I'll kick your black arse for you.'

'I didn't say nothing.' Job tried to smile, but it was a weak and transient grimace.

'Good,' said Sean grimly, and picked up the nylon sling seat and straps.

'Claudia, give us a hand here.'

Between them, they got Job on his feet and Sean rigged the nylon slings around his waist and under his crotch like a parachute harness, and looped them over his own shoulders. Then he supported Job with an arm around the waist.

'One more river, there's one more river to cross,' he sang hoarsely and untunefully, and grinned at Job. They moved forward. Although Job's feet touched the ground and he tried to take as much of his own weight as possible, he was mainly supported by the straps that crossed over Sean's shoulders and they were locked together like a pair in a harness.

Within the first hundred paces they had established some sort of rhythm, but still their progress was unsteady and painfully slow, set by Job's uncertain footsteps. There could be no attempt at stealth or anti-tracking for Sean had to pick the easiest and most obvious route. They stuck to the open game trails, that complex network that like the veins in a dried leaf meshes the African veld.

Behind them Claudia followed laden with the medical pack and the rest of the water-bottles, but still she carried a leafy branch with which she tried to sweep their tracks. Her efforts might conceal their passing from a casual observer, but a Frelimo tracker would follow them as though he were on the Ml motorway. It was hardly worth the effort, but Sean did not discourage her, he knew how important it was to her to feel that she was pulling her weight and making a useful contribution to their escape.

Sean counted their paces against the second hand of his wristwatch and estimated that they were down to less than a mile an hour, eight miles a day was all the progress they could hope for, and he started to divide that into three hundred but gave up before he reached the depressing answer.

Both Matatu and Alphonso had disappeared into the combretum forest ahead of them and Sean glanced at his watch again.

They had only been going a little over thirty minutes, but already their momentum was winding down. Job's weight was heavier, the straps cutting painfully into the flesh of Sean's shoulders, and Job's footsteps were dragging and catching on every irregularity of the game path.

'I'm cutting down to thirty-minute stages,' he told Job. 'We'll take five minutes now.'

When Sean lowered him to a sitting position against the bole of a tree, Job leant his head back against the rough bark and closed his eyes. His breathing sobbed in his chest, and droplets of sweat made slow runnels down his cheeks. Like tiny black pearls, the drops reflected the colour of his skin.

Sean let the five minutes run over to ten and then told Job cheerfully, 'On your feet, soldier, let's eat some ground.'

Getting Job up on his feet again was torture for both of them and Sean realized that trying to be gentle on him, he had allowed Job to rest too long. The wound had begun to stiffen.

The next thirty-minute stage endured so long that Sean was convinced that his watch had stopped. He had to check the sweep of the second hand to reassure himself.

When at last, he lowered him to a sitting position, Job grimaced. 'Sorry, Sean, cramps. Left calf.'

Sean squatted in front of him and felt the knots of tortured muscle in Job's leg. While he massaged it, he spoke quietly to Claudia. 'There are salt tablets in the medic pack, front pocket.'

Job swallowed them and Claudia held the water-bottle to his lips. After two swallows, he pushed it away.

'More,' Claudia urged him, but he shook his head.

'Don't waste it,' he murmured.

'How's that feel?' Sean gave his calf a couple of hard slaps.

'Good for another few miles.'

'Let's go,' Sean said. 'Before it seizes up again.'

It amazed Claudia how the two of them kept going through the night with only those five-minute breaks and the frugal draughts from the water-bottles.

'Three hundred miles of this,' she thought. 'It simply is not possible. Flesh and blood can't take it. It will kill both of them.'

A little before dawn, Matatu popped up like a small black shadow out of the forest and whispered to Sean.

'He has found a waterhole about two or three miles ahead,' Sean told them. 'Can you make it, Job?'

The sun had risen and cleared the tops of the trees and the day's heat was building up like a stoked furnace. When Job collapsed and hung suspended at Sean's side, dangling with his full weight on the cross straps, they were still half a mile from the waterhole.

Sean lowered him to the ground and sat beside him. He was so exhausted himself that, for a few minutes, he could not find the energy to talk or move.

'Well, at least you picked a good place to pass out,' he congratulated Job in a hoarse whisper. They were in a patch of thick thorn bush that would give them shade and cover for the rest of the day.

They made a bed of cut grass for Job in the shade and settled him on it. He was only half conscious, his speech slurred and wandering, and his eyes continually slipping out of focus. Claudia tried to feed him, but he turned his face away. However, he drank thirstily when at last Matatu and Alphonso returned from the waterhole with all the water-bottles refilled. After he had drunk, Job lapsed back into coma and they waited out the heat of the day in the thorn patch.

Sean and Claudia lay in each other's arms, she had become so accustomed to falling asleep in his embrace. She realized that Sean was near the end of his tether. She had never imagined that he could be so finely stretched, that even his strength which she had come to believe was inexhaustible had a limit upon it.

When she woke a little after noon, he lay like a dead man beside her and she studied his face lovingly, almost greedily. His beard was full and beginning to curl and she picked out two curly silver hairs in the dense bush. His features were gaunt, all trace of fat and superfluous flesh burned away and there were lines and weathered creases in his skin that she had never noticed before. She studied them as though his life history were chiselled into them like cuneiform writing on a tablet that she could read. 'God, but I love him,' she thought, amazed at the depth of her own feelings. His skin was burned to the colour of dark mahogany by the sun, and yet it retained a lustre like that of fine leather, well used but polished with care over the years, 'like Papa's polo boots'. She smiled at the simile, but it was somehow apt. She had watched her father in his dressing-room lovingly applying dubbin to the leather with his fingers and polishing it to a dull glow with his own bare palm.

'Boots!' she whispered. 'That's a good name for you,' she told Sean as he slept, and she remembered how her father's boots had flexed and wrinkled at the ankle, almost as supple as silk as he stepped up into the stirrup. 'Wrinkled just like you, my old boot.' She smiled and kissed the lines in his forehead so softly as not to wake him.

She realized then to just what extent the memory of her father had been absorbed in this man who lay for once like a child in her arms. The two men seemed to have merged

527

in one body, and she could concentrate all her love in a single place. Gently she moved Sean's sleeping head until it nestled against her shoulder, and she burrowed her fingers into the dense springing curls at the back of his head and rocked him gently.

Up until this moment, he had succeeded in evoking the full spectrum of her emotions, from anger to sensual passion, everything except tenderness. Now, however, it was complete. 'My baby,' she whispered, as tenderly as a mother. For once she truly felt that he belonged to her completely.

A soft groan shattered her fragile mood, and she raised her head and glanced across at where Job lay beneath the thorn bush nearby, but he relapsed into silence once again.

She thought about the two of them, Job and Sean and their special masculine relationship in which she knew she could never share. She should have been jealous, but instead in some strange way, it made her feel more secure. If Sean could be so constant and self-sacrificing in his love for another man, then she hoped that she could expect the same constancy from him in their own different but even more intense relationship.

Job groaned again and began to thrash about restlessly. She sighed and then gently disentangled herself from Sean's sleeping form, stood up and crossed to where Job lay.

A cloud of metallic-green flies buzzed around the blood-soaked bandage that covered his shoulder. They settled on the soiled dressing and tasted it with their long proboscises, then rubbed their front legs together with delight. Claudia saw that they had laid their rice-grain eggs in thick rafts on the bloody cloth, and with an exclamation of disgust, she fanned them away, and then scraped the loathsome white eggs from the folds of the bandage.

Job opened his eyes and looked up at her. She realized that he was fully conscious once again and she smiled encouragingly at him. 'Would you like another drink?'

'No.' His voice was so low that she had to lean closer to him. 'You have to make him do it,' he said.

'Who? Sean?' she asked, and Job nodded.

'He can't go on like this. He's killing himself. Without him, none of you will survive. You must make him leave me here.' She had begun to shake her head before he stopped speaking.

'No,' she said firmly. 'He would never do it, and I wouldn't let him, even if he wanted to. We are in this together, pardner.' She touched his arm. 'Now, how about that drink?' He subsided, too weak to argue further. Like Sean, Job also seemed to have deteriorated alarmingly in the last few hours. She sat beside him fanning the flies away with an ilala palm frond while the sun slid slowly down the western sky.

In the cool of the afternoon Sean stirred and sat up, instantly wide awake, taking in his surroundings with a quick glance. Sleep revived and fortified him.

'How is he?' he asked, and when she shook her head, he came to squat beside her.

'We'll have to get him up again pretty soon.'

'Give him a few more minutes,' she pleaded, and then went on. 'Do you know what I've been thinking about while I've been sitting here?'

'Tell me,' he invited, and put his arm around her shoulders.

'I've been thinking about that waterhole out there. I've been fantasizing about pouring water over myself, washing my clothes, getting rid of this stink.'

'Have you heard about Napoleon?' he asked.

'Napoleon?' She looked puzzled. 'What does he have to do with bathing?'

'Whenever he returned from a campaign, he would send a galloper ahead of him to Josephine with the message, "*Je rentre, ne te lave pas.*" "I'm coming home, don't bathe." You see he liked his ladies the way he liked his cheese, full bodied. He would have loved you the way you are now!'

'You're disgusting.' She punched his shoulder, and Job groaned.

'Hey, there.' Sean turned his attention to him. 'What's going down, man?'

'I'll take you up on your offer now,' Job whispered.

'Morphine?' Sean asked, and Job nodded.

'Just a little shot, okay?'

'You've got it,' Sean agreed, and reached for the medical pack.

After the injection, Job lay with his eyes closed and they watched the taut lines of pain around his mouth slowly relax.

'Better?' Sean asked, and Job smiled softly without opening his eyes. 'We'll give you a few minutes more,' Sean told him. 'While we make the radio sched. with Banana Tree.'

Sean stood up and went across to where Alphonso was already rigging the radio aerial.

'*N'gulube*, this is Banana Tree.' The response to Alphonso's first call was so strong and clear that Sean started.

Alphonso adjusted the gain and then thumbed the microphone and gave another fictitious position report, as though he were still on the return march to the river area.

There was a pause, filled only by the drone and crackle of static, and then another voice equally clear and loud. 'Let me speak to Colonel Courtney!' The intonation was unmistakable and Alphonso looked up at Sean.

'General China,' he whispered, and he offered Sean the microphone but Sean pushed it aside and frowned with concentration as he waited for the next transmission.

In the silence that followed, Claudia left Job's side and crossed quickly to Sean. She squatted beside him and he placed his arm around her protectively; they both stared at the radio.

'The deserters,' she said softly. 'China knows.'

'Listen!' Sean cautioned. They waited.

'Very well.' China's voice again. 'I can understand that you do not wish to reply. However, I will presume that you are listening, Colonel.'

All their attention was on the radio, and Job opened his eyes. He had heard every word that China spoke quite clearly and rolled his head. Alphonso had left his pack and webbing piled on his blanket not ten paces from where Job lay. The butt of the Tokarev pistol protruded from the side pocket of the pack.

'You have yet to disappoint me, Colonel.' China's voice was mellow and affable. 'It would have been too simple and totally unsatisfying if you had merely blundered into the arms of the reception committee I had arranged for you at the Zimbabwean border.'

Job eased himself up on his good elbow. There was no pain, merely a sensation of weakness and drowsiness. The morphine was working. It was difficult to think clearly. He focused all his attention on the pistol, and he wondered if Alphonso had chambered a round. He began to move towards it extending his legs, digging in his heels, then lifting his buttocks clear and jack-knifing his legs. He made no sound and the others were all concentrating on the voice from the radio.

'So the game is still on, Colonel, or should we rather call it the hunt? You are a great hunter, a great white hunter. You glory in the pursuit of wild animals. You call it sport, and you pride yourself on what you term "fair chase".'

Job was halfway across the clearing. There was still no pain, and he moved a little quicker. At any moment, one of them might turn their head and see him.

'I have never understood your white man's passion for this pursuit. To me it always seemed so pointless. My people have always believed that if you want meat, you should kill it as efficiently and with as little effort as possible.'

Job reached the pile of equipment on Alphonso's blanket

and stretched out to touch the hilt of the pistol. However, when he tried to withdraw it from the pocket, his fingertips were numb and it slipped from his hand; but instead of clattering on the hard earth, the pistol dropped soundlessly onto a fold of the blanket and he saw with a rush of relief that the action was cocked and the safety-catch engaged. Alphonso had loaded it, ready for instant use.

Behind him, China's voice still echoed from the radio set, 'Perhaps you have corrupted me, Colonel. Perhaps I am acquiring your decadent European ways, but for the first time, I understand your passion. Perhaps it is simply that at last the game is big enough to excite me. I wonder how you must feel at this change of role, Colonel. You are the game and I am the hunter. I know where you are, but you don't know where I am. Perhaps, I am closer than you believe possible. Where am I, Colonel? You must guess. You must run and hide. When will we meet, and how?'

Job settled his fingers carefully around the butt of the Tokarev. He lifted it and was surprised by the effort it required. He placed his thumb upon the slide of the safety-catch, and it would not budge. He felt panic rising in him. His hand was too weak and numb to move the slide forward into the firing position.

'I do not promise you "fair chase", Colonel. I will hunt you in my own African way, but it will be good sport. I promise you that at least.'

Job exerted all his strength and felt the slide of the safety-catch begin to move under his thumb.

'The time is now 1800 hours Zulu. I will call you on this frequency at the same time tomorrow, Colonel. That is if we have not already met. Until then watch the sky, Colonel Courtney, look behind you. You do not know from which direction I will come. But be sure, I will come!'

There was a faint click as China unkeyed his microphone and Sean reached over and switched off the radio set to conserve the battery. None of them spoke or moved, until another sharper metallic click broke the silence. To Sean the sound was unmistakable, the sound of a safety-catch being disengaged, and he reacted instinctively, pushing Claudia flat and whirling round to face it.

For a moment, he was paralysed and then he screamed, 'No! Job, for Christ's sake! No!!' and hurled himself forward, like a sprinter from the blocks.

Job was lying on his side facing Sean, but well beyond his reach. Sean drove himself across the space that separated them, but he seemed to be wading through honey, sticky and slow, it impeded his movements. He watched Job raise the pistol, and he tried to prevent him by the force of his gaze. They were looking into each other's eyes, Sean trying to dominate and command him, but Job's eyes were sad, filled with a deep regret and yet unwavering.

Sean saw him open his lips and heard the muzzle of the pistol click against his teeth as Job thrust it deeply into his own mouth and closed his lips around the muzzle, like a child sucking a frozen lollipop. Sean reached out desperately, straining with all his strength to reach Job's pistol hand and rip the stubby black barrel out of his mouth. His fingertips had only touched Job's wrist when the pistol fired.

The sound was muffled, damped down by the flesh and bone of Job's skull.

In his extremity of effort, Sean's vision was enhanced to unnatural clarity and it seemed that time had been suspended so that everything happened very slowly, like a movie reel run at half speed.

Job's head altered shape, it swelled before Sean's eyes, like a rubber hallowe'en mask filled with high-pressure gas. His eyelids flew wide open and for an instant his eyeballs bulged from their sockets exposing a wide rim of white around their dark iris and then rolling upwards into his skull.

His shattered head changed shape again, elongating backwards, stretching his skin tightly over his cheekbones, and flattening his nostrils as the bullet drew the contents of his skull out through the back of his head, whiplashing his neck to its full stretch so that even in the aftermath of the shot, Sean heard the vertebrae creak and click.

Job was jerked backwards, his arm flung away from his head in a debonair salute with the Tokarev pistol still gripped in his clenched fist, but Sean was quick enough to catch him before his mutilated head hit the hard earth.

He caught Job in his arms and held him to his chest with all his strength. His body was heavy and hot with fever, but slack and plastic as though it contained no bone. It seemed to overflow Sean's enfolding arms, and he held him hard. He felt Job's muscles shiver and shudder, and his legs kicked in a macabre little jigging movement and he tried to hold him still.

'Job,' he whispered, and reached up behind him and cupped his hand over the back of his head, covering the terrible exit wound, as though he were trying to hold it together, to press the spilled contents back into the ruptured skull.

'You fool,' he whispered. 'You shouldn't have done it.' He laid his own cheek against Job's, and held him like a lover.

'We would have made it. I would have got you out.' Still hugging Job's quiescent body, he began to rock him gently, murmuring to him softly, pressing his cheek to Job's, his eyes closed tightly.

'We have come so far together, it wasn't fair to end it here.'

Claudia came to them and went down on one knee beside Sean. She reached out to touch his shoulder and searched desperately for something to say, but there were no words, and she stopped her hand before she touched him. Sean was oblivious of her and everything else around him.

His grief was so terrible to see that she felt she should not watch it. It was too private, too vulnerable, and yet she could not tear her eyes from his face. Her own feelings were overshadowed entirely by the magnitude of Sean's sorrow. She had developed a deep affection for Job, but it was as nothing compared to the love that she now saw laid naked before her.

It was as though that pistol shot had destroyed a part of Sean himself, and she experienced no sense of shock or surprise when he began to weep. Still holding Job in his arms, Sean felt the last involuntary tremors of dying nerves and muscle grow still and the first chill of death sap the heat from this body he hugged so tightly to his chest.

The tears seemed to well up from very deep inside of Sean and they came up painfully, burning all the way, scalding his eyelids when at last they forced their way between them and rolled slowly down his darkly weathered cheeks into his beard.

Even Alphonso could not watch it. He stood up and walked away into the thorn scrub, but Claudia could not move. She went on kneeling beside Sean, and her own tears rose in sympathy with his. Together they wept for Job.

Matatu had heard the shot from a mile out where he was guarding their rear, lying up on their back-spoor to watch for a following patrol.

He came in quickly and from the bush at the perimeter of the camp watched for only a few seconds before he deduced exactly what had happened. Then he crept in quietly and crouched behind Sean. Like Claudia, he respected Sean's mourning, waiting for him to master its first unbearably bitter pangs.

Sean spoke at last, without looking round, without opening his eyes.

'Matatu,' he said.

'*Ndio, Bwana.*'

'Go and find the burial place. We have neither tools nor time to dig a grave, yet he is a Matabele and he must be buried sitting up facing the direction of the rising sun.'

'Ndio, Bwana.' Matatu slipped away into the darkling forest and at last Sean opened his eyes and laid Job gently back upon the grey wool blanket. His voice was steady, almost conversational.

'Traditionally we should bury him in the centre of his own cattle kraal.' He wiped the tears from his cheeks with the back of his hand, and went on quietly, 'But we are wanderers, Job and I, he had no kraal nor cattle to call his own.'

She was not certain that Sean was speaking to her, but she replied, 'The wild game were his cattle, and the wilderness his kraal. He will be content here.'

Sean nodded, still without looking at her. 'I am grateful that you understand.'

He reached down and closed Job's eyelids. His face was undamaged except for the chips from his front teeth, and with a fold of the blanket, Sean wiped the blood from the corner of his mouth. Now he looked peaceful and at rest. Sean rolled him on his side and began to wrap him in the blanket, using the nylon webbing and the rifle slings to bind his body tightly into a sitting position, with his knees up under his chin.

Matatu returned before he had finished. 'I have found a good place,' he said, and Sean nodded without looking up from his task.

Claudia broke the silence. 'He gave his life for us,' she said quietly. 'Greater love hath no man.' It sounded so trite and unworthy of the moment that she wished she had not said it, but Sean nodded again.

'I was never able to square the account with him,' he said. 'And now I never will.'

He was finished. Job was trussed securely into the grey blanket, only his head was exposed.

Sean stood up and went to his own small personal pack. He took out the only spare shirt it contained and came back to where Job lay. He knelt beside him again.

536

'Goodbye, my brother. It was a good road we travelled. I only wish we could have reached the end of it together,' he said softly, and leaned forward and kissed Job's forehead. He did it so unaffectedly that it seemed completely natural and right.

Then with the clean shirt, he wrapped Job's head, hiding the ghastly wound, and he picked him up in his arms and walked with him into the forest, cradling Job's head against his shoulder.

Matatu led him to an abandoned ant-bear hole in the thorn forest nearby. It was the work of a few minutes to enlarge the entrance just enough to slide Job's body down into it. With Matatu assisting him, Sean turned him until he was facing east, with his back to the evening star.

Before they covered the grave, Sean knelt beside it and took the fragmentation grenade from the pocket on his webbing. Matatu and Claudia watched as he cautiously rigged a booby trap with the grenade and a short length of bark twine. As he stood up, Claudia looked at him enquiringly, and he answered her shortly, 'Grave robbers.'

Matatu helped him pack stones around Job's shoulders to hold him in a sitting position. Then with larger boulders, they covered him completely, building a cairn over his grave that would keep the hyena out. When it was done, Sean did not linger. He had said his farewell. He walked away without looking back, and after a few moments Claudia followed him.

Despite her sorrow, in some strange way she felt privileged and sanctified by what she had witnessed. Her respect and love for Sean had been reinforced a hundredfold by the emotions he had displayed at the loss of his friend. She felt that his tears had proved his strength rather than betrayed his weakness, and that rare demonstration of love had only pointed up his manhood. From this terrible tragedy, she had learned more about Sean than she might otherwise have done in a lifetime.

They marched hard that night. Sean forged on as though he were trying to outrun his grief. Claudia did not try to slow him. Although she was now lean and fit as a coursing greyhound, she had to put out all her strength to stay with him, but she did not complain. By sunrise, they had covered almost forty miles from where they had buried Job, and ahead of them lay a wide alluvial plain.

Sean found a grove of tall trees to give them a little shade and while Claudia and Matatu prepared their meal, Sean slung his binoculars across his back and stuffed the field map into his back pocket and went to the base of the tallest tree.

Claudia watched him anxiously as he began to climb, but he was as nimble as a squirrel and as powerful as a bull baboon, using the brute strength of his arms to haul himself up the smooth stretches of the bole where there were no footholds.

When he neared the top of the tree, a white-backed vulture launched herself from her shaggy nest of dried branches and circled anxiously overhead while Sean settled into the fork of a branch only a few feet from the nest.

The vulture's nest contained two large chalky-white eggs and Sean murmured soothingly to the bird still cruising high above. 'Don't worry, old girl. I'm not going to steal them.' Sean did not share the popular distaste for these birds. They performed a vital function in cleansing the veld of carrion and disease, and while grotesque in repose, they were models of elegance and beauty in the air, masters of the sky and of natural flight, revered as gods by the ancient Egyptians and other peoples with a close affinity to nature.

Sean smiled up at the bird. The first smile that had bent his lips since Job had gone, and then he gave his full attention to the terrain spread out below him. The alluvial plain ahead had been intensively cultivated, only scattered groves of trees still stood between the open fields. Sean knew that these would mark the sites of the small family villages shown on his map. He turned his binoculars upon them.

He saw at once that the fields had not been tilled nor planted for many seasons. They were thick with the rank secondary growth that invades abandoned cultivation in Africa. He recognized the tall harsh stems of *Hibiscus irritans* named for the sharp fine hairs that cover the leaves and which brush off on anyone that touches them. He saw castor-oil bush and cotton gone wild, and the orange-coloured blossoms of wild cannabis, whose narcotic properties had first so delighted Jack Kennedy's peace corps boys and girls and which over the years since then, had given solace to the hordes of other European and American youngsters who had followed them out to Africa equipped only with back-packs, dirty blue jeans, good intentions and a hazy belief in beauty, peace and the brotherhood of man. Recently fear of Aids had slowed their arrival to a trickle and Sean was grateful for that. He realized his thoughts were wandering and he pulled himself up and panned his binoculars slowly across the scene of desolation ahead.

He could just make out the roofless ruins of the villages. On some of the huts, the roof timbers were still intact but skeletal and blackened by flames; the thatch burned away. Though he scrutinized the area meticulously, he could make out no sign of recent human presence. The paths between the fields were all overgrown, there was no sign of domestic stock, no chicken nor goat and no tell-tale tendrils of smoke rising from a cooking-fire.

'Somebody. Frelimo or Renamo, has worked this area over pretty thoroughly,' he thought, and then looked away to the east to the distant blue hills of the interior. This early in the morning, the air was still clear and bright and he was able to recognize some of the features and cross-reference them to the topography of his field map. Within fifteen minutes he was able to mark in their position with reasonable accuracy and confidence.

They had made a little better progress than he had estimated. Those mountains out on the right-hand side were the Chimanimani; they formed the border between Mozambique and Zimbabwe but their nearest peaks were almost forty kilometres distant. His map was marked in kilometres, and Sean still liked to work in miles rather than the metric scale.

The larger village of Dombe should be a few kilometres out on his left flank, but he could pick out no indication of its exact whereabouts. He guessed that like the other family villages ahead, it had long ago been abandoned and allowed to return to bush and forest, in which case there would be little prospect of finding food there. With so many feeding from it, the small quantity of maize-meal they had been able to bring with them was almost expended. By tomorrow they would need to begin foraging and that would slow them up. On the other hand, if Dombe was still inhabited, it would certainly be either a Frelimo or a Renamo stronghold. Prudently he resolved to avoid any contact with all other humans. Nobody, not even Alphonso, could say which territory was held by the opposing forces and which was a destruction area devastated equally by both sides. Even those boundaries would be fluid and would alter on a daily, if not an hourly basis, like the amorphous body of an amoeba.

He looked directly southward along their intended route. In that direction, there were no features rising above the plain. This was a part of the littoral that stretched down to the shores of the Indian Ocean, and no mountain nor deep valley ruffled it. The only natural obstacles ahead were the dense hardwood forests, the rivers and the swamps that guarded the approaches to them.

The largest river was the Sabi, or the Rio Save as the Portuguese named it as it flowed in across their border with the land that was to become Zimbabwe and down towards the ocean. It was broad and deep and they would probably need some sort of craft to make the crossing.

The last river, Rudyard Kipling's great grey-green, greasy Limpopo river, all set about with fever-trees, was the final obstacle they would face. It was still three hundred kilometres further south. Three national borders converged and met upon its banks, Zimbabwe, Mozambique, and the Republic of South Africa. If they were able to reach that point then they had reached the northern boundary of the celebrated Kruger National Park, heavily guarded and patrolled by the South African military. Sean studied the map longingly – South Africa and safety, South Africa and home, where the rule of law still held sway and men did not walk each moment in the shadow of death.

A soft whistle brought him out of his reverie, and he looked down. Matatu was at the base of the tree, sixty feet below where he sat. He gesticulated up at Sean.

'Listen!' he signalled. 'Danger!' And Sean felt his pulse trip and accelerate. Matatu did not use the danger signal lightly. He cocked his head and listened, but still it was almost a full minute before he heard it. As a bushman Sean's senses, especially eyesight and hearing, were honed and acute, but compared to Matatu, he was a blind mute.

As he heard and recognized the sound at last, even though it was faint and faraway. Sean's pulse jumped again and he swivelled round in the fork of the branch and looked back northwards, in the direction from which they had come.

Apart from a few high streaks of cirro-stratus cloud, the morning sky was empty blue. Sean put up his binoculars and searched it, looking low along the horizon, close to the tops of the tall hard-wood trees. The distant sound, increasing in volume, gave him a direction in which to search, until suddenly the shape appeared in the field of his binoculars and he felt the slide of dread in his guts.

Like some gigantic and noxious insect, the Hind cruised humpbacked and nose low above the forest tops. It was still some miles distant, but coming on directly towards Sean's tree-top perch.

General China sat in the flight engineer's seat under the forward canopy of the Hind and looked ahead through the armoured windscreen. This early in the morning the air had a crystalline lucidity through which the rays of the low sun lit every detail of the landscape below him with a radiant golden light.

Although he had already flown many hours in the captured machine, he had not yet grown accustomed to the extraordinary sense of power that his seat under the forward canopy aroused in him. The earth and everything in it lay below him, he could look down on mankind and know that he held the power of life and death over them.

He reached out now and gripped the control lever of the Gatling-cannon. The pistol grip fitted neatly into his right hand, and as the heel of his hand depressed the cocking plunger, the remote aiming screen lit on the control panel directly in front of him. As he moved the control lever, traversing, depressing or elevating, so the multiple barrels of the cannon faithfully duplicated each movement and the image of the target was reflected on the screen.

With the slightest pressure of his forefinger, he could send a dense stream of cannon shell hosing down to obliterate any target he chose. Then by simply throwing a switch on the weapons console, he could select any of the Hind's alternative armaments, the rockets in their pods or the banks of missiles.

It had not taken China long to master the complex weapons control system, for the basic training he had received in the Siberian guerrilla training camp so long ago, at the beginning of the Rhodesian war of liberation, had stood him in good stead down the years. However, this was the most awe-inspiring fire power he had ever had at his fingertips and the most exhilarating vantage point from which to deploy it.

At a single word of command, he could soar aloft like an eagle in a thermal, or plunge like a stooping peregrine, he could hover on high or dance lightly on the leafy tops of the forest. The power that this machine had bestowed upon him was truly godlike.

At first there had been serious problems to surmount. He could not work with the captured Russian pilot and crew. They were sullen and unreliable. Despite the threat of horrible death that hung over them he realized that they would seize the first opportunity to escape, or to sabotage his precious new Hind. One of the Russian ground crew need only drain the lubricant from a vital part of the machine, or loosen a bolt, or burn out a section of wiring, and neither China nor any of his Renamo had the technical expertise to recognize the sabotage attempt until it was too late. In addition, the Russian pilot had from the very beginning made communication between them difficult. He had played dumb and deliberately misunderstood China's commands. Trading on the knowledge that China could not do without him, he had become progressively more defiant and recalcitrant.

China had solved that problem swiftly. Within hours of the destruction of the Russian squadron and the capture of the Hind, he had radioed a long coded message to a station two hundred miles further north across the national boundary between Mozambique and Malawi. The message had been received and decoded at the headquarters of a large tea plantation on the slopes of Mlanje mountain, the proprietor of which was a member of the central committee of the Mozambique National Resistance and the deputy director of Renamo intelligence. He had telexed China's report and requests directly to the director general of the central committee at his headquarters in Lisbon, and within six hours a crack Portuguese military helicopter pilot with many thousands of hours flying experience and two skilled aeronautical engineers were aboard a TAP airliner southward bound for Africa. From Nairobi they changed to an Air Malawi commercial flight scheduled directly for Blantyre, the capital of Malawi. There a driver and Land-Rover from the tea plantation were waiting to whisk them out to the private airstrip on the tea estate.

That night the tea company's twin-engined Beechcraft, made a midnight crossing of Lake Cabora Bassa, a perilous journey that the pilot had undertaken many times before, and a single red flare guided him to the secret bush strip that General China's men had hacked out of the wilderness just west of the mountains of Gorongosa.

A double line of Renamo guerrillas, each holding aloft a burning torch of paraffin-soaked rags, provided a flare path and the Beechcraft pilot landed smoothly and without shutting down his engines deposited his passengers, turned and taxied back to the end of the rough airstrip and then roared away, climbed clear and turned northwards again into the night.

There had been a time not long ago when such a complicated route for bringing in men and material would not have been necessary. Only a year previously China's request would have been radioed southwards, rather than north, and the delivery vehicle, instead of a small private aircraft, would have been a Puma helicopter with the South African air-force markings.

In those days when the Marxist President of Frelimo, Samora Machel, had hosted the guerrillas of the African National Congress, and allowed them to use Mozambique as a staging post for their terror attacks with limpet mines and car bombs on the civilian population of South Africa, the South Africans had retaliated by giving their full support to the Renamo forces that were attempting to topple Machel's Frelimo government.

Then to the dismay of the Renamo command, Samora Machel and P. W. Botha, the South African president, had signed an accord at the little town of Nkomati on the border between their two countries, the direct result of which had been a drastic reduction of South African aid to Renamo in exchange for the expulsion of the ANC terror squads from Mozambique.

Both sides had cheated on the agreement, with a wink and a nudge. Machel had closed the ANC offices in Maputo but allowed them to continue their terror campaign without official Frelimo support or approval, and the South Africans had cut back on their support of Renamo, but still the Pumas made their clandestine cross-border flights.

Then the deck had been reshuffled when Samora Machel died in the wreck of his personal aircraft, an antiquated Tupolev which had been retired from airline service in the USSR and magnanimously given to Machel by his Russian allies. The Tupolev's instrumentation was decrepit, and on the night of the crash both the Russian pilots had been so full of vodka that they had neglected to file a flight plan. They were almost two hundred kilometres off-course when they crashed on the South African border, actually striking on the Mozambique side and then by some improbable chance bouncing and sliding across into South Africa.

Despite the evidence of the flight recorder, the Tupolev's black box, which contained a recording of the two Russian pilots' repeated requests for more vodka from the air hostess and an animated and anatomically precise discussion of exactly what they were going to do to her after they had landed, the Russians and the Frelimo government insisted that the South Africans had lured Machel to his death. The Nkomati accord died with Machel on that remote African hillside, and the Pumas resumed their cross-border flights, ferrying supplies to the Renamo guerrillas.

Then gradually news began to filter out of the Mozambiquan wilderness. At first a few dedicated missionaries
emerged from the bush to describe the appalling destruction,
the misery and the starvation, and the atrocities that were
being perpetrated by the ravaging Renamo guerrilla armies
over an area the size of France.

A few intrepid journalists managed to get into the battle
zone, and one or two of them survived and emerged to
relate their accounts of the holocaust that was raging. Some
of their reports put the estimate of civilian casualties as
high as half a million dead of starvation, disease and geno-
cide.

Refugees, tens of thousands of them, began to stream
across the border into South Africa. Terrified, starving,
riddled with disease, they told their harrowing stories. The
South Africans realized to their horror that they had been
nourishing a monster in Renamo.

At the same time, the more moderate Chissano, who
had replaced Samora Machel as president of the government
of Mozambique, and Frelimo began making placatory over-
tures. The two presidents met and the Nkomati accord was
hurriedly revived, this time with honest intent. Overnight,
the flow of South African aid to Renamo was cut off.

This had all taken place only months before, and General
China and his fellow Renamo commanders were angry and
desperate men, their stores of food and weapons dwindling
rapidly without prospect of resupply. Soon they would be
reduced to surviving on plunder and loot, foraging and
scavenging from a countryside already ravaged by twelve
years of guerrilla warfare. It was inevitable that they would
turn their fury on what remained of the civilian population
and on any foreigner that they could capture. The world
was against them, and they were against the world.

Sitting up in the high seat of the Hind, General China
let all this run through his mind. From here he seemed to
have an over-view of the chaos and confusion. The entire

country was in a state of flux, and always in a situation such as this, there was opportunity for the cunning and the ruthless to seize upon.

Of the Renamo field commanders, General China had proved himself over the years to be the most resourceful. With each victory and success he had established his power more firmly. His army was the most powerful of the three Renamo divisions. The external central committee was nominally the high command of the resistance movement, but paradoxically General China's prestige and influence was becoming progressively greater with each setback that the movement received. More and more the central committee acceded to his wishes. The alacrity with which they had reacted to his request for a Portuguese pilot and engineers demonstrated this most aptly. Of course, the destruction of the Russian squadron and the capture of the Hind had enormously inflated his prestige and importance, while possession of the extraordinary vehicle in which he now soared over the wilderness placed him in a unique position of power.

General China smiled contentedly and spoke into the microphone of his hard helmet. 'Pilot, can you see the village yet?'

'Not yet, General. I estimate four minutes' more flying time.'

The Portuguese pilot was in his early thirties. Young enough still to have dash and fire, but old enough to have accumulated experience and discretion. He was handsome in a swarthy olive-skinned fashion, with a drooping gunslinger moustache and the dark bright eyes of a predatory bird. From the first he handled the controls of the Hind with precision and confidence, and his skill had increased with each hour flown as he came to terms with every nuance of the Hind's flying characteristics.

The two Portuguese engineers had taken command of the Russian ground crew and supervised every move they made. One of the Hind's principal advantages was that it could be serviced and maintained in all conditions without the need for sophisticated equipment, and the chief engineer assured General China that the spares and tools he had captured at the laager were sufficient to keep the Hind airborne indefinitely. The only shortages were of missiles for the Swatter system and assault rockets, but this was amply compensated for by almost a million rounds of 12.7mm cannon shells they had captured in the laager.

It had taken a hundred and fifty porters to carry the munitions away, while another five hundred porters had each carried a twenty-five-litre drum of Avgas. Renamo used mainly women porters, trained since girlhood to carry weights on their heads. That quantity of Avgas was sufficient to keep the Hind flying for almost two hundred hours, and by then there would be a good chance of capturing a Frelimo fuel tanker, either on the railway line or on one of the roads nearer the coast that were still open to traffic.

However, General China's main concern at that moment was to keep the rendezvous which he had arranged by radio with General Tippoo Tip, the commander of Renamo's southern division.

'General, I have spotted the village,' the pilot spoke in China's headphones.

'Ah, yes, I see it,' China answered. 'Turn towards it, please.'

As the Hind approached Sean shifted his perch, creeping behind a densely leafed bough and flattening himself against the branch. Although he knew it was dangerous to turn his face towards the sky, he relied on the bush of his beard and his deep tan to prevent the sun reflecting off his face and he watched the helicopter avidly.

He realized that their ultimate survival depended on being able to elude this monster, and he studied its shape to estimate the view that the pilot and his gunner commanded from behind their canopies. It might be vital for Sean to know the blind spots of the flight engineer and the field of fire of his weapons.

He saw the cannon in the remote turret below the nose abruptly traverse left and right, almost as though the gunner was demonstrating them for him. Sean could not know that General China was merely gloating on his own power and playing with the weapon controls, but the movement illustrated the Gatling-cannon's restricted field of fire. The barrel could only swing through an arc of thirty degrees from lock to lock, beyond that the pilot was obliged to swivel the entire aircraft on its own axis in order to bring the cannon to bear.

The Hind was very close now. Sean could make out every minute detail of the hull, from the crimson 'Excellent' logo on the nose to the rows of rivet heads that stitched the titanium armour sheets. He looked for some weakness, some flaw in the massive armour, but in the few seconds, before she was overhead, he saw that she was impregnable, except for the air intakes to the turbo engines, like a pair of hooded eyes above the upper pilot's canopy. The intakes were screened by debris suppressors, bossed light metal discs that inhibited the dust and debris thrown up by the down-draught of the rotors when the helicopter hovered close to the ground from being sucked into the turbines. However, the debris suppressors were not so substantial as to prevent the Stinger missiles flying clearly into the intakes, and Sean saw that there was a necessary gap around the edge of the metal boss wide enough for a man to stick his head through. At the correct angle and from very close range an expert marksman might just be able to aim a burst of machine-gun fire through that gap so as to damage the turbine vanes. Sean knew that even a chip from one of those vanes would unbalance the turbine and set up such vibrations in the engine that it would fly to pieces within seconds.

'A hell of a shot, and a hell of a lot of luck,' Sean muttered, staring upwards through slitted eyes. Suddenly the light reflected from the armoured glass canopy altered so that he could see into the interior of the cockpit.

As he recognized General China, despite the hard plastic flying-helmet and the mirrored aviator glasses shielding his eyes, hatred flushed fiercely through Sean's guts. Here was the man on whom he could firmly set the blame for Job's death and all their other woes and hardships.

'I want you,' Sean muttered. 'God, how badly I want you.'

China seemed to sense the force of his hatred for he turned his head slightly and looked down directly at Sean's perch, staring at him evenly through the mirrored lens of his sunglasses, and Sean shrank down upon the branch.

Then abruptly the Hind banked away, exposing its blotched grey belly. The down-draught lashed the tree-top, shaking the branches, and throwing Sean about in the hurricane of disrupted air, and Sean realized that it had been an illusion and that China had not spotted him in his tree-top bower.

He watched the huge machine skitter away on its new heading and then a few miles distant the engine beat changed, the sound of the rotors whined in finer pitch and the Hind hovered briefly above the forest and then sank from view.

Sean clambered down the tree. Matatu had doused the small cooking-fire at the first sound of the Hind's approach, but the canteen of maize porridge had already cooked through.

'We'll eat on the march,' Sean ordered.

Claudia groaned softly, but pulled herself to her feet. Every muscle in her legs and back ached with fatigue.

'Sorry, beautiful.' Sean put an arm around her shoulders and squeezed her. 'China landed only a mile or two east of here. Probably at the village of Dombe, we can be pretty sure he has troops there. We've got to move on.'

They ate the last handfuls of hot sticky salted maize

porridge on the march and washed it down with water from the bottles that tasted of mud and algae. 'From now on, we are living off the land,' Sean told her. 'And China is breathing down our necks.'

The Hind hovered a hundred feet above the road that ran through the village of Dombe.

It was the only road, and the village was merely a collection of twenty or so small buildings that had been long abandoned. The glass was broken from the window frames and the whitewashed plaster had fallen from the adobe walls in leprous patches. Termites had devoured the roof timbers so that the corroded corrugated sheeting sagged from the roof. Those buildings fronting onto the road had all once been small general dealers' stores, the ubiquitous *dukas* of Africa, owned by Hindu traders. One faded sign hung at a drunken angle. 'Patel & Patel', it proclaimed between the crimson trademarks of the Coca-Cola company.

The road itself was dirt-surfaced and littered with rubbish and debris, weeds growing rankly in the unused ruts.

'Take us down,' China ordered, and the helicopter sank towards the roadway, lifting a whirlwind thick with dead leaves, scraps of paper, discarded plastic bags and other rubbish.

There were men on the verandah of 'Patel & Patel' and armed men amongst the derelict buildings, fifty or more, all heavily armed and dressed in an assortment of camouflage, military and civilian clothing, the eclectic uniform of the African guerrilla.

The Hind settled to the rutted road and the pilot throttled back the turbos; the rotors slowed and the engine noise sank to a low whistle. General China opened the armoured canopy, jumped down lightly to earth and turned to face the group of men on the stoep of the general dealer's store.

'Tippoo Tip,' he said, and opened his arms wide in fraternal greeting. 'How good to see you again.' He raised his voice above the engine whistle.

General Tippoo Tip came down the steps to meet him, his own thick arms held wide as a crucifix. They embraced with the utmost insincerity of two fierce rivals who knew that they might one day have to kill each other.

'My old friend,' said China, and held him at arm's length, smiling warmly and lovingly upon him.

Tippoo Tip was not his real name, he had taken that as his *nom de guerre* from one of the most notorious of the old Arab slave-traders and ivory-runners of the previous century. However, the name and its associations suited him to perfection, China thought as he looked down upon him. Here stood a rogue and brigand cast in the classic mould, a man to admire and to treat with great caution.

He was short, the top of his head on a level with China's chin, but everything else about him was massive. His chest was like that of a bull gorilla, and his thick arms hung in similar fashion, so his knuckles were at the level of his knees. His head was like one of those gigantic Rhodesian granite boulders balanced on the pinnacle of a rocky kopje. He had shaved his pate, but his beard was a thick mattress of woolly black curls, that hung onto his chest. The forehead and nose above it were broad and his lips full and fleshy.

He wore a gaily coloured strip of cotton cloth bound around his forehead, while a gilet of tanned kuku-hide over his naked torso was open down the front to expose his chest. His chest was covered with black peppercorns of wool, and his naked arms protruding from the short sleeves were thick and roped with muscle.

He smiled back at China and his teeth were brilliant as mother-of-pearl, in contrast to the smoky yellow whites of his eyes, laced with a network of veins.

'Your presence has perfumed my day with the scent of mimosa blossom,' he said in Shangane, but his eyes slid past China's face and returned to the huge helicopter from which he had disembarked. Tippoo Tip's envy was so unconcealed that China felt he could smell it and taste it like burning sulphur in the air.

That machine had altered the fine trim and balance of the relationship between these two most powerful of all the Renamo warlords. Tippoo Tip could not keep his eyes off it. It was obvious that he wanted to examine it more closely but China took his arm and led him back towards the shade of the verandah. The pilot had not killed the engines and as China and his host stepped out of the circle of the rotors he gunned the Hind and pulled on his collective. The great machine rose, and turned away.

Tippoo Tip twisted out of China's grip and shaded his eyes to watch it. His smoked yellow eyes were as hungry as though he were watching a beautiful naked woman performing an obscene act. China let him yearn after it until it passed out of sight. He had sent the Hind away purposely because he knew and understood Tippoo Tip. He knew that if the machine had remained, the temptation might have become too strong for him to resist, and treachery was as natural to both of them as breathing was to other men. The Hind was China's joker, his wild card.

Tippoo Tip shook himself and laughed for no apparent reason. 'They told me that you had destroyed the squadron and captured one of those, and I said, "China is a lion among men and he is my brother."'

'Come, my brother,' China agreed. 'It is hot in the sun.'

There were stools ready for them on the verandah in the shade and two of Tippoo Tip's young women brought them clay pots of beer, thick as gruel and refreshingly tart. The girls were both in their teens, pretty little things with eyes like fawns. Tippoo Tip liked women and always surrounded himself with them. It was one of his weaknesses, China thought, and smiled a cold superior smile. He himself could take a boy or a girl with equal enjoyment, but only as a brief diversion and not as a necessity of life, and the women engaged his attention for only a fleeting moment before he turned back to his host.

The bodyguards had retired out of earshot, and Tippoo Tip waved the girls away.

'And you, my brother?' China asked. 'How goes the battle? I hear that you have taken the head of Frelimo and pushed it down between their knees to give them a close-up view of their own fundament. Is that true?'

It was not true, of course. As commander of the southern division of Renamo, Tippoo Tip was closer to the capital and port of Maputo which was the centre of government power. He was, therefore, more prejudiced by the withdrawal of South African military assistance and he stood in the front line of Frelimo counter-attacks and reprisals. China knew that in the last few months Tippoo Tip had experienced heavy reversals and lost many men and much territory in the south, but now Tippoo Tip chuckled and nodded.

'We have eaten everything that Frelimo has sent against us. Swallowed them without a belch or a fart.'

They sparred lightly over the beer pots, smiling and laughing, but watching each other like lions over a kill, on guard and ready at any instant to pounce or defend themselves until, at last, China murmured, 'I am pleased to hear that all goes so well with you. I had come to see if my Hind gunship could assist you against Frelimo.' He spread his hands in a deprecating gesture. 'But I see you have no need of help from me.'

It was a machiavellian ploy, and China watched as the point slid through Tippoo Tip's guard and his expression changed. China knew that it would have been a serious tactical error to ask a man like this for assistance. Tippoo Tip had the nose of a hyena to smell out weakness. Instead China had offered the bait of the Hind, dangled it for an instant before his eyes, and then with a crafty sleight of hand made it disappear again.

Tippoo blinked and behind his grin he searched for a response. He also hated to admit failure or weakness to one who he knew would exploit it ruthlessly, but still he craved and lusted after that fabulous machine.

'The help of a brother is always welcome,' he contradicted pleasantly, 'especially a brother who rides the skies in his own *henshaw*.' And then he went on swiftly, 'And perhaps there is some small service that I can offer in return for your help?'

'Crafty rogue,' China thought, admiring his style. 'He knows I haven't come here out of compassion. He knows I want something.' And both of them retreated, in the African manner, behind another screen of pleasantries and trivialities, coming back only circuitously and almost flirtatiously to the main subject.

'I laid a trap for Frelimo,' Tippoo Tip boasted. 'I pulled back from the Save forests.' In truth he had been driven out of those infinitely valuable indigenous forests only after hard fighting, in the face of the most determined Frelimo attacks since the beginning of the long campaign.

'That was cunning of you,' China agreed, letting the razor edge of sarcasm flash in his tone. 'What a trap to leave the forests to Frelimo and how stupid of them to fall for it.'

The Save forests were a treasure house – seventy-foot-tall leadwoods, which were also called ivory tusk trees for their dense finely grained timber; magnificent Rhodesian mahogany which yielded logs five feet in diameter; and the most rare and valuable of all African trees, the tamboti or African sandalwood with its richly figured and scented timber.

Probably nowhere on the continent was there such a concentration of these precious hardwoods. They constituted the last natural resource of this ravaged land. First the great elephant herds had been wiped out, then the rhinoceros and the buffalo had been machine-gunned from the air. The Soviets and the North Koreans had plundered the vast natural prawn-beds and fisheries of the rich warm Mozambique current along the eastern coast, while foreign adventurers with Frelimo licences and approval had decimated the crocodile population of Lake Cabora Bassa. Only the forests still remained intact.

Even more so than the other newly independent African states, the government of Mozambique was desperately short of foreign exchange. For over a decade they had been fighting a drawn-out guerrilla war that had bled their economy white. Those forests were the last assets they had to sell for hard cash.

'They have moved in with labour battalions, twenty, perhaps thirty thousand slaves,' Tippoo Tip told China.

'So many?' China asked with interest. 'Where did they find them?'

'They have swept the last peasants off the land, they have raided the refugee camps, gathered the vagrants and the unemployed from the slums and streets of Maputo. They call it the "democratic People's Full Employment Programme", and the men and women work from dawn to sundown for ten Frelimo escudos a day, and the single meal they are fed costs them fifteen Frelimo escudos.' Tippoo Tip threw back his head and laughed, more in admiration than amusement. 'Sometimes Frelimo is not so stupid,' he admitted. 'The labour battalions pay five escudos a day for the privilege of cutting the government timber, a most admirable arrangement.'

'And you have allowed Frelimo to do this?' China asked. It was not the plight of the labour battalions that concerned him. A single sixty-foot log of tamboti was valued at approximately fifty thousand US dollars, and the forests extended for hundreds of thousands of acres.

'Of course I allow them to do this,' Tippoo Tip agreed. 'They cannot move the timber out until the roads and the railway are reconstructed, and until then they are piling the logs in dumps along the old line of rail. My scouts count each log that is added to the stock pile.' Tippoo Tip took a grubby plastic-covered notebook from the pocket of his kudu-skin gilet and showed China the figures that he had neatly noted down in blue ballpoint pen on the back page.

China kept his face impassive as he read the total, but his eyes glittered behind the gold-rimmed sunglasses. That sum of dollars was sufficient to finance the war chest of both armies for a further five years, enough to buy the alliance of nations or to elevate a small warlord to the estate of president over the entire nation for life.

'The time is almost ready for me to return to the forests of Save and collect the harvest that Frelimo has gathered in ready for me.'

'How would you export this harvest? A log of tamboti weighs a hundred tons, who would buy it from you?'

Tippoo Tip clapped his hands and shouted to one of his aides who was squatting in the shade of the building across the street. The guerrilla jumped up and hurried to where the two generals sat. He knelt to unroll a field map on the cracked concrete floor of the verandah between their stools and placed lumps of broken concrete on the corners of the map to hold it flat. Tippoo Tip and China leaned forward to study it.

'Here are the forests.' Tippoo Tip traced out the boundaries of that vast area between the Rio Save and Limpopo rivers, directly south of their own position. 'Frelimo have set up their timberyards, here and here and here.'

'Go on,' China encouraged him.

'The most southerly dump is only thirty miles from the north bank of the Limpopo, thirty miles from the South African border.'

'The South Africans have disavowed us, they have signed an accord with Chissano and Frelimo,' China pointed out.

'Treaty and accords are merely pieces of paper.' Tippoo Tip waved them aside. 'Here, we are discussing half a billion

US dollars' worth of timber. I have already received assurances from our erstwhile allies in the south that if I can make good delivery, they will arrange transport to their border and payment in Lisbon or Zurich.' He paused. 'Frelimo has cut and stacked the goods for me, it remains only for me to collect and deliver.'

'And my new helicopter gunship will assist your collection?' China suggested.

'Assist, yes, although I could achieve the same result with my own forces.'

'Perhaps, but a joint operation would be quicker and more certain,' China told him. 'We share the fighting and the spoils. With my *henshaw* and reinforcements from the north it would take a week or less to drive the Frelimo forces out of the forests.'

Tippoo Tip pretended to consider the proposition, and then nodded and asked delicately, 'Of course, I could reward you for your help, with a modest percentage of the value of the timber we capture.'

'Modest is not a word I greatly favour,' China sighed. 'I prefer the good socialist word equal, let us say an equal share?' And Tippoo Tip looked pained and threw up his hands in protest.

'Be reasonable, my brother.' For an hour longer they haggled and argued, slowly drawing closer to striking a bargain over the private distribution of a nation's wealth and the fate of tens of thousands of wretched individuals in the labour battalions.

'My scouts tell me that the people in the logging camps are near the end of their usefulness,' Tippoo Tip remarked at one point. 'Frelimo have fed them on such rations that nearly all of them are sick and starving. They are dying by hundreds each day and they are cutting half the timber that they were two months ago. Frelimo have run out of replacements for the logging gangs and the whole business is running down. There is not much to be gained by waiting any longer, we should attack immediately, before the beginning of the rains.'

China looked at his digital wristwatch, a badge of rank as significant as the star upon his epaulettes. The Hind would be returning to pick him up within half an hour, he must conclude the negotiations and strike the bargain. Within minutes, they had agreed on the last details of the combined operation and then China mentioned casually, 'There is one other matter.' And his tone alerted Tippoo Tip to the importance of the next request. He leaned forward on the stool and placed his hands, as broad and powerful as the paws of a grizzly bear, on his knees. 'I am chasing a small party of white fugitives. It seems that they are attempting to reach the South African border.' Briefly China sketched out a description of Sean's party and ended, 'I want you to alert all your forces between here and the Limpopo to be on the look-out for them.'

'A white man and a white woman, a young white woman. It sounds interesting, my brother,' Tippoo Tip said thoughtfully.

'The man is the most important. The woman is an American and may have some value as a hostage, but otherwise she means little.'

'To me a woman always has value,' Tippoo Tip contradicted him. 'Especially if she is white and young. I like a change of flesh occasionally. Let us make another bargain, my brother, once again equal shares. If I help you to capture these runaway whites, you may have the man, but I will keep the woman. Is it agreed?'

China thought for a moment and then nodded. 'Very well, you may have her, but I want the man alive and uninjured.'

'That is exactly how I want the woman,' Tippoo Tip chuckled. 'So again, we are in accord.' He stretched out his right hand, and China took it. Both of them knew as they stared into each other's eyes that the gesture was meaningless, that their agreement would be honoured only as long as it favoured both of them, and it could be broken without warning by either of them as circumstances altered.

'Now tell me about this young white woman,' Tippoo Tip invited. 'Where was she last seen, and what are you doing to catch her?'

China returned immediately to the map spread between them and Tippoo Tip took note of the new animation in his expression and the eagerness in his voice as he explained how Sean and his party had avoided the trap he had set on the border and how the Shangane deserters had reported their position and their intention of heading southwards.

'We know their last definite position was here.' China touched a spot just north of the railway line. 'But that was three days ago. They could be anywhere along here.' He spread his hand and drew it down across the map. 'One of the party is badly wounded so they have probably not reached this far south. I have patrols, almost three hundred men quartering the ground south of the railway looking for their spoor, but I want you to lay a net, like this, in front of them. How many men can you spare?'

Tippoo Tip shrugged. 'I have already placed three companies here along the Rio Save keeping watch on the logging in the forests. There are five more companies spread across here, further north. If these whites are trying to reach the Limpopo border, they will have to pass right through my lines and the Frelimo guards in the forest. I will radio my company commanders to be fully alert for them.'

General China's tone was sharp and authoritative. 'They must cover every trail, every river crossing. They must stake out a stop line with no gaps in it, and my sweep line coming down from the north will drive them onto it. But warn your section commanders that the white man is a soldier and a good one. He commanded the Ballantyne Scouts at the end of the war.'

'Courtney,' Tippoo Tip broke in. 'I remember him well.'

And then he chuckled. 'Of course, it was Courtney who led the raid on your base. No small wonder that you want him so badly. You and Colonel Courtney go back many years. You have a long memory, my brother.'

'Yes,' China nodded, and touched the lobe of his deaf ear. 'Many years and a long memory, but then revenge is a dish that tastes best if it is eaten cold.'

They both looked up as the sound of the Hind's turbos whistled in from the north of the village and China checked his wristwatch. The pilot was precisely on time for the pickup and China felt his confidence in the young Portuguese reinforced. He stood up from the stool.

'We will maintain radio contact on 118.4 MHZ,' he told Tippoo Tip. 'Three schedules daily, six a.m., noon and six in the evening.' But Tippoo Tip was not looking at him, he was looking up longingly at the shape of the Hind as it hovered above the village like some mutated monster from a horror movie.

General China settled himself into the flight engineer's seat and closed the armoured-glass canopy. He raised his right thumb towards where Tippoo Tip stood on the verandah of the derelict *duka* and as he returned the salute, the Hind rose vertically above the village and swung its nose towards the north.

'General, one of the patrols has been calling you urgently on the radio.' The pilot spoke in China's earphones. 'They are using the call sign "Twelve Red".'

'Very well, please switch to the patrol frequency,' China ordered, and watched the digital display on the panel of his radio transmitter.

'"Twelve Red" this is "Banana Tree". Do you read?' he spoke into his helmet microphone. 'Twelve Red' was one of his crack scouting groups sweeping for spoor south of the railway line. Glancing at the map on his knee China tried to guess the scouts' exact position. The section leader answered his call almost immediately.

'"Banana Tree", this is "Twelve Red". We have a confirmed contact.'

China felt the excitement and triumph rise in his chest, but he kept his voice level.

'Report your position,' he ordered, and as the section leader read out the co-ordinates China checked them on his field map, and saw that the patrol was about thirty-five miles due north of the village.

'Have you got that, pilot?' he asked. 'Get there as fast as you can.' And as the engine tone of the Hind rose sharply he called ahead, '"Twelve Red", give us a red flare when you have us in sight.'

Seven minutes later the flare arced up out of the forest almost directly under the Hind's nose, and the pilot slowed the machine and let it drift down towards the tree-tops.

The Renamo patrol had cleared a landing zone with their machetes and the pilot manoeuvred the Hind into it and let her settle in a cloud of dust and debris. He saw with satisfaction that the scouts had thrown out a protective screen around the landing zone. They were crack bush fighters. China leapt eagerly out of the cockpit and the section leader came forward to salute him. He was a lean veteran, festooned with weapons and water-bottles and bandoliers of ammunition.

'They passed this way sometime yesterday,' he reported.

'Are you sure it's them?' China demanded.

'The white man and woman,' the section leader nodded. 'But they buried something over there.' He pointed with his chin. 'We have not touched it, but I think it is a grave.'

'Show me,' China ordered, and followed him into the thorn thicket. The section leader stopped beside a cairn of boulders.

'Yes, a grave,' China said with finality. 'Open it up.'

The section leader snapped an order at two of his men and they laid aside their weapons and went forward. They kicked away the top stones and rolled them down the slope.

'Hurry!' China called. 'Work faster!' And the ironstone boulders rang against each other and struck sparks as they were hurled aside.

'There is the corpse,' the section leader called, as Job's bundled head was exposed. He stepped forward and jerked aside the stained shirt that covered it.

'It's the Matabele.' China recognized Job's features immediately, 'I didn't think he'd get this far. Dig him out and feed him to the hyena,' he ordered.

Two of the scouts reached down and seized Job's blanket-wrapped shoulders and China watched with ghoulish interest. Mutilation of the enemy dead was an ancient Nguni custom, the ritual disembowelment allowed the spirit of the vanquished to escape so that it would not plague the victor. There was, however, a vindictive satisfaction in watching his men exhume the Matabele. He understood what grief this act would cause Sean Courtney, and he relished how he would describe it to him on his next radio transmission.

At that moment, he spotted the short length of bark twine. It was twisted lightly around the blanket-wrapped shoulders of the corpse. For a moment he stared at it with puzzlement and then as he saw it tighten and heard the click of the grenade primer, he realized what it was and he screamed a warning and hurled himself face forward to the earth.

The explosion crushed his eardrums and filled his head with pain. He felt the blast wave hit him and something struck him in the cheek with numbing force. He rolled into a sitting position, and for a moment thought that he had lost his eyesight; then the stars and Catherine wheels of light that filled his head dissipated, and with a rush of relief he realized that he could see again.

Blood was streaming down the side of his face, and dribbling from his chin onto the front of his battledress blouse. He whipped the kerchief from around his neck and wadded it into the deep gash that a fragment from the grenade had opened across his cheekbone.

Unsteadily he came to his feet and stared down into the grave. The grenade had gutted one of his men like a fish. He was kneeling and trying to push his own bowels back into the hole, but the wet lining was sticking to his bare hands. The second guerrilla had been killed cleanly. The section leader sprang to China's side and tried to examine the gash in his cheek, but China struck his hands away.

'You white bastard,' his voice was shrill. 'You will pay dearly for that, Colonel Courtney. I swear it to you.'

The wounded guerrilla was still fumbling with his own entrails, but they bulged out between his fingers. He was making a dreadful cawing bubbling sound that only increased General China's fury.

'Get that man out of here!' he screamed. 'Take him away and shut him up!'

They dragged the wounded man away and still China was not satisfied. He was shaking wildly with shock and fury, looking around for something on which to vent his rage.

'You men!' He pointed with a trembling finger. 'Bring your pangas.' Two guerrillas ran forward to obey. 'Pull that Matabele dog out of his hole! That's right. Now use the pangas. Chop him into hyena food. That's it. Small pieces, don't stop! Mincemeat! I want him turned into mincemeat!'

All that morning Matatu led them southwards through the abandoned fields and past the deserted villages. The weeds and rank secondary growth gave them good cover and they avoided the footpaths and skirted the burnt-out huts.

Claudia was having difficulty keeping up. They had been going with only brief rests since the previous evening and she was reaching the limits of her endurance. There was no sensation of pain. Even the devilish little red-tipped thorns that left red weeping lines across the exposed skin of her arms merely tugged painlessly at her as she passed. Her steps were leaden and mechanical, and though she tried to keep the rhythm of the march, she felt herself running down like a clockwork toy. Slowly Sean drew ahead of her and she could not lengthen her stride to hold him. He glanced over his shoulder and saw how she was lagging and slowed for her to catch up.

'I'm sorry,' she blurted, and he glanced at the sky.

'We have to keep going,' he answered, and she toiled on behind him.

A little after midday they heard the Hind again. The sound of its engines were very faint and grew fainter still, dwindling away into the north.

Sean put out an arm to steady Claudia as she swayed on her feet.

'Well done,' he told her gently. 'I'm sorry I had to do that to you, but we've made good ground. China will never expect us to have got so far south. He has headed back northwards, and we can rest now.'

He led her to a cluster of low thorn acacia which formed a natural shelter. She sobbed with exhaustion as she sank to the hard ground and lay quietly as Sean squatted in front of her to remove her shoes and socks.

'Your feet have hardened up beautifully,' he told her as he massaged them gently. 'Not a sign of a blister. You're as tough as a Scout and twice as gutsy.' She couldn't even raise a smile at the compliment. Sean pulled her sock over his hand, stuck one finger through the hole in the toe and wiggled it like a ventriloquist's dummy.

'Okay. She walks good,' he made the sock speak like Miss Piggie, 'but, buster, you should see her in the sack.'

Claudia giggled weakly and he smiled down at her gently. 'That's better,' he said. 'Now go to sleep.'

For a few minutes longer she watched him working on her sock.

'Which of your trollops taught you to darn?' she murmured drowsily.

'I was a virgin until I met you. Go to sleep.'

'I hate her whoever she was,' Claudia said, and closed her eyes. It seemed to her that she opened them again immediately but the light had changed to soft shades of evening and the midday heat had cooled. She sat up.

Sean was cooking over a small fire of dry sticks, and he looked across at her.

'Hungry?' he asked.

'Starving.'

'Dinner.' He brought the metal billy to her.

'What is it?' she asked suspiciously, and peered down at the heap of scorched black sausages, each the size of her little finger.

'Don't ask,' he said. 'Eat.'

Gingerly she picked one out and sniffed at it. It was still hot from the cooking-fire.

'Eat!' he repeated, and to set an example popped one into his own mouth, chewed and swallowed.

'Damned good,' he gave his opinion. 'Go ahead.'

Carefully she bit into it and it squelched between her teeth and burst, filling her mouth with the consistency of warm custard that tasted like creamed spinach. She forced it down.

'Have another.'

'No thanks.'

'They're full of protein. Eat.'

'I couldn't.'

'You won't last out the next march on an empty stomach. Open your mouth.' He fed her and then himself alternately.

When the billy was empty, she asked again, 'Now tell me, what have I been eating?' But he grinned and shook his head and turned to Alphonso who was squatting across the fire devouring his share of the meal.

'Rig the radio,' Sean ordered. 'Let's hear if China has anything to say.'

While Alphonso was busy stringing the radio aerial, Matatu slipped quietly into camp. He was carrying a cylinder of freshly peeled bark whose ends were stoppered with plugs of dried grass. He and Sean exchanged a few words, and Sean looked serious.

'What is it?' Claudia asked with concern.

'Matatu has seen a lot of sign up ahead. It looks like there is a great deal of patrol activity. Frelimo or Renamo, he can't tell which.'

That made her uneasy and Claudia moved a little closer to where Sean sat and leaned against his shoulder. Together they listened to the radio, and here again there seemed to be a much higher level of traffic, most of it in Shangane or African-accented Portuguese.

'There is something brewing,' Alphonso grunted, as he concentrated on the set. 'They are moving patrols into a stop line.'

'Renamo?' Sean asked, and Alphonso nodded.

'Sounds like General Tippoo Tip's men.'

'What does he say?' Claudia asked, but Sean didn't want to alarm her further.

'Routine traffic,' he lied, and Claudia relaxed and watched Matatu at the cooking-fire as he carefully unstoppered the bark cylinder and shook out its contents onto the coals. As she realized what he was cooking, she stiffened with horror.

'Those are the most disgusting . . . !' She couldn't finish and she stared in awful fascination at the huge hairy caterpillars writhing and wriggling on the coals. Their long ginger hair frizzled off in little puffs of smoke and gradually the worms stopped moving and curled into little crisp black sausages.

Claudia let out a tiny strangled cry and clutched at

Sean's arm as she recognized them. 'They aren't . . . !' she gasped. 'I didn't! You didn't make me! Oh! No! I can't believe . . . !'

'Highly nutritious,' Sean assured her, and Matatu seeing the direction of her gaze picked one of the caterpillars out of the coals and passing it quickly from hand to hand to cool it, offered it to her with a magnanimous flourish.

'I think I'm going to throw up,' Claudia said faintly, and turned her face away. 'I can't believe I actually ate one of those.'

At that moment the radio crackled sharply and a voice spoke very faintly in a guttural language that Claudia could not understand. However, Sean's sudden interest in the transmission distracted her from her feelings of nauseous disgust and she asked, 'What language is that?'

'Afrikaans,' he replied shortly. 'Quiet! Listen!' But the transmission faded out abruptly.

'Afrikaans?' she asked. 'South African Dutch?'

'That's right,' Sean nodded. 'We must be getting within extreme range. That was almost certainly a South African military transmission, probably a border patrol on the Limpopo.' Sean spoke briefly to Alphonso and then told Claudia, 'He agrees. South African border patrol. Alphonso says they sometimes pick up skip transmissions like that even further north.' Sean checked his wristwatch. 'Well, it doesn't look as though General China is going to entertain us this evening. We had better pack up and get ready to march.' Sean had half risen when suddenly the radio burst into life again. This time the voice was so clear that they could hear every intake of General China's breath.

'Good evening, Colonel Courtney. Please forgive me for the late schedule, but I have had urgent business to attend to. Come in please, Colonel Courtney.'

In the silence that followed Sean made no move towards the microphone, and General China chuckled softly across the ether.

'Still at a loss for words, Colonel. Never mind. I'm sure you are listening, so I will congratulate you on the ground you have covered to date. Quite remarkable, especially in view of Miss Monterro's brake upon your progress.'

'Arrogant bastard,' Claudia whispered bitterly. 'He is everything and a male chauvinist pig to boot.'

'Quite frankly, Colonel Courtney, you took me by surprise. We have been forced to redeploy our stop lines further south to welcome you.'

Again there was a short silence and then suddenly General China's voice was full of malice.

'You see, Colonel, we have found where you buried your Matabele.' Claudia felt Sean stiffen beside her and the silence drew out until China spoke again. 'We dug up the body and we were able to judge how long it had been in the earth by the extent of putrefaction.' Sean began to tremble and China went on affably. 'A Matabele can stink like a dead hyena and your friend was no exception. Tell me, Colonel, did you put that bullet in his head? Very sensible thing to do. He wasn't going to make it anyway.'

'The swine! The bloody swine!' It was wrung out of Sean.

'Oh and by the way, the booby trap didn't work. Very amateurish effort, I'm afraid.' China laughed easily. 'And don't worry about the Matabele. I made it easier for the hyena. I put two of my men to work on him with pangas. Bite-size chunks, Colonel, Matabele goulash!'

Sean lunged for the microphone and snatched it to his mouth. 'You depraved bloody animal!' he yelled into it. 'You filthy ghoul! By Christ, you'd better pray I never get my hands on you!'

Sean broke off, panting with the strength of his outrage.

'Thank you, Colonel.' There was a smile in General China's voice, 'I was getting bored with talking to myself. It's good to be in contact again, I've missed you.'

With a huge effort Sean resisted the temptation to reply and instead switched off the set.

'Pack up.' His voice was still trembling with fury. 'China will have us pretty well pinpointed after that little outburst. We've got to move fast now.'

'Like we were dragging our heels before?' Claudia asked with resignation, but stood up obediently.

Yet their progress was slower this night. Twice before midnight Matatu cautioned them to wait, warned by his animal sixth sense of danger ahead. He went forward to scout the track and found the ambush that had been set for them, and each time they were forced to make a slow and stealthy detour to avoid the trap.

'General Tippoo Tip's men,' Alphonso muttered. 'He must be helping General China. There are men waiting for us on every path.'

However, after midnight their luck changed for the better. Matatu came across a well-used path running almost directly southwards, and discovered that only a short time before a large detachment of men had passed along it in the same direction as they were headed.

'We'll use their spoor to cover our own.' Sean seized the opportunity and put Matatu in the lead, with Claudia following him, while he and Alphonso took the drag, deliberately treading over the small distinctive footmarks of the leading pair, obliterating them and losing them in the heavy sign which the party of Tippoo Tip's men had left behind them.

They hurried along the path until Matatu's sharp ears picked out the tiny sounds that the Renamo patrol was making as it moved forward in the silence of the night. Then they moderated their pace and trailed them at a discreet distance, letting the patrol run interference for them.

Keeping in contact with the enemy, maintaining the strict interval that was the line between discovery and concealment was a delicate and eerie business for which they had to rely completely on Matatu's hearing and night sight, but they were moving at almost double the pace they could have hoped for without this assistance.

A little before dawn the Renamo patrol stopped just ahead of them and they crouched in the darkness and listened to them setting up an ambush on both sides of the pathway. Once the ambush party was settled in, Matatu led them on another detour to meet the path again further on and they struck out southwards once more.

'We have covered twenty-five miles by my reckoning,' Sean murmured with grim satisfaction, as the first delicate light of dawn paled the eastern stars. 'But we cannot risk moving further in daylight, the country is crawling with Renamo. Matatu, find us a place to lie up for the day.'

During that night march, they had moved into an area of wet vlei ground on the approaches to the Save river and now Matatu led them deliberately into the tall swamp grass. They waded knee-deep across the flood plains that guarded the river, picking their way between shallow open lagoons from which the mosquitos rose in grey clouds. The water covered their tracks and Sean brought up the rear of the file, meticulously closing the swamp grass and brushing it upright behind him to disguise their passing.

A few hundred yards off the path Matatu discovered a small dry island only inches above the level of the flood waters and as he stepped onto it there was a violent upheaval in the reeds as a heavy body rushed through it.

Claudia screamed with shock, certain they had blundered into another murderous Renamo ambush. However. Matatu whipped out his skinning knife and with a shrill war-cry dived into the grass; there was a wild commotion as he wrestled with a writhing scaly body twice his own size.

Sean rushed forward to help him and between them they clubbed and stabbed the creature and dragged it out of the grass on to the island. Claudia shuddered with horror as she realized that it was a huge grey lizard, almost seven feet long, with a speckled yellow belly and a long whip of a tail that still twitched and lashed from side to side.

With squeaks of glee, Matatu began immediately to peel off the scaly skin.

'What is it?'

'Matatu's favourite delicacy, leguan.' Sean whetted the blade of his trench knife on the palm of his hand and then helped Matatu butcher the monitor lizard.

The flesh from the tail was white as the fillets of Dover sole, but Claudia grimaced when Sean offered her a strip.

'You and Matatu would eat your own offspring,' she accused.

'That from the girl who dines regularly on mopane caterpillars!'

'Sean, I couldn't, I really couldn't force myself. Not raw.'

'We haven't any dry wood for a fire and you have eaten Japanese sashimi, haven't you? You told me you loved it.'

'That's raw fish, not raw lizard!'

'Same difference, think of it as a kind of African sashimi,' he coaxed her gently. When at last she gave in and tasted it, she found it surprisingly palatable, and her hunger overcame her squeamishness.

For once there was no shortage of water and they filled their bellies with sweet white meat and flood water and then curled up on their blankets. With the tall swamp grass swaying over their heads to protect them from the burning sunlight and the eyes in the sky, Claudia felt secure and gave in to her fatigue.

Once in the middle of the day, she woke and lay in Sean's arms to listen to the sound of the searching Hind.

'China is working the riverbanks ahead of us,' Sean whispered. The sound of the Hind's turbos rose and fell as it turned on each leg of the search pattern, and Claudia felt her stomach muscles knotting and contracting as it grew louder, passing only a short distance south of where they lay, and then finally faded into silence.

'He's gone,' Sean hugged her. 'Get some sleep.'

She woke again with a sense of panic upon her, but when she tried to move she found herself held down firmly and the palm of someone's hand clamped painfully across her mouth. She turned her eyes sideways and Sean's face was close to hers.

'Quiet!' he breathed in her ear. 'Not a peep out of you.'

When she nodded he released her and rolled over to look out through the screen of swamp grass. She did the same and peered out across the shallow waters of the lagoon.

At first she saw nothing and then she heard someone singing. It was a sweet girlish treble softly piping a Shangane love song, and with it came the sound of light footfalls in the shallow lagoon water. The singing came very close, so close that Claudia instinctively shrank nearer to Sean and held her breathe.

Then suddenly the singing girl stepped into the line of her vision through the aperture in the grass before Claudia's eyes. She was a slim and graceful lass, just past puberty, for though her features were sweet and childlike, her breasts were big and round as tsama melons. She wore only a ragged loin-cloth pulled up between her long coltish legs and her skin glowed in the late afternoon sunlight like burnt molasses. She seemed as wild and fey as a spirit of the forest and Claudia was instantly enchanted by her.

In her right hand the girl carried a light reed fishing spear with multiple barbed grains, and as she waded softly through the lucid warm waters she held the spear poised to strike.

Abruptly the song died on her lips and she froze for an instant and then lunged with the grace of a dancer. The shaft of the spear twitched in her hands and with a happy little cry she lifted a long slimy catfish clear of the water. It wriggled on the end of the spear, its wide whiskered mouth gulping and grunting and the girl clubbed its flattened skull and dropped it into the plaited-reed bag at her waist.

She washed the fish slime from her small pink-palmed hands, picked up the spear and resumed her fishing, coming on directly towards where they lay in the patch of swamp grass. Sean reached out and squeezed Claudia's arm, cautioning her not to move, but the black girl was already so close that with a few more paces, she would stumble over them.

Suddenly she looked up, directly into Claudia's eyes. The two of them stared at each other for only a moment, and then the girl whirled and darted away. In an instant, Sean was up and racing after her, and from the grass on either side both Alphonso and Matatu rushed out to join the chase.

The girl was halfway across the lagoon before they caught up with her; she tried to dodge and double back, but each way she turned there was one of them ready to cut her off and, at last, she stood at bay. Wild-eyed and panting with terror, but holding the fishing spear determinedly in front of her. Her courage and spirit were wasted against the three men facing her; like a cat surrounded by Alsatians she had no chance of escape.

Matatu feinted at her flank and the instant she turned the point of the spear towards him, Sean knocked it out of her hands and swept her up under his arm. Kicking and clawing, he carried her back to the island and dumped her on the dry land. She had lost both her straw bag and loin-cloth in the struggle, and she crouched naked and trembling, staring up at the men who surrounded her.

Sean spoke to her in soft soothing tones, but at first she would not reply. Then Alphonso questioned her, and as soon as the girl realized that he was of her own tribe, she seemed to relax slightly, and after another few gentle questions, made a hesitant breathless response.

'What does she say?' Claudia could not restrain her concern for the child.

'She is living here in the swamps to hide from the

soldiers,' Sean answered. 'Renamo killed her mother and Frelimo took her father and the rest of her family away to cut trees in the forest. She escaped.'

They questioned the girl for almost an hour. How far ahead was the river? Was there a crossing? How many soldiers were there at the river? Where were the Frelimo cutting trees? And as she replied to each question, the girl's terror abated and she seemed to sense Claudia's sympathy and looked towards her with a pathetic childlike trust.

'I speak English a little, miss,' she whispered at last, and Claudia was startled.

'How did you learn?'

'At the mission, before the soldiers came and burned it and killed the nuns.'

'Your English is good,' Claudia smiled at her. 'What is your name, child?'

'Miriam, miss.'

'Don't get too chummy,' Sean warned Claudia grimly.

'She's a darling little thing.'

Sean seemed about to reply but then thought better of it and looked up at the sunset instead. 'Damn it, we have missed China's radio schedule. Let's get ready to move out. Time to get cracking.'

It took only minutes for them to gird up for the march, and with her pack on her back, Claudia asked, 'What about the girl?'

'We'll leave her here,' Sean said, but something in his voice and the way he looked away worried Claudia. She started to follow Sean as he stepped off the island into the water, and then she stopped and looked back. The black girl still squatted naked, staring after Claudia unhappily, but behind her stood Matatu, and he had the skinning knife in his right hand.

Realization dashed over Claudia like a huge wave of icy anger.

'Sean!' Her voice shook as she called him back. 'What are you going to do to this child?'

'Don't worry about it,' he told her brusquely.

'Matatu!' She began to tremble. 'What are you going to do?' And he grinned at her. 'Are you going to . . . ?' She drew her finger across her own throat, and Matatu nodded merrily and showed her the knife.

'Ndio,' he agreed. 'Kufa.' She knew that Swahili word. Matatu had used it whenever her father had shot down an animal and Matatu had slit its throat. Suddenly she was shaking with anger. She rounded on Sean.

'You're going to murder her!' Her voice was shrill with outrage and horror.

'Wait, Claudia, listen. We can't leave her here. If they catch her . . . It would be suicide.'

'You bastard!' she screamed at him. 'You're as bad as any Renamo thug, as bad as China himself!'

'It's our lives, don't you understand? It's survival.'

'I can't believe what I'm hearing!'

'This is a hard, cruel land. If we are to survive, we have to live by those standards. We can't afford the folly of compassion.'

She wanted to attack him physically, she balled her fists in the effort of self-control, but her voice was still shrill.

'Compassion and conscience are all that separate us from the animals.' She drew a deep breath. 'If you value what there is between us, you won't say anything more, you won't try to rationalize what you almost did to this child.'

'You prefer to be captured by General China?' he demanded. 'This child, as you call her, won't hesitate to give them our exact whereabouts.'

'Don't, Sean! I'm warning you, everything you say is causing damage to our relationship that can never be repaired.'

'All right then.' Sean reached out to take her hands and draw her to him. 'What do you want us to do with her? I'll do whatever you say. You want us to turn her loose to report to the first Renamo patrol that comes along, I'll do it.'

Claudia was standing rigid in the circle of his arms and though the strident edge was gone from her voice, it was cold and determined.

'We'll take her with us.'

Sean dropped his arms. 'With us?'

'That's what I said. If we can't leave her, then that is the only solution.'

Sean stared at her and she went on firmly, 'You said you'd do whatever I say. You gave me a promise.'

He opened his mouth and then closed it and looked at the black girl. She had understood some of the argument, enough to know that her life was at stake and that Claudia was her champion, her saviour. When Sean saw the expression on the child's face, suddenly he was filled with shame and self-disgust. It was an alien sensation. During the bush war the Scouts had left no witnesses. This woman of his was turning him soft, he thought, and then smiled and shook his head – or perhaps she was simply humanizing him.

'All right.' He was still smiling. 'The girl comes with us, on condition that you forgive me.'

The kiss was brief, cool. Claudia's lips were tightly closed. Sean understood it would take time for her to recover from her outrage. She turned from Sean and lifted the black girl to her feet. Miriam clung to her thankfully.

'Fetch her loin-cloth,' Sean ordered Matatu. 'And put your knife away. The girl is coming with us.' Matatu rolled his eyes in disapproval. But he went to find the girl's single item of clothing.

While Miriam rewound the scrap of rag around her waist, Sergeant Alphonso leaned on his rifle and watched her with interest. It was obvious that he was not unhappy with the decision to spare the girl. Claudia did not approve of his appraisal of her protégée and she opened her small personal pack and dug out her one spare shirt, a camouflage Renamo sweat-shirt from General China's stores.

The shirt hung half down Miriam's thighs and satisfied Claudia's sense of decorum. The black girl was delighted, her terror of a few minutes before forgotten as she preened in her new finery.

'Thank you, Donna, thank you very much. You good lady.'

'All right,' Sean intervened. 'The fashion show is over, let's move out.' And Alphonso took Miriam's arm.

Only then the girl realized that she was being abducted, and she pulled away and broke into a passionate protest.

'Damn it!' Sean exploded. 'Now we are really in trouble!'

'What is it?' Claudia demanded.

'She isn't alone. She's got others with her.'

'I thought she had lost her parents!'

'That's right, but she's got a brother and sister hidden in the swamps. Two kids so young that they can't fend for themselves. Damn it! Damn it!' Sean repeated bitterly. 'Now what the hell do we do?'

'We fetch the children and take them with us also,' Claudia stated simply.

'Two brats! Are you crazy? We aren't running an orphanage.'

'Do we have to go over this one more time?' Claudia turned her back on him in exasperation and took Miriam's hand. 'It's all right. You can trust me. We'll look after all of you.'

The black girl quietened and stared at Claudia with a puppy's trust and adoration.

'Where are the children? We'll fetch them.'

'Come, Donna. I show you.' Miriam led her by the hand into the swamp.

It was almost dark when they reached the tiny island where Miriam had hidden the children in a clump of papyrus. When she parted the thick green stems, two pairs of huge dark eyes stared out at them like owlets from the nest.

'A boy.' Claudia lifted him out. He was five or six years of age, skinny and shivering with fright. 'And a girl.' She was younger, not more than four years old and Claudia exclaimed as she touched her.

'She's burning up, this child is very sick!' She was too weak to stand and she lay curled like a dying kitten, trembling and mewling softly.

'Malaria,' said Sean, and squatted beside the child. 'She's riddled with it.'

'We've got chloroquine in the medical pack.' Claudia reached for it briskly.

'This is madness!' Sean growled. 'We can't lumber ourselves with this bunch. It's a nightmare!'

'Do shut up!' Claudia snapped. 'How many chloroquine do I give her? The instructions say, "For children under six years, consult a physician." Thanks a lot, we'll try two tablets.'

As they worked over the child, Claudia asked Miriam, 'What are their names? What do you call the children?'

The answer was so long and complicated that even Claudia looked daunted, but she recovered quickly.

'I'll never pronounce that,' she said finally. 'We'll call them Mickey and Minnie.'

'Walt Disney will sue,' Sean warned, but she ignored him and wrapped Minnie in her own blanket.

'You'll have to carry her,' she told Sean matter-of-factly.

'If the little bugger pees on me, I'll wring her neck,' he protested.

'And Alphonso can carry Mickey.'

Sean could see that Claudia's maternal instincts were thoroughly aroused, and his resentment of this additional burden that had been thrust upon them was tempered by the tonic the new responsibilities had been to her. Claudia had sloughed off her exhaustion and lethargy and was more vigorous and incisive than she had been since Job's death.

Sean lifted the child's almost weightless little body on to his back and strapped it there with a strip of the blanket. The heat of the fever soaked through the blanket as though she were a hot-water bottle. However, it was a familiar experience to the child who had been carried since infancy in this fashion, and she was immediately quiet and somnolent, 'I still can't believe what's happening to me,' Sean muttered. 'A goddamned unpaid nursemaid at my age.' But he plunged once more into the swamp.

Before the night had half run, Miriam had proved an asset that far outweighed the additional burden that the two children had placed upon them. She knew the river area with the intimacy of a swamp creature. She went ahead with Matatu and guided him through the labyrinth of islands and lagoons, picking out the secret pathways that saved them hours of wearisome exploration.

A little after midnight, when Orion the great hunter stood directly overhead with his bow at full draw, Miriam led them out onto the bank of the Rio Save and pointed out the ford through which a man could wade to the far bank.

They rested and the women tended the children and fed them morsels of the leguan meat. The chloroquine had taken effect and the little girl was cooler and less fretful. After a hurried meal, the men concealed themselves in the reed-beds and stared out across the black waters in which the stars were reflected like drowning fireflies.

'This is the most dangerous point,' Sean whispered. 'China was patrolling the river all day yesterday in the Hind and he'll be back at first light. We don't dare waste time here. We have to get across and get clear before sunrise.'

'They'll be waiting on the far side,' Alphonso demurred. 'They'll be expecting us.'

'That's right,' Sean agreed. 'They are here, but we know they are here. We'll leave the women on this side and go across to clear the far bank. We can't use firearms, it will have to be knives and wire. It's wet work tonight.' He used the old Scouts' term for it. '*Sebenza enamanzi*. In more ways than one, it will be wet work tonight.'

Sean's wire was a four-foot length of stainless steel, the single strand that he had cut from the winch cable of the Hercules aircraft before abandoning it. Job had carved two hardwood buttons and fixed them to either end of the wire to form grips. It rolled into a coil the size of a silver dollar and slipped easily into the grenade pocket of his webbing. Now Sean fished it out and unrolled it. He tested it, settling the wooden buttons between his fingers and jerking it tight, grunting with satisfaction at the familiar tension in the single resilient strand. Then he recoiled the wire and slipped it over his left wrist like a bangle.

The three of them stripped completely naked, wet clothing dripped water to alert an enemy or give him a hold in a hand-to-hand struggle. Each of them wore his knife on a short cord around his bare neck.

Sean went to where Claudia waited with the children in the reeds. When he kissed her, her lips were soft and warm and she clung to him briefly.

'Have you forgiven me?' he asked. For an answer she kissed him again.

'Come back soon,' she whispered.

The three men slid into the water soundlessly, keeping close contact, and dog-paddled quietly out from the bank letting the current carry them well down below the ford.

They landed in a bed of papyrus on the south bank and slid ashore on their bellies. Sean's naked white body gleamed in the starlight. He rolled in the sticky black swamp mud until it coated every inch of his skin, and then he scooped a double handful and rubbed it over his face.

'Ready?' he asked quietly, and freed the trench knife in its sheath at his throat.

'Let's go!'

They moved out away from the river and circled back upstream towards the ford. The swamps were confined to the north bank, while this side of the river was drier, and the forests grew almost to the river's edge. They stayed in the shadows beneath the trees for concealment. As they drew closer to the ford they moved more cautiously, spreading out, Sean in the middle and Alphonso and Matatu on the flanks.

Sean smelt Renamo before he saw them. It was the odour of stale native tobacco smoke and dried sweat in unwashed clothing and he froze, listening and staring ahead with all his soul concentrated on it.

A little ahead of him in the darkness, a man coughed softly and cleared his throat, and Sean placed him accurately. He sank down and touched the earth, sweeping a clear spot with his fingertips for his next footstep, so that no twig or dry leaf would betray him. One step at a time, he moved forward until he had the Renamo's head silhouetted against the starry sky. He was sitting behind an RPD machine-gun on its bipod, staring out across the river.

Sean waited and the minutes drew out, five then ten, each one a separate age. Then someone else yawned and stretched out on the left flank and immediately a third voice cautioned him to silence in an angry whisper.

'Three of them.' Sean memorized each position, and then withdrew as quietly and cautiously as he had come in.

On the edge of the forest Alphonso was waiting for him, and minutes later Matatu crept back to join them.

'Three,' Alphonso whispered.

'Yes, three,' Sean agreed.

'Four,' Matatu contradicted them both. 'There is another one just below the bank.' Matatu missed nothing and Sean accepted his estimate without reservation.

Only four Renamo in the ambush, Sean was relieved. He had expected more, but China must be spreading his men thinly to cover every path and every ford of the river.

'No noise,' Sean warned them. 'One shot and we'll have the entire army doing a war dance on our backs. Matatu, you take the one you found below the bank. Alphonso, the one in the reeds who spoke. I'll take the two in the centre.' He slipped the wire bangle off his left wrist and unrolled it, once more stretching and testing it between his hands to get the feel of it.

'Wait until you hear my man blow before you strike yours.' He reached out and lightly touched their shoulders, the ritual benediction, and then they separated and drifted away into the night, back towards the river.

The machine-gunner was exactly where Sean had left him, but as Sean moved in behind him a few scattered clouds obscured the stars, and Sean had to wait for them to clear. Every second's delay increased the chance of discovery and he was tempted to work only by sense of touch, but he restrained himself. As the sky cleared, he was glad he had done so. The sentry had removed his cap and was scratching the back of his head; that raised hand would have blocked the wire and prevented a clean kill. There would have been a scream, gunshots, and every Renamo within miles would have come down upon him.

He waited while the sentry relieved his itch, and re-adjusted his cap, then as he dropped his hands. Sean reached forward and looped the wire noose around his throat in one swift wrap. In the same movement he hauled back with the full strength of both his arms and shot his right knee between the man's shoulder-blades. The wire sliced through flesh and windpipe as though they were cheddar cheese. Sean felt the momentary check as the wire came up hard against the vertebrae of the neck, but he sawed with both hands, keeping all his weight on the wire, pushing with his knee.

The wire found the gap between the vertebrae and snicked clearly through it. The man's head fell forward, and tumbled into his own lap and the man blew. The air from his lungs rushed out through the open windpipe, in a soft

583

sigh. It was the sound he had told Matatu and Alphonso to wait for. He knew they would be taking their victims at this moment, but there was no sound until the man Sean had killed flopped forward and his carotid artery discharged onto the earth with a regular hiss like milk from the teat jetting into the bucket under the milkmaid's practised fingers.

The sound alerted the fourth Renamo, the only one still alive, and he called out in a puzzled tone.

'What is it, Alves? What are you doing?'

The question guided Sean to him, and he had the knife out of its sheath, holding it under-hand so the point went up at an acute angle under the man's ribs. Sean pinned him down with his left hand, holding his throat closed to prevent him screaming, working the knife with his other hand, opening the wound, twisting and turning the blade with all the strength of his right wrist.

In thirty seconds, it was over. The last tremors shook the body beneath him and Sean released him and stood up. Matatu was already beside him, with his skinning knife ready. The knife and his hands were wet. His own work was done and he had come to help Sean, but it was not necessary.

They waited for a full minute, listening for any alarm, perhaps there was another sentry that even Matatu might have overlooked, but apart from the croaking of the frogs in the reed-beds and the whine of mosquitos there was no sound.

'Search them,' Sean ordered. 'Take whatever we can use.'

One of the rifles, all of the ammunition, half a dozen grenades, spare clothing, all the food. They gathered it up swiftly.

'That's it,' Sean said. 'Dump the rest of it.' They dragged the bodies down the bank and pushed them out into the current, then dropped the heavy machine-gun and the rest of the discarded equipment into the deep water beyond the reeds.

Sean glanced at his watch. 'We are running out of time, we must bring the others across.'

Claudia and Miriam and the children were still in the reed-beds on the south bank where they had left them.

'What happened? We didn't hear anything.' Claudia hugged Sean's naked wet chest with relief.

'Nothing to hear,' Sean told her, and picked up the sleeping children, one on each arm.

Across the current, they formed a human stanchion, locking arms together, bracing each other against the heavy pull of the water that was as deep as Claudia's chin. Without this support the women would have been swept away. Even with it the crossing was arduous and they dragged themselves onto the south bank near exhaustion.

Sean would not let them rest longer than the few minutes it took to dry Minnie and wrap her in a jacket they had looted from one of the dead Renamo; then he had them up again and chivvied them onwards into the forest.

'We have to get clear of the river before sunrise. China will be back as soon as it is light.'

General China picked out the group of men on the riverbank at two hundred feet. As the helicopter slanted in towards them, the down-draught of its rotors furred the surface of the Save river with a dark ruffle.

The Portuguese pilot set the machine down at the edge of the forest on the south bank and China clambered out of the weapons cockpit and went striding down towards the river. Although his face was an expressionless mask, his anger boiled behind it and glinted in his eyes. He took the dark glasses from his breast pocket and concealed his eyes behind the lens.

The circle of men opened respectfully and China stepped through and looked down at the disembodied human head that lay on the muddy bank. It had been washed up amongst the reeds, the fresh-water crabs had nibbled it, and the water had leached the exposed flesh white and clouded the open eyes to opaque marbles, but the clean cut that had severed the neck was still as unmistakable as a hand-written signature.

'That's the white man's work,' China said softly. 'His Scouts called it "wet work", the wire was their trade-mark. When did it happen?'

'Last night.' Tippoo Tip tugged at his own beard with agitation. There had been no survivors of the ambush party, no one of which to make an example.

'You let them get through,' China accused coldly. 'You promised me they would never cross the river.'

'These dogs,' Tippoo Tip snarled. 'Those useless pigs.'

'They are your men,' China pointed out. 'And men take after those who command them. Their failure is your failure, General.'

It was said in front of his own staff, and Tippoo Tip growled with humiliation. He had made the promise and failed, and he shook with anger. He glared round at his men, looking for a victim, but they dropped their eyes and their faces were abject and obsequious. There was no relief there.

Suddenly he drew back his foot and swung a vicious kick at the severed head. The steel toe-cap of his boot crushed in the pulpy waterlogged nose.

'Dog!' he shouted, and booted the head again, sending it rolling down the bank. He followed it shouting with anger, aiming wild kicks at it, until it bounced like a football and plopped over the bank into the river.

He came back to General China, panting with rage.

'Very good, General,' China applauded him ironically. 'Very brave, what a pity you could not do the same to the white man.'

'I had every crossing of the river guarded,' Tippoo Tip

started, and then broke off as he noticed the crudely stitched gash on China's cheek for the first time and he grinned viciously. 'You have been wounded. What misfortune. It wasn't the fault of the white man, was it? Surely not. You are too cunning to let him injure you, General China, apart from your ear, of course.'

It was China's turn to bridle with fury. 'If only I had my own men here. These stupid dogs of yours couldn't wipe their own backsides.'

'One of your men is a stooge,' Tippoo Tip roared back at him. 'He's running with the white man, my men are not traitors. I have them in my hands.' He showed those great paws, shaking them in China's face, and General China closed his eyes for a moment and drew a deep breath. He realized that they were on the brink of an irretrievable breach, a few more words like those exchanged and he would have no further co-operation from this great bearded ape. One day he would kill him, but he needed him today.

Today the most important thing in General China's world was getting his hands on the white man, alive if possible, but dead if it had to be. Without Tippoo Tip's help, there was no chance of that. His anger and retribution must wait for another time and opportunity.

'General Tippoo Tip,' his tone was conciliatory, almost humble, 'please forgive me. I let my disappointment run over my good sense. I know you did your best for me. We are, both of us, victims of our own people's incompetence. I ask you to ignore my bad manners.'

Tippoo Tip was taken off-balance as China had intended and the angry words died in his open mouth.

'Even though these fools were unable to stop them, now at last we know exactly where they are. We have their fresh spoor, and a full day in which to follow it. Let us make the most of this opportunity. Let's get this tiresome business over with. Then I, and my helicopter, will be entirely at your disposal for the more important task ahead of us.'

He saw that he had picked the right words. Tippoo Tip's rage gradually gave way to that sly and avaricious expression that China knew so well.

'I have already called up my best trackers,' he agreed. 'I'll have fifty of my men on their spoor within the hour, men who can run an eland off its feet. The white man will be in your hands before the sun sets this evening. This time there will be no mistake.'

'Where are these trackers?' China demanded.

'I have radioed.'

'I will send the helicopter to fetch them.'

'That will save valuable time.'

They watched the Hind rise and bear away northwards, low across the darkly flowing waters of the Save river. As it disappeared they both turned to stare towards the south.

'You no longer control the territory south of the river,' China pointed out. 'These are the forests that you so cunningly relinquished to the Frelimo.' He pointed at the dense stands of hardwoods that stood tall against the southern sky.

'The river is my front line.' Tippoo Tip conceded reluctantly. 'But the nearest Frelimo forces are still many miles further south. My patrols cover this ground without interference from them. The men I am sending after the white man will catch him long before he gets into Frelimo-held territory.' Tippoo Tip broke off and then pointed along the riverbank. 'Ah, here they come.' A long double file of heavily armed guerrillas came trotting down the footpath towards them. 'Fifty of my best men. You will eat white chickens for dinner tonight. Don't worry, my friend. They are as good as on your plate already.'

The two platoons of Renamo halted and fell out on the bank, waiting for their trackers. China was a good judge of troops. He walked amongst them, and he recognized in them that eagerness and enthusiasm tempered by discipline and professionalism that is the peculiar mark of first-class bush fighters. For once he agreed with Tippoo Tip. These were hard men who could be relied upon to get the job done. China beckoned the section leaders across to him.

'You know who you are chasing?' he asked, and they nodded. 'The white man is as dangerous as a wounded leopard, but I want him alive. Do you understand?'

'We understand, General.'

'You have a radio. I want a report of your progress every hour on the command frequency.'

'Yes, General.'

'And when you have the quarry in sight, call me. I will come in the *henshaw*. I want to be there at the death.'

The section leaders looked across the river, their expressions alert, and moments later even with his impaired hearing, China picked up the whistle of the Hind's turbos returning from the north.

'If you do your job, you will be rewarded. But if you fail me, you will regret it. You will regret it deeply,' General China promised them.

As soon as the helicopter landed the two trackers clambered down with alacrity from the small rear cabin and Tippoo Tip shouted at them and pointed to the outgoing spoor that Sean and his party had left.

Watching the trackers begin their task, China was even more confident of the outcome. These two were good. They made a quick cast ahead and then came back to the centre and squatted over the spoor, whispering together softly, touching the faint tracks with the supple wands of wild willow they each carried, intent as a pair of bloodhounds taking the scent of the chase. When they stood up again a change had come over them. They were determined and businesslike. They turned to face the southern forests and went away at a run.

Behind them, the two full platoons of camouflaged Renamo assault troopers fanned out into their running formation and set their pace to match the trackers.

'The white woman can never keep up that speed,' Tippoo

Tip exulted. 'We will overtake them before they reach the Frelimo lines, we will have them before the end of this day. This time they'll not escape.' He turned back to China. 'Why don't we follow them in the helicopter?'

China hesitated. He did not want to explain the Hind's short-comings. It was better to let Tippoo Tip go on believing in its infallibility. He would not discuss with him the difficulty of bringing up sufficient fuel, nor the Hind's limited range even with full tanks, nor the fact that his Portuguese engineer had warned him that the turbos were long overdue for service, that the pilot had already reported a malfunction and loss of power in the starboard engine.

'I will wait here,' he said. 'When your men catch up with the white man, they will call on the radio. That is when I will follow them.'

China adjusted his dark glasses and sauntered across to the Hind. The pilot was waiting for him, leaning with assumed nonchalance against the camouflaged fuselage below the main cockpit.

'How is the engine behaving?' China asked in Portuguese.

'It is beginning to surge and miss. It needs to be worked on.'

'Fuel?'

'Main tanks are down to quarter. However, I still have the auxiliary.'

'The convoy of porters with the fuel will be at our forward base by tomorrow morning. The engineer can work on her tonight, but I have to have her on standby until dark. I'll need her when they catch up with the runaways.'

The pilot shrugged. 'I'll fly her, if you are willing to take the chance on that engine,' he agreed.

'Keep a listening watch on the radio,' China ordered. 'With luck it will all be over in a few hours.'

*

Sean realized that Claudia could not maintain this pace much further. She was running just ahead of him so he could study the changes in her that privation and hard living had brought about. She was so lean and wispy that her scanty threadbare shirt flapped around her flanks, and the legs of her trousers had been reduced by thorns and razor-edged grass to a fringe of tatters that hung halfway down her thighs; below that, the length of her legs was exaggerated by their extreme thinness, yet somehow they had retained their elegant high-bred lines. However, the thorns and sharp grass had wrought havoc on the exposed skin of her arms and legs. It looked as though she had been scourged by a cat-o'-nine-tails, some of the scratches were healed, others scabbed over, but a few still bled.

Her hair had grown into a lank sweat-tangled mop that thumped between her prominent bony shoulder-blades with each pace, and her back was so thin that he could have counted the knobs of her vertebrae beneath her shirt. The perspiration had soaked through in a dark line down her spine, and hard exercise had firmed her buttocks into a pair of Indiarubber balls in the sun-bleached cotton pants; through a tiny three-cornered tear a tender flash of her white bottom winked at him with each pace. Her legs were floppy with exhaustion, throwing out sideways, and her ankles were loose and wobbled under her.

He would have to let her rest very soon and yet she had not complained, not once in all the long tortured hours since they had left the river, and he grinned fondly as he remembered the spoilt arrogant bitch that had stepped off the Boeing at Harare airport so many aeons ago. This was a different woman, tough, determined and with a spirit as resilient as a Damascus steel blade. He knew that she would never give up, she would keep going until she killed herself. He reached forward and tapped her shoulder.

'Ease up, wench. We'll take ten.'

When she pulled up she was unsteady on those long legs and he put an arm around her shoulders to steady her. 'You're a ruddy marvel do you know that?' He eased her down to sit with her back against one of the leadwood trees and unscrewed the stopper on his water-bottle and passed it to her.

'Give Minnie to me. It's time for her chloroquine.' Claudia's voice was husky with tiredness. Sean swung the little girl off his back and placed her in Claudia's lap.

'Remember, ten minutes, that's all.'

Alphonso had taken the break to rig the radio, Mickey was squatting on one side of him, Miriam on the other. They watched with fascination as he tuned the set and began searching the bands. There was the crackle and buzz of static followed by some faint extraneous snatches of Afrikaans, and then an excited voice speaking in Shangane, very close and loud.

'Very close now,' it said, and the reply came immediately.

'Keep going hard. Push them. Don't let them escape. Call me as soon as you catch them.' That voice was unmistakable and they did not need the acknowledgement to confirm it.

'Very well, General China.'

The transmission ended and Sean and Alphonso exchanged a quick hard frown.

'Very close,' said the Shangane. 'We can't outrun them.'

'You might be able to get away,' Sean said, 'on your own.'

Alphonso hesitated and looked sideways at Miriam. The Shangane maid returned his glance with open trusting eyes and Alphonso coughed and scratched himself with embarrassment.

'I'll stay,' he muttered, and Sean laughed bitterly and said in English, 'Join the club, mate. That little witch didn't take long to hook you. These ruddy sheilas will be the death of all of us yet, you mark my words.'

Alphonso frowned, he did not understand and Sean

switched back into Shangane. 'Pack up the radio. If you are going to stand with us, we'd best find a good place to do it. Your dung-eating Renamo brothers are going to be with us very soon.'

Sean turned and looked across at Matatu, and instantly he was on his feet.

'That was China on the radio,' he told him in Swahili.

'He hisses like a cobra,' Matatu nodded.

'His men are on our spoor, they boast to him that they are very close. Are there any more tricks we can use now, old friend?'

'Fire?' Matatu suggested, but without conviction, and Sean shook his head.

'The wind is against us, we'd cook ourselves if we torched the forest.'

Matatu hung his head. 'If we keep the women and children with us, there are no more tricks,' he admitted. 'We are slow, and we leave a spoor that a blind man can follow in a moonless night.' He shook his small grizzled head miserably. 'The only trick we have left is to fight them, and after that we are dead, my *Bwana*.'

'Go back, Matatu. Find how close behind us they really are. We will go ahead and find a good place to fight them.' He touched the little man's shoulder, and then let him go. Sean watched him disappear amongst the tree-trunks and then deliberately altered his expression before he turned to Claudia, striking a lighter more carefree pose and putting a lift in his tone.

'How's our patient?' he asked. 'She looks pretty chirpy to me.'

'The chloroquine has done wonders.' Claudia bounced the child on her lap and as if to confirm her improvement, Minnie stuck her thumb in her mouth and smiled shyly around it at Sean. He felt that smile tug at him with wholly unexpected poignancy.

Claudia laughed. 'No female is immune to your fatal charms. You have collected yourself another fan.'

'Typical woman, all she really wants is a free ride.' But he stroked the child's soft woolly little head. 'All right, sweetness, your horsey is ready to go.'

Trustingly Minnie held out both arms and he swung her up on to his back and strapped her there.

Claudia pulled herself stiffly to her feet and for a moment leaned against him. 'Do you know something? You are a much nicer person than you pretend to be.'

'Fooled you, didn't I?'

'I'd like to see you with a baby of your own,' she whispered.

'Now you really terrify me. Let's go before you come up with any more crazy ideas like that one.'

But the idea lingered with him as they ran on through the forest, a son of his own from this woman.

He had never even thought about that before, and then, as though to complement the idea, he felt a tiny hand reach across his shoulder from behind and touch his beard, stroking it as lightly as an alighting butterfly. Minnie was reciprocating that caress he had bestowed on her a few minutes earlier and for a moment his throat closed up and made it difficult for him to breathe. He took her tiny hand in his, and it was silken and fragile as the wing of a humming-bird and he was overcome with a feeling of terrible regret. Regret that there would never be a son, he accepted that at last, nor a daughter. It was almost over. The hunting pack was very close behind. They could never outrun them. There was no escape, all they could hope for was a good place in which to make the final stand. After that there was nothing, no escape, no future.

He was so wrapped up in his melancholy that he had run out into the open before he realized it. Claudia pulled up so sharply in front of him that he almost ran into her.

He stopped at her side and they looked about them with puzzled uncertainty.

The forest had been laid waste. For as far ahead as they could see the great hardwoods had been swept away as though by a hurricane. Only the stumps remained, raw and bleeding gum as red as heart's blood. The earth was torn and scarred, where the huge trunks had come crashing down. Bright piles of sawdust remained where their branches had been stripped and the logs cut into lengths, and then between the windrows of discarded branches and wilting boughs were the drag roads along which the precious timber had been hauled away.

Miriam stopped beside Sean. 'This is where my people were forced to work,' she said softly. 'Frelimo came and took them to cut the trees. They chained them together and made them work until the meat was torn from the bones of their hands. They beat them like oxen and worked them until they fell and could not rise.'

'How many people?' Sean asked. 'So many trees have been destroyed.'

'Perhaps a man or woman died for every tree,' Miriam whispered. 'They took everybody, thousands upon tens of thousands.' She pointed to the horizon. 'They work far south now and they leave no tree standing.'

Sean felt the anger beginning to rise through his amazement. This was destruction on a scale that affronted the law of nature and the sanctity of life itself. It was not just that those trees had taken three hundred years to reach their full majesty, and had been destroyed with a few hours' callous work with the axe blades. It was more, much more. This forest was the source and fountain of myriad forms of life, insect and bird and mammal and reptile, of man himself. In this vast devastation, all would perish.

It did not end there. With his own fate determined, with a term and a number of the hours that remained of his own life, Sean was overtaken by a prophetic melancholia. He realized that the destruction of this forest was symbolic of the predicament of the entire continent. In a few fleeting decades, Africa had been overtaken by its own inherent savagery. The checks that had been placed upon it by a century of colonialism had been struck off. Chains perhaps those checks had been, but once freed of them, the peoples of Africa were rushing headlong, with almost suicidal abandon, towards their own destruction.

Sean felt himself shaking with impotent rage at the folly of it and at the same time saddened, sickened almost unto death, by the terrible tragedy of it all.

'If I have to die,' he thought, 'then it's best to do so before I see everything I love, the land, the animals, the people, all of it destroyed.'

With his arm round Claudia's thin shoulders and the little black girl strapped on his back, he turned and looked back the way they had come and, at that moment, Matatu came scampering out of the forest behind them.

There was desperate urgency in his gait and the fear of death in his small wizened features.

'They are very close, my *Bwana*. They have two trackers leading them. I watched them work, we will not throw them off. They are good.'

'How many troopers with them?' With an effort Sean cast off the oppressive mantle of dejection.

'As many as the grass on the plains of Serengeti,' Matatu replied. 'They ran like a pack of wild dogs on the hunt and they are hard men and fierce. Even the three of us will not stand too long against them.'

Sean roused himself and looked around him. The cut line in which they stood was a natural killing ground, devoid of cover except for the knee-high stumps of hardwood. The open ground stretched two hundred metres wide to where the dead wood was piled in untidy windrows, the leaves long withered and browned, the branches forming a natural barricade.

'We'll make our stand there,' Sean decided swiftly and signalled Alphonso forward. They crossed the open ground at a run, bunched up with the two women in the middle. Miriam was dragging her little brother along by one arm. Alphonso ran protectively beside them. The big Shangane was heavily burdened with the radio and the packs of ammunition and stores they had picked up from the ambush at the Save river, nevertheless he had also carried Mickey whenever the boy tired, only setting him down on his own feet for short intervals. The three Shanganes, man, woman and boy child, had very swiftly formed their own distinct core within the band, drawn together by tribal loyalties and natural physical attraction. Sean knew he could rely on Alphonso to take care of his own, and that allowed him to concentrate on his particular charges, Claudia and Matatu and now the little girl.

Alphonso needed no orders. Like Sean he had a soldier's eye for terrain and he ran unerringly towards a section of the tumble of discarded branches that formed a natural redoubt, and which commanded the best field of fire across the cut line.

Swiftly they settled in, dragging some of the heavier branches into place to strengthen the position, laying out their weapons and spare ammunition, making their very limited preparations to stand off the first rush of the attackers.

Claudia and Miriam had taken the children a little further back to where a hollow in the earth and two especially large tree-stumps formed some sort of shelter. His own preparations complete, Sean crossed to them quickly, and squatted beside Claudia.

'As soon as the shooting starts, I want you to take Miriam and the children and run for it,' he told her. 'Keep heading south.' He broke off as he realized that she was shaking her head, and her jaw was clenched obstinately.

'I've run far enough,' she told him. 'I'm staying with

you.' She laid her hand on his arm. 'No, don't argue. It would be a waste of time.'

'Claudia!'

'Please don't,' she forestalled him. 'There isn't much time left, don't spend it arguing.'

She was right, of course. To try and run further on her own was pointless, not with two children to care for and a team of fifty Renamo on her spoor. He nodded.

'All right,' he agreed, and took the Tokarev pistol from his belt, cocked it and carefully engaged the safety-catch. 'Take this.'

'What's that for?' She stared at the weapon with distaste.

'I think you know what it's for.'

'The same way as Job?'

He nodded. 'It would be easier than going China's way.'

She shook her head. '1 couldn't,' she whispered. 'If there is no other way, at the end, won't you do it for me?'

'I'll try,' he said. 'But I don't think I'll have the guts. Here, take it, just in case.' Reluctantly she accepted the pistol and tucked it into her belt.

'Now kiss me,' she said.

Matatu's whistle interrupted their embrace. 'I love you,' Sean murmured in her ear.

'I'll love you . . .' she replied, 'through all eternity.'

He left her and crawled back into the piles of dead wood. At Matatu's side he sank down and peered out through the chink between two branches towards the edge of the forest.

For many minutes he saw nothing, and then there was a shadowy flit of movement amongst the boles of the standing hardwood, and Sean laid his right hand on the pistol grip of the AKM rifle and raised it until the buttstock touched his cheek.

The silence drew out in the languorous sunlit afternoon while they waited. No bird sang, no creature moved, until at last there was a muted bird whistle from the edge of the forest and a man shape detached itself and flitted into the opening, showing for just a small part of a second and then disappearing behind one of the thick tree-stumps. As soon as it was gone another broke from the tree-line a hundred metres further to the left and darted forward. This one also disappeared and almost immediately, out on the right, a third Renamo guerrilla emerged.

'Three only,' Sean murmured, they were not going to expose more men than that and these were good. They advanced in fleeting rushes, never two together, widely spread out and wary as old tom-leopards coming in to the bait.

'What a pity,' Sean thought. 'We are only going to get one out of this lot. I had hoped for a better killing to get us off the mark.' He concentrated on the advancing scouts, trying to pick the most dangerous of their enemies.

'Probably the one in the centre,' he decided, and almost immediately had his choice confirmed as he saw the flick of the man's hand from behind the stump that hid him. He was signalling one of the others forward, co-ordinating the advance, and that marked him as the main man, the one to take out first.

'Let him come in close,' Sean told himself. The AKM was no sniping rifle and he didn't trust its accuracy over a hundred metres. He waited, willing the man in, watching for him over the sights of the rifle.

The Renamo jumped up and kept coming. Sean saw that he was young, mid-twenties, with bandoliers of ammunition over both shoulders, and a Rastafarian hairstyle, ribbons of camouflage rag braided into his hair. There was an Arabian cast to his features, and an amber patina to his skin, a good-looking lad except that his left eye was a little askew and it gave his face a sly knowing expression.

Close enough to see the cast in his eye was close enough. Sean lined up carefully on the tree-stump behind which the Renamo had disappeared and drew a breath, exhaled half of it and let the first joint of his right forefinger rest lightly on the trigger.

The Renamo popped up into his sights. Sean took him low, deliberately declining a clean kill. He knew what damage the 7.62 bullet would do as it plunged through his belly at over three thousand feet a second, and he knew from bitter experience just how unnerving it was to have one of your comrades lying in no-man's land with his guts shot out screaming for water and mercy. In the Scouts they called them 'warblers', and a warbler in good voice could inhibit an attack almost as effectively as a well-placed RPD machine-gun.

Sean heard the bullet hit the Renamo in the stomach, that meaty thump like a watermelon dropped on a stone floor, and he went down out of sight in the trash and debris.

Instantly there was a heavy volley of rifle fire from the edge of the forest, but it was obvious from the wild aim that they had not spotted Sean and the firing stuttered swiftly into silence. Renamo was conserving ammunition, a sure sign of their discipline and training. Second-rate African troops started firing at the beginning of a contact and kept shooting until their last round was expended.

'These lads know their business,' Sean confirmed Matatu's estimate. 'We aren't going to hold them long.' The two guerrillas were still pinned down in the middle of the cut line, and there was a low hollow groan from out there as the first pangs of the belly wound hit the downed man.

'Sing to us, Daddy-oh!' Sean encouraged him. 'Let your pals know how it hurts.' But he was studying the forest edge, trying to get some hint of the next play before it developed.

'Now, they'll make a pincer move to try to out-flank us,' he guessed. 'But which flank, left or right?' And as if in answer he saw a tiny blur of movement in the forest. One of them was moving right.

'Alphonso,' Sean called softly. 'They are going to try the right. Stay here. Hold the centre.'

Sean crawled back, until he was hidden by the high

windrow of brush. Then he rose to his feet, and ran doubled over, out to the right flank.

Four hundred metres out he dropped to his knees and crawled forward, finding another position facing the forest wall. He wriggled in behind a protective stump and marshalled his breathing, watching the tree-line, the AKM set on automatic fire, and his thumb on the safety-catch.

He had anticipated the next move almost perfectly, the flanking movement came out of the forest only a hundred metres further to his right. A detachment of eight troopers, they came all together, trying to reach the cover of the windrow in a single concerted rush, and Sean let them get halfway across the cut line.

'This is better. I should be able to get a brace out of this covey,' he told himself. He had them in enfilade, his fire would be coming in from their flank and sweeping the line. He picked out the section leader who was running slightly ahead of the line. Sean led him by a man's length so that he would run into the stream of fire, taking him at knee height because the AKM rode up brutally in automatic and he held the trigger down.

The section leader dropped as though he had fallen over a trip wire, and the two men following him ran into the same burst. Sean saw the bullets hit them. One of them took it in the shoulder, and a puff of dust flew from his camouflage tunic to mark the strike. The other was a head shot, a clean hit in the temple and as he went down his baseball cap fluttered from his head like a maimed dove.

'Three.' Sean changed magazines, pleased with the result. He had expected one and hoped for two.

The rest of them had turned and were racing back for the forest, the attack broken completely. Sean got off another quick burst before they reached the trees, and thought he saw one of them hunch his shoulders and lurch to the shot, but he kept going and disappeared.

Almost immediately there was another burst of firing

back in the centre, and Sean jumped up from behind his stump and ran back to help Alphonso.

As he ran somebody opened up on him from the forest. Shot passed close to his head with that vicious whiplashing sound that made his adrenalin spurt hotly into his bloodstream. He ducked his head and ran on. He was enjoying himself, riding the curling wave of his terror.

In the centre there was a sharp fire-fight raging. Renamo was trying to rush the open ground, and they were almost across when Sean fell flat in the brush near Alphonso and added the weight of his fire to the defence. The attack wavered and broke, just short of the row of deadwood behind which they lay. The Renamo went ducking and dodging back between the tree-stumps with AK fire kicking up dust around them.

'Two!' Alphonso shouted across at Sean. 'I put two of them down.' But Matatu was tugging at Sean's arm and pointing out to the left flank. Sean was just able to get a glimpse of another group of Renamo cutting across the cut line and reaching cover on this side. The attacks on the right and centre had been diversions. Now there were a dozen or so Renamo coming in behind them, within minutes they would be surrounded, pinned down helplessly.

'Alphonso, they have got in our rear,' Sean called across.

'There was nothing we could do to stop them,' Alphonso answered. 'There are too many, we are too few.'

'I am going back to hold the rear, I'll be with the women.'

'They won't attack again,' Alphonso told him flatly. 'Now that they have us surrounded they will wait for the *henshaw* to come.'

A burst of automatic fire raked the pile of deadwood, and they ducked instinctively.

'They are only shooting to hold us,' Alphonso called. 'They don't have to risk losing more men.'

'How long until the helicopter arrives?' Sean wanted his own estimate confirmed.

'Not more than an hour,' Alphonso told him with finality. 'Then it will all be over very quickly.'

Alphonso was right. Against the Hind, there was no defence, no more tricks to play.

'I'm leaving you here,' Sean repeated, and crawled back to the hollow in which the women were concealed.

Claudia had Minnie on her lap, but she looked up expectantly as Sean slid down the shallow side of the hollow.

'They've got in behind us,' Sean told her shortly. 'We are surrounded.' He dumped the empty AK magazines in front of her. 'There are boxes of spare ammo in Alphonso's pack. You know how to fill these.'

It would keep her busy. The next hour was going to be difficult to live through. Sean crawled to the back lip of the hollow and peered over the edge.

He saw something move in the dried brown leaves fifty paces ahead of him and he fired a quick burst into the brush. His fire was returned from three or four positions in their rear. AK bullets cracked overhead and behind him Minnie wailed with fright. The minutes dragged past slowly, the silence broken every few seconds by sporadic bursts of holding fire from the Renamo positions.

Claudia crawled up beside Sean and stacked the replenished magazines at his right elbow.

'How many boxes left?' he asked.

'Ten,' she told him, and pressed a little closer to him.

It didn't really matter that there were only two hundred rounds remaining in Alphonso's pack. Sean looked up at the sky, any moment now they would hear the whistle of the Hind's turbos.

Claudia read his thoughts, and she groped for his hand. Lying in the hot African sun, they held hands and waited. There was nothing left to say, nothing more that they could do. No defence, however feeble. All that remained was to wait for the inevitable.

Matatu touched Sean's leg. It wasn't necessary to say

anything. Sean cocked his head and picked up the sound. It was higher and steadier than the soughing of the afternoon breeze in the forest-tops.

Claudia squeezed his hand very hard, digging her fingernails into his palm. She had heard it also.

'Kiss me,' she whispered. 'One last time.' And he laid the rifle down and rolled onto his side to take her in his arms. They strained together, holding with all their strength.

'If I have to die,' Claudia whispered, 'I'm glad it will be like this.' And Sean felt her press the loaded Tokarev into his hand.

'Goodbye, my darling,' she said.

He knew that he had to do it, but he did not know where he would find the courage.

The sound of the Hind's engines was rising into a high penetrating shriek.

He slid the safety-catch to the 'off' position and lifted the Tokarev gently. Claudia's eyes were tightly closed and she had turned her head half away. A little sweat-damp tendril of dark hair hung down in front of her ear, and he could see the artery beating under the creamy skin of her temple that the curl had protected from the sun. It was the most difficult task he had ever set himself, but he raised the muzzle of the Tokarev towards her temple.

There was a shattering explosion of a shell-burst on the lip of their shelter. Instinctively Sean pulled Claudia down to protect her. He thought for a moment that the Hind had opened fire, but that was impossible, it was still out of sight and range.

A further series of explosions crashed out in rapid succession, and Sean lowered the pistol and released Claudia. He rolled to the lip of the hollow, and saw that a heavy barrage of fire was sweeping the Renamo positions. Mortar fire, Sean recognized the characteristic bursts of three-inch mortar shells and then the rushing smoke trails of RPG rockets amongst the trees of the forest. The rattling din of small arms drowned out even the sound of the approaching Hind. The entire situation had changed.

Suddenly they were in the midst of a battle, and Sean saw figures running wildly amongst the windrows and stumps, firing as they ran.

'Frelimo!' Matatu was tugging at Sean's arm and screeching with excitement. 'Frelimo!'

Only then Sean understood. Their desultory exchange of fire with the Renamo pursuers must have called up a large force of Frelimo troops who had been massed in the immediate vicinity, probably preparing to attack the Save river line.

Now the fifty Renamo guerrillas suddenly found themselves attacked by a vastly superior Frelimo force. Judging by the intensity of fire, Sean estimated that there were several hundred Frelimo out there in the forest, front-line regular troops in battalion strength.

He saw the small party of Renamo who had cut them off abandon their positions amongst the dead wood of the cut line, and scuttle away in wild disorder with mortar shells bursting amongst them. Sean snatched up the AKM and helped them on their way with a long burst. One of the running men fell and flopped around into the brush like a beached catfish.

Then he spotted a sweep line of Frelimo infantry coming in from the left at a run. Their camouflage field dress was East German issue, the blotches of green and brown distinctly different from the Renamo tiger-stripes.

Renamo or Frelimo were equally dangerous for them. Sean pulled Claudia down beside him.

'Don't move. The Frelimo probably don't know we are here. They might just chase off the Renamo and overlook us. We've still got a chance.'

Minnie was wailing loudly, terrified by the uproar. Sean called urgently to Miriam, 'Keep her quiet. Stop her screaming.'

The Shangane girl pulled the child down beside her and covered her mouth and nose with her hand, cutting off her wails abruptly.

Sean raised one eye above the lip of the hollow and saw the Frelimo sweep line still bearing down on them, tough-looking troopers, firing from the hip as they came. They would overrun the hollow within seconds. He raised the AKM. Their salvation had been fleeting, the only real change was that now they would be killed by Frelimo rather than by Renamo.

As he raised the AKM and aimed at the belly of the nearest of the oncoming Frelimo troopers, the target was blotted out by a tall curtain of flying dust and from the sky above came the thunderous roll of the heavy 12.7mm cannon. The Frelimo sweep line dissolved before Sean's eyes, blown away by the Hind's concentrated fire, and the dust rolled over the hollow in which they lay, concealing them from the air in those crucial seconds that the Hind hovered above them.

Now all was chaos, two forces inextricably mixed up in the deep forest, mortar and rocket fire crashing through the trees, while over the battlefield the Hind hovered, sending in rockets and bursts of cannonfire to make the confusion complete.

Sean slapped Matatu on the shoulder. 'Fetch Alphonso,' he ordered, and the little Ndorobo disappeared into the dust and gunfire, to emerge only a minute later with the huge Shangane close behind him.

'Alphonso, get ready to make another run for it,' Sean told him tersely. 'Frelimo and Renamo are giving each other a full go out there. We'll try to sneak away before the Hind spots us.' Sean broke off and sniffed the air, and then raised himself quickly on his knees to look back.

Already the air around them was turning a dirty grey, and above the din of battle and the whine of turbos, Sean heard the first faint crackle of burning brush.

'Fire!' he snapped. 'And it's upwind of us!'

One of the exploding rockets had ignited the rows of piled deadwood, and now a dense cloud of smoke rolled down over the hollow where they lay, stinging their eyes and making them cough and choke.

'Now, we have no choice, it's run or cook.' The crackle and roar of the flames was already drowning out the din of battle. Dimly they heard the shrieks of wounded men caught up in the path of the surging fire.

'Let's go!' Sean swept Minnie onto his back and the child locked both arms around his neck and clung to him like a little black flea. Sean pulled Claudia to her feet. Alphonso had Mickey sitting perched on his shoulders, his legs dangling over the bulky radio pack. Miriam was at his side clinging to the arm which held his rifle.

The smoke rolled over them, thick as oil, and they ran with the wind, bunched up to keep contact with each other. The smoke filled their lungs and blotted out the sky, screening them from the fighting men in the forest around them and from the helicopter gunship that hovered above them, and the fire raged close behind them driving them on wildly, but gaining on them with every second.

Sean felt the heat fan the back of his neck, and Minnie squeaked as a flying spark touched her cheek. Gasping for breath, Claudia stumbled and sank to her knees, but Sean hauled her to her feet and dragged her onwards.

Sean was suffocating, each breath burned all the way down into his lungs. They couldn't go much farther. The heat licked their skin and flying sparks dashed against them and the child on Sean's back screamed in agony and pawed ineffectually at her tortured body as though assailed by a swarm of wasps. She lost her grip and would have fallen, but Sean snatched her off his back and carried her under one arm.

Suddenly, they were into another open cut line. Only dead stumps surrounded them, standing like tombstones in the dense banks of rolling smoke, and the sandy earth beneath their feet had been ploughed up by the teams of loggers.

'Down!' Sean pushed Claudia flat on the ground and placed Minnie in her arms.

The child was struggling wildly. 'Hold her still!' Sean shouted and stripped off his shirt.

'Lie flat, face down!' he ordered and obediently Claudia rolled on her stomach, holding Minnie under her. Sean wrapped the shirt around both their heads to filter out the smoke and sparks and soot. He tore the stopper out of his water-bottle and soaked the shirt, splashing their hair and soaking their clothing.

Minnie was still shrieking and struggling, but Claudia held her down firmly. Sean knelt beside them and scooped loose sand over them, burying them under a mound of earth, like one of those beach games that children play. The smoke was thinner closer to the earth, they could still breathe. Alphonso had seen what he was doing and followed his example, burying Miriam and her little brother in the sand nearby.

Live sparks swirled through the blinding clouds of smoke and settled on Sean's bare skin. They stung like the poisonous bites of safari ants. Sean felt his beard begin to frizzle and his eyeballs drying out in the heat. He emptied his pack on to the ground and pulled the empty canvas bag over his head, poured the contents of the second water-bottle over his torso, and then fell on his back and scooped the loose sand over himself and lay still.

With his head low to the ground the air was breathable, just sufficient oxygen in it to keep him conscious, but his head buzzed and swirled dizzily and the heat came at him in crushing blasts. He smelled the canvas bag over his head begin to smoulder and the thin layer of sand that covered his body scalded him like a pot fresh from the furnace. He heard the roar of the flames rise to a crescendo, the dry branches crackled like rifle fire in the inferno. The fire was in the windrows all around them, but the wind, generated by its own heat, drove it swiftly onwards.

It swept past them, the roaring subsided, and for an instant the smoke clouds opened allowing them a fleeting gasp of sweet air, but the heat around them was still so fierce that Sean dared not shake off the protective layer of sand that covered his body.

Gradually the heat dissipated, and the gusts of cooler sweeter air became more frequent. Sean sat up and lifted the canvas pack from his head. His skin burned as though acid had been splattered upon it, and the bright red spots where sparks had touched him would soon be blisters.

He crawled to the mound of earth that covered Claudia and the child and scraped it away from their heads. The shirt had kept their mouths and noses clear, and when they sat up and shook off the sand, he saw that they had come off much better than either he or Alphonso had. The fire had run past them, but the air around them was still so thick with smoke that the sky was blotted out.

Sean hauled them to their feet. 'We have to get well away before the smoke clears,' he croaked hoarsely. His throat felt as though he had swallowed a handful of crushed glass, and tears spilled down his sooty scorched cheeks.

Clinging together, picking their way through the blackened, smouldering landscape, like a party of bedraggled soot-covered phantoms, they limped through the swirling fog of smoke. The earth was hot as a flow of volcanic lava, scorching the soles of their boots, but they carried the children, and avoided the piles of glowing ash.

Twice they heard the Hind above them, but although they peered up with red and weeping eyes, they caught not a glimpse of it through the drifting blue clouds and there was no sign of pursuit by either Renamo or Frelimo. The opposing forces had been scattered and swept away by the flames.

'The little bugger has asbestos-lined feet,' Sean muttered, as he watched Matatu dance ahead of them through the thinning smoke. On Sean's back, Minnie whimpered fretfully with the pain of her blisters and at their first rest stop Sean gave her half an aspirin and a swallow from their one remaining bottle of water.

The sunset that evening filled the heavens with flaming crimsons and sombre purples. In the darkness, they lay huddled together, too exhausted and weakened by the smoke to post sentries, and their sleep was interrupted by bouts of painful lung-tearing coughing.

In the dawn, the wind veered into the south but the smoke still hung over the land like a heavy river-mist, reducing visibility to a few hundred feet.

Sean and Claudia treated the children first, smearing their blisters and burns with yellow iodine paste, and though Mickey bore it with the stoicism of a Shangane warrior, the little girl whined with the sting of the iodine and Sean had to take her on his lap and blow on her injuries to cool them.

Once the children were taken care of, the women tended their men. The burns on Sean's chest and back were all superficial, but Claudia treated them with a gentleness that reflected her gratitude and her complete love.

Neither of them spoke of that moment when he had lifted the Tokarev pistol to her temple. They probably never would, but both of them would be conscious of it for ever more. It would always be there between them: for Sean the most horrific moment of his life, worse even than that of Job's death; for Claudia, an affirmation of his devotion to her. She knew that he would have found the strength to do it, but she knew also that it would have cost him dearer than the sacrifice of his own life. She needed no more proof of his love.

The children needed water desperately, they were

desiccated by the heat of the flames and the smoke. Sean gave half the remaining water to them, and shared the remainder disproportionately amongst the adults, most of it to the two women and a bare taste to the men.

'Matatu,' he said in a harsh gravelly whisper, 'if you don't find us water before nightfall, then we are as dead as if the *henshaw* had blown us into dust with its cannons.'

They limped on through the blackened and smouldering forest, and in the late afternoon Matatu led them to a shallow clay pan, surrounded by the smoking stumps of burned-out trees. In the centre of the pan, thick with black ash and the charred bodies of small creatures, of snakes and rats and civet cats that had fled there for protection from the flames, was a puddle of filthy water.

Sean strained it through his shirt and they drank it as though it were nectar, groaning with the pleasure through their scorched and smoke-abraded throats. When they had drunk until their bellies ached, they scooped the water over their heads and let it soak their clothing, and they laughed weakly with the joy of it.

A mile beyond the waterhole, they reached the line at which the wind had changed and held the fire, driving it back upon itself. They left behind them the devastation of black ash and smouldering stumps and camped that night amongst the confusion of withered dead branches where the logging gangs had wrought almost as much destruction as the flames had done.

For the first time since the fire, Alphonso rigged the radio aerial, and they gathered round the set and listened for General China's taunts and threats. They all stiffened instinctively as they recognized his voice, but he was talking in Shangane and they could hear the sound of the helicopter's engines in the background. His transmissions were terse and enigmatic, and the replies from his subordinates were equally abrupt and business-like.

'What do you think he is up to?' Sean asked Alphonso, and the Shangane shook his head.

'It sounds like he is moving troops into fresh positions.' But there was no conviction in his tone.

'He hasn't given up?' Sean said. 'He may have lost our spoor in the burn, but I don't think he has given up.'

'No,' Alphonso agreed. 'I know him well. He has not given up. He will follow us all the way. General China is a man who hates very well. He will not let us go.'

'We are in Frelimo-held territory now. Do you think he will follow us in here?'

Alphonso shrugged. 'He has the *henshaw*, he does not have to worry too much about Frelimo. I think he will follow us wherever we go.'

General China made his last transmission and it was obvious he was arranging for refuelling. He had changed to Portuguese and the reply seemed to be from a ground engineer in the same language. Alphonso translated.

'The porters have arrived. We now have reserves of two thousand litres.'

China's voice, 'What about the spare booster pump?'

'It's here, my General,' the engineer again. 'I can change it tonight.'

'We must be airworthy again by first light tomorrow.'

'I will have it ready by then. I guarantee it, General.'

'Very well, I'll be landing in a few minutes. Be ready to begin work immediately,' China ordered and then signed off.

They listened for another ten minutes, until it was fully dark, but there were no further transmissions and Alphonso reached across to turn off the radio. On an impulse Sean prevented him doing so and instead switched frequencies. Almost at once, he picked up the South African military traffic. It was much stronger now, they were that much closer to the border on the Limpopo river, and to Sean the sound of Afrikaans was a comfort and a promise.

After a few minutes, Sean sighed and switched off the set. 'Alphonso, you take the first sentry. Go!' he ordered.

With the threat of aerial surveillance reduced, Sean decided to resume daylight travel, and every mile they covered towards the south the signs left by the logging gangs were fresher and more numerous.

On the third day after the fire, Matatu led them on a wide detour. The hardwood stumps had been cut very recently and they were still weeping sap. The leaves on the discarded branches piled in tall windrows had not dried out and were still green and pliant. Matatu cautioned them to silence and as they trudged on between the piled rows of trash, they heard not far off, the whine of chain saws, and the doleful work chant of the labour gangs.

The forest around them was full of human activity, and the soft soil carried the prints of thousands of bare feet and the skid marks of heavy logs being dragged and man-handled towards the rough logging roads. However, so skilfully did Matatu shepherd them through the torn and despoiled forests that it wasn't until the fourth day of travel that they actually caught sight of any other human beings.

Leaving the others to eat and rest well concealed under a shaggy pile of newly cut branches, Sean and Matatu sneaked forward to the edge of a natural open glade in the forest and through the binoculars Sean lay and watched the Frelimo logging gangs at work on the far side of the opening. Hundreds of black men and women, some of them no more than children, were toiling in teams, supervised by guards in Frelimo camouflage battledress.

The guards all carried AK rifles slung on their shoulders, but they wielded the long hippo-hide whips, the savage African sjambok, which they plied to the naked backs and legs of their charges. The snap of the lash on bare flesh and the agonized yelps carried across five hundred yards of open ground to where Sean and Matatu lay.

The labour gangs were piling the roughly trimmed logs into tall pyramid-shaped stacks, half of them straining and heaving on the heavy ropes while the others pushed against the huge timber baulks from the lower side. The guards urged them to greater effort, calling out the verses of the work-chant to which the gangs responded with a deep melancholy chorus and a concerted heave on the heavy manila ropes.

While Sean watched through his binoculars, one of the huge logs was laboriously hoisted towards the pinnacle of the stack, but before it could be rolled securely into place, one of the ropes parted and the log slewed sideways and went bouncing and rumbling down the side of the pyramid. Wailing with terror the labour gang broke and fled before it, but some of the weaker ones were not fast enough and the log steamrolled over them. Sean heard their shrill shrieks snuffed out and the crackle of their bones like dried twigs being fed through a clothes mangle.

It was too much even for a soldier's hardened stomach, and he touched Matatu's shoulder and they crept away, back to where they had left the others.

That afternoon they passed close to the labour camps, a vast collection of primitive lean-to huts that stank of wood-smoke, open latrines and human misery.

'The cheapest African commodity these days is black flesh,' Sean told Claudia grimly.

'If you told people back home about this, they just simply wouldn't understand what you were talking about. It's just so contrary to our own experience,' said Claudia.

At this time of day, the camps were almost deserted. All the able-bodied were at work in the forest and only the sick and the dying lay under the crude open shelters. Sean sent Matatu into the camp to scavenge, and he must have found one of the field kitchens and eluded the cooks. He returned with a half sack of uncooked maize-meal slung over his shoulder.

They ate handfuls of maize porridge that evening, huddled round the radio, listening to General China's voice on the Renamo command frequency.

Once again after General China had made his last transmission at nightfall, Sean switched to the South African military frequency and listened for almost half an hour, learning the voices and call signs of the various units within range. At last, he felt he had identified the South African border headquarters. It was using the call-sign 'Kudu', that beautiful spiral-horned antelope of the bushveld.

Sean waited patiently for a lull in the military traffic and then he keyed the microphone and spoke in Afrikaans.

'"Kudu", this is "Mossie". This is a storm sending. Do you read me, "Kudu"? This is "Mossie"!'

A storm sending was the call for a top priority message. It was the radio procedure that they had used back in the days of the Rhodesian bush war. He hoped that the South African commander's military experience went back that far. 'Mossie' in Afrikaans was a sparrow and had been Sean's call-sign in those far-off days.

A long silence followed Sean's transmission, in which the static echoed in the void of the stratosphere, and Sean thought that his call had been lost. He lifted the microphone to call again just as the radio came to life.

'Station calling "Kudu",' said a voice, heavy with suspicion. 'Say again your call-sign.'

'"Kudu", this is "Mossie". I repeat "Mossie". Mike Oscar Sierra Sierra India Echo. I request a relay to General De La Rey, the deputy minister of law and order.'

Lothar De La Rey had been Sean's control back in the seventies. Since then he had risen to high political office. 'Kudu' would surely know who he was, and hesitate to refuse a request for relay to such a source.

It was clear that 'Kudu' must be thinking the same

thoughts, but taking longer to reach a decision. At last he called again, '"Mossie", standby. We are relaying you to De La Rey.'

Almost an hour later, long after dark, 'Kudu' called again. 'Mossie, this is "Kudu". De La Rey is unobtainable.'

'"Kudu", this is life and death. I will call you on this frequency every six hours until you reach De La Rey.'

'*Dood reg*, "Mossie". We'll keep a six-hour listening watch for you. *Totsiens*.'

They had abandoned their blankets when they fled before the fire, and tonight it was frosty. Sean and Claudia lay in each other's arms and whispered together softly.

'I didn't understand what you were saying on the radio. Who were you speaking with?' Claudia used the Americanism 'with', and Sean corrected it as he replied.

'I was speaking to a South African military base, probably on the border where we are headed.'

'Will they give us assistance?' she asked hopefully.

'I don't know. They might, if I can contact someone I know. I have asked them to try, but they can't get hold of him.'

'Who?'

'During the bush war, although I was in command of the Rhodesian Scouts, I was also reporting to the South African military intelligence,' he explained.

'A spy?' she asked.

'No,' he answered too quickly. 'The South Africans and the Rhodesians were allies, both on the same side. I am a South African, so I was neither a spy nor a traitor.'

'A double agent, then?' she teased him.

'Call it whatever you like, but De La Rey was my South African control. Since the war, I have continued sending him reports from time to time; whenever I have been able to pick up pieces of information about ANC terrorist activity or sanctioneering moves by hostile governments, I pass it on to him.'

'He owes you, does he?' she asked.

'He owes me plenty, besides which we are related. He's a cousin, a first cousin on my grandmother's side.' Sean broke off as a small body insinuated itself between them. 'Well, look who's here! If it isn't Minnie Mouse herself!'

Claudia wriggled around to make room for the child and Minnie settled down happily in the warm cradle formed by their bodies and pillowed her head on Sean's arm. He drew the child's body a little closer.

'She's so cute.' Claudia stroked the child's head. 'I could just eat her up.'

They were silent for so long that Sean thought she had fallen asleep, but Claudia spoke again, softly and thoughtfully.

'If we get out of here, do you think we could adopt Minnie?'

The simple question was fraught with snares and pitfalls. It presupposed a life together thereafter, a settled existence with home and children and responsibilities, all the things that Sean had avoided over a lifetime. It should have startled him, but instead it made him feel warm and comfortable.

The portable Honda generator clattered noisily and its light bulbs were strung on poles around the grounded helicopter.

The engine hatches were open and the debris suppressors had been removed from over the turbo intakes. The Portuguese engineer in blue overalls supervised and checked every task performed by his Russian prisoners. The Portuguese had very soon come to know and understand General China, and to appreciate just how vulnerable was his own position. During the short time he had been with the Renamo force he had on more than one occasion been a witness to the punishment that General China dealt out to anyone who failed or offended him, and he was conscious now of those dark fanatical eyes upon him as he worked.

It was after midnight, but General China had not yet retired to rest. He had been flying all the previous day, from first light to dusk, only landing to refuel the helicopter. A normal man would have been exhausted by now, certainly the Portuguese pilot had slouched off to his tent many hours before, but General China was indefatigable. He prowled around the helicopter, watching every move, every action, asking questions, demanding haste, as restless as though he were possessed by some dark passion.

'You must have her ready to fly at dawn,' he repeated, it seemed for the hundredth time that night, and then he went striding back to the open canvas-roofed shelter that he was using as his forward headquarters and pored over the large-scale map, studying once more his troop dispositions, brooding over them and muttering to himself.

On the map he had noted the features he had observed from the air, the location of the Frelimo logging camps and the rough roads they had hacked out of the forest. He had very soon realized the scope of the deforestation, and the numbers employed in the forced labour battalions. He had swiftly realized the futility of trying to find such a small party amongst such multitudes. He knew any sign of Sean's progress would have been obliterated by the intense activity in the area. He dared not send trackers or a pursuit into the logging area. He had already lost almost forty men in the Frelimo attack and the subsequent fire.

'No, I must be patient,' he told himself.

He moved his hand down across the map.

The Frelimo logging operation had not yet reached as

far south as the hills that guarded the approaches to the Limpopo river-basin; between the hills and the river the forest thinned out and gave way to open mopane veld. It was a strip fifty kilometres wide, good ground for tracking the fugitives, ground that they would be forced to traverse in order to reach the Limpopo and the border.

General China had decided to set his final stop line there. All that day he had ferried in the fresh troops that Tippoo Tip had placed at his disposal. In its rear cabin the Hind was able to carry fourteen men in full field kit, and they had made eleven sorties. They had hopped over the forest, fully laden with assault troops, and landed them along the line of hills with orders to set up observation posts on each hill crest and to patrol the gaps between them. He now had almost a hundred and fifty men in place to cut Sean Courtney off from the Limpopo.

General China stared at the map as though it were a portrait of the white man's face. Once again he experienced the bitter disappointment and frustration. He had almost had the white man in his grasp, pinned down by his pursuit troops, with no possible avenue of escape, and then had come the Frelimo intervention; the forest below him had been obliterated by the roiling clouds of smoke and the screaming of his men on the radio, crying for help as the flames engulfed them.

Tippoo Tip had tried in vain to convince him that Sean Courtney had perished with them in the forest fire, but General China knew better than that. He had dropped his own trackers from the Hind into the blackened ashes as soon as they had cooled sufficiently for men to walk upon them. They had found the spot where the white man had buried his people to evade the heat, the marks of their bodies were still imprinted in the soft earth, and they had found the tracks leading away southwards, ever southwards.

For the rest of that day, China had searched from the low-flying Hind, but the smoke had hampered him, limiting his vision to the small circle directly beneath the Hind's belly.

If anything, this additional failure had intensified his determination. The white man's cunning and his outrageous good fortune in evading all China's best efforts only aggravated his hatred and inflamed his longing for revenge. During those long hours when they had ferried his last line of assault troops into position, China had sustained himself with fantasies of vengeance, dreaming up the most bizarre ordeals for Sean Courtney and his woman once he had them in his power.

There would be no haste then. He would draw out the pleasure, eking out their suffering and pain as jealously as a miser his shekels. He would begin with the woman, of course, and the white man would watch it all. After Tippoo Tip had enjoyed her to the full, they would hand her over to the men. China would personally select the most repulsive, those with hideous features, deformed bodies and elephantine members. Some of his men were truly remarkable in their physical development. He would let them have the woman after Tippoo Tip, and when they were done, he would bring on the sick and diseased, the men with open venereal ulcers and virulent skin disorders, covered with scabs and tropical sores. Then at last he would give her to the men with the slim sickness, the most dreaded of all. Yes, it would be marvellous sport. He wondered how strong the American woman was, how many she could take. Would her mind go before her body? It would be fascinating to find out, and of course, the white man would be forced to watch every second of it.

Only when the woman was finished, would he begin on Colonel Sean Courtney. He had not yet decided what it would be, there were so many possibilities. However, the man was tough, he could be expected to last for days, perhaps even weeks. Planning it, gloating on it, brought a smile to General China's lips and calmed his frustration enough to allow him to drop into his canvas chair, draw the lapels of his greatcoat around him and sink at last into sleep.

He awoke in confusion, unable to orientate himself. Somebody was shaking him urgently, and he threw off the hands and struggled out of his chair, glaring around him wildly. It was morning, the trees around his temporary base were grey skeletons against the paler grey of the dawn sky. The light bulbs still glowed on their poles above the squatting helicopter and the radio on the rough table of hand-planed logs in front of him was squawking urgently.

'Contact! General China, we have a live contact!' It was the commander of the line of men that he had placed upon the hills at the approaches to the Limpopo. He was calling in clear language, proof of his agitation.

Still half asleep, China stumbled to the radio set and seized the microphone. 'This is "Banana Tree", report your position and status correctly,' he snapped, and at the sound of his voice the distant patrol leader steadied himself and corrected his radio procedure.

The fugitives had run into his stop line, at almost precisely the point which China had predicted. There had been a brief fire-fight and then the fugitive band had taken refuge on the crest of a small kopje, almost within sight of the Limpopo river.

'I have called for the mortars to come up,' the patrol leader exulted. 'We'll blow them off the top of that hill.'

'Negative.' China spoke very clearly, 'I say again, negative. Do not open fire on the position with mortars. Do not attack. I want them taken alive. Surround the hill and wait for my arrival.' He glanced across at the helicopter. The titanium engine hatches were back in place, and the Portuguese engineer was overseeing the last of the refuelling. A line of porters, each of them with a twenty-five-litre drum balanced on his head, were queued up, waiting their turns to empty the drums into the helicopter's main tanks.

China shouted to the engineer in Portuguese and he came striding across to the tent.

'We must take off immediately,' he ordered.

'I will complete the refuelling in half an hour.'

'That's too long. How much fuel have you got on board right now?'

'Auxiliary tanks are full, main tank is three quarters.'

'That will do, call the pilot. Tell him we must take off right away.'

'I must replace the debris suppressors over the turbo intakes,' the engineer protested.

'How long will that take?'

'Not more than half an hour.'

'Too long!' China shouted with agitation. The pilot was stumbling along the pathway from his tent. Not yet fully awake, he was pulling on his leather flying jacket and the flaps of his helmet dangled loosely around his ears.

'Hurry!' China yelled at him. 'Get her started!'

'What about the suppressors?' the engineer insisted.

'We can fly without them, they are only precautionary.'

'Yes, but . . . !'

'No!' China pushed him away. 'I can't wait! Forget about the suppressors! We fly at once! Get the engines started!'

With the tails of his greatcoat flapping around his legs, General China ran to the helicopter and scrambled up into his seat in the weapons cockpit.

Sean Courtney lay on his belly between two rocks just below the crest of the kopje and looked out over the tops of the mopane forest. Away towards the south, the dark green belt of trees was just visible in the uncertain light. It marked the position of the Limpopo river.

'So close,' he lamented. 'We so very nearly made it.'

It was against all the odds that they had survived this

far, almost three hundred kilometres through a devastated war-torn land and two murderous opposing armies, only to be stopped here in sight of their goal. There was a burst of AK fire from down the slope of the hill, and a ricochet sang away into the dawn sky.

Matatu lay amongst the rocks nearby, and he was still berating himself. 'I am a stupid old man, my *Bwana*. You must send me away and get yourself a clever young one who is not blind and decrepit with age.'

Sean guessed that a Renamo observation post must have spotted them as they crossed one of the open glades between the hills. There had been no warning, no obvious pursuit, no set ambush. Without warning a sweep line of tiger-striped figures had rushed at them from out of the mopane.

They had all been weary after travelling hard all night, perhaps their concentration had been eroded, perhaps they should have stayed in the trees instead of cutting across the open vlei, but it was pointless to think about what they might have done.

There had only been sufficient time to snatch up the children and drag the women up the side of the kopje with poorly aimed Renamo fire whining off the rocks around them. Perhaps the Renamo aim had been deliberately wild, Sean pondered. He could guess what General China's orders to his men had been. 'Take them alive!'

'Where is China now?' he wondered. One thing was certain, he was not far away and coming as fast as the Hind would fly. He looked out at the Limpopo river again and there was the foul taste of failure and disappointment on the back of his tongue.

'Alphonso,' he called out. 'Have you got the radio rigged?' It was more for something to occupy his mind than with any real hope of making contact.

Twice during the night he had attempted to make the prearranged radio schedule with the South African army. Once he had even heard 'Kudu' calling him very faintly;

however, the batteries of their radio had finally begun to fail. The battery test needle had dropped back deeply into the red quadrant of the dial.

'If I try to raise the aerial those baboons down there will shoot my testicles off,' Alphonso growled from amongst the rocks.

'It's almost line of sight to the river,' Sean told him brusquely. 'Give me the aerial.' He raised himself on one elbow and threw the bundle of insulated wire as far out down the slope as he could reach and then stooped to the radio set. When he turned on the power, the control panel glowed feebly.

'"Kudu", this is "Mossie",' he sent out his despairing call, '"Kudu", do you read me? "Kudu", this is "Mossie"!'

A stray bullet hit the rock above his head, but Sean ignored it.

'"Kudu", this is "Mossie"!'

The two women, white and black, were holding the children and watching him wordlessly.

'"Kudu", this is "Mossie".' He adjusted the gain knob, and then unbelievably, so faintly that he could barely catch the words, a voice answered him.

'"Mossie", this is "Oubaas". I read you strength three.'

'"Oubaas", Oh God,' he breathed '"Oubaas"!'

Oubaas, the grandfather, was General Lothar De La Rey's code name.

'"Oubaas". We are in deep shit here. Request an immediate hot extraction.' He was asking for a removal while under enemy fire. 'We are seven pax, five adults and two children. Our position is . . .' He read out the map co-ordinates of his dead-reckoning position. 'We are holding a small kopje approximately twenty kilometres north of the Limpopo.' He raised his head and glanced around quickly. 'There are two large kopjes approximately two miles due east of our position. Do you read me, "Oubaas"?'

'I read you "Mossie".' The voice faded and then came back. 'What was your grandmother's maiden name?'

'Oh, sod you!' Sean snarled frustration. Lothar was double-checking his identity at a time like this. 'My grandmother's maiden name was Centaine De Thiry and she is your grandmother also, Lothar, you rotten bastard!'

'Okay, "Mossie". I'm sending a Puma in for a hot extraction. Can you hold out for one hour longer?'

'Pull finger, "Oubaas". We've got gooks all over us.'

'Wilco, "Mossie".' Sean had to put his ear close to the set to catch the last words. Give them hell, Sean . . .' And then the signal faded and the last flicker of the battery died.

'They are coming!' Sean looked up from the radio and grinned across at Claudia. 'They are sending a Puma helicopter in to take us out.' Then his grin faded and all their faces turned slowly towards the north. There was a new sound in the dawn, still faint and far off, but they all recognized it. It was the sound of death.

They watched the Hind come down from the north, sweeping in low over the forest, a great hunchbacked monster, blotched with camouflage paint, the first rays of the rising sun reflecting off the cockpit canopy like huge glowing red eyes.

Out of the mopane forest at the foot of the kopje a signal rocket sailed up in a lazy red parabola, calling the Hind in, and it altered course slightly and headed directly towards the crest of the hill on which they lay.

Claudia was at Sean's side and he placed his arm over her shoulders.

'It's so cruel,' she whispered. 'It's like dying twice over.' She pulled the Tokarev pistol from her belt and tried to place it in his hand.

'No!' he rejected. 'I can't do it! I can't screw myself up to that again!' He pushed the pistol away.

'What then?' she asked, and he showed her the fragmentation grenade he held in his right hand.

She glanced at the deeply chequered black metal orb. It looked like some evil poisonous fruit, and she shuddered and averted her eyes.

'It will be as quick and more certain,' he whispered reassuringly. 'And we'll go together, at the very same moment.'

He knew what he had to do. He would hold the grenade between them as they lay chest to chest.

He looked up again at the approaching Hind. It was very close. It was almost time. He would not warn her. He would simply kiss her one last time and then . . .

Suddenly Sean's eyes narrowed. Something about the Hind's silhouette was different. It was coming in swiftly, swelling in size before his eyes and he felt the first stirring of a new excitement as he realized what had been changed on the helicopter.

'There is still a chance,' he whispered to her. 'A small chance, but we are going to take it. Come here, Minnie. Come quickly!' he called in Shangane, and the tiny black girl tottered across to where they lay.

'Hold her,' Sean whispered, and lifted the back of the child's short ragged skirt. Under the skirt, she wore a pair of blue knickers.

Sean pulled open the elastic top of the knickers and pushed something down into them, something as round and black as one of her little buttocks between which it nestled.

'Keep that for me, little one,' he whispered to the child in Shangane as he adjusted the waistband. 'It's a secret. Don't take it out. Just keep it there. Will you do that for me, my little flower?'

Minnie stared at him with dark adoring eyes and nodded solemnly and Sean gave her a hug.

The sound of the Hind's turbos was almost unbearably

shrill as it came in towards them at the level of the hilltop. When it was two hundred metres out, Alphonso opened fire with his AK rifle, pouring a full magazine into the front canopy. The light bullets left no mark on the armoured glass, and the helicopter slowed and hung motionless on its shining rotor. General China was sitting up in the high-backed seat of the weapons cockpit, so close that they could clearly see the triumphant smirk on his face as he lifted the microphone to his mouth.

His grossly magnified voice boomed out of the speakers of the 'sky shout' system that were slung below the helicopter's stubby wings.

'Good morning, Colonel Courtney. You have led me a merry dance, but the chase is over. Tell your men to lay down their weapons, please.'

'Do it!' Sean shouted at Alphonso, but he snarled a protest and clipped a fresh magazine onto his rifle. 'Do as I tell you!' Sean's voice hardened, 'I have a plan. Trust me.'

Still Alphonso hesitated, and suddenly the Hind's Gatling-cannon thundered, deafening them and kicking a storm of rock chips and dust from the side of the kopje just below where they lay.

'Don't try my patience, Colonel. Tell your men to stand up, with their hands high above their heads.'

'Do it!' Sean repeated, and first Matatu and then Alphonso rose slowly to their feet with arms held high.

'Tell them to turn around. I want to make sure they have no surprises for me.'

They shuffled in a circle and China's voice boomed out again.

'Take your clothes off, all of them.'

Slowly they stripped themselves and stood naked before him.

'All right, now move down the hill into the open.'

Still with their hands held high they walked down into the open ground below the crown of rocks.

'Now the two women.'

'Be brave,' Sean whispered to Claudia. 'We've still got a chance, a good chance.'

Claudia stood up slowly.

'Miss Monterro,' China's voice echoed across the forest tops, 'will you be good enough to remove your clothing?'

Briskly, defiantly Claudia unbuttoned her ragged shirt and pulled it over her tousled head. Her breasts were white in the early sunlight.

'Now your trousers,' China encouraged her. She let them drop around her ankles and kicked them off.

'Very good, and now the rest of it.'

Claudia's lace panties had been washed and worn until they were wispy as spider web, her pubic triangle was a dark shadow under the filmy cloth.

'No.' She shook her head, 'I won't do it.' She crossed her hands in front of her. Her refusal was unmistakable.

'Very well. We'll allow you your modesty for the time being. My men will enjoy it all the more later.' China chuckled. 'Move down into the open, please.'

Claudia walked down the hill, her chin and her small pert breasts held high, and stood between Alphonso and Matatu.

'Now you, woman,' China spoke in Shangane, and Miriam stood up. She did not have a European's shame of nudity and quickly stripped herself naked. Holding her little brother's hand, she went down to join the others.

'And now, Colonel Courtney. The last is the best of all the game.'

Sean rose to his feet and carelessly threw aside his tattered clothing.

'Very impressive, Colonel,' China taunted him. 'For a white man, that is.'

Sean stood and stared up at him impassively, but he was trying to judge the distance to the helicopter. Sixty yards, he estimated, much too far.

'Please come down into the open where I can keep an eye on you, Colonel. We don't want any misunderstanding now, do we?'

Sean took Minnie's hand and led her down the hill. The lump under the little girl's skirt wobbled from side to side like a Victorian bustle, and with her free hand she tugged at the waistband of her knickers to prevent them being pulled down around her knees by the weight.

Ten, fifteen, twenty paces, Sean counted as he moved towards the hovering Hind. He could clearly see the pupils of General China's eyes, forty yards, still too far. He stopped beside Claudia and they stood in a row, naked and vulnerable.

China gave an order in Shangane, and at the foot of the hill his men burst out of the forest and came swarming up the slope, whooping with triumph. The Portuguese pilot edged the huge machine in closer, and then closer still, showing off his prowess at the controls.

Thirty yards, twenty-five yards, Sean was concentrating on the opening of the air-intakes to the turbo engines. They were the size of garbage bins with the covers missing: he could just make out deep in the circular openings the velvety blur of the rotor blades spinning at incredible speed.

The Hind steadied in the air and hung in front of them. In the cockpit General China twisted his head to peer down the hill at the line of advancing Renamo guerrillas. He was distracted and Sean seized the moment.

He stooped slightly and jerked up the back of Minnie's skirt. In the same movement, he thrust his hand under the waistband of her knickers and closed his fist over the grenade. As it came out, he pulled the pin and let the firing handle fly free. He heard the pin fall on the primer. There was a delay of five seconds. He counted off three under his breath and then reared back like a baseball pitcher just as China looked back at him.

He concentrated on the starboard engine intake, and hurled the grenade. It went up in a flat arc and he willed its flight, trying by sheer force of his mind to steer it into the small circle of the intake.

The grenade struck the bottom of the intake rim, and bounced on the edge, like a million-dollar putt quivering on the lip. Then the tremendous draught of air created by the rotor blades sucked it in, and it popped into the throat of the open duct.

The grenade exploded as it hit the spinning blades, and the great turbo's energy was thrown out of balance, all its mighty power directed upon itself, in an orgy of self-destruction.

As Sean seized Claudia and Minnie under each arm and hurled them face down, the Hind's engine tore itself to pieces in one fatal instant.

The Hind lurched heavily, throwing General China's aim so that the burst he fired from the Gatling-cannon flew almost straight into the sky, and the helicopter rolled on to its back. Smoke and fragments of metal blew in a screaming cloud from its maimed engines.

It struck the side of the hill, and bounced high, fell again, and cart-wheeled down the slope, directly on top of the climbing line of Renamo. They broke and scattered, but most of them could not escape, and the shattered fuse-lage of the Hind rolled over them and swept them away down the slope.

At last the Hind slithered on its belly like a gigantic toboggan to the bottom of the kopje and came up hard against the tree-line. Avgas, as clear as water, fountained from its ruptured main tanks and sprayed over the hull, sparkling in the sunlight.

Sean and Claudia rose shakily to their knees and watched in awe the magnificent destruction.

Then, incredibly, the canopy of the weapons cockpit opened like the half shell of an enormous oyster and General China crawled out from under it. The Hind's fuel sprayed high in the morning sunlight as innocuous-seeming as a garden sprinkler, and fell upon him in a gentle rain. It soaked his uniform and ran in thin rivulets down his face, but China pushed himself away from the shattered fuselage and set off down the hill at a shambling run.

He had not gone ten shaky paces when the Hind went up in a sheet of flame, and the flames jumped the gap and ignited China's sodden uniform. It turned him into a human torch and he ran on down the slope with the yellow flames streaking out behind him. They could hear his screams even from the top of the hill, it was a high inhuman sound.

China did not reach the trees. He fell at the edge of the forest and his burning flesh touched off the thick brown grass in which he lay. The hillside became his pyre, but still they could hear him screaming in the heart of the flames.

'Back!' Sean shouted, and his voice aroused them from their mesmerized horror. He hauled Claudia to her feet and picked Minnie up in his arms.

In a bunch they fled back into the circle of rocks that crowned the kopje just as a renewed Renamo fusillade whined about them. They lay behind the rocks, not yet bothering to cover their naked bodies and watched the Hind burn, and the flames sweep through the grass at the edge of the forest.

When the flames had passed, a dark charred mound lay on the blackened slope. It might have been merely a pile of discarded sacking, except that when the wind shifted, the odour of burned flesh carried up to them on the crest of the hill.

The shift in the wind carried a new sound to them, and Sean roused himself and looked towards the green Limpopo river on the horizon.

The Puma helicopter was still a dark speck out there, but it was coming on swiftly, the sound of its engines rising on the wind.

'Put your pants on, darling,' Sean hugged Claudia a little closer. 'It looks as though we've got company dropping in on us!'

VICIOUS CIRCLE

On the far side of the boggy hollow Hazel's Ferrari was just topping the crest of the hill. Hector realized that they had been neatly cut off from each other by the van and bike.

'Hazel!' Hector shouted her name as all his feral instincts kicked in at full force. 'They are after Hazel!' He grabbed his mobile phone and punched in her number.

A disembodied voice answered the call, 'The person you have called is presently unavailable. Please try again later.'

When Hector Cross's new life is overturned, he immediately recognizes the ruthless hand of an enemy he has faced many times before: a terrorist group has re-emerged – like a deadly scorpion from beneath its rock.

Determined to fight back, Hector draws together a team of his most loyal friends from his former life in Cross Bow Security, a company originally contracted to protect his beloved wife, Hazel Bannock, and her company, the Bannock Oil Corp. They travel to the remotest Middle East, to hunt down those who pursue him and his loved ones.

For Hazel and Hector have a child, a precious daughter, who he will go to the ends of the earth to protect. And brutal figures from the Bannock family's past – thought long-gone – are returning, with an agenda so sinister that Hector realizes he is facing a new breed of enemy. One whose shifting attack and dark, shocking secrets take Hector to the heart of Africa and to a series of crimes so shocking they demand revenge.

LOVE. LOSS. REVENGE.